Ruth Rendell

INSPECTOR WEXFORD

Ruth Rendell

INSPECTOR WEXFORD

A New Lease of Death

The Best Man to Die

Wolf to the Slaughter

Put On By Cunning

This edition first published by Cresset Editions in 1994
an imprint of the Random House Group
20 Vauxhall Bridge Road
London SW1V 2SA

First published by Hutchinson Ltd

ISBN 0 7529 0425 6

Jacket illustration by Tony Nutley

Typeset in 11.5 on 12.25 pts Baskerville by
Pure Tech Corporation, Pondicherry, India
Printed and bound in Australia by
Griffin Paperbacks

CONTENTS

A New Lease
of Death

For my Father and Simon

CHAPTER ONE

The laws of the Realm may punish Christian men with death for heinous and grievous offences.

The Thirty-nine Articles

It was five in the morning. Inspector Burden had seen more dawns than most men, but he had never quite become jaundiced by them, especially summer dawns. He liked the stillness, the sight of the little country towns in a depopulated state, the hard blue light that was of the same shade and intensity as the light at dusk but without dusk's melancholy.

The two men they had been questioning about last night's fight in one of Kingsmarkham's cafés had confessed separately and almost simultaneously just a quarter of an hour before. Now they were locked into two stark white cells on the ground floor of this incongruously modern police station. Burden stood by the window in Wexford's office, looking at the sky which had the peculiar greenish tint of aquamarine. A flock of birds flying in dense formation crossed it. They reminded Burden of his childhood when, as at dawn, everything had seemed bigger, clearer and of more significance than it did today. Tired and a little sickened, he opened the window to get rid of cigarette smoke and the sweaty smell of youths who wore leather jackets in the height of summer.

Outside in the corridor he could hear Wexford saying good night — or good morning — to Colonel Griswold, the Chief Constable. Burden wondered if Griswold had guessed when he arrived just before ten with a long spiel about stamping out hooliganism that he was in for an all-night session. That, he thought unfairly, was where meddling got you.

The heavy front door clanged and Griswold's car started. Burden watched it move off the forecourt, past the great stone urns filled with pink geraniums and into Kingsmarkham High

Street. The Chief Constable was driving himself. Burden saw with approval and grudging amusement that Griswold drove at just about twenty-eight miles per hour until he reached the black and white derestriction sign. Then the car gathered speed and flashed away out of sight along the empty country road that led to Pomfret.

He turned round when he heard Wexford come in. The Chief Inspector's heavy grey face was a little greyer than usual, but he showed no other sign of tiredness and his eyes, dark and hard as basalt, showed a gleam of triumph. He was a big man with big features and a big intimidating voice. His grey suit — one of a series of low fastening, double-breasted affairs — appeared more shabby and wrinkled than ever today. But it suited Wexford, being not unlike an extension of his furrowed pachydermatous skin.

'Another job jobbed,' he said, 'as the old woman said when she jobbed the old man's eye out.'

Burden bore with such vulgarisms stoically. He knew that they were meant to horrify him; they always succeeded. He made his thin lips crease into a tight smile. Wexford handed him a blue envelope and he was glad of the diversion to hide his slight embarrassment.

'Griswold's just given me this,' Wexford said. 'At five in the morning. No sense of timing.'

Burden glanced at the Essex postmark.

'Is that the man he was on about earlier, sir?'

'Well, I don't have fanmail from beautiful olde worlde Thringford as a general rule, do I, Mike? This is the Rev. Mr Archery all right, taking advantage of the Old Pals' Act.' He lowered himself into one of the rather flimsy chairs and it gave the usual protesting creak. Wexford had what his junior called a love-hate relationship with those chairs and indeed with all the aggressively modern furnishings of his office. The glossy black floor, the square of nylon carpet, the chairs with their sleek chrome legs, the primrose venetian blinds — all these in Wexford's estimation were not 'serviceable', they were dust-traps and they were 'chi-chi'. At the same time he took in them an enormous half-secret pride. They had their effect. They served to impress visiting strangers such as the writer of this letter Wexford was now taking from its envelope.

It too was written on rather thick blue paper. In a painfully authentic upper-class accent, the Chief Inspector said affectedly, 'May as well get on to the Chief Constable of Mid-Sussex, my dear. We were up at Oxford together, don't you know?' He squeezed his face into a kind of snarling grin. 'All among the bloody dreaming spires,' he said. 'I hate that sort of thing.'

'Were they?'

'Were they what?'

'At Oxford together?'

'I don't know. Something like that. It may have been the playing fields of Eton. All Griswold said was, "Now we've got those villains wrapped up, I'd like you to have a look at a letter from a very good friend of mine called Archery. Excellent fellow, one of the best. This enclosure's for you. I'd like you to give him all the help you can. I've a notion it's got something to do with that scoundrel Painter." '

'Who's Painter?'

'Villain who got the chop about fifteen or sixteen years ago,' said Wexford laconically. 'Let's see what the parson has to say, shall we?'

Burden looked over his shoulder. The letter was headed St Columba's Vicarage, Thringford, Essex. The greek e's awakened in him a small hostility. Wexford read it aloud.

' "Dear sir, I hope you will forgive me for taking up your valuable time . . ." Don't have much choice, do I? " . . . but I regard this matter as being of some urgency. Col. Griswold, the Chief Constable of blah blah and so on, has very kindly told me you are the gentleman who may be able to assist me in this problem so I am taking the liberty, having first consulted him, of writing to you." ' He cleared his throat and loosened his crumpled grey tie. 'Takes a hell of a time coming to the point, I must say. Ah, here we go. "You will remember the case of Herbert Arthur Painter . . ." I *will.* "I understand you were in charge of it. I therefore supposed I should come to you before pursuing certain enquiries which, much against my will, I am compelled to make." '

'Compelled?'

'That's what the man says. Doesn't say why. The rest's a load of compliments and can he come and see me tomorrow —

3

no, today. He's going to phone this morning, but he "anticipates my willingness to meet him".' He glanced at the window to see where the sun was coming up over York Street and with one of his distorted quotations, said, 'I suppose he's sleeping in Elysium at this moment, crammed with distressful cold mutton or whatever parsons go to bed on.'

'What's it all about?'

'O God, Mike, it's obvious, isn't it? You don't want to take any notice of this "being compelled" and "against his will" stuff. I don't suppose his stipend amounts to much. He probably writes true crime stories in between early Communion and the Mothers' Meeting. He must be getting desperate if he reckons on titillating the mass appetite by resurrecting Painter.'

Burden said thoughtfully, 'I seem to remember the case. I'd just left school . . .'.

'And it inspired your choice of a career, did it?' Wexford mocked. ' "What are you going to be, son?" "I'm going to be a detective, Dad." '

In his five years as Wexford's right-hand man, Burden had grown immune to his teasing. He knew he was a kind of safety valve, the stooge perhaps on whom Wexford could vent his violent and sometimes shocking sense of humour. The people of this little town, indiscriminately referred to by Wexford as 'our customers', had, unless suspected of felony, to be spared. Burden was there to take the overflow of his chief's rage, ridicule and satire. Now he was cast as the sponge to soak up the scorn that was rightly the due of Griswold and Griswold's friend.

He looked shrewdly at Wexford. After a trying, frustrating day and night, this letter was the last straw. Wexford was suddenly tense with irritation, his skin more deeply wrinkled than usual, his whole body flexed with the anger that would not suffer fools gladly. That tension must find release.

'This Painter thing,' Burden said slyly, slipping into his role of therapist, 'a bit run of the mill, wasn't it? I followed it in the papers because it was the big local sensation. I don't remember it was remarkable in any other way.'

Wexford slipped the letter back into its envelope and put it in a drawer. His movements were precise and under a tight control. One wrong word, Burden thought, and he'd have torn it up, chucked the pieces on the floor and left them to the mercy of the cleaner. His words had apparently been as right as possible under the circumstances for Wexford said in a sharp cool voice, 'It was remarkable to me.'

'Because you handled it?'

'Because it was the first murder case I ever handled on my own. It was remarkable to Painter because it hanged him and to his widow, I daresay. I suppose it shook her a bit as far as anything could shake that girl.'

Rather nervously Burden watched him observe the cigarette burn one of the men they had been interviewing had made in the lemon-coloured leather of a chair seat. He waited for the explosion. Instead Wexford said indifferently:

'Haven't you got a home to go to?'

'Too late now,' said Burden, stifling a yawn that threatened. 'Besides, my wife's away at the seaside.'

A strongly uxorious man, he found his bungalow like a morgue when Jean and the children were absent. This was a side of his character that afforded Wexford many opportunities for quips and snide remarks, this coupled with his comparative youth, his solid stick-in-the-mud nature and a certain primness of outlook. But all Wexford said was, 'I forgot.'

He was good at his job. The big ugly man respected him for that. Although he might deride, Wexford appreciated the advantage of having a deputy whose grave good looks were attractive to women. Seated opposite that ascetic face, warmed by a compassion Wexford called 'softness', they were more inclined to open their hearts than to a majestic fifty-five-year-old heavyweight. His personality, however, was not strong and his superior effaced him. Now, in order to channel off that sharp-edged vitality, he was going to have to risk a rebuke for stupidity.

He risked it. 'If you're going to have to argue the toss with this Archery, wouldn't it be a good idea if we had a re-cap of the facts?'

'We?'

'Well, you then, sir. You must be a bit rusty yourself on the case after so long.'

The outburst came with an undercurrent of laughter. 'God

Almighty! D'you think I can't see your brain working? When I want a psychiatrist I'll hire a professional.' He paused and the laughter became a wry grin. 'O.K., it might help me . . .' But Burden had made the mistake of relaxing too soon. 'To get the facts straight for Mr Bloody Archery, I mean,' Wexford snapped. 'But there's no mystery, you know, no cunning little red herrings. Painter did it all right.' He pointed eastwards out of the window. The broad Sussex sky was becoming suffused with rose and gold, bands of soft creamy pink like strokes from a water-colour brush. 'That's as sure as the sun's rising now,' he said. 'There never was any doubt. Herbert Arthur Painter killed his ninety-year-old employer by hitting her over the head with an axe and he did it for two hundred pounds. He was a brutal savage moron. I read in the paper the other day that the Russians call anti-social people 'unpersons' and that just about describes him. Funny sort of character for a parson to champion.'

'If he's championing him.'

'We shall see,' said Wexford.

They stood in front of the map that was attached to the yellow 'cracked ice' wallpaper.

'She was killed in her own home, wasn't she?' Burden asked. 'One of those big houses off the Stowerton road?'

The map showed the whole of this rather sleepy country district. Kingsmarkham, a market town of some twelve thousand inhabitants, lay in the centre, its streets coloured in brown and white, its pastoral environs green with the blotches of dark veridian that denoted woodland. Roads ran from it as from the meshy heart of a spider's web, one leading to Pomfret in the south, another to Sewingbury in the north-east. The scattered villages, Flagford, Clusterwell and Forby, were tiny flies on this web.

'The house is called Victor's Piece,' said Wexford. 'Funny sort of name. Some general built it for himself after the Ashanti Wars.'

'And it's just about here.' Burden put his finger on a vertical strand of the web that led from Kingsmarkham to Stowerton, lying due north. He pondered and light dawned. 'I

6

think I know it,' he said. 'Hideous dump with a lot of green woodwork all over it. It was an old people's home up until last year. I suppose they'll pull it down.'

'I daresay. There are a couple of acres of land to it. If you've got the picture we may as well sit down.'

Burden had moved his chair to the window. There was something consoling and at the same time rejuvenating in watching the unfolding of what was going to be a lovely day. On the fields tree shadows lay long and densely blue and bright new light glinted on the slate roofs of ancient houses. Pity he hadn't been able to get away with Jean. The sunlight and the fresh heady air turned his thoughts towards holidays and prevented him from recalling details of this case that had long ago shocked Kingsmarkham. He searched his memory and found to his shame that he could not even remember the murdered woman's name.

'What was she called?' he asked Wexford. 'A foreign name, wasn't it? Porto or Primo something?'

'Primero. Rose Isabel Primero. That was her married name. Far from being foreign, she'd been brought up at Forby Hall. Her people were by way of being squires of Forby.'

Burden knew Forby well. What tourists there were in this agricultural country with neither seaside nor downs, castles nor cathedrals, made a point of going to Forby. The guide books listed it absurdly as the fifth prettiest village in England. Every local newsagent's contained postcards of its church. Burden himself regarded it with a certain affection because its inhabitants had shown themselves almost totally devoid of criminal tendencies.

'This Archery could be a relative,' he suggested. 'Maybe he wants some gen for his family archives.'

'I doubt it,' Wexford said, basking in the sun like a huge grey cat. 'The only relatives she had were her three grandchildren. Roger Primero, the grandson, lives at Forby Hall now. Didn't inherit it, had to buy it. I don't know the details.'

'There used to be a family called Kynaston at Forby Hall, or so Jean's mother says. Mind you, that was years and years ago.'

'That's right,' Wexford said with a hint of impatience in his rumbling bass voice. 'Mrs Primero was born a Kynaston and she was going on for forty when she married Dr Ralph Primero. I imagine her people looked on it a bit askance — this was at the turn of the century, remember.'

'What was he, a G.P.?'

'Some sort of specialist, I think. It was when he retired that they came to live at Victor's Piece. They weren't all that well-off, you know. When the doctor died in the thirties Mrs Primero was left with about ten thousand pounds to live on. There was one child of the marriage, a son, but he'd died soon after his father.'

'D'you mean she was living alone in that great place? At her age?'

Wexford pursed his lips, reminiscing. Burden knew his chief's almost supernatural memory. When he was sufficiently interested he had the nearest thing to total recall. 'She had one maid,' Wexford said. 'Her name was — is, she's still alive — her name was Alice Flower. She was a good bit younger than her employer, seventy odd, and she'd been with Mrs Primero for about fifty years. A real ancient retainer of the old school. Living like that, you might think they'd have become friends rather than mistress and servant, but Alice kept to her place and they were 'Madam' and 'Alice' to each other till the day Mrs Primero died. I knew Alice by sight. She was quite a local character when she came into town to do their shopping, particularly when Painter started bringing her in in Mrs Primero's Daimler. D'you remember how nursemaids used to look? No, you wouldn't. You're too young. Well, Alice always wore a long navy coat and what's called a 'decent' navy felt hat. She and Painter were both servants, but Alice put herself miles above him. She'd pull her rank on him and give him his orders just like Mrs Primero herself. He was Bert to his wife and his cronies but Alice called him 'Beast'. Not to his face, mind. She wouldn't have quite dared that.'

'You mean she was frightened of him?'

'In a way. She hated him and resented his being there. I wonder if I've still got that cutting.' Wexford opened the bottom drawer of his desk, the one where he kept personal, semi-official things, grotesqueries that had interested him. He hadn't much hope of finding what he sought. At the time of Mrs Primero's murder Kingsmarkham police had been housed in an old yellow brick building in the centre of town. That had been pulled down four or five years ago and replaced by this block of startling modernity on the outskirts. The cutting had very probably got lost in the move from the high pitch pine desk to this one of lacquered rosewood. He leafed through notes, letters, odd little souvenirs, finally surfacing with a grin of triumph.

'There you are, the "unperson" himself. Good-looking if you like the type. Herbert Arthur Painter, late of the Fourteenth Army in Burma. Twenty-five years old, engaged by Mrs Primero as chauffeur, gardener and odd-job man.'

The cutting was from the *Sunday Planet,* several columns of type surrounding a double-column block. It was a clear photograph and Painter's eyes were staring straight at the camera.

'Funny, that,' said Wexford. 'He always looked you straight in the eye. Supposed to denote honesty, if you've ever heard such a load of rubbish.'

Burden must have seen the picture before, but he had entirely forgotten it. It was a large well-made face with a straight though fleshy nose, spread at the nostrils. Painter had the thick curved lips that on a man are a coarse parody of a woman's mouth, a flat high brow and short tightly waving hair. The waves were so tightly crimped that they looked as if they must have pulled the skin and pained the scalp.

'He was tall and well-built,' Wexford went on. 'Face like a handsome overgrown pug, don't you think? He'd been in the Far East during the war, but if the heat and the privation had taken it out of him it didn't show by then. He had a sort of glistening good health about him like a shire horse. Sorry to use all these animal metaphors, but Painter was like an animal.'

'How did Mrs Primero come to take him on?'

Wexford took the cutting from him, looked at it for a moment and folded it up.

'From the time the doctor died,' he said, 'until 1947 Mrs Primero and Alice Flower struggled to keep the place going, pulling up a few weeds here and there, getting a man in when they wanted a shelf fixed. You can imagine the kind of thing.

They had a succession of women up from Kingsmarkham to help with the housework but sooner or later they all left to go into the factories. The place started going to rack and ruin. Not surprising when you think that by the end of the war Mrs Primero was in her middle eighties and Alice nearly seventy. Besides, leaving her age out of it, Mrs Primero never touched the place as far as housework went. She hadn't been brought up to it and she wouldn't have known a duster from an antimacassar.'

'Bit of a tartar, was she?'

'She was what God and her background had made her,' Wexford said gravely but with the faintest suspicion of irony in his voice. 'I never saw her till she was dead. She was stubborn, a bit mean, what nowadays is called "reactionary", inclined to be an autocrat and very much monarch of all she surveyed. I'll give you a couple of examples. When her son died he left his wife and kids very badly off. I don't know the ins and outs of it, but Mrs Primero was quite willing to help financially provided it was on her terms. The family was to come and live with her and so on. Still, I daresay she couldn't afford to keep up two establishments. The other thing was that she'd been a very keen churchwoman. When she got too old to go she insisted on Alice going in her place. Like a sort of whipping boy. But she had her affections. She adored the grandson, Roger, and she had one close friend. We'll come to that later.

'As you know, there was an acute housing shortage after the war and a hell of a servant problem too. Mrs Primero was an intelligent old woman and she got to thinking how she could use one to solve the other. In the grounds of Victor's Piece was a coach house with a sort of loft over the top of it. The place for the coach was used to house the aforesaid Daimler. No one had driven it since the doctor died — Mrs Primero couldn't drive and, needless to say, Alice couldn't either. There was precious little petrol about but you could get your ration, enough to do the shopping and take a couple of old dears for a weekly jaunt around the lanes.'

'So Alice was that much of a friend?' Burden put in.

Wexford said solemnly, 'A lady can be accompanied by her maid when she goes driving. Anyway, Mrs Primero put an advert in the *Kingsmarkham Chronicle* for a young able-bodied man, willing to do the garden, perform odd jobs, maintain and drive the car in exchange for a flat and three pounds a week.'

'*Three pounds?*' Burden was a non-smoker and no lover of extravagant living, but he knew from doing his wife's weekend shopping what a little way three pounds went.

'Well, it was worth a good bit more in those days, Mike,' Wexford said almost apologetically. 'Mrs Primero had the loft painted up, divided into three rooms and piped for water. It wasn't Dolphin Square but, God, people were glad of one room back in 1947! She got a lot of answers but for some reason — God knows *what* reason — she picked Painter. At the trial Alice said she thought the fact that he had a wife and a baby daughter would keep him steady. Depends what you mean by steady, doesn't it?'

Burden shifted his chair out of the sun. 'Was the wife employed by Mrs Primero too?'

'No, just Painter. She'd got this little kid, you see. She was only about two when they came. If she'd worked up at the house she'd have had to bring the child with her. Mrs Primero would never have stood for that. As far as she was concerned between her and the Painters there was a great gulf fixed. I gathered she'd hardly exchanged more than a couple of words with Mrs Painter all the time Painter was there and as for the little girl — her name was Theresa, I think — she barely knew of her existence.'

'She doesn't sound a very nice sort of woman,' Burden said doubtfully.

'She was typical of her age and class,' Wexford said tolerantly. 'Don't forget she was a daughter of the lord of the manor when lords of the manor still counted for something. To her Mrs Painter was comparable to a tenant's wife. I've no doubt that if Mrs Painter had been ill she'd have sent old Alice over with a bowl of soup and some blankets. Besides, Mrs Painter kept herself to herself. She was very pretty, very quiet and with a sort of deadly respectability about her. She was a bit scared of Painter which wasn't hard to understand, she being so small and Painter such a great hulking brute. When I talked to her after the murder I noticed she'd got bruises on her arm, too many bruises for her just to have got them through the usual kitchen accidents, and I wouldn't mind betting her husband used to knock her about.'

'So, in fact,' Burden said, 'they were two completely separate units. Mrs Primero and her maid living alone at Victor's Piece, the Painter family in their own home at the bottom of the garden.'

'I don't know about "bottom of the garden". The coach house was about a hundred feet from the back door of the big house. Painter only went up there to carry in the coal and receive his instructions.'

'Ah,' said Burden, 'there was some complicated business about coal, I seem to remember. Wasn't it more or less the crux of the whole thing?'

'Painter was supposed to chop wood and carry coal,' Wexford continued. 'Alice was past carrying coal and Painter was supposed to bring a scuttleful at mid-day — they never lit a fire before that — and another one at six-thirty. Now, he never objected to the gardening or the car maintenance, but for some reason he drew the line at the coal. He did it — apart from frequent lapses — but he was always grumbling about it. The mid-day duty cut across his dinner time, he said, and he didn't like turning out on winter evenings. Couldn't he bring two scuttles at eleven? But Mrs Primero wouldn't have that. She said she wasn't going to have her drawing room turned into a railway yard.'

Burden smiled. His tiredness had almost worn off. Given breakfast, a shave and a shower down, he would be a new man. He glanced at his watch, then across the High Street to where the blinds were going up on the Carousel Café.

'I could do with a cup of coffee,' he said.

'Two minds with but a single thought. Root someone out and send them over.'

Wexford stood up and stretched, tightened his tie and smoothed back the hair that was too sparse to become untidy. The coffee arrived in wax cups with plastic spoons and little cubes of wrapped sugar.

'That's better,' said Wexford. 'D'you want me to go on?' Burden nodded.

'By September 1950 Painter had been working for Mrs Primero for three years. The arrangement appeared to work pretty well apart from the difficulties Painter made about the coal. He never brought it in without complaining and he was always asking for a rise.'

'I suppose he thought she was rolling in money?'

'Of course, he couldn't have known what she'd got in the bank or in shares or whatever it was. On the other hand it was an open secret she kept money in the house.'

'In a safe, d'you mean?'

'Not on your life. You know these old girls. Some of it was in drawers stuffed into paper bags, some of it in old handbags.'

With a feat of memory Burden said suddenly, 'And one of those handbags contained *the* two hundred pounds?'

'It did,' Wexford said grimly. 'Whatever she might have been able to afford, Mrs Primero refused to raise Painter's wages. If he didn't like the set-up he could go, but that would mean giving up the flat.

'Being a very old woman, Mrs Primero felt the cold and she liked to start fires in September. Painter thought this unnecessary and he made the usual fuss about it . . .'

He stopped as the telephone rang and he took the receiver himself. Burden had no idea from Wexford's reiterated, 'Yes, yes . . . all right,' who it could be. He finished his coffee with some distaste. The rim of the wax cup had become soggy. Wexford dropped the phone.

'My wife,' he said. 'Am I dead? Have I forgotten I've got a home of my own? She's run out of housekeeping and she can't find the cheque book.' He chuckled, felt in his pocket and produced it. 'No wonder. I'll have to nip back.' He added with sudden kindness, 'Go home and have a bit of shut-eye, why don't you?'

'I don't like being left in the air,' Burden grumbled. 'Now I know how my kids feel when I break off in the middle of a bedtime story.'

Wexford began bundling things into his briefcase.

'Leaving out all the circumstantial stuff,' he said, 'there isn't much more. I told you it was straightforward. It was the evening of September 24th it happened, a cold wet Sunday. Mrs

13

Primero had sent Alice off to church. She went at about a quarter past six, Painter being due to bring the coal at half past. He brought it all right and departed two hundred pounds to the good.'

'I'd like to hear the circumstantial stuff,' Burden said.

Wexford was at the door now.

'To be continued in our next,' he grinned. 'You can't say I'm leaving you in suspense.' The grin faded and his face hardened. 'Mrs Primero was found at seven. She was in the drawing room lying on the floor by the fireplace in a great pool of blood. There was blood on the walls and on her armchair, and in the hearth was a blood-stained wood chopper.'

CHAPTER TWO

When sentence is given upon him let him be condemned ...
let his children be fatherless and his wife a widow.

Psalm 109, appointed for the 22nd Day

The nap Wexford had prescribed for him would have been
attractive on a dull day, but not this morning when the sky was
blue and cloudless and the sun promised tropical heat by midday.
Moreover, Burden remembered that he had not made his bed for
three days. Better have that shower and that shave instead.

After a canteen breakfast of two eggs and a couple of
rashers of the greenback he liked, he had made up his mind
what he was going to do. An hour could easily be spared. He
drove northwards along the High Street with all the car
windows down, past the shops, over the Kingsbrook Bridge,
past the Olive and Dove and out on to the Stowerton road.
Apart from a new house here and there, a supermarket on the
site of the old police station, and aggressive road signs all over
the place, things had not changed much in sixteen years. The
meadows, the tall trees burdened with the heavy foliage of July,
the little weatherboard cottages were much the same as when
Alice Flower had seen them on her shopping trips in the
Daimler. There would have been less traffic then, he thought.
He braked, pulled in and raised his eyebrows at the youth on a
motor-bike who, overtaking the oncoming stream, had missed
him by inches.

The lane where Victor's Piece was must be somewhere
about here. Those circumstantial details Wexford had been so
tantalising about were coming back to him from his own
memory. Surely he had read about a bus stop and a telephone
box at the end of the lane? Would these be the meadows he
remembered reading that Painter had crossed, desperate to
conceal a bundle of bloodstained clothing?

Here was the phone box now. He indicated left and turned slowly into the lane. For a short way its surface was metalled, then it petered out into a track ending in a gate. There were only three houses: a white-plastered semi-detached pair and opposite them the late Victorian pile he had described as 'a hideous dump'.

He had never been as near to it as this before, but he saw nothing to make him change his opinion. The roof of grey slates had been constructed — tortured almost — into a number of steep gables. Two of these dominated the front of the house, but there was a third on the right hand side and out of it grew another smaller one that apparently overlooked the back. Each gable was criss-crossed with timbering, some of it inexpertly carved into chevrons and all painted a dull bottle green. In places the plaster between the wood had fallen away, exposing rough pinkish brickwork. Ivy, the same shade of green, spread its flat leaves and its rope-like grey tendrils from the foot of the downstairs windows to the highest gable where a lattice flapped open. There it had crept and burrowed into the mealy wall, prising the window frame away from the bricks.

Burden observed the garden with a countryman's eye. Never had he seen such a fine selection of weeds. The fertile black soil, cultivated and tended for many years, now nourished docks with leaves as thick and glossy as rubber plants, puce-headed thistles, nettles four feet tall. The gravel paths were choked with grass and mildewed groundsel. Only the clarity of the air and the soft brilliance of sunlight prevented the place from being actually sinister.

The front door was locked. No doubt this window beside it belonged to the drawing room. Burden could not help wondering with a certain wry humour what insensitive administrator had decreed that this scene of an old woman's murder should be for years the home — indeed the last refuge — of other old women. But they were gone now. The place looked as if it had been empty for years.

Through the window he could see a large shadowy room. In the grate of the amber-coloured marble fireplace someone had prudently placed crumpled newspaper to catch the drifts of soot. Wexford had said there had been blood all over that

16

fireplace. There, just in front of the copper kerb, was where the body must have lain.

He made his way round the side, pushing through a shrubbery where elders and strong little birches were threatening to oust the lilac. The panes in the kitchen casement were blurred with dirt and there was no kitchen door, only a back door that apparently opened off the end of the central passage. The Victorians, he reflected, were not too hot on design. Two doors with a straight passage between them! The draught would be appalling.

By now he was in the back garden but he literally could not see the wood for the trees. Nature had gone berserk at Victor's Piece and the coach house itself was almost totally obscured by creeper. He strolled across the shady flagged yard, made cool by the jutting walls of the house, and found himself skirting a conservatory, attached apparently to a kind of morning or breakfast room. It housed a vine, long dead and quite leafless.

So that was Victor's Piece. Pity he couldn't get inside, but he would, in any case, have to get back. Out of long habit — and partly to set a good example — he had closed all the windows of his car and locked the doors. Inside it was like an oven. He drove out of the broken gateway, into the lane and joined the traffic stream on the Stowerton road.

A greater contrast between the building he had left and the building he entered could hardly have been found. Fine weather suited Kingsmarkham Police Station. Wexford sometimes said that the architect of this new building must have designed it while holidaying in the South of France. It was white, boxy, unnecessarily vast and ornamented here and there with frescoes that owed something to the Elgin marbles.

On this July morning its whiteness glared and glistened. But if its façade seemed to welcome and bask in the sun its occupants did not. There was far too much glass. All right, said Wexford, for hothouse plants or tropical fish, but a mixed blessing for an elderly Anglo-Saxon policeman with high blood pressure and a low resistance to heat. The telephone receiver slid about in his large hand and when he had finished talking to Henry Archery he pulled down the venetian blinds.

'Heat wave's coming,' he said to Burden. 'I reckon your wife's picked a good week.'

Burden looked up from the statement he had begun to read. Lean as a greyhound, his face thin and acute, he often had the hound's instinct for scenting the unusual, coupled with a man's eager imagination.

'Things always seem to happen in a heat wave,' he said. 'Our sort of things, I mean.'

'Get away,' said Wexford. 'Things are always happening around here.' He raised his spiky toothbrush brows. 'What's happening today,' he said, 'is Archery. He's coming at two.'

'Did he say what it's all about?'

'He's leaving that for this afternoon. Very la-di-da manner he's got with him. All part of the mystique of how to be a gentleman on nothing a year. One thing, he's got a transcript of the trial so I shan't have to go through the whole thing again.'

'That'll have cost him something. He must be keen.'

Wexford looked at his watch and rose. 'Got to get over to the court,' he said. 'Polish off those villains who lost me my night's sleep. Look, Mike, I reckon we deserve a bit of gracious living and I don't fancy the Carousel's steak pie for my lunch. What about popping into the Olive and booking a table for one sharp?'

Burden smiled. It suited him well enough. Once in a blue moon Wexford would insist on their lunching or even dining in comparative style.

'It shall be done,' he said.

The Olive and Dove is the best hostelry in Kingsmarkham that can properly be called an hotel. By a stretch of the imagination the Queen's Head might be described as an inn, but the Dragon and the Crusader cannot claim to be more than pubs. The Olive, as locals invariably call it, is situated in the High Street at the Stowerton end of Kingsmarkham, facing the exquisite Georgian residence of Mr Missal, the Stowerton car dealer. It is partly Georgian itself, but it is a hybrid structure with lingering relics of Tudor and a wing that claims to be pre-Tudor. In every respect it conforms to what nice middle-class people mean when they talk about a 'nice' hotel. There are always three waiters, the chambermaids are staid and often elderly, the bath water is hot, the food as well as can be expected and the A.A. Guide has given it two stars.

Burden had booked his table by phone. When he walked into the dining room just before one he saw to his satisfaction that he had been placed by the High Street window. Here it was just out of the sun and the geraniums in the window box looked fresh and even dewy. Girls waiting on the other side of the street for the Pomfret bus wore cotton frocks and sandals.

Wexford marched in at five past. 'I don't know why he can't get up at half twelve like they do in Sewingbury,' he grumbled. 'He', Burden knew, meant the chairman of the Kingsmarkham bench. 'God, it was hot in court. What are we going to eat?'

'Roast duck,' said Burden firmly.

'All right, if you twist my arm. As long as they don't mix a lot of rubbish up with it. You know what I mean, sweet corn and bananas.' He took the menu, scowling. 'Look at that, Polynesian chicken. What do they think we are, aborigines?'

'I went and had a look at Victor's Piece this morning,' said Burden while they waited for the duck to come.

'Did you now? I see it's up for sale. There's a card in the agent's window with a highly misleading photograph. They're asking six thousand. Bit steep when you think Roger Primero got less than two for it in 1951.'

'I suppose it's changed hands several times since then?'

'Once or twice before the old folks moved in. Thanks,' he said to the waiter. 'No we don't want any wine. Two halves of bitter.' He spread his napkin over his capacious lap and to Burden's controlled distaste sprinkled wing and orange sauce liberally with pepper.

'Was Roger Primero the heir?'

'One of the heirs. Mrs Primero died intestate. Remember I told you she'd only got ten thousand to leave and that was divided equally between Roger and his two younger sisters. He's a rich man now, but however he got his money it wasn't from his grandmother. All kinds of pies he's got his finger in — oil, property development, shipping — he's a real tycoon.'

'I've seen him around, I think.'

'You must have. He's very conscious of his status as a landowner since he bought Forby Hall. Goes out with the Pomfret hounds and all that.'

'How old is he?' Burden asked.

'Well, he was twenty-two when his grandmother was killed. That makes him about thirty-eight now. The sisters were much younger. Angela was ten and Isabel nine.'

'I seem to remember he gave evidence at the trial.'

Wexford pushed his plate away, signalled rather imperiously to the waiter and ordered two portions of apple pie. Burden knew that his chief's notion of gracious living was somewhat limited.

'Roger Primero had been visiting his grandmother that Sunday,' Wexford said. 'He was working in a solicitor's office in Sewingbury at the time and he used to make quite a habit of having Sunday tea at Victor's Piece. Maybe he had his eye on a share of the loot when Mrs Primero went — God knows he hadn't a bean in those days — but he seemed genuinely fond of her. It's certainly a fact that after we'd seen the body and sent for him from Sewingbury as next of kin, we had to restrain him forcibly from going over to the coach house and laying violent hands on Painter. I daresay his grandmother and Alice made a lot of him, you know, buttered him up and waited on him. I told you Mrs Primero had her affections. There'd been a family quarrel but apparently it didn't extend to the grandchildren. Once or twice Roger had taken his little sisters down to Victor's Piece and they'd all got on very well together.'

'Old people usually do get on well with kids,' said Burden.

'They had to be the right kind of children, Mike. Angela and Isabel, yes, and she had a very soft spot for young Liz Crilling.'

Burden put down his spoon and stared at the Chief Inspector.

'I thought you said you'd read all this up at the time?' Wexford said suspiciously. 'Don't say it was a long time ago. My customers are always saying that to me and it makes me see red. If you read the account of that trial you must remember that Elizabeth Crilling, aged precisely five at the time, found Mrs Primero's body.'

'I assure you I can't remember, sir.' That must have been the day he'd missed, the day he hadn't bothered with the papers because he'd been nervous about an interview. 'She didn't appear at the trial, surely?'

'Not at that age — there are limits. Besides, although she was actually the first to go into the drawing room and come upon the body, her mother was with her.'

'Digressing a little,' Burden said, 'I don't quite get this stuff about the right kind of children. Mrs Crilling lives over there in Glebe Road.' He turned to the window and waved his hand in the direction of the least attractive part of Kingsmarkham where long streets of small terraced brown houses had sprung up between the wars. 'She and the girl live in half a house, they haven't a penny to bless themselves with . . .'

'They've come down a lot,' said Wexford. 'In September 1950 Crilling himself was still alive — he died of T.B. soon after — and they lived opposite Victor's Piece.'

'In one of those white semi-detached places?'

'That's right. A Mrs White and her son lived next door. Mrs Crilling was about thirty at the time, little bit over thirty.'

'You're joking,' said Burden derisively. 'That makes her only in her late forties now.'

'Look, Mike, people can say what they like about hard work and childbearing and all that. I tell you there's nothing like mental illness to make a woman look old before her time. And you know as well as I do Mrs Crilling's been in and out of mental hospitals for years.' He paused as their coffee came and pursed his lips censoriously at the anaemic brown liquid.

'You did say black, sir?' the waiter asked.

Wexford gave a sort of grunt. The church clock struck the last quarter. As the reverberation died away, he said to Burden:

'Shall I keep the parson waiting ten minutes?'

Burden said neutrally, 'That's up to you, sir. You were going to tell me how Mrs Primero and the Crilling woman became friends. I suppose they were friends?'

'Not a doubt of it. Mrs Crilling was ladylike enough in those days and she had a way with her, sycophantic, sucking up, *you* know. Besides, Crilling had been an accountant or something, just enough of a professional man, anyway, in Mrs

Primero's eyes to make his wife a lady. Mrs Crilling was always popping over to Victor's Piece and she always took the child with her. God knows, they must have been pretty close. Elizabeth called Mrs Primero "Granny Rose" just as Roger and his sisters did.'

'So she "popped over" that Sunday night and found Granny Rose dead?' Burden hazarded.

'It wasn't as simple as that. Mrs Crilling had been making the kid a party frock. She finished it by about six, dressed Elizabeth up and wanted to take her over and show her off to Mrs Primero. Mind you, she and Alice Flower were always at loggerheads. There was a good bit of jealousy there, spheres of influence and so on. So Mrs Crilling waited until Alice had gone off to church and went over alone, intending to go back and fetch the child if Mrs Primero was awake. She dozed a good bit, you see, being so old.

'That first time — it was about twenty past six — Mrs Primero *was* asleep and Mrs Crilling didn't go in. She just tapped on the drawing room window. When the old woman didn't stir she went back and returned again later. By the way, she saw the empty scuttle through the window so she knew Painter hadn't yet been in with the coal.'

'You mean that Painter came in and did the deed between Mrs Crilling's visits?' Burden asked.

'She didn't go back again till seven. The back door had to be left unlocked for Painter, so she and the child went in, called out "yoo-hoo" or some damn' thing, and marched into the drawing room when they didn't get an answer. Elizabeth went first — more's the pity — and Bob's your uncle!'

'Blimey,' said Burden, 'that poor kid!'

'Yes,' Wexford murmured, 'yes ... Well, much as I should like to while away the rest of the afternoon, reminiscing over the coffee cups, I do have to see this clerical bloke.'

They both got up. Wexford paid the bill, leaving a rather obviously exact ten per cent for a tip.

'I can't see where the parson comes into it at all,' Burden said when they were in the car.

'He can't be an abolitionist because they've done away with the death penalty. As I say, he's writing a book, expects to make a big thing out of it and that's why he's laid out good money on a transcript.'

'Or he's a prospective buyer of Victor's Piece. He's a haunted house merchant and he thinks he's got another Borley Rectory.'

An unfamiliar car stood on the forecourt of the police station. The numberplate was not local and beside it was a little metal label that bore the name Essex with the county coat of arms of three scimitars on a red field.

'We shall soon know,' said Wexford.

CHAPTER THREE

There are false witnesses risen up against me and such as speak wrong.

Psalm 27, appointed for the 5th Day

In general Wexford disliked the clergy. To him the dog collar was like a slipped halo, indicating a false saintliness, probable hypocrisy and massive self-regard. As he saw it vicars were not vicarious enough. Most of them expected you to worship God in them.

He did not associate them with good looks and charm. Henry Archery, therefore, caused him slight surprise. He was possibly not much younger than Wexford himself, but he was still slim and exceedingly good-looking, and he was wearing an ordinary rather light-coloured suit and an ordinary collar and tie. His hair was thick enough and fair enough for the grey not to show much, his skin was tanned and his features had a pure evenly cut regularity.

During the first preliminary small-talk remarks Wexford had noticed the beauty of his voice. You felt it would be a pleasure to hear him read aloud. As he showed him to a chair and sat down opposite him, Wexford chuckled to himself. He was picturing a group of tired ageing female parishioners working their fingers to the bone for the pitiful reward of this man's smile. Archery was not smiling now and he looked anything but relaxed.

'I'm familiar with the case, Chief Inspector,' he began. 'I've read the official transcript of the trial and I've discussed the whole thing with Colonel Griswold.'

'What exactly do you want to know, then?' Wexford asked in his blunt way.

Archery took a deep breath and said rather too quickly:

'I want you to tell me that somewhere in your mind there

24

is just the faintest doubt, the shadow of a doubt, of Painter's guilt.'

So that was it, or part of it. Burden with his theories that the parson was a Primero relative or seeking to buy the Primero house couldn't have been more wrong. This man, whatever axe he might be grinding, was bent on whitewashing Painter.

Wexford frowned and after a moment said, 'Can't be done. Painter did it all right.' He set his jaw stubbornly. 'If you want to quote me in your book you're quite welcome. You can say that after sixteen years Wexford still maintains that Painter was guilty beyond the shadow of a doubt.'

'What book is this?' Archery inclined his handsome head courteously. His eyes were brown and now they looked bewildered. Then he laughed. It was a nice laugh and it was the first time Wexford had heard it. 'I don't write books,' he said. 'Well, I did once contribute a chapter to a work on Abyssinian cats but that hardly . . .'

Abyssinian cats. Bloody great red cats, thought Wexford. Whatever next? 'Why are you interested in Painter, Mr Archery?'

Archery hesitated. The sun showed up lines on his face that Wexford had not realised were there. Funny, he thought ruefully, how dark women age slower than fair ones but the reverse was true of men.

'My reasons are very personal, Chief Inspector. I can't suppose that they would interest you. But I can assure you that there's no possibility of my publishing anything you tell me.'

Well, he had promised Griswold — as to that, he didn't have much choice. Hadn't he, in any case, already resigned himself to giving up most of the afternoon to this clergyman? Weariness was at last beginning to gain a hold on him. He might be equal to reminiscing, going over past familiar words and scenes; on this hot afternoon he was quite unequal to anything more exacting. Probably the personal reasons — and he confessed mentally to an almost childish curiosity about them — would emerge in due course. There was something frank and boyish in his visitor's face which made Wexford think he would not be particularly discreet.

'What d'you want me to tell you?' he asked.

'Why you are so determined Painter was guilty. Of course I don't know any more about this sort of thing than the average layman, but it seems to me there were a good many gaps in the evidence. There were other people involved, people who had quite definite interests in Mrs Primero's death.'

Wexford said coldly, 'I'm fully prepared to go over any points with you, sir.'

'Now?'

'Certainly now. Have you got that transcript with you?'

Archery produced it from a very battered leather briefcase. His hands were long and thin but not womanish. They reminded Wexford of saints' hands in what he called "churchy" paintings. For five minutes or so he scanned the papers in silence, refreshing his memory on tiny points. Then he put them down and raised his eyes to Archery's face.

'We have to go back to Saturday, September 23rd,' he said, 'the day before the murder. Painter didn't appear with the coal at all that evening. The two old women waited until nearly eight o'clock when the fire was almost out, and Mrs Primero said she would go to bed. Alice Flower was incensed at this and went out to get what she called "a few lumps".'

'That was when she hurt her leg,' Archery said eagerly.

'It wasn't a serious injury but it made Mrs Primero angry and she blamed Painter. At about ten on the following morning she sent Alice down to the coach house to tell Painter she wanted to see him at eleven-thirty sharp. He came up ten minutes late, Alice showed him into the drawing room and afterwards she heard him and Mrs Primero quarrelling.'

'This brings me to the first point I want to raise,' Archery said. He flipped through the transcript and, putting his finger at the beginning of a paragraph, passed it to Wexford. 'This, as you know, is part of Painter's own evidence. He doesn't deny the quarrel. He admits that Mrs Primero threatened him with dismissal. He also says here that Mrs Primero finally came round to see his point of view. She refused to give him a rise because she said that would put ideas into his head and he would only ask for another increase in a few months' time. Instead she'd give him what she understood was called a bonus.'

'I remember all that well,' Wexford said impatiently. 'He

said she told him to go upstairs and into her bedroom where he'd find a handbag in her wardrobe. He was to bring that handbag down to her and this, he said, he did. There was about two hundred pounds in the handbag and this he could have, take it away in the handbag and look upon it as a bonus on condition he was absolutely circumspect about bringing the coal at the required times.' He coughed. 'I never believed a word of it and neither did the jury.'

'Why not?' Archery asked quietly.

God, thought Wexford, this was going to be a long session.

'Firstly, because the stairs at Victor's Piece run up between the drawing room and the kitchen. Alice Flower was in the kitchen cooking the lunch. She had remarkably good hearing for her age, but she never heard Painter go up those stairs. And, believe me, he was a big heavy lout if ever there was one.' Archery winced faintly at this but Wexford went on, 'Secondly, Mrs Primero would never have sent the gardener upstairs to poke about in her bedroom. Not unless I'm very mistaken in her character. She would have got Alice to have fetched the money on some pretext or other.'

'She might not have wanted Alice to know about it.'

'That's for sure,' Wexford retorted sharply. 'She wouldn't have. I said on some pretext or other.' That made the parson draw in his horns. Wexford said very confidently, 'In the third place Mrs Primero had a reputation for being rather mean. Alice had been with her for half a century but she'd never given Alice anything bar her wages and an extra pound at Christmas.' He jabbed at the page. 'Look, she says so here in black and white. We know Painter wanted money. The night before when he hadn't brought the coal he'd been drinking up at the Dragon with a pal of his from Stowerton. The pal had a motor-bike to sell and he'd offered it to Painter for a bit less than two hundred pounds. Apparently Painter hadn't a hope of getting the money but he asked his friend to hold on to the bike for a couple of days and he'd contact him the minute anything came up. You're saying he got the money before noon on Sunday. I say he stole it after he brutally murdered his employer in the evening. If you're right, why didn't he get in touch with his friend on Sunday afternoon? There's a phone box at the bottom of the lane. We checked with the pal, he didn't move out of his house all day and the phone never rang.'

It was a very tempest of fact and Archery yielded, or appeared to yield, before it. He said only:

'You're saying, I think, that Painter went to the wardrobe after he'd killed Mrs Primero in the evening. There was no blood on the inside of the wardrobe.'

'For one thing he wore rubber gloves to do the deed. Anyway, the prosecution's case was that he stunned her with the flat side of the axe blade, took the money, and when he came downstairs, finished her off in a panic.'

Archery gave a slight shiver. 'Doesn't that strike you as odd,' he then said, 'that if Painter did it he should have been so transparent about it?'

'Some are. They're stupid, you see.' Wexford said it derisively, his mouth curling. He still had no notion what Archery's interest in Painter might be, but that he was pro-Painter was apparent. 'Stupid,' he said again, intent on flicking the clergyman on the raw. Another wince from Archery rewarded him. 'They think you'll believe them. All they've got to say is it must have been a tramp or a burglar and you'll go away satisfied. Painter was one of those. That old tramp thing,' he said. 'When did you last *see* a tramp? More than sixteen years ago, I'll bet.'

'Let's come to the murder itself,' Archery said quietly.

'By all means.' Again Wexford took the transcript, gathering with a quick glance the information he needed. 'Now, then,' he began, 'Painter said he went over to fetch the coal at half past six. He remembered the time — twenty-five past six when he left the coach house — because his wife said five minutes to go before the child's bedtime. The time's not all that important, anyway. We know it was between twenty past six and seven o'clock that she was killed. Painter went over, chopped some wood and cut his finger. Or so he said. He certainly did cut his finger — cut it deliberately.'

Archery ignored this last. 'He and Mrs Primero belonged to the same blood group,' he said.

'They were both Group O. They weren't quite so accurate about the minute grouping of blood sixteen years ago as they are now. It was handy for Painter, that. But it didn't do him any real good.'

The clergyman crossed his legs and leaned back. Wexford could see he was trying to appear relaxed and making a poor job of it. 'I believe you personally went to interview Painter after the crime was discovered?'

'We were round at the coach house by a quarter to eight. Painter was out. I asked Mrs Painter where he was and she said he'd come back from the big house some time after six-thirty, washed his hands and gone straight out again. He'd told her he was going to Stowerton to see his friend. We'd only been there about ten minutes when he came in. His story didn't stand up, there was far too much blood around to have come from a cut finger and — well, you know the rest. It's all down there. I charged him on the spot.'

The transcript fluttered a little in Archery's hand. He could not keep his fingers quite steady. 'In evidence,' he said, speaking slowly and evenly, 'Painter said he hadn't been to Stowerton. "I waited at the bus stop at the end of the lane, but the bus never came. I saw the police cars turn into the lane and I wondered what was up. Presently I felt a bit faint on account of my finger bleeding a lot. I came back to my flat. I thought my wife might know what it was all about." ' After a pause, he added with a kind of pleading eagerness, 'That doesn't sound like the evidence of the complete moron you make him out to be.'

Wexford answered him patiently as if he were talking to a precocious teenager. 'They edit these things, Mr Archery. They condense them, make them sound coherent. Believe me. You weren't in court and I was. As to the truth of that statement, I was in one of those police cars and I was keeping my eyes open. We overtook the Stowerton bus and turned left into the lane. There wasn't anyone waiting at the bus stop.'

'I imagine you mean that while he said he was at the bus stop he was in fact hiding some clothes.'

'Of course he was hiding the clothes! When he was working he habitually wore a raincoat. You'll see that in Mrs Crilling's evidence and in Alice's. Sometimes it hung in the coach house and sometimes on a hook behind the back door of Victor's Piece. Painter said he had worn it that evening and had left it hanging on the back door. The raincoat couldn't be found. Both Alice and Roger Primero said they remembered having seen it on the back door that afternoon, but Mrs Crilling was certain it wasn't there when she brought Elizabeth in at seven.'

'You finally found the raincoat rolled up in a ball under a hedge two fields away from the bus stop.'

'The raincoat plus a pullover,' Wexford retorted, 'and a pair of rubber gloves. The lot was sodden with blood.'

'But anyone could have worn the raincoat and you couldn't identify the pullover.'

'Alice Flower went so far as to say it looked like one Painter sometimes wore.'

Archery gave a deep sigh. For a time he had been firing questions and statements briskly at Wexford, but suddenly he had fallen silent. Little more than indecision showed on his face. Wexford waited. At last, he thought, Archery had reached a point where it was going to become necessary to reveal those 'personal reasons'. A struggle was going on within him and he said in an artificial tone:

'What about Painter's wife?'

'A wife cannot be compelled to give evidence against her husband. As you know, she didn't appear at the trial. She and the child went off somewhere and a couple of years later I heard she married again.'

He stared at Archery, raising his eyebrows. Something he had said had made the clergyman's mind up for him. A slight flush coloured Archery's even tan. The brown eyes were very bright as he leaned forward, tense again.

'That child . . .'

'What of her? She was asleep in her cot when we searched Painter's bedroom and that's the only time I saw her. She was four or five.'

Archery said jerkily, 'She's twenty-one now and she's a very beautiful young woman.'

'I'm not surprised. Painter was a nice enough looking fellow if you like the type, and Mrs Painter was pretty.' Wexford stopped. Archery was a clergyman. Had Painter's daughter taken after her father and somehow come into his care as a result of her transgressions? Archery could be a prison visitor.

It was right up his street, Wexford thought nastily. Anger rose in his throat as he wondered if all this sparring discussion had been engineered merely because Archery wanted his help in getting the right psychological approach to a convicted thief or confidence woman. 'What about her?' he snapped. Griswold could go to hell! 'Now come on, sir, you'd better tell me and have done.'

'I have a son, Chief Inspector, an only child. He also is twenty-one . . .'

'Well?'

Obviously the clergyman had difficulty in framing the words. He hesitated and pressed his long hands together. At last he said diffidently and in a low voice, 'He wishes to marry Miss Painter.' When Wexford started and stared at him, he added, 'Or Miss Kershaw, as her legal name now is.'

Wexford was all at sea. He was astonished, a rare thing for him, and he felt a sharp-edged excitement. But he had shown all the surprise he thought consistent with policy and now he spoke soberly.

'You must excuse me, Mr Archery, but I can't see how your son, the son of an Anglican clergyman, came to meet a girl in Miss Painter's — er, Miss Kershaw's — position.'

'They met at Oxford,' Archery said easily.

'At the *university*?'

'That is so. Miss Kershaw is quite an intelligent young woman.' Archery gave a slight smile. 'She's reading Modern Greats. Tipped for a First, I'm told.'

CHAPTER FOUR

If any of you know cause or just impediment why these two persons should not be joined together in holy matrimony, ye are to declare it.

The Banns of Marriage

If he had been asked to predict the future of such a one as Theresa Painter, what would he have foreseen for her? Children like her, Wexford reflected as he recovered from his second shock, children like Painter's little girl started life with a liability and a stain. The surviving parent, well-meaning relatives and cruel schoolfellows often made matters worse. He had hardly thought about the fate of the child until today. Now, thinking quickly, he supposed he would have counted her lucky to have become an anonymous manual worker with perhaps already a couple of petty convictions.

Instead to Theresa Painter had apparently come the greatest blessings of civilised life: brains, advanced education, beauty, friendship with people like this vicar, an engagement to this vicar's son.

Wexford cast his mind back to the first of only three encounters with Mrs Painter. A quarter to eight it had been on that Sunday in September. He and the sergeant with him had knocked on the door at the foot of the coach house stairs and Mrs Painter had come down to let them in. Whatever might have been fashionable in London at that time, the young women of Kingsmarkham were still doing their hair in a big pile on the forehead with tight curls falling to the shoulders. Mrs Painter was no exception. Hers was naturally fair, her face was powdered and her mouth painted diffidently red. Respectable provincial matrons did not go in for eye make-up in 1950 and Mrs Painter was of all things respectable. There seemed to be very little else to her. On her dry fine skin lines had already begun to form, little indentations which marked a regular prudish pursing of the lips, a setting of the chin that accompanied an outraged flounce.

She had the same attitude to the police as others might have to bugs or mice. When they came upstairs she alternated her replies to their questions with reiterated remarks that it was a disgrace to have them in the house. She had the blankest, most obtuse blue eyes he had ever seen on anyone. At no time, even when they were about to take Painter away, did she show the least pity or the least horror, only this fixated dread of what people would think if they found the police had been questioning her husband.

Perhaps she had not been so stupid as he had thought. Somewhere in that pretty respectable mouse and that great hunk of sub-humanity, her husband, must have been the spring from which their daughter drew her intelligence. 'Quite an intelligent girl,' Archery had said casually. Good God, thought Wexford, remembering how he had boasted when his own daughter got eight O Level passes. Good God! What were Modern Greats, anyway? Were they the same as Mods and did that mean Modern Languages? He had a vague idea that this might be the esoteric and deliberately deceptive name given to Philosophy and Political Economy! He almost whistled. Painter's daughter reading — yes, that was the term, reading — philosophy! It made you think all right. Why, it made you doubt . . .

'Mr Archery,' he said, 'you're quite sure this *is* Herbert Arthur Painter's girl?'

'Of course I'm sure, Chief Inspector. She told me.' He looked almost defiantly at Wexford. Perhaps he thought the policeman would laugh at his next words. 'She is as good as she is beautiful,' he said. Wexford's expression remained unaltered. 'She came to stay with us at Whitsun. It was the first time we'd seen her, though naturally our son had written and told us about her. We took to her at once.

'Chief Inspector, times have changed since I was at college. I had to face the possibility that my son would meet some girl at Oxford, perhaps want to marry her at an age when I'd thought of myself as still a boy and when Orders were a lifetime away. I'd see my friends' children marry at twenty-one and I was prepared to try and manage something for him, give him something to start life on. All I hoped was that the girl would be someone we could like and understand.

'Miss Kershaw — I'll use that name if you don't mind — is just what I would have chosen for him myself, beautiful, graceful, well-mannered, easy to talk to. Oh, she does her best to hide her looks in the uniform they all wear nowadays, long shaggy hair, trousers, great black duffel coat — you know the kind of thing. But they all dress like that. The point is she can't hide them.

'My wife is a little impulsive. She was hinting about the wedding before Theresa had been with us for twenty-four hours. I found it hard to understand why the young people were so diffident about it. Charles's letters had been paeans of praise and I could see they were deeply in love. Then she told us. She came out with it quite baldly. She said — I remember the very words — 'I think you ought to know something about me, Mrs Archery. My father's name was Painter and he was hanged for killing an old woman.'

'At first my wife didn't believe it. She thought it was some sort of game. Charles said, "It's true. It doesn't matter. People are what they are, not what their parents did." Then Theresa — we call her Tess — said, "It wouldn't matter if he had done it, only he didn't. I told you *why* he was hanged. I didn't mean he'd done it." Then she began to cry.'

'Why does she call herself Kershaw?'

'It's her stepfather's name. He must be a very remarkable man, Chief Inspector. He's an electrical engineer, but . . .' You needn't come that rude mechanicals stuff with me, thought Wexford crossly. '. . . but he must be a most intelligent, perceptive and kind person. The Kershaws have two children of their own, but as far as I can gather, Mr Kershaw has treated Tess with no less affection than his own son and daughter. She says it was his love that helped her to bear — well, what I can only call the stigma of her father's crime when she learnt about it at the age of twelve. He followed her progress at school, encouraged her in every way and fostered her wish to get a County Major Scholarship.'

34

'You mentioned "the stigma of her father's crime". I thought you said she thinks he didn't do it?'

'My dear Chief Inspector, she *knows he didn't do it.*'

Wexford said slowly, 'Mr Archery, I'm sure I don't have to tell a man like yourself that when we talk of somebody *knowing* something we mean that what they know is a fact, something that's true beyond a reasonable doubt. We mean that the majority of other people *know* it too. In other words, it's history, it's written down in the books, it's common knowledge.' He paused. 'Now I and the Law Lords and the official records and what your son means when he talks about the Establishment, know beyond any reasonable doubt, that Painter did kill Mrs Rose Primero.'

'Her mother told her so,' said Archery. 'She told her that she had absolute irrefutable personal knowledge that Tess's father did not kill Mrs Primero.'

Wexford shrugged and smiled. 'People believe what they want to believe. The mother thought it was the best thing for her daughter. If I'd been in her shoes I daresay I'd have said the same.'

'I don't think it was like that,' Archery said stubbornly. 'Tess says her mother is a very unemotional woman. She never talks about Painter, never discusses him at all. She just says quite calmly, "Your father never killed anybody" and beyond that she won't say any more.'

'Because she can't say any more. Look, sir, I think you're taking a rather romantic view of this. You're visualising the Painters as a devoted couple, kind of merry peasants, love in a cottage and all that. It wasn't like that. Believe me, Painter was no loss to her. I'm certain in my own mind he was in the habit of striking her just when the fancy took him. As far as he was concerned, she was just his woman, someone to cook his meals, wash his clothes and — well,' he added brutally, 'someone to go to bed with.'

Archery said stiffly, 'I don't see that any of that's material.'

'Don't you? You're picturing some sort of declaration of innocence plus incontrovertible proof made to the one person he loved and whom he knew would believe in him. Forgive me, but that's a load of rubbish. Apart from the few minutes when he came back to the coach house to wash his hands — and incidentally hide the money — he was never alone with her. And he couldn't have told her then. He wasn't supposed to know about it. D'you understand me? He could have told her he had done it, he couldn't have told her he had *not*.

'Then we came. We found blood flecks in the sink and faint blood marks on the kitchen wall where he'd stripped off that pullover. As soon as he came back he took the bandage off his hand to show us the cut and he handed the bandage to his wife. But he didn't speak to her, didn't even appeal to her for support. He made just one reference to her . . .'

'Yes?'

'We found the handbag with the money in it under the mattress in their double bed. Why hadn't Painter told his wife if he'd been given that money in the morning? Here it is, find it in your transcript. "I knew the wife would want to get her hooks on it. She was always nagging me to buy things for the flat." That's all he said and he didn't even look at her. We charged him and he said, "O.K., but you're making a big mistake. It was a tramp done it." He came straight down the stairs with us. He didn't kiss his wife and he didn't ask to go in and see his child.'

'She must have seen him in prison?'

'With a prison officer present. Look, sir, you appear to be satisfied and so do all the parties concerned. Surely that's the main thing. You must forgive me if I can't agree with you.'

Silently Archery took a snapshot from his wallet and laid it on the desk. Wexford picked it up. Presumably it had been taken in the vicarage garden. There was a great magnolia tree in the background, a tree as tall as the house it partly concealed. It was covered with waxen cup flowers. Under its branches stood a boy and a girl, their arms round each other. The boy was tall and fair. He was smiling and he was plainly Archery's son. Wexford wasn't particularly interested in him.

The girl's face was in sad repose. She was looking into the camera with large steady eyes. Light-coloured hair fell over her forehead in a fringe and down to the shoulders of a typical undergraduate's shirtwaister, faded, tightly belted and with a crumpled skirt. Her waist was tiny, her bust full. Wexford saw the mother again, only this girl was holding a boy's hand instead of a bloody rag.

'Very charming,' he said dryly. 'I hope she'll make your son happy.' He handed the photograph back. 'No reason why she shouldn't.'

A mixture of emotions, anger, pain, resentment, flared in the clergyman's eyes. Interestedly, Wexford watched him.

'I do not know what or whom to believe,' Archery said unhappily, 'and while I'm in this state of uncertainty, Chief Inspector, I'm not in favour of the marriage. No, that's putting it too coolly.' He shook his head vehemently. 'I'm bitterly, bitterly against it,' he said.

'And the girl, Painter's daughter?'

'She believed — perhaps accepts is the better word — in her father's innocence, but she realises others may not. When it comes to it, I don't think she would marry my son while his mother and I feel as we do.'

'What are you afraid of, Mr Archery?'

'Heredity.'

'A very chancy thing, heredity.'

'Have you children, Chief Inspector?'

'I've got two girls.'

'Are they married?'

'One is.'

'And who is her father-in-law?'

For the first time Wexford felt superior to this clergyman. A kind of *Schadenfreude* possessed him. 'He's an architect, as a matter of fact, Tory councillor for the North Ward here.'

'I see.' Archery bowed his head. 'And do your grandchildren already build palaces with wooden bricks, Mr Wexford?' Wexford said nothing. The only sign of his first grandchild's existence was so far evinced in its mother's morning sickness. 'I shall watch mine from their cradle, waiting to see them drawn towards objects with sharp edges.'

'You said if you objected she wouldn't marry him.'

'They're in love with each other. I can't . . .'

'Who's going to know? Palm Kershaw off as her father.'

'I shall know,' said Archery. 'Already I can see Painter when I look at her. Instead of her mouth and her eyes I can see his thick lips and bloodlust. It's the same blood, Chief Inspector, the blood that mingled with Mrs Primero's, on the floor, on the clothes, down the water pipes. That blood will be in my grandchild.' He seemed to realise that he had allowed himself to be carried away, for he stopped suddenly, blushed, and shut his eyes briefly as if wincing at the sight he had described.

Wexford said gently, 'I wish I could help you, Mr Archery, but the case is closed, over, finished. There is nothing more I can do.'

Archery shrugged and quoted softly, almost as if he could not stop himself, ' "He took water and washed his hands before the multitude, saying, I am innocent of the blood of this just person . . ." ' Then he jumped up, his expression suddenly contrite. 'Forgive me, Chief Inspector. That was an appalling thing to say. May I tell you what I intend to do?'

'Pontius Pilate, that's me,' said Wexford. 'So see you show more respect in future.'

Burden grinned. 'What exactly did he want, sir?'

'Firstly for me to tell him Painter may have been unjustly executed, which I can't. Damn it all, it would be tantamount to saying I didn't know my job. It was my first murder case, Mike, and it was fortunate for me it was so straightforward. Archery's going to do a spot of enquiry on his own. Hopeless after sixteen years but it's useless telling him. Secondly, he wanted my permission to go round hunting up all the witnesses. Wanted my support if they came round here, complaining and foaming at the mouth.'

'And all he's got to go on,' said Burden thoughtfully, 'is Mrs Painter's sentimental belief in her husband's innocence?'

'Aah, that's nothing! That's a load of hooey. If you got the chop, wouldn't Jean tell John and Pat you were innocent? Wouldn't my wife tell the girls? It's natural. Painter didn't make any last-minute confessions — you know what the prison authorities are like for watching out for things like that. No, she dreamed it up and convinced herself.'

'Has Archery ever met her?'

'Not yet, but he's making a day of it. She and her second husband live in Purley and he's got himself an invite for tea.'

'You say the girl told him at Whitsun. Why has he waited so long? It must be a couple of months.'

'I asked him that. He said that for the first couple of weeks he and his wife just let it ride. They thought the son might see reason. But he wouldn't. He got his father to get hold of a transcript of the trial, nagged him into working on Griswold. Of course he's an only child and as spoilt as they come. The upshot was that Archery promised to start poking his nose into it as soon as he got his fortnight's holiday.'

'So he'll be back?'

'That will depend on Mrs Painter,' said Wexford.

CHAPTER FIVE

... That they may see their children christianly and virtuously brought up.

The Solemnisation of Matrimony

The Kershaws' house was about a mile from the town centre, separated from shops, station, cinema and churches by thousands of other large suburban villas. For number 20 Craig Hill was large, half-heartedly Georgian and built of raspberry red brick. The garden was planted with annuals, the lawn was clover-free and the dead heads had been nipped off the standard rose bushes. On the concrete drive a boy of about twelve was washing down a large white Ford.

Archery parked his car at the kerb. Unlike Wexford he had not yet seen the coach house at Victor's Piece, but he had read about it and it seemed to him that Mrs Kershaw had climbed high. Sweat started on his forehead and his upper lip as he got out of the car. He told himself that it was unusually hot and that he had always been prone to feel the heat.

'This is Mr Kershaw's house, isn't it?' he asked the boy.

'That's right.' He was very like Tess, but his hair was fairer and his nose was freckled. 'The front door's open. Shall I give him a shout?'

'My name is Archery,' said the clergyman and he held out his hand.

The boy wiped his hands on his jeans. 'Hallo,' he said.

By now a little wrinkled man had come down the porch steps. The bright hot air seemed to hang between them. Archery tried not to feel disappointment. What had he expected? Certainly not someone so small, so unfinished looking and so wizened as this scrawny creature in old flannels and tieless knitted shirt. Then Kershaw smiled and the years fell from him. His eyes were a bright sparkling blue and his uneven teeth white and clean.

40

'How do you do?'

'Good afternoon, Mr Archery. I'm very happy to meet you. As a matter of fact I've been sitting in the window, looking out for you.'

In this man's presence it was impossible not to feel hope, cheerfulness almost. Archery detected at once a rare quality in him, a quality he had come upon perhaps only half a dozen times in his life. This was a man who was interested in all things. Energy and enthusiasm radiated from him. On a winter's day he would warm the air. Today, in this heat, his vitality was overwhelming.

'Come inside and meet my wife.' His voice was a hot breeze, a cockney voice that suggested fish and chips, eels and mash and East End pubs. Following him into the square panelled hall, Archery wondered how old he was. Perhaps no more than forty-five. Drive, the fire of life, lack of sleep because sleep wasted time, could prematurely have burnt away his youth. 'We're in the lounge,' he said, pushing open a reeded glass door. 'That's what I like about a day like this. When I get home from work I like to sit by the french windows for ten minutes and look at the garden. Makes you feel all that slogging in the winter was worthwhile.'

'To sit in the shade and look upon verdure?' After the words were out Archery was sorry he had spoken. He didn't want to put this suburban engineer in a false position.

Kershaw gave him a quick glance. Then he smiled and said easily, 'Miss Austen certainly knew what she was talking about, didn't she?' Archery was overcome. He went into the room and held out his hand to the woman who had got up from an armchair.

'My wife. This is Mr Archery, Rene.'

'How do you do?'

Irene Kershaw said nothing, but holding out her hand, smiled a tight bright smile. Her face was Tess's face as it would be when time had hardened it and finished it. In her youth she had been blonde. Now her hair, evidently set that day and perhaps in his honour, was dyed a dull leaf-brown and arranged in unreal feathery wisps about her forehead and ears.

'Sit down, Mr Archery,' said Kershaw. 'We won't keep you a minute for your tea. Kettle's on, isn't it, Rene?'

Archery sat in an armchair by the window. Kershaw's garden was full of experimental rose pergolas, eruptions of rockery and stone sporting geraniums. He gave the room a quick glance, noting at once its cleanliness and the enormous mass of things which had to be kept clean. Books abounded, Readers' Digests, encyclopaedias, dictionaries, works on astronomy, deep sea fishing, European history. There was a tank of tropical fish on a corner table, several model aircraft on the mantelpiece; stacks of sheet music covered the grand piano, and on an easel was a half-finished, rather charming, portrait in oils of a young girl. It was a large room, conventionally furnished with Wilton carpet and chintz covers, but it expressed the personality of the master of the house.

'We've had the pleasure of meeting your Charlie,' said Kershaw. 'A nice unassuming boy. I liked him.' Charlie! Archery sat very still, trying not to feel affronted. Charles's eligibility, after all, was not in question.

Quite suddenly Rene Kershaw spoke. 'We all like him,' she said. Her accent was just the same as Wexford's. 'But I'm sure I don't know how they plan to manage, what with everything being such an awful price — the cost of living, you know — and Charles not having a job in line . . .' Archery felt amazement. Was she really concerned with this trivia? He began to wonder how he would broach the subject that had brought him to Purley. 'I mean where will they live?' Mrs Kershaw asked primly. 'They're just babies really. I mean, you've got to have a home of your own, haven't you? You've got to get a mortgage and . . .'

'I think I can hear the kettle, Rene,' said her husband.

She got up, holding her skirt modestly to cover her knees. It was a very suburban skirt of some permanently pleated material banded in muted blue and heather pink and of dead sexless respectability. With it she wore a short-sleeved pink jumper and around her neck a single string of cultured pearls. If cultured meant tended and nurtured, Archery thought he had never seen such obviously cultured pearls. Each night, he was sure, they were wrapped in tissue and put away in the dark. Mrs Kershaw smelt of talcum powder, some of which lingered in the lines of her neck.

'I don't think we've got to the mortgage stage yet,' said Kershaw when she had gone. Archery gave a wry smile. 'Believe me, Mr Archery, I know you haven't come here just for an inlaws' get-together over the tea cups.'

'I'm finding it more awkward than I thought possible.'

Kershaw chuckled. 'I daresay. I can't tell you anything about Tess's father that isn't common knowledge, that wasn't in the papers at the time. You know that?'

'But her mother?'

'You can try. At times like this women see things through a cloud of orange blossom. She's never been very keen on Tess being an educated woman. She wants to see her married and she'll do her best to see nothing stands in her way.'

'And you, what do you want?'

'Me? Oh, I want to see her happy. Happiness doesn't necessarily begin at the altar.' Suddenly he was brisk and forthright. 'Frankly, Mr Archery, I'm not sure if she can be happy with a man who suspects her of homicidal tendencies before she's even engaged to him.'

'It isn't like that!' Archery hadn't expected the other man to put him on the defensive. 'Your stepdaughter is perfect in my son's eyes. I'm making the enquiries, Mr Kershaw. My son knows that, he wants it for Tess's sake, but he doesn't even know I'm here. Put yourself in my position . . .'

'But I *was* in your position. Tess was only six when I married her mother.' He looked quickly at the door, then leaned closer to Archery. 'D'you think I don't watch her, look out for the disturbance to show itself? When my own daughter was born Tess was very jealous. She resented the baby and one day I found her leaning over Jill's pram striking her on the head with a celluloid toy. Luckily, it *was* a celluloid toy.'

'But, good heavens . . . !' Archery felt the pallor drawing at his face muscles.

'What could I do? I had to go to work and leave the children. I had to trust my wife. Then we had a son — I think you bumped into him outside cleaning the car — and Jill resented him in just the same way and with just the same violence. All children behave like this, that's the point.'

'You never saw any more — any more of these tendencies?'

'Tendencies? A personality isn't made by heredity, Mr Archery, but by environment. I wanted Tess to have the best sort of environment and I think I can say, with all due modesty, that she has.'

The garden shimmered in the heat haze. Archery saw things he hadn't noticed at first, chalk lines on the lawn, where, regardless of herbaceous borders, the glass had been marked out for a tennis court; a shambles of rabbit hutches attached to the garage wall; an ancient swing. Behind him on the mantelpiece he saw propped against ornaments two party invitations. A framed photograph above it showed three children in shirts and jeans sprawled on a haystack. Yes, this had been the best of all possible environments for the murderer's orphan.

The door was pushed open and the girl in the portrait came in pushing a tea trolley. Archery, who was too hot and troubled to feel hungry, saw with dismay that it was laden with home-baked pastries, strawberries in glass dishes, fairy cakes in paper cases. The girl looked about fourteen. She was not so beautiful as Tess and she wore a bunchy school tunic, but her father's vitality illuminated her face.

'This is my daughter Jill.'

Jill sprawled in a chair, showing a lot of long leg.

'Now, sit nicely, dear,' said Mrs Kershaw sharply. She gave the girl a repressive look and began to pour tea, holding the pot with curled fingers. 'They don't realise they're young women at thirteen these days, Mr Archery.' Archery was embarrassed but the girl didn't seem to care. 'You must have one of these cakes. Jill made them.' Unwillingly he took a pastry. 'That's right. I've always said to both my girls, schooling is all very well in its way, but algebra won't cook the Sunday dinner. Tess and Jill are both good plain cooks . . .'

'Mummy! I'm not plain and Tess certainly isn't.'

'You know what I mean. Now don't take me up on everything. When they get married their husbands won't be ashamed to have anybody for a meal.'

'This is my managing director, darling,' said Jill pertly. 'Just cut a slice off him and put it under the grill, will you?'

Kershaw roared with laughter. Then he took his wife's hand. 'You leave Mummy alone.' All this jollity and family intimacy was making Archery nervous. He forced a smile and knew it looked forced.

'What I really mean is, Mr Archery,' said Mrs Kershaw earnestly, 'is that even if your Charlie and my Tessie have their ups and downs at first, Tess hasn't been brought up to be an idle wife. She'll put a happy home before luxuries.'

'I'm sure she will.' Archery looked helplessly at the lounging girl, firmly entrenched in her chair and devouring strawberries and cream. It was now or never. 'Mrs Kershaw, I don't doubt Theresa's suitability as a wife...' No, that wasn't right. That was just what he did doubt. He floundered. 'I wanted to talk to you about...' Surely Kershaw would help him? Jill's brows drew together in a small frown and her grey eyes stared steadily at him. Desperately he said, 'I wanted to speak to you alone.'

Irene Kershaw seemed to shrink. She put down her cup, laid her knife delicately across her plate and, folding her hands in her lap, looked down at them. They were poor hands, stubby and worn, and she wore just one ring, her second wedding ring.

'Haven't you got any homework to do, Jill?' she asked in a whisper. Kershaw got up, wiping his mouth.

'I can do it in the train,' said Jill.

Archery had begun to dislike Kershaw, but he could not help admiring him. 'Jill, you know all about Tess,' Kershaw said, 'what happened when she was little. Mummy has to discuss it with Mr Archery. Just by themselves. We have to go because, although we're involved, it's not quite our business. Not like it is theirs. O.K.?'

'O.K.,' said Jill. Her father put his arm round her and took her into the garden.

He had to begin, but he was hot and stiff with awkwardness. Outside the window Jill had found a tennis racquet and was practising shots against the garage wall. Mrs Kershaw picked up a napkin and dabbed at the corners of her mouth. She looked at him, their eyes met, and she looked away. Archery felt suddenly that they were not alone, that their thoughts concentrated on the past had summoned from its prison grave a presence of brute strength that stood behind their chairs, laying a bloody hand on their shoulders and listening for judgement.

'Tess says you have something to tell me,' he said quietly. 'About your first husband.' She was rolling the napkin now, squashing it, until it was like a golf-ball. 'Mrs Kershaw, I think you ought to tell me.'

The paper ball was tipped soundlessly on to an empty plate. She put her hand up to her pearls.

'I never speak of him, Mr Archery. I prefer to let the past be the past.'

'I know it's painful — it must be. But if we could discuss it just once and get it over, I promise I'll never raise the subject again.' He realised that he was speaking as if they would meet again and often, as if they were already connected by marriage. He was also speaking as if he had confidence in her word. 'I've been to Kingsmarkham today and . . .'

She clutched at the straw. 'I suppose they've built it all up and spoiled it.'

'Not really,' he said. Please God, don't let her digress!

'I was born near there,' she said. He tried to stifle a sigh. 'A funny little sleepy place it was, my village. I reckon I thought I'd live and die there. You can't tell what life will bring forth, can you?'

'Tell me about Tess's father.'

She dropped her hands from fidgeting with the pearls and rested them in her respectable blue lap. When she turned to him her face was dignified, almost ridiculously prim and shuttered. She might have been a mayoress, taking the chair at some parochial function, clearing her throat preparatory to addressing the Townswomen's Guild. 'Madam chairman, ladies . . .' she should have begun. Instead she said:

'The past is the past, Mr Archery.' He knew then that it was hopeless. 'I appreciate your difficulty, but I really can't speak of it. He was no murderer, you'll have to take my word. He was a good kind man who wouldn't have harmed a fly.' It was curious, he thought, how she jumbled together old village phrases with platform jargon. He waited, then burst out:

'But how do you know? How *can* you know? Mrs Kershaw, did you see something or hear something . . . ?'

The pearls had gone up to her mouth and her teeth closed over the string. As it snapped pearls sprayed off in all directions,

into her lap, across the tea things, on to the carpet. She gave a
small refined laugh, petulant and apologetic. 'Look what I've
done now!' In an instant she was on her knees, retrieving the
scattered beads and dropping them into a saucer.

'I'm very keen on a white wedding.' Her face bounced up
from behind the tea trolley. Politeness demanded that he too
should get on his knees and help in the hunt. 'Get your wife to
back me up, will you? Oh, thanks so much. Look, there's
another one, just by your left foot.' He scrambled round after
her on all fours. Her eyes met his under the overhanging cloth.
'My Tess is quite capable of getting married in jeans if the fancy
takes her. And would you mind if we had the reception here?
It's such a nice big room.'

Archery got up and handed her three more pearls. When
the tennis ball struck the window he jumped. The sound had
been like a pistol shot.

'Now, that's quite enough, Jill,' said Mrs Kershaw sharply.
Still holding the saucer full of pearls, she opened the window.
'If I've told you once, I've told you fifty times, I don't want any
more breakages.'

Archery looked at her. She was annoyed, affronted, even
slightly outraged. He wondered suddenly if this was how she
had looked on that Sunday night long ago when the police had
invaded her domain at the coach house. Was she capable of any
emotion greater than this, of mere irritation at disturbance of
her personal peace?

'You just can't settle to a quiet discussion with children
about, can you?' she said.

Within an instant, as if at a cue, the whole family was
upon them, Jill truculent and protesting, the boy he had encountered on the drive now demanding tea, and Kershaw
himself, vibrant as ever, his little lined face showing a certain
dry acuteness.

'Now, you're to come straight out and give me a hand with
these dishes, Jill.' The saucer was transferred to the mantelpiece
and stuck between an Oxfam collecting box and a card inviting
Mrs Kershaw to a coffee morning in aid of Cancer Relief. 'I'll
say good-bye now, Mr Archery.' She held out her hand. 'You've
such a long way to go, I know you'll want to be on your way.'

It was almost rude, yet it was queenly. 'If we don't meet again before the great day — well, I'll see you in church.'

The door closed. Archery remained standing.

'What am I to do?' he said simply.

'What did you expect?' Kershaw countered. 'Some sort of incontrovertible evidence, an alibi that only she can prove?'

'Do *you* believe her?' Archery countered.

'Ah, that's another matter. I don't care, you see. I don't care one way or the other. It's so easy *not* to ask, Mr Archery, just to do nothing and accept.'

'But I care,' said Archery. 'If Charles goes ahead and marries your stepdaughter, I shall have to leave the church. I don't think you realise the sort of place I live in, the sort of people . . .'

'Aah!' Kershaw wrinkled up his mouth and spread his hands angrily fanwise. 'I've no patience with that sort of out-dated rubbish. Who's to know? Everybody round here thinks she's my kid.'

'I shall know.'

'Why the hell did she have to tell you? Why couldn't she keep her mouth shut?'

'Are you condemning her for her honesty, Kershaw?'

'Yes, by God I am!' Archery winced at the oath and shut his eyes against the light. He saw a red haze. It was only eyelid membrane, but to him it seemed like a lake of blood. 'It's discretion, not honesty, that's the best policy. What are you worrying about, anyway? You know damn well she won't marry him if you don't want it.'

Archery snapped back, 'And what sort of relationship should I have with my son after that?' He controlled himself, softened his voice and his expression. 'I shall have to try to find a way. Your wife is so sure?'

'She's never weakened.'

'Then I shall go back to Kingsmarkham. It's rather a forlorn hope, isn't it?' He added with an absurdity he realised after the words had come, 'Thanks for trying to help and — and for an excellent tea.'

CHAPTER SIX

Yet, forasmuch as in all appearance the time of his dissolution draweth near, so fit and prepare him . . . against the hour of death.

The Visitation of the Sick

The man lay on his back in the middle of the zebra crossing. Inspector Burden, getting out of the police car, had no need to ask where he was or to be taken to the scene of the accident. It was all there before his eyes like a horrible still from a Ministry of Transport warning film, the kind of thing that makes women shudder and turn quickly to the other channel.

An ambulance was waiting, but nobody was making any attempt to move the man. Inexorably and with a kind of indifference the twin yellow beacons went on winking rhythmically. Up-ended, with its blunt nose poking into the crushed head of a bollard, was a white Mini.

'Can't you get him away?' asked Burden.

The doctor was laconic. 'He's had it.' He knelt down, felt the left wrist and got up again, wiping blood from his fingers. 'I'd hazard a guess the spine's gone and he's ruptured his liver. The thing is he's still more or less conscious and it'd be hell's own agony to shift him.'

'Poor devil. What happened? Did anybody see it?'

His eye roved across the knot of middle-aged women in cotton dresses, late homegoing commuters and courting couples on their evening stroll. The last of the sun smiled gently on their faces and on the blood that gilded the black and white crossing. Burden knew that Mini. He knew the stupid sign in the rear window that showed a skull and the words: *You have been Mini-ed.* It had never been funny and now it was outrageous, cruel in the way it mocked the man in the road.

A girl lay sprawled over the steering wheel. Her hair was

short, black and spiky, and she had thrust her fingers through it in despair or remorse. The long red nails stuck out like bright feathers.

'Don't worry about her,' said the doctor contemptuously. 'She's not hurt.'

'You, madam . . .' Burden picked out the calmest and least excited looking of the bystanders. 'Did you happen to see the accident?'

'Ooh, it was awful! Like a beast she was, the little bitch. Must have been doing a hundred miles an hour.'

Picked a right one there, thought Burden. He turned to a white-faced man holding a sealyham on a lead.

'Perhaps you can help me, sir?'

The lead was jerked and the sealyham sat down at the kerb.

'That gentleman . . .' Blanching afresh, he pointed towards the crumpled thing lying on the stripes. 'He looked right and left like you're supposed to. But there was nothing coming. You can't see all that well on account of the bridge.'

'Yes, yes. I get the picture.'

'Well, he started to cross to the island like, when that white car came up out of nowhere. Going like a mad thing she was. Well, not a hundred, but sixty, I reckon. Those Minis can go at a terrible lick when they've had their engines hotted up. He sort of hesitated and then he tried to go back. You know, it was all in a flash. I can't rightly go into details.'

'You're doing very well.'

'Then the car got him. Oh, the driver slammed on her brakes for all she was worth. I'll never forget the noise to my dying day, what with the brakes screaming and him screaming too, and sort of throwing up his arms and going down like a ninepin.'

Burden set a constable to take names and addresses, turned away and took a step in the direction of the white car. A woman touched his arm.

'Here,' she said, 'he wants a priest or something. He kept on asking before you came. Get me Father Chiverton, he says, like he knew he was going.'

'That right?' said Burden sharply to Dr Crocker.

Crocker nodded. The dying man was covered now, a folded

mac under his head, two policemen's jackets across his body. 'Father Chiverton is what he said. Frankly, I was more concerned for his physical than his spiritual welfare.'

'R.C. then, is he?'

'God, no. Bunch of atheists, you cops are. Chiverton's the new vicar here. Don't you ever read the local rag?'

'*Father?*'

'He's very high. Genuflecting and Sung Eucharist and all that jazz.' The doctor coughed. 'I'm a Congregationalist myself.'

Burden walked over to the crossing. The man's face was blanched a yellowish ivory, but his eyes were open and they stared back. With a little shock Burden realised he was young, perhaps no more than twenty.

'Anything you want, old chap?' He knew the doctor had given him a pain-killing injection. With his own bent body he shielded him from the watchers. 'We'll get you away from here in a minute,' he lied. 'Anything we can get you?'

'Father Chiverton . . .' It was a toneless whisper, as detached and inhuman as a puff of wind. 'Father Chiverton . . .' A spasm crossed the waning face. 'Confess . . . atone . . . spare Thou them which are penitent.'

'Bloody religion,' said the doctor. 'Can't even let a man die in peace.'

'You must be an asset to the Congregationalists,' Burden snapped. He got up, sighing. 'He obviously wants to confess. I suppose they do have confession in the Church of England?'

'You can have it if you want it but you needn't if you don't fancy it. That's the beauty of the C of E.' When Burden looked murderous, he added. 'Don't get in a tiz with me. We've been on to Chiverton, but he and his curate are off at some conference.'

'Constable Gates!' Burden beckoned impatiently to the man noting down the addresses. 'Nip into Stowerton and fetch me a — a vicar.'

'We've tried Stowerton, sir.'

'O God,' said Burden quietly.

'Excuse me, sir, but there's a clergyman got an appointment with the Chief Inspector now. I could get on to the station and . . .'

Burden raised his eyebrows. Kingsmarkham police station had apparently become the battleground of the Church Militant.

'You do that, and quick . . .'

He murmured something useless to the boy, and moved towards the girl who had begun to sob.

She was not crying because of what she had done, but because of what she had seen two hours before. It was two or three years now since she had what she called a waking nightmare — though at one time they were more real than reality — and she was crying because the nightmares were going to begin again and the remedy she had tried had not erased the picture from her mind.

She had seen it in the estate agent's window when she was coming home from work. It was a photograph of a house, but not as it was now, dirty and weathered, set in a tangled wilderness. The estate agents deceived you, they meant you to think it was like it had once been long ago . . . You? As soon as she found she was addressing herself as 'You' she knew it was beginning again, the re-telling of the nightmare. So she had got into the Mini and driven to Flagford, away from associations and memories and the hateful You voice, to drink and drink and try to send it away.

But it would not go away and you were back in the big house, listening to the voices that went on coaxing, cajoling, arguing until you were bored, so bored until you went out into the garden and met the little girl.

You went up to her and said, 'Do you like my dress?'

'It's pretty,' she said, and she didn't seem to mind that it was much nicer than her own.

She was playing with a heap of sand, making pies in an old cup without a handle. You stayed and played and after that you came to the sand every day, down there out of sight of the big windows. The sand was warm and nice and you could understand it. You could understand the little girl too, even though she was the only little girl you had ever known. You knew a lot of grown-ups, but you could not understand them, nor the ugly words and the funny wheedling way the talk was always about money, so that you seemed to see coins dropping out of wriggling lips and sliding dirtily through twitching fingers.

The little girl had some magic about her, for she lived in a tree. Of course it was not really a tree but a house inside a kind of bush all shivering with leaves.

The sand was not dry like the desert you lived in now, but warm and moist, like beach sand washed by a tepid sea. It was dirty too and you were afraid of what would happen if you got it on your dress . . .

You cried and stamped your foot, but you never cried as you were crying now as the good-looking inspector came up to the car, his eyes full of anger.

Did he seriously imagine he was going to find anything new after so long? Archery considered Wexford's question. It was, he decided, more a matter of faith than of any real belief in Painter's innocence. But faith in what? Not, surely, in Mrs Kershaw. Perhaps it was just a childlike certainty that such things could not happen to anyone connected with him, Archery. The child of a murderer could not be as Tess was, Kershaw would not have loved her, Charles would not want to marry her.

'It can't do any harm to see Alice Flower,' he said. He felt he was pleading, and pleading weakly. 'I'd like to talk to the Primero grandchildren, particularly the grandson.'

For a moment Wexford said nothing. He had heard of faith moving mountains, but this was simply absurd. To him it was almost as ridiculous as if some crank had come to him with the suggestion that Dr Crippen was the innocent victim of circumstances. From bitter experience he knew how difficult it was to hunt a killer when only a week had elapsed between a murder and the beginning of an investigation. Archery was proposing to open an enquiry a decade and a half too late and Archery had no experience at all.

'I ought to put you off,' he said at last. 'You don't know what you're attempting.' It's pathetic, he thought, it's laughable. Aloud he said, 'Alice Flower's in the geriatric ward at Stowerton Infirmary. She's paralysed. I don't even know if she could make herself understood.'

It occurred to him that Archery must be totally ignorant of

the geography of the place. He got up and lumbered over to the wall map.

'Stowerton's there,' he said, pointing with the sheathed tip of a ballpoint pen, 'and Victor's Piece is about here, between Stowerton and Kingsmarkham.'

'Where can I find Mrs Crilling?'

Wexford made a wry face. 'In Glebe Road. I can't recall the number off-hand, but I'll get it looked up or you could find it on the electoral register.' He turned round ponderously and fixed Archery with a grey glare. 'You're wasting your time, of course. I'm sure I don't have to tell you to be very careful when it comes to throwing out a lot of unfounded accusations.'

Under those cold eyes it was difficult for Archery not to drop his own. 'Chief Inspector, I don't want to find someone else guilty, just prove that Painter was innocent.'

Wexford said briskly, 'I'm afraid you may find the former consequent upon the latter. It would be a wrong conclusion, of course — I don't want trouble.' At a knock on the door he spun round testily. 'Yes, what is it?'

Sergeant Martin's bland face appeared. 'That fatal on the zebra in the High Street, sir?'

'What of it? It's hardly my province.'

'Gates has just been on, sir. A white Mini, LMB 12M, that we've had our eye on — it was in collision with a pedestrian. It appears they want a clergyman and Gates recalled that Mr Archery was . . .'

Wexford's lips twitched. Archery was in for a surprise. In the courtly manner he sometimes assumed, he said to the vicar of Thringford, 'It looks as if the secular arm needs some spiritual assistance, sir. Would you be so good . . . ?'

'Of course I will.' Archery looked at the sergeant. 'Someone has been knocked down and is — is *dying*?'

'Unfortunately, yes, sir,' said Martin grimly.

'I think I'll come with you,' said Wexford.

As a priest of the Anglican Church Archery was obliged to hear confession if a confessor was needed. Until now, however, his only experience of this mystery concerned a Miss Bayliss, an elderly female parishioner of his who, having been (according to Mrs Archery) for many years in love with him, demanded that he should listen to a small spate of domestic sins mumbled out each Friday morning. Hers was a masochistic, self-abasing need, very different from the yearning of the boy who lay in the road.

Wexford shepherded him across the black and white lines to the island. Diversion notices had been placed in the road, directing the traffic around Queen Street, and the crowd had been induced to go home. There were several policemen buzzing and pacing. For the first time in his life Archery realised the aptness of the term 'bluebottles'. He glanced at the Mini and averted his eyes hastily from the bright bumper with its ribbon of blood.

The boy looked at him doubtfully. He had perhaps five minutes to live. Archery dropped to his knees and put his ear to the white lips. At first he felt only fluttering breath, then out of the soft sighing vibration came something that sounded like 'Holy orders . . .', with the second word rising on a high note of enquiry. He bent closer as the confession began to flow out, jerky, toneless, spasmodic, like the gulping of a sluggish stream. It was something about a girl, but it was utterly incoherent. He could make nothing of it. We fly unto Thee for succour, he thought, in behalf of this Thy servant, here lying under Thy hand in great weakness of body . . .

The Anglican Church provides no order quite comparable to that of Extreme Unction. Archery found himself saying urgently over and over again, 'It will be all right, it will be all right.' The boy's throat rattled and a stream of blood welled out of his mouth, splashing Archery's folded hands. 'We humbly commend the soul of this Thy servant, our dear brother, into Thy hands . . .' He was tired and his voice broke with compassion and with horror. 'Most humbly beseeching Thee that it may be precious in Thy sight . . .'

It was the doctor's hand that appeared, mopping with a handkerchief at Archery's fingers, then feeling a still heart and an inert pulse. Wexford looked at the doctor, gave an infinitesimal shrug. Nobody spoke. Across the silence came the sound of brakes, a horn braying and an oath as a car, taking the diversion too late, veered into Queen Street. Wexford pulled the coat up over the dead face.

Archery was shattered and cold in the evening heat. He got up stiffly, feeling an utter loneliness and a terrible desire to weep. The only thing to lean on now the bollard was gone was the rear of that lethal white car. He leaned on it, feeling sick.

Presently he opened his eyes and moved slowly along the body of the car to where Wexford stood contemplating a girl's shaggy black head. This was no business of his, Archery's. He wanted no hand in it, only to ask Wexford where he could find an hotel for the night.

Something in the other man's expression made him hesitate. The big Chief Inspector's face was a study in irony. He watched Wexford tap on the glass. The window was slid back and the girl inside lifted to them a face drowned in tears.

'This is a bad business,' he heard Wexford say, 'a very bad business, Miss Crilling.'

'God moves in a mysterious way,' said Wexford as he and Archery walked over the bridge, 'His wonders to perform.' He hummed the old hymn tune, apparently liking the sound of his rather rusty baritone.

'That's true,' said Archery very seriously. He stopped, rested his hand on the granite parapet and looked down into the brown water. A swan sailed out from under the bridge, dipping its long neck into the drifting weed. 'And that is really the girl who found Mrs Primero's body?'

'That's Elizabeth Crilling, yes. One of the wild young things of Kingsmarkham. A boy friend — a very *close* friend, I may add — gave her the Mini for her twenty-first and she's been a menace in it ever since.'

Archery was silent. Tess Kershaw and Elizabeth Crilling were the same age. Their lives had begun together, almost side by side. Each must have walked with their mother along the grass verges of the Stowerton Road, played in the fields behind Victor's Piece. The Crillings had been comfortably off, middle-class people; the Painters miserably poor. In his mind's eye he saw again that tearwrecked face down which grease and mascara ran in rivulets, and he heard again the ugly words she had used to Wexford. Another face superimposed itself on Elizabeth Crilling's, a fair aquiline face with steady intelligent

eyes under a page-boy's blonde fringe. Wexford interrupted his
thoughts.

'She's been spoilt, of course, made too much of. Your Mrs
Primero had her over with her every day, stuffing her with
sweets and what-have-you, by all accounts. After the murder
Mrs Crilling was always taking her to psychiatrists, wouldn't let
her go to school till they had the kid-catcher down on her. God
knows how many schools she *has* been to. She was what you
might call the female lead in the juvenile court here.'

But it was Tess whose father had been a murderer, Tess who
might have been expected to grow up like that. 'God knows how
many schools she's been to . . .' Tess had been to one school and
to one ancient, distinguished university. Yet the daughter of the
innocent friend had become a delinquent; the killer's child a
paragon. Certainly God moved in a mysterious way.

'Chief Inspector, I want very much to talk to Mrs Crilling.'

'If you care to attend the special court in the morning, sir,
she'll in all likelihood be there. Knowing Mrs Crilling, I'd say
you might again be called upon in your professional capacity
and then, who knows?'

Archery frowned as they walked on. 'I'd rather it was all
above-board. I don't want to do anything underhand.'

'Look, sir,' said Wexford in a burst of impatience, 'if you're
coming in on this lark you'll have to be underhand. You've no
real authority to ask questions of innocent people and if they
complain I can't protect you.'

'I'll explain everything frankly to her. May I talk to her?'

Wexford cleared his throat. 'Are you familiar with *Henry the
Fourth,* Part One, sir?'

Slightly puzzled, Archery nodded. Wexford stopped under
the arch that led to the coaching yard of the Olive and Dove.
'The quotation I had in mind is Hotspur's reply to Mortimer
when he says he can call spirits from the vasty deep.' Startled
by Wexford's deep voice, a little cloud of pigeons flew out from
the beams, fluttering rusty grey wings. 'I've found that reply
very useful to me in my work when I've been a bit too
optimistic.' He cleared his throat and quoted, ' "And so can I
and so can any man. But will they come when you do call to
them?" Good night, sir, I hope you find the Olive comfortable.'

CHAPTER SEVEN

Into how high a dignity . . . ye are called, that is to say to be
Messengers, Watchmen and Stewards . . .

The Ordering of Priests

Two people sat in the public gallery of Kingsmarkham court,
Archery and a woman with sharp, wasted features. Her long
grey hair, oddly fashionable through carelessness rather than
intent, and the cape she wore gave her a medieval look.
Presumably she was the mother of this girl who had just been
charged with manslaughter, the girl whom the clerk had named
as Elizabeth Anthea Crilling, of 24A Glebe Road, Kingsmarkham in the County of Sussex. She had a look of her mother and
they kept glancing at each other, Mrs Crilling's eyes flicking
over her daughter's string-thin body or coming to rest with
maudlin watery affection on the girl's face. It was a well-made
face, though gaunt but for the full mouth. Sometimes it seemed
to become all staring dark eyes as a word or a telling phrase
awakened emotion, sometimes blank and shuttered like that of
a retarded child with an inner life of goblins and things that
reach out in the dark. An invisible thread held mother and
daughter together but whether it was composed of love or
hatred Archery could not tell. Both were ill-dressed, dirty-look-
ing, a prey, he felt, to cheap emotion, but there was some
quality each had — passion? Imagination? Seething memory?
— that set them apart and dwarfed the other occupants of the
court.

He had just enough knowledge of the law to know that this
court could do no more than commit the girl to the Assizes for
trial. The evidence that was being laboriously taken down on a
typewriter was all against her. Elizabeth Crilling, according to
the licensee of the Swan at Flagford, had been drinking in his
saloon bar since six-thirty. He had served her with seven double

whiskies and when he had refused to let her have another, she had abused him until he had threatened to call the police.

'No alternative but to commit you for trial at the Assizes at Lewes,' the chairman was saying. ' . . . Nothing to hope for from any promise of favour, and nothing to fear from any threat which may be . . .'

A shriek came from the public gallery. 'What are you going to do to her?' Mrs Crilling had sprung up, the tent-like cape she wore billowing out and making a breeze run through the court. 'You're not going to put her in prison?'

Hardly knowing why he did so, Archery moved swiftly along the form until he was at her side. At the same time Sergeant Martin took half a dozen rapid strides towards her, glaring at the clergyman.

'Now, madam, you'd far better come outside.'

She flung herself away from him, pulling the cape around her as if it were cold instead of suffocatingly hot.

'You're not going to put my baby in gaol!' She pushed at the sergeant who stood between her and her view of the bench. 'Get away from me, you dirty sadist!'

'Take that woman outside,' said the magistrate with icy calm. Mrs Crilling spun round to face Archery and seized his hands. 'You've got a kind face. Are you my friend?'

Archery was horribly embarrassed. 'You can ask for bail, I think,' he muttered.

The policewoman who stood by the dock came over to them. 'Come along now, Mrs Crilling . . .'

'Bail, I want bail! This gentleman is an old friend of mine and he says I can have bail. I want my rights for my baby!'

'We really can't have this sort of thing.' The magistrate cast an icy scornful look upon Archery who sat down, wrenching his hands from Mrs Crilling's. 'Do I understand you wish to ask for bail?' He turned his eyes on Elizabeth who nodded defiantly.

'A nice cup of tea, Mrs Crilling,' said the policewoman. 'Come along now.' She shepherded the demented woman out, her arm supporting her waist. The magistrate went into conference with the clerk and bail was granted to Elizabeth Crilling in her own recognisance of five hundred pounds and that of her mother for a similar sum.

'Rise, please!' said the warrant officer. It was over.

On the other side of the court Wexford shovelled his papers into his briefcase.

'A friend in need, that one,' he said to Burden, glancing in Archery's direction. 'You mark my words, he'll have a job getting out of old Mother Crilling's clutches. Remember when we had to cart her off to the mental unit at Stowerton that time? You were her friend then. Tried to kiss you, didn't she?'

'Don't remind me,' said Burden.

'Funny affair altogether last night, wasn't it? Him being on hand, I mean, to show that poor kid his way to heaven.'

'It was lucky.'

'I only remember that happening once before, except in the case of R.C.s, of course.' He turned as Archery slipped between the wooden forms and came up to them. 'Good morning, sir. I hope you slept well. I was just saying to the inspector, there was a fellow killed out Forby way soon after I came here. Must be all of twenty years. I've never forgotten it. He was just a kid too and got it in the neck from an army lorry. But he wasn't quiet, he was screaming. All about a girl and a kid it was.' He paused. 'Did you speak, sir? Sorry, I thought you did. He wanted a clergyman, too.'

'I hope and trust he got what he wanted.'

'Well, no he didn't as a matter of fact. He died — unshriven is the word, I think. The vicar's car broke down on the way. Funny, I've never forgotten it. Grace was his name, John Grace. Shall we go?'

The Crillings had departed. As they came out into the sunshine, the policewoman came up to Wexford.

'Mrs Crilling left a note with me, sir. She asked me to give it to a Mr Archery.'

'Take my advice,' said Wexford. 'Tear it up. She's as mad as a hatter.' But Archery had already opened the envelope.

Dear Sir, he read.

They tell me that you are a man of God. Blessed is he that sitteth not in the seat of the scornful. God has sent you to me and my baby. I will be at home this afternoon, waiting to thank you in person.

Your affectionate friend, Josephine Crilling

*

Archery's bedroom combined charmingly the best of old and new. The ceiling was beamed, the walls painted pink and decorated with a tooled design of chevrons, but there was also a fitted carpet, an abundance of lights on walls and bedhead and a telephone. He rinsed his hands at the pink washbasin (a private bathroom he felt to be an unwarranted extravagance), lifted the receiver and asked for a call to Thringford in Essex.

'Darling?'

'Henry! Thank heaven you've phoned. I've been trying over and over again to get you at that Olive Branch place or whatever it's called.'

'Why, what's the matter?'

'I've had a dreadful letter from Charles. Apparently poor darling Tess phoned her people late yesterday afternoon and now she's told Charles the engagement's definitely off. She says it wouldn't be fair on him or us.'

'And . . . ?'

'And Charles says if Tess won't marry him he's going to come down from Oxford and go out to Africa to fight for Zimbabwe.'

'How utterly ridiculous!'

'He says if you try and stop him he'll do something dreadful and get sent down.'

'Is that all?'

'Oh, no. There's lots and lots of it. Let me see. I've got the letter here. 'What's the use of Father always ballsing on' — sorry, darling, does that mean something awful? — 'on about faith and taking things on trust if he won't take Tess's word and her mother's? I've been into the whole fiasco of the case myself and it's full of holes. I think Father could get the Home Secretary to have the case re-opened if he would only make some sort of effort. For one thing there was an inheritance involved but it never came up at the trial. Three people inherited vast sums and at least one of them was buzzing around the place the day Mrs Primero died . . .'

'All right,' said Archery wearily. 'If you remember, Mary, I have a transcript of the trial myself and it cost me two hundred pounds. How are things apart from that?'

'Mr Sims is behaving rather oddly.' Mr Sims was Archery's

curate. 'Miss Bayliss says he keeps the communion bread in his pocket, and this morning she got a long blonde hair in her mouth.'

Archery smiled. This parish chit-chat was more in his wife's line than solving murders. It brought her to him visually, a handsome strong woman who minded the lines on her face that he never noticed. He was beginning to miss her mentally and physically.

'Now, listen, darling. Write back to Charles — be diplomatic. Tell him how well Tess is behaving and say I'm having some very interesting talks with the police. If there's the slightest chance of getting the case re-opened I'll write to the Home Secretary.'

'That's wonderful, Henry. Oh, there go your second lot of pips. I'll ring off. By the way, Rusty caught a mouse this morning and left it in the bath. He and Tawny are missing you.'

'Give them my love,' said Archery to please her.

He went downstairs into the dark cool dining room, ordered something called a *Navarin d'agneau,* and in a burst of recklessness, a half-bottle of Anjou. All the windows were open but on some of them the green shutters had been closed. A table in one of these embrasures reminded him with its white cloth, its tilted cane chairs and its vaseful of sweet peas of a Dufy that hung on the wall of his study at home. Filtered sunlight lay in primrose-pale bars across the cloth and the two places laid with silver.

But for himself and half a dozen elderly residents, the dining room was deserted, but presently the door from the bar opened and the head waiter ushered in a man and a woman. Archery wondered if the management would object to the apricot poodle the woman fondled in her arms. But the head waiter was smiling deferentially and Archery saw him pat the tiny woolly head.

The man was small and dark and would have been good-looking but for his glassy, red-rimmed eyes. Archery thought he might be wearing contact lenses. He sat down at the Dufy table, ripped open a packet of Peter Stuyvesant and poured the contents into a gold cigarette case. In spite of the man's obvious polish — his sleek hair, svelte suit, taut bone-smooth skin —

there was something savage in the way his white fingers tore the paper. A wedding ring and a big bold signet gleamed in the soft light as he tossed the mutilated packet on to the cloth. Archery was amused to see how much jewellery he wore, a sapphire tie pin and a watch as well as the rings.

By contrast the woman wore none. She was plainly dressed in a cream silk suit that matched her hair, and everything about her from the gauzy hat and hair to her crossed ankles was the colour of faint sunlight, so that she seemed to glow with a pale radiance. Outside the cinema and the pictures in Mary's magazines, she was the most beautiful woman he had seen for years. Compared to her Tess Painter was just a pretty girl. Archery was reminded of an ivory orchid or a tea rose which, when lifted from the florist's cube of cellophane, still retains its patina of dew.

He gave himself a little shake and applied himself determinedly to his *Navarin*. It had turned out to be two lamb chops in a brown sauce.

Between Kingsmarkham High Street and the Kingsbrook Road lies an estate of ugly terraced houses covered with that mixture of mortar and grit builders call pebble dashing. On a hot day when the roads are dusty and flickering with heat mirage these rows of dun-coloured houses look as if they have been fashioned out of sand. A giant's child might have built them, using his crude tools unimaginatively.

Archery found Glebe Road by the simple and traditional expedient of asking a policeman. He was getting into the habit of asking policemen and this one was low in the hierarchy, a young constable directing traffic at the crossroads.

Glebe Road might have been designed by the Romans, it was so straight, so long and so uncompromising. The sand houses had no woodwork about them. Their window frames were of metal and their porch canopies excrescences of pebbly plaster. After every fourth house an arch in the façade led into the back and through these arches sheds, coal bunkers and dustbins could be seen.

The street was numbered from the Kingsbrook Road end and Archery walked nearly half a mile before he found twenty-four. The hot pavements running with melted tar made his feet burn. He pushed open the gate and saw that the canopy covered not one front door but two. The house had been converted into two surely tiny flatlets. He tapped the chromium knocker on the door marked 24A and waited.

When nothing happened he tapped again. There was a grinding trundling sound and a boy on roller skates came out from under the arch. He took no notice at all of the clergyman. Could Mrs Crilling be asleep? It was hot enough for a siesta and Archery felt languid himself.

He stepped back and looked through the arch. Then he heard the door open and slam shut. So somebody was at home. He rounded the sandy wall and came face to face with Elizabeth Crilling.

At once he sensed that she had not answered, nor probably even heard, his knock. Evidently she was going out. The black dress had been changed for a short blue cotton shift that showed the outlines of her prominent hip bones. She wore backless white mules and carried a huge white and gilt handbag.

'What d'you want?' It was obvious she had no idea who he was. He thought she looked old, finished, as if somehow she had been used and wrecked. 'If you're selling something,' she said, 'you've come to the wrong shop.'

'I saw your mother in court this morning,' Archery said. 'She asked me to come and see her.'

He thought she had rather a charming smile, for her mouth was well-shaped and her teeth good. But the smile was too brief.

'That,' she said, 'was this morning.'

'Is she at home?' He looked helplessly at the doors. 'I — er — which one is it, which flat?'

'Are you kidding? It's bad enough sharing a house with her. Only a stone-deaf paralytic could stick living *underneath* her.'

'I'll go in, shall I?'

'Suit yourself. She's not likely to come out here.' The bag strap was hoisted on to the right shoulder, pulling the blue stuff tight across her breasts. Without knowing why, Archery remembered the exquisite woman in the dining room of the Olive and Dove, her petal skin and her easy grace.

Elizabeth Crilling's face was greasy. In the bright afternoon light the skin had the texture of lemon peel. 'Well, go on in,' she said sharply, unlocking the door. She pushed it open and turned away, her mules flapping and clacking down the path. 'She won't bite you,' she said over her shoulder. 'At least, I shouldn't think so. She bit me once, but there were — well, extenuating circumstances.'

Archery went into the hall. Three doors led off it but they were all closed. He coughed and said tentatively, 'Mrs Crilling?' The place was stuffy and silent. He hesitated for a moment, then opened the first of the doors. Inside was a bedroom divided into two by a hardboard partition. He had been wondering how the two women managed. Now he knew. The middle room must be where they lived. He tapped on the door and opened it.

Although the french windows were ajar the air was thick with smoke and the two ashtrays on a gateleg table were filled with stubs. Every surface was covered with papers and debris and the debris with dust. As he entered a blue budgerigar in a tiny cage broke into a stream of high brittle chatter. The cage swung furiously.

Mrs Crilling wore a pink nylon dressing gown that looked as if it had once been designed for a bride. The honeymoon, Archery thought, was long over, for the dressing gown was stained and torn and hideous. She was sitting in an armchair looking through the window at a fenced-in piece of land at the back. It could hardly be called a garden for nothing grew in it but nettles, three feet high, rose-pink fireweed, and brambles that covered everything with fly-infested tendrils.

'You hadn't forgotten I was coming, Mrs Crilling?'

The face that appeared round the wing of the chair was enough to intimidate anyone. The whites of the eyes showed all the way round the black pupils. Every muscle looked tense, taut and corrugated as if from some inner agony. Her white hair, fringed and styled like a teenager's, curtained the sharp cheek-bones.

'Who are you?' She dragged herself up, clinging to the chair arm, and came slowly round to face him. The vee at the dressing gown front showed a ridged and withered valley like the bed of a long-dried stream.

'We met in court this morning. You wrote to me . . .'

He stopped. She had thrust her face within inches of his and seemed to be scrutinising it. Then she stepped back and gave a long chattering laugh which the budgerigar echoed.

'Mrs Crilling, are you all right? Is there anything I can do?'

She clutched her throat and the laugh died away in a rising wheeze. 'Tablets . . . asthma . . . ,' she gasped. He was puzzled and shocked, but he reached behind him for the bottle of tablets on the littered mantelpiece. 'Give me my tablets and then you can . . . you can get out!'

'I'm sorry if I've done anything to distress you.'

She made no attempt to take a tablet but held the bottle up against her quaking chest. The movement made the tablets rattle and the bird, fluttering its wings and beating against the bars, began a frenzied crescendo, half song and half pain.

'Where's my baby?' Did she mean Elizabeth? She must mean Elizabeth.

'She's gone out. I met her in the porch. Mrs Crilling, can I get you a glass of water? Can I make you a cup of tea?'

'Tea? What do I want with tea? That's what she said this morning, that police girl. Come and have a cup of tea, Mrs Crilling.' A terrible spasm shook her and she fell back against the chair, fighting for breath. 'You . . . my baby . . . I thought you were my friend . . . Aaah!'

Archery was really frightened now. He plunged from the room into the dirty kitchen and filled a cup with water. The window ledge was stacked with empty chemist's bottles and there was a filthy hypodermic beside an equally dirty eye dropper. When he came back she was still wheezing and jerking. Should he make her take the tablets, dare he? On the bottle label were the words: *Mrs J. Crilling. Take two when needed.* He rattled two into his hand and, supporting her with his other arm, forced them into her mouth. It was all he could do to suppress the shudder of distaste when she dribbled and choked over the water.

'Filthy . . . nasty,' she mumbled. He half-eased, half-rolled her into the chair and pulled together the gaping edges of the dressing gown. Moved with pity and with horror, he knelt down beside her.

'I will be your friend if you want me to be,' he said soothingly.

The words had the opposite effect. She made a tremendous effort to draw breath. Her lips split open and he could see her tongue rising and quivering against the roof of her mouth.

'Not my friend . . . enemy . . . police friend! Take my baby away . . . I saw you with them . . . I watched you come out with them.' He drew back from her, rising. Never would he have believed her capable of screaming after that spasm and when the scream came, as clear and ear-splitting as a child's, he felt his hands go up to his face. '. . . Not let them get her in there! Not in the prison! They'll find it out in there. She'll tell them. . . my baby . . . She'll have to tell them!' With a sudden galvanic jerk she reared up, her mouth open and her arms flailing. 'They'll find it all out. I'll kill her first, kill her . . . D'you hear?'

The french windows stood open. Archery staggered back into the sun against a stinging prickling wall of weeds. Mrs Crilling's incoherent gasps had swollen into a stream of obscenity. There was a gate in the wire netting fence. He unlatched it, wiping the sweat from his forehead, and stepped into the cool dark cave of the sand-walled arch.

'Good afternoon, sir. You don't look very well. Heat affecting you?'

Archery had been leaning over the bridge parapet, breathing deeply, when the detective inspector's face appeared beside him.

'Inspector Burden, isn't it?' He shook himself, blinking his eyes. There was comfort in this man's steady gaze and in the shoppers who flowed languidly across the bridge. 'I've just come from Mrs Crilling's and . . .'

'Say no more, sir. I quite understand.'

'I left her in the throes of an asthma attack. Perhaps I should have got a doctor or an ambulance. Frankly, I hardly knew what to do.'

There was a crumb of stony bread on the wall. Burden flicked it into the water and a swan dived for it.

'It's mostly in the mind with her, Mr Archery. I should have warned you what to expect. Threw one of her scenes on you,

67

did she?' Archery nodded. 'Next time you see her I daresay she'll be as nice as pie. That's the way it takes her, up one minute, down the next. Manic-depressive is the term. I was just going into the Carousel for a cup of tea. Why don't you join me?'

They walked up the High Street together. Some of the shops sported faded striped sunblinds. The shadows were as black as night, the light cruelly bright under a Mediterranean blue sky. Inside the Carousel it was darkish and stuffy and it smelt of aerosol fly spray.

'Two teas, please,' said Burden.

'Tell me about the Crillings.'

'There's plenty to tell, Mr Archery. Mrs Crilling's husband died and left her without a penny, so she moved into town and got a job. The kid, Elizabeth, was always difficult and Mrs Crilling made her worse. She took her to psychiatrists — don't ask me where the money came from — and then when they made her send her to school it was one school after another. She was in St Catherine's, Sewingbury, for a bit but she got expelled. When she was about fourteen she came up before the juvenile court here as being in need of care and protection and she was taken away from her mother. But she went back eventually. They usually do.'

'Do you think all this came about because she found Mrs Primero's body?'

'Could be.' Burden looked up and smiled as the waitress brought the tea. 'Thanks very much, miss. Sugar, Mr Archery? No, I don't either.' He cleared his throat and went on, 'I reckon it would have made a difference if she'd had a decent home background, but Mrs Crilling was always unstable. In and out of jobs, by all accounts, until she ended up working in a shop. I think some relative used to give them financial assistance. Mrs Crilling used to take days off from work ostensibly on account of the asthma but really it was because she was crazy.'

'Is she certifiable?'

'You'd be surprised how difficult it is to get anyone certified, sir. The doctor did say that if ever he saw her in one of her tantrums he could get an urgency order, but they're cunning, you see. By the time the doctor gets there she's as normal as you or me. She's been into Stowerton once or twice as a voluntary patient. About four years ago she got herself a man friend. The whole place was buzzing with it. Elizabeth was training to be a physiotherapist at the time. Anyway, the upshot of it all was that the boy friend preferred young Liz.'

'*Mater pulchra, filia pulchrior,*' Archery murmured.

'Just as you say, sir. She gave up her training and went to live with him. Mrs Crilling went off her rocker again and spent six months in Stowerton. When she came out she wouldn't leave the happy couple alone, letters, phone calls, personal appearances, the lot. Liz couldn't stand it so eventually she went back to mother. The boy friend was in the car trade and he gave her that Mini.'

Archery sighed. 'I don't know if I ought to tell you this, but you've been very kind to me, you and Mr Wexford . . .' Burden felt the stirring of guilt. It wasn't what he would call kind. 'Mrs Crilling said that if Elizabeth — she calls her her baby — went to prison . . . it might mean prison, mightn't it?'

'It might well.'

'Then she'd tell you something, you or the prison authorities. I got the impression she'd feel compelled to give you some information Mrs Crilling wanted kept secret.'

'Thank you very much, sir. We shall have to wait and see what time brings forth.'

Archery finished his tea. Suddenly he felt like a traitor. Had he betrayed Mrs Crilling because he wanted to keep in with the police?

'I wondered,' he said, justifying himself, 'if it could have anything to do with Mrs Primero's murder. I don't see why Mrs Crilling couldn't have worn the raincoat and hidden it. You admit yourself she's unbalanced. She was there, she had just as much opportunity as Painter.'

Burden shook his head. 'What was the motive?'

'Mad people have motives which seem very thin to normal men.'

'But she dotes on her daughter in her funny way. She wouldn't have taken the kid with her.'

Archery said slowly, 'At the trial she said she went over the first time at twenty-five past six. But we've only her word for it.

Suppose instead she went at twenty to seven when *Painter* had already been and gone. Then she took the child back later because no-one would believe a killer would wittingly let a child discover a body she knew was there.'

'You've missed your vocation, sir,' said Burden, getting up. 'You should have come in on our lark. You'd have been a superintendent by now.'

'I'm letting my fancy run away with me,' Archery said. To avoid a repetition of the gentle teasing, he added quickly, changing the subject, 'Do you happen to know the visiting times at Stowerton Infirmary?'

'Alice Flower's next on your list, is she? I'd give the matron a ring first, if I were you. Visiting's seven till seven-thirty.'

CHAPTER EIGHT

The days of our age are threescore years and ten; and though men be so strong that they come to fourscore years, yet is their strength then but labour and sorrow.

Psalm 90. *The Burial of the Dead*

Alice Flower was eighty-seven, almost as old as her employer had been at the time of her death. A series of strokes had battered her old frame as tempests batter an ancient house, but the house was strong and sturdily built. No gimcrack refinements of decoration or delicacy had ever belonged to it. It had been made to endure wind and weather.

She lay in a narrow high bed in a ward called Honeysuckle. The ward was full of similar old women in similar beds. They had clean pink faces and white hair through which patches of rose-pink scalp showed. Every bed trolley held at least two vases of flowers, the sops to conscience, Archery supposed, of visiting relatives who only had to sit and chat instead of handling bed-pans and tending bed-sores.

'A visitor for you, Alice,' said the sister. 'It's no use trying to shake hands with her. She can't move her hands but her hearing's perfectly good and she'll talk the hind leg off a donkey.'

A most un-Christian hatred flared in Archery's eyes. If she saw it the sister took no notice.

'Like a good gossip, don't you, Alice? This is the Reverend Archery.' He winced at that, approached the bed.

'Good evening, sir.'

Her face was square with deeply ridged rough skin. One corner of her mouth had been drawn down by the paralysis of the motor nerves, causing her lower jaw to protrude and reveal large false teeth. The sister bustled about the bed, pulling the old servant's nightgown higher about her neck and arranging on

71

the coverlet her two useless hands. It was terrible to Archery to have to look at those hands. Work had distorted them beyond hope of beauty, but disease and oedema had smoothed and whitened the skin so that they were like the hands of a misshapen baby. The emotion and the feel for the language of 1611 that was with him always welled in a fount of pity. Well done, thou good and faithful servant, he thought. Thou hast been faithful over a few things, I will make thee ruler over many things . . .

'Would it upset you to talk to me about Mrs Primero, Miss Flower?' he asked gently, easing himself into a bentwood chair.

'Of course it wouldn't,' said the sister, 'she loves it.'

Archery could bear no more. 'This is rather a private matter, if you don't mind.'

'Private! It's the whole ward's bedtime story, believe me.' She flounced away, a crackling navy and white robot.

Alice Flower's voice was cracked and harsh. The strokes had affected her throat muscles or her vocal cords. But her accent was pleasant and correct, learnt, Archery supposed, in the kitchens and nurseries of educated people.

'What was it you wanted to know, sir?'

'First tell me about the Primero family.'

'Oh, I can do that. I always took an interest.' She gave a small rattling cough and turned her head to hide the twisted side of her mouth. 'I went to Mrs Primero when the boy was born . . .'

'The boy?'

'Mr Edward, her only child he was.'

Ah, thought Archery, the father of rich Roger and his sisters.

'He was a lovely boy and we always got on a treat, him and me. I reckon it really aged me and his poor mother when he died, sir. But he'd got a family of his own by then, thanks be to God, and Mr Roger was the living spit of his father.'

'I suppose Mr Edward left him pretty well off, did he?'

'Oh, no, sir, that was the pity of it. You see, old Dr Primero left his money to madam, being as Mr Edward was doing so well at the time. But he lost everything on something in the city and when he was taken Mrs Edward and the three kiddies were quite badly off.' She coughed again, making Archery wince. He fancied he could see a terrible vain effort to raise those hands and cover the rattling lips. 'Madam offered to help — not that she had more than she needed — but Mrs Edward was that proud, she wouldn't take a penny from her mother-in-law. I never shall know how she managed. There was the three of them, you see. Mr Roger he was the eldest, and then there was the two little mites, ever so much younger than their brother, but close together if you take my meaning. No more than eighteen months between them.'

She rested her head back on the pillows and bit at her lip as if trying to pull it back into place. 'Angela was the oldest. Time flies so I reckon she'd be twenty-six now. Then there was Isabel, named after madam. They was just babies when their Daddy died and it was years before we saw them.

'It was a bitter blow to madam, I can tell you, not knowing what had become of Mr Roger. Then one day just out of the blue he turned up at Victor's Piece. Fancy, he was living in digs just over at Sewingbury, studying to be a solicitor with a very good firm. Somebody Mrs Edward knew had got him in. He hadn't no idea his granny was still alive, let alone in Kingsmarkham, but he was looking up somebody in the phone book, in the line of business, sir, and there it was: Mrs Rose Primero, Victor's Piece. Once he'd come over there was no stopping him. Not that we wanted to stop him, sir. Pretty nearly every Sunday he came and once or twice he fetched his little sisters all the way from London and brought them with him. Good as gold they were.

'Mr Roger and madam, they used to have some laughs together. All the old photographs they'd have out and the tales she used to tell him!' She stopped suddenly and Archery watched the old face swell and grow purple. 'It was a change for us to have a nice gentlemanlike young fellow about the place after that Painter.' Her voice changed to a shrill whistling shriek. 'That dirty murdering beast!'

Across the ward another old woman in a bed like Alice Flower's smiled a toothless smile as of one hearing a familiar tale retold. The ward's bedtime story, the sister had said.

Archery leant towards her. 'That was a dreadful day, Miss

Flower,' he said, 'the day Mrs Primero died.' The fierce eyes flickered, red and spongey blue. 'I expect you feel you'll never forget it . . .'

'Not to my dying day,' said Alice Flower. Perhaps she thought of the now useless body that had once been so fine an instrument and was already three-quarters dead.

'Will you tell me about it?'

As soon as she began he realised how often she must have told it before. It was likely that some of these old women were not absolutely bedridden, that sometimes in the evenings they got up and gathered round Alice Flower's bed. A tale, he thought, paraphrasing, to draw children from play and old women from the chimney corner.

'He was a devil,' she said, 'a terror. I was scared of him but I never let him know it. Take all and give nothing, that was his motto. Six pounds a year, that was all I got when I first went out into service. Him, he had his home and his wages, a lovely motor to drive. There's some folks want the moon. You'd think a big strong young fellow like that'd be only too glad to fetch the coal in for an old lady, but not Mr Bert Painter. Beast Painter was what I called him.

'That Saturday night when he never come and he never come madam had to sit all by herself in the icy cold. Let me go over and speak to him, madam, I said, but she wouldn't have it. The morning's time enough, Alice, she said. I've said to myself over and over again, if he'd come that night I'd have been in there with them. He wouldn't have been able to tell no lies then.'

'But he did come the next morning, Miss Flower . . .'

'She told him off good and proper. I could hear her giving him a dressing down.'

'What were you doing?'

'Me? When he come in first I was doing the vegetables for madam's lunch, then I popped on the oven and put in the meat tin. They asked me all that at the court in London, the Old Bailey it was.' She paused and there was suspicion in the look she gave him. 'You writing a book about it all, are you, sir?'

'Something like that,' said Archery.

'They wanted to know if I was sure I could hear all right.

My hearing's better than that judge's, I can tell you. Just as well it is. If I'd been hard of hearing we might have all gone up in smoke that morning.'

'How was that?'

'Beast Painter was in the drawing room with madam and I'd gone into the larder to get the vinegar for the mint sauce, when all of a sudden I heard a kind of plop and sizzle. That's that funny old oven, I said, and sure enough it was. I popped back quick and opened the oven door. One of the potatoes had kind of spat out, sir, and fallen on the gas. All in flames it was and sizzling and roaring like a steam engine. I turned it off quick and then I did a silly thing. Poured water on it. Ought to have known better at my age. Ooh, the racket and the smoke! You couldn't hear yourself think.'

There had been nothing about that in the trial transcript. Archery caught his breath in the excitement. 'You couldn't hear yourself think...' While you were choked with smoke and deafened by hissing you might not hear a man go upstairs, search a bedroom and come down again. Alice's evidence in this matter had been one of the most important features of the case. For if Painter had been offered and had taken the two hundred pounds in Mrs Primero's presence in the morning, what motive could he have had for killing her in the evening?

'Well, we had our lunch and Mr Roger came. My poor old leg was aching from where I'd bruised it the night before getting a few lumps in on account of Beast Painter being out on the tiles. Mr Roger was ever so nice about it, kept asking me if there was anything he could do, wash up or anything. But that isn't man's work and I always say it's better to keep going while you can.

'It must have been half past five when Mr Roger said he'd have to go. I was up to my neck what with the dishes and worrying if Beast would turn up like he'd promised. "I'll let myself out, Alice," Mr Roger said, and he come down to the kitchen to say good-bye to me. Madam was having a little snooze in the drawing room, God rest her. It was the last she had before her long sleep.' Aghast, Archery watched two tears well into her eyes and flow unchecked down the ridged sunken cheeks. 'I called out, "Cheeri-by, Mr Roger dear, see you next

Sunday", and then I heard him shut the front door. Madam was sleeping like a child, not knowing that ravening wolf was lying in wait for her.'

'Try not to upset yourself, Miss Flower.' Doubtful as to what he should do — the right thing is the kind thing, he thought — he pulled out his own clean white handkerchief and gently wiped the wet cheeks.

'Thank you, sir. I'll be all right now. You do feel a proper fool not being able to dry your own tears.' The ghastly cracked smile was almost more painful to witness than the weeping. 'Where was I? Oh, yes. Off I went to church and as soon as I was out of the way along comes Madam Crilling, poking her nose in . . .'

'I know what happened next, Miss Flower,' Archery said very kindly and quietly. 'Tell me about Mrs Crilling. Does she ever come to see you in here?'

Alice Flower gave a kind of snort that would have been comical in a fit person. 'Not she. She's kept out of my way ever since the trial, sir. I know too much about her for her liking. Madam's best friend, my foot! She'd got one interest in madam and one only. She wormed that child of hers into madam's good books on account of she thought madam might leave her something when she went.'

Archery moved closer, praying that the bell for the end of visiting would not ring yet.

'But Mrs Primero didn't make a will.'

'Oh, no, sir, that's what worried Mrs Clever Crilling. She'd come out into my kitchen when madam was sleeping. "Alice," she'd say, "we ought to get dear Mrs Primero to make her last will and testament. It's our duty, Alice, it says so in the Prayer Book." '

'Does it?'

Alice looked both shocked and smug. 'Yes, it does, sir. It says, "But men should often be put in remembrance to take order for the settling of their temporal estates whilst they are in health." Still I don't hold with everything that's in the Prayer Book, not when in comes to downright interference — saving your presence, sir. "It's in your interest too, Alice," she says. "You'll be turned out into the streets when she goes."

'But madam wouldn't have it, anyway. Everything was to go to her natural heirs, she said, them being Mr Roger and the little girls. It'd be theirs automatically, you see, without any nonsense about wills and lawyers.'

'Mr Roger didn't try to get her to make a will?'

'He's a lovely person is Mr Roger. When Beast Painter had done his murdering work and poor madam was dead Mr Roger got his bit of money — three thousand it was and a bit more. "I'll take care of you, Alice," he said, and so he did. He got me a nice room in Kingsmarkham and gave me two pounds a week on top of my pension. He was in business on his own then and he said he wouldn't give me a lump sum. An allowance, he called it, bless his heart, out of his profits.'

'Business? I thought he was a solicitor.'

'He always wanted to go into business on his own, sir. I don't know the ins and outs of it, but he came to madam one day — must have been two or three weeks before she died — and he said a pal of his would take him in with him if he could put up ten thousand pounds. "I know I haven't got a hope," he said, speaking ever so nice. "It's just a castle in the air, Granny Rose." "Well, it's no good looking at me," says madam. "Ten thousand is all I've got for me and Alice to live on and that's tucked away in Woolworth's shares. You'll get your share when I'm gone." I don't mind telling you, sir, I thought then, if Mr Roger liked to do his little sisters down he could try getting round madam to make that will and leave him the lot. But he never did, never mentioned it again, and he'd always made a point of bringing the two mites just whenever he could. Then Beast Painter killed madam and the money went like she said it would, to the three of them.

'Mr Roger's doing very well now, sir, very well indeed, and he comes to see me regular. I reckon he got the ten thousand from somewhere or maybe another pal came up with something else. It wasn't for me to ask, you see.'

A nice man, Archery thought, a man who had needed money perhaps desperately, but would do nothing underhand to get it; a man who provided for his dead grandmother's domestic while he was struggling to get a business going, who still visited her and who doubtless listened patiently over and over again to the tale Archery had just heard. A very nice man. If love, praise and devotion could reward such a man, he had his reward.

'If you should see Mr Roger, sir, if you want to see him about the story you're writing, would you give him my best respects?'

'I won't forget, Miss Flower.' He put his hand over her dead one and pressed it. 'Good-bye and thank you.' Well done, thou good and faithful servant.

It was gone eight when he got back to the Olive and Dove. The head waiter glared at him when he walked into the dining room at a quarter past. Archery stared about him at the empty room, the chairs arranged against the walls.

'Dance on tonight, sir. We did make a point of asking residents to take their dinner at seven sharp, but I expect we can find you something. In here, if you please.'

Archery followed him into the smaller of the two lounges that led off the dining room. The tables had been crammed in and people were hastily gobbling their meal. He ordered, and through the glass doors, watched the band take its place on the dais.

How was he to spend this long hot summer evening? The dancing would probably go on until half-past twelve or one and the hotel would be unbearable. A quiet stroll was the obvious thing. Or he could take the car and go and look at Victor's Piece. The waiter came back with the braised beef he had ordered, and Archery, resolutely economical, asked for a glass of water.

He was quite alone in his alcove, at least two yards from the next table, and he jumped when he felt something soft and fluffy brush against his leg. Drawing back, he put his hand down, lifted the cloth and met a pair of bright eyes set in a golden woolly skull.

'Hallo, dog,' he said.

'Oh I'm so sorry. Is he being a nuisance?'

He looked up and saw her standing beside him. They had evidently just come in, she, the man with the glassy eyes and another couple.

'Not a bit.' Archery's poise deserted him and he found himself almost stammering. 'I don't mind, really. I'm fond of animals.'

'You were here at lunch, weren't you? I expect he recognised you. Come out, Dog. He doesn't have a name. We just call him Dog because he is one and it's just as good a name as Jock or Gyp or something. When you said, "Hallo, dog," he thought you were a personal friend. He's very intelligent.'

'I'm sure he is.'

She gathered the poodle up in her arms and held him against the creamy lace of her dress. Now that she wore no hat he could see the perfect shape of her head and the high unshadowed brow. The head waiter minced over, no longer harassed.

'Back again, Louis, like the proverbial bad pennies,' said the glassy-eyed man heartily. 'My wife took a fancy to come to your hop, but we must have a spot of dinner first.' So they were married, these two. Why hadn't it occurred to him before, what business was it of his and, above all, why should it cause him this faint distress? 'Our friends here have a train to catch, so if you can go all out with the old speed we'll be eternally grateful.'

They all sat down. The poodle mooched between diners' legs, scavenging for crumbs. Archery was faintly amused to see how quickly their dinner was brought to them. They had all ordered different dishes, but there was little delay and at the same time little hustle. Archery lingered over his coffee and his bit of cheese. Surely he was no bother to anyone in his small corner. People were coming in to dance now, passing his table and leaving in their wake the faint scent of cigars and floral perfume. In the dining room, a ballroom, now, the garden doors had been opened and couples stood on the terrace listening to the music in the tranquillity of the summer night.

The poodle sat on the threshold, bored, watching the dancers.

'Come here, Dog,' said his owner. Her husband got up.

'I'll take you to the station, George,' he said. 'We've only got ten minutes, so get a wiggle on, will you?' He seemed to have a variety of expressions to imply the making of haste. 'You don't have to come, darling. Finish your coffee.'

The table was veiled in smoke. They had smoked

throughout the courses. He would be gone perhaps only half an hour but he bent over and kissed his wife. She smiled at him, lit another cigarette. When they had gone, she and Archery were alone. She moved into her husband's chair from where she could watch the dancers, many of whom she seemed to know, for she waved occasionally and nodded as if promising she would soon join them.

Archery suddenly felt lonely. He knew no one in this place except two rather hostile policemen. His stay might be for the whole fortnight. Why hadn't he asked Mary to join him? It would be a holiday for her, a change, and — heaven knew — she needed a change. In a minute, when he had finished his second cup, he would go upstairs and telephone her.

The girl's voice startled him. 'Do you mind if I have your ashtray? Ours are all full.'

'Of course not, take it.' He lifted the heavy glass plate and as he handed it to her the tips of her cool dry fingers touched his own. The hand was small, childlike, with short unpainted nails. 'I don't smoke,' he added rather foolishly.

'Are you staying here long?' Her voice was light and soft, yet mature.

'Just a few days.'

'I asked,' she said, 'because we come here so often and I hadn't seen you before today. Most of the people are regulars.' She put out the cigarette carefully, stubbing it until the last red spark was dead. 'They have these dances once a month and we always come. I love dancing.'

Afterwards Archery wondered what on earth had induced him, a country vicar nearly fifty years old, to say what he did. Perhaps it was the mingled scents, the descending twilight or just that he was alone and out of his environment, out of his identity almost.

'Would you like to dance?'

It was a waltz they were playing. He was sure he could waltz. They waltzed at church socials. You simply had to make your feet go one, two, three in a sort of triangle. And yet, for all that, he felt himself blush. What would she think of him at his age? She might suppose he was doing what Charles called 'picking her up'.

'I'd love to,' she said.

Apart from Mary and Mary's sister, she was the only woman he had danced with in twenty years. He was so shy and so overcome by the enormity of what he was doing, that for a moment he was deaf to the music and blind to the hundred or so other people who circled the floor. Then she was in his arms, a light creature of scent and lace whose body so incongruously touching his had the fluidity and the tenuousness of a summer mist. He felt that he was dreaming and because of this, this utter unreality, he forgot about his feet and what he must make them do, and simply moved with her as if he and she and the music were one.

'I'm not very good at this sort of thing,' he said when he found his voice. 'You'll have to overlook my mistakes.' He was so much taller than she that she had to lift her face up to him.

She smiled. 'Hard to make conversation when you're dancing, isn't it? I never know what to say but one must say something.'

'Like "Don't you think this is a good floor?" ' Strange, he remembered that one from undergraduate days.

'Or "Do you reverse?" It's absurd really. Here we are dancing together and I don't even know your name.' She gave a little deprecating laugh. 'It's almost immoral.'

'My name's Archery. Henry Archery.'

'How do you do, Henry Archery?' she said gravely. Then as they moved into a pool of sunset light, she looked steadily at him, the glowing colour falling on her face. 'You really don't recognise me, do you?' He shook his head, wondering if he had made some terrible *faux pas*. She gave a mock sigh. 'Such is fame! Imogen Ide. Doesn't it ring a bell?'

'I'm awfully sorry.'

'Frankly, you don't look as if you spend your leisure perusing the glossy magazines. Before I married I was what they call a top model. The most photographed face in Britain.'

He hardly knew what to say. The things that came to mind all had some reference to her extraordinary beauty and to speak them aloud would have been impertinent. Sensing his predicament, she burst out laughing, but it was a companionable laugh, warm and kind.

He smiled down at her. Then over her shoulder he caught sight of a familiar face. Chief Inspector Wexford had come on to the floor with a stout pleasant-looking woman and a young couple. His wife, his daughter and the architect's son. Archery supposed, feeling a sudden pang. He watched them sit down and just as he was about to avert his eyes, Wexford's met his. The smiles they exchanged were slightly antagonistic and Archery felt hot with awkwardness. Wexford's expression held a mocking quality as if to say that dancing was a frivolity quite out of keeping with Archery's quest. Abruptly he looked away and back to his partner.

'I'm afraid I only read *The Times*,' he said, feeling the snobbishness of the remark as soon as the words were out.

'I was in *The Times* once,' she said. 'Oh, not my picture. I was in the High Court bit. Somebody mentioned my name in a case and the judge said "Who is Imogen Ide?".'

'That really is fame.'

'I've kept the cutting to this day.'

The music that had been so liquid and lullaby-like suddenly jerked into a frightening tempo with a stormy undertone of drums.

'I haven't a hope of doing this one,' Archery said helplessly. He released her quickly, there in the middle of the floor.

'Never mind. Thank you very much anyway. I've enjoyed it.'

'So have I, very much indeed.'

They began to thread their way between couples who were shuddering and bounding about like savages. She was holding his hand and he could hardly withdraw it without rudeness.

'Here's my husband back,' she said. 'Won't you join us for the evening if you've nothing better to do?'

The man called Ide was coming up to them, smiling. His evenly olive face, dead black hair and almost feminine standard of grooming gave him the look of a waxwork. Archery had the absurd notion that if you came upon him at Madame Tussaud's the old joke of the naive spectator mistaking a model for a flesh and blood attendant would be reversed. In this case you would pass the real man by, thinking him a figure in wax.

'This is Mr Archery, darling. I've been telling him he ought to stay. It's such a beautiful night.'

'Good idea. Perhaps I can get you a drink, Mr Archery?'

'Thank you, no.' Archery found himself shaking hands, astonished because of his fantasy at the warmth of Ide's hand. 'I must go. I have to phone my wife.'

'I hope we shall see you again,' said Imogen Ide. 'I enjoyed our dance.' She took her husband's hand and they moved away into the centre of the floor, their bodies meeting, their steps following the intricate rhythm. Archery went upstairs to his bedroom. Earlier he had supposed that the music would annoy him but here in the violet-coloured dusk it was enchanting, disturbing, awakening in him forgotten, undefined longings. He stood at the window, looking at the sky with its long feathery scarves of cloud, rose pink as cyclamen petals but less substantial. The strains of the music had softened to match this tranquil sky and now they seemed to him like the opening bars of an overture to some pastoral opera.

Presently he sat down on the bed and put his hand to the telephone. It rested there immobile for some minutes. What was the point of ringing Mary when he had nothing to tell her, no plans even for what he would do in the morning? He felt a sudden distaste for Thringford and its small parochial doings. He had lived there so long, so narrowly, and outside all the time there had been a world of which he knew little.

From where he sat he could see nothing but sky, broken continents and islands on a sea of azure. 'Here will we sit and let the sound of music creep in our ears . . .' He took his hand from the telephone and lay back, thinking of nothing.

CHAPTER NINE

The words of his mouth were softer than butter, having war in his heart: his words were smoother than oil, and yet be they very swords.

Psalm 55, appointed for the Tenth Day.

'I suppose there isn't anything in it?'

'In what, Mike? Liz Crilling having some dark secret her mother doesn't want extorted from her under the third degree?'

Burden lowered the blinds against the brazen morning sky.

'Those Crillings always make me uneasy,' he said.

'They're no more kinky than half our customers,' Wexford said breezily. 'Liz'll turn up at the Assizes all right. If not for any other reason simply because Mrs Crilling doubts her ability to get a thousand quid out of her brother-in-law, or whoever it is supports them. And then if she's got something to tell us, she'll tell us.'

Burden's expression, though apologetic, was obstinate.

'I can't help feeling it's got some connection with Painter,' he said.

Wexford had been leafing through a thick orange-coloured trade directory. Now he dropped it on the desk with a deliberate bang.

'By God, I won't have any more of this! What is it, anyhow, some sort of conspiracy to prove I can't do my job?'

'I'm sorry, sir, you know I didn't mean that.'

'I don't know a damn' thing, Mike. I only know the Painter case was an open and shut affair, and nobody's got a hope in hell of showing he didn't do it.' He began to calm down slowly, and he spread his hands in two large implacable fans on the directory cover. 'Go and question Liz by all means. Or tell Archery to do it for you. He's a fast worker that one.'

'Is he? What makes you say so?'

'Never mind. I've got work to do if you haven't and . . .' said Wexford, splendidly co-ordinating his metaphors, 'I'm fed up to my back teeth with having Painter rammed down my throat morning, noon and night.'

Archery had slept deeply and dreamlessly. It occurred to him that he had done all his dreaming while he was awake and there was none left for sleep. The telephone roused him. It was his wife.

'Sorry it's so early, darling, but I've had another letter from Charles.'

There was a cup of cold tea by the bed. Archery wondered how long it had been there. He found his watch and saw that it was nine.

'That's all right. How are you?'

'Not so bad. You sound as if you're still in bed.'

Archery grunted something.

'Now, listen. Charles is coming down tomorrow and he says he's coming straight over to Kingsmarkham.'

'Coming *down*?'

'Oh, it's all right, Henry. He's going to cut the last three days of term. Surely it can't matter much.'

'As long as it isn't the thin end of the wedge. Is he coming to the Olive?'

'Well, naturally. He's got to stay somewhere. I know it's expensive, darling, but he's got himself a job for August and September — something in a brewery. It sounds awful but he's going to get sixteen pounds a week and he says he'll pay you back.'

'I hadn't realised I made such an avaricious impression on my son.'

'You know he doesn't mean that. You *are* touchy this morning . . .'

After she had rung off he still held the receiver for some moments in his hand. He wondered why he hadn't asked her to join him as well. He had meant to last night and then . . . Of course, he had been so drowsy while she was speaking that he hardly knew what he was saying. The operator's voice broke in.

'Have you finished or did you want to make a call?'

'No thank you. I've finished.'

The little sandy houses in Glebe Road seemed to have been bleached and dried up by the sun. This morning they looked even more like desert dwellings, each surrounded by its own scanty oasis.

Burden went first to number a hundred and two. An old acquaintance of his lived there, a man with a long record and a nasty sense of humour called by some 'Monkey' Matthews. Burden thought it more than likely that he was responsible for the home-made bomb, a bizarre affair of sugar and weed killer stuffed into a whisky bottle that a blonde woman of easy virtue had received that morning through her letter box. The bomb had done no more than wreck the hall of her flat, she and her current lover being still in bed, but Burden thought it might amount to attempted murder just the same.

He knocked and rang but he was sure the bell didn't work. Then he went round the back and found himself ankle-deep in garbage, pram wheels, old clothes, newspapers and empty bottles. He looked through the kitchen window. There was a packet of weed killer — sodium chlorate crystals — on the window sill and the top had been torn off. How confident could you get, or how stupid? He went back up the street to a call box and told Bryant and Gates to pick up the occupant of a hundred and two Glebe Road.

Twenty-four was on the same side. Now he was so near there would be no harm in having a chat with Liz Crilling. The front door was closed but the latch was down. He coughed and walked in.

In the back room a plastic transistor was playing pop music. Elizabeth Crilling sat at the table reading the Situations Vacant in last week's local paper and she was wearing nothing but a slip, its broken shoulder strap held together with a safety pin.

'I don't remember inviting you in.'

Burden looked at her distastefully. 'D'you mind putting something on?' She made no move but kept her eyes on the paper. He glanced around the dismal, untidy room, and from the various miscellaneous heaps of clothes, selected something that might have been a dressing gown, a pink floppy thing whose flounces recalled withered petals. 'Here,' he said, and he wondered if she were not quite well, for she shuddered as she put the dressing gown round her. It was far too big, obviously not her own.

'Where's your mother?'

'I don't know. Gone out somewhere. I'm not her keeper.' She grinned suddenly, showing her beautiful teeth. 'Am I my mother's keeper? That's good, don't you think? Which reminds me . . .' The smile died and she exclaimed sharply, 'What's that clergyman doing here?'

Burden never answered a question if he could help it.

'Looking for a new post, are you?'

She gave a sulky pout. 'I phoned my firm yesterday when I got back from that bloody court and they gave me the push. I've got you lot to thank for that.' Burden inclined his head politely. 'Well, I've got to have a job, haven't I? They want girls at the raincoat factory and they say you can pick up twenty quid a week with overtime.'

Burden remembered her education, the expensive schools the Crilling relatives had paid for. She stared at him boldly.

'I may as well go and see them,' she said. 'What's the harm? Life's hell anyway.' She gave a strident laugh, walked to the mantelpiece and leaned against it, looking down at him. The open dressing gown, the tatty underclothes were provocative in a raw, basic way, that seemed to go with the hot weather and the dishevelled room. 'To what do I owe the honour of this visit? Are you lonely, Inspector? I hear your wife's away.' She took a cigarette and put it between her lips. Her forefinger was rusty with nicotine, the nail yellow, the cuticle bitten. 'Where the hell are the matches?'

There was something in the quick wary look she gave over her shoulder that impelled him to follow her to the kitchen. Once there, she turned to face him, grabbed a box of matches and stood as if barring his way. He felt a thrill of alarm. She thrust the matches into his hand.

'Light it for me, will you?'

He struck the match steadily. She came very close to him and as the flame shrivelled the tobacco, closed her fingers over his hand. For a split second he felt what his rather prudish nature told him was vile, then that nature, his duty and a swift suspicion took over. She was breathing hard, but not, he was certain, because of his nearness to her. From long practice he side-stepped neatly, freeing the long bare leg from between his own, and found himself confronting what she perhaps had hoped to hide from him.

The sink was crammed with dirty crocks, potato peelings, tea leaves, wet paper, but the Crillings were long past middle-class concealment of squalor.

'You could do with a few days off, I should think,' he said loudly. 'Get this place in some sort of order.'

She had begun to laugh. 'You know, you're not so bad-looking on the other side of a smoke-screen.'

'Been ill, have you?' He was looking at the empty pill bottles, the one that was half full and the syringe. 'Nerves, I daresay.'

She stopped laughing. 'They're hers.'

Burden read labels, saying nothing.

'She has them for her asthma. They're all the same.' As he put out his hand to find the hypodermic she seized his wrist. 'You've no business to turn things over. That amounts to searching and for searching you need a warrant.'

'True,' said Burden placidly. He followed her back to the living room and jumped when she shouted at him:

'You never answered my question about the clergyman.'

'He's come here because he knows Painter's daughter,' said Burden guardedly.

She went white and he thought she looked like her mother.

'Painter that killed the old woman?'

Burden nodded.

'That's funny,' she said. 'I'd like to see her again.' He had a queer feeling she was changing the subject, and yet her remark was not inconsequential. She turned her eyes towards the garden. But it wasn't, he thought, the nettles, the brambles and the mean wire fence she could see. 'I used to go over to the coach house and play with her,' she said. 'Mother never knew. She said Tess wasn't my class. I couldn't understand that. I thought, how can she have a class if she doesn't go to school?' She reached up and gave the birdcage a vicious push. 'Mother was always with the old woman — talk, talk, I'll never forget it — and she used to send me into the garden to play. There wasn't anything to play with and one day I saw Tessie, mucking about with a heap of sand . . . Why are you looking at me like that?'

'Am I?'

'Does she know about her father?' Burden nodded. 'Poor kid. What does she do for a living?'

'She's some kind of student.'

'*Student?* My God, I was a student once.' She had begun to tremble. The long worm of ash broke from her cigarette and scattered down the pink flounces. Looking down at it, she flicked uselessly at old stains and burn marks. The movement suggested the uncontrollable jerking of chorea. She swung round on him, her hate and despair striking him like a flame. 'What are you trying to do to me?' she shouted. 'Get out! Get out!'

When he had gone she grabbed a torn sheet from a stack of unironed linen and flung it over the birdcage. The sudden movement and the gust of breeze it had caused fluttered the thing her mother called a negligee but that she had never feared until it touched her own skin. Why the hell did he have to come here and rake it all up again. Perhaps a drink would help. True, it hadn't done so the other day . . . There never was a drink in this house, anyway.

Newspapers, old letters and unpaid bills, empty cigarette packets and a couple of old laddered stockings tumbled out when she opened the cupboard door. She rummaged in the back among dusty vases, Christmas wrapping paper, playing cards with dog-eared corners. One vase had an encouraging shape. She pulled it out and found it was the cherry brandy Uncle had given her mother for her birthday. Filthy, sweet cherry brandy . . . She squatted on the floor among the debris and poured some of it into a grimy glass. In a minute she felt a lot better, almost well enough to get dressed and do something about the bloody job. Now she had begun she might as well finish the bottle — it was wonderful how little it took to do the trick provided you started on an empty stomach.

The neck of the bottle rattled against the glass. She was concentrating on keeping her hand steady, not watching the liquid level rise and rise until it overbrimmed, spilt and streamed over the spread pink flounces.

Red everywhere. Good thing we're not houseproud, she thought, and then she looked down at herself, at red on pale pink . . . Her fingers tore at the nylon until they were red and sticky too. O God, God! She trampled on it, shuddering as if it were slimy, alive, and threw herself on the sofa . . . You had nothing pretty on now, nothing to show to Tessie. She used to worry in case you got yourself dirty and one day when Mummy was indoors with Granny Rose and the man they called Roger she took you upstairs to see Auntie Rene and Uncle Bert, and Auntie Rene made you put an old apron on over your frock.

Uncle Bert and Roger. They were the only men you knew apart from Daddy who was always ill — 'ailing' Mummy called it. Uncle Bert was rough and big and once when you came upstairs quietly you heard him shouting at Auntie Rene and then you saw him hit her. But he was kind to you and he called you Lizzie. Roger never called you anything. How could he when he never spoke to you, but looked at you as if he hated you?

It was in the autumn that Mummy said you ought to have a party frock. Funny really, because there weren't any parties to go to, but Mummy said you could wear it on Christmas day. Pink it was, three layers of pale pink net over a pink petticoat, and it was the most beautiful dress you had ever seen in your life . . .

Elizabeth Crilling knew that once it had begun it would go on and on. Only one thing could stop it now. Keeping her eyes from the pink thing, all spattered with red, she stumbled out into the kitchen to find her temporary salvation.

Irene Kershaw's voice on the telephone sounded cold and distant. 'Your Charlie seems to have had a bit of a tiff with Tessie, Mr Archery. I don't know what it's all about, but I'm sure it can't be her fault. She worships the ground he treads on.'

'They're old enough to know what they're doing,' said Archery insincerely.

'She's coming home tomorrow and she must be upset if she's cutting the last days of term. All the people round here keep asking when the wedding is and I just don't know what to say. It puts me in a very awkward position.'

Respectability, always respectability.

'Did you ring me up about something special, Mr Archery, or was it just for a chat?'

'I wondered if you'd mind giving me your husband's business number?'

'If you two think you can get together,' she said more warmly, 'and have a go at patching things up, that would suit me down to the ground. I really can't contemplate the idea of my Tess being — well, thrown over.' Archery did not answer. 'The number's Uplands 62234,' she said.

Kershaw had an extension of his own and a bright cockney secretary.

'I want to write to Painter's commanding officer,' Archery said when the civilities had been exchanged.

Kershaw seemed to hesitate, then said in his usual eager vital voice, 'Don't know the bloke's name, but it was the Duke of Babraham's Light Infantry he was in. Third Battalion. The War Office'll tell you.'

'The defence didn't call him at the trial, but it might help me if he could give Painter a good character.'

'If. I wonder why the defence didn't call him, Mr Archery?'

The War Office was helpful. The Third Battalion had been commanded by a Colonel Cosmo Plashet. He was an old man now living in retirement in Westmorland. Archery made several attempts to write to Colonel Plashet. The final letter was not what he would have wished, but it would have to do. After lunch he went out to post it.

He strolled up towards the Post Office. Time hung heavy on his hands and he had no notion what to do next. Tomorrow Charles would come, full of ideas and extravagant plans, but comforting, an assistant. Or, knowing Charles, a director. He badly needed someone to direct him. Police work is for policemen, he thought, experts who are trained and have all the means for detection at their disposal.

Then he saw her. She was coming out of the florist's next door to the Post Office and her arms were full of white roses. They matched and mingled with the white pattern on her black dress so that you could not tell which were real and which a mere design on silk.

RUTH RENDELL

'Good afternoon, Mr Archery,' said Imogen Ide.

Until now he had hardly noticed the beauty of the day, the intense blue of the sky, the glory of perfect holiday weather. She smiled.

'Would you be very kind and open the car door for me?'

He jumped to do her bidding like a boy. The poodle, Dog, was sitting on the passenger seat and when Archery touched the door, he growled and showed his teeth.

'Don't be such a fool,' she said to the dog and dumped him on the back seat. 'I'm taking these up to Forby cemetery. My husband's ancestors have a sort of vault there. Very feudal. He's in town so I said I'd do it. It's an interesting old church. Have you seen much of the country round here yet?'

'Very little, I'm afraid.'

'Perhaps you don't care for clerestories and fonts and that sort of thing.'

'Quite the contrary, I assure you. I'll get the car and go over to Forby tonight if you think it's worth seeing.'

'Why not come now?'

He had meant her to ask him. He knew it and he was ashamed. Yet what was there to be ashamed about? In a way he was on holiday and holiday acquaintances were quickly made. He had met her husband and it was only by chance her husband was not with her now. In that case there was no harm in a man going on a little excursion with a woman. How many times had he picked up Miss Bayliss in Thringford village and driven her into Colchester to do her shopping? Imogen Ide was much farther removed from him in age than Miss Bayliss. She couldn't be more than thirty. He was old enough to be her father. Suddenly he wished he hadn't thought of that, for it put things in an unpleasant perspective.

'It's very good of you,' he said. 'I'd like to.'

She was a good driver. For once he didn't mind being driven, didn't wish he was at the wheel. It was a beautiful car, a silver Lancia Flavia, and it purred along the winding roads. All was still and they passed only two other cars. The meadows were rich green or pale yellow where they had been shorn of hay, and between them and a dark ridge of woodland ran a glittering brown stream.

'That's the Kingsbrook,' she said, 'the same one that passes under the High Street. Isn't it strange? Man can do almost anything, move mountains, create seas, irrigate deserts, but he can't prevent the flow of water. He can dam it, channel it, pass it through pipes, make bridges over it . . .' He watched her, remembering with wonder that she had been a photographic model. Her lips were parted and the breeze blew her hair. 'But still it springs from the earth and finds its way to the sea.'

He said nothing and hoped she could sense if not see his nod. They were coming into a village. A dozen or so cottages and a couple of big houses surrounded a sprawling green; there was a little inn and through a mass of dark green foliage. Archery could see the outlines of the church.

The entrance to the churchyard was by way of a kissing gate. He followed Imogen Ide and he carried the roses. The place was shady and cool but not well-tended and some of the older gravestones had tumbled over on their backs into the tangle of nettles and briars.

'This way,' she said, taking the left-hand path. 'You mustn't go widdershins around a church. It's supposed to be unlucky.'

Yews and ilexes bordered the path. Underfoot it was sandy, yet green with moss and the delicate tufts of arenaria. The church was very old and built of rough-hewn oaken logs. Its beauty lay in its antiquity.

'It's one of the oldest wooden churches in the country.'

'There's one like it in my county,' said Archery. 'At Greensted. I believe it's ninth century.'

'This one's Nine something. Would you like to see the leper squint?'

They knelt down side by side and, bending forward, he peered through the small triangular gap at the base of the log wall. Although it was not the first of its kind he had seen, it pained him to think of the outcast, the unclean, who came to this tiny grille and listening to the Mass, received on his tongue the bread that some believe is the body of God. It made him think of Tess, herself an outcast, condemned like the leper to an undeserved disease. Within he could see a little stone aisle, wooden pews and a pulpit carved with saints' faces. He shivered and he felt her shiver beside him.

They were very close together under the yew boughs. He had a strange feeling that they were quite alone in the world and that they had been brought here for the working out of some destiny. He lifted his eyes, and turning to her, met hers. He expected her to smile but instead her face was grave, yet full of wonder and a kind of fear. He felt in himself, without analysing it, the emotion he saw in her eyes. The scent of the roses was intoxicating, fresh and unbearably sweet.

Then he got to his feet quickly, a little quelled by the stiffness of his knees. For a moment he had felt like a boy; his body betrayed him as bodies always do.

She said rather brightly, 'Have a look inside while I put these flowers on the grave. I won't be long.'

He went softly up the aisle and stood before the altar. Anyone watching him might have taken him for an atheist, so cool and appraising was his glance. Back again to look at the unassuming little font, the inscriptions on the wall plaques. He put two half-crowns in the box and signed his name in the visitors' book. His hand was shaking so badly that the signature looked like that of an old man.

When he came out once more into the churchyard she was nowhere to be seen. The lettering on the older stones had been obliterated by time and weather. He walked into the new part, reading the last messages of relatives to their dead.

As he came to the end of the path where the hedge was and on the other side of the hedge a meadow, a name that seemed familiar caught his eye. Grace, John Grace. He reflected, searching his mind. It was not a common name and until quite recently he had associated it only with the great cricketer. Of course — a boy had lain dying in the road and that death and that boy's request had reminded Wexford of another similar tragedy. Wexford had told him about it in the court. 'Must be all of twenty years . . .'

Archery looked to the engraved words for confirmation.

Sacred to the Memory of
John Grace
Who departed This Life
February 16th, 1945

In the Twenty-First Year
of His Age

Go, Shepherd, to your rest;
Your tale is told.
The Lamb of God takes
Shepherds to his fold.

A pleasant, if not brilliant, conceit, Archery thought. It was apparently a quotation, but he didn't recognise it. He looked round as Imogen Ide approached. The leaf shadows played on her face and made a pattern on her hair so that it looked as if it was covered by a veil of lace.

'Are you reminding yourself of your mortality?' she asked him gravely.

'I suppose so. It's an interesting place.'

'I'm glad to have had the opportunity of showing it to you. I'm very patriotic — if that's the word — about my country though it hasn't been mine for long.'

He was certain she was going to offer herself as his guide on some future occasion and he said quickly: 'My son is coming tomorrow. We'll have to explore together.' She smiled politely. 'He's twenty-one,' he added rather fatuously.

Simultaneously their eyes turned to the inscription on the stone.

'I'm ready to go if you are,' she said.

She dropped him outside the Olive and Dove. They said good-bye briskly and he noticed she said nothing about hoping to see him again. He didn't feel like tea and he went straight upstairs. Without knowing why he took out the photograph he had of Painter's daughter. Looking at the picture, he wondered why he had thought her so lovely. She was just a pretty girl with the prettiness of youth. Yet while he looked he seemed to realise for the first time why Charles longed so passionately to possess her. It was a strange feeling and it had little to do with Tess, with Tess's appearance or with Charles. In a way it was a universal diffused empathy, but it was selfish too and it came from his heart rather than from his mind.

CHAPTER TEN

And if he hath not before disposed of his goods, let him be
admonished to make his will . . . for the better discharging of his
conscience and the quietness of his executors.

The Visitation of the Sick

'You don't seem to have got very far,' said Charles. He sat down
in an armchair and surveyed the pleasant lounge. The maid
who was operating a floor polisher thought him very handsome
with his rather long fair hair and his scornful expression. She
decided to give the lounge a more than usually thorough do.
'The great thing is to be businesslike about it. We haven't got
all that long. I start at the brewery on Monday week.' Archery
was rather nettled. His own parochial duties were being overlooked. 'I'm sure there's something fishy about that fellow
Primero, Roger Primero. I rang him up before I got here last
night and I've got a date to see him this morning at half eleven.'
  Archery looked at his watch. It was almost ten.
  'You'd better get a move on, then. Where does he live?'
  'You see? Now if I'd been in your shoes that's the first thing
I'd have found out. He lives at Forby Hall. I suppose he fancies
himself as the lord of the manor.' He glanced at his father and
said quickly, 'Be all right if I have the car?'
  'I suppose so. What are you going to tell him, Charles? He
might have you thrown out.'
  'I don't think he will,' Charles said thoughtfully. 'I've found
out a bit about him and it seems he's mad keen on publicity.
Always trying to create an image.' He hesitated, then added
boldly, 'I told him I was the top features man on the *Sunday
Planet* and we were doing a series on tycoons. Rather good,
don't you think?'
  'It doesn't happen to be true,' said Archery.
  Charles said rapidly, 'The end justifies the means. I thought

96

I could put across the line about his early life being dogged by misfortune, father dying, grandmother murdered, no prospects — that sort of thing. And look at him now. You never know what will come out. He's supposed to be very forthcoming to the Press.'

'We'd better go and get the car out.'

It was as hot as ever, but more sultry. A thin mist covered the sun. Charles wore an open necked white shirt and rather tapering trousers. Archery thought he looked like a Regency duellist.

'You won't want to start yet,' he said. 'Forby's only about four miles away. Would you like to look round the place?'

They walked up the High Street and over the Kingsbrook bridge. Archery was proud to have his son beside him. He knew they were very much alike but he didn't for a moment deceive himself they might be taken for brothers. The heavy muggy weather had brought on a twinge of lumbago and today he had utterly forgotten what it felt like to be twenty-one.

'You're reading English,' he said to Charles. 'Tell me where this comes from.' His memory hadn't begun to fail, at any rate. He was word perfect in the little verse.

> ' "Go, Shepherd, to your rest;
> Your tale is told.
> The lamb of God takes
> Shepherds to his fold." '

Charles shrugged. 'Sounds vaguely familiar, but I can't place it. Where did you see it?'

'On a gravestone in Forby churchyard.'

'You really are the end, Father. I thought you wanted to help me and Tess and all you've been doing is messing about in cemeteries.'

Archery controlled himself with difficulty. If Charles was going to take everything into his own hands there seemed no reason why he shouldn't just go back to Thringford. There was nothing to keep him in Kingsmarkham. He wondered why the prospect of returning to the vicarage seemed ineffably dull. Suddenly he stopped and nudged his son's arm.

'What's the matter?'

'That woman outside the butcher's, the one in the cape —
it's that Mrs Crilling I told you about. I'd rather not come face
to face with her.'

But it was too late. She had evidently seen them already,
for with her cape flying, she came bearing down upon them like
a galleon.

'Mr Archery! My dear friend!' She took both his hands in
hers and swung them as if she were about to partner him in an
eightsome reel. 'What a lovely surprise! I was only saying to my
daughter this morning, I do hope I shall see that dear man
again so that I can thank him for ministering to me in my
wretched affliction.'

This was a new mood. She was like a dowager at a
successful garden party. The cape was familiar but the dress she
wore under it was an ordinary cotton frock, simple and dowdy,
somewhat splashed with gravy stains on its front. She gave a
broad, calm and gracious smile.

'This is my son, Charles,' Archery muttered. 'Charles, this
is Mrs Crilling.'

To his surprise Charles took the outstretched, none-too-
clean hand and half-bowed over it.

'How do you do?' Over her head he gave his father an
angry glance. 'I've heard so much about you.'

'Nice things, I hope.' If it occurred to her that Archery had
seen nothing nice about her to relate she gave no sign of it. She
was quite sane, gay, even frivolous. 'Now, don't refuse to gratify
my little whim. I want you both to come into the Carousel and
take a wee cup of coffee with me. My treat, of course,' she
added archly.

'Our time,' said Charles grandiloquently — absurdly, Archery thought, 'is quite at your disposal. Until eleven fifteen, that
is. Don't let us discuss anything so absurd as treats in the
company of a lady.'

Evidently it was the right line to take with her. 'Isn't he
sweet?' she gurgled. They went into the cafe. 'Children are such
a blessing, don't you think? The crown of the tree of life. You
must be proud of him, even though he quite puts you in the
shade.'

Charles pulled out a chair for her. They were the only customers and for a while no one came to take their order. Mrs Crilling leant confidingly towards Archery.

'My baby has got herself a situation and she starts to-morrow. An operative in a ladies' wear establishment. I understand the prospects are excellent. With her intelligence there's no knowing how far she can go. The trouble is she's never had a real chance.' She had been speaking in a low genteel voice. Suddenly she turned her back on him, banged the sugar basin on the table and screamed loudly in the direction of the kitchen:

'Service!'

Charles jumped. Archery shot him a glance of triumph.

'Always having her hopes raised and then it comes to nothing,' she went on just as if the scream had never happened. 'Her father was just the same — struck down with T.B. in the flower of his age and dead within six months.' Archery flinched as she jerked away from him once more. 'Where the flaming hell are those bloody girls?' she shouted.

A woman in a green uniform with Manageress embroidered on the bodice came out of the kitchen. The look she gave Mrs Crilling was bored and withering.

'I asked you not to come in here again, Mrs Crilling, if you can't behave yourself.' She smiled frostily at Archery. 'What can I get you, sir?'

'Three coffees, please.'

'I'll have mine black,' said Charles.

'What was I talking about?'

'Your daughter,' said Archery hopefully.

'Oh, yes, my baby. It's funny really she should have had such a bad break because when she was a little tot it looked as if everything in the garden was lovely. I had a dear old friend, you see, who simply doted on my baby. And she was rolling in money, kept servants and all that kind of thing . . .'

The coffee came. It was the espresso kind with foam on the top.

'You can bring me some white sugar,' said Mrs Crilling sulkily. 'I can't stomach that demerara muck.' The waitress flounced away, returned with another sugar bowl and banged it down on the table. Mrs Crilling gave a shrill little shriek as soon as she was out of earshot. 'Silly bitch!'

Then she returned to her theme. 'Very old my friend was and beyond being responsible for her actions. Senile, they call it. Over and over again she told me she wanted to do something for my baby. I passed it off, of course, having an absolute revulsion about stepping into dead men's shoes.' She stopped suddenly and dropped four heaped teaspoonfuls of sugar into her coffee.

'Naturally,' said Charles. 'The last thing anyone would call you is mercenary, Mrs Crilling.'

She smiled complacently and to Archery's intense amusement, leant across the table and patted Charles's cheek.

'You dear,' she said. 'You lovely, understanding dear.' After a deep breath she went on more practically, 'Still, you have to look after your own. I didn't press it, not till the doctor told me Mr Crilling had only got six months to live. No insurance, I thought in my despair, no pension. I pictured myself reduced to leaving my baby on the steps of an orphanage.'

For his part, Archery was unable to picture it. Elizabeth had been a sturdy youngster of five at the time.

'Do go on,' said Charles. 'It's most interesting.'

'You ought to make a will, I said to my friend. I'll pop down the road and get you a will form. A thousand or two would make all the difference to my baby. You know how she's gladdened your last years, and what have those grandchildren of yours ever done for you? Damn all, I thought.'

'But she didn't make a will?' Archery said.

'What do you know about it? You let me tell it in my own way. It was about a week before she died. I'd had the will form for weeks and weeks and all the time poor Mr Crilling was wasting away to a shadow. But would she fill it in? Not her, the old cow. I had to use all my most winning powers of persuasion. Every time I said a word that crazy old maid of hers would put her spoke in. Then that old maid — Flower, her name was — she got a bad cold and had to keep to her bed. "Have you thought any more about disposing of your temporal estates?" I said to my friend in a light-hearted, casual manner. "Maybe I should do something for Lizzie," she said and I knew my opportunity was at hand.

'Back across the road I flew. I didn't like to witness it myself, you know, on account of my baby being a beneficiary. Mrs White, my neighbour, came over and the lady who helped with her housework. They were only too delighted. You might say it brought a ray of sunshine into their humdrum lives.'

Archery wanted to say, 'But Mrs Primero died intestate.' He didn't dare. Any hint that he knew whom she was talking about and the whole narrative might be brought to a halt.

'Well, we got it all written out. I'm a great reader, Mr Archery, so I was able to put it in the right language. "Blood is thicker that water," said my old friend — she was wandering in her mind — but she only put the grandchildren down for five hundred apiece. There was eight thousand for my baby and I was to have charge of it till she was twenty-one, and a bit left over for the Flower woman. My friend was crying bitterly. I reckon she realised how wicked she'd been in not doing it before.

'And that was that. I saw Mrs White and the other lady safely off the premises — more fool I, though I didn't know it at the time. I said I'd keep the will safe and I did. She wasn't to mention it to anybody. And — would you believe it? — a week later she met with her death.'

Charles said innocently, 'That was a good start for your daughter, Mrs Crilling, whatever misfortunes came afterwards.'

He started as she got up abruptly. Her face had blanched to the whiteness it had worn in court and her eyes blazed.

'Any benefits she got,' she said in a choking voice, 'came from her dead father's people. Charity it was, cold charity. "Send me the school bills, Josie," her uncle'd say to me. "I'll pay them direct, and her auntie can go with her to get her uniform. If you think she needs treatment for her nerves her auntie can go with her to Harley Street, too." '

'But what about the will?'

'That bloody will!' Mrs Crilling shouted. 'It wasn't legal. I only found out after she was dead. I took it straight round to Quadrants, the solicitors that were in the High Street. Old Mr Quadrant was alive then. "What about these alterations?" he said. Well, I looked and, lo and behold, the old cow had scribbled in a lot of extra bits while I was at the front door with

101

Mrs White. Scribbled in bits and scratched out bits too. "These invalidate the whole thing," said Mr Quadrant. "You have to get the witnesses to sign them, or have a codicil. You could fight it," he said, looking me up and down in a nasty way, knowing I hadn't got a bean. "But I wouldn't say much for your chances." '

To Archery's horror she broke into a stream of obscenities, many of which he had never heard before. The manageress came out and took her by the arm.

'Out you go. We can't have this in here.'

'My God,' said Charles, after she had been hustled away. 'I see what you mean.'

'I must confess her language shook me a bit.'

Charles chuckled. 'Not fit for your ears at all.'

'It was most enlightening, though. Are you going to bother with Primero now?'

'It can't do any harm.'

Archery had to wait a long time in the corridor outside Wexford's office. Just as he was beginning to think he would have to give up and try again later, the main entrance doors opened and a little bright-eyed man in working clothes came in between two uniformed policemen. He was plainly some sort of criminal, but everyone seemed to know him and find him a source of ironic amusement.

'I can't stand these contemporary-type nicks,' he said impudently to the station sergeant. Wexford came out of his office, ignoring Archery, and crossed to the desk. 'Give me the old-fashioned kind every time. I've got a slummy mind, that's my trouble.'

'I'm not interested in your views on interior decoration, Monkey,' said Wexford.

The little man turned to him and grinned.

'You've got a nasty tongue, you have. Your sense of humour's sunk as you've gone up. Pity, really.'

'Shut up!'

Archery listened in admiration. He wished that he had the power and the authority to talk like that to Mrs Crilling, or that such authority could be vested in Charles, enabling him to question Primero without the inhibitions of subterfuge. Wexford, talking silkily about bombs and attempted murder, ushered the little man into his office and the door closed on them. Such things did go on, Archery thought. Perhaps his own new-forming theories were not so far-fetched after all.

'If I could just see Inspector Burden for a moment,' he said more confidently to the station sergeant.

'I'll see if he's free, sir.'

Eventually Burden came out to him himself.

'Good morning, sir. Doesn't get any cooler, does it?'

'I've got something rather important to tell you. Can you spare me five minutes?'

'Surely.'

But he made no move to take him into a more private place. The station sergeant occupied himself with perusing a large book. Sitting on a ridiculous spoon-shaped chair outside Wexford's office, Archery felt like a school boy who, having waited a long time to see the headmaster, is compelled to confide in and perhaps take his punishment from an underling. Rather chastened, he told Burden briefly about Mrs Crilling.

'Most interesting. You mean that when Mrs Primero was murdered the Crilling woman thought the will was valid?'

'It amounts to that. She didn't mention the murder.'

'We can't do anything. You realise that?'

'I want you to tell me if I have sufficient grounds to write to the Home Secretary.'

A constable appeared from somewhere, tapped on Wexford's door and was admitted.

'You haven't any circumstantial evidence,' Burden said. 'I'm sure the Chief Inspector wouldn't encourage it.'

A roar of sardonic laughter sounded through the thin dividing wall. Archery felt unreasonably piqued.

'I think I shall write just the same.'

'You must do as you please, sir.' Burden got up. 'Been seeing much of the country round here?'

Archery swallowed his anger. If Burden intended to terminate the interview with small talk, small talk he should have. Hadn't he promised his old friend Griswold and, for that matter, the Chief Inspector, not to make trouble?

'I went to Forby yesterday,' he said. 'I was in the churchyard and I happened to notice the grave of that boy Mr Wexford was talking about in court the other day. His name was Grace. Do you remember?'

Burden's face was a polite blank but the station sergeant glanced up.

'I'm a Forby man myself, sir,' he said. 'We make a bit of a song and dance about John Grace at home. They'll tell you all about him in Forby for all it was twenty years ago.'

'All about him?'

'He fancied himself as a poet, poor kid, wrote plays too. Sort of religious mystic he was. In his day he used to try and sell his verses from door to door.'

'Like W. H. Davis,' said Archery.

'I daresay.'

'Was he a shepherd?'

'Not as far as I know. Baker's roundsman or something.'

Wexford's door swung open, the constable came out and said to Burden, 'Chief Inspector wants you, sir.'

Wexford's voice roared after him, 'You can come back in here, Gates, and take a statement from Guy Fawkes. And give him a cigarette. He won't blow up.'

'It seems I'm wanted, sir, so if you'll excuse me . . .'

Burden went with Archery to the entrance doors.

'You had your chat with Alice Flower just in time,' he said. 'If you had it, that is.'

'Yes, I talked to her. Why?'

'She died yesterday,' said Burden. 'It's all in the local rag.'

Archery found a newsagent. The *Kingsmarkham Chronicle* had come out that morning and fresh stacks of papers lay on the counter. He bought a copy and found the announcement at the bottom of the back page.

'Death of Miss A. Flower.'

He scanned it and took it back with him to the terrace of the hotel to read it properly.

'The death occurred today . . .' That meant yesterday, Archery thought, looking at the dateline. He read on. 'The death occurred today of Miss Alice Flower at Stowerton Infirmary. She was eighty-seven. Miss Flower, who had lived in the district for twenty-five years, will be best remembered for the part she played in the notorious Victor's Piece murder trial. She was for many years maid and trusted friend of Mrs Primero . . .'

There followed a brief account of the murder and the trial.

'The funeral will take place at Forby parish church on Monday. Mr Roger Primero has expressed a wish that the last rites may be celebrated quietly and that there will be no sightseers.'

Roger Primero, faithful to the end, Archery thought. He found himself hoping that Charles had done nothing to distress this kindly and dutiful man. So Alice Flower was dead at last, death had waited just long enough to let her tell him, Archery, all she knew. Again he seemed to feel the working of destiny. Well done, thou good and faithful servant. Enter thou into the joy of thy Lord!

He went in to lunch, feeling jaded and depressed. Where on earth was Charles? He had been gone more than two hours. By now Primero had probably seen through that absurd cover story and . . .

His imagination showing him his son being interrogated by Wexford at his nastiest, he was just picking at his fruit salad and warm ice-cream when Charles burst into the dining room, swinging the car keys.

'I was wondering where you'd got to.'

'I've had a most instructive morning. Anything happened here?'

'Nothing much. Alice Flower is dead.'

'You can't tell me anything about that. Primero was full of it. Apparently he was at her bedside for hours yesterday.' He threw himself into a chair next to his father's. 'God, it was hot in that car! As a matter of fact, her dying like that was a help if anything. Made it easier to get him on to the murder.'

'I didn't think you could be so callous,' said Archery distastefully.

'Oh, come off it, Father. She'd had her allotted span plus seventeen. She can't have wanted to live. Don't you want to hear what I got out of him?'

'Of course.'

'You don't want any coffee, do you? Let's go outside.'

There was no one on the terrace. A yellow climbing rose

had shed its petals all over the ground and the battered cane chairs. What residents there were had left possessions out here as if to reserve permanent perches, magazines, library books, a roll of blue knitting, a pair of glasses. Ruthlessly Charles cleared two chairs and blew away the rose petals. For the first time Archery noticed that he looked extremely happy.

'Well,' he said when they had sat down, 'the house first. It's quite a place, about ten times the size of Thringford Manor, and it's built of grey stone with a kind of pediment thing over the front door. Mrs Primero lived there when she was a girl and Roger bought it when it came up for sale this spring. There's a park with deer in it and a vast drive coming up from a pillared entrance. You can't see the house from the road, only the cedars in the park.

'They've got an Italian butler — not so classy as an English one, d'you think? But I suppose they're a dying race. Anyway, this butler character let me in and kept me hanging about for about ten minutes in a hall the size of the ground floor of our house. I was a bit nervous because I kept thinking, suppose he's rung up the *Sunday Planet* and they've said they've never heard of me? But he hadn't and it was all right. He was in the library. Superb collection of books he's got and some of them looked quite worn, so I suppose someone reads them, though I shouldn't think he does.

'It was all furnished in leather, black leather. You know that rather sexy modern stuff. He asked me to sit down and have a drink . . .'

'A bit early, wasn't it?'

'People like that, they slosh it down all day. If they were working class they'd be alcoholics, but you can get away with anything when you've got a butler and about fifty thousand a year. Then his wife came in. Rather a nice-looking woman — a bit past it, of course — but magnificent clothes. Not that I'd want Tess to dress like that . . .' His face fell and Archery's heart moved with pity. 'If I ever get a say in what Tess wears,' he added dolefully.

'Go on.'

'We had our drinks. Mrs Primero wasn't very talkative, but her husband was most expansive. I didn't have to ask him much, so you needn't get all steamed up about your conscience, and he got on to the murder, quite naturally. He kept saying he wished he hadn't left Victor's Piece so early that Sunday evening. He could easily have stayed.

' "I was only going to meet a couple of chaps I knew at a pub in Sewingbury," he said. "And, as it happened, it was a dead loss because they never turned up. Or, at least, they did turn up but I got the wrong pub. So I waited about for an hour or so and then I went back to my lodgings. I wonder," he said, "how many times I've cursed myself for not staying at Victor's Piece." '

'What d'you think of that? I thought it was fishy.'

'He didn't have to tell you,' Archery said. 'In any case the police must have questioned him.'

'Maybe they did and maybe they didn't. He didn't say.' Charles lounged back in his chair, and swinging his feet up poked them through the trellis. 'Then we got on to money,' he said. 'Money, I may add, is the mainspring of his existence.'

Inexplicably, Archery felt himself marked out as Primero's defender. Alice Flower had painted him in such glowing colours. 'I had the impression he was rather a nice sort of man,' he said.

'He's all right,' Charles said indifferently. 'He's very modest about his success and about his money.' He grinned. 'The kind of character who cries all the way to the bank. Anyway, now we come to the crux of the whole thing.

'Just before Mrs Primero was killed some mate of his asked him if he'd like to go into business with him. Importing or exporting. I don't quite know what it was but it doesn't matter. The friend was to put up ten thousand and so was Primero. Well, Primero hadn't got it, hadn't got a smell of it. As far as he was concerned it was hopeless. Then Mrs Primero died.'

'We know all this,' Archery objected. 'Alice Flower told me as much . . .'

'All right, wait for it. Alice Flower didn't know this bit. "That was the making of me," he said very breezily. "Not that I wasn't devastated by my grandmother's death," he added as a sort of hasty afterthought. His wife was sitting there all the time with a blank look on her face. He kept looking at her uneasily.

' "I put up the money and we were away," he said, talking rather fast. "And since then I've never looked back." '

'I was in a bit of a dilemma. Everything was going so smoothly and I didn't want to mess things up. I thought he was looking defiant and suddenly I realised why. *He didn't know how much I knew about Mrs Primero's money.* She died intestate, it was sixteen years ago, I was a newspaper reporter and for all he knew I was interested in him, not his grandmother.'

'A lot to read into a defiant look,' said Archery.

'Perhaps there was a bit of hindsight in that. But just wait a minute. Then I asked a question. It was a shot in the dark but it came off.

' "So you got your ten thousand just when you needed it?" I said casually. Primero didn't say anything, but his wife looked at me and said, "Just the exact sum after death duties. You should really be asking me. Roger's told me about it so often I know it better than he does."

'Well, I couldn't leave it there. I persisted. "I understand you've got two sisters, Mr Primero," I said. "I suppose they inherited similar amounts?" He began to look terribly suspicious. After all, it wasn't my business and it had nothing to do with the story I was supposed to be writing. "Are they successful in business too?" I asked, trying to justify myself. It was a stroke of genius. Sorry to be big-headed but it was. I could actually see him relax.

' "I really don't see much of them," he said. "Oh, Roger," said his wife, "you know me *never* see them." Primero gave her an icy look. "One's married," he said, "and the other has a job in London. They're much younger than I am." "It must be nice to inherit ten thousand pounds when you're still a child," I said. "I imagine it's always nice," he said, "but I've never had the pleasure of inheriting any more. Shall we leave the subject and get on with the story of my life?"

'I pretended to take notes. I was doodling really but he thought it was shorthand. When we'd finished he got up and shook hands and said he'd keep his eye open for the *Sunday Planet.* I felt a bit awkward at that and I didn't quite know what to say but his wife saved me by asking me to lunch. So I accepted and we had a splendid lunch, smoked salmon and enormous steaks, great sides of oxen they were, and raspberries in framboise liqueur.'

'You've got a nerve,' said Archery in grudging admiration. He pulled himself up. 'It was very wrong of you. Most unethical.'

'All in a good cause. You do see the point, don't you?'

Why do one's children always think one senile yet childish, dully practical yet irrational, capable of supporting them but unintelligent to the point of imbecility?

'Of course I do,' Archery said irritably. 'Alice Flower and Mrs Crilling both said Mrs Primero had only ten thousand to leave, but apparently Roger Primero didn't get only a third of that, he got the whole ten thousand.'

Charles jerked round to face him, scattering more rose petals from the trellis. 'Now, why? There definitely wasn't a will. I've checked on that. And there were just the three heirs, Roger, Angela and Isabel. Mrs Primero hadn't another relative in the world and according to the law it should have been divided between the three grandchildren. But Roger got the lot.'

'I can't understand it.'

'Neither can I — yet. Maybe I shall when I've seen the sisters. I couldn't ask Roger where they lived, but Primero isn't a common name and the single one may be in the London phone directory. I haven't quite made up my mind about the line I'll take with them, but I've got the glimmerings of an idea. I might say I've come from the Inland Revenue . . .'

'Facilis descensus Averni.'

'In matters of this kind,' Charles said crisply, 'you have to be bloody, bold and resolute. Can I have the car again tomorrow?'

'If you must.'

'I thought you might like to go out to Victor's Piece,' Charles said in a hopeful tone, 'and just have a look round. See if you can see if Primero could have hidden himself anywhere, sneaked upstairs or something instead of letting himself out of the front door that Sunday night.'

'Aren't you letting your imagination run away with you?'

'It's a family failing.' His eyes clouded suddenly and to Archery's dismay he put his head in his hands. Archery didn't know what to do. 'Tess hasn't spoken to me for two days,' the boy said. 'I can't lose her, I can't.' If he had been ten years younger his father would have taken him in his arms. But if he had been ten years younger the whole thing would never have happened.

'I don't give a damn,' Charles said, controlling himself, 'what her father was or what he did. I don't care if every one of her ancestors were hanged. But you do and she does and . . . Oh, what's the use?' He got up. 'Sorry to make an exhibition of myself.' Still looking down, he scuffed his feet against the eddies of petals. 'You're doing all you can,' he said with a dreadful prim gravity, 'but you can't be expected to understand at your age.' Without looking at his father, he turned and went into the hotel.

CHAPTER ELEVEN

From fornication, and all other deadly sin; and from all the
deceits of the world, the flesh and the devil,
Good Lord, deliver us.

The Litany

Angela Primero lived in a flat at Oswestry Mansions, Baron's
Court. She was twenty-six years old and the elder of Mrs
Primero's granddaughters. That was all Charles Archery knew
about her — that and her telephone number which he had
easily found. He rang her up and asked if he could see her on
the following morning. Thinking better of his original plan, he
said he represented the *Sunday Planet*, and the death of Alice
Flower having brought once more into prominence Mrs Primero's murder, his newspaper were running a feature on the fate
of the other people concerned in the case. He was rather
pleased with that. It had the ring of verisimilitude.

Miss Primero had a grim voice for so young a woman. It
was gravelly, abrupt, almost masculine. She would be glad to
see him, but he did realise, didn't he, that her recollection of
her grandmother was slight? Just a few childhood memories
were what he wanted, Miss Primero, little touches to add colour
to his story.

She opened the door to him so quickly that he wondered if
she had been waiting behind it. Her appearance surprised him
for he had kept a picture of her brother in his mind and he had
therefore expected someone small and dark with regular features. He had seen a photograph of the grandmother too, and
though the old face was both wizened and blurred by age, there
were still to be seen vestiges of an aquiline beauty and a strong
resemblance to Roger.

The girl whose flat this was had a strong plain face with
bad skin and a big prognathous jaw. Her hair was a dull flat

111

brown. She wore a neat dark blue frock bought at a chain store and her figure, though over-large, was good.

'Mr Bowman?'

Charles was pleased with the name he had invented for himself. He gave her a pleasant smile.

'How do you do, Miss Primero?'

She showed him into a small very sparsely furnished sitting room. He could not help adding to the mystery by contrasting this with the library at Forby Hall. Here there were no books, no flowers, and the only ornaments were framed photographs, half a dozen perhaps, of a young blonde girl and a baby.

She followed his gaze towards the studio portrait of the same girl that hung above the fireplace. 'My sister,' she said. Her ugly face softened and she smiled. As she spoke there came from the next room a thin wail and the murmur of a voice. 'She's in my bedroom now, changing the baby's napkin. She always comes over on Saturday mornings.'

Charles wondered what Angela Primero did for a living. A typist perhaps, or a clerk? The whole set-up seemed too scanty and poor. The furniture was brightly coloured but it looked cheap and flimsy. In front of the hearth was a rug woven out of woollen rags. Needy nothing trimmed in jollity . . .

'Please sit down,' said Angela Primero.

The little orange chair creaked as it took his weight. A far cry, he thought, from the brother's voluptuous black leather. From the floor above he could hear music playing and someone pushing a vacuum cleaner.

'What do you want me to tell you?'

There was a packet of Weights on the mantelpiece. She took one and handed them to him. He shook his head.

'First, what you remember of your grandmother.'

'Not much. I told you.' Her speech was brusque and rough. 'We went there to tea a few times. It was a big dark house and I remember I was afraid to go to the bathroom alone. The maid used to have to take me.' She gave a staccato, humourless laugh and it was an effort to remember she was only twenty-six. 'I never even saw Painter if that's what you mean. There was a child across the road we used to play with sometimes and I believe Painter had a daughter. I asked about her once but my grandmother said she was common, we weren't to have anything to do with her.'

Charles clenched his hands. He felt a sudden desperate longing for Tess, both for himself, and also to set her beside this girl who had been taught to despise her.

The door opened and the girl in the photographs came in. Angela Primero jumped up at once and took the baby from her arms. Charles's knowledge of babies was vague. He thought this one might be about six months old. It looked small and uninteresting.

'This is Mr Bowman, darling. My sister, Isabel Fairest.'

Mrs Fairest was only a year younger than her sister, but she looked no more than eighteen. She was very small and thin with a pinkish-white face and enormous pale blue eyes. Charles thought she looked like a pretty rabbit. Her hair was a bright gingery gold.

Roger's hair and eyes were black, Angela's hair brown and her eyes hazel. None of them was in the least like either of the others. There was more to genetics than met the eye, Charles thought.

Mrs Fairest sat down. She didn't cross her legs but sat with her hands in her lap like a little girl. It was difficult to imagine her married, impossible to think of her as having given birth to a child.

Her sister scarcely took her eyes off her. When she did it was to coo at the baby. Mrs Fairest had a small soft voice, tinged with cockney.

'Don't let him tire you, darling. Put him down in his cot.'

'You know I love holding him, darling. Isn't he gorgeous? Have you got a smile for your auntie? You know your auntie, don't you, even if you haven't seen her for a whole week?'

Mrs Fairest got up and stood behind her sister's chair. They both gurgled over the baby, stroking its cheeks and curling its fingers round their own. It was obvious that they were devoted to each other, but whereas Angela's love was maternal to both sister and nephew, Isabel showed a clinging dependence on the older girl. Charles felt that they had forgotten he was there and he wondered how Mr Fairest fitted into the picture. He coughed.

'About your early life, Miss Primero . . . ?'

'Oh, yes. (Mustn't cry, sweetie. He's got wind, darling.) I really can't remember any more about my grandmother. My mother married again when I was sixteen. This is the sort of thing you want, is it?'

'Oh, yes.'

'Well, as I say, my mother married again and she and my stepfather wanted us to go out to Australia with them. (Up it comes! There, that's better.) But I didn't want to go. Isabel and I were still at school. My mother hung it out for a couple of years and then they went without us. Well, it was their life, wasn't it? I wanted to go to training college but I gave that up. Isabel and I had the house, didn't we, darling? And we both went out to work. (Is he going to have a little sleep, then?)'

It was an ordinary enough tale, fragmentary and very clipped. Charles felt that there was far more to it. The hardship and the privation had been left out. Money might have changed it all but she had never mentioned money. She had never mentioned her brother either.

'Isabel got married two years ago. Her husband's in the Post Office. I'm a secretary in a newspaper office.' She raised her eyebrows, unsmiling. 'I'll have to ask them if they've ever heard of you.'

'Yes, do,' said Charles with a suavity he didn't feel. He must get on to the subject of the money but he didn't know how to. Mrs Fairest brought a carry-cot in from the other room, they placed the baby in it, bending tenderly over him and cooing. Although it was nearly noon neither of them had mentioned a drink or even coffee. Charles belonged to a generation that has accustomed itself to almost hourly snacks, cups of this, glasses of that, bits and pieces from the refrigerator. So, surely, did they. He thought wistfully of Roger's hospitality.

Mrs Fairest glanced up and said softly, 'I do like coming here. It's so quiet.' Above them the vacuum cleaner continued to whirr. 'My husband and me, we've only got one room. It's nice and big but it's awfully noisy at weekends.'

Charles knew it was impertinent but he had to say it.

'I'm surprised your grandmother didn't leave you anything.'

Angela Primero shrugged. She tucked the blanket round the baby and stood up. 'That's life,' she said in a hard voice.

'Shall I tell him, darling?' Isabel Fairest touched her arm and looked timidly into her face, waiting for guidance.

'What's the point? It's of no interest to him.' She stared at Charles and then said intelligently, 'You can't put that sort of thing in newspapers. It's libel.'

Damn, damn, damn! Why hadn't he said he was from the Inland Revenue? Then they could have got on to money at once.

'But I think people ought to know,' said Mrs Fairest, showing more spirit than he had thought her capable of. 'I do, darling. I always have, ever since I understood about it. I think people ought to know how he's treated us.'

Charles put his notebook away ostentatiously.

'This is off the record, Mrs Fairest.'

'You see, darling? He won't say anything. I don't care if he does. People ought to know about Roger.'

The name was out. They were all breathing rather heavily. Charles was the first to get himself under control. He managed a calm smile.

'Well, I *will* tell you. If you put it in the paper and I have to go to prison for it, I don't care! Granny Rose left ten thousand pounds and we should all have had a share, but we didn't. Roger — that's our brother — he got it all. I don't quite know why but Angela knows the ins and outs of it. My mother had a friend who was a solicitor where Roger worked and he said we could try and fight it, but Mother wouldn't on account of it being awful to have a court case against your own son. We were just little kids, you see, and we didn't know anything about it. Mother said Roger would help us — it was his moral duty, even if it wasn't legally — but he never did. He kept putting it off and then Mother quarrelled with him. We've never seen him since I was ten and Angela was eleven. I wouldn't know him now if I saw him in the street.'

It was a puzzling story. They were all Mrs Primero's grandchildren, all equally entitled to inherit in the event of there being no will. And there had been no will.

'I don't want to see all this in your paper, you know,'

Angela Primero said suddenly. She would have made a good teacher, he thought, reflecting on waste, for she was tender with little children, but stern when she had to be.

'I won't publish any of it,' Charles said with perfect truth.

'You'd better not, that's all. The fact is, we couldn't fight it. We wouldn't have stood a chance. In law Roger was perfectly entitled to it all. Mind you, it would have been another story if my grandmother had died a month later.'

'I don't quite follow you,' said Charles, by now unbearably excited.

'Have you ever seen my brother?'

Charles nodded, then changed it to a shake of the head. She looked at him suspiciously. Then she made a dramatic gesture. She took her sister by the shoulders and pushed her forward for his inspection.

'He's little and dark,' she said. 'Look at Isabel, look at me. We don't look alike, do we? We don't look like sisters because we aren't sisters and Roger isn't our brother. Oh, Roger is my parents' child all right and Mrs Primero was his grandmother. My mother couldn't have any more children. They waited eleven years and when they knew it was no good they adopted me. A year later they took Isabel as well.'

'But . . . I . . .' Charles stammered. 'You were legally adopted, weren't you?'

Angela Primero had recovered her composure. She put her arm round her sister who had begun to cry.

'We were legally adopted all right. That didn't make any difference. Adopted children can't inherit when the dead person has died without making a will — or they couldn't in September 1950. They can now. They were making this Act at the time and it became law on October 1st, 1950. Just our luck, wasn't it?'

The photograph in the estate agent's window made Victor's Piece look deceptively attractive. Perhaps the agent had long given up hope of its being sold for anything but its site value, for Archery, enquiring tentatively, was greeted with almost fawning exuberance. He emerged with an order to view, a bunch of keys and permission to go over the house whenever he chose.

No bus was in sight. He walked back to the stop by the Olive and Dove and waited in the shade. Presently he pulled the order to view out of his pocket and scanned it. 'Splendid property of character,' he read, 'that only needs an imaginative owner to give it a new lease of life . . .' There was no mention of the old tragedy, no hint that violent death had once been its tenant.

Two Sewingbury buses came and one marked Kingsmarkham Station. He was still reading, contrasting the agent's euphemisms with the description in his transcript, when the silver car pulled into the kerb.

'Mr Archery!'

He turned. The sun blazed back from the arched wings and the glittering screen. Imogen Ide's hair made an even brighter silver-gold flash against the dazzling metal.

'I'm on my way to Stowerton. Would you like a lift?'

He was suddenly ridiculously happy. Everything went, his pity for Charles, his grief for Alice Flower, his sense of helplessness against the juggernaut machinery of the law. An absurd dangerous joy possessed him and without stopping to analyse it, he went up to the car. Its bodywork was as hot as fire, a shivering silver blaze against his hand.

'My son took my car,' he said. 'I'm not going to Stowerton, just to a place this side of it, a house called Victor's Piece.'

She raised her eyebrows very slightly at this and he supposed she knew the story just as everyone else did, for she was looking at him strangely. He got in beside her, his heart beating. The continual rhythmic thudding in his left side was so intense as to be physically painful and he wished it would stop before it made him wince or press his hand to his breast.

'You haven't got Dog with you today,' he said.

She moved back into the traffic. 'Too hot for him,' she said. 'Surely you're not thinking of buying Victor's Piece?'

His heart had quietened. 'Why, do you know it?'

'It used to belong to a relative of my husband's.'

Ide, he thought, Ide. He couldn't remember hearing what had become of the house after Mrs Primero's death. Perhaps it had been owned by some Ides before it became an old people's home.

117

'I have a key and an order to view, but I'm certainly not going to buy. It's just — well . . .'

'Curiosity?' She could not look at him while she was driving but he felt her thoughts directed on him more powerfully than any eyes. 'Are you an amateur of crime?' It would have been natural to have used his name, to end the question with it. But she didn't. It seemed to him that she had omitted it because 'Mr Archery' had suddenly become too formal, his Christian name still too intimate. 'You know, I think I'll come over it with you,' she said. 'I don't have to be in Stowerton until half-past twelve. Let me be your guide, may I?'

Imogen Ide will be my guide . . . It was a stupid jingle and it tinkled in his ears on a minor key like an old, half-forgotten madrigal. He said nothing but she must have taken his silence for assent, for instead of dropping him at the entry she slowed and turned into the lane where dark gables showed between the trees.

Even on this bright morning the house looked dark and forbidding. Its yellow-brown bricks were crossed with fretted half-timbering and two of its windows were broken. The resemblance between it and the agent's photograph was as slight as that of a holiday postcard to the actual resort. The photographer had cunningly avoided or else subsequently removed the weeds, the brambles, the damp stains, the swinging rotted casements and the general air of decay. The gates were broken down and she drove straight through the gap, up the drive and stopped directly before the front door.

This moment should have been important to him, his first sight of the house where Tess's father had committed — or had not committed — his crime. His senses should have been alert to absorb atmosphere, to note details of place and distance that the police in their jaded knowledge had overlooked. Instead he was conscious of himself not as an observer, a note-taker, but only as a man living in the present, dwelling in the moment and discarding the past. He felt more alive than he had done for years and because of this he became almost unaware of his surroundings. Things could not affect him, not recorded fact. His emotions were all. He saw and experienced the house only as a deserted place into which he and this woman would soon go and would be alone.

As soon as he had thought this in so many words he knew that he should not go in. He could easily say that he only wanted to look at the grounds. She was getting out of the car now, looking up at the windows and wrinkling her eyelids against the light.

'Shall we go in?' she said.

He put the key in the lock and she was standing close beside him. He had expected a musty smell from the hall but he was hardly aware of it. Shafts of light crossed the place from various dusty windows and motes danced in the beams. There was an old runner on the tiled floor and catching her heel in it, she stumbled. Instinctively he put out his hand to steady her and as he did so he felt her right breast brush his arm.

'Mind how you go,' he said, not looking at her. Her shoe had sent up a little cloud of dust and she gave a nervous laugh. Perhaps it was just a normal laugh. He was beyond that kind of analysis, for he could still feel the soft weight against his arm as if she had not stepped quickly away.

'Terribly stuffy in here,' she said. 'It makes me cough. That's the room where the murder was committed — in there.' She pushed open a door and he saw a deal board floor, marble fireplace, great bleached patches on the walls where pictures had hung. 'The stairs are behind here and on the other side is the kitchen where poor old Alice was cooking the Sunday dinner.'

'I don't want to go upstairs,' he said quickly. 'It's too hot and dusty. You'll get your dress dirty.' He drew a deep breath and, moving far from her, stood against the mantelpiece. Here, just on this spot, Mrs Primero had felt the first blow of the axe; there the scuttle had stood, here, there, everywhere, the old blood had flowed. 'The scene of the crime,' he said fatuously.

Her eyes narrowed and she crossed to the window. The silence was terrible and he wanted to fill it with chatter. There was so much to say, so many remarks even mere acquaintances could make to each other on such a spot. The noonday sun cast her shadow in perfect proportion, neither too tall nor grossly dwarfed. It was like a cut-out in black tissue and he wanted to fall to his knees and touch it, knowing it was all he would get.

It was she who spoke first. He hardly knew what he had expected her to say, but not this — certainly not this.

'You are very like your son — or he's like you.'

The tension slackened. He felt cheated and peeved.

'I didn't know you'd met,' he said.

To this she made no reply. In her eyes was a tiny gleam of fun. 'You didn't tell me he worked for a newspaper.'

Archery's stomach turned. She must have been there, at the Primeros'. Was he expected to sustain Charles's lie?

'He's so very like you,' she said. 'It didn't really click, though, until after he'd gone. Then, taking his appearance and his name together — I suppose Bowman's his pseudonym on the *Planet*, is it? — I guessed. Roger hasn't realised.'

'I don't quite understand,' Archery began. He would have to explain. 'Mrs Ide . . .'

She started to laugh, stopped when she saw the dismay in his face. 'I think we've both been leading each other up the garden,' she said gently. 'Ide was my maiden name, the name I used for modelling.'

He turned away, pressing the hot palm of his hand against the marble. She took a step towards him and he smelt her scent. 'Mrs Primero was the relative who owned this house, the relative who's buried at Forby?' There was no need to wait for her answer. He sensed her nod. 'I don't understand how I can have been such a fool,' he said. Worse than a fool. What would she think tomorrow when the *Planet* came out? He offered up a stupid ashamed prayer that Charles had found out nothing from the woman who was her sister-in-law. 'Will you forgive me?'

'There's nothing to forgive, is there?' She sounded truly puzzled, as well she might. He had been asking pardon for future outrages. 'I'm just as much to blame as you. I don't know why I didn't tell you I was Imogen Primero.' She paused. 'There was no deceit in it,' she said. 'Just one of those things. We were dancing — something else came up . . . I don't know.'

He raised his head, gave himself a little shake. Then he walked away from her into the hall. 'You have to go to Stowerton, I think you said. It was kind of you to bring me.'

She was behind him now, her hand on his arm. 'Don't look

like that. What are you supposed to have done? Nothing, nothing. It was just a — a social mistake.'

It was a little fragile hand but insistent. Not knowing why, perhaps because she too seemed in need of comfort, he covered it with his own. Instead of withdrawing it, she left her hand under his and as she sighed it trembled faintly. He turned to look at her, feeling shame that was as paralysing as a disease. Her face was a foot from his, then only inches, then no distance, no face but only a soft mouth.

The shame went in a wave of desire made the more terrible and the more exquisite because he had felt nothing like it for twenty years, perhaps not ever. Since coming down from Oxford he had never kissed any woman but Mary, scarcely been alone with any but the old, the sick or the dying. He did not know how to end the kiss, nor did he know whether this in itself was inexperience or the yearning to prolong something that was so much more, but not enough more, than touching a shadow.

She took herself out of his arms quite suddenly, but without pushing or struggling. There was nothing to struggle against. 'Oh, dear,' she said, but she didn't smile. Her face was very white.

There were words to explain that kind of thing away. 'I don't know what made me do that' or 'I was carried away, the impulse of the moment . . .' He was sick of even the suggestion of lying. Truth itself seemed even more compelling and urgent than his desire and he thought he would speak it even though tomorrow and in the days to come it too would appear to her as a lie.

'I love you. I think I must have loved you from the first moment I saw you. I think that's how it was.' He put his hands up to his forehead and his fingertips, though icy cold, seemed to burn just as snow can burn the skin. 'I'm married,' he said. 'You know that — I mean my wife is living — and I'm a clergyman. I've no right to love you and I promise I'll never be alone with you again.'

She was very surprised and her eyes widened, but which of his confessions had surprised her he had no idea. It even occurred to him that she might be amazed at hearing from him

121

lucid speech, for up to now he had been almost incoherent. 'I mustn't suppose,' he said, for his last sentence seemed like vanity, 'that there's been any temptation for you.' She started to speak, but he went on in a hurry, 'Will you not say anything but just drive away?'

She nodded. In spite of his prohibition, he longed for her to approach him again, just touch him. It was an impossible hunger that made him breathless. She made a little helpless gesture as if she too were in the grip of an overpowering emotion. Then she turned, her face held awkwardly away from him, ran down the hall and let herself out of the front door.

After she had gone it occurred to him that she had asked no questions as to his reasons for coming to the house. She had said little and he everything that mattered. He thought that he must be going mad, for he could not understand that twenty years of discipline could fall away like a lesson imparted to a bored child.

The house was as it had been described in the transcript of the trial. He noticed its layout without emotion or empathy, the long passage that ran from the front door to the door at the back where Painter's coat had hung, the kitchen, the narrow, wall-confined stairs. A kind of cerebral paralysis descended on him and he moved towards that back door, withdrawing the bolts numbly.

The garden was very still, overgrown, basking under a brazen sky. The light and the heat made him dizzy. At first he could not see the coach house at all. Then he realised he had been looking at it ever since he stepped into the garden, but what he had taken for a great quivering bush was in fact solid bricks and mortar hidden under a blanket of virginia creeper. He walked towards it, not interested, not in the least curious. He walked because it was something to do and because this house of a million faintly trembling leaves was at least a kind of goal.

The doors were fastened with a padlock. Archery was relieved. It deprived him of the need for any action. He leant against the wall and the leaves were cold and damp against his face. Presently he went down the drive and through the gateless entrance. Of course, the silver car would not be there. It wasn't.

A bus came almost immediately. He had quite forgotten that he had omitted to lock the back door of Victor's Piece.

Archery returned the keys to the estate agent and lingered for a while looking at the photograph of the house he had just come from. It was like looking at the portrait of a girl you had known only as an old woman, and he wondered if it had perhaps been taken thirty years before when Mrs Primero had bought the house. Then he turned and walked slowly back to the hotel.

Half-past four was usually a dead time at the Olive and Dove. But this was a Saturday and a glorious Saturday at that. The dining room was full of trippers, the lounge decorously crowded with old residents and new arrivals, taking their tea from silver trays. Archery's heart began to beat as he saw his son in conversation with a man and a woman. Their backs were towards him and he saw only that the woman had long fair hair and that the man's head was dark.

He made his way between the armchairs, growing hot with trepidation and weaving among beringed fingers holding tea-pots, little asthmatic dogs, pots of cress and pyramids of sandwiches. When the woman turned he should have felt relief. Instead bitter disappointment ran through him like a long thin knife. He put out his hand and clasped the warm fingers of Tess Kershaw.

Now he saw how stupid his first wild assumption had been. Kershaw was shaking hands with him now and the man's lively face, seamed all over with the wrinkles of animation, bore no resemblance at all to Roger Primero's waxen pallor. His hair was not really dark but thin and sprinkled with grey.

'Charles called in on us on his way back from town,' Tess said. She was perhaps the worst dressed woman in the room in her white cotton blouse and a navy serge skirt. As if explaining this, she said quickly, 'When we heard his news we dropped everything and came back with him.' She got up, threaded her way to the window and looked out into the bright hot afternoon. When she came back she said, 'It feels so strange. I must have walked past here lots of times when I was little, but I can't remember it at all.'

Hand in hand with Painter perhaps. And while they

walked, the murderer and his child, had Painter watched the traffic go by and thought of the way he could become part of that traffic? Archery tried not to see in the fine pointed face opposite his own, the coarse crude features of the man Alice Flower had called Beast. But then they were here to prove it had not been that way at all.

'News?' he said to Charles and he heard the note of distaste creep into his voice.

Charles told him. 'And then we all went to Victor's Piece,' he said. 'We didn't think we'd be able to get in, but someone had left the back door unlocked. We went all over the house and we saw that Primero could easily have hidden himself.'

Archery turned away slightly. The name was now invested with many associations, mostly agonising.

'He said good-bye to Alice, opened and closed the front door without actually going out of it, then he slipped into the dining room — nobody used the dining room and it was dark. Alice went out and . . .' Charles hesitated, searching for a form of words to spare Tess. 'And, after the coal was brought in, he came out, put on the raincoat that was left hanging on the back door and — well, did the deed.'

'It's only a theory, Charlie,' said Kershaw, 'but it fits the facts.'

'I don't know . . .' Archery began.

'Look, Father, don't you want Tess's father cleared?'

Not, thought Archery, if it means incriminating *her* husband. Not that. I may already have done her an injury, but I can't do her that injury.

'This motive you mentioned,' he said dully.

Tess broke in excitedly, 'It's a marvellous motive, a *real* motive.' He knew exactly what she meant. Ten thousand pounds was real, solid, a true temptation, while two hundred pounds . . . Her eyes shone, then saddened. Was she thinking that to hang a man wrongfully was as bad as killing an old woman for a bag of notes? And would that too remain with her all her life? No matter which way things fell out, could she ever escape?

'Primero was working in a solicitor's office,' Charles was saying excitedly. 'He would have known the law, he had all the facilities for checking. Mrs Primero might not have known about it, not if she didn't read the papers. Who knows about all the various Acts of Parliament that are going to be passed anyway? Primero's boss probably had a query about it from a client, sent him to look it up, and there you are. Primero would have known that if his grandmother died intestate before October 1950 all the money would come to him. But if she died after the Act his sisters would get two-thirds of it. I've been looking it all up. This is known as the Great Adoption Act, the law that gave adopted children almost equal rights with natural ones. *Of course* Primero knew.'

'What are you going to do?'

'I've been on to the police but Wexford can't see me before two on Monday. He's away for the weekend. I'll bet the police never checked Primero's movements. Knowing them, I'd say it's likely that as soon as they got hold of Painter they didn't trouble with anyone else.' He looked at Tess and took her hand. 'You can say what you like about this being a free country,' he said hotly, 'but you know as well as I do that everyone has a subconscious feeling that "working class" and "criminal class" are more or less synonymous. Why bother with the respectable, well-connected solicitor's clerk when you've already got your hands on the chauffeur?'

Archery shrugged. From long experience he knew it was useless to argue with Charles when he was airing his quasi-communist ideals.

'Thank you for your enthusiastic reception,' Charles said sarcastically. 'What is there to look so miserable about?'

Archery could not tell him. A load of sorrow seemed to have descended on him and in order to answer his son, he sorted out from conflicting pain something he could express to them all.

'I was thinking of the children,' he said, 'the four little girls who have all suffered from this crime.' He smiled at Tess. 'Tess, of course,' he went on, 'those two sisters you saw — and Elizabeth Crilling.'

He did not add the name of the grown woman who would suffer more than any of them if Charles was right.

CHAPTER TWELVE

Is it not lawful for me to do what I will with mine own?

The Gospel for Septuagesima Sunday

The man who was shown into Wexford's office at nine on Monday morning was small and slender. The bones of his hands were particularly fine and with narrow delicate joints like a woman's. The dark grey suit he wore, very expensive looking and very sleek, made him look smaller than he actually was. He seemed to be surrounded, even so early in the morning and away from his own home, with a great many adjuncts of elegance. Wexford, who knew him well, was amused by the sapphire tie-pin, the two rings, the key chain with its heavy drop of chased — amber, was it? — the briefcase of some kind of reptile skin. How many years, he asked himself, was Roger Primero going to need to get used to wealth?

'Lovely morning,' said Wexford. 'I've just had a couple of days at Worthing and the sea was like a millpond. What can I do for you?'

'Catch a con man,' said Primero, 'a lousy little squirt posing as a journalist.' He unclipped his briefcase and flicked a Sunday newspaper across Wexford's desk. It slipped on the polished surface and fell to the floor. Raising his eyebrows, Wexford let it lie.

'Hell,' said Primero. 'There's nothing for you to see, anyway.' His glazed eyes had a sore look in the handsome expressionless face. The man's vanity had made him rebel against glasses at last, Wexford thought, blinking slightly behind his own heavy tortoise-shell frames. 'Look here, Chief Inspector, I don't mind telling you, I'm hopping mad. This is how it was. Mind if I smoke?'

'Not at all.'

A gold cigarette case spilled out from his pocket, followed

126

by a holder and a lighter in peculiar black and gold mosaic. Wexford watched this production of props, wondering when it was going to end. The man is furnished like a room, he thought.

'This is how it was,' he said. 'Character rang me up on Thursday, said he was on the *Planet* and wanted to do an article about me. My early life. You get the picture? I said he could come along on Friday and he did. I gave him a hell of a long interview, all the dope and the upshot of it was my wife asked him to lunch.' He screwed up his mouth and nose like a man smelling something offensive. 'Hell,' he said, 'I don't suppose he's ever seen a lunch like that in all his life . . .'

'But no article appeared and when you rang the *Planet* this morning they'd never heard of him.'

'How did you know?'

'It happens,' said Wexford dryly. 'I'm surprised at you, sir, a man of your experience. The time to ring the *Planet* was *Friday* morning.'

'It makes me feel such a frightful ass.'

Wexford said airily, 'No money passed, I daresay?'

'Hell, no!'

'Just the lunch, then, and you told him a lot of things you'd rather have left unsaid.'

'That's the thing.' His expression had been sulky, but suddenly he smiled and it was a likeable smile. Wexford had always rather liked him. 'Oh hell's bells, Chief Inspector . . .'

'Hell's bells, as you say. Still, you were wise to come to us, though I don't know that we can do anything unless he makes a move . . .'

'A move? What d'you mean, a move?'

'Well, let me give you an example. Nothing personal, you understand. Just supposing a wealthy man, a man who is somewhat in the public eye, says something a shade indiscreet to a reputable journalist. Ten to one he can't use it because he's laying his paper open to libel action.' Wexford paused and gave the other man a penetrating look. 'But if he says those same indiscreet things to an impostor, a confidence trickster . . .' Primero had grown very pale. 'What's to stop the impostor following a few leads and ferreting out something really damaging. Most people, Mr Primero, even decent law-abiding people, have something in their pasts they'd rather not have known. You have to ask yourself, if he's not on the level, what's he up to? The answer is either he's after your money or else he's crazy.' He added more kindly, 'In my experience nine out of ten of them are just crazy. Still, if it'll help to set your mind at rest perhaps you could give us a description. I suppose he gave you his name?'

'It wouldn't be his real name.'

'Naturally not.'

Primero leant confidingly towards him. During the course of his long career Wexford had found it valuable to make himself *au fait* with perfumes and he noticed that Primero smelt of Lentheric's Onyx.

'He seemed nice enough,' Primero began. 'My wife was quite taken with him.' His eyes had begun to water and he put his fingers very cautiously up to them. Wexford was reminded of a weeping woman who dare not rub her eyes for fear of smudging mascara. 'I haven't told her about this, by the way. I passed it off. Wouldn't want to upset her. He was well-spoken, Oxford accent and all that. A tall fair fellow, said his name was Bowman, Charles Bowman.'

'A-ha!' said Wexford but not aloud.

'Chief Inspector?'

'Mr Primero?'

'I've just remembered something. He was — well, he was extraordinarily interested in my grandmother.'

Wexford almost laughed.

'From what you've told me I think I can assure you there won't be any serious repercussions.'

'You think he's a nut?'

'Harmless, anyway.'

'You've taken a load off my mind.' Primero got up, retrieved his briefcase and picked up the newspaper. He did it rather awkwardly as if he was unused to performing even so simple a service for himself. 'I'll be more careful in future.'

'An ounce of prevention, you know.'

'Well, I won't take up any more of your time.' He pulled a long, but possibly sincerely sad face. The watering eyes added to his look of melancholy. 'Off to a funeral, as a matter of fact. Poor old Alice.'

Wexford had noticed the black tie on which the sapphire glowed darkly. He showed Primero to the door. Throughout the interview he had kept a solemn face. Now he permitted himself the indulgence of gargantuan, though almost silent, laughter.

There was nothing to do until two o'clock except sight-seeing. Charles had been out early and bought a guide book. They sat in the lounge studying it.

'It says here,' said Tess, 'that Forby is the fifth prettiest village in England.'

'Poor Forby,' said Charles. 'Damned with faint praise.'

Kershaw began organising them.

'How about all piling into my car . . .' He stuck his finger on the map '. . . and going down the Kingsbrook road to Forby — keep clear of Forby Hall, eh, Charlie? — have a quick look at the church, and then on to Pomfret. Pomfret Grange is open every weekday in the summer — we might have a look over it — and back into Kingsmarkham along the main road.'

'Lovely,' said Tess.

Kershaw drove and Archery sat beside him. They followed the same route he had taken with Imogen Ide when she had come to put flowers on old Mrs Primero's grave. As they came within sight of the Kingsbrook he remembered what she had said about the implacability of water and how, notwithstanding the efforts of man, it continues to spring from the earth and seek the sea.

Kershaw parked the car by the green with the duckpond. The village looked peaceful and serene. Summer was not as yet so far advanced as to dull the fresh green of the beech trees or hang the wild clematis with its frosty greyish beard. Knots of cottages surrounded the green and on the church side was a row of Georgian houses with bow windows whose dark panes glistened, showing chintz and silver within. There were just three shops, a post office, a butcher's with a canopy and white colonnade, and a place selling souvenirs for tourists. The cottagers' Monday morning wash hung drying in the windless warm air.

They sat on the seat on the green and Tess fed the ducks from a packet of biscuits she had found on the shelf under the dashboard. Kershaw produced a camera and began taking photographs. Suddenly Archery knew he did not want to go any further with them. He almost shivered with distaste at the thought of trailing round the galleries of Pomfret Grange, gasping with false pleasure at the china and pretending to admire family portraits.

'Would you mind if I stayed here? I'd like to have another look at the church.'

Charles glared. 'We'll all go and look at the church.'

'I can't, darling,' said Tess. 'I can't go into a church in jeans.'

'Not in these trousers,' Kershaw quipped. He put away his camera. 'We'd better get moving if we're going to see the stately home.'

'I can easily go back on the bus,' said Archery.

'Well, for God's sake, don't be late, Father.'

If it was going to be any more than a sentimental journey, he too would need a guide. When the car had gone he made his way into the souvenir shop. A bell rang sweetly as he opened the door and a woman came out from a room at the back.

'We don't keep a guide to St Mary's, but you'll find them on sale inside the church door.'

Now he was here he ought to buy something. A postcard? A little brooch for Mary? That, he thought, would be the worst kind of infidelity, to commit adultery in your heart every time you saw your wife wearing a keepsake. He looked drearily at the horse brasses, the painted jugs, the trays of costume jewellery.

A small counter was devoted entirely to calendars, wooden plaques with words on them in pokerwork, framed verses. One of these, a little picture on a card, showing a haloed shepherd with a lamb, caught his eye because the words beneath the drawing were familiar.

'Go, Shepherd, to your rest . . .'

The woman was standing behind him.

'I see you're admiring the efforts of our local bard,' she said brightly. 'He was just a boy when he died and he's buried here.'

'I've seen his grave,' said Archery.

'Of course a lot of people who come here are under the impression he was a shepherd, you know. I always have to explain that at one time shepherd and poet meant the same thing.'

'Lycidas,' said Archery.

She ignored the interruption. 'Actually he was very well-educated. He'd been to High School and everyone said he should have gone to college. He was killed in a road accident. Would you like to see his photograph?'

She produced a stack of cheap framed photographs from a drawer beneath the counter. They were all identical and each bore the legend: John Grace, Bard of Forby. Those whom God loves, die young.

It was a fine ascetic face, sharp-featured and ultra-sensitive. It also, Archery considered, gave the impression that its owner suffered from pernicious anaemia. He had a curious feeling that he had seen it somewhere before.

'Was any of his work published?'

'One or two bits in magazines, that's all. I don't know the ins and outs of it because I've only been here ten years, but there was a publisher who had a weekend cottage here and he was very keen on making his poetry into a book when the poor boy died. Mrs Grace — his mother, you know — was all for it, but the thing was most of the stuff he'd written had disappeared. There were just these bits you see here. His mother said he'd written whole plays — they didn't rhyme, if you know what I mean, but they were kind of like Shakespeare. Anyway, they couldn't be found. Maybe he'd burnt them or given them away. It does seem a shame, though, doesn't it?'

Archery glanced out of the window towards the little wooden church. 'Some mute inglorious Milton here may rest . . .' he murmured.

'That's right,' said the woman. 'You never know, they may turn up, like the Dead Sea Scrolls.'

Archery paid five and sixpence for the picture of the shepherd and the lamb and strolled up towards the church. He opened the kissing gate and, walking in a clockwise direction, made for the door. What was it she had said? 'You must never go widdershins around a church. It's unlucky.' He needed luck for Charles and for himself. The irony was that however things fell out, one of them would lose.

There was no music coming from the church, but as the door opened he saw that some sort of service was in progress. For a moment he stood, looking at the people and listening to the words.

'If after the manner of men I have fought with beasts at Ephesus, what advantageth it me, if the dead rise not?'

It was a funeral. They were almost exactly halfway through the service for the burial of the dead.

'Let us eat and drink for tomorrow we die . . .'

The door gave a slight whine as he closed it. Now, as he turned, he could see the funeral cars, three of them, outside the other gate. He went to look again at Grace's grave, passed the newly dug trench where this latest coffin was to be laid, and finally sat down on a wooden seat in a shady corner. It was a quarter to twelve. Give it half an hour, he thought, and then he would have to go for his bus. Presently he dozed.

The sound of gentle footfalls awakened him. He opened his eyes and saw that they were carrying the coffin out of the church. It was supported by four bearers, but it was a small coffin, a child's perhaps or a short woman's. On it were a few bunches of flowers and a huge wreath of madonna lilies.

The bearers were followed by a dozen people, the procession being headed by a man and a woman walking side by side. Their backs were towards Archery and besides that the woman, dressed in a black coat, wore a large black hat whose brim curved about her face. But he would have known her anywhere. He would have known her if he were blind and deaf, by her presence and her essence. They could not see him, had no idea they were watched, these mourners who had come to bury Alice Flower.

The other followers were mostly old, friends of Alice's perhaps, and one woman looked as if she must be the matron of the Infirmary. They gathered at the graveside and the vicar began to speak the words that would finally commit the old servant to the ground. Primero bent down and, taking rather fastidiously a handful of black earth, cast it on to the coffin. His shoulders shook and a little hand in a black glove reached out and rested on his arm. Archery felt a savage stab of jealousy that took away his breath.

The vicar spoke the Collect and blessed them. Then Primero went a little way apart with him, they spoke together and shook hands. He took his wife's arm and they walked slowly towards the gate where the cars were. It was all over.

When they were out of sight Archery got up and approached the gradually filling grave. He could smell the lilies five yards off. A card was attached to them and on it someone had written simply: 'From Mr and Mrs Roger, with love.'

'Good day,' he said to the sexton.

'Good day, sir. Lovely day.'

It was gone a quarter past twelve. Archery hurried towards the kissing gate, wondering how often the buses ran. As he came out from under the arch of trees, he stopped suddenly. Charles was striding towards him up the sandy lane.

'Good thing you didn't come,' Charles called. 'The place was shut for redecorating. Can you beat it? We thought we might as well drift back and pick you up.'

'Where's the car?'

'Round the other side of the church.'

They would be gone by now. Just the same Archery wished he were safely back at the Olive and Dove eating cold beef and salad. As they rounded the yew hedge a black car passed them. He forced himself to look towards the gate. The Primeros were still there, talking to the matron. His throat grew suddenly dry.

'Let's cut across the green,' he said urgently.

'Mr Kershaw happens to be waiting on this side.'

They were now only a few yards from the Primeros. The matron shook hands and stepped into a hired limousine. Primero turned and his eyes met those of Charles.

He grew first white, then a curious vinegary purple. Charles went on walking towards him and then Primero too began to move. They were approaching each other menacingly, ridiculously, like two gunmen in a Western.

'Mr Bowman, of the *Sunday Planet*, I believe?'

Charles stopped and said coolly, 'You can believe what you like.'

She had been talking to the women in the car. Now she withdrew her head and the car began to move off. They were alone, the four of them, in the centre of the fifth prettiest village in England. She looked at Archery first with embarrassment, then with a warmth that conquered her awkwardness.

'Why, hallo, I . . .'

Primero snatched at her arm. 'Recognise him? I shall need you for a witness, Imogen.'

Charles glared. 'You what?'

'Charles!' said Archery sharply.

'Do you deny that you made your way into my home under false pretences?'

'Roger, Roger . . .' She was still smiling, but her smile had grown stiff. 'Don't you remember we met Mr Archery at the dance? This is his son. He's a journalist, but he uses a pseudonym, that's all. They're here on holiday.'

Charles said rigidly, 'I'm afraid that isn't quite true, Mrs Primero.' She blinked, her lashes fluttering like wings, and her gaze came to rest softly on Archery's face. 'My father and I came here with the express purpose of collecting certain information. That we have done. In order to do it we had to make our way into your confidence. Perhaps we have been unscrupulous, but we thought the end justified the means.'

'I'm afraid I don't understand.' Her eyes were still on Archery and he was unable to draw his own away. He knew that his face registered a tremendous plea for forgiveness, a disclaimer of Charles's statement and also registered the agony of love. There was, however, no reason why she should read there anything but guilt. 'I don't understand at all. What information?'

'I'll tell you . . .' Charles began, but Primero interrupted him.

'Since you're so frank, you won't have any objection to coming down to the police station right now and laying your "information" before Chief Inspector Wexford.'

'None at all,' Charles drawled, 'except that it happens to be my lunchtime and in any case I have an appointment with the Chief Inspector already. At two sharp. I intend to tell him, Mr Primero, just how opportunely for you your grandmother died, how — oh, perfectly legally, I admit — you managed to cheat your sisters out of their inheritance, and how you concealed yourself in Victor's Piece on a certain evening in December sixteen years ago.'

'You're out of your mind!' Primero shouted.

Archery found his voice. 'That's enough, Charles.' He heard her speak, a tiny disembodied sound.

'It isn't true!' And then, terribly afraid, 'It isn't true, is it?'

'I'm damned if I'll argue it out in the street with this crook!'

'Of course it's true.'

'It was all above board.' Primero suddenly broke. They were all hot, standing there in the noon sun, but only Primero's face showed actual sweat, water drops on the cheesy sallow skin. 'Hell, it was a matter of law,' he blustered. 'What's it got to do with you, anyway? Who *are* you?'

Without taking her gaze from Archery, she took her husband's arm. All the gaiety had left her face and she looked almost old, a faded blonde who was effaced by her black clothes. Because she had become ugly she suddenly seemed for the first time within Archery's reach, yet she had never been farther from it. 'Let's go home, Roger.' Her mouth trembled and cobweb lines had appeared at its corners. 'In the course of your enquiries, Mr Archery,' she said, 'I hope you managed to combine pleasure with business.'

Then they were gone. Charles gave a great gasp.

'I must say I rather enjoyed that. I suppose by pleasure she meant the lunch they gave me. You can rely on these tycoons' wives to tot up every egg in the caviare. Still it was hard on her. You needn't look so shattered, Father. It's awfully middle-class to have a phobia about scenes.'

CHAPTER THIRTEEN

I deal with the thing that is lawful and right . . . and all false
ways I utterly abhor.

Psalm 119, appointed for the 26th Day

'Public General Acts and Measures, 1950. Wexford took the
book — was it a White Paper? Archery was ashamed to confess
that he did not know — and read the title aloud. 'There's
something here you want me to look at?'

Charles found the page for him. 'Here.' Wexford began
to read. The silence was tense, almost agonised. Archery
looked surreptitiously at the others, Charles who was flushed
with eagerness, Kershaw trying to sit casually, but whose
bright darting eyes betrayed his anxiety, Tess who looked
confident, serene. Was it her mother in whom she trusted
so completely or was it Charles? A good deal of Charles's
poise had deserted him when on entering the office five
minutes before he had had to introduce Tess to the Chief
Inspector.

'Miss Kershaw,' he had said, 'my . . . the girl I'm going to
marry. I . . .'

'Ah, yes.' Wexford had been very urbane. 'Good afternoon,
Miss Kershaw, Mr Kershaw. Won't you sit down? Heat wave's
coming to an end at last, I'm afraid.'

And indeed a change had come over the bright blue
un-English sky. It had begun just after lunch with the appearance of a cloud that was truly no bigger than a man's hand, and
this cloud had been followed by more, driven by a sudden wind.
Now, as Wexford, frowning a little, read steadily, Archery
contemplated the window from which the yellow blind had
been fully raised, and through it the lumpy blotchy mass of
cumulus, hollowed and pock-marked with grey.

'Very interesting,' said Wexford, 'and new to me. I didn't

know the Primero sisters were adopted. Convenient for Primero.'

'Convenient?' said Charles. Archery sighed within himself. He could always tell when his son was going to be rude or what Charles himself called forthright. 'Is that all you've got to say?'

'No,' said Wexford. Few people have the confidence and the restraint to say 'yes' or 'no' without qualification. Wexford was big and heavy and ugly; his suit had seen better days, too many wet ones and too many hot dusty ones, but he radiated strength. 'Before we go any further on this tack, Mr Archery,' he said to Charles, 'I'd like to say that I've had a complaint about you from Mr Primero.'

'Oh, that.'

'Yes, that. I've been aware for some days that your father had made the acquaintance of the Primeros. Perhaps it wasn't a bad idea and I'm sure it wasn't an unpleasant one to do so through Mrs Primero.' Archery knew his face had become white. He felt sick. 'And let me say in all fairness,' Wexford went on, 'that I told him it was all right as far as I was concerned to make contact with the people concerned in the Primero case.' He glanced briefly at Tess, who didn't move. 'Make contact, I said, not make trouble. Your little escapade on Friday is what I call making trouble and that I won't have!'

Charles said sulkily, 'All right, I'm sorry.' Archery saw that he had to justify himself before Tess. 'You're not going to tell me that your people don't occasionally invent a cover story to get what they want.'

'My people,' Wexford snapped, 'happen to have the law on their side.' He added grandiloquently, 'They *are* the law.' The frown thawed. 'Now we've got the lecture over you'd better tell me just what you and your father have found out.'

Charles told him. Wexford listened patiently, but as the evidence against Primero mounted, instead of surprise, his face registered a strange blankness. The heavy features had become brutish, like those of an old bull.

'Of course, you'll say he had an alibi,' said Charles. 'I realise your people would have checked his alibi and after all these years it's going to be difficult to crack, but . . .'

'His alibi was not checked,' said Wexford.

'What did you say?'

'His alibi was not checked.'

'I don't understand.'

'Mr Archery . . .' Wexford got up and rested his massive hands on the desk, but he didn't move away from behind it. 'I am quite happy to discuss this whole matter with you, answer any questions you may like to ask.' He paused. 'But not in the presence of Miss Kershaw. If I may say so, I think you were unwise to bring her with you.'

Now it was Charles's turn to get to his feet.

'Miss Kershaw is going to be my wife,' he said hotly. 'Anything you say to me you can say to her. I won't have any secrets from her in this.'

Casually Wexford sat down again. He drew a bunch of papers from a desk drawer and began to study them. Then he lifted his eyes slowly and said: 'I'm sorry this has been a fruitless interview for you. With a little co-operation I think I could have saved you a lot of useless enquiry. But, if you'll forgive me, I'm a very busy man so I'll say good afternoon.'

'No,' said Tess suddenly. 'I'll go. I'll wait in the car.'

'Tess!'

'Of course I'm going, darling. Don't you see? He can't talk about my father in front of me. Oh, darling, be your age!'

He is being his age, thought Archery miserably. Wexford knew something — something that was going to be horrible. But why was he playing this pouncing cat and mouse game with them all, why had he played it with Archery all along? Confidence and strength — but did it cover a fierce inverted snobbism, a fear that the Archerys might shake his authority and trouble the still waters of his district? And yet the man held such sway and was, beyond a doubt, a good, just man. He would never lie or even shift truth to cover a lapse. 'His alibi was not checked . . .' If only they would stop fencing!

Then suddenly, Wexford stopped it.

'No need to leave the building, Miss Kershaw,' he said. 'If your — your father would care to take you upstairs — straight along the corridor and turn left when you come to the double doors — you'll find we've got quite a reasonable canteen, even for a lady. I suggest a cup of strong tea and an eccles cake.'

'Thanks.' Tess turned and just touched Kershaw's shoulder. He rose at once. Wexford closed the door after them.

Charles took a deep breath, and making a brave attempt to lounge casually in his chair, said, 'All right, then. What about this alibi that for some mysterious reason was never investigated?'

'The reason,' said Wexford, 'was not mysterious. Mrs Primero was killed between six-twenty-five and seven o'clock on the evening of Sunday, September 24th, 1950.' He paused to allow Charles's inevitable interruption of 'Yes', yes', uttered with fierce impatience. 'She was killed in Kingsmarkham and at six-thirty Roger Primero was seen in Sewingbury five miles away.'

'Oh, he was seen, was he?' Charles scoffed, crossing his legs. 'What do you think, Father? Doesn't it seem remotely possible to you that he could have fixed beforehand that he'd be "seen"? There's always some shifty mate who'll perjure himself and say he's seen you for twenty quid.'

'Some shifty mate, eh?' Wexford was now hardly bothering to conceal his amusement.

'Somebody saw him. All right. Who saw him?'

Wexford sighed and the smile was erased.

'I saw him,' he said.

It was a blow in the face. Archery's love for his son, dormant over the past days, rose within his breast in a hot tide. Charles said nothing, and Archery who had been doing this sort of thing rather a lot lately, tried hard not to hate Wexford. He had taken an unconscionable time coming to the point, but this, of course, was his revenge.

The big elbows rested on the desk, the fingers meeting and pressing together in an implacable pyramid of flesh. The law incarnate. If Wexford had seem Primero that night, there was no gainsaying it, for here was incorruptibility. It was almost as if God had seen him. Horrified, Archery pulled himself up in his chair and gave a dry painful cough.

'You?' said Charles at last.

'I,' said Wexford, 'with my little eye.'

'You might have told us before!'

'I would have,' said Wexford mildly and, oddly enough,

believably, 'if I'd had the remotest idea you suspected him. Chatting up Primero about his grandmother was one thing, pinning murder on him quite another.'

Polite now, stiff and very formal, Charles asked, 'Would you mind telling us the details?'

Wexford's courtesy matched his. 'Not at all. I intend to. Before I do, however, I'd better say that there was no question of hindsight. I knew Primero. I'd seen him in court with his chief on a good many occasions. He used to go along with him to learn the ropes.' Charles nodded, his face set. Archery thought he knew what was going on in his mind. Loss was something he knew about, too.

'I was in Sewingbury on a job,' Wexford continued, 'and I'd got a date to meet a man who sometimes gave us a bit of information. What you might call a shifty mate, but we never got twenty quidsworth out of him. The appointment was for six at a pub called the Black Swan. Well, I had a word with my — my friend, and I was due back in Kingsmarkham at seven. I walked out of the public bar at just on half past six and ran slap bang into Primero.

' "Good evening, Inspector," he said, and I thought he looked a bit lost. As well he might. I found out afterwards that he'd been going to meet some pals, but he'd got the wrong pub. They were waiting for him at the Black Bull. "Are you on duty?" he said. "Or can I buy you a short snort?" '

Archery nearly smiled. Wexford had given a very fair imitation of the absurd slang Primero still affected after sixteen years of affluence.

' "Thanks all the same," I said, "but I'm late as it is." "Good night to you, then," he said and he went up to the bar. I'd only been in Kingsmarkham ten minutes when I got called out to Victor's Piece.'

Charles got up slowly and extended a stiff, mechanical hand.

'Thank you very much, Chief Inspector. I think that's all anyone can say on the subject, don't you?' Wexford leaned across the desk and took his hand. A faint flash of compassion softened his features, weakened them, and was gone. 'I'm sorry I wasn't very polite just now,' Charles said.

'That's all right,' said Wexford. 'This is a police station, not a clerical garden party.' He hesitated and added, 'I'm sorry, too.' And Archery knew that the apology had nothing to do with Charles's ill manners.

Tess and Charles began to argue even before they had all got into the car. Certain that they had said it all or something very like it before, Archery listened to them indifferently. He had kept silent for half an hour and still there was nothing he could say.

'We have to be realistic about it,' Charles was saying. 'If I don't mind and Mother and Father don't mind, why can't we just get married and forget you ever had a father?'

'Who says they don't mind? That's not being realistic, anyway. I'm being realistic. One way or another I've had a lot of luck . . .' Tess flashed a quick watery smile at Kershaw. 'I've had more than anyone would have thought possible, but this is one bit I have to dip out on.'

'And what does that mean exactly?'

'Just that — well, it was ridiculous ever to imagine we could be married, you and I.'

'You and I? What about all the others who'll come along and fancy you? Are you going to go through the same melodrama with them or d'you think you'll weaken when the thirties rear their ugly heads?'

She winced at that. Archery thought Charles had almost forgotten they were not alone. He pushed her into the back seat of the car and banged the door.

'I'm curious, you see,' Charles went on, bitterly sarcastic. 'I'd just like to know if you've taken a vow of perpetual chastity. O God, it's like a feature in the *Sunday Planet* — Condemned to lonely spinsterhood for father's crime! Just for the record, since I'm supposed to be so far above you morally, I'd like to know the qualifications the lucky man has to have. Give me a specification, will you?'

Her mother had built up her faith, but the Archery family with their doubts had knocked it down; still it had lived until Wexford had killed it. Her eyes were fixed on Kershaw who had given her reality. Archery was not surprised when she said hysterically:

'I suppose he'd have to have a murderer for a father.' She gasped, for she was admitting it to herself for the first time. 'Like me!'

Charles tapped Archery's back. 'Just nip out and knock someone off,' he said outrageously.

'Oh, shut up,' said Kershaw. 'Give it a rest, Charlie, will you?'

Archery touched his arm. 'I think I'll get out, if you don't mind. I need some air.'

'Me too,' said Tess. 'I can't stand being boxed up in here any longer and I've got a ghastly head. I want some aspirins.'

'Can't park here.'

'We'll walk back to the hotel, Daddy. If I don't get out I'll pass out.'

Then they were all three on the pavement, Charles's face as black as thunder. Tess swayed a little and Archery caught her arm to steady her. Several passers-by gave them curious looks.

'You said you wanted aspirins,' said Charles.

It was only a few yards to the nearest chemist's, but Tess was shivering in her thin clothes. The air was heavy and cloying. Archery noticed that all the shopkeepers had furled their sunblinds.

Charles seemed about to begin again but she gave him a pleading look. 'Don't let's talk about it any more. We've said it all. I needn't see you again till October, not then if we're careful . . .'

He frowned silently, made a little gesture of repudiation. Archery held the shop door open for Tess to pass through.

There was no one inside but the assistant and Elizabeth Crilling.

She did not appear to be buying anything, just waiting and gossiping with the shop girl. It was the middle of a weekday afternoon and here she was shopping. What had become of the job in the 'ladies' wear establishment'? Archery wondered if she would recognise him and how he could avoid this happening, for he did not want to have to introduce her to Tess. It gave him a little thrill of awe when he realised what was happening in this small town shop, a meeting after sixteen years of the child who was Painter's daughter and the child who had discovered Painter's crime.

While he hovered near the door Tess went up to the counter. They were so close together that they were almost touching. Then Tess reached across in front of Liz Crilling to select one of the aspirin bottles, and in doing so brushed her sleeve.

'I beg your pardon.'

'That's O.K.'

Archery could see Tess had nothing smaller than a ten shilling note. His trepidation, his fears for the effect of illumination on Tess at this moment were so great, that he almost cried aloud, 'Never mind. Leave it! Only, please God, let us all get away and hide ourselves!'

'Haven't you anything smaller?'

'I'm sorry.'

'I'll just go and see if we've got any change.'

The two young women stood side by side in silence. Tess stared straight in front of her, but Liz Crilling was playing nervously with two little scent bottles displayed on a glass shelf, moving them about as if they were chessmen.

Then the pharmacist in his white coat came out from the back.

'Is there a Miss Crilling waiting for a prescription?'

Tess turned, her face flooded with colour.

'This is a repeat prescription, but I'm afraid it's no longer valid . . .'

'What d'you mean, no longer valid?'

'I mean that it can only be used six times. I can't let you have any more of these tablets without a fresh prescription. If your mother . . .'

'The old cow,' said Liz Crilling slowly.

The swift animation on Tess's face died as if she had been struck. Without opening her purse she tumbled the change loose into her handbag and hurried out of the shop.

The old cow. It was her fault, everything bad that had ever happened to you was her fault — beginning with the beautiful pink dress.

She was making it for you and she worked at the sewing machine all day that cold wet Sunday. When it was finished you put it on and Mummy brushed your hair and put a ribbon in it.

'I'll just pop over and show you off to Granny Rose,' Mummy said and she popped over, but when she came back she was cross because Granny Rose was asleep and hadn't heard when she'd tapped on the window.

'Give it half an hour,' Daddy said, 'and maybe she'll be awake then.' He was half asleep himself, lying in bed, white and thin on the pillows. So Mummy had stayed upstairs with him, giving him his medicine and reading to him because he was too weak to hold a book.

'You stay in the sitting room, Baby, and mind you don't get that frock dirty.'

You had done as you were told but it made you cry just the same. Of course you didn't care about not seeing Granny Rose, but you knew that while she was talking to Mummy you could have slipped out into the passage and down the garden to show it to Tessie, now, while it was brand-new.

Well, why not? Why not put on a coat and run across the road? Mummy wouldn't come down for half an hour. But you would have to hurry, for Tessie always went to bed at half-past six. Auntie Rene was strict about that. 'Respectable working class,' Mummy said, whatever that meant, and although she might let you into Tessie's bedroom she wouldn't let you wake her up.

But why, why, why had you gone?

Elizabeth Crilling came out of the shop and walked blindly towards the Glebe Road turning, bumping into shoppers as she went. Such a long long way to go, past the hateful little sand houses that were like desert tombs in this spectral storm light, such a long way . . . And there was only one thing left to do when you got to the end of the road.

CHAPTER FOURTEEN

It is lawful for Christian men . . . to wear weapons and serve in the wars.

The Thirty-nine Articles

The letter with the Kendal postmark was awaiting Archery on the hall table when they got back to the Olive and Dove. He glanced at it uncomprehendingly, then remembered. Colonel Cosmo Plashet, Painter's commanding officer.

'What now?' he said to Charles when Tess had gone upstairs to lie down.

'I don't know. They're going back to Purley tonight.'

'Do we go back to Thringford tonight?'

'I don't know, Father. I tell you I don't know.' He paused, irritable, pink in the face, a lost child. 'I'll have to go and apologise to Primero,' he said, the child remembering its manners. 'It was a bloody awful way to behave to him.'

Archery said it instinctively, without thinking. 'I'll do that, if you like. I'll ring them.'

'Thanks. If he insists on seeing me I'll go. You've talked to her before, haven't you? I gathered from something Wexford said.'

'Yes, I've talked to her, but I didn't know who she was.'

'That,' said Charles, severe again, 'is you all over.'

Was he really going to ring her up and apologise? And why should he have the vanity to suppose that she would even come to the phone? 'In the course of your enquiries, Mr Archery, I hope you managed to combine pleasure with business.' She was bound to have told her husband what she had meant by that. How the middle-aged clergyman had suddenly gone sentimental on her. He could hear Primero's reply, his colloquialism, 'Didn't actually make the old pass, did he?' and her light dismissive laughter. His soul cringed. He went into the empty lounge and ripped open Colonel Plashet's letter.

It was handwritten on rough white vellum almost as thick as cartridge paper. By the occasional fading of the ink from deep black to pale grey Archery could tell that the writer had not used a fountain pen. An old man's hand, he thought, a military man's address, 'Srinagar', Church Street, Kendal...

Dear Mr Archery, he read,

I was interested to receive your letter and will do my best to provide you with what information I can on Private Herbert Arthur Painter. You may be aware that I was not called to give evidence as to character at Painter's trial, though I held myself in readiness to do so should it have been necessary. Fortunately I have retained in my possession certain notes I then made. I say fortunately, for you will appreciate that Private Painter's war service covered a period of from twenty-three to twenty years ago, and my memory is no longer what I should like it to be. Lest you should be under the impression, however, that I am the possessor of information sympathetic to Painter's relatives, I must reluctantly disabuse your mind. In deciding not to call me, Painter's defending counsel must have been aware that any statements I could truthfully have made would, instead of assisting their cause, have merely made the task of prosecution easier.

That was it, then. There would follow only another loathsome catalogue to Painter's propensities. Colonel Plashet's very idiosyncratic style of writing brought home to him, more forcibly than the cold print of the transcript had done, the kind of man Charles was prepared to accept as a father-in-law. Curiosity, not hope, made him read on.

Painter had been serving with His Majesty's Forces for one year when he entered my regiment. This was shortly prior to our embarkation for Burma as part of the Fourteenth Army. He was a most unsatisfactory soldier. We saw no action until we had been in Burma for three months, during which time Painter was twice put on a charge for being drunk and disorderly and sentenced to seven days' detention for gross insolence on an officer.

In action his manner and bearing improved considerably. He was a naturally pugnacious man, brave and aggressive. Soon after this, however, an incident occurred in the village in which we had our camp and a young Burmese woman was killed. A Court Martial was held before which

Painter was charged with her manslaughter. He was found not guilty. I think I had better say no more on this matter.

In February 1945, six months before the cessation of hostilities in the Far East, Painter succumbed to a certain tropical affliction which manifests itself in severe ulceration of the legs, accelerated, I am told, by his complete disregard of certain elementary hygienic precautions and his refusal to take a proper diet. He became seriously ill and responded badly to treatment. There was at this time a troopship lying off Calcutta, and as soon as Painter's condition allowed, he and certain other sick men were transported there by air. This troopship reached a United Kingdom port during the latter part of March, 1945.

I have no further information as to Painter's fate except that I believe he was shortly afterwards demobilised on health grounds.

If you have any other questions whatsoever to put to me regarding Painter's war service, you may be assured of my willingness to answer them to the best of my ability and discretion. You have my full permission to publish this letter. May I, however, ask your indulgence to an old man's whim, and request a copy of your book when it comes out?

Yours sincerely,

Cosmo Plashet

They all assumed he was writing a book. Archery smiled a little at the colonel's grandiose style, but there was nothing to smile at in the brief lines about the Burmese woman's death. The colonel's guarded, 'I think I had better say no more on this matter . . .' told him more than a page of explanations

Nothing new, nothing vital. Why, then, did he have this urgent sensation of having missed something of importance? But no, he couldn't see it . . . He looked again, not knowing what he was looking for. Then, as he stared at the spidery loops and whorls, he was engulfed by a hot wave of trepidation and longing. He was afraid to speak to her, yet he longed to hear her voice.

He looked up, surprised to find how dark it had become. The summer afternoon sky simulated dusk with its covering of slate-coloured cloud. Over the housetops away to the east it was leaden tinged with angry purple and as Archery began to fold the letter, a vivid flash of lightning shocked across the room, flashing the words on the paper into relief and bleaching his hands livid white. The thunder followed it as he reached the stairs, and echoes were still curling and growling round the old building when he entered his bedroom.

She could only refuse to speak to him. She wouldn't even have to do that herself, for she could send the Italian butler. There was no question of her berating or reproaching him personally — she could do it with far more crushing effect by proxy.

'Forby Hall. Mr Primero's residence.'

It *was* the butler. The Italian accent distorted every word except the name to which it gave true Latin emphasis.

'I should like to speak to Mrs Primero.'

'What name shall I say, sir?'

'Henry Archery.'

Perhaps she would not be with her husband when the message came. People situated as they were in an enormous house of many rooms tended to live individual lives, he in the library, she in the drawing room. She would send the butler back with a message. As a foreigner the butler would be without that intimate feel for the nuances of English and that would give her scope. She could tell him to say something subtle and apparently polite and he would not appreciate the cutting sting that underlay the words. He heard footsteps, echoing footsteps across the big hall Charles had described. The phone crackled, perhaps because of the storm.

'Hallo?'

Out of a bone-dry throat he tried to speak. Why hadn't he rehearsed something? Because he had been so sure she wouldn't come?

'Hallo, are you still there?'

'Mrs Primero . . .'

'I thought you might have got fed-up with waiting. Mario took so long about it.'

'Of course I waited.' Rain burst against his window, smacking and sobbing at the glass. 'I want to apologise to you for this morning. It was unforgivable.'

'Oh, no,' she said. 'I've forgiven you — for this morning. You didn't really take any part in it, did you? It was the other times that seem so — well, not forgivable, just incomprehensible.'

He could imagine her little helpless gesture, the white hands spreading out.

'One doesn't like to feel one's been used, you see. It's not that I'm hurt. I'm not likely to be hurt because I'm really very tough, much tougher than Roger. But I am a bit spoilt and I feel as if I've been kicked off my pedestal. Good for me, I expect.'

Archery said slowly, 'There's so much to explain, I thought I could explain on the phone, but now I find I can't.' And yet the violence of the storm made it easier for him. He could hardly hear his own words. 'I want to *see* you,' he said, forgetting his promise.

Apparently she had forgotten it too. 'You can't come here,' she said practically, 'because Roger's somewhere about and he might not look on your apology in the same light as I do. And I can't come to you because the Olive and Dove, being a respectable hostelry, doesn't allow visitors in residents' bedrooms.' He made an inarticulate murmur. 'That's the second cheap thing I've said to you today,' she said. 'Oh, my dear, you wouldn't want me to talk in the lounge among all the fuddy-duddies, would you? I know, what about Victor's Piece?'

'It's locked,' he said, adding stupidly, 'and it's raining.'

'I've got a key. Roger's always kept one. Shall we say eight? The Olive will be only too happy if you have an early dinner.'

He dropped the receiver almost guiltily as Charles put his head round the door. And yet the telephone call had not been clandestine but made at Charles's instigation.

'I think I've made it all right with the Primeros,' he said, and he reflected on words from an unremembered source. God gave men tongues that they might conceal their thoughts.

But Charles, with the quixotry of youth, had lost interest. 'Tess and her father are just off,' he said.

'I'll come down.'

They were standing in the hall, waiting. For what? Archery wondered. The storm to cease? A miracle? Or just to say goodbye?

'I wish we hadn't seen Elizabeth Crilling,' Tess said. 'And yet now I wish I'd talked to her.'

'Just as well you didn't,' said Archery. 'You're worlds apart.

The only thing you'd have in common is your age. You're both twenty-one.'

'Don't wish away my life,' Tess said oddly and he saw there were tears in her eyes. 'I'm not twenty-one till October.' She picked up the duffel bag that served her as a weekend case and held out her hand to Archery.

'We must love you and leave you,' said Kershaw. 'Doesn't seem anything more to be said, does there, Mr Archery? I know you hoped things would work out, but it wasn't to be.'

Charles was gazing at Tess. She kept her eyes averted.

'For God's sake say I can write to you.'

'What's the use?'

'It would give me pleasure,' he said tightly.

'I shan't be at home. I'm going to Torquay to stay with my aunt the day after tomorrow.'

'You won't be camping on the beach, will you? This aunt, doesn't she have an address?'

'I haven't got a piece of paper,' said Tess and Archery saw that she was near to tears. He felt in his pocket, pulled out first Colonel Plashet's letter — not that, not for Tess to see — then the illuminated card with the verse and the picture of the shepherd. Her eyes were misted and she scrawled the address quickly, handing it to Charles without a word.

'Come on, lovey,' said Kershaw. 'Home, and don't spare the horses.' He fished out his car keys. 'All fifteen of them,' he said, but no one smiled.

CHAPTER FIFTEEN

If he hath offended any other . . . ask them forgiveness; and where he hath done injury or wrong to any man . . . make amends to the uttermost of his power.

The Visitation of the Sick

It was raining so heavily that he had to dash from the car into the dilapidated porch and even there the rain caught him, blown by the gusty wind and tossed in icy droplets off the evergreens. He leant against the door and staggered because it gave with his weight and swung noisily open.

She must have arrived already. The Flavia was nowhere to be seen and he felt a shiver of self-disgust and trepidation when it occurred to him that she was being purposely discreet. She was well known in the district, she was married and she was having a secret meeting with a married man. So she had hidden her conspicuous car. Yes, it was cheap, cheap and sordid, and he, a priest of God, had engineered it.

Victor's Piece, dry and rotten in drought, smelt wet and rotten now the rain had come. It smelt of fungus and dead things. There were probably rats under these knotted flaking floorboards. He closed the door and walked a little way down the passage, wondering where she was and why she had not come out to him when she heard the door. Then he stopped, for he was facing the back door where Painter's raincoat had hung, and there was a raincoat hanging there now.

Certainly nothing had hung there on his previous visit to the house. He moved up to the raincoat, fascinated and rather horrified.

Of course, it was obvious what had happened. Someone had bought the place at last, the workmen had been in and one of them had left his raincoat. Nothing to be alarmed about. His nerves must be very bad.

'Mrs Primero,' he said, and then, because you do not call women with whom you have secret assignations by their surnames, 'Imogen! Imogen!'

There was no answer. And yet he was sure he was not alone in the house. What about knowing her if you were deaf and blind, jeered a voice within him, what about knowing her by her essence? He opened the dining room door, then the drawing room. A damp cold smell came to meet him. Water had leaked under the window sill and formed a spreading pool, dark in colour, hideously evocative. This and the rusty veining on the marble of the fireplace recalled to him splashed blood. Who would buy this place? Who could bear it? But someone had bought it for there was a workman's coat hanging behind the door . . .

Here she had sat, the old woman, and bade Alice go to church. Here she had sat, her eyes closing easily into sleep, when Mrs Crilling had come tapping at the window. Then he had come, whoever he was, with his axe and perhaps she had still been sleeping, on and on over the threats and the demands, over the blows of the axe, on and on into endless sleep. Endless sleep? *Mors janua vitae.* If only the gateway to life had not been through an unspeakable passage of pain. He found himself praying for what he knew was impossible, that God should change history.

Then Mrs Crilling tapped on the window.

Archery gave a start so violent and galvanic that he seemed to feel a hand squeeze his heart with slippery fingers. He gasped and forced himself to look.

'Sorry I'm late,' said Imogen Ide. 'What a ghastly night.'

She should have been on the inside, he thought, pulling himself together. But she had been outside, tapping, tapping, because she had seen him standing there like a lost soul. This way it altered the aspect of things, for she had not hidden the car. It stood on the gravel beside his own, wet, silver, glittering, like something alive and beautiful from the depths of the sea.

'How did you get in?' she said in the hall.

'The door was open.'

'Some workman.'

'I suppose so.'

She wore a tweed suit and her pale hair was wet. He had

been silly enough — bad enough, he thought — to imagine that
when they met she would run to him and embrace him. Instead
she stood looking at him gravely, almost coldly, two little frown
lines between her brows.

'The morning room, I think,' she said. 'There's furniture in
there and besides it doesn't have — associations.'

The furniture consisted of two kitchen stools and a cane-
back chair. From the window, heavily encrusted with grime, he
could see the conservatory to whose walls of cracked glass the
tendrils of a dead vine still clung. He gave her the chair and sat
down on one of the stools. He had a strange feeling — but a
feeling not without a charm of its own — that they had come
here to buy the house, he and she, had come early and were
reduced to wait thus uncomfortably until the arrival of the
agent who would show them round.

'This could be a study,' he would say. 'It must be lovely on
a fine day.'

'Or we could eat in here. Nice and near the kitchen.'

'Will you able to bear getting up in the morning to cook
my breakfast?' (My love, my love . . .)

'You were going to explain,' she said, and of course, there
would never be a shared bed or a shared breakfast or any future
at all. This was their future, this interview in a damp morning
room, looking at a dead vine.

He began to tell her about Charles and Tess, about Mrs
Kershaw's belief. Her face grew even harder and colder when
he came to the bit about the inheritance and before he had
finished, she said:

'You really meant to pin the murder on Roger?'

'What could I do? I was torn between Charles,' he said,
'and you.' She shook her head quickly, the blood running into
her face. 'I beg you to believe I didn't try to know you because
you were his wife.'

'I believe you.'

'The money . . . his sisters . . . you didn't know about that?'

'I knew nothing. Only that they existed and that he never
saw them. Oh God!' She screwed up her face, pushed her hands
over her cheeks, across her eyes and up to the temples. 'We've
been talking about it all day. He can't see that he was morally

obliged to help them. Only one thing matters to him, that Wexford won't take it seriously as a motive for murder.'

'Wexford saw him himself that night at the crucial time in Sewingbury.'

'He doesn't know or he's forgotten. He's going to go through hell until he can pluck up courage to ring Wexford. Some people might say that's his punishment.' She sighed. 'Are his sisters very badly off?'

'One of them is. She lives in a single room with her husband and her baby.'

'I've got Roger to agree to let them have what they should have had in the first place, three thousand, three hundred odd each. I think I'd better go to see them myself. He won't even notice it's gone. It's funny, you know, I knew he was unscrupulous. You can't make that amount of money without being, but I didn't know he'd stoop to that.'

'It hasn't made you . . . ?' He hesitated, wondering what he had destroyed.

'Never feel the same about him again? Oh, my dear, you are funny. Listen, I'll tell you something. Seven years ago it was the month of June. My face was on the cover of six separate magazines that month. The most photographed girl in Britain.'

He nodded, puzzled and out of his depth.

'If you reach a peak there's nothing left but to go downhill. In June of the next year I had my face on one magazine. So I married Roger.'

'You didn't love him?'

'I liked him, you know. He saved me in a way and all the time I'm saving him.' Archery knew what she meant, recalling her soft tranquillity in the Olive dining room, her hand touching a mourner's trembling arm. He expected always from her calm serenity and he was shocked when she raged suddenly: 'How was I to know there was a middle-aged clergyman waiting for me — a clergyman with a wife and a son and a guilt complex as big as a mountain?'

'Imogen!'

'No, you're not to touch me! It was stupid to come here and I should never have done it. O God, how I hate these sentimental scenes!'

He got up and walked as far from her as the little room allowed. It had stopped raining but the sky was sludge-coloured and the vine was as dead as a doornail.

'What will they do now,' she said, 'your son and this girl?'

'I don't think they know themselves.'

'And you, what will you do?'

' "Go to the wife of my bosom," ' he quoted, ' "the same as I ought to go." '

'Kipling!' She gave a hysterical laugh, and he was pained by the depths he was discovering too late. 'Kipling! That's all I need.'

'Good-bye,' he said.

'Good-bye, dear Henry Archery. I've never known what to call you. Do you know that?' She lifted his hand, kissed the palm.

'Perhaps it's not a name for dalliance,' he said ruefully.

'But it sounds well with Rev. in front of it.'

She went out, closing the door soundlessly behind her.

'Jenny kissed me,' he said to the vine. Jenny could just be short for Imogen. 'So what?'

Presently he came out into the hall and he wondered why the place seemed emptier and more lifeless than before. Perhaps it was his own fresh sense of loss. He turned towards the back door and then he saw. It was not an imagined but an actual diminishing. The raincoat had gone.

Had it ever been there or was his fancy, morbid and hypersensitive, creating hallucinations? It was a vision that might naturally come to someone involved as he was in Painter's story. But if the raincoat had never been there what would account for those penny-sized puddles on the floor, made surely by rain rivulets running from a sleeve?

He had no belief in the vulgar supernatural. But now as he stood looking at the hook where the raincoat had hung, he remembered how he had jumped at the tap on the window and had likened the marble veining to blood. It was not impossible that some evil hung over places such as this, fermenting the imagination and re-creating on the mind's retina images from a past tragedy.

The door was glazed in square panes. All were dirty yet all glinted faintly in the evening light — all but one. He peered, then smiled wryly at his absurd fancies. The glass had been completely removed from the frame nearest to the lock. An arm could have passed through it to turn the key and slide back the bolts.

It was unbolted now. He stepped out on to the flagged yard. Beyond, the garden lay enveloped in thin wet mist. The trees, the bushes, the lush blanket of weed sagged under their weight of water. Once he would have felt the responsible citizen's anxiety as to the whereabouts of whoever had broken that window, might even have considered going to the police. Now he was simply apathetic, indifferent.

Imogen filled his mind, but even on this subject, his thoughts were no longer passionate or ashamed. He would give her five more minutes to get away and then he would return to the Olive. Mechanically he stooped down and for something to do began carefully picking up the shards of broken glass, stacking them against the wall where no one, not even the burglar, might tread on them.

His nerves were bad, he knew that, but surely that was a footfall, the sound of indrawn breath.

She was coming back! But she must not — it was more than he could stand. The sight of her would be joy, but anything she said could only mean a fresh parting. He set his teeth, tightened the muscles of his hands and before he could stop himself his fingers had closed on a sliver of glass.

The blood came before the pain. He stood up, looking stupidly at his hand and saying, 'I've cut myself' aloud in that empty place, and he turned to meet the tap-tap of high heels.

Her scream burst in his face.

'Uncle Bert! Uncle Bert! Oh, my God!'

His hand was all bloody but he put it out, the hurt hand and the other, to catch Elizabeth Crilling as she fell.

'You ought to have it stitched,' she said. 'You'll get tetanus. You'll have an awful scar.'

He wrapped the handkerchief more tightly about the wound and sat grimly on the step, watching her. She had come round in seconds but her face was still white. A little gust of wind flicked through the tangled mass of green and showered them with water drops. Archery shivered.

'What are you doing here?' he asked.

She lay back in the chair he had fetched her from the morning room, her legs stretched out and limp. He noticed how thin they were, thin as the legs of an Oriental, the stockings wrinkled at the ankles.

'I've had a row with my mother,' she said.

He said nothing, waiting. For a moment she remained inert, then her body seemed to snap forwards, a trap with a steel spring. Instinctively, he shifted a little away from her, for she had brought her face towards his, her hands clutching each other between knees and breast. Her mouth moved before the words found sound.

'Oh Christ!' He kept still, controlling his inevitable reaction to the oath. 'I saw you with blood on you,' she said, 'and then you said it, what he said. "I've cut myself." ' A great shudder rocked her as if she had been grasped and shaken by an invisible force. Amazed, he watched her slacken again and heard her say in cold contrast, 'Give me a cigarette.' She tossed her bag to him. 'Light it!' The flame guttered in the damp air and the tugging wind. She cupped her thin hands with their big knuckles around it. 'Always snooping, aren't you?' she said, drawing back. 'I don't know what you thought you'd find, but this is it.'

Bewildered, he found himself staring at the garden, up at the overhanging gables, down at the wet broken paving.

'Me, I mean,' she said with savage impatience. 'You've been telling tales to the police about me and you don't even know what it's all about.' Again she snapped forward and shamelessly — he was horrified — pulled up her skirt and exposed her thigh above her stocking top. The white skin was covered all over with needle punctures. 'Asthma, that's what it's about. Asthma tablets. You dissolve them in water — and that's a hell of a job on its own — and then you fill up a hypodermic.'

Archery did not think himself easily shocked. But he was shocked now. He felt the blood run into his face. Embarrassment silenced him, then gave place to pity for her and a kind of diffused indignation with humanity.

'Does it have any effect?' he asked as coolly as he could.

'It gives you a lift, if you follow me. Much the same as you get from singing psalms, I expect,' she jeered. 'There was this man I lived with, he put me on to it. I was in the right place

157

for getting supplies, you see. Until you sent that bastard Burden down and he put the fear of God into my mother. She's got to get a new prescription every time she wants them now and she's got to collect them herself.'

'I see,' he said, and hope went. So that was what Mrs Crilling had meant. In prison there would be no tablets, no syringe, and because she had become addicted to them she would have to reveal her addiction or . . .

'I don't think the police can do anything to you,' he said, not knowing whether they could or not.

'What would you know about it? I've got twenty left in a bottle so I came here. I've made myself a bed upstairs and . . .'

He interrupted her. 'It's your raincoat?'

The question surprised her, but only for a moment, then scorn returned to make her look twice her age.

'Sure it is,' she said scathingly. 'Whose did you think it was, Painter's? I went out for a bit to get something from my car, left the door on the latch and when I came back you were here with that tarty piece.' He kept his eyes on her, controlling himself. For the only time in his life he felt an urge to strike another person's face. 'I didn't dare come back for a bit,' she said, returning to the only other mood she had, a self-pitying childishness. 'But I had to get my raincoat — the tablets were in the pocket.'

She inhaled deeply and flung the cigarette away from her into the wet bushes.

'What the hell were you doing, returning to the scene of the crime? Trying to get under his skin?'

'Whose skin?' he whispered urgently.

'Painter's of course. Bert Painter's. My Uncle Bert.' She was defiant again, but her hand shook and her eyes glazed. It was coming now. He was like a man awaiting bad news, knowing it was inevitable, knowing even exactly what it was going to be, but still hoping that there would be some detail, some facts to mitigate it. 'That night,' she said, 'he stood there just like you. Only he was holding a piece of wood and there was blood on it and all over him. "I've cut myself," he said. "Don't look, Lizzie, I've cut myself."'

CHAPTER SIXTEEN

When the unclean spirit is gone out of a man, he walketh through dry places seeking rest and finding none. He saith, I will return unto my house whence I came out.

The Gospel for the Fourth Sunday in Lent

She told it in the second person, 'You did this,' 'You did that.' Archery realised he was hearing what no parent and no psychiatrist had ever heard, and he marvelled. The peculiar use of the pronoun seemed to draw his own mind into the child's body so that he could see with her eyes and feel with her overweening terror.

She sat down in the damp dusk on the spot where it had all begun for her, utterly still now. Only her eyelids moved. Sometimes, at agonising moments in the narrative, she would close her eyes then open them again with a slow exhalation of breath. Archery had never been to a seance — would indeed disapprove of such a thing as being theologically untenable — but he had read of them. Elizabeth Crilling's steady outpouring of terrible events told in a flat monotone was reminiscent, he thought, of mediumistic revelation. She was coming to the end now and a weary relief crossed her face as of one shedding a load.

. . . You put your coat on, your best coat because it was your best frock, and you ran across the road, down the sideway and past the greenhouse. Nobody saw you because there was no one about. Or was there? Surely that was the back door closing softly.

You came very quietly around the side of the house and then you saw it was only Uncle Bert who had come out of the house into the garden.

'Uncle Bert, Uncle Bert! I've got my best frock on. Can I go and show it to Tessie?'

Suddenly you were very frightened, more frightened than you had ever been in all your life, because Uncle Bert was breathing in such a funny way, gasping and coughing like Daddy did when he had one of his attacks. Then he turned round and there was red stuff all over him, on his hand and all down the front of his coat.

'I've cut myself,' he said. 'Don't look, Lizzie. I've just cut myself.'

'I want Tessie! I want Tessie!'

'Don't you go up there!'

'You're not to touch me. I've got my new dress on. I'll tell my mummy.'

He just stood there with the red stuff on him and his face was like the face of a lion, big thick mouth, thick nose, curly tawny hair. Yes, it was like the lion in that picture book Mummy said you must not look at . . .

The red stuff had splashed on to his face and trickled to the corner of his mouth. He brought that dreadful face down close to yours and shouted right at you:

'You tell her, Lizzie Crilling, you stuck-up little snob, and d'you know what I'll do? Wherever I am — wherever, d'you hear me? — I'll find you and I'll give you what I gave the old girl.'

It was over. He could tell that by the way she came out of her trance, sat up and gave a kind of moan.

'But you went back,' Archery murmured. 'You went back with your mother?'

'My mother!' Weeping would not have surprised him. This violent bitter laughter did. On a high discordant peal, she stopped suddenly and rushed into her answer. 'I was only five, only a kid. I didn't know what he meant, not then. I was much more frightened of letting her know I'd been over there.' He noted that 'her' and knew intuitively she would not mention her mother by name again. 'You see, I didn't even know it was blood and I reckon I must have thought it was paint.

'Then we went back. I wasn't afraid of the house and I didn't know what he meant by the old girl. I think when he said about giving me what he'd given the old girl I thought he meant his wife, Mrs Painter. He knew I'd seen him hit her. I found the body. You knew that? God, it was terrible. I didn't understand, you see. D'you know what I thought at first? I thought she'd sort of burst.'

'Don't,' said Archery.

'If you can't take it now, what d'you think it was like for me? I was *five*. Five, my Christ! They put me to bed and I was ill for weeks. Of course, they'd arrested Painter, but I didn't know that. You don't tell children that sort of thing. I didn't know what had happened at all, only that Granny Rose had burst open and he had made it happen and if I said I'd seen him he'd do the same to me.'

'But afterwards. Didn't you tell anyone then?'

She had talked about finding the body and said it was terrible, but then there had been affectation in her voice. A child finding a murdered woman, he thought. Yes, all the world would recoil in shock from that. Yet for her that had not been the worst. Now as he asked her about afterwards he saw the trance begin once more to mist her face as the spectre of Painter — Painter on this very spot — rose before it.

'He'd find you,' she mumbled. 'He'd find you wherever you were, wherever he was. You wanted to tell *her,* but she wouldn't listen to you. 'Don't think about it, Baby, put it out of your mind.' But it wouldn't go *out* . . .' Her features worked and the blank eyes flickered.

'Miss Crilling, let me take you home.'

She was standing up now, moving mechanically towards the house wall, a robot whose programming has failed. When her hands touched the bricks she stopped and spoke again, talking to him but into the house itself.

'It wouldn't go out. It went in and in, till it was just a little black wheel spinning and playing the same thing over and over again.'

Had she realised she was speaking in metaphor? He had thought of a medium's utterances, but now he knew it had been more like a discordant record, playing the same horror each time it was pricked by the stylus of association. He touched her arm and was surprised when she followed him meekly and limply back to the chair. They sat in silence for some minutes. She was the first to speak and she was almost her normal self.

'You know Tessie, don't you? She's going to marry your son?' He shrugged. 'I think she was the only real friend I ever had,' she said quietly. 'It was her birthday the next week. She was going to be five, and I thought I'd give her one of my old dresses. Sneak it round when *she* was with the old girl. Generous little beast, wasn't I? I never saw her again.'

Archery said gently, 'You saw her this afternoon in the chemist's.'

Her new tranquillity was very finely balanced. Had he pushed it too far?

'In the white blouse?' she said in a dead even voice, so low that he had to lean forward and strain to catch it. He nodded.

'That girl who hadn't got any change?'

'Yes.'

'She was standing beside me and I never knew.' There was a long silence. The only sound was the faint rustling of wet bushes, water-loaded gleaming leaves on the coach-house walls. Then she tossed her head. 'I reckon I don't notice women much,' she said. 'I saw you all right and the boy that was with you. I remember I thought the talent's looking up in this dump.'

'The talent,' Archery said, 'is my son.'

'Her boy friend? I never would have told you!' She gave a low cry of exasperation. 'And, my God, I never would have told her — not if you hadn't caught me out like that.'

'It was chance, coincidence. Perhaps it's better that I do know.'

'You!' she said. 'That's all you think about, you and your precious son. What about me?' She stood up, looked at him and moved towards the door with the broken pane. It was true he thought, ashamed. He had been prepared to sacrifice all these other people to save Charles — the Crillings, Primero, even Imogen — but his quest had been doomed from the beginning because history could not be changed.

'What will they do to me?' Her face was turned away from him and she spoke softly. But there was such urgency and such fear in those six short words that their impact was as if she had shouted.

'Do to you?' He could do no more than get to his feet and stand helplessly behind her. 'Why should they do anything to you?' He remembered the dead man on the crossing and he remembered the needle punctures, but he said only, 'You've been more sinned against than sinning.'

'Oh, the Bible!' she cried. 'Don't quote the Bible to me.' He said nothing for he had not done so. 'I'm going upstairs now,' she said strangely. 'When you see Tess would you give her my love? I wish,' she said, 'I wish I could have given her something for her birthday.'

By the time he had found a doctor's house he felt all hand, nothing but hand, a throbbing thing that beat like a second heart. He recognised Dr Crocker at once and saw that he, too, was remembered.

'You must be enjoying your holiday,' Crocker said. He stitched the finger, filled a syringe with anti-tetanus serum. 'First that dead boy and now this. Sorry, but this may hurt. You've got thick skin.'

'Really?' Archery could not help smiling as he bared his upper arm. 'I want to ask you something.' Without stopping to explain he put the question that had been troubling him all the way from Victor's Piece. 'Is it possible?'

'Beginning of October?' Crocker looked closely and not unsympathetically at him. 'Look, how personal is this?'

Archery read his thoughts and managed a laugh. 'Not that personal,' he said. 'I am, as they say, enquiring for a friend.'

'Well, it's extremely unlikely.' Crocker grinned. 'There have been cases, very few and far between. They make minor medical history.'

Nodding, Archery got up to go.

'I shall want to see that finger again,' the doctor said. 'Or your local G.P. will. You'll need another couple of injections. See to it when you get home, will you?'

Home . . . yes, he would be home tomorrow. His stay in Kingsmarkham had not been a holiday, anything but that, yet he had that curious end-of-a-holiday feeling when the resort one has stayed in becomes more familiar than home.

He had walked along this High Street every day, more frequently even than he trod the main village street at Thringford. The order of the shops, chemist, grocer, draper, was as

well known to him as to the housewives of Kingsmarkham. And
the place was certainly pretty. Suddenly it seemed sad that he
should hardly have noticed its prettiness — more than that
really, for prettiness does not go with grace and dignity — but
would associate it for ever with a lost love and a failed search.

Street lamps, some of them of ancient design and with
wrought iron casings, showed him alleys winding between stone
walls, coaching yards, flowers in a few cottage gardens. The
weak yellow light bleached these flowers to a luminous pallor.
Half an hour ago it had been just light enough to read print by;
now the darkness had come down and lamps appeared in
windows fronting the street. The sky had a rainy look and the
stars showed only in the crevices between bulbous bloated
cloud. There was no moon.

The Olive and Dove was brightly lit and the car park full.
Glass doors separated the hall from the cocktail bar and he saw
people sitting on high stools, gathered round the small black oak
tables. Archery thought he would give everything he possessed
to see Charles among them, throwing back his head in laughter,
his hand resting on the shoulder of a pretty girl. Not a beautiful,
intellectual, tainted girl — just someone pretty and dull and
uncomplicated. But Charles was not there. He found him alone
in the lounge writing letters. Only a few hours had elapsed since
his parting from Tess, but already he was writing . . .

'What on earth have you done to your hand and where
have you been?'

'Hacking away at the past.'

'Don't be cryptic, Father. It doesn't suit you.' His tone was
bitter and sullen. Archery wondered why people say that suffering
improves the character, why indeed he had sometimes thought-
lessly said it to his own parishioners. He listened to his son's voice,
carping, querulous and selfish. 'I've been wanting to address this
envelope for the past two hours, but I couldn't because I don't
know where Tess's aunt lives.' Charles gave him a sour accusing
look. 'You wrote it down. Don't say you've lost it.'

'Here.' Archery took the card from his pocket and dropped
it on the table. 'I'm going to phone your mother, tell her we'll
be home in the morning.'

'I'll come up with you. This place goes dead at night.'

Dead? And the bar crowded with people, some of whom were surely as exacting as Charles. If Tess had been with them it would not have been dead. Quite suddenly Archery made up his mind that Charles must be made happy, and if happiness meant Tess, he should have Tess. Therefore the theory he was formulating would have to be made to work.

He paused on the threshold of his bedroom, put his hand to the light switch but did not press it. There in the darkness with Charles behind him there flashed across his brain a picture of himself and Wexford that first day at the police station. He had been firm then. 'Bitterly, bitterly against this marriage,' he had told the Chief Inspector. How utterly he had come round! But then he had not known what it was to crave for a voice and a smile. To understand all was not merely to forgive all, it was utter identification of the spirit and the flesh.

Over his shoulder Charles said, 'Can't you find the switch?' His hand came up and met his father's on the dry cold wall. The room flooded with light. 'Are you all right? You look worn-out.'

Perhaps it was the unaccustomed gentleness in his voice that did it. Archery knew how easy it is to be kind when one is happy, how nearly impossible to feel solicitude in the midst of one's own misery. He was suddenly filled with love, an overflowing diffused love that for the first time in days had no specific object but included his son — and his wife. Hoping unreasonably that her voice would be soft and kind, he moved towards the telephone.

'Well, you are a stranger,' were the first words he heard and they were sharp with resentment. 'I was beginning to wonder what had happened to you. Thought you must have eloped.'

'I wouldn't do that, darling,' he said, sick at heart. And then, because he had to set his foot back on the path of constancy, he took a grotesque echo, 'Kingsmarkham isn't conspicuous for its talent. I've missed you.' It was untrue and what he was going to say next would also be a lie. 'It'll be good to be home with you again.' That lie would have to be changed into truth. He clenched his hand till the hurt finger burned with pain, but as he did so he thought that he and time could make it true . . .

'You do use some extraordinary expressions,' Charles said when he had rung off. 'Talent, indeed. Very vulgar.' He was still holding the card, staring at it with utter absorption. A week ago Archery would have marvelled that a woman's address and a woman's handwriting could provide such fascination.

'You asked me on Saturday if I'd ever seen this before. You asked me if I'd heard it. Well, now I've *seen* it, it's rung a bell. It's part of a long religious verse play. Part of it's in prose but there are songs in it — hymns really — and this is the last verse of one of them.'

'Where did you see it? In Oxford? In a library?'

But Charles was not listening to him. He said as if he had been meaning to say it for the past half-hour, 'Where did you go tonight? Had it any connection with me and — and Tess?'

Must he tell him? Was he obliged to root out those last vestiges of hope before he had anything real and proven to put in their place?

'Just to have a last look at Victor's Piece.' Charles nodded. He appeared to accept this quite naturally. 'Elizabeth Crilling was there, hiding.' He told him about the drugs, the wretched attempts to secure more tablets, but he did not tell him everything.

Charles's reaction was unexpected. 'Hiding from what?'

'The police, I suppose, or her mother.'

'You didn't just leave her there?' Charles asked indignantly. 'A crazy kid like that? God knows what she might do. You don't know how many of those tablets would poison her. She might take them deliberately to that end. Have you thought of that?'

She had accused him of not considering her but even that taunt had not prompted him. It had simply not crossed his mind that he was doing something irresponsible in leaving a young girl alone in an empty house.

'I think we ought to go to Victor's Piece and try to get her to come home,' Charles said. Observing the sudden animation on his son's face, Archery wondered how sincere he was and how much of this spurt of energy was due to a desire to do something, anything, because he knew that if he went to bed he would not sleep. Charles put the card away in his pocket. 'You won't like this,' he said, 'but I think we ought to take the mother with us.'

'She's quarrelled with her mother. She behaves as if she hates her.'

'That's nothing. Have you ever seen them together?'

Only a glance across a courtroom, a glance of indecipherable passion. He had never seen them together. He knew only that if Charles were alone somewhere and miserable, on the verge perhaps of taking his own life, he, Archery, would not want strangers to go to his succour.

'You can drive,' he said and he tossed the keys to his son. Mrs Crilling would be in bed. Then it occurred to him for the first time that she might be worrying about her daughter. He had never attributed to the Crillings ordinary emotions. They were different from other people, the mother deranged, the girl delinquent. Was that why, instead of being merciful, he had merely used them? As they turned into Glebe Road he felt a new warmth stir within him. It was not too late — especially now she had found some release — to bring Elizabeth back, to heal that old wound, to retrieve something out of chaos.

Outwardly he was cold. He was coatless and the night was chilly. You expect a winter's night to be cold, he thought. There was something depressing and wrong about a cold summer night. November with flowers, a November wind that ruffled the ripe leaves of summer. He must not find omens in nature.

'What d'you call it,' he said to Charles, 'when you ascribe emotions to nature? What's the expression?'

'The Pathetic Fallacy,' Charles said. Archery shivered.

'This is the house,' he said. They got out. Number twenty-four was in darkness upstairs and down.

'She's probably in bed.'

'Then she'll have to get up,' said Charles and rang the bell. He rang again and again. 'Pointless,' he said. 'Can we get round the back?'

Archery said, 'Through here,' and led Charles through the sandy arch. It was like a cavern, he thought, touching the walls. He expected them to be clammy but they were dry and prickly to the touch. They emerged into a dark pool among patches of light which came from french windows all along the backs of houses. A yellow square segmented by black bars lay on each shadowed garden but none came from Mrs Crilling's window.

'She must be out,' said Archery as they opened the little gate in the wire fence. 'We know so little about them. We don't know where she'd go to or who her friends are.'

Through the first window the kitchen and the hall showed dark and empty. To reach the french windows they had to push through a tangle of wet nettles which stung their hands.

'Pity we didn't bring a torch.'

'We haven't *got* a torch,' Archery objected. He peered in. 'I've got matches.' The first he struck showed him the room as he had seen it before, a muddle of flung-down clothes and stacked newspapers. The match died and he dropped it on wet concrete. By the light of a second he saw that on the table were the remains of a meal, cut bread still in its paper wrappings, a cup and saucer, a jam jar, a single plate coated with something yellow and congealed.

'We might as well go,' he said. 'She isn't here.'

'The door's not locked,' said Charles. He lifted the latch and opened it quietly. There came to them at once a peculiar and unidentifiable odour of fruit and of alcohol.

'You can't go in. There isn't the slightest justification for breaking in.'

'I haven't broken anything.' Charles's foot was over the threshold, but he stopped and said over his shoulder to his father, 'Don't you think there's something odd here? Don't you feel it?'

Archery shrugged. They were both in the room now. The smell was very strong but they could see nothing but the dim outlines of cluttered furniture.

'The light switch is on the left by the door,' he said. 'I'll find it.' He had forgotten that his son was a man, that his son's adult sense of responsibility had brought them there. In that dark, evilly scented place, they were just a parent and his child. He must not do as Mrs Crilling had done and let the child go first. 'Wait there,' he said. He felt his way along the side of the table, pushed a small armchair out of his path, squeezed behind the sofa and felt for the switch. 'Wait there!' he cried again, much more sharply and in a spasm of real fear. Previously in his passage across the room his feet had come into contact with debris on the floor, a shoe, he thought, a book dropped face-downwards. Now the obstruction was larger and more solid. His scalp crept. Clothes, yes, and within those clothes something heavy and inert. He dropped to his knees, thrusting forward hands to palpate and fumble. 'Dear God . . . !'

'What is it? What the hell *is* it? Can't you find the light?'

Archery could not speak. He had withdrawn his hands and they were wet and sticky. Charles had crossed the room. Light pouring into and banishing that darkness was a physical pain. Archery closed his eyes. Above him he heard Charles make an inarticulate sound.

He opened his eyes and the first thing he saw was that his hands were red. Charles said, 'Don't look!' and he knew that his own lips had been trying to frame those words. They were not policemen, not used to sights such as this, and each had tried to save the other from seeing.

Each had to look. Mrs Crilling lay spread on the floor between the sofa and the wall and she was quite dead. The chill of her body came up to Archery's hands through the pink flounces that covered it from neck to ankles. He had seen that neck and at once had looked away from the stocking that made a ligature around it.

'But she's got blood all over,' said Charles. 'It's as if — God! — as if someone had sprinkled her with it.'

CHAPTER SEVENTEEN

I held my tongue and spake nothing; I kept silence, yea, even from good words; but it was pain and grief to me.

Psalm 39. *The Burial of the Dead*

'It isn't blood,' said Wexford. 'Don't you know what it is? Couldn't you smell it?' He lifted the bottle someone had found under the sideboard and held it aloft. Archery sat on the sofa in Mrs Crilling's living room, worn, tired, utterly spent. Doors banged and footsteps sounded as Wexford's two men searched the other room. The people upstairs had come in at midnight, Saturday night happy, the man a little drunk. The woman had had hysterics during Wexford's questioning.

They had taken the body away and Charles moved his chair round so that he could not see the crimson splashes of cherry brandy.

'But why? Why did it happen?' he whispered.

'Your father knows why!' Wexford stared at Archery, his grey gimlet eyes deep and opaque. He squatted opposite them on a low chair with wooden arms. 'As for me, I don't know but I can guess. I can't help feeling I've seen something like this before, a long, long time ago. Sixteen years to be exact. A pink frilly dress that a little girl could never wear again because it was spoilt with blood.'

Outside the rain had begun again and water lashed against the windows making them rattle. It would be cold now inside Victor's Piece, cold and eerie like a deserted castle in a wood of wet trees. The Chief Inspector had an extra uncanny sense that almost amounted to telepathy. Archery willed his thoughts to alter course lest Wexford should divine them, but the question came before he could rid his mind of its pictures.

'Come on, Mr Archery, where is she?'

'Where is who?'

'The daughter.'

'What makes you think I know?'

'Listen to me,' said Wexford. 'The last person we've talked to who saw her was a chemist in Kingsmarkham. Oh, yes, we went to all the chemists first, naturally. This one remembers that when she was in the shop there were two men and a girl there too, a young man and an elder one, tall, fair, obviously father and son.'

'I didn't speak to her then,' Archery said truthfully. The smell sickened him. He wanted nothing but sleep and peace and to get out of this room where Wexford had kept them since they had telephoned him.

'Mrs Crilling's been dead six or seven hours. It's ten to three now and you left the Olive at a quarter to eight. The barman saw you come in at ten. Where did you go, Mr Archery?'

He sat silent. Years and years ago — Oh, centuries ago! — it had been like this in school. You own up, you betray someone, or everyone suffers. Funny, once before he had thought of Wexford as a kind of headmaster.

'You know where she is,' Wexford said. His voice was loud, threatening, ominous. 'D'you want to be an accessory? Is that what you want?'

Archery closed his eyes. Quite suddenly he knew why he was prevaricating. He wanted the very thing that Charles had warned him might happen and although it was contrary to his religion, wicked even, he wanted it with all his heart.

Charles said, 'Father . . .' and when he got no reply shrugged, turned his dull shocked eyes to Wexford. 'Oh, what the hell? She's at Victor's Piece.'

Archery realised that he had been holding his breath. He let it out in a deep sigh. 'In one of the bedrooms,' he said, 'looking at the coach house and dreaming of a heap of sand. She asked what they would do to her and I didn't understand. What will they do to her?'

Wexford got up. 'Well, sir . . .' Archery noted that 'sir' as one might notice the re-assuming of a velvet glove. 'You know as well as I do that it's no longer lawful to punish with death for certain . . .' His eyes flickered over the place where Mrs Crilling had lain. ' . . . certain heinous and grievous offences.'

'Will you let us go now?' Charles asked.

'Until tomorrow,' said Wexford.

The rain met them at the front door like a wave or a wall of spray. For the past half-hour it had been drumming on the roof of the car and seeping in through the half-open quarter light. There was water laying in a small pool at Archery's feet but he was too tired to notice or care.

Charles came with him into his bedroom.

'I shouldn't ask you now,' he said. 'It's almost morning and God knows what we'll have to go through tomorrow, but I have to know. I'd rather know. But what else did she tell you, that girl at Victor's Piece?'

Archery had heard of people pacing a room like caged beasts. He had never imagined himself so strung with tension that in spite of utter exhaustion he would have to find release by crossing and re-crossing a floor, picking up objects, replacing them, his hands shaking. Charles waited, too wretched even for impatience. His letter to Tess lay in its envelope on the dressing table and beside it the card from the gift shop. Archery picked it up and kneaded it in his hands, crumpling the deckle edging. Then he went up to his son, put his hands gently on his shoulders and looked into the eyes that were young replicas of his own.

'What she told me,' he said, 'needn't matter to you. It would be like — well, someone else's nightmare.' Charles did not move. 'If you will only tell me where you saw the verse that is printed on this card.'

The morning was grey and cool, such a morning as occurs perhaps three hundred times a year out of the three hundred and sixty-five, when there is neither rain nor sun, frost nor fog. It was a limbo of a morning. The policeman on the crossing had covered his shirt sleeves with his dark jacket, the striped shop blinds were rolled up and sluggish steps had grown brisk.

Inspector Burden escorted Archery along the drying pavements to the police station. Archery was ashamed to answer Burden's kindly question as to how he had slept. He had slept heavily and soundly. Perhaps he would also have slept dreamlessly had he known what the inspector now told him, that Elizabeth Crilling was alive.

'She came with us quite willingly,' Burden said and added rather indiscreetly, 'To tell you the truth, sir, I've never seen her so calm and sane and — well, at peace, really.'

'You want to go home, I suppose,' Wexford said when Burden had left them alone in the blue and yellow office. 'You'll have to come back for the inquest and the magistrates' court hearing. You found the body.'

Archery sighed. 'Elizabeth found a body sixteen years ago. If it hadn't been for her mother's self-seeking vanity, greed for something she had no claim to — that would never have happened. You might say that the greed reached out and destroyed long after its original purpose had been frustrated. Or you might say that Elizabeth bore her mother a grudge because Mrs Crilling would never let her talk about Painter and bring her terrors to the light of day.'

'You might,' said Wexford. 'It could be all those things. And it could be that when Liz left the chemist's she went back to Glebe Road, Mrs Crilling was afraid to ask for another prescription, so Liz, in the addict's frenzy, strangled her.'

'May I see her?'

'I'm afraid not. I'm beginning to guess just what she saw sixteen years ago and what she told you last night.'

'After I talked to her I went to see Dr Crocker. I want you to look at this.' Archery gave Wexford Colonel Plashet's letter, silently indicating the relevant passage with his bandaged finger. 'Poor Elizabeth,' he murmured. 'She wanted to give Tess a dress for her fifth birthday. Unless Tess has changed a lot it wouldn't have meant much to her.'

Wexford read, closed his eyes briefly and then gave a slight smile. 'I see,' he said slowly and restored the letter to its envelope.

'I am right, aren't I? I'm not juggling things, imagining things? You see, I can't trust my own judgement any more. I have to have an opinion from an expert in deduction. I've been to Forby, I've seen a photograph, I've got a letter and I've talked to a doctor. If you had the same clues would you have come to the same conclusions?'

'I'm sure you're very kind, Mr Archery.' Wexford gave a broad ironic grin. 'I get more complaints than compliments.

Now, as to clues and conclusions, I would, but I'd have been on to it a whole lot sooner.

'You see, it all depends on what you're looking for and the fact is, sir, you didn't know what you *were* looking for. All the time you were trying to disprove something in the face of — well, you said it — expert deduction. What you've found now achieves the same results as the other thing would have. For you and your son, that is. But it hasn't changed what for justice is the *status quo*. We would have made sure we knew precisely what we were looking for at the start, the basic thing. When you come down to that, it doesn't matter a damn to you who committed the crime. But you were looking through a pair of spectacles that were too big for you.'

'A glass darkly,' said Archery.

'I can't say I envy you the coming interview.'

'Strange,' said Archery thoughtfully as he got up to go, 'that although we both held such opposing opinions in the end we were both right.'

Wexford had said he must come back. He would make his visits short, though, short and blind, his eyes opening only in the court he could see out of this window, his words mere evidence. He had read stories of people transported to strange places, blindfolded and in shuttered cars, so that they should not see the country through which they passed. In his case he would be prevented from seeing visions and associations with those visions, by the presence of those he was legitimately allowed to love. Mary should come with him and Charles and Tess to be his shutters and his hood. Certainly he would never see this room again. He turned to give it a last glance, but if he hoped to have the last word he was disappointed.

'Both right,' said Wexford, giving Archery's hand a gentle clasp. 'I by reason and you by faith. Which, taken all in all,' he added, 'is only what one might expect.'

She opened the door to them carefully, grudgingly, as if she expected to see gypsies or a brush salesman from a disreputable firm.

'I hope you'll forgive us, Mrs Kershaw,' Archery said with

too loud heartiness, 'Charles wanted to see Tess and as we were coming this way . . .'

It is difficult to greet callers, even unwelcome callers, without some kind of a smile. Irene Kershaw did not smile, but she made muttering noises in which he caught the occasional word: 'very welcome, I'm sure,' 'unexpected . . .' and 'not really prepared . . .' They got into the hall, but it was an awkward manoeuvre and it almost involved pushing past her. She had grown rather red and she said to Charles, now quite coherently:

'Tess has popped down to the shops to get a few last-minute things for her holiday.' Archery could see that she was angry and that she did not know how to vent her anger on people who were at the same time adults and from a different background from her own. 'You've quarrelled, haven't you?' she said. 'What are you trying to do, break her heart?' Apparently she was capable of emotion, but once she had shown it, not capable of control. Tears welled into her eyes. 'Oh dear . . . I didn't mean to say that.'

Archery had explained everything to Charles in the car. He was to find Tess, get her alone and tell her. Now he said, 'You might go down the hill, Charles, and see if you can meet her coming up. She'll be glad of a hand with her basket.'

Charles hesitated, possibly because he was at a loss to answer Mrs Kershaw's accusation and could not bring himself to echo so exaggerated an expression as 'a broken heart'. Then he said, 'I'm going to marry Tess. That's what I've always wanted.'

The colour died out of her face and now that there was no occasion for them the tears trickled down her cheeks. Archery would, under no other circumstances, have been embarrassed. Now he realised that this mood of hers, tears, a lukewarm resentment that might be her nearest approach to passion, would make her receptive to what he had to say. A tired tigress apparently lurked under that dull suburban exterior, a mother beast capable of being roused only when its young was threatened.

Charles let himself out of the front door. Archery, left alone with her, wondered where the other children were and how soon Kershaw himself would return. Again he was finding himself, when in the sole company of this woman, at a loss for words. She made no effort to help him, but stood stiff and expressionless, dabbing at the tearmarks with the tips of her fingers.

'Perhaps we could sit down?' He made a vague gesture towards the glass door. 'I should like to have a talk, settle things, I . . .'

She was recovering fast, tunnelling back into the sanctuary of her respectability. 'You'd like some tea?'

The mood must not be allowed to peter out into small talk over the cups. 'No,' he said, 'no, really . . .'

She went before him into the living room. There were the books, the Reader's Digests, the dictionaries and the works on deep sea fishing. The portrait of Jill on the easel was finished and Kershaw had made the amateur's mistake of not knowing when to stop, so that the likeness had been lost in last-minute touches. In the garden which was spread before him with the unreality and the garish colours of a cushion cover in gros point, the Paul Crampel geraniums burned so brightly that they hurt his eyes.

Mrs Kershaw sat down genteelly and crimped her skirt over her knees. Today, now that it was cold again, she wore a cotton dress. She was that kind of woman, Archery thought, who would wear her winter clothes on and on cautiously until she was sure a heat wave was fully established. Then just as the hot weather was ending and the storm about to break, then at last the carefully laundered thin dress would be brought out.

The pearls had been restrung. She put her hand up to them and drew it away quickly, curbing temptation. Their eyes met and she gave a tiny nervous giggle, perhaps aware that he had noticed her tiny vice. He gave a small inner sigh, for all her emotion had gone and her face showed only the natural bewilderment of a hostess who does not know the purpose of a call and is too discreet to question the caller.

He must — he *must* — awaken something from behind that pale lined brow. All his carefully prepared openings died. In a moment she would begin on the weather or the desirability of white weddings. But she did not quite do that. He had forgotten the other stock remark that is so handy a conversation starter between strangers.

'And how did you enjoy your holiday?' said Irene Kershaw. Very well. That would do as well as anything.

'Forby is your native village, I believe,' he said. 'I went to see a grave while I was there.'

She touched the pearls with the flat of her hand. 'A grave?' For an instant her voice was as raw as when she had talked of a broken heart, then all passionless Purley again as she added, 'Oh, yes, Mrs Primero is buried there, isn't she?'

'It wasn't her grave I saw.' Softly he quoted, ' "Go, Shepherd, to your rest . . ." ' Tell me, why did you keep all the works he left behind him?'

That there would be reaction and that that reaction might be anger he had expected. He was prepared for a flouncing hauteur or even the damning, dulling response so dear to the heart of the Mrs Kershaws of this world: 'We needn't discuss that.' He had not thought she would be frightened and at the same time stricken with a kind of awe. She cowered a little in the armchair — if cowering is compatible with perfect stillness — and her eyes, wide and glistening now, had the utter immobility of the dead.

Her fear had the effect of frightening him. It was as communicable as a yawn. Suppose she were to have a fit of hysterics? He went on very gently:

'Why did you keep them hidden away in the dark? They might have been published, they might have been acted. He could have had posthumous fame.'

She made no answer at all, but now he knew what to do, the answer came to him like a gift of God. He only had to go on talking, gently, mesmerically. The words tumbled out, platitudes and clichés, praise of work he had never seen and had no reason to suppose he would admire, assurances and unfounded promises he might never be able to honour. All the time, like a hypnotist, he kept his eyes on her, nodding when she nodded, breaking into a wide fatuous smile when for the first time a tiny vague one trembled on her lips.

'May I see them?' he dared. 'Will you show me the works of John Grace?'

He held his breath while with torturing slowness she mounted a stool and reached for the top of the book case. They were in a box, a large cardboard grocer's box that had apparently once contained a gross of tinned peaches. She handled it with a peculiar reverence, her care all concentrated on it, so that she let the magazines which had been stacked on it cascade to the floor.

There must have been a dozen of them but only one cover picture splashed at Archery like acid on the eyes. He blinked away from the beautiful photographed face, the pale hair under a hat of June roses. He had waited for Mrs Kershaw to speak now and her words pulled him out of shock and misery.

'I suppose Tess told you,' she whispered. 'It was supposed to be our secret.' She lifted the lid of the box so that he was able to read the writing on the topmost sheet of manuscript. *'The Fold. A Prayer in Dramatic Form* by John Grace.' 'If you'd told me before I would have shown them to you. Tess said I should show them to anyone who would be interested and would — would understand.'

Again their eyes met and Irene Kershaw's tremulous stare was caught and steadied in his strong one. He knew his face was mobile and expressive of his thoughts. She must have read them for she said, thrusting the box towards him, 'Here, have them. You can have them.' He drew away his hands and his body, horrified and ashamed. At once he had realised what she was doing, that she was trying to pay him off with her most precious material possession. 'Only don't ask me.' She gave a little thin cry. 'Don't ask me about him!'

Impulsively, because he could not bear those eyes, he covered his own with his hands. 'I've no right to be your inquisitor,' he murmured.

'Yes, yes . . . It's all right.' Her fingers touching his shoulder were firm with a new strength. 'But don't ask me about him. Mr Kershaw said you wanted to know about Painter — Bert Painter, my husband. I'll tell you everything I can remember, anything you want to know.'

Her inquisitor and her tormentor . . . Better a swift knife thrust than this interminable twisting on the rack. He clenched his hands till the only pain he could feel came from the wound where the glass had gone in and he faced her across the yellowing sheets of verse.

'I don't want to know about Painter any more,' he said. 'I'm not interested in him. I'm interested in Tess's father ...' The moan she gave and the feel of those fingers scrabbling at his arm could not stop him now. 'And I've known since last night,' he whispered, 'that Painter *couldn't* have been her father.'

CHAPTER EIGHTEEN

...As ye will answer at the dreadful day of judgement when
the secrets of all hearts shall be disclosed...

The Solemnisation of Matrimony

She lay on the floor and wept. To Archery, standing by helpless,
it was some measure of her total breakdown that she had come
so far wide of her conventional limits as to lie there prone and
shake with sobs. Archery had never in his life reached such a
nadir of despair. He pitied with an anxiety that had something
of panic in it this woman who cried as if the power to weep had
long fallen into disuse, as if she were experimenting with some
new and shattering exercise.

He did not know how long this abandonment to grief had
lasted or would last. This room with all its apparatus for living
what some call a 'full life' contained no clock and he had
removed his watch to make room for the wrist anchorage of the
bandage. Just as he was beginning to feel that she would never
stop, she made a curious humping movement so that she rested
like a flogged overburdened beast.

'Mrs Kershaw...' he said. 'Mrs Kershaw, forgive me.'

She got up slowly, her breast still heaving. The cotton dress
was creased into a faded rag. She said something but he could
not hear her at all and he realised what had happened. She had
utterly exhausted her voice.

'Can I get you a glass of water, some brandy?'

Her head shook as if it were not part of her body but a
separate thing quivering on a pivot. Her voice came in a hoarse
croak. 'I don't drink.' Then he knew that nothing could fully
pierce the layers of respectability. She fell into the chair from
which his questions had prised her and let her arms hang limply
over its sides. When he came back from the kitchen and gave
her the glass of water she had recovered sufficiently to sip it and

to rub with the old refinement at the corners of her lips. He was afraid to speak.

'Does she have to know?' The words had a hollow sound to them but the roughness had gone. 'My Tessie, does she have to know?'

He did not dare to tell her that Charles would have told her already. 'It's nothing these days,' he said, and shed with a word two thousand years' teaching of his faith. 'Nobody thinks anything of it any more.'

'Tell me what you know.'

He knelt at her feet, praying that all his guesses would approximate to the truth and that there would be few gaps for her to fill. If only he could deal well with this and save her the shame of confession. 'You and John Grace,' he said, 'lived close together in Forby. You were in love, but he was killed . . .'

On an impulse he took the manuscript in his hands and laid it gently on her lap. She took it as a religious takes a talisman or a relic and she said softly:

'He was so clever. I couldn't understand the things he wrote, but they were beautiful. His teacher wanted him to go to college but his mother wouldn't let him. You see, his father had a bakery business and he had to go into that.' Let her go on, he prayed, edging away to squat on the edge of his chair. 'He still wrote his poems and his plays,' she said, 'and in the evenings he used to study for some exam. He wasn't strong enough to go into the force, anaemia or something he had.' Her fingers tightened on the manuscript but her eyes were dry and drained. Archery had a quick vision of the pale pointed face in the souvenir shop picture, only now it was blending into and becoming one with Tess's.

He let his eyes linger on Irene Kershaw for a brief moment with painful compassion. They had reached a point in this telling where she must, unless he could save her, touch on that which would humiliate her most.

'You were going to be married,' he said.

Perhaps she was afraid to hear the words he might choose. 'We never did anything wrong but the once,' she cried. 'After-wards — well, he wasn't nasty like other boys, and he was just as ashamed as me.' Justifying herself, her head turned from him, she whispered, 'I've had two husbands and then there was John, but I've never been so much for that side of things.' Her head swung back and her face was aflame. 'We were engaged, we were going to be married . . .'

Archery knew he must rush on with his conjectures. 'After he was killed you knew you were going to have a child?' She nodded, silent now with the enormity of her embarrassment. 'You had nowhere to go, you were afraid so you married Painter. Let me see, John Grace was killed in February 1945 and Painter got home from Burma at the end of March. You must have known him before,' he said, guessing, improvising. 'Perhaps he was stationed at Forby before he went to the Far East?' A tiny nod rewarded him and he was prepared to go on, drawing someone else's story out of an inspired imagination, out of a letter from Kendal, a photographed face, the bruises on a woman's arm. He lifted his eyes from her and clasped his hands tightly to stop the sound that might have been no more than a sigh. Even a sigh would tell her. At the open french window, against the blaze of red petals, Kershaw was standing, silent, still and powerfully alert. How long had he been there? How much had he heard? Archery, transfixed, sought momentarily in his expression for suffering or anger and saw a sweetness that brought a sudden strength to his heart.

Perhaps he was betraying this woman, perhaps he was doing the unforgivable. It was too late for such recriminations.

'Let me try to finish,' he said, and he had no idea whether he kept his voice on the same level he had used before. 'You were married and you let him think he was Tess's father. But he suspected and that was why he never loved her as a father loves his child? Why didn't you tell Mr Kershaw?'

She leant forward and he could tell she had not heard the man behind her move almost soundlessly into the room. 'He never asked me about my life with Bert,' she said. 'But I was so ashamed of it, of being married to a man like that. Mr Kershaw's so good — you don't know him — he never asked me, but I had to tell him some of it, didn't I?' She was suddenly eloquent. 'Think what I had to tell him, think what I had to bring him — nothing! People used to point to me out in the street like I was a freak. He had to take that on his shoulders

— Mr Kershaw who'd never touched dirt in all his life. He said he'd take me away and give me a new life where no one'd know, he said I wasn't to blame, I was innocent. D'you think I was going to give up the one chance I'd ever had by telling him Tess was — was illegitimate?'

Archery gasped and staggered to his feet. By the power of his eyes and his will he had been trying to force the man behind her chair to retreat the way he had come. But Kershaw remained where he was, still, a man apparently without breath or heartbeats. His wife had been rapt, her own story dulling all outer stimuli, but now she seemed to sense the atmosphere in the room, the soundless passion of two other people whose sole desire was to help her. She twisted in her chair, sketched a strange little gesture of pleading and rose to confront her husband.

The scream Archery expected never came. She lurched a little, but whatever she was trying to gasp out was lost and muffled by Kershaw's strong embrace. He heard her say only, 'Oh, Tom, oh, Tom!' but his energy was so drained that his brain was filled with just one foolish thought. It was the first time he had ever heard Kershaw's christian name.

She did not come downstairs again for that time. Archery supposed that he would not see her again until they all met among flowers and bridesmaids and wedding cake. Tess sat pale-faced and almost shy, her hand clasped in that of Charles, the manuscript on her knees.

'I feel so strange,' she said. 'I feel I have a new identity. It's as if I had three fathers and the most remote of them was really my father . . .'

Charles said tactlessly, 'Well, wouldn't you choose to have had this one, a man who could write like this?' But Tess lifted her eyes momentarily to the man Archery would have to learn to call Tom and he knew she had made her choice.

Then she thrust the heavy stack of paper towards Archery. 'What can we do with them?'

'I could show them to a publisher I know. I once wrote part of a book myself . . .' He smiled. 'On Abyssinian cats. I do know someone who might be interested. Something I can do to make amends,' he said.

'You? You've got nothing to reproach yourself with.' Kershaw moved to stand between him and the lovers. Only marred one marriage to make another, Archery thought. 'Listen,' said Kershaw, his face scored with the lines of effort to make himself understood. 'You did nothing but what I should have done years ago, talked to her. I couldn't you see. I wanted to get off on the right foot. Now I can see you can be too tactful, too damned diplomatic. Oh, there were a thousand little things, how she'd never cared for Painter but he'd been pestering her to marry him. I never asked her what made her change her mind when he came home from Burma. God help me, I thought it wasn't my business! She didn't want me to tell Tess about Painter and I went through agony trying to put that across to a kid of twelve.' Here, unafraid of sentimentality, he caught his stepdaughter's free hand and held it briefly. 'I remember I even got mad at Rene because she seemed to be contradicting every blessed word I said.'

Tess quoted softly, ' "Never mind what Daddy says. Your father was no murderer." '

'And she was right but I turned a deaf ear. She'll talk to me now as she's never talked in all these years. She'll talk to you, Tess, if you'll go up to her now.'

Like a child she hesitated and her lips trembled into a nervous smile of indecision. But obedience — happy, reasonable obedience — was natural in that house. Archery had seen an instance of it before.

'I don't know what to say, how to begin,' she said, getting slowly to her feet. 'I'm so desperately afraid of hurting her.'

'Begin with your wedding, then,' Kershaw said robustly. Archery watched him stoop to the floor where the magazines had fallen. 'Show her this and let her dream of seeing you in something like it.'

Tess was in jeans and a white shirt, an Olivia or a Rosalind finding her lost birthright and with it a new womanhood. She took the magazine from Kershaw and glanced at the cover picture, the hat that was a pyramid of flowers crowning the most photographed face in Britain.

'That's not for me,' she said, but she took it with her and Archery watched them depart together, Charles's flesh and blood love and his own, a paper fantasy. Not for me, not for me . . .

'We must go soon,' he said to his son. 'It's time we shared all this with your mother.'

The Best Man to Die

For George and Dora Herbert,
in gratitude for their
helpful advice

CHAPTER ONE

Jack Pertwee was getting married in the morning and the Kingsmarkham and District Darts Club were in the Dragon to give him what George Carter called a send-off.

'I don't like the sound of that, George,' said Jack. 'I'm getting married, not buried.'

'It comes to the same thing.'

'Thanks very much. I'll buy you another drink for that.' He moved up to the bar but the darts club chairman intercepted him.

'My round, Jack. Don't you take any notice of George. Marilyn's a lovely girl and you're a lucky man. I know I speak for us all when I say there's no one here who wouldn't like to be in your shoes tomorrow.'

'His pyjamas more like,' said George. 'You ought to see them. Black nylon they are with a karate top. Cor!'

'Keep the party clean, George.'

'What's it to be then, gentlemen?' said the barman patiently. 'Same again?'

'Same again, Bill, and have one yourself. No, Jack, man is a monogamous animal and there's no partnership on earth to touch a happy marriage. Especially when you're starting off on the right foot like you and Marilyn. Bit of money in the Post Office, nice little flat and nothing to reproach yourselves with.'

'You reckon?' Jack was in a hurry to gloss over that right foot and reproaching stuff. The chairman's homily called to mind the short — but too long — talk he and Marilyn had suffered two days before in the vicar's study. He downed his beer, looking around him uncomfortably.

'The first ten years are the worst,' he heard someone say, and he turned, suddenly nettled. 'Well, damn it,' he said, 'you are a bloody cheerful mob. I notice it's the bachelors who don't have a good word to say for marriage.'

'That's right,' the chairman concurred. 'Pity there aren't a few more husbands to back me up, eh, Jack? Charlie Hatton now. There's an ux-ux-what's the word I want?'

'Don't ask me. What the hell does it matter, anyway? You and your words. This is supposed to be a stag party, not an annual general meeting. What we need is someone to liven things up.'

'Like Charlie. Where d'you reckon he's got to?'

'He said he'd be late. He's bringing the lorry down from Leeds.'

'Maybe he's gone home first.'

'He wouldn't do that. The last thing he said to me on Wednesday, "Jack," he said, "I'll get along to your rave-up on Friday even if I have to knock the guts out of her. I've told Lilian to expect me when she sees me." No, he'll come here first all right.'

'I hope nothing's happened to him, that's all.'

'Like what?'

'Well, he's had that lorry hi-jacked twice, hasn't he?'

'Bloody old woman you are, George,' said Jack, but he too had begun to feel uneasy. It was nine-thirty, only an hour to go before the Dragon closed. Charlie was going to be his best man. Marvellous wedding he'd have if they found his best man at midnight somewhere in the Midlands with his head bashed in.

'Drink up,' said the darts club wit, 'and I'll tell you the one about the girl who married the sailor.'

'I've heard it,' Jack said dolefully.

'Not this one you haven't. Same again, please, Bill. There was this girl, you see, and the night before she got married her mother said, "Now whatever you do, don't let him . . ." '

'Hold your horses, mate. Here's Charlie now.'

They were all big men, topping six feet, but Charlie Hatton was a little fellow with a brown face and very brilliant sharp eyes. They flashed quickly and calculatingly over the assembled company before Charlie smiled. He showed a set of perfect white teeth which no one there but Jack knew were false. Charlie was sensitive about having false teeth at thirty — why hadn't all that wartime milk and orange juice set him up for life as it had his contemporaries? — but he didn't mind Jack knowing. He didn't mind what Jack knew about him, within reason, that is, although he had ceased to confide in him as

absolutely as he had in the days when they had passed through
Kingsmarkham Primary School together. They were friends. In
another age and another society it might have been said that
they loved each other. They were as David and Jonathan, but
if anyone had hinted such Jack would have poked him on the
nose, and as for Charlie . . . The drinkers in the Dragon all
privately and rather proudly believed that Charlie was capable
of anything.

Marilyn Thompson was Charlie's wife's best friend; Charlie
was to be Jack's best man and one day he thought he would be
godfather to Jack's first child. Many a time they had drunk thus
together, as boys, as youths, as men, and come out under the
same starlit sky to walk beside each other up the familiar High
Street where every house was a landmark and every face part
of a shared history. There might have been no one else in the
pub tonight but the two of them. The others were but background and audience. Jack was passing through a door tonight,
dying a little, and as always Charlie would die with him too.

If these emotions stirred under the stubbly balding crown,
Charlie showed none of them. His grin wide, he slapped Jack
on the back and peered six inches up into the bridegroom's
handsome red face.

'I made it then, me old mate. My brother Jonathan, very
pleasant hast thou been unto me; thy love to me was wonderful,
passing the love of women . . .'

'I reckoned you would,' said Jack and his heart was filled
with joy. 'I'd have had it in properly for you if you hadn't.
What're you going to have?'

'Not that gnat's piss, for a start. Eleven bloody hours I've
driven today. You're a mean devil if you can't run to scotch,
Jack.'

'Give me a chance, I . . .'

'Put it away. It's only my fun, you know me. Seven doubles,
Bill, and you needn't look like that. No wonder they reckon the
beer's on the turn in here. I've taken the lorry back to the depot
and I'm walking home if that's what's worrying you. Happy
days, Jack, and may all your troubles be little ones!'

Charlie had opened his wallet with a flourish, taking care

that its contents were visible to all the patrons of the bar. His pay packet was there unopened and he didn't open it now but paid for his round from a wad of notes held together with an elastic band. It was a thick wad and although most of the notes were green, some were blue.

'How the rich live,' said George Carter.

'You want to make something of it, do you?'

'No need to get touchy with me, mate. I must want my head tested sorting mail all day when I could be picking up wads of it on the lorries.'

'You ought to know. It's your bloody head. Take it along to a trick cyclist if it bothers you.'

'Break it up,' said the club wit. 'I was just telling you about this girl and what her mother said on the night before she got married to the sailor.'

'Who got married?' said Charlie. 'Her mother? Bit late in the day for that, wasn't it? O.K., mate, it's only my fun, but Jack and me heard that one our last term at school. And the sailor said, "Have it your own way but if we don't we'll never have kids." Right? That the pay-off?'

'Thank you and good night.'

'Don't be like that,' said Jack. Charlie had a knack for rubbing people up the wrong way. Funny *he* never fell foul of him. 'My round, I think.'

'Can't have that, Jack. Seven more doubles, Bill. Jack, I said *put it away*. I can afford it. There's plenty more where that came from. I come in late, didn't I, so I've got lee-way to make up?'

'No more for me,' said the man whose joke Charlie had spoiled. He patted Jack's shoulder and said good night while the others drank their whisky in an awkward silence.

'Last orders, gentlemen, please,' said the barman.

George Carter dipped his hand into his pocket and brought out some silver. 'One for the road then, Jack?'

Charlie looked at the coins. 'What's that? Your missus's housekeeping?'

George flushed. He wasn't married; Charlie knew he wasn't married; knew moreover that his steady had chucked him two weeks before. George had got the deposit ready for a house and made the first down payment on a dining suite. 'You bastard,' he said.

Charlie bristled at him, a smart little fighting cock.

'Nobody calls me a bastard.'

'Gentlemen, gentlemen,' said the barman.

'Yes,' said the chairman, 'pack it in. Talk about folks being touchy, Charlie. No wonder they're touchy when you pick on them the way you do.' He smiled breezily, struck an orator's attitude. 'Now the evening's drawing to a close, and I reckon we ought to take the opportunity of conveying to Jack here the heartiest good wishes of the Kingsmarkham and District Darts Club. I for one . . .'

'We'll take it as said then, shall we?' said Charlie. 'A hearty vote of thanks for the chairman.' He put another fiver on the counter. As red as George had been, the chairman shrugged and gave Jack a nod which was meaningful and sympathetic but which Jack ignored. Then he went, taking another man with him.

The barman wiped the counter in silence. Charlie Hatton had always been cocky but in the past weeks he'd become insufferable and most of the meetings had broken up like this.

Of the stag party now only Jack, Charlie, George and one other remained. He was a lorry driver like Charlie, his name was Maurice Cullam and until now he had scarcely opened his mouth except to pour alcohol down it. Now, having witnessed the rout and ignominy of his friends, he took his last drink and said:

'Been seeing much of McCloy lately, Charlie?'

Charlie made no reply and it was Jack who said, 'Why, have you?'

'Not me, Jack. I keep my hands clean. Money's not everything. I like to sleep in my bed.'

Instead of the expected explosion, Charlie said softly and mildly, 'Time you did. Time you slept for a change.'

Maurice had five children born in six years. Charlie's crack could be taken as a compliment and as such, to the relief of George and Jack, Maurice took it. He smiled sheepishly at this tribute to his virility. Considering Maurice's wife was an exceptionally plain woman, there were a good many ripostes Charlie could have made, ripostes which might have been transparently insulting. Instead he had chosen to flatter.

'Time, gentlemen,' said the barman. 'Here's wishing you all you wish yourself, Mr Pertwee.' The barman usually called Jack by his Christian name and Jack knew 'Mr Pertwee' was a mark, never to be repeated, of the respect due to a bridegroom.

'Thanks a lot,' he said, 'and for a grand evening. I'll be seeing you.'

'Let's be toddling, Jack,' said Charlie, and he tucked his fat wallet away.

The air was soft and mild and the sky scattered with many stars. Orion rode above them, his belt crossed by a wrack of midsummer cloud.

'Lovely night,' said Charlie. 'Going to be a fine day tomorrow, Jack.'

'You think?'

'Happy is the bride that the sun shines on.' Drink had made George sentimental and he turned his mouth down lugubriously as he remembered his steady and the down payment on the furniture.

'You have a good cry, mate,' said Charlie. 'Nothing like a bit of a weep to make a girl feel better.'

George led the Kingsmarkham group of Morris dancers and in the past Charlie had fripped him when he appeared in his motley suit, his cap and bells. He bit his lip, clenching his fists. Then he shrugged and turned away. 'Get stuffed,' he muttered. The others watched him cross the road and make his unsteady way down York Street. Jack raised one hand in a feeble salute.

'You shouldn't have said that, Charlie.'

'Ah, he makes me sick. Let's have a bit of a sing-song then, shall we?' He put one arm around Jack's waist and the other, after a barely discernible pause, around Maurice's.

'One of them old music-hall ballads of yours, Charlie.'

They meandered along under the old overhanging house fronts and Jack had to duck his head to avoid cracking it on a lamp in an iron cage. Charlie cleared his throat and sang:

> 'Mabel dear, listen here!
> There's robbery in the park.

I sat alone in the Y.M.C.A.,
Singing just like a lark —
There's no place like ho-ome,
But I couldn't go home in the dark!'

'Yoo-hoo!' yelled Jack in Wild Western imitation, but his voice tailed away as Inspector Burden of Kingsmarkham C.I.D. emerged from Queen Street and approached them across the forecourt of the Olive and Dove. ' 'Evening, Mr Burden.'

' 'Evening.' The inspector viewed them with cool distaste. 'We wouldn't want to do anything likely to lead to a breach of the peace, would we?' He passed on and Charlie Hatton sniggered.

'Copper,' he said. 'I reckon I've got more in this pocket than he gets in a month.'

Maurice said stiffly, 'I'll say good night then, Jack.' They had come to the Kingsbrook bridge and the beginning of the footpath to Sewingbury that followed the waters of the river. Maurice lived in Sewingbury, Charlie in one of the new council flats on the far side of the Kingsbrook Road. The footpath was a short cut home for both of them.

'Wait for Charlie. He's going your way.'

'I won't, thanks. I promised the missus I'd be home by eleven.' Charlie had turned his back, making it plain he didn't want Maurice's company. 'Powerful stuff, that,' Maurice said, his face pale in the lamplight. 'I don't reckon I should have mixed it.' He belched and Charlie sniggered. 'Cheers, Jack, see you in church.'

'Cheers, mate.'

Maurice vaulted the stile and, by a miracle, landed steadily on his feet. He passed the wooden seats, ducked under the willows, and the last they saw of him was his undulating shadow. Jack and Charlie were alone.

They had drunk a great deal and the night was warm, but on a sudden they were both stone-cold sober. Both of them loved women and in that love as in every emotion they were inarticulate, yet in no impulse of the heart were they so tongue-tied as in this great and pure friendship of theirs.

As with the Greeks, they had found in each other an all-embracing spiritual compatibility. Their women were their pride and treasure, for bed, for hearth and home, for showing off, for their manhood. But without each other their lives would be incomplete, lacking, as it were, the essence and the fuse. They had never heard of the Greeks, unless you counted the man who kept the Acropolis restaurant in Stowerton, and neither could now understand the emotion which held each of them, preserving him in silence and a kind of despair.

If Charlie had been a different man, a cultivated man or effeminate or living in a bygone age when tongues were more freely unloosed, he might now have embraced Jack and told him from a full heart how he entered wholly into his joy and would die for his happiness. And if Jack had been such another he would have thanked Charlie for his unstinted friendship, his generous loans, his hospitality and for bringing him Marilyn Thompson. But Charlie was a sharp little lorry driver and Jack was an electrician. Love was between a man and a woman, love was for marriage, and each would have died before admitting to anything more than that they 'got on well' together. They hung over the bridge, dropping stone chippings into the water, and then Charlie said:

'I reckon you need your beauty sleep, so I'll be on my way.'

'We got your present, Charlie. I wasn't going to say nothing till the others had gone, but it's a real grand job that record-player. It quite knocked me back when I saw it. Must have set you back a bit.'

'I got it cost, mate.' Another stone dropped and splashed in the darkness beneath.

'Marilyn said she'd be writing to Lilian.'

'She has, too. A lovely letter come from her before I went up north. A real educated girl you got there, Jack. She knows how to put a letter together all right. You don't grudge the outlay when you get a letter like that. I brought you two together and don't you ever forget it.'

'Ah, you know how to pick them, Charlie. Look at Lilian.'

'Well, I'd better get looking at her, hadn't I?' Charlie turned to face his friend and his shadow was short and black against Jack's long one. He raised his hard little hand and brought it down on Jack's resoundingly. 'I'll be off, then.'

'I reckon you'd better, Charlie.'

'And if I don't get the chance tomorrow — well, I'm no speechmaker like Brian, but all the very best, Jack.'

'You'll get the chance all right. You'll have to make a speech.'

'Save it up till then, eh?' Charlie wrinkled his nose and winked quickly. The shadows parted, he negotiated the stile. 'Good night, me old love.'

' 'Night, Charlie.'

The willows enclosed him. His shadow appeared again as the path rose and dipped. Jack heard him whistling, 'Mabel dear, listen here' under the stars and then as the shadow was absorbed and lost in the many tree shadows, the whistle too faded and there was no sound but the gentle chatter of the stream, the Kingsbrook that flowed everlastingly over its bed of thin round stones.

Many waters cannot quench love, nor the floods drown it.

CHAPTER TWO

Detective Chief Inspector Wexford didn't care for dogs. He had never had a dog and now that one of his daughters was married and the other a student at drama school, he saw no reason why he should ever give one house-room. Many an anti-dog man joins the ranks of dog lovers because he is too weak to resist the demands of beloved children, but in Wexford's household the demands had never been more than half-hearted, so he had passed through this snare and come out unscathed.

When therefore he arrived home late on Friday night to find the grey thing with ears like knitted dishcloths in his favourite chair he was displeased.

'Isn't she a darling?' said the drama student. 'Her name's Clytemnestra. I knew you wouldn't mind having her for just a fortnight.' And she whisked out to answer the telephone.

'Where did Sheila get it from?' Wexford said gloomily.

Mrs Wexford was a woman of few words.

'Sebastian.'

'Who in God's name is Sebastian?'

'Some boy,' said Mrs Wexford. 'He's only just gone.'

Her husband considered pushing the dog on to the floor, thought better of it, and went sulkily off to bed. His daughter's beauty had never ceased to surprise the chief inspector. Sylvia, the elder married one, was well-built and healthy, but that was the best that could be said for her; Mrs Wexford had a magnificent figure and a fine profile although she had never been of the stuff that wins beauty contests. While he . . . All he needed, he sometimes thought, was a trunk to make him look exactly like an elephant. His body was huge and ponderous, his skin pachydermatous, wrinkled and grey, and his three-cornered ears stuck out absurdly under the sparse fringe of colourless hair. When he went to the zoo he passed the elephant house quickly lest the irreverent onlooker should make comparisons.

Her mother and sister were fine-looking women, but the odd thing about Sheila was that her beauty was not an enlargement or enhancement of their near-handsomeness. She looked like her father. The first time Wexford noticed this — she was then about six — he almost hooted aloud, so grotesque was the likeness between this exquisite piece of doll's flesh and her gross progenitor. And yet that high broad forehead was his, the little tilted nose was his, his the pointed — although in her case, flat — ears, and in her huge grey eyes he saw his own little ones. When he was young his hair had been that flaxen gold too, as soft and as fine. Only hope she doesn't end up looking like her dad, he thought sometimes with a rich inner guffaw.

But on the following morning his feelings towards his younger daughter were neither tender nor amused. The dog had awakened him at ten to seven with long-drawn howls and now, a quarter of an hour later, he stood on the threshold of Sheila's bedroom, glowering.

'This isn't a boarding kennels, you know,' he said. 'Can't you hear her?'

'The Acrylic Swoofle Hound, Pop? Poor darling, she only wants to be taken out.'

'What did you call her?'

'The Acrylic Swoofle Hound. She's a mongrel really, but that's what Sebastian calls her. She looks as if she's made of man-made fibres you see. Don't you think it's funny?'

'Not particularly. Why can't this Sebastian look after his own dog?'

'He's gone to Switzerland,' said Sheila. 'His plane must have gone by now.' She surfaced from under the sheets and her father saw that her hair was wound on huge electrically heated rollers. 'I felt awful letting him walk all that way to the station last night.' She added accusingly, 'But you had the car.'

'It's my car,' Wexford almost shouted. This argument he knew of old was hopeless and he listened to his own voice with a kind of horror as a note of pleading crept into it. 'If the dog wants to go out, hadn't you better get up and take her?'

'I can't. I've just set my hair.' Downstairs Clytemnestra let out a howl that ended in a series of urgent yelps. Sheila threw back the bedclothes and sat up, a vision in pink baby doll pyjamas.

'God almighty!' Wexford exploded. 'You can't take your

friend's dog out but you can get up at the crack of dawn to set your hair.'

'Daddy . . .' The wheedling tone as well as the now seldom-used paternal appellation told Wexford that a monstrous request was to be made of him. He glared, drawing his brows together in the manner that made Kingsmarkham's petty offenders tremble. 'Daddy, duck, it's a gorgeous morning and you know what Dr Crocker said about your weight and I *have* just set my hair . . .'

'I am going to take a shower,' Wexford said coldly.

He took it. When he emerged from the bathroom the dog was still howling and pop music was issuing from behind Sheila's door. A degenerate male voice exhorted its hearers to give it love or let it die in peace.

'There seems to be an awful lot of noise going on, darling,' said Mrs Wexford sleepily.

'You're joking.'

He opened Sheila's door. She was applying a face pack.

'Just this once, then,' said the chief inspector. 'I'm only doing it because I want your mother to have a quiet lie-in, so you can turn that thing off for a start.'

'You are an angel, Daddy,' said Sheila, and she added dreamily, 'I expect Clytemnestra has spent a penny by now.'

Clytemnestra. Of all the stupid pretentious names for a dog . . . But what else could you expect of someone called Sebastian? She had not, however, yet 'spent a penny'. She flung herself on Wexford, yelping frenetically, and when he pushed her away, ran round him in circles, wildly gyrating her tail and flapping her knitted ears.

Wexford found the lead, obligingly left by Sheila in a prominent position on top of the refrigerator. Undoubtedly it was going to be a beautiful day, a summer's day such as is unequalled anywhere in the world but in the South of England, a day that begins with mists, burgeons into tropical glory and dies in blue and gold and stars.

'Full many a glorious morning,' quoted Wexford to Clytemnestra, 'have I seen, flatter the mountain tops with sovereign eye.'

Clytemnestra agreed vociferously, leaping on to a stool and screeching hysterically at sight of her lead.

'Bear your body more seemly,' said Wexford coldly, switching from sonnet to comedy without varying his author. He looked out of the window. The sovereign eye was there all right, bright, molten and white-gold. Instead of mountain tops it was flattering the Kingsbrook meadows and turning the little river into a ribbon of shimmering metal. It wouldn't do him any harm to take this ungoverned creature for a short jaunt in the fields and the experience would give him a splendid ascendancy over Inspector Burden when he walked into the station at nine-thirty.

'Lovely morning, sir.'

'It was, Mike. The best of it's over now, of course. Now when I was down by the river at half seven . . .'

He chuckled. Clytemnestra whimpered. Wexford went to the door and the dog screamed for joy. He clipped on the lead and stepped forth into the sweet peace of a summer Saturday in Sussex.

It was one thing to boast afterwards of pre-breakfast hiking, quite another to be actually seen leading this freak of nature, this abortion, about the public streets. Observed in uncompromising midsummer light, Clytemnestra looked like something that, having long lain neglected at the bottom of an old woman's knitting basket, has finally been brought out to be mended.

Moreover, now that she had achieved the heart's desire for which she had turned on her shameless, neurotic display, she had become dejected, and walked along meekly, head and tail hanging. Just like a woman, Wexford thought crossly. Sheila would be just the same. Hair out of curlers, face cleaned up, she was in all probability downstairs now calmly making her mother a cup of tea. When you get what you want you don't want what you get . . . *On a fait le monde ainsi.*

He would, however, eschew the public streets.

From this side of town, the footpath led across the fields to the bank of the stream where it divided, one branch going to the new council estate and Sewingbury, the other to the centre of Kingsmarkham High Street, at the Kingsbrook bridge. Wexford certainly wasn't going to embark on a sabbath day's journey to Sewingbury, and now they had mucked up the Kingsbrook Road with those flats, there was no longer any point in going there. Instead he would walk down to the river, take the path to the bridge and pick up his *Police Review* at Braddan's on his way home. They always forgot to send it with the papers.

In agricultural districts pastureland is usually fenced. These meadows were divided by hedges and barbed wire and in them great red cattle were grazing. Mist lay in shallow patches over the hollows and where the fields were lying fallow the hay was nearly ready to be cut, but it was not yet cut. Wexford, very much a countryman at heart, marvelled that the townsman calls grass green when in reality it is as many-coloured as Joseph's coat. The grass heads hung heavy with seed, ochre, chestnut and powdery grey, and all the thick tapestry of pasture was embroidered and interlaced with the crimson thread of sorrel, the bright acid of buttercups and the creamy dairy-maid floss of meadowsweet. Over it all the fanning whispering seed and the tenuous mist cast a sheen of silver.

The oak trees had not yet lost the vivid yellow-green of their late springtime, a colour so bright, so fresh and so unparalleled elsewhere in nature or in art that no one has ever been able to emulate it and it is never seen in paint or cloth or women's dresses. In such things the colour would be crude, if it could be copied, but against this pale blue yet fixedly cloudless sky it was not crude. It was exquisite. Wexford drew in lungfuls of scented, pollen-laden air. He never had hay fever and he felt good.

The dog, who had perhaps feared a pavement perambulation, sniffed the air too and became frisky. She poked about in the brambles and wagged her tail. Wexford undid the lead clip and let her run.

With a kind of stolid tranquillity he began to reflect on the day's work ahead. That grievous bodily harm thing was coming up at a special court this morning, but that ought to be all wrapped up in half an hour. Then there was the possibility of the silver on sale at the Saturday morning market being stolen goods. Someone had better go down and have a word. . . . No doubt there'd been the usual spate of Friday night burglaries, too.

Mrs Fanshawe had regained consciousness in Stowerton Royal Infirmary after her six-week-long coma. They would have to talk to her today. But that was the uniformed branch's pigeon, not his. Thank God, it wasn't he who had to break the news to the woman that her husband and daughter had both been killed in the car crash that had fractured her skull.

Presumably they would now resume the adjourned inquest on that unfortunate pair. Burden said Mrs Fanshawe might just recall why her husband's Jaguar had skidded and overturned on the empty fast lane of the twin track road, but he doubted it. A merciful amnesia usually came with these comas and who could deny it was a blessing? It seemed downright immoral to torment the poor woman with questions now just for the sake of proving the Jaguar's brakes were faulty or Fanshawe was driving over the seventy limit. It wasn't as if any other vehicle had been involved. No doubt there was some question of insurance. Anyway, it wasn't his worry.

The sun shone on the rippling river and the long willow leaves just touched its bubbling golden surface. A trout jumped for a sparkling iridescent fly. Clytemnestra went down to the water and drank greedily. In this world of clean fast-running water, of inimitable oaks and meadows which made the Bayeux tapestry look like a traycloth, there was no place for somersaulted cars and carnage and broken bodies lying on the wet and bloody tarmac.

The dog paddled, then swam. In the sunshine even grey knitted Clytemnestra was beautiful. Beneath her flat furry belly the big shallow stones had the marble veining of agate. Upon the water the mist floated in a golden veil, spotted with the dancing of a myriad tiny flies. And Wexford who was an agnostic, a profane man, thought, Lord, how manifold are thy works in all the earth.

There was a man on the other side of the river. He was walking slowly some fifty yards from the opposite bank and parallel to it, walking from the Sewingbury direction to Kingsmarkham. A child was with him, holding his hand, and he too had a dog, a pugnacious-looking black dog. Wexford had an idea, drawn partly from experience in looking out of his office window, that when two dogs meet they inevitably fight. Clytemnestra would come out badly from a fight with that black devil. Wexford couldn't bring himself to call his charge by her name. He whistled.

Clytemnestra took no notice. She had gained the opposite bank and was poking about in a great drifting mass of torn grass and brushwood. Further upstream a cache of rubbish had been washed against the bank. Wexford, who had been lyrical, felt positively pained by this evidence of man's indifference to nature's glories. He could see a bundle of checked cloth, an old blanket perhaps, an oil drum and, a little apart from the rest, a floating shoe. Clytemnestra confirmed his low opinion of everything canine by advancing on this water-logged pocket of rubbish, her tail wagging and her ears pricked. Filthy things, dogs, Wexford thought, scavengers and dustbin delvers. He whistled again. The dog stopped and he was just about to congratulate himself on his authoritative and successful method of summoning her, when she made a plunging dart forward and seized the mass of cloth in her mouth.

It moved with a heavy surge and the dog released it, her hackles rising. The slow and somehow primeval erecting of that mat of grey hairs brought a curious chill to Wexford's blood. The sun seemed to go in. He forgot the black dog, coming ever nearer, and his joy in the morning went. Clytemnestra let out an unearthly keening howl, her lips snarling back and her tail a stiff prolongation of her backbone.

The bundle she had disturbed eddied a few inches into the deeper water and as Wexford watched, a thin pale hand, lifeless as the agate-veined stones, rose slowly from the sodden cloth, its fingers hanging yet pointing towards him.

He took off his shoes and socks and rolled his trousers to his knees. The man and the child on the other side watched him with interest. He didn't think they had yet seen the hand. Holding his shoes, he stepped on to the stones and crossed the river carefully. Clytemnestra came to him quickly and put her face against his bare leg. Wexford pushed aside the willows that hung like a pelmet and came to the rubbish pocket, where he knelt down. One shoe floated empty, the other was still on a foot. The dead man lay face-downwards and someone had smashed in the back of his head with a heavy smooth object. One of these very stones, Wexford guessed.

The brambles shivered behind him and a footstep crunched.

'Keep back,' Wexford said. 'Keep the child back.'

He turned shielding what lay in the water with his own big body. Downstream the child was playing with both dogs, throwing stones for them into the water.

'Christ!' said the man softly.

'He's dead,' said Wexford. 'I'm a police officer and . . .'

'I know you. Chief Inspector Wexford.' The man approached and Wexford couldn't stop him. He looked down and gasped. 'My God, I . . .'

'Yes, it isn't a pleasant sight.' The thought came to Wexford that something very out of the way had happened. Not so much that here on a fine June morning a man lay murdered, but that he, Wexford, had found him. Policemen don't find bodies unless they are sent to look for them or unless someone else has found them first. 'Will you do something for me?' he asked. The newcomer's face was green. He looked as if he was about to be sick. 'Will you go down to the town, to the nearest phone box and get on to the station? Just tell them what you've seen. They'll do the rest. Come on, man, pull yourself together.'

'O.K., it's just that . . .'

'Perhaps you'd better let me have your name.'

'Cullam, Maurice Cullam. I'll go, I'll go right away. It's just that — well, last night I was having a drink with him at the Dragon.'

'You know who it is then? You can't see his face.'

'I don't need to. I'd know Charlie Hatton anywhere.'

CHAPTER THREE

He looked a right Charlie in those tails and striped trousers. That would be something funny to say to his best man when he came.

'You and me, we look a pair of right Charlies, Charlie Hatton.'

Quite witty really. Jack often thought he wasn't quick enough to match Charlie's easy repartee, but now he had thought of something that would make his friend smile.

Dear old Charlie, he thought sentimentally, the best friend a man ever had. Generous to a fault, and if he wasn't always strictly above-board — well, a man had to live. And Charlie knew how to live all right. The best of everything he had. Jack was ready to bet all the crisp honeymoon pound notes he had in his pocket that Charlie would be one of the few guests not wearing a hired morning coat. He had his own and not off the peg, either.

Not that he looked half bad himself, he thought, admiring his reflection. At his age boozing didn't have much visible effect and he always had a red face anyway. He looked smashing, he decided, shyly proud, as good as the Duke of Edinburgh any day. Probably the Duke used an electric shaver though. Jack put another bit of cotton wool on the nick on his chin and he wondered if Marilyn was ready yet.

Thanks to Charlie boy, they'd been able to splash a bit on the wedding and Marilyn could have the white satin and the four bridesmaids she'd set her heart on. It would have been a different story if they'd had to find the key money for the flat themselves. Trust Charlie to come up with a long-term interest-free loan. That way they'd be able to blue some of their own savings on having the flat done up nicely. How well it had all worked out! A fortnight away by the sea and when they came back, the flat all ready and waiting for them. And it was all thanks to Charlie.

Moving away from the mirror, Jack looked into the future,

twenty, thirty years hence. Charlie would be a really rich man by then. Jack would be very much surprised if his friend wouldn't be living in one of those houses in Ploughman's Lane like the one where he sometimes did electrical jobs with real old French furniture and real oil paintings and the kind of china you looked at but didn't eat off. He and Charlie had had a good laugh over that particular house, but there had been something serious in Charlie's laughter and Jack had guessed he aimed high.

They'd still be mates of course, for there was no side to Charlie Hatton. It wouldn't be beer and a hand of solo then, but dinner parties and bridge games with their wives in cocktail gowns and real jewellery. Jack grew dizzy as he thought of it, seeing them sitting with tall glasses on a shady patio and, strangely, seeing them too as they were now, untouched by the hand of time.

Abruptly he came back to the present day, his wedding day. Charlie was taking a hell of a time about coming. Maybe there was some difficulty about Lilian's dress or he was waiting for her to get back from the hairdresser's. Charlie was dead keen on Lilian doing him credit and she always did, always looked as if she'd just stepped out of a bandbox. After Marilyn, she'd be the best dressed woman at the wedding, blonde, shapely, in the green dress Marilyn had got so superstitious about. Jack dabbed at his chin again and went to the window to watch for Charlie.

It was ten-thirty and the wedding was fixed for an hour's time.

She was blonde, shapely, pretty in Sheila Wexford's style but without Sheila's transcending beauty. Her face was rather blunt, the features unfinished putty dabs, and now it was swollen with crying. After they had told her Wexford and Burden sat helplessly while she flung herself face-downwards on the sofa and sobbed into the cushions.

Presently Wexford moved over to her and touched her shoulder. She reached for his hand, and clutched it and dug in her long nails. Then she struggled up, burying her face in his hand and her own. The expensive velvet cushions were blotched with her tears.

Wexford glanced quickly around the smartly, even luxuriously, furnished room. Over the back of one of the chairs hung a blue and green flowered dress, a green coat, long wrist-buttoning gloves. In the middle of the long teak dining table lay Lilian Hatton's wedding hat, an elaborate confection of satin leaves and tulle as green and fresh as the real leaves he could see through the picture window in the Kingsbrook meadows.

'Mrs Hatton,' he said gently and she raised her face obediently, 'Mrs Hatton, weren't you worried when your husband didn't come home last night?'

She didn't speak. He repeated the question, and then she said in a voice choked with sobs, 'I didn't expect him home. I only half-expected him.' She dropped Wexford's hand, recoiling as if in taking it she had done something indecent.

'When he didn't come,' she said, 'I thought He hasn't made it, he hasn't made Jack's party. He's stopping off on the road, he'll be in in the morning, I . . .' The sobs were uncontrollable and she gave a long piteous cry.

'I won't trouble you any more now, Mrs Hatton. You say your mother's coming? If I could just have Mr Pertwee's address . . .'

'Jack, yes,' she said. 'Jack'll take this hard.' She drew a long breath, twisting her hands. 'They'd been pals since they were schoolkids.' Suddenly she stood up, staring wildly. 'God, Jack doesn't know! It's his wedding day and Charlie was going to be his best man. Oh, Jack, Jack, poor Jack!'

'Leave it to us, Mrs Hatton,' said Inspector Burden. 'We'll tell Mr Pertwee. Bailey Street, is it? We'll tell him. There's your front door bell now. I expect that'll be your mother.'

'Mum,' said Lilian Hatton. 'What am I going to do, Mum?' The older woman looked past her, then put her arms around the shaking shoulders. 'Marilyn said I shouldn't wear green to a wedding, she said it was unlucky.' Her voice was very low, a slurring mumble. 'I bought that green coat just the same. I never got as far as the wedding, Mum, but it was unlucky, wasn't it?' Suddenly she broke into a terrible, loud and demented scream. 'Charlie, Charlie, what am I going to do, Charlie?' She held on to her mother, clawing at the lapels of her coat. 'Oh my God, Charlie!' she screamed.

*

'I never get used to it, you know,' said Burden quietly.

'Do you think I do?' Wexford had amiable, sometimes distinctly fond feelings for his subordinate, but occasionally Burden made him impatient, especially when he instituted himself keeper of the chief inspector's conscience. He had a smug parsonical face, Wexford thought unkindly, and now his thin mouth turned piously down. 'The worst is over anyway,' he said crossly. 'The bridegroom won't go into transports of grief and you don't put off your wedding because your best man's been done in.'

You callous devil, said Burden's look. Then the neat, well-modelled head was once more averted and the inspector re-entered his silent, respectful reverie.

It took only ten minutes to get from the Hattons' flat to Bailey Street where, at number ten, Jack Pertwee lived with his widowed father. The police car stopped outside a tiny terraced house with no garden to separate its front door from the pavement. Mr Pertwee senior answered their knock, looking uneasy in a too large morning coat.

'Thought you were our missing best man come at last.'

'I'm afraid Mr Hatton won't be coming, sir.' Wexford and Burden edged themselves courteously but firmly past him into the narrow hall. 'I'm very sorry to tell you we have bad news.'

'Bad news?'

'Yes, sir, Mr Hatton died last night. He was found down by the river this morning and he'd been dead since midnight or before.'

Pertwee went pale as chalk. 'By gum,' he said, 'Jack'll take this hard.' His mouth trembling, he looked at them both and then down at the knife-edge creases in his trousers. 'D'you want me to go up and tell him?' Wexford nodded. 'Well, if that's the way you want it. He's getting married at eleven-thirty. But if I've got to tell him, I suppose I've got to tell him.'

They both knew Jack Pertwee by sight. Most Kingsmark-ham faces were familiar to Wexford and Burden remembered seeing him the night before arm-in-arm with the dead man, singing and disturbing decent citizens. A happily married man himself, he had the deepest sympathy for the widow, but in his heart he thought Jack Pertwee a bit of a lout. You didn't have to tread softly with such as he and he wondered scornfully why the fellow's face was lard-coloured.

Impatiently he watched him lumber blindly down the steep narrow staircase and when the bridegroom reached the bottom, Burden said curtly:

'Your father's told you? Hatton was murdered last night. We want to know the lot, where you'd been and what time you left him.'

'Here, go easy,' said the father. 'It's been a shock. They were old mates, my boy and Charlie.'

Jack pushed past him into the poky front parlour and the others followed. The wedding flowers had come. Jack had a white rose in his buttonhole and there were two more, their stems wrapped in silver foil, on the fumed oak sideboard. One was for the bridegroom's father and the other would never be worn. Jack plucked the flower out of his morning coat and closed his fist slowly over it, crushing it into a pulp.

'I'll get you a drop of whisky, son.'

'I don't want it,' Jack said with his back to them. 'We was drinking whisky last night. I never want to touch it again.' He pulled his black immaculate sleeve across his eyes. 'Who did it?' he shouted.

'We hoped you'd be able to tell us that,' said Burden.

'Me? Are you out of your bloody mind? Just show me the bastard who killed Charlie Hatton and I'll . . .' He sat down heavily, spread his arms on the table and dropped his head.

'Charlie,' he said.

Wexford didn't pursue it. He turned to the father. 'What was it last night, a stag party?' Pertwee nodded. 'D'you know who was there?'

'Jack, of course, and poor old Charlie. Then there was all the darts club lot, George Carter, fellow called Bayles, Maurice Cullam from Sewingbury and a couple of others. That right, Jack?'

Jack nodded dumbly.

'Charlie got there late, Jack said. They left at closing time, split up outside, I reckon. Charlie and Cullam'll have walked home across the fields. That right, Jack?'

This time Jack lifted his head. Burden thought him a weak womanish fool, despising his red eyes and the muscle that twitched in his cheek. But Wexford spoke gently.

'I realise this has been a blow to you, Mr Pertwee. We won't bother you much longer. Did Mr Cullam and Mr Hatton walk home together?'

'Maurice went first,' Jack muttered. 'About twenty to eleven it was. Charlie . . . Charlie stayed for a bit of a natter with me.' A sob caught his throat and he coughed to mask it. 'He said he wished me luck in case he didn't get the chance today. Christ, he didn't know he'd never get another chance.'

'Come on, son, bear up. Let me give you a little drop of scotch. You owe it to Marilyn to keep going you know. It's your wedding day, remember?'

Jack shook off his father's hand and lurched to his feet.

'There isn't going to be no wedding,' he said.

'You don't mean that, Jack, think of that girl of yours, think of all them folks coming. They'll be getting to the church in a minute. Charlie wouldn't have wished it.'

Stubbornly Jack said, 'I'm not getting married today. D'you think I don't know what's right, what's proper?' He wrenched off his tie and flung his morning coat over the back of a chair.

His father, with a working man's regard for hired finery, picked it up, smoothed it and stood draping it over his arm like an outfitter's assistant. Bewildered by the holocaust of events, by death that had suddenly changed a world, he began apologising, first to the policemen: 'I don't know what to say, his best man to die like that . . .' and then to his son: 'I'd give my right hand to have things different, Jack. What can I do for you, son? I'll do anything you say.'

Jack dropped his handful of bruised petals. A sudden dignity made him straighten his back and hold his head high. 'Then get down to that church,' he said, 'and tell them the wedding's off.' He faced Wexford. 'I'm not answering any more questions now. I've got my grief. You ought to respect my grief.' Still the old man hesitated, biting his lip. 'Go on, Dad,' Jack said fiercely. 'Tell them it's all off and tell them why.' He gasped as if suddenly, at this moment, it had come home to him. 'Tell them Charlie Hatton's dead!'

Oh, Jonathan, thou wast slain in thy high places . . . How are the mighty fallen and the weapons of war perished!

'A best man, indeed,' said Burden. 'Everyone's best man.'

You callous devil, thought Wexford. 'Naturally Pertwee'd be upset. What did you expect?'

Burden made a moue of disgust. 'That sort of grief, that's the widow's province. A man ought to have more self-control.' His pale ascetic face flushed unbecomingly. 'You don't suppose there was anything . . . ?'

'No I don't,' said Wexford. 'And why can't you call a spade a spade? They were friends. Don't you have friends, Mike? A pretty pass we've come to if a man can't have a friend without being labelled queer.' He stared aggressively at Burden and declaimed loudly and meaningfully, 'O brave new world, that has such people in it!'

Burden gave a stiff repressive cough and maintained silence until they reached York Street. Then he said coldly, 'George Carter's place is down here, old Pertwee said.'

'He's a Morris dancer, isn't he? I've seen him cavorting about on summer nights outside the Olive and Dove.'

'Lot of affected nonsense.'

But George Carter wasn't wearing his cap and bells this morning. From the brilliantined hair and smart lounge suit, Wexford gathered that he was a wedding guest.

He hinted at the unlikelihood of Jack Pertwee's being married that day and was inwardly amused to observe that this piece of information — the fact that Carter would be deprived of his cold chicken and champagne — distressed him more than Hatton's death. The wedding guest did not exactly beat his breast but he looked considerably crestfallen.

'All that money wasted,' he said. 'I know, I was making plans for my own wedding, but then you won't want to know about that. Pity Jack had to be told, really. I don't seem to be able to take it in. Charlie Hatton dead! He was always so full of life, if you know what I mean.'

'And very well liked, I gather.'

George Carter's eyebrows went up. 'Charlie? Oh well, mustn't speak ill of the dead.'

'You'd better speak the truth, Mr Carter,' said Burden, 'and never mind whether it's ill or not. We want to know all about this party last night. The lot, please. You can take your time.'

Like Jack Pertwee and yet utterly unlike him, Carter took off his jacket and loosened his tie. 'I don't know what you mean by the lot,' he said. 'It was just a bunch of mates having a drink.'

'What happened? What did you talk about?'

'O.K.' He gave them an incredulous glance and said sarcastically, 'Stop me if I'm boring you. Charlie come into the Dragon at about half nine, maybe a quarter to ten. We was drinking beer so, of course, Charlie has to make us all feel small by paying for whiskies all round. A crack hand at that, was Charlie Hatton. I made some comment and he bit my head off. This the sort of thing you want to know?'

'Exactly the sort of thing, Mr Carter.'

'Seems a bit mean, that's all, with the poor geezer dead. Then someone else was telling a joke and he sort of — well, humiliated him, if you know what I mean. He was like that, always had to be top dog. He drank my drink because I said something about all the money he was always flashing around and then he made a dirty crack about . . . Well, that doesn't matter. It was personal. He got at our chairman too and he left with a couple of the others. Geoff had already gone. There was me and Charlie and Maurice and Jack left and we went when they closed. And that's the lot.'

'You're sure?'

'I told you there was nothing much. I can't think of any more . . . Oh, wait a minute. But it was nothing.'

'We'll have it just the same, Mr Carter.'

George Carter shrugged impatiently. 'I don't even know what it was about. Nothing, I reckon. Maurice said — it was after the others had gone — Maurice said, "Seen much of McCloy lately, Charlie?" I think those were his words. I know the name was McCloy but it didn't mean nothing to me. Jack didn't like it and he was a bit shirty with Maurice. I reckon Charlie looked a bit sick. God, it was all so . . . well, it was nothing. But Charlie'd always rise. I expected him to rise. I don't know why. He didn't. He just made a crack about Maurice needing to sleep quiet in his bed. Said it was time he did, meaning Maurice had so many kids and . . . well, you can get the message.'

'Not altogether,' said Wexford. 'Had Cullam suggested that Hatton couldn't sleep quiet in *his*?

'That's right. I forget that bit. I wish I could remember his words. Something like "I don't have nothing to do with McCloy, I like to sleep quiet in my bed." '

Very interesting, Wexford thought. Far from being popular, Hatton had evidently had a host of enemies. He had spent less than an hour in the Dragon and during that time he had succeeded in needling at least four men.

'You mentioned all the money Hatton used to flash around,' he said. 'What money?'

'He always had wads of it,' said Carter. 'I've known him three years and he was always flush. But he'd had more lately. He bought four rounds of double scotches last night and it didn't even make a hole in what he'd got.'

'How much had he got, Mr Carter?'

'I didn't count it, you know,' Carter said with asperity. He blew his nose on his clean white wedding handkerchief. 'He'd got his pay packet, but he didn't touch that. Then he had this roll of notes. I told you I didn't count them. How could I?'

'Twenty pounds, thirty, more?'

Carter wrinkled his forehead in an effort of concentration. 'He paid for the first round out of a fiver and the third with another fiver. He'd got two fivers left, then. As well as that there was a wad of oncers.' He indicated with two parted fingers a quarter of an inch. 'I reckon he was carrying a hundred quid besides his pay.'

CHAPTER FOUR

By lunchtime Wexford and Burden had interviewed all those members of the darts club that had been present at Jack Pertwee's stag party with the exception of Maurice Cullam, but none of them had been able to do more than confirm that Hatton had been aggressive, vain and malicious and that he had been carrying a great deal of money.

They returned to the police station, passing the parish church on whose steps a June bride and her attendants were being photographed. The bridegroom moved out of the throng and Wexford felt a strange sentimental pang because it was not Jack Pertwee. Then he pulled himself together and said, as they mounted the station steps under the concrete canopy:

'Now if we were cops inside the covers of a detective story, Mike, we'd know for sure that Hatton was killed to stop Pertwee getting married today.'

Burden gave a sour smile. 'Easier to kill Pertwee, I'd have thought.'

'Ah, but that's your author's subtlety. Still, we aren't and he wasn't. The chances are he was killed for the money he was carrying. There was nothing in his wallet when I found him.'

The foyer of the police station enclosed them. Behind the long black sweep of counter Sergeant Camb sat fanning himself with a newspaper, the sweat dripping down his forehead. Wexford made for the stairs.

'Why not use the lift, sir?' said Burden.

The police station was not yet half a dozen years old, but ever since its completion the powers that be, like fussy housewives, had been unable to let well alone, adding innovation after innovation, perpetually trying to improve their handiwork. First there had been the stone tubs on the forecourt, a constant temptation to vandals who got a more than commonly satisfying kick from ravishing these particular flowers. Then came the consignment of houseplants for the offices, *tradescantia* and *sanseveria* and *ficus elastica* that were doomed from the start to

217

dehydration and ultimately to have their pots serve as repositories for cigarette ash.

Last year it had been glass sculpture, a strange green tree, a very Ygdrasil, for Burden's sanctum, and for Wexford an inky-blue, amorphous pillar that in some lights grossly resembled the human figure. These, too, had been fated, Wexford's broken by a pretty young woman who was helping him with his enquiries and Burden's one day inadvertently put out with the rubbish.

That should have been the end of it. And then, just as the foyer was beginning to take on a shabby, comfortable look, the lift arrived, an elegant black and gilt box with a sliding door.

'It isn't working yet,' Wexford said, a shade nervously.

'That's where you're wrong. Been operating since this morning. Shall we try it?'

'I should just like to know what's wrong with the stairs,' Wexford exploded. 'It's a downright disgrace wasting the rate-payers' money like this.' He stuck out his lower lip. 'Besides, Crocker says walking upstairs is the best exercise in the world for me with my blood pressure.'

'Just as you like,' said Burden, turning his face away so that Wexford should not see him smile.

By the time they reached the third floor they were both out of breath. The flimsy yellow chair behind Wexford's rosewood desk creaked as he lowered his heavy body into it.

'For God's sake open a window, Mike.'

Burden grumbled that opening windows upset the air conditioning but he complied, raising the yellow venetian blind and letting in a powerful shaft of noonday sunshine.

'Well, sir,' he said. 'Shall we re-cap on what we know about Charlie Hatton?'

'Thirty years old, born and bred in Kingsmarkham. Two years ago he got married to a Miss Lilian Bardsley, sister of the man he's in business with. Bardsley's got his own firm, transporting small electrical goods.'

'Was Hatton a full partner?'

'We'll have to find out. Even if he was, I can't see he could get that flush driving loads of irons and heaters up to Leeds and Scotland a couple of times a week. Carter says he had a hundred quid on him, Mike. Where did he get the money from?'

'Maybe this McCloy.'

'Do we know any McCloys?'

'Not that I can recall, sir. We shall have to ask Maurice Cullam.'

Wexford wiped his brow with his handkerchief and, following Camb's example, began to fan himself with the morning paper. 'The philoprogenitive Cullam,' he said. 'He had one of his quiverful with him when I found Hatton this morning. He's a lorry driver too, Mike. I wonder . . . Hatton had his lorry hijacked twice this year.'

Burden opened his pale blue eyes wide. 'Is that so?'

'I remembered,' said Wexford, 'as soon as Cullam told me whose the body was. Both times were on the Great North Road and no one was ever done for it. Hatton got knocked on the head the first time but the second time he wasn't hurt, only tied up.'

'Once,' said Burden thoughtfully, 'is fair enough. Occupational hazard. Twice looks fishy. I want to hear what the doctor has to say. And if I'm not mistaken that's him outside now.'

Dr Crocker and Wexford had been at school together. Like Jack Pertwee and Charlie Hatton, they were lifelong friends, but their friendship was a casual business and their manner to each other dry, irreverent, often caustic. Crocker, some six years the chief inspector's junior, was the only man Burden knew who could get the better of Wexford and match his acid tongue. A tall lean figure with deep lines carved vertically down his brown cheeks, he came into the office looking as cool as he did on a winter's day.

'I used the lift,' said the doctor. 'Very smart. Whatever will they think of next?'

'Pictures are threatened,' said Wexford. 'The inspector here is to have a suitable flower piece and I a Constable landscape.'

'I don't know much about art,' said Crocker, sitting down and crossing one elegant lean leg over the other, 'but there's one painting I *would* like to have. Rembrandt, The Anatomy Lesson. Lovely thing it is. There's this poor devil, this corpse, you see, lying on the table with his guts laid open and all these students . . .'

'Do you mind,' said Wexford. 'I'm just going to have my lunch. You doctors bring your revolting trade into everything. We can hear your ideas on interior decoration another time. Now I want to know about Charlie Hatton.'

'Perfectly healthy bloke,' said the doctor, 'bar the fact that he's dead.' He ignored Burden's glance of reproof. 'Someone bashed him on the back of the head with a heavy smooth object. I'd say he was dead by eleven but it's impossible to be accurate about these things. What did you say he did for a living?'

'He was a lorry driver,' said Burden.

'I thought that's what you said. He'd got a marvellous set of teeth.'

'So what?' said Wexford. 'He ought to have good teeth.' Rather ruefully he ran his tongue over the two stumps that held in place his upper plate. 'He was only thirty.'

'Sure,' said Crocker, 'he ought to have had his own being a war baby and a cog in the welfare state. The point is he didn't. What I mean was he'd got just about the finest set of *false* teeth I've ever seen. Lovely ivory castles. Very nifty grinders Charlie Hatton had, all cunningly contrived to look more real than the real thing. I'd be surprised if they cost less than two hundred quid.'

'Rich man,' said Wexford ruminatively. 'A hundred pounds in his wallet and two hundred in his mouth. I wish I could believe he'd come by it honestly, driving his lorry up and down the Great North Road.'

'That's your problem,' said the doctor. 'Well, I'm away to my lunch. Tried the lift yet?'

'In your capacity as my medical adviser, you advised me to walk upstairs. Physician, heal thyself. About all the exercise you get is pressing the button on your automatic gear change. You want to watch your blood pressure, too.'

'I should worry,' said Crocker. He went to the door where the sunshine showed off his elegant figure and absence of paunch to best advantage. 'All a matter of metabolism,' he said airily. 'Some have it rapid.' He looked back at Wexford. 'Others slow. The luck of the draw.'

Wexford gave a snort. When the doctor had gone, he opened the top drawer of his desk and took from it the contents of Charlie Hatton's pockets. The wallet was there, but it was empty of money. It was still soaking wet and now Wexford carefully removed from its leather partitions a photograph of Lilian Hatton, a driving licence and a darts club membership card and spread them in the sun to dry.

In the pocket also there had been a clean handkerchief with a small card caught between its folds. You couldn't see the card until you unfolded the handkerchief and now Wexford looked at it for the first time. It was too wet and the ink writing on it indecipherable, but it was still recognisable as the pasteboard square dentists use to remind patients of their appointments. On the top was printed: *Jolyon Vigo, B.D.S., L.D.S., R.C.S., Eng., Dent. Surg., 19 Ploughman's Lane, Kingsmarkham, Sussex. Tel: Kingsmarkham 384.*

Wexford held it up in the bright shaft of sunlight.

'The source of the delectable dentures, d'you reckon?'

'Maybe Vigo can tell us where the money came from if Cullam can't,' said Burden. 'My wife goes to Vigo. He's a good dentist.'

'A fly one too, if you ask me, getting a sharp little customer like Charlie Hatton to part with two hundred for thirty-two teeth. No wonder he can afford to live in Ploughman's Lane. We're in the wrong job here, Mike, and no mistake. I'm going for my lunch now. Join me? And then we'll go and root Cullam out of his domestic bliss.'

'May as well use the lift,' said Burden with a trace of self-consciousness.

It was more than Wexford's life was worth to admit his craven fear of the lift. Although a notice inside clearly stated its capacity to carry three persons, he was secretly afraid that it would be inadequate to bear his vast bulk. But he hesitated for no more than a moment before stepping inside and when the door was closed he took refuge in clowning.

'Soft furnishings, table linen, cutlery,' he said, facetiously, pressing the button. The lift sighed and began to sink. 'First floor for ladies' underwear, stockings . . . Why's it stopping, Mike?'

'Maybe you pressed the wrong button.'

Or it won't stand my weight, Wexford thought, alarmed.

The lift came to rest at the first floor and the door slid open. Sergeant Camb hesitated apologetically on the threshold.

'Sorry, sir. I didn't know it was you. I can walk down.'

'*Three* persons are permitted, Sergeant,' Wexford said, hoping his now very real trepidation didn't show. 'Come along.'

'Thank you, sir.'

'Not bad, is it? The tribute of a grateful government.' Come on, come on, he thought, and pictured the three of them plummeting down the last thirty feet into the basement.

'You off to see Mrs Fanshawe, I suppose?' he said superfluously. The lift floated lightly, steadied and the door opened. Must be stoutly built, thought Wexford, like me. 'I heard she'd regained consciousness.'

'I'm hoping the doctors'll have broken the news about her husband and her daughter, sir,' said Camb as they crossed the black and white checkerboard foyer of the station. 'It's not a job I fancy. They were all the family she'd got. She hasn't a soul in the world barring her sister who came down and identified the bodies.'

'How old is she?'

'Mrs Fanshawe, sir? Fifty odd. The sister's a good bit older. Horrible business for her having to identify Miss Fanshawe. She was a nasty mess, I can tell you. Face all . . .'

'I'm just off for my lunch,' said Wexford firmly.

He marched through the swing doors in front of the others and Camb got into his car. The stone flowerpots on the forecourt sported bright pink bouquets of *pelargoniums,* their magenta-splashed faces turned gratefully to the noonday sun.

'What was that all about?' asked Burden.

'Mrs Fanshawe? It's not our cup of tea. She and her husband were driving home from Eastbourne in Fanshawe's Jaguar. It overturned in the fast lane on the twin-track road on the other side of Stowerton. Their home was in London and Fanshawe must have been in a hurry. God knows how it happened, there wasn't another thing on the road, but the Jag overturned and caught fire. Mrs Fanshawe was flung clear, the other two killed outright. Badly burned too.'

'And this Mrs Fanshawe doesn't know?'

'She's been in a coma since it happened six weeks ago.'

'I remember now,' said Burden, lifting the plastic strip curtain the Carousel Café hung up in hot weather to keep out wasps. 'The inquest was adjourned.'

'Till Mrs F. regained consciousness. Presumably Camb's going to try and get her to tell him just why a seasoned driver like Fanshawe overturned his car on an empty road. Some hopes! What d'you fancy for lunch, Mike? I'm going for the salad myself.'

'Two ham salads,' said Burden to the waitress. He poured himself some water from a chilled carafe.

'Getting quite transatlantic the old Carousel,' said Wexford. 'And about time too. Not so long ago the water used to steam away like a perishing engine on these tables in hot weather. What's the betting this McCloy's running a big racket, paying Charlie Hatton to leave his lorry unattended and paying him to keep other lorry drivers occupied whenever the chance presents itself? Lorries are always getting hi-jacked. They leave them in these lay-bys while they have a little kip or a cup of tea. Hatton could have done a nice little distracting job there. Fifty or a hundred quid a lorry depending on the load.'

'In that case, why does McCloy kill the goose that lays the golden eggs?'

'Because Hatton gets scared or fed-up and threatens to rat on him. He may even have tried blackmail.'

'I shouldn't be a bit surprised,' said Burden, spreading butter on his roll. The butter was almost liquid. Like the rest of humanity, he reflected, the Carousel staff were disappointingly inconsistent.

CHAPTER FIVE

'But my daughter wasn't in the car.'

Seldom had Sergeant Camb felt so sorry for anyone as he did for this woman who lay against the piled pillows. His heart ached for her. And yet she was in one of the nicest private rooms in the hospital; she had a telephone and a television; her nightgown was a silly frou-frou of frills and spilling lace and on her thin fingers the rings — diamonds and sapphires in platinum — rattled as she clasped and unclasped the sheet.

It's true what they say, money can't buy happiness, thought the simple sergeant. He had noticed there were no flowers in the room and only one 'get well' card on the table by the chair where the policewoman sat. From her sister, he supposed. She hadn't anyone else now, not a soul in the world. Her husband was dead and her daughter . . .

'I'm very very sorry, Mrs Fanshawe,' he said 'but your daughter *was* in the car. She was travelling back to London with you and your husband.'

'They didn't suffer,' put in the young policewoman quickly. 'They can't have felt a thing.'

Mrs Fanshawe touched her forehead where the dyed hair showed half an inch of white at the roots. 'My head,' she said. 'My head aches. I can't remember things, not details. Everything's so vague.'

'Don't you worry,' said Camb heartily. 'You'll find you'll get your memory back in time. You're going to get quite well, you know.' For what? For widowhood, for childlessness?

'Your sister's been able to supply us with most of the details we need.'

They had been close, Mrs Fanshawe and Mrs Browne, and there wasn't much about the Fanshawes Mrs Browne hadn't known. From her they had learned that Jerome Fanshawe had a bungalow at Eastover between Eastbourne and Seaford and that he and his wife and daughter had driven down there for a week's holiday on May 17th. The daughter Nora had left her

post as an English teacher in a German school before Easter.
She was between jobs, at a loose end, Camb had gathered,
otherwise nothing would have induced her to accompany her
parents. But she had accompanied them. Mrs Browne had been
at the Mayfair flat and seen them all off together.

They had left Eastover days earlier than had been expected. Mrs Browne couldn't account for that, unless it had
been because of the wet weather. Perhaps no one would ever
know the reason, for Jerome Fanshawe's Jaguar had skidded,
crashed and caught fire five miles from the hospital where the
sole survivor now lay.

'I won't bother you for long,' Camb said gently. 'Perhaps
you can't remember much about the crash. Do you think you
could try and tell me what you do remember?'

Dorothy Fanshawe had forgotten who these kind though tiresome people were, just as she had again forgotten where she
was. Her sister had been to see her and made her very tired and
various strangers had moved her and pummelled her in a
familiar manner that made her angry. Then someone had told
her that Jerome was dead and had waited for her to cry. Mrs
Fanshawe had twisted her rings — they were a great comfort to
her, those rings — and said:

'Then it's all mine now, mine and Nora's.'

They thought she was wandering and they went away. She
was glad to see the back of them with their interfering ways and
their lack of respect. There was only one person she wanted to
see and that was why she stared so searchingly into the young
pretty face of the policewoman. But she had been in a coma,
she wasn't mad. She knew very well this wasn't the right face.
'Am I in London?' she asked clearly and briskly.

'No, Mrs Fanshawe,' said the sergeant, thinking how
quavering and weak her voice was. 'You're in Stowerton Royal
Infirmary, Stowerton in Sussex.'

'You seem very well-informed,' said Mrs Fanshawe, pleased
because she had succeeded so well in pulling herself together.
'Perhaps you can tell me why my daughter doesn't come to see
me? Haven't they told her I'm here? Nora would want to know.
She'd come home.'

'Oh, Mrs Fanshawe . . .' The policewoman sounded very wretched, almost distraught, and catching her eye, Sergeant Camb gave her a sharp reproving glance. Better leave it, the look said. Maybe it's more merciful this way. Let her learn about it by degrees. The mind has its own way of softening blows, he thought sententiously.

'Now back to the — er, accident,' he said. 'Just try and see if you can tell me what happened when you left Eastover. It was getting dark and there wasn't much traffic on the road, it being a Monday. It had been raining and the road was wet. Now, Mrs Fanshawe?'

'My husband was driving,' she began and she wondered why the man's face wore such a sloppy expression. Perhaps he had noticed her rings. She slid them up and down her fingers, suddenly remembering that the five of them were worth nearly twenty thousand pounds. 'Jerome was driving . . .' What a silly name it was. Like *Three Men in a Boat*. That made her giggle, although the sound came out like a harsh cackle. 'I sat beside him, of course, and I was knitting. I must have been knitting. I always do when Jerome drives. He drives so fast,' she said querulously. 'Much too fast and he never takes any notice when I tell him to go slower, so I do my knitting. To keep my mind off it, you know.'

Mean and selfish Jerome was. A man of fifty-five hadn't any business to drive like a crazy teenager. She had told him that, but he had ignored her like he ignored everything else she ever said. Still, she was used to being ignored. Nora never took any notice of what she said either. When she came to think of it, the only thing she and Jerome had ever agreed about was what a difficult, trying and utterly maddening creature Nora was. It was exactly like her to go away and not get in touch with her parents. Jerome would have something to say about that . . . Then there swam pleasantly into her muddled mind the recollection that Jerome would never have anything to say about anything again, never drive at eighty-five or pick on Nora or do those other terrible and humiliating things. Tonight, when she felt better, she would write to Nora and tell her her father was dead. With Jerome out of the way and all that money for themselves, she felt they would have a much happier relationship . . .

'I was knitting a jumper for Nora,' she said. What a marvellous constitution she must have to remember that after all she'd been through! 'Not that she deserved it, the naughty girl.' Now, why had she said that? Nora had been naughty, much naughtier than ever before, but for the life of her Dorothy Fanshawe couldn't remember of what the naughtiness had consisted. She wished the policeman or whoever he was would wipe that mawkish sheeplike expression off his face. There was no need for anyone to feel sorry for her, Dorothy Fanshawe, of Astbury Mews, Upper Grosvenor Street, W.I. She was a merry widow now, rich in her own right, soon to be well again, the mother of a good-looking talented only daughter. 'I don't remember what we talked about,' she said 'my *late* husband and I. Nothing, probably. The road was wet and I kept telling him to go slower.'

'Your daughter was in the back seat, Mrs Fanshawe?'

Oh! really, how absurd the man was! 'Nora was *not* in the car. I keep telling you. Nora went back to Germany. No doubt she is in Germany now.'

To the sergeant the jerky bumbling words sounded like the raving of a madwoman. In spite of what the doctors said, it seemed to him probable that the accident had irremediably damaged her brain. He didn't take it upon himself to enlighten her further. God knew what harm he might do! Sooner or later, if she ever got her reason back, she would realise that her daughter had resigned from this German job six weeks before the accident, and she hadn't breathed a word to her aunt or her friends about the possibility of her returning to Europe. The girl's body had been identified by her aunt, Mrs Browne. She was dead and buried.

'I expect she is,' he said soothingly. 'No doubt she is. What made your husband swerve, Mrs Fanshawe?'

'I was knitting.'

'Did you hit something, did a tyre burst?'

'I told you, I didn't look. I was knitting.'

'Did your husband cry out, say anything?'

'I think he said "My God",' said Mrs Fanshawe. She couldn't really remember anything, only that she had been knitting and then she had woken up in this bed with her nosy, bossy sister sitting beside her. But Jerome was always saying 'My God' or even 'My Christ'. He had a limited vocabulary and she had stopped telling him not to be blasphemous twenty years ago. 'I don't remember anything else,' she said. That was all they were going to get out of her. She wasn't going to waste her strength. She needed it for the letter she was going to write in a minute to Nora.

Camb looked compassionately at the quivering febrile mouth and the long unfiled nails that played with those rings. Mrs Fanshawe had told him nothing. Perhaps he ought to have realised it was too soon, or his superiors ought to have realised. They would have to go now anyway. The young lady doctor had said ten minutes, but they must have been here twenty. Here was the nurse coming now. Funny uniforms they wear these days, he thought, eyeing the girl's navy-blue nylon overall and a hat like a white forage cap. Poor Mrs Fanshawe was staring at her desperately. No wonder, exhausted and broken-hearted as she was.

No, it wasn't Nora. Just for a split second Mrs Fanshawe had thought it was. But Nora never wore an overall, she despised housework — and this girl was wearing an overall, not the rather smart dress for which Mrs Fanshawe had first taken it. She had a cap on her head too. Was it possible that her sister had taken on a new maid for the Fanshawes' flat and not said anything about it? More than possible, considering how inter-fering her sister was. Interfering but irresponsible. A responsible person would have sent for Nora by now.

'What's your name?' Mrs Fanshawe said sharply.

'Rose, Mrs Fanshawe. Nurse Rose. I've come to make you more comfy and bring you your tea. You could drink a nice cup of tea, couldn't you? I'm afraid you'll have to run along now Sergeant. I can't allow my patient any setbacks, you know.'

Very talkative, thought Mrs Fanshawe. Takes a lot upon herself. She tried to sit up.

'Rose,' she said, 'I want to write a letter to my daughter, my daughter in Germany. Will you fetch me writing paper and a pen, please?'

She doesn't know, Camb thought, she's new. Nobody's told

her. Just as well. He intercepted the policewoman's glance and crushed it with a frown.

'We *are* getting better, aren't we?' said the nurse skittishly. 'Writing letters! Well, I don't know, I'm sure. I'm certain you haven't got any paper of your own. I'll tell you what I'll do, I'll just pop down the corridor and borrow some from Mrs Goodwin in number four. Then I'll post your letter when I go off duty, shall I?'

'That will be very kind of you,' said Mrs Fanshawe austerely. 'Then you can bring the tea.'

A pert girl and probably untrainable, she thought. Time would show. At any rate, Jerome wouldn't be there to upset this one, catch her in corners and smack her bottom like he had the Danish *au pair*. Jerome was dead. She'd always said he'd kill himself driving like that and now he had. Why hadn't he killed her too? What good fortune had decreed that she be saved and be sitting here in her own bed in her own flat?

But it wasn't her own bed and her own flat. Very carefully Mrs Fanshawe marshalled her thoughts and her memories. Jerome was dead, Nora was in Germany and she was in Something-or-other Royal Infirmary. A hospital. Very thoughtful of someone to have engaged a maid for her in hospital.

Unless this Rose was a nurse. Of course, she must be a nurse. What a fool I am, thought Mrs Fanshawe. I feel exactly as if I were having a very prolonged dream but every time I come out of it I'm so tired I fall back into it again.

The inaccurate information given by all these busybodies didn't help at all. People were so inefficient these days. First her sister had forgotten to inform Nora, then this policeman said Nora had been with her and Jerome in the Jaguar. They must all think she was out of her mind. As if a mother didn't know where her own daughter was! Why, she even remembered Nora's address.

Goethestrasse 14, Köln, West Germany. Mrs Fanshawe was very proud of the way she wrote Köln like that instead of Cologne. What reserves of strength and intellect she must have to remember details like that! And after all she'd been through. Presently the nurse came back with the paper.

'Thank you, Nurse,' said Mrs Fanshawe to show what a

fine grasp of things she had. She tried to hold the pen, but it zigzagged all over the paper like that Planchette thing her father had used long ago.

'Why not let me write it for you?' said Nurse Rose.

'Perhaps it would be better. I'll dictate. Shall I begin?'

Nurse Rose had to exercise all her powers of concentration to sort out from the mumblings and digressions exactly what Mrs Fanshawe wanted to say. But she was a kind-hearted girl and, besides, it always paid to be attentive to patients in the private wing. Last year when one of them had left after only a fortnight she had given Nurse Rose a travelling clock and a nearly full bottle of *Rochas' Femme*.

' "Dearest Nora," ' she read aloud. ' "I am almost well again and think you should come and see me. Poor Daddy would have wished it. I expect auntie has told you everything and you have been too busy to come, but please come now. We will let bygones be bygones. Love from Mummy." That all right, Mrs Fanshawe? I've got some stamps, enough to make up to ninepence. I think I'll pop it in the post now when I go for my tea.'

Coming back from the pillar box at the end of Charteris Road, Nurse Rose met the Private Wing sister.

'I've just been posting a letter for poor Mrs Fanshawe, Sister,' she said virtuously. 'I like to do what I can, you know. Anything to cheer them up. She was so keen to get a letter to her daughter off tonight.'

'Her daughter's dead.'

'Oh, Sister, you don't mean it! Oh God, how dreadful! I never dreamt, I never guessed . . . Ooh, Sister!'

'You'd better get back on duty, Nurse, and do try not to be so impulsive.'

CHAPTER SIX

The child who opened the door to him was the one that had been out in the fields with his father. He was a boy of about seven, big for his age, aggressive looking and with food adhering to his face in greasy red and brown streaks.

'Who is it, Dominic?' came a voice from the sleazy depths of this small and totally inadequate council house.

'A man,' said Dominic simply.

'What does he want?'

To put an end to all this pointless colloquy, Wexford stepped into the hall, then the living room. Three more children were watching athletics on television. The remains of lunch were still on the stained crumb-scattered tablecloth and a woman sat at the table feeding a baby from a bottle. She might have been any age between thirty and sixty and Wexford set the lower limit so low only because of her young children. Her hair was thin and fair and long, caught back with an elastic band, and her face was thin and long too, wizened and pinched. A weariness that was as much chronic boredom as physical tiredness seemed the most dominant thing about her. It was the sordid exhaustion of poverty, of overwork, of perpetual near-incarceration, of eternal nagging demands, and to be left alone just to sit for perhaps only five minutes in unthinking apathy was her sole remaining desire. To this end she never wasted a word or a gesture and when she saw Wexford she neither greeted him nor even lifted her head, but said to one of her little girls:

'Go and fetch your dad, Samantha.'

Samantha jerked a thick black cat off her lap and trailed listlessly via the kitchen to the back garden. A middle-class woman, a woman with more money and fewer children, might have apologised for the squalor and the smell of a hundred stale meals. Mrs Cullam didn't even look at him and when he asked her at what time her husband had come home on Friday night she said laconically, 'Quarter past eleven.'

'How can you be so sure of the time?'

'It was a quarter past eleven.' Mrs Cullam put the baby on the table among the crumbs, removing its napkin which she dropped on the floor, and said in the same low economical tone, 'Get me another nappie, Georgina.' A strong smell of ammonia fought with the cabbage. The baby, which was female, began to cry. Mrs Cullam lit a cigarette and stood against the table, her hands hanging by her sides, the cigarette dangling from her mouth. Georgina came back with a grey rag, sat down and watched her brother poke his fingers in the cat's ears. 'Leave the cat alone, Barnabus,' said Mrs Cullam.

Her husband came in, drying his hands on a tea cloth, the black dog cowering at his heels. He nodded to Wexford and then he turned off the television.

'Get up, Samantha, and let the gentleman sit down.' The child took no notice and made no sound when her father slapped one arm and yanked her up by the other. He viewed the room helplessly, paying particular attention to the discarded napkin, but there was no disgust on his face, only vaguely resentful acceptance.

Wexford didn't take the vacant seat and something in his expression must have told Cullam he wanted privacy, for he said to his wife, 'Can't you get them kids out of here?'

Mrs Cullam shrugged and the ash from her cigarette fell into a plate of congealing gravy. She hoisted the baby on to her hip and dragging a chair close up to the television set, sat down and stared at the blank screen. 'Leave the cat alone, I said,' she remarked without heat.

'What were you wanting?' Cullam asked.

'We'll go into your kitchen, if you don't mind, Mr Cullam.'

'It's in a right old mess.'

'Never mind.'

Mrs Cullam made no comment. She switched on the television without looking up. Two of the children began to fight in the depths of their armchair. Wexford followed their father into the kitchen. There was nowhere to sit so, pushing aside the handles of four encrusted saucepans, he leant against the gas cooker.

'I only want to know who McCloy is,' he said mildly.

Cullam gave him a look of not altogether comfortable cunning. 'How d'you know about McCloy, anyway?'

'Come on now, you know I can't tell you that.' The children were screaming now above the sound of the racy athletics commentary. Wexford closed the door and he heard Mrs Cullam say, 'Leave the bleeding cat alone, Barnabus.' She had wasted a word. 'You know who he is,' Wexford said. 'Now you can tell me.'

'I don't know. Honest I don't.'

'You don't know who he is, but last night in the pub you asked Mr Hatton if he'd been seeing much of McCloy lately. You wouldn't touch McCloy because you like to sleep quiet in your bed.'

'I tell you, I don't know who he is and I never saw him.'

Wexford removed his elbow from its dangerous proximity to a half-full plate of cold chips. 'You didn't like Mr Hatton very much, did you? You wouldn't walk home with him, though he was going your way. So you went on ahead and maybe you hung about a bit under those trees.' Pursuing the line, he watched Cullam's beefy face begin to lose colour. 'I reckon you must have done, Cullam. A strong young fellow like you doesn't take thirty-five minutes to get here from the Kingsbrook bridge.'

In a low resentful voice, Cullam said, 'I was sick. I was nearly home and I come over queer. I'm not used to scotch and I went into the gents by the station to be sick.'

'Let me congratulate you on your powers of recovery. You were fit enough to be out on a country walk at seven-thirty this morning. Or were you just popping back to see you'd left Hatton neat and tidy? I want to see the clothes you wore last night.'

'They're out on the line.'

Wexford looked at him, his eyebrows almost vanishing into the vestiges of his hair, and the implications in that look were unmistakable. Cullam fidgeted, he moved to the crock-filled sink, leaning on it compressing his lips.

'I washed them,' he said. 'Pullover and trousers and a shirt. They was — well, they were in a bit of a state.' He shifted his feet.

'Charming,' Wexford said unkindly. '*You* washed them?

What d'you have a wife for?' For the first time he noticed the washing machine, a big gleaming automatic affair, and the only object in that kitchen that was not stained or chipped or coated with clotted food drips. He opened the back door and eyed the sagging clothesline from which the three garments Cullam had named hung between a row of napkins. 'The blessings of modern mechanisation,' he said. 'Very nice too. I often remark these days how the roles of the sexes have been reversed.' His voice became deceptively friendly and Cullam licked his thick lips. 'A man can be dead tired after a week's work but he can still give his wife a helping hand. One touch of a button and the family wash comes out whiter than white. In fact, a gadget like that turns chores into a pleasure, you might say. Men are all little boys at heart, when all's said and done, and it's not only women that like to have these little play-things about to make a break in the daily round. Besides, they cost so much, you might as well get some fun out of them. Don't tell me that little toy cost you less than a hundred and twenty, Cullam.'

'A hundred and twenty-five,' said Cullam with modest pride. He was quite disarmed and, advancing upon the machine, he opened the gleaming porthole. 'You set your programme . . .' A last uneasy look at the chief inspector told him his visitor was genuinely interested, paying no more than a routine call. 'Put in your powder,' he said. 'and Bob's your uncle.'

'I knew a fellow,' Wexford lied ruminatively, 'a lorry driver like yourself. Big family too and we all know what inroads a big family makes. He got in bad company, I'm sorry to say. His wife kept on at him, you see, wanting more gear about the house. He'd already turned a blind eye when a couple of his lorries got hijacked. Well, you can't call it a crime, can you, looking the other way in a cafe when somebody's nicking your vehicle from a layby?' Cullam closed the porthole, keeping his head turned. 'They paid well, this bad company. Mind you, this fellow jibbed a bit when they offered him two hundred to knock off a bloke who wouldn't play along with them, but not for long. He reckoned he'd a right to nice things the same as this bad company he'd got in with. And why not? We're all equal these days. Share and share alike, this fellow said. So he hung about in a lonely spot one night, just where the other fellow was due to pass by and — well, Bob's your uncle, as you so succinctly put it. He's doing twelve years, as a matter of fact.'

Cullam looked at him, truculently disillusioned.

'I saved up my overtime for that washer,' he said.

'Sure it wasn't McCloy's little dropsy for services rendered? Isn't a man's life worth a hundred and twenty nicker, Cullam? There's a sump on that machine of yours, you know. I can't help asking myself if there's blood and hair and brains in that sump, you know. Oh, you needn't look like that. We could find it. We can take that machine apart this afternoon, and your drains. They're a funny council, Sewingbury. I knew a family — six children in that case there were — they got evicted neck and crop just because they cracked a drainpipe. Vandalism, the council called it. We'll get your drains up, Cullam, but we're busy right now. I don't reckon we could find the labour to get them put back again.'

'You bastard,' said Cullam.

'I didn't hear that. My hearing's not what it was, but I haven't got one foot in the grave. I'd like to sit down, though. You can take that rubbish off that chair and wipe it, will you?'

Cullam sat on his washing machine, his long legs dangling. Behind the closed door the programme had changed from athletics to wrestling and once more the baby had begun to cry.

'I told you,' said its father, 'I don't know who McCloy is and I don't. I just said that to Charlie to needle him. Always bragging and boasting, he got on my wick.'

Wexford didn't have to absorb any more of the squalor to see what Cullam meant. This house was the very embodiment of sleazy noisy discomfort. It was a discomfort which would have brief pause only while its inhabitants slept and it extended from the top to the lowest level. The man and his wife were weighed down by almost every burden known to the philoprogenitive, ill-paid artisan; their children were miserable, badly brought up and perhaps ill-treated; their home overcrowded, even their animals wretchedly tormented. The parents had neither the character nor the love to make coping and organisation tenable. He remembered Charlie Hatton's brand-new flat, the pretty young wife with her smart clothes. These two men did the same sort of job. Or did they?

'If I tell you how it was,' Cullam said, 'you won't believe me.'

'Maybe not, try me.'

Cullam put his elbows on his knees and leant forward.

'It was in a café,' he said. 'One of them places where they have rooms for drivers to kip down for the night. Up on the A.1 between Stamford and Grantham. I was coming up to my eleven hours — we're not supposed to drive for more than eleven hours — and I went in and there was Charlie Hatton. I'd seen his lorry in the lay-by. We had a bite to eat and got talking.'

'What load do you carry?'

'Tyres, rubber tyres. While we was having our meal I looked out of the window and there was a fellow there — in the lay-by — sitting in a black car. I don't know why, but I didn't much like the look of him. I said so to Charlie, but all he said was I was like an old woman. He was always saying that to folks. Then he got me and two more drivers to go into his room for a hand of pontoon. He said it was quieter in there, but I couldn't see the lay-by from his room and after a bit I went outside. The fellow in the car was still there.'

'Did you take the number? Could you describe him?'

'I don't know.' Cullam gave him a shifty look. 'I never took the number. I sat in the cab for half an hour and then this fellow went off. Charlie'd said he wanted to phone Lilian and when I come back over the road he was in the phone box. I wanted a light for my fag — I'd run out of matches — so I opened the door of the box and just asked Charlie for a light. Well, I don't reckon he'd heard me coming. "Tell Mr McCloy it's no dice," I heard him say and it was then I said had he got a match? He jumped out of his skin like he'd been stung. "What the hell are you up to," he shouts at me, "interfering with my private phone calls?" He was as white as a sheet.'

'You connected this call with the man in the car?'

'I reckon I did,' Cullam said. 'I did afterwards when I thought about it. My mind went back a couple of months to when Charlie'd asked me if I'd like to make a bit on the side. I wasn't interested and that was all there was. But I never forgot the name McCloy and when Charlie got so cocky in the pub I thought I'd needle him a bit. That's all.'

'When was the café incident, Cullam?'

'Come again?'

'When did you overhear Hatton's phone conversation?'

'Way back in the winter. January, I reckon. Not long after Charlie had his lorry pinched and got hit on the head.'

'All right. That'll do for now, but I may want to talk to you again.'

Wexford went back through the Cullams' living room. The children had disappeared. Mrs Cullam still sat in front of the television, the baby asleep now in her lap, the dog lying across her slippered feet. She moved her head as he crossed the room and for a moment he thought she was going to speak to him. Then he saw that the movement was a mere craning of the neck because for an instant he had obstructed her view of the screen.

Dominic, Barnabas, Samantha and Georgina were sitting on the kerb poking sticks through the drain cover. Wexford wasn't inclined to be sentimental over the Cullams but he couldn't help being faintly touched that they who were poor in everything had been affluent, extravagant and imaginative in one respect. If they never gave their children another thing, they had at least endowed them with names usually reserved to the upper classes.

Dominic, whose face was still coated with food, looked up truculently as he passed and Wexford said, because he couldn't resist it:

'What's the baby called?'

'Jane,' said Dominic simply and without surprise.

When Wexford got home for his tea Clytemnestra wagged her darning-wool tail at him but she didn't get out of his chair. Wexford scowled at her.

'Where's Sheila?' he asked his wife.

'Dentist's.'

'She never said anything about toothache.'

'You don't go to the dentist's because you've got toothache any more. You go for a check-up. She's having that molar of hers crowned.'

'So I suppose she won't feel up to taking that creature out

in the morning. Well, she needn't put it on me. I've got enough on my plate.'

But Sheila danced in gaily at six o'clock and smiled at her father to show off the triumph of orthodontics.

'There, isn't that great?' To satisfy her Wexford peered into the perfect mouth. 'That filling was getting a bit of a drag,' she said. 'Very shy-making for close-ups. An actress has to think about these things.'

'I bet Bernhardt never bothered about her teeth,' said Wexford to annoy her.

Sheila opened her eyes wide and fixed her father with a precisely constructed look of wistful adoration. 'Did you often see Bernhardt when you were a young man, Pop?' she asked.

Wexford's reply was an ill-tempered snort. He pushed a cup of tea to his daughter who rejected it in favour of cold milk. This she sipped slowly, very conscious of the picture she made in her cream linen dress, her pale hair slightly but attractively disordered, Roman sandal thongs binding her long legs to the knee. Wexford wondered what life held for her. Would she succeed and the future be a succession of triumphs, starring parts, world tours, fame, the increasing terror of growing old? Or would she marry some young idiot like this Sebastian and forget all her aspirations in the possession of two children and a semi? Because he was a father and no longer young he confessed to himself that he would prefer the latter. He wanted her to be safe. Nothing on earth would have made him tell her so.

No such thoughts troubled her, he fancied. Living in the moment, she drank her milk and began to prattle on about her visit to the dentist.

'If I ever settle down . . .' Sheila said this in much the same tone of incredulity as she might have said, 'If I ever die.' 'If I ever settle down, I wouldn't mind a house like his. Not in Kingsmarkham of course. Stratford might be nice or the Cotswolds near Stratford.'

'Within commuting distance,' Wexford put in slyly.

His daughter ignored him. 'One of those black and white houses it is. Terribly ancient and full of atmosphere. Of course, the surgery part's all modern. New copies of *Nova* and *Elle*. I thought that progressive.'

'Thoughtful too,' said Wexford, 'what with everyone in Kingsmarkham being bi-lingual.'

'Your generation just wasn't educated, Pop, but I can tell you I hardly know *anyone* who doesn't read French. Anyway, the old fuddy-duddies can look at the antiques.' Sheila put her glass down and tossed her head. 'Gorgeous paintings on the walls, and some marvellous glass sculpture.'

Sounds like the police station, Wexford thought. 'And where is this shrine of culture?' he said aloud.

'Ploughman's Lane.'

'He wouldn't be called Vigo would he?'

'Mm-hm, he would.' Sheila sat on the sofa and began painting shiny black lines on her eyelids. 'It's about time you and Mummy stopped going to that dreary old Richardson in the High Street and switched to Mr Vigo.' The most difficult feat of her artistry completed, she started to stroke her lashes with a mascara wand. 'Mr Vigo is an absolute dream. One of those fair-haired characters with a craggy face. Madly sexy.' Wexford winced and hoped she hadn't seen. His daughters were still little girls to him. Who the hell did this craggy fair fellow think he was, projecting his dreamy sexiness at his little girl? 'Of course he's not *young*,' said Sheila serenely.

'All of thirty-five, I daresay. One foot in the grave and the other on a bar of soap.'

'About thirty-five,' said Sheila seriously. She held her eyelashes up with two fingers to curl them. 'He's got a baby of six months and — something rather tragic. His older child's a mongol. Ghastly, isn't it? It's eight now and Mr Vigo hasn't seen it for years. He and his wife tried and tried to have another one and they did, but it took them all those years. Of course he worships the baby.'

'How do you know all this?' Wexford asked. She was a detective's daughter all right. 'I thought you went to get your tooth done, not do a survey.'

'Oh, we had a long talk,' Sheila said airily. 'I don't suppose you can understand, but I'm interested in human nature. If I'm going to be a real actress I'll have to know what makes people tick. I'm getting quite good at summing people up.'

'Bully for you,' said her father sourly. 'I've been trying

for forty years and the margin of error's still about eighty per cent.'

Shelia looked at herself in her handbag mirror. 'Mr Vigo's got a very smooth sophisticated manner. Cool, if you know what I mean. I sometimes think dentists have a very interesting relationship with their patients. They've got to be nice, have the right psychological approach, otherwise you'd never go back to them again, would you? It's such an intimate thing. I mean, can you think of any other situation, Pop, when a man gets so close to a woman except when he's actually making love to her?'

'I sincerely hope nothing like that happened.'

'Oh, Pop . . . I was just saying what it was *like*. I was making a sort of comparison.' Sheila giggled and twisted a strand of hair around one finger. 'Although, when I was going he did give me a sort of squeeze and said I'd got the loveliest mouth he'd ever seen.'

'My God!' said Wexford, getting up. 'If you don't mind what you say to your father, you might remember he's also a detective chief inspector.' He paused and then said, not realising the effect his words would have, 'I may go along and see this Vigo.'

'Oh, Pop!' Sheila wailed.

'Not because of your lovely mouth, my dear. In pursuance of an enquiry of my own.'

'Well, don't you dare . . .'

All this time Mrs Wexford had been placidly eating ginger biscuits, but now she looked up and said calmly:

'What a silly girl you are. I often think it's a blessing intelligence isn't necessary in the interpretive arts. If you've finished with your face you'd better take that dog out.'

At the word dog, Clytemnestra uncurled herself.

'All right,' said Sheila meekly.

CHAPTER SEVEN

They stood under the willow trees, looking at the river. Anyone who didn't know them might have taken them for a couple of businessmen out for a Sunday afternoon stroll.

But almost everyone in Kingsmarkham knew them and knew also by now that this was the spot where Charlie Hatton had been murdered.

'I said we'd have to talk to everyone in the darts club,' said Burden, stopping down at the water's edge, 'and I reckon we have. Funny, isn't it? Pertwee's the only one who could put up with Hatton for a moment, but no one's willing to come out with it. It's always the others who were daggers drawn with him. The one you're talking to is all tolerance and forbearance. The farthest he'll go is to admit a sort of resentment. Does a man do murder because a mate of his riles him in a pub or because he's got more money than he has?'

'He might if he was going to get some of the money,' said Wexford. 'A hundred pounds is a lot to a man like Cullam. We're going to have to watch Cullam, see if he does some big spending in the next few days. I'm not at all happy about the way he washed the clothes he was wearing on Friday night.'

Burden was advancing gingerly across the river, trying not to get his feet wet. He trod on the projecting stones which the water lapped without covering. Then he bent down and said, 'There's your weapon.'

From the bank Wexford followed the direction of his pointing finger. All but one of the stones was furred at their perimeters and partly on their surfaces with green weed. Burden was pointing to the only one that looked bare, as if until very recently it had lain with its exposed area embedded in the river's gravelly floor. He squatted precariously and lifted the stone in both hands. Then he eased himself to his feet and scrambled back to Wexford.

It was a big stone, not round, but elongated and shaped rather like a mandolin. The side which had lain on the river bed was green and moss-grown and there was nothing about it except for its shape and its anomalous position in the water to show that it might have been used as a lethal weapon. Wexford grasped it in both his hands, raised it high and brought it down hard to meet the empty air. Hatton had been walking along in the dark and someone had waited for him among the willows and the brambles, the stone ready for use. Full of whisky, his thoughts fuddled and far away, Hatton had given warning of his approach. He had been whistling and probably not bothering to tread softly. The stone had been raised high just as Wexford was raising it now but brought down that time on the back of Hatton's skull. Once, twice, more than that? As many times as it took to kill. Then Hatton had rolled into the water. His killer had rifled his wallet before casting the stone into the stream.

Wexford thought all these things and he knew Burden was following his thoughts, matching them, so he didn't bother to say anything. He dropped the stone and it rolled a little before falling into the water with a soft plop.

Across the meadows he could see the flats of the council estate, the sun striking their plate-glass windows and making them blaze as if the whole place was on fire.

'Since we've come so far,' he said, 'we may as well have another chat with Mrs Hatton.'

Her mother was with her and three other people. Jack Pertwee sat on the smart checked tweed sofa holding the hand of a girl with a monumental pile of black hair and eyelashes like shoe brushes. Mrs Hatton and her mother were both in black, smart unseasonable black relieved with a great deal of showy costume jewellery. The widow's suit looked brand-new and Wexford couldn't help wondering if she had actually been out the previous afternoon to buy it. She wore a white blouse with an ostentatious frilly jabot and a big paste spray on one lapel. Her stockings were dark and her shoes, though also apparently new, the outdated stiletto-heeled pointed kind of gleaming black patent. She looked as if she were about to set off for a provincial cocktail party, an office party of female executives.

At first Wexford felt a curious distaste and then he thought about the dead man and what he knew of him. This was the way Charlie Hatton would have liked his widow to look, brave, defiant, bedizened. The last thing a cocky little man like Hatton would want was a kind of spiritual suttee.

He surveyed the rest of the company. Plainly they had interrupted a mourning tea party. The girl on the sofa must be the bride whose nuptials Hatton's death had deferred. And the other man?

'My brother, Mr Bardsley,' said Mrs Hatton. 'Him and Mum came to keep me company. This gentleman is Mr Pertwee.'

'We've met,' said Wexford graciously.

'And Miss Thompson,' said Mrs Hatton. She spoke in a low dutiful voice. Her eyes were swollen under the thick green and black make-up. 'They were all very fond of Charlie. Would you like a cup of tea? You can if you want. You're welcome.'

'We won't, thanks, Mrs Hatton.'

'Well, sit down then, there's plenty of room.' She said it proudly, indicating the several empty chairs. They were good chairs, upholstered and cared for, not the uncomfortable dining seats with hard backs a less affluent hostess would be obliged to offer latecomers. Looking at the branched hanging lamp of teak and smoky glass, the velvet curtains and the big colour television set, Wexford decided that Hatton had done his wife proud. Cullam and he were both lorry drivers, both lived in council accommodation, but that was all they had in common. He glanced at Bardsley, the brother, a fair rabbity man, like his sister but less well-favoured, and he observed his suit. It was very likely his best suit — today of all days he would surely wear his best suit — but it was a cheap off-the-peg affair.

'Please forgive me, Mrs Hatton, if I ask you a few routine questions,' he said. She gave him a pleased earnest nod. 'You and Mr Hatton were in business together, I understand, Mr Bardsley?'

'That's right.'

'Was it a full partnership?'

Bardsley put his teacup down and said in a melancholy voice, 'I was thinking of taking him into partnership, but business hasn't been that good lately. As it was, he just worked for me.'

'Would you mind telling me what wages you paid him?'

'Well, I don't know . . . I don't rightly like to.'

'Of course he don't,' Jack Pertwee suddenly interrupted belligerently. 'What's it got to do with what happened on Friday?'

'That's right, Jack,' murmured the girl and she squeezed his hand.

'You can see Charlie did all right for himself. You've only got to look around you.'

'Don't make trouble, Jack," Mrs Hatton said with that peculiar intense control of hers. 'The officers are only doing what they have to.' She fingered her brooch uneasily. 'Charlie usually brought home a bit over twenty pounds a week. That's right, isn't it, Jim?'

Jim Bardsley looked unhappy about it and his voice became aggressive. 'I've been lucky to make that much myself lately,' he said. 'Charlie was one of the sort that make a little go a long way. I reckon he was careful.'

Marilyn Thompson tossed her head and a lock of hair drifted from the elaborate structure. 'He wasn't mean, anyway,' she flared, 'if that's what you mean by careful. There's not many men who aren't even relations that'd give someone a record player for a wedding present.'

'I never said he was mean, Marilyn.'

'It makes me sick. What you want to do is find who killed him.' The girl's hands trembled and she clenched them. 'Give us a cig, Jack.' Her hands enclosed Pertwee's wrist as he held the lighter and they were no more steady than his. 'You lot,' she muttered, 'you lot don't reckon nothing to a working man. If he hasn't got a nice home you call him a layabout.' She glared at Wexford, pushing back her hair. 'And if he's got things like your class take for granted you jump right on him, say he must have nicked them. Class, class, class,' she said, tears trembling on the brush-bristle lashes. 'That's all you think about.'

'Wait till the revolution comes,' said Bardsley nastily.

'Oh, shut up the pair of you,' Mrs Hatton said shrilly. She turned to Wexford, her controlled dignity returning. 'My husband did overtime,' she said, 'and he had his side lines.'

Side lines, Wexford thought. He got a little overtime and he made it go a long way. The man had colour television, false teeth worth two hundred pounds; he gave his friend a record player for a wedding present. Wexford had seen that glass and teak lamp in a Kingsmarkham shop and noted it had been priced at twenty-five pounds, one and a quarter times Hatton's weekly wage. When he was killed he had had a hundred pounds on him.

'If he's got things like your class take for granted,' the girl had said, 'you say he must have nicked them.' Curious, really, Wexford reflected, watching her huddled now in the crook of Pertwee's arm. Of course she was very young, probably got a Communist shop steward for a father, and doubtless went about sneering at people better-educated and better-spoken than herself. It was an aggressive type that had even reached Kingsmarkham, a type that talked pacifism and the rights of man and brotherly love without the energy or courage to do anything that might bring these desirable conditions nearer.

And yet he had said nothing to provoke her outburst. Neither for that matter had Bardsley beyond hinting that Hatton had been prudent. Had she risen to this intangible slight bait because she knew Hatton's wealth had been dishonestly come by? If she knew it, green and uncouth as she was, Pertwee would know it also. Everyone in this room but Burden and himself might know it. Not for the first time he reflected on the power of grief. It is the perfect unassailable defence. Pertwee had already employed it the previous morning effectively to terminate interrogation. Mrs Hatton, even more expertly, kept it under a piteous control that only a brute would have the brashness to disregard. She was moving about the room now, balancing painfully but stoically on her high heels, taking empty cups and plates from each of her guests with a gentle murmur for every one of them. Wexford took in the looks that passed to her from each of her visitors, her mother's merely solicitous, Pertwee's indicative of deep affection, Bardsley's shifty, while the thwarted bride leaned forward, stuck out her chin and nodded her utter committed partisanship.

'Did your husband have a bank account, Mrs Hatton?' Burden asked as she passed his chair.

The sun was full on her face, showing every stroke and grain of make-up, but at the same time driving expression from it. She nodded, 'At the Midland,' she said.

'I'd like to see his paying-in book.'

'What for?'

The truculent harsh voice was Pertwee's. Wexford ignored him and followed the widow to the sideboard from a drawer of which she took a long cream-coloured book. He handed it to Burden and said, apparently inconsequentially:

'When did your husband get his false teeth, Mrs Hatton?'

Pertwee's muttered 'Bloody nosy-parker' made her flinch a little and throw a desperate glance over her shoulder. 'He'd always had them. Had them since he was twenty,' she said.

'This present set?'

'Oh, no. They were new. He went to Mr Vigo for them about a month back.'

Nodding, Wexford eyed the paying-in book over Burden's shoulder and what he saw astonished him far more than any of Hatton's prodigality. Some three-quarters of all the slips in the book had been torn out and with the exception of three, all the stubs had been torn too.

On the most recent remaining stub the date was April and on that occasion Hatton had paid into his bank account the modest sum of five and fourpence.

'Fourth dividend on the pools that was,' Mrs Hatton said with a miserable gulp.

The other two stubs were filled in each with amounts of two pounds.

'Mrs Hatton,' he said, beckoning her into a corner. 'The purpose of these stubs in a paying-in book is for the holder to have a record of the amount of money he has deposited in his bank. Can you suggest to me why Mr Hatton tore them out? They must have been filled in at the bank either by Mr Hatton himself or else by the cashier who was attending to him.'

'It's a mystery to me. Charlie never talked about money to me. He always said . . .' She gulped again and a tear trickled through the make-up. 'He always said, "Don't worry your head about that. When we got married I promised I'd give you everything you want and so I will. You name it, you can have it." ' She bent her head and began to sob. 'He was one in a million was Charlie. He'd have got me the moon out of the sky if I'd wanted it.' The girl Marilyn got up and put her arms around her friend. 'Oh, Charlie, Charlie . . . !'

The drawer was open, Hatton's cheque book exposed. Wexford leafed through it and saw that Hatton had paid twenty-five pounds for the lamp on May 22nd. Thirty pounds had been paid to Lucrece Ltd., High Street, Kingsmarkham (his wife's wedding outfit?), and another thirty in the same week, the last week of May, to Excelsior Electrics, Stowerton (Pertwee's record player?).

Then came three blank stubs, lastly one filled in for fifty pounds cash. There was no stub for Vigo, the dentist. Hatton must have paid for his teeth in cash.

He put the books back in the drawer and stood waiting for Mrs Hatton to recover. Her mother and brother had departed to the kitchen from where Wexford could hear their muted whisperings and the funereally careful clink of cups.

The widow's eye make-up had transferred itself to Marilyn Thompson's handkerchief. 'I keep breaking down,' she said. 'I can't seem to stop myself.'

'Yeah, but just reckon what you've been through, love.'

'I don't know what I'd do without you two.'

Pertwee said nothing but his baleful pugnacious look was absurd in its intensity and Wexford was almost embarrassed. He said lightly, 'Does the name McCloy mean anything to you, Mr Pertwee?'

That it meant nothing, less than nothing, to Mrs Hatton he was sure at once. Of Pertwee and the girl he was less certain. The latter's lower lip stuck out and her eyes flickered. For an instant she was a primitive creature looking for a hole to hide in. Pertwee had reddened, possibly only with anger at Wexford's persistence. 'Sounds Irish,' was all he said.

'Doesn't it also sound familiar?'

'Not to me, I don't know any McCloy. Never heard of him.'

'Strange then that you should have discussed this Mr McCloy with your friends in the Dragon on Friday. Is he a local man?'

'I told you I'd never heard of him.' Pertwee bit his lip and looked down at his knees. Wexford watched him feel for the girl's hand, but she was occupied with Mrs Hatton, dabbing at her face and smoothing her hair. Forsaken, deserted, the hand came up to Pertwee's brow and pushed into the greasy black waves. 'Can't you leave us alone now?' he pleaded and Wexford felt impotently that once again the man was enclosing himself within the unimpregnable defence of grief. 'I never knew what went on on the lorries,' he said. 'I wasn't Charlie's only friend. He had hundreds of friends. Ask Jim Bardsley, ask Cullam.' Pertwee's eyes were glazed and dull. 'Let someone else do dirt on his memory.'

Jim Bardsley had an apron tied round his waist. He moved gingerly about the kitchen, putting away crockery, as if he were afraid his touch might damage or contaminate the pristine glory of its equipment. The Hatton flat and the Cullam house had one thing in common, an automatic washing machine. Mrs Hatton had plenty besides, mixers, electric tin-openers, a steam iron as well as the huge scarlet refrigerator and the cooker with eye-level grill.

'You transport this kind of stuff, don't you, Mr Bardsley?' Burden asked. 'I suppose Mr Hatton got it wholesale.'

'I daresay,' Bardsley said cagily.

'Irons, electric fires and so on, was that the load you lost when Mr Hatton's lorries were hi-jacked?' Bardsley nodded unhappily. 'Doubtless you were insured?'

'Not the second time, not in March when they knocked it off at Stamford. I had to stand the loss myself.' Bardsley untied his apron and hung up the tea cloth that, appropriately enough in this flat, was a large linen facsimile of a pound note. 'Set me back, I can tell you. I reckon poor old Charlie was glad I hadn't taken him into partnership. Mind you, they found the lorry both times. It wasn't damaged, just the stuff gone, that's all. That second time Charlie'd pulled into a lay-by and gone to sleep at the wheel. The villains didn't harm him, thank God. Just tied him up and put a gag in his mouth.'

'But he was injured on the previous occasion?'

'Had a bit of concussion,' Bardsley said. 'There wasn't any mark to show, bar a bit of a bruise.'

'Ever heard of the name McCloy, Mr Bardsley?'

'It doesn't ring a bell,' said Bardsley and Burden believed him. 'Mind you,' he added, 'I've seen my own stuff flogged off in the market here. Known it was mine but couldn't prove it. You know what them stallholders are, up to all the tricks.' He scratched his head. 'I was a bit too nosy that time and I haven't seen the stall here since.'

'If you do, Mr Bardsley, come straight to us. Don't argue about it, come straight to us.'

'O.K.,' said Bardsley, but without hope. Burden left him contemplating the printed tea cloth as if, were it possible to transmute it to paper, reduce its size and multiply it manifold, he would be a happy man.

'First of all,' said Wexford. 'I'd like to know exactly how much there is in the account.'

The bank manager became pedantic and precise. 'Exactly six hundred and nine pounds, four and sevenpence.'

'I take it that's a current account? He didn't have anything on deposit, did he?'

'Unfortunately, no. When Mr Hatton began paying large sums in I did attempt to persuade him to open one, the rate of interest being so desirable, you understand. Five per cent, as you doubtless know. But Mr Hatton wouldn't. "I'm one for the ready, Mr Five Per Cent," he said to me in his amusing way.' The manager sighed. 'A very likeable, amusing man, poor Mr Hatton. One of the best.'

That's a matter of opinion, Wexford thought. 'What were these large sums?'

'Really, it seems most unorthodox, but if you insist.' A large ledger was opened and horn-rimmed glasses set on the manager's nose. 'Mr Hatton opened this account in November of last year,' he began, 'with the sum of one hundred pounds.' Payment for the first lorry hi-jacking, Wexford thought, a nice little bit of compensation for his concussion. 'Nothing was added to it until January when two separate payments of fifty pounds were made.' Two more hi-jackings, set up by Hatton, who had kept the drivers occupied at pontoon in a carmen's café? Wexford felt rather pleased. All the pieces in his puzzle were falling neatly into place. 'Then in March, March 15th, a further hundred was paid in, but no more after that until May 22nd.'

The manager paused and Wexford made a mental note to find out whether any lorries had been hi-jacked on Hatton's A.1

route during the penultimate week of May. Evidently Hatton got a hundred when he was personally involved, fifty when it was someone else to be knocked on the head and left in a ditch. Such a likeable, amusing man!

'How much?' he said coldly.

The manager readjusted his glasses.

'Er . . . let me see . . . Good heavens. No, it isn't an error. Really, I wasn't aware . . . As a matter of fact, Mr Hatton paid five hundred pounds into his current account on May 22nd.'

And what in God's name, Wexford thought flabbergasted, did Hatton have in his power to do that was worth five hundred pounds? What could a lorry be carrying that its load was so valuable to a thief as to make Hatton's a feasible reward? There would have to be several men involved in the racket, McCloy himself, two or three men to commandeer the lorry and incapacitate the driver as well as Hatton. McCloy would want the lion's share of whatever the load realised and if Hatton, a mere decoy, got five hundred, the three henchmen would be worth at least five hundred apiece. Four times five and what for McCloy? A thousand, two thousand? That meant a cargo to the value of four or five thousand pounds. At least. For McCloy wouldn't get anything like the cargo's true value in his under-world market.

Well, it should be easy enough to find out. A hi-jacking of that magnitude wouldn't be likely to be quickly forgotten by the police in whose district it had occurred. He couldn't understand why he didn't recall it himself. It must have made front-page news. The last week but one in May, he repeated to himself. Presumably they'd never done anyone for the job. They certainly hadn't done Hatton.

'And after that?' he said calmly.

'Regular payments of fifty pounds a week over the past six weeks.'

Wexford checked an explosion of astonishment. 'But no more large sums?'

'No more large sums,' said the bank manager.

It was obvious what had happened. Hatton had done his jobs for McCloy and the last one had been something spectacular. So spectacular — perhaps involving great injury or death. Why the hell couldn't he *remember* it? That Hatton, finding some weak spot in McCloy's armour, had commenced to blackmail him. A lump sum down on May 22nd and then fifty pounds a week.

It must have been nice while it lasted, Wexford reflected amorally. What was more exhilarating to a poor man than a sudden influx of unearned cash, springing from a seemingly limitless fertile source? How could such a one as Hatton restrain himself from making a splash? It came into Wexford's mind that money metaphors often have to do with water, gushing, springing, and that businessmen talk of liquidity and cash flow.

He came to the Kingsbrook bridge and paused for a moment on the parapet, listening to the soft suck and chatter of the stream. Everlastingly the Kingsbrook rattled over its stones, hindered here and there by tree roots or a growth of weed, but ultimately unimpeded, always moving, glittering in the sun as if gold pieces gleamed beneath its ripples.

By the water's edge Hatton had met his death. Because a source less abundant and less generous than this river had dried up?

CHAPTER EIGHT

'There are only three McCloys in this district,' Burden said on the following morning. 'I've seen them all and they struck me as perfectly ordinary honest citizens. A couple in Pomfret are brothers. One's a teacher at the comprehensive school and the other's a lab assistant. James McCloy, who lives here in town, runs a very small unsuccessful sort of decorating business.'

'Small fry?' said Wexford, still thinking of his fish and water metaphors.

'Very small. No sign of any more money than is needed to keep the wolf from the door. Still, I've been through the trade directory and come up with something a bit more hopeful. There's a firm in London, in Deptford, calling themselves McCloy & Son Ltd., and what d'you think their line of business is?'

'*Etonne-moi,*' said Wexford after the manner of Diaghilev to Cocteau. Burden looked at him suspiciously, so he said with amused impatience, 'I don't know, Mike, and I'm not in the mood for this suspense stuff.'

'They spray the laminated surfaces on to small electrical equipment.'

'Do they, indeed?'

'I've put through a call to London and I'm waiting for them to ring me up. If there's anything at all promising I'm off to Deptford.'

'While you're waiting,' said Wexford, 'you might get on to Stamford police, Stamford in Lincolnshire. I'd like to know just what did happen when Hatton's lorry was hi-jacked on the 15th of March and if they've got any McCloys in their district.'

'Stamford, sir? Isn't there a bridge there where poor old Harold won a victory before coming a cropper at Hastings?'

'Wrong one,' said Wexford. 'This is a charming little ancient town of grey stone which the A.1 now fortunately by-passes. Shakespeare mentions it. "How a good yoke of bullocks

at Stamford fair?" You might also ask them if they had a big hi-
jacking at the end of May. It might not have been near them,
of course, but it was so big they'll likely have heard of it.'

The pretty toy of a lift had borne his weight serenely on
four occasions by this time and he no longer felt much trepidation on entering it. As it sank obediently to the ground floor, he
thought again about McCloy's mysterious feat of modern high-
waymanship. He had checked the file of that period and found
nothing. Now he too was waiting for a phone call, promised for
the afternoon. Scotland Yard would enlighten him when they
had consulted their records. But how could it have escaped his
knowledge and the newspapers?

Sergeants Camb and Martin were gossiping in the foyer
when he emerged from the lift. He gave a low cough.

'Just discussing this Fanshawe inquest, sir,' said Camb
respectfully.

'I thought it had been adjourned.'

'The coroner wants to resume now, but I've told him we've
nothing to go on. I'm all for waiting till Mrs Fanshawe perks up
a bit.'

'In a bad way, is she?' said Martin. Like an old woman in
a supermarket queue, Wexford thought derisively.

'That accident's turned her brain, I reckon. She's no more
fit to appear in court than she was six weeks ago. God knows, I
can sympathise. Her husband's dead and her only child. It's not
funny, I can tell you, trying to tell a sick woman her daughter's
dead when she keeps insisting she's alive and in Germany.'

'Maybe she is alive,' said Wexford, more from a mischie-
vous desire to throw a spanner in the works than from conviction. He was sick and tired of the name Fanshawe. He didn't
burden the uniformed branch with his problems and he didn't
see why he should have to listen to Camb's maunderings.
'Maybe it was someone else in the car.'

'Oh, no sir; the aunt identified the girl.'

'Well, it's your problem, Sergeant. You're the coroner's
officer.' Wexford added annoyingly, 'We all have our troubles
and we must deal with them as best we can.' He swung open
the door and said over his shoulder, 'I don't know what you
think you're doing, Martin, distracting the coroner's officer in

the execution of his duty. If you want a job just run upstairs and say McCloy to Mr Burden. I'm away to the dentist myself.'

'Not in much pain, sir, I hope?'

'You're behind the times,' said Wexford, chuckling. 'You don't go to the dentist these days because you've got toothache, you go for a check-up.'

It was too fine a day for the car. Wexford crossed the road to Grover's newspaper shop and turned into York Street. In the display window of Joy Jewels the sun set the rhinestone ropes and little gilt collarets ablaze, and the plane tree leaves shadowed the pavement in damask tablecloth patterns. After the petrol station and the little houses, in one of which George Carter lived, were left behind, the street petered out into a country lane. Such was the incline of the hills at this point and the arrangement of the trees that, looking straight ahead, nothing that was not absolutely pastoral could be seen. A stranger to the district, coming over the brow of the hill, would have stopped astonished and perhaps a little peeved to see Ploughman's Lane lying beneath him.

Not that there was anything to dismay the aesthetic purist. Through the centuries about twenty-five houses had been built in Ploughman's Lane, first of all for the minor gentry, the widows and kinsmen, for instance, of the lord of the manor; in more recent times equally large and widely spaced dwellings had been put up for the professional class.

From where he stood Wexford could see roofs, a yellow patch of new thatch on the far left, red tiles some fifty yards from it, then the pinnacled and turreted grey slate so dear to the heart of the Victorian bourgeoisie; next, half lost among the spread arms of a black cedar, the pinned-down tarred fabric that roofed a split-level ranch bungalow.

He descended briskly, glad of the shade the thickening trees afforded. A Bentley swam out from behind the ranch house's tamarisk hedge, accelerated arrogantly and, passing him, drove him back flat against the hedge.

'And if I should chance to run over a cad,'

Wexford quoted,

'I can pay for the damage if ever so bad.
So pleasant it is to have money, heigh ho . . .'

God Almighty, he was getting as bad as Maurice Cullam!
He had noted the number of the Bentley. Very nice cars they
all had around here. There was another Bentley outside the
grey slate Gothic place with a smart yellow Cortina snuggling
up against it. Married bliss, thought Wexford, grinning to
himself. Even the wives' cars were sizeable. No minis and no
second- or third-hand jalopies. But women would never be
equal, he reflected, pleased to have discovered a new profund-
ity, until the day came when men stopped thinking it natural
that their wives should always have the smaller car. And they
always did, no matter how rich they were; no matter, come to
that, if the wives were richer or bigger than the husbands. He
tried to think of a wife who had a larger car than her husband's
and he couldn't think of one. Not that he particularly wanted
women to be equal. As far as that went, he was quite satisfied
with the *status quo*. But to have lighted upon a new yet universal
truth amused him and he went on thinking about it until he
came to Jolyon Vigo's house.

The tall dark girl got off the London train and as she passed
through the barrier at Stowerton station she asked the woman
collecting tickets where she could get a taxi.

'There's only one. But he won't be busy at this time of day.
You might be lucky. There you are! I can just see him, waiting
on the rank.'

She watched the girl march briskly down the steps. Very
few women as smart and cocksure as that one arrived at
Stowerton station, even from London, even in the height of
summer. The ticket collector, who had just had a new perm,
thought the girl's geometrically cut and excessively short hair
awful. It made her look like a boy, or how boys used to look in
the days when men had some self-respect and went to the
barber's. Flat-chested and skinny too, like a stick all the way
down. You had to admit, though, that that kind made a good
clothes prop. The suit she was wearing was the colour and
texture of sacking, a foreign-looking suit somehow with those

buttoned pockets, but the ticket collector was willing to bet it hadn't cost a penny less than forty guineas. It hardly seemed fair that a kid of — what would she be? Twenty-three? Twenty-four? — had forty quid to throw away on a bit of sacking. Money talks all right, she thought. It was money that gave that snooty lift of the chin, too, that masterful stance and walk and that stuck-up voice.

The girl approached the taxi and said to the driver:

'Will you take me to Stowerton Royal Infirmary, please?'

When they got to the hospital she opened her brown leather bag to pay him and he noticed that, as well as the English money, she had some funny-looking foreign notes in her wallet. He half hoped she would give him one of them by mistake so that he could make a scene, but she didn't. He summed her up as a sharp little piece with a head on her shoulders. She was a stranger to the place but she knew where she was going. As he reversed, he saw her march confidently into the porter's office.

'Can you direct me to the private wing?'

'Straight down the drive, madam, and you'll see a notice with an arrow.' The porter called her madam because she had asked the way to the private wing. If she had asked for Ward Five he would have told her morning visiting in the public wards was forbidden and he might, because he was feeling benevolent, have called her love. On the other hand, he couldn't imagine anyone like this ever wanting a public ward. She was madam, all right, a proper little madam.

Nurse Rose was late with her bed-making on Tuesday morning. She had seen to Mrs Goodwin by nine o'clock and stopped for a chat and a bit of buttering-up. You were half-way to being a lady's maid with these private patients and if they wanted you to paint their fingernails while they told you their life histories you couldn't choose but obey. Just the same, she would have been well ahead but for those policemen turning up again and wanting to ask poor Mrs Fanshawe more questions. Of course she couldn't make Mrs Fanshawe's bed while they were poking about and it was nearly twelve before she managed to get the poor deluded creature into a chair and the sheets whipped off.

'It might take a letter a week to get to Germany, mightn't it?' said Mrs Fanshawe, taking her rings off and amusing herself by making them flash in the sunlight into Nurse Rose's eyes.

'Weeks and weeks,' said Nurse Rose, blinking. 'You don't want to worry about that.'

Once bitten, twice shy, thought Nurse Rose. She wasn't even going to humour Mrs Fanshawe any more. Stick her neck out and her life would be a succession of errands for Mrs Fanshawe, running about the town sending crazy messages to a girl who didn't exist.

'Would you like me to brush your hair?' she asked, pummelling the pillows.

'Thank you very much, my dear. You're a good girl.'

'Back into bed then. Ooh! You're as light as a feather. Don't leave those lovely rings on the table, now.'

Nurse Rose had really been very helpful, Mrs Fanshawe thought. She didn't seem or look very intelligent, but she must be. She was the only one who didn't keep up this nonsense about Nora being dead. And how she envied her those rings! Funny little thing . . . When Nora came she would get her to run up to the flat and root out that paste thing she'd once bought on a whim at Selfridges. It wasn't worth more than thirty shillings, but Nurse Rose wouldn't know that and she decided she would definitely give it to Nurse Rose.

She lay back comfortably while her hair was brushed.

'While you're getting my lunch,' she said, 'I'll think how I'm going to word my telegram. Oh, and you might take my sister's card away. It's getting on my nerves.'

Nurse Rose was glad to escape. She came out of the room, pulling her bag of soiled linen, and because she wasn't looking where she was going, almost cannoned into a tall dark girl.

'Can you tell me where I can find Mrs Dorothy Fanshawe?'

'She's in there,' said Nurse Rose. She had never seen anything like the shoes the girl was wearing. They were brown calf with a copper beech leaf on the instep and their shape was so strange and outlandish that Nurse Rose decided they must be the extreme of fashion. Nothing like them had ever been seen in Stowerton, nor, for that matter, Nurse Rose believed, in

London. 'Mrs Fanshawe's just going to have her lunch,' she said.

'I don't suppose it matters if that's held up for ten minutes.'

Not to you, Nurse Rose thought indignantly, whoever you may be. But she couldn't let those desirable shoes vanish without any comment and she said impulsively, 'I hope you don't mind my asking, but I do think your shoes are super. Where did you get them?'

'Nobody minds a compliment,' said the girl coldly. 'They were made in Florence but I bought them in Bonn.'

'Bonn? Bonn's in Germany, isn't it? Ooh, you can't be! You can't be Nora. You're dead!'

Earlier that morning Wexford had quoted Justice Shallow and now, as he contemplated Jolyon Vigo's house, he thought that this was just the sort of place Shallow might have lived in. It would have been a mature house already in Shakespeare's time, a 'black and white' house, timbered, solid, so perfect a place to live in that it seemed in advance to confer upon its owner grace and taste and superiority. A climbing rose with yellow satiny flowers spread across the black striped gables and nestled against the tudor roses, carved long ago by some craftsmen on every square inch of oak. On either side of the front path a knot garden had been planted with low hedges and tufts of tiny blossom. It was so neat, so unnatural in a way, that Wexford had the notion the flowers had been embroidered on the earth.

A coach-house of slightly later vintage served as a double garage. It had a small belvedere and a vertical sundial under its pediment. The garage doors were open — a single untidy touch — and within Wexford saw two cars. Again it amused him to note the general application of what he was beginning to think of as Wexford's Law. A woman was in the act of opening the door of a pale blue Minor. She slammed it and, carrying a child in her arms, squeezed between the small vehicle and the huge, finned Plymouth, dragonfly blue, that stood a foot from it.

The phrase 'a woman with a child' somehow suggested a peasant and a shawled baby. Eyeing her, Wexford thought that to say a lady with an infant would be better.

'What d'you want?' she said in the sharp high-pitched voice

of the local gentry. Before she could add, as she was evidently about to, that she never bought anything at the door, he announced himself hurriedly and asked for her husband.

'He's in the surgery. You go round by the pleached walk.'

Marvellous that anyone could say this without a trace of selfconsciousness or humour, Wexford looked her up and down. She was a plain young woman, thin and dark with a worn face. She put the child into a pram and wheeled it down the path. The boy was big and handsome, blue-eyed and fair-headed. He looked as though by being born he had sapped his mother's strength and left her a used-up husk. Wexford was reminded of a butterfly, fresh and lusty, that has escaped from a dried chrysalis.

He was not precisely sure what a pleached walk was, but when he came upon it there was no mistaking it and, smiling to himself, he descended a flagged step and passed into a green tunnel. The trees whose branches met and interwove above his head were apples and pears and already the young green fruit hung abundantly. The walk led to some greenhouses and what had once been a stable, now converted into a surgery. Amid all this sylvan glory the notice giving the dentist's working hours struck a discordant note. Wexford opened a latched horse-box door and entered the waiting room.

A pretty girl in a white coat came out to him and he reminded her of his appointment. Then, having no inclination for *Elle* or *Nova*, he sat down and viewed the room.

It was a funny place for Charlie Hatton to have found himself in and Wexford wondered why he hadn't attended the dentist in the town. On these walls were none of the usual posters bidding young mothers to drink milk in pregnancy and bring their toddlers for a twice-yearly check-up. Nor was there any notice explaining how to get dental treatment on the National Health Service. You couldn't imagine anyone sitting here with a handkerchief pressed to a swollen jaw.

The walls were papered in a Regency stripe and the one or two pieces of upholstered furniture looked like genuine antiques. The curtains were of dark chintz patterned with medallions. A small chandelier caught the sun and made rainbow spot patterns on the ceiling. Wexford thought the place was just like the sitting room of a person of taste. There were dozens like it in Kingsmarkham. But this was just a dentist's waiting room and it made him wonder what the rest of the house would be like. He was in for a surprise. He was admiring a stylish flower arrangement, observing how cunningly a spray of jasmine had been made to tremble half in, half out of the vase and trail against the console table, when the girl came back and told him Mr Vigo would see him now.

Wexford followed her into the surgery.

There was nothing out of the ordinary here, just the usual chairs and trays of instruments and contraptions of tubes and clamps and wires. Ice-blue blinds were lowered to keep out the noonday sun.

Vigo was standing beside one of the windows, fingering some instruments in a tray, and when Wexford came in he didn't look up. Wexford smiled dryly to himself. This air of being always overworked, preoccupied by esoteric matters was, he knew, characteristic of some doctors and dentists. It was part of the mystique. In a moment Vigo would glance round, show surprise and make some swift apology for being engaged on matters beyond a policeman's comprehension.

The dentist had a fine leonine head, the hair fair and abundant. His jaw was strong and prominent, the mouth thin. One day when he was old this would be a nutcracker face but that was a long way off. He seemed to be counting and when he had finished he turned and reacted as Wexford had expected he would.

'Do forgive me, Chief Inspector. A little matter that couldn't be left. I understand you want to talk to me about the late Mr Hatton. I've no more patients after lunch, so shall we go into the house?'

He took off his white coat. Under it he was wearing a slate-blue suit in tussore, the cut, material and colour not quite masculine enough for his height and heavily muscled chest. He had the figure of a rugby international and he made Wexford, who was just on six feet, feel short.

Wexford followed him through the pleached walk and they entered the house by a glazed garden door. It was like stepping into a museum. Wexford hesitated, dazzled. He had heard of

Chinese rooms, heard of Chinese Chippendale, but he had never seen a room furnished in the style. The brilliance of its colours turned the remembered garden outside into monochrome. His feet sank into the carpet whose blues and creams evoked a summer sky and, at Vigo's behest, he lowered himself uneasily into a chair with a yellow satin seat and legs of rearing dragons. The dentist moved with apparent carelessness between tables and cabinets loaded with china and jade and stood, a faint smile on his thin lips, under a long picture of red fish painted on silk.

'I don't know what you can have to ask me about Mr Hatton's teeth,' he said. 'He didn't have his own teeth.'

Wexford had come to talk business and yet for a moment he could not. Talk of false teeth in this setting? His eye fell on a set of chessmen ranged on a table in a far corner. They were two armies, one of ivory, one of red jade, and the pawns were on horseback, the white armed with spears, the red with arrows. One of the red knights on a panoplied charger had a contemporary Western face, a raw sharp face which called to mind absurdly that of Charlie Hatton. It grinned at Wexford, seeming to prompt him.

'We know that, Mr Vigo,' he said, wrenching his eyes away and fixing them on an eggshell thin service, made to contain jasmine tea. 'What surprises us is that a man of his means should have such superb false ones.'

Vigo had an attractive, rather boyish laugh. He checked it with a shake of his head. 'A tragedy, wasn't it? Have you any idea who could have . . . ? No, I mustn't ask that.'

'I've no objection to your asking, but no, we've no idea yet. I've come to you because I want you to tell me everything you can about Mr Hatton with particular reference to anything you may know about the source of his income.'

'I only know that he drove a lorry.' Vigo was still savouring with pride and joy his caller's astonishment. 'But yes, I see what you mean. It surprised me too. I don't know much but I'll tell you what I can.' He moved to a cabinet whose door handles were the long curved tails of dragons. 'Will you join me in a pre-luncheon sherry?'

'I don't think so, thank you.'

'Pity.' Vigo didn't press him but poured a glass of Manzanilla for himself and sat down by the window. It gave on to a shadowed court whose centerpiece was an orrery on a stone plinth. 'Mr Hatton made an appointment with me at the end of May. He had never been a patient of mine before.'

The end of May. On the 22nd of May Hatton had paid five hundred pounds into his bank account, his share, no doubt, of the mysterious and elusive hi-jacking haul.

'I can tell you the precise date, if you like. I looked it up before you came. Tueday, 21st May. He telephoned me at lunchtime on that day and by a fluke I had a cancellation, so I was able to see him almost immediately. He'd had dentures since he was twenty, very bad ill-fitting ones, by the way. They made him selfconscious and he wanted a new set. I asked him if he realised this would involve him in considerable expense. He said that money was no object — those were his actual words — and he wanted the most expensive teeth I could provide. We finally arrived at a figure of two hundred and fifty pounds and he was perfectly agreeable.'

'You must have been surprised.'

Vigo sipped his sherry reflectively. He touched one of the chessmen, a crenellated castle, caressing it with pride. 'I was astonished. And I don't mind telling you I was a little uneasy.' He didn't elaborate on this unease but Wexford thought he must have been worried lest the two hundred and fifty wasn't forthcoming. 'However, the teeth were made and fitted at the beginning of June. About a month ago it would have been.'

'How did Mr Hatton pay you?'

'Oh, in cash, he paid me on the same day, insisted on doing so. The money was in five-pound notes which I'm afraid I paid straight into my bank. Chief Inspector, I understand what you're getting at, but I couldn't ask the man where he got his money from, could I? Just because he came here in his working clothes and I knew he drove a lorry . . . I couldn't.'

'Did you ever see him again?'

'He came back once for a check. Oh, and a second time to tell me how pleased he was.'

Again Wexford was becoming bemused by the colours, by the seductive spectrum that caught and held his eye wherever he looked. He bent his head and concentrated on his own big ugly hands. 'On any of his visits,' he said stolidly, 'did he ever mention someone called McCloy?'

'I don't think so. He spoke about his wife and his brother-in-law that he was in business with.' Vigo paused and searched his memory. 'Oh, and he mentioned a friend of his that was getting married. I was supposed to be interested because the chap had sometimes been here doing electrical repairs. Hatton said something about buying him a record player for a wedding present. The poor fellow's dead and I don't know whether I ought to say this . . .'

'Say on, Mr Vigo.'

'Well, he did rather harp on what a lot of money he spent. I don't want to sound a snob but I thought it vulgar. He only mentioned his wife to tell me he'd just bought her something new to wear and he tried to give me the impression his brother-in-law was something of a poor fish because he couldn't make ends meet.'

'But the brother-in-law was in the same line of business.'

'I know. That struck me. Mr Hatton did say he had a good many irons in the fire and that sometimes he brought off a big deal. But frankly, if I thought about that at all, I imagined he had some line, painting people's houses perhaps or cleaning windows.'

'Window cleaners don't speak of bringing off big deals, Mr Vigo.'

'I suppose not. The fact is I don't have many dealings with people of Mr Hatton's . . .' Vigo paused. Wexford was sure he had been about to say 'class'. 'Er, background,' said the dentist. 'Of course you're suggesting the side lines weren't legitimate and this may be hindsight, but now I look back Mr Hatton did perhaps occasionally have a shady air about him when he talked of them. But really it was only the merest nuance.'

'Well, I won't trouble you any further.' Wexford got up. It must be his over-sensitive suspicious mind that made him see a relieved relaxing of those muscled shoulders. Vigo opened the carved oak door for him.

'Let me see you out, Chief Inspector.' The hall was a largish square room, its flagged floor dotted with thin soft rugs, and every inch of burnished ancient wood caught the sunlight. There were Blake prints on the walls, the Inferno scenes, Nebuchadnezzar with his eagle's talons, the naked Newton with his golden curls. Stripped of his blue tussore, Vigo himself might look rather like that, Wexford thought. 'I had the pleasure of a visit from your daughter the other day,' he heard the dentist say. 'What a very lovely girl she is.'

'I'm told she's much admired,' Wexford said dryly. The compliment slightly displeased him. He interpreted it as spurious and ingratiating. Also there had been a note of incredulity in Vigo's voice as if he marvelled at such an old goose begetting a swan.

The front door swung open and Mrs Vigo came in, holding the child. For the first time since his arrival, Wexford remembered that there was another child, a mongol, confined somewhere in an institution.

The baby which Vigo now took in his arms was perhaps six or seven months old. No one could have doubted its paternity. Already it had its father's jaw and its father's athletic limbs. Vigo lifted the boy high, laughing as he chuckled, and there came into his face an intense besotted adoration.

'Meet my son, Mr Wexford. Isn't he splendid?'

'He's very like you.'

'So they tell me. Looks more than seven months, doesn't he?'

'Going to be a big chap,' said the chief inspector. 'Now that we've each complimented the other on his handsome offspring, I'll take my leave, Mr Vigo.'

'A mutual admiration society, eh?' Vigo laughed heartily but his wife's face remained grave. She took the boy from him roughly as if so much exaggerated worship offended her. Again Wexford thought of the mongol whose fate no amount of money could change. Grief fills the room up of my absent child, lies in his bed, walks up and down with me . . .

Wexford went out into the sunshine and the knot garden.

CHAPTER NINE

The call from Scotland Yard came through half an hour after Wexford got back to the station. In the whole country only two lorries had been hi-jacked during the latter part of May and neither was on Hatton's regular route. One had been in Cornwall, the other in Monmouthshire, and they had been loaded with margarine and tinned peaches respectively.

Wexford looked at the memo Burden had left him before departing for Deptford:

'Stamford say no records of any thefts from lorries in their area during April or May.'

It was unlikely that Hatton could have had a hand in the Cornwall or Monmouthshire jobs. Margarine and tinned fruit! Even if there had been tons of it, a fourth or fifth share couldn't have amounted to five hundred pounds. Besides, wasn't he understimating Hatton's haul? He had banked five hundred on May 22nd, *drawn out* twenty-five pounds for the lamp. Another sixty had gone on clothes and the record player. And all this while, Wexford guessed, Hatton had been living like a king. True, the first and perhaps the second blackmail payments had come in before he was obliged to pay for his teeth at the beginning of June, but he had blithely paid two hundred and fifty for them in cash when the demand came.

Surely that meant that although Hatton had banked only five hundred on May 22nd, he had in fact received more, perhaps even twice that sum. He carried notes about with him in his wallet, on one occasion, at any rate about a hundred pounds.

Suppose there had been no mammoth hi-jacking at the end of May? That would mean that all Hatton's wealth had been acquired through blackmail, and blackmail entered into not as the consequence of hi-jacking but of something else.

There was a lot more to this, Wexford thought with frustration, than met the eye.

*

'There seems to be a lot more to this than meets the eye,' said Sergeant Camb indignantly. 'Mrs Fanshawe's own sister identified the dead young lady as Miss Nora Fanshawe.'

'Nevertheless,' the girl said, 'I am Nora Fanshawe.' She sat down on the red spoon-shaped chairs in the station foyer and placed her feet neatly together on the black and white tiles, staring down at the shoes Nurse Rose had so gushingly admired. 'My aunt was probably very strung up and you say the girl was badly burned. Very disfigured, I suppose?'

'Very,' said Camb unhappily. His immediate superior and his superintendent had departed ten minutes before for a conference at Lewes and he was more than somewhat at a loss. What the coroner was going to say to all this he dreaded to think.

'Mrs Fanshawe's sister seemed quite certain.' But had she? He remembered the scene quite vividly, taking the woman into the mortuary and uncovering the faces, Jerome Fanshawe's first and then the girl's. Fanshawe had been lying on his face and the fire had scarcely touched him. Besides, the woman had recognised the silver pencil in his breast pocket, his wrist-watch and the tiny knife scar, relic of some schoolboy ritual, on that wrist. Identifying the girl had been so extremely distasteful. All her hair had been burnt away but for the black roots and her features hideously charred. It made him shudder to think of it now, hardened as he was.

'Yes, that's my niece,' Mrs Browne had said, recoiling and covering her own face. Of course he had asked her if she was quite certain and she had said she was, quite certain, but now he wondered if it was mere association that had made her agree, association and horror. She had said it was her niece because the girl was young and had black hair and because who else but Nora Fanshawe could have been in that car with her parents? Yet someone else had been . . . And what the hell was the coroner going to say?

His eyes still seeing the charred appalling face, he turned to the young hard untouched face in front of him and said:

'Can you prove you're Nora Fanshawe, miss?'

She opened the large hide handbag she was carrying and produced a passport, handing it to Camb without a word. The photograph wasn't much like the girl who sat on the other side of the desk, but passport photographs seldom are much like their originals. Glancing up at her uneasily and then back to the document in front of him he read that Nora Elizabeth Fanshawe, by profession a teacher, had been born in London in 1945, had black hair, brown eyes and was five feet nine inches tall with no distinguishing marks. The girl in the mortuary hadn't been anything like five feet nine, but you couldn't expect an aunt to tell the height of a prone corpse.

'Why didn't you come back before?' he asked.

'Why should I? I didn't know my father was dead and my mother in hospital.'

'Didn't you write? Didn't you expect them to write to you?'

'We were on very bad terms,' the girl said calmly. 'Besides, my mother did write. I got her letter yesterday and I took the first plane. Look here, my mother knows me and that ought to be enough for you.'

'Your mother . . .' Camb corrected himself. 'Mrs Fanshawe's a very sick woman . . .'

'She's not mad if that's what you mean. The best thing will be for me to phone my aunt and then perhaps you'll let me go and have something to eat. You may not know it, but I haven't had a thing to eat since eight o'clock and it's half-past two now.'

'Oh, I'll phone Mrs Browne,' Camb said hastily. 'It wouldn't do for her to hear your voice just like that. Oh dear, no.' He was half convinced.

'Why me?' said Wexford. 'Why do I have to see her? It's nothing to do with me.'

'You see, sir, the super and Inspector Letts have gone to Lewes . . .'

'Did the aunt recognise her voice?'

'Seemed to. She was in a bit of a way, I can tell you. Frankly, I don't have much faith in the aunt.'

'Oh, bring her up,' Wexford said impatiently. 'Anything to make a change from lorries. And, Camb — use the lift.'

He had never seen her mother or her aunt so he couldn't look for family resemblances. But she was a rich man's daughter. He looked at the bag, the shoes, the platinum watch and, more than anything, he sensed about her an air, almost repellent, of arrogance. She wore no scent. He took from her in silence the passport, the international driver's licence and Mrs Fanshawe's letter. It occurred to him as he turned them over that Nora Fanshawe — if she was Nora Fanshawe — probably stood to inherit a vast sum of money. Jerome Fanshawe had been an affluent stockbroker. It might be that this girl was a con woman and he and Camb the first victims of a colossal deception.

'I think we had better have an explanation,' he said slowly.

'Very well. I don't quite know what you want.'

'Just a moment.' Wexford took Camb aside. 'Was there nothing but this Mrs Browne's word to identify the dead girl?' he asked rather grimly.

Camb looked downcast. 'There was a suitcase in the car with clothes in it,' he said. 'We went through the contents of two handbags we found in the road. One was Mrs Fanshawe's. The other had nothing in it but some make-up, a purse containing two pounds and some silver and a packet of cigarettes.' He added defensively, 'It was a good expensive handbag from Mappin and Webb.'

'My God,' said Wexford in disgust, 'I just hope you haven't landed us with a female Tichborne claimant.' He went back to the girl, sat down on the opposite side of the desk and gave a brisk nod. 'You went on holiday with Mr and Mrs Fanshawe to Eastover?' he asked. 'On what date was that?'

'May the 17th,' the girl said promptly. 'I am a teacher of English at a school in Cologne and I gave up my job at the end of March and returned to England.'

'Since when you have been living with Mr and Mrs Fanshawe?'

If the girl noticed that he didn't refer to them as her parents she gave no sign. She sat stiff and tense with her finely sculpted head held high. 'Not at first,' she said and he sensed a faint diffidence creep into her voice. 'My parents and I hadn't been on good terms for some time. I went back to live with them — or rather, to stay with them — in the middle of May. My mother wanted me to go down to the bungalow with them and because I wanted — I wanted our relations to improve — well, I said I would.' Wexford nodded noncomittally and she went on. 'We all drove down to Eastover on Friday, May 17th...' Her shoulders stiffened and she looked down at her folded hands. 'That night I had a disagreement with my parents. Is there any need for me to go into details?' Without waiting for Wexford's consent to her reticence, she swept the quarrel aside and said, 'I felt it was useless to try and patch things up. We were worlds apart, we... The result was that on the Saturday morning, I told my mother there was nothing for me in England and I was going back to Germany to try and get my old job back. I took one of the suitcases of clothes I had brought with me and went to Newhaven to get the boat for Dieppe.'

'And did you get your old job back?'

'Fortunately I did. There's a shortage of teachers in Germany as well as here and they were only too glad to see me. I even got my old room back in the *Goethestrasse.*'

'I see. Now I should like the name and address of the authority who employ you, the name of your landlady and that of the school in which you've been teaching.'

While the girl wrote this information down for him, Wexford said:

'Weren't you surprised to hear nothing from Mr and Mrs Fanshawe during the past six weeks?'

She looked up and raised her straight, rather heavy, black eyebrows. 'I told you we'd quarrelled. My father would have expected an abject apology from me, I assure you, before he condescended to write.' It was the first show of emotion she had made and it did more to make Wexford believe her story than all the documentary evidence she had furnished him with. 'These silences were commonplace with us,' she said, 'especially after a set-to like the one we had that night. Six months could have gone by. Why should I imagine any harm had come to them? I'm not a clairvoyant.'

'But you came as soon as Mrs Fanshawe wrote.'

'She is my mother, after all. Now do you suppose I might go and get myself some lunch?'

'In a moment,' Wexford said. 'Where are you planning to stay?'

'I was going to ask you to recommend somewhere,' the girl said a shade sardonically.

'The Olive and Dove is the best hotel. I suggest you get in touch immediately with your late father's solicitors.'

The girl got up and not a crease marked the skirt of her suit. Her self-confidence was almost stupefying. Camb opened the door for her and with a crisp 'Good afternoon' she took her leave of them. As her footsteps died away, the sergeant burst out miserably:

'If she's Nora Fanshawe, sir, who, for God's sake, was the girl in the road?'

'That's your problem, Sergeant,' Wexford said, unkindly.

'It could well be yours, sir.'

'That's what I'm afraid of. Haven't I got enough with a murder on my hands?'

Lilian Hatton was an easier nut to crack than the girl who called herself Nora Fanshawe. She broke down and wept bitterly when Wexford told her that her husband's supplementary income had come from a criminal source. He was almost sure that it was all a revelation to her and he watched her in sad silence as she covered her face and shook with sobs.

'I have been given your husband's log book by your brother, Mrs Hatton,' he said gently as she recovered herself. 'Now I also want to know if you keep any sort of diary or engagement book yourself.'

'Just a pad by the phone,' she gulped, 'where I kind of jot things down.'

'I'm going to ask you if you'll kindly let me borrow that.'

'You think,' she began, dabbing at her eyes as she came back with the pad, 'you think someone — someone killed my Charlie because he wouldn't go on — go on doing these jobs for them?'

'Something like that.' Now was not the time to suggest to this woman that her husband had been a blackmailer as well as a thief. 'Who knew Mr Hatton would pass along the Kingsbrook path that night?'

She twisted the damp handkerchief in hands whose nails were still pitifully and bravely painted the way Charlie Hatton had liked them, red and shiny and glittering. 'All the darts club,' she said. 'And me — I knew. My mum knew and my brother, Jim. Charlie always came that way back from the pub.'

'Mrs Hatton, did your husband ever receive any callers in this flat that you didn't know? Strangers, I mean, that he wanted to talk to alone?'

'No, he never did.'

'Perhaps when you were out? Can you ever remember your husband asking you to go out and leave him alone with anyone?'

The handkerchief was torn now, sopping wet and useless as an absorbent. But she put it to her eyes and brought it away streaked black and green. 'When he was home,' she said, 'I never went out. We always went out together. We was like — like inseparable. Mr Wexford . . .' She gripped the arms of her chair and two red flame-like spots burned in her cheeks. 'Mr Wexford, I've heard all you've said and I've got to believe it. But whatever Charlie did, he did it for me. He was a husband in a million, a good kind man, a wonderful man to his friends. You ask anyone, ask Jack . . . He was one in a million!'

Oh! withered is the garland of war! The soldier's poll is fallen . . . Strange, Wexford thought, that when you considered Charlie Hatton you thought of war and soldiers and battles. Was it because life itself is a battle and Hatton had waged it with unscrupulous weapons, winning rich spoils and falling as he marched home with a song on his lips?

How sentimental he was getting! The man was a black-mailer and a thief. If life was a battle and Charlie Hatton a soldier of fortune he, Wexford, stood in the position of a United Nations patrol whose job it was to prevent incursions on the territory of the defenceless.

'I don't want to ask you anything more now, Mrs Hatton,' he said to the widow as he left her weeping among the dead man's ill-gotten glories.

In the High Street he encountered Dr Crocker emerging from Grover's with a copy of the *British Medical Journal*.

'Been making any good arrests lately?' asked the doctor cheerfully. 'Now, now, mind your hypertension. Want me to take your blood pressure? I've got my sphyg in the car.'

'You know what you can do with your sphyg,' said

Wexford, proceeding to tell him in lurid detail. 'I reckon just about the whole population of Kingsmarkham knew Charlie Hatton would be taking the field path home that night.'

'No reason why it should be a local man, is there?'

'I may not be a wizard with a sphygmomanometer,' said Wexford derisively, 'but I'm not daft. Whoever killed Charlie Hatton knew the lie of the land all right.'

'How come? He'd only got to be told by Charlie that he'd be leaving the High Street by the bridge and walking along the local river.'

'You think? You reckon Hatton would also have told him the river bed was full of stones one of which would make a suitable weapon for knocking off his informant?'

'I see what you mean. There could be one or more brains behind the killing but whoever struck the blow, albeit a henchman, was Kingsmarkham born and bred.'

'That's right, Watson. You're catching on. My old mate,' Wexford remarked to no one in particular, 'albeit a sawbones, is coming on.' Suddenly his voice dropped and tapping the doctor's arm, his face hardening, he said, 'D'you see what I see? Over there by the Electricity Board?'

Crocker followed his gaze. From Tabard Road a woman wheeling a pram had emerged in Kingsmarkham High Street and stopped outside a plate-glass display window of the Southern Electricity Board. Presently two more children joined her, then a man holding a third child by the hand and another in his arms. They remained in a huddle on the pavement, staring at the dazzling array of kitchen equipment as if hypnotised.

'Mr and Mrs Cullam and their quiverful,' said Wexford.

The family were too far away for their conversation, an apparently heated and even acrimonious discussion, to be audible. But it was evident that an argument was taking place between the adults, possibly as to whether their need of a refrigerator was greater than their desire for a mammoth room heater. The children were taking sides vociferously. Cullam shook one of his daughters, cuffed his elder son on the head, and then they all plunged into the showroom.

'Will you do something for me?' Wexford asked the doctor.

'Go in there and buy a light bulb or something. I want to know what that lot are up to.'

'What, spy on them and report back, d'you mean?'

'Charming way you put it. That's what I spend my life doing. I'll sit in your car. Can I have the keys?'

'It's not locked,' Crocker said awkwardly.

'Is that so? Well, don't come screaming to me next time one of the local hippies pinches a load of your acid off you. Go on. A forty watt bulb and we'll reimburse you out of petty cash.'

The doctor went unwillingly. Wexford chuckled to himself in the car. Crocker's cautious approach to the electricity showroom, his quick sidelong glances, called to mind days long gone by when Wexford, then a sixth-form boy, had witnessed this same man as a child of ten, scuttling up to front doors playing 'Knocking Down Ginger'. In those days the infant Crocker had run up paths lightly and gleefully to bang on a knocker or ring a bell and, elated with an enormous naughtiness, hidden behind a hedge to see the angry householder erupt and curse. There was no hedge here and Crocker was fifty. But as he entered the showroom, had he too experienced a flash of memory, a stab of nostalgia?

Jesu, Jesu, thought Wexford, once more evoking Justice Shallow, the mad days that I have spent! And to see how many of my old acquaintance are dead . . . Enough of that. On the lighter side it reminded him of Stamford and he wondered how Burden had got on. Somehow a little business in Deptford didn't quite match up with his own ideas of McCloy's origins.

Samantha Cullam scuttled out on to the pavement. Her mother came next, lugging the pram. When the whole brood were assembled their father regimented them with a series of fortunately ill-aimed blows and they all trailed off the way they had come. Then Crocker appeared, duplicity incarnate.

'Well?'

'Don't snap at me like that, you saucy devil,' said the doctor, immensely pleased with himself. 'I set traps, as the Psalmist says, I catch men.'

'What did Cullam buy?'

'He didn't exactly *buy* anything, but he's after a refrigerator.'

'Getting it on the H.P., is he?'

'Money wasn't mentioned. They had a bit of a ding-dong, Mr and Mrs, and one of the kids knocked a Pyrex dish off a cooker. That brute Cullam fetched him a fourpenny one, poor little devil. They're all dead keen on getting this fridge, I can tell you.'

'Well, what about these traps you laid?'

'That was just a figure of speech,' said the doctor. 'Didn't I do all right? I bought the bulb like you said. One and nine if you don't mind. I'm not in this for my health.'

CHAPTER TEN

'They call themselves McCloy Ltd.,' Burden said wearily, 'but the last member of the firm of that name died twenty years ago. It's an old established set-up, but I reckon it's on its last legs now. In this so-called affluent society of ours folks buy new stuff, they don't want this reconditioned rubbish.'

'You can say that again,' said Wexford, thinking of Cullam.

'The Yard put me on to six other McCloys all more or less in the hardware business or on its fringes. Not a smell of anything fishy about one of them. Stamford have given me a list of local McCloys and there again not a sniff as far as they know. But I'll be off to Stamford in the morning to have a scent round. The local force have promised me all the help I need.'

Wexford lounged back in his swivel chair and the dying sun played on his face. 'Mike,' he said, 'I wonder if we haven't been starting from the wrong end. We've been looking for McCloy to lead us to his hired assassin. We might do better to find the hired assassin and let him lead us to McCloy.'

'Cullam?'

'Maybe. I want Martin to be Cullam's shadow and if he goes and pays cash for that refrigerator we're really getting somewhere. Meanwhile I'm going to make Hatton's log book and Mrs Hatton's engagement book my homework for tonight. But first, how about a quick one at the Olive and Dove?'

'Not for me thanks, sir. I haven't had an evening in for a week now. Divorce is against my wife's principles but she might get ideas as to a legal separation.'

Wexford laughed and they went down in the lift together. The evening was warm and clear, the light and the long soft shadows more flattering to this market town High Street than the noonday sun. The old houses were at their best in it, their shabbiness, the cracks in their fabric veiled, as an ageing face is veiled and smoothed by candlelight. By day the alleys that ran into a scruffy hinterland were rat-hole rubbish traps but now they seemed romantic lanes where lovers might meet under the bracket lamps and as the sun departed, watch the moon ride over a Grimm's fairy tale huddle of pinnacled rooftops.

As yet it was only eight o'clock and the sun reluctant to leave without treating its worshippers to a pyrotechnic display of rose and gold flames that burnt up the whole western sky. Wexford stood on the south side of the bridge and listened to the river chuckling. Such an innocent river, for all that it knew a secret, for all that one of its stones had put a man out of sight of the sunset!

All the street windows of the Olive and Dove were open, the curtains fanning out gently over window boxes and over fuchsias that dripped red flowers. On the forecourt a band of Morris dancers had assembled. They wore the motley coat of jesters and one of them was hopping around on a hobby horse. To his amusement Wexford picked out George Carter among the company.

'Lovely night, Mr Carter,' he said jovially. Rather shame-facedly Carter waved at him a stick with ribbons and bells on. Wexford went into the saloon bar.

At a table in the alcove on the dining-room wall sat the girl Camb had brought to him earlier in the day, an elderly woman and a man. Wexford bought his beer and as he passed them the man got up as if to take his leave.

'Good evening,' Wexford said. 'Have you decided to stay at the Olive?'

The girl was sparing with her smiles. She nodded sharply to him and said, naming his rank precisely, 'I'd like you to meet my father's solicitor, Mr Updike. Uncle John, this is Detective Chief Inspector Wexford.'

'How do you do?'

'And I don't think you've met my aunt, Mrs Browne?'

Wexford looked from one to the other. Marvellous the way he always had to do Camb's work for him! The aunt was looking pale but excited, the solicitor gratified. 'I'm quite prepared to accept that you're Miss Fanshawe now, Miss Fanshawe,' Wexford said.

'I've known Nora since she was so high,' said Updike. 'You need have no doubt that this is Nora.' And he gave Wexford a card naming a London firm. Updike, Updike and Sanger of Ave

Maria Lane. The chief inspector looked at it, then again at Mrs Browne who was Nora Fanshawe grown old. 'I'm satisfied.' He passed on to an empty table.

The solicitor went to catch his train and presently Wexford heard the aunt say:

'I've had a long day, Nora, I think I'll just give the hospital a ring and then I'll go up to bed.'

Wexford sat by the window, watching the Morris dancers. The music was amateurish and the performers self-conscious, but the evening was so beautiful that if you shut your eyes to the cars and the new shop blocks you might imagine yourself briefly in Shakespeare's England. Someone carried out to the nine men a tray of bottled beer and the spell broke.

'Come into the lounge,' said a voice behind him.

Nora Fanshawe had removed the jacket of her suit and in the thin coffee-coloured blouse she looked more feminine. But she was still a creature of strong straight lines and planes and angles and she was still not smiling.

'May I get you a drink, Miss Fanshawe?' Wexford said, rising.

'Better not.' Her voice was abrupt and she didn't thank him for the offer. 'I've had too much already.' And she added with a dead laugh, 'We've been what my aunt calls celebrating. The resurrection of the dead, you see.'

They went into the lounge, sat down in deep cretonne-covered armchairs and Nora Fanshawe said:

'Mr Updike wouldn't tell me the details of the accident. He wanted to spare me.' She beckoned to the waiter and said without asking Wexford first, 'Bring two coffees.' Then she lit a king-size cigarette and slipped it into an amber holder. 'You tell me about it,' she said.

'You don't want to be spared?'

'Of course not. I'm not a child and I didn't like my father.'

Wexford gave a slight cough. 'At about ten o'clock on May 20th,' he began, 'a man driving a petrol tanker on the north to south highway of Stowerton by-pass saw a car overturned and in flames on the fast lane of the south to north track. He reported it at once and when the police and ambulance got there they found the bodies of a man and a girl lying on the road and partially burned. A woman — your mother — had been flung clear on to the soft shoulder. She had multiple injuries and a fractured skull.'

'Go on.'

'What remained of the car was examined but, as far as could be told, there was nothing wrong with the brakes or the steering and the tyres were nearly new.'

Nora Fanshawe nodded.

'The inquest was adjourned until your mother regained consciousness. The road was wet and your mother has suggested that your father may have been driving exceptionally fast.'

'He always drove too fast.' She took the coffee that the waiter had brought and handed a cup to Wexford. He sensed that she would take it black and sugarless and he was right. 'Since the dead girl wasn't I,' she said with repellently faultless grammar, 'who was she?'

'I'm hoping you'll be able to tell us that.'

She shrugged, 'How should I know?'

Wexford glanced at the curled lip, the hard direct eyes. 'Miss Fanshawe,' he said sharply, 'I've answered your questions, but you haven't even met me half-way. This afternoon you came to my office as if you were doing me a favour. Don't you think it's time you unbent a little?'

She flushed at that and muttered. 'I don't unbend much.'

'No, I can see that. You're twenty-three, aren't you? Don't you think all this upstage reserve is rather ridiculous?'

Her hand was small, but, ringless and with short nails as it was, it was like a man's. He watched it move towards the cup and saucer and for a moment he thought she was going to take her coffee, get up and leave him. She frowned a little and her mouth hardened.

'I'll tell you about my father,' she said at last. 'It might just help. I first knew about his infidelities when I was twelve,' she began. 'Or, let me say, I knew he was behaving as other people's fathers didn't behave. He brought a girl home and told my mother she was going to stay with us. They had a row in my presence and when it was over my father gave my mother five hundred pounds.' She took the cigarette stub from her holder and replaced it with a fresh one. This sudden chain smoking was the only sign she gave of emotion. 'He bribed her, you understand. It was quite direct and open. 'Let her stay and you can have this money.' That was how it was. The girl stayed six months. Two years later he bought my mother a new car and at just the same time I caught him in his office with his secretary.' She inhaled deeply. 'On the floor,' she said coldly. 'After that it was an understood thing that when my father wanted a new mistress he paid my mother accordingly. By that I mean what he thought the girl was worth to him. He wanted my mother to stay because she was a good hostess and kept house well. When I was eighteen I went up to Oxford.

'After I got my degree I told my mother I could keep her now and she should leave my father. Her response was to deny everything and to tell my father to stop my allowance. He refused to stop it — mainly because my mother had asked him to, I suppose. I haven't drawn it for two years now, but . . .' She glanced swiftly at her bag, her watch. 'You can't always refuse to take presents,' she said tightly, 'not when it's your own mother, not when you're an only child.'

'So you took a job in Germany?' Wexford asked.

'I thought it would be as well to get away.' The flush returned, an unbecoming mottled red. 'In January,' she said hesitantly, 'I met a man, a salesman who made business trips to Cologne from this country.' Wexford waited for her to talk of love and instead heard her say with a strange sense of shock, 'I gave up my job, as I told you, and came back to London to live with him. When I told him that if we were to be married I wouldn't ask my father for a penny he . . . well, he threw me out.'

'You returned to your parents?'

Nora Fanshawe raised her head and for the first time he saw her smile, an ugly harsh smile of self-mockery. 'You're a cold fish, aren't you?' she said surprisingly.

'I was under the impression you despised sympathy, Miss Fanshawe.'

'Perhaps I do. Want some more coffee? No, nor do I. Yes, I went back to my parents. I was still sorry for my mother, you see. I thought my father was older now and I was older. I knew

I could never live with them again, but I thought . . . Family quarrels are uncivilised, don't you think? My mother was rather pathetic. She said she'd always wanted a grown-up daughter to be real friends with.' Nora Fanshawe wrinkled her nose in distaste. 'Even upstage reserved characters like myself have their weak spots, Chief Inspector. I went to Eastover with them.'

'And the quarrel, Miss Fanshawe?'

'I'm coming to that. We'd been on surprisingly good terms up till then. My father called my mother darling once or twice and there was a kind of Darby and Joan air about them. They wanted to know what I was doing about getting another job and all was serene. So serene, in fact, that after we'd had a meal at the bungalow and a few drinks my mother did something she'd never done before. My father had gone off up to bed and she suddenly began to tell me what her life with him had been, the bribery and the humiliation and so on. She really talked as if I were a woman friend of her own age, her confidante. Well, we had about an hour of this and then she asked me if I had any romantic plans of my own. Those were her words. Like a fool I told her about the man I'd been living with. I say like a fool. Perhaps if I hadn't been a fool I would have been the dead girl in the road.'

'Your mother reacted unsympathetically?'

'She goggled at me,' said Nora Fanshawe, emphasising the verb pedantically. 'Then, before I could stop her she got my father out of bed and told him the whole thing. They both raved at me. My mother was hysterical and my father called me a lot of unpleasant names. I stood it for a bit and then I'm afraid I said to him that what was sauce for the gander was sauce for the goose and at least I wasn't married.' She sighed, moving her angular shoulders. 'What do you think he said?'

'It's different for men,' said Wexford.

'How did you guess? At any rate, for once my parents presented a united front. After my mother had obligingly betrayed all my confidences to him in my hearing, he said he would find the man — Michael, that is — and compel him to marry me. I couldn't stand any more, so I locked myself in my bedroom and in the morning I went to Newhaven and got on the boat. I parted from my mother just about on speaking terms. My father had gone out.'

'Thank you for unbending, Miss Fanshawe. Have you been suggesting that the dead girl might have been your father's mistress?'

'You think it impossible that my father would drive his wife and mistress together to London? I assure you it's not unlikely. For him it would simply have been a matter of bringing the girl along, telling my mother she was coming with them and paying her handsomely for the hardship occasioned.'

Wexford kept his eyes from Nora Fanshawe's face. She was as unlike his Sheila as could be. They had in common only their youth and health and the fact, like all women, of each being someone's daughter. The girl's father was dead. In a flash of unusual sentimentality, Wexford thought he would rather be dead than be the man about whom a daughter could say such things.

In a level voice he said, 'You gave me to understand that as far as you know there was no woman at the time but your mother. You have no idea who this girl could be?'

'That was the impression I had. I was evidently wrong.'

'Miss Fanshawe, this girl clearly could not have been a friend or neighbour at Eastover whom your parents were simply driving to London. In that case her relatives would have enquired for her, raised a hue and cry at the time of the accident.'

'Surely that would apply whoever she was?'

'Not necessarily. She could be a girl with no fixed address or someone whose landlady or friends expected her to move away about that particular weekend. She may be listed some-where among missing persons and no search has begun for her because the manner of her life showed that occasional apparent disappearances were not unusual. In other words, she could be a girl who led a somewhat itinerant life in the habit of taking jobs in various parts of the country or moving about to live with different men. Suppose, for instance, she had spent the weekend in some South Coast resort and tried to hitch a lift back to London from your father?'

'My father wouldn't have given a lift to anyone. Both he and my mother disapproved of hitch-hiking. Chief Inspector, you're talking as if everyone in that car is now dead. Aren't you forgetting that my mother is very much alive? She's well on the way to recovery and her brain isn't affected. She insists there was no one in the car but my father and herself.' Nora Fanshawe lifted her eyes and her voice lost some of its confidence. 'I suppose it's possible she could be having some sort of psychological block. She wants to believe my father was a changed man, that no girl was with them, so she's convinced herself they were alone. That could be it.'

'I'm sure it must be.' Wexford got up. 'Good night, Miss Fanshawe. Thank you for the coffee. I take it you'll be staying here a few days?'

'I'll keep in touch. Good night, Chief Inspector.'

The next step, he thought as he walked home, would be to investigate the missing persons list in the holiday towns and London too, if those proved fruitless. That was routine stuff and not for him. Why, anyway, was he allowing this road accident that wasn't even properly his province to distract his mind from the urgency of the Hatton affair? Because it had features so distracting and so inexplicable that no-one could simply explain them away?

Of course it would turn out that the dead girl was merely someone Jerome Fanshawe had come across that weekend and who had taken his fancy. Nothing so dramatic as Nora Fanshawe had suggested need have happened. Why shouldn't Fanshawe just have said to his wife, 'This young lady has missed her last train and since she lives in London I said we'd give her a lift'? But in that case Mrs Fanshawe would hardly deny the girl's presence.

There was more to it than that. There was the handbag. Camb had searched that handbag and found in it nothing but make-up and a little money. That wasn't natural, Wexford reflected. Where were her keys? Come to that, where were all the other things women usually stuff into bags, handkerchiefs, dress shop bills, receipts, tickets, pen, letters? The things which were there were anonymous, the things which were not there were the objects by which someone might be identified.

Wexford let himself into his own house and the dog Clytemnestra galloped to meet him.

'What would you do,' Wexford said to his wife, 'if I brought a young girl home and offered you a thousand pounds to let her stay?'

'You haven't got a thousand pounds,' said Mrs Wexford.

'True. There's always a fly in the ointment.'

'On the subject of young girls and money, Mr Vigo has sent a whacking bill for your daughter's tooth.'

Wexford looked at it and groaned. 'Pleached walks!' he said. 'Chinese Chippendale! I just hope one of my customers pinches his orrery, that's all. Is there any beer in the house?'

Suppressing a smile, his wife stepped over the now recumbent form of the knitted dog and went into the kitchen to open a can.

A pewter tankard at his elbow, Wexford spent the next couple of hours studying Hatton's log book and Mrs Hatton's engagement diary.

It was the week immediately preceding May 21st which interested him. On the 22nd Hatton had paid five hundred pounds into his bank and two days prior to that had either been in possession of a large sum of money or confident of acquiring it, for on the 21st, a Tuesday, he had ordered his new set of teeth.

Mrs Hatton's engagement diary was a calendar in the shape of a rectangular book. The left-hand pages bore a coloured photograph of some English beauty spot with an appropriate verse, both for the picture and the time of the year, while the right-hand pages were each divided into seven sections. The days of the week were listed on the left side and a space of perhaps one inch by five was allowed for brief jottings.

Wexford opened it at Sunday, May 12th.

The photograph was of Kentish fruit orchards and the lines beneath it from *As You Like It*: 'Men are April when they woo, December when they wed. Maids are May while they are maids, but the sky changes when they are wives.' Not true of the Hattons, he thought. Now to see how Mrs Hatton had occupied herself during that particular week.

Nothing for Sunday. Monday May 13th: *C. left for Leeds. Mother to tea.* Tuesday May 14th: *Rang Gas Board. C. home 3 p.m.*

Pictures. And here in Hatton's log book was the Leeds trip confirmed. He had stopped twice on the way up, at Norman Cross for lunch at the Merrie England café, and at Dave's Diner near Retford for a cup of tea. His room in Leeds was with a Mrs Hubble at 21 Ladysmith Road, and on the return journey he had stopped only once and again at the Merrie England. There was nothing in the log book at this stage to make Wexford even pause. Hatton had done the journey in the shortest possible time, leaving no possible spare moment for undercover activities. He turned back to the diary.

Wednesday, May 15th: *C. off work. Rang doctor. Mem, N.H.S., not private*. Interesting. Hatton had been ill and at that time apparently not in funds. Thursday May 16th: *C. summer flu. Ring Jack and Marilyn put off dinner*. There was no entry for Friday May 17th.

Saturday, May 18th: *C. better. Doctor called again. Jim and mother came*.

That completed the week. Wexford turned the page to Sunday, May 18th: *C. left for Leeds. Mem, will ring me 8 p.m. J and M came for drinks and solo game*. Opposite was a photograph of a large country house and the lines: 'It is a truth universally acknowledged that a single man in possession of a good fortune must be in want of a wife.' Wexford smiled grimly to himself. Monday, May 20th: *C. bad again. Left Leeds late. Home 10 p.m.*

Quickly Wexford checked with the log book. Yes, here was Hatton's entry that he had been too ill to start the return journey until noon. He had driven home slowly and stopped twice on the way at the Hollybush at Newark and at the Merrie England. But had he really been ill or had he been shamming, crafty sick to give himself extra time in Leeds? For however he acquired that money he must have acquired it, Wexford was certain, during the 19th or the 20th of May.

Tuesday, May 21st: *C. fit again. Day off. Saw Jack and Marilyn. Appointment 2 p.m. with dentist*.

A precise little woman, Lilian Hatton, if not exactly verbose. Impossible to tell if she knew anything. The last place to which she would have confided her secrets was this calendar diary.

It didn't look as if Hatton had been up to much on that Monday morning in Leeds, but you never knew. There was always the night between Sunday and Monday to be considered. For all Wexford knew or could remember there might have been a bank robbery in that city at that time. It would all have to be checked. He wondered why the Fanshawe business kept intruding and upsetting his concentration, and then suddenly he knew.

Fanshawe had crashed his car on Monday, May 20th; an unidentified girl had died on May 20th and also on May 20th something big had happened to Charlie Hatton.

But there couldn't be a connection. Fanshawe was a wealthy stockbroker with a flat in Mayfair and, apart from a bit of moral nastiness, not a stain on his character. Charlie Hatton was a cocky little lorry driver who had probably never set foot in Mayfair all his life.

It was just a curious coincidence that Hatton had been killed on the day following that of Mrs Fanshawe's regaining consciousness.

Wexford closed the books and emptied his tankard for the third time. He was tired and fanciful and he had drunk too much beer. Yawning ponderously, he put Clytemnestra outside the back door and while he waited for her, stood staring emptily at the cloudless, star-filled sky.

CHAPTER ELEVEN

'Good morning, Miss Thompson,' Wexford said with a heartiness he didn't feel.

'Mrs Pertwee, if you don't mind.' She picked up one of the wire baskets that were stacked outside the supermarket and gave him a self-conscious, defiant stare. 'Jack and me got married very quietly yesterday afternoon.'

'May I be among the first to offer my congratulations?'

'Thanks very much, I'm sure. We didn't tell no one about it, just went off to church quietly by ourselves. Jack's been so cut up about poor Charlie. When are you going to catch his killer, that's what I want to know? Not putting yourselves out, I reckon, on account of him being a working fella. Been different if he was one of your upper crust. This capitalist society we live in makes me spit, just spit it does.'

Wexford backed a little, fearing she might suit the action to the word. The bride snapped her bootbrush eyelashes at him. 'You want to pull your socks up,' she said relentlessly. 'Whoever killed Charlie, hanging'd be too good for him.'

'Dear, oh dear,' said Wexford mildly, 'and I thought you progressives were dead against capital punishment.'

She banged into the supermarket and Wexford went on his way, smiling wryly. Camb eyed him warily as he entered the police station.

'Getting interested in this Fanshawe business, I gather, sir. I met Miss Fanshawe on my way in.'

'So interested,' Wexford said, 'that I'm sending Detective Constable Loring down to find out who's missing in the holiday towns and it might be worth our while to check with London too.'

Burden had left for Stamford. Stepping into the lift, Wexford decided to do the London checking himself. Young women were beginning to get on his nerves. There were so many of them about, and it seemed to him they caused as much trouble to a policeman as burglars. Now to see how many of them were missing in London. This task was for him somewhat *infra dig,* but until Burden and Sergeant Martin brought him some information he had little else to do, and this way he could, at any rate, be certain it was well done.

By lunchtime he had narrowed his search down to three out of the dozens of girls missing in the London area. The first was a Carol Pearson, of Muswell Hill, interesting to him because she had worked as a hairdresser's improver at a shop in Eastcheap. Jerome Fanshawe's office was in Eastcheap and the hairdresser's had a barber's shop attached to it. Hers was also a significant name because she had black hair and her disappearance was reported on May 17th.

The second girl, Doreen Dacres, was like Carol Pearson, black-haired and aged twenty, and his interest was aroused because she had left her room in Finchley on May 15th to take a job in Eastbourne. Nothing further had been heard of her either in Finchley or at the Eastbourne club address.

Bridget Culross was the last name with which he felt he need concern himself. She was twenty-two years old and had been a nurse at the Princess Louise Clinic in New Cavendish Street. On Saturday May 18th she had gone to spend the weekend with an unnamed boy friend in Brighton, but had not returned to the clinic. It was assumed that she had eloped with her boy friend. Her hair was also dark, her life erratic and her only relative an aunt in County Leix.

Young women! Wexford thought irritably, and he thought also of his own daughter who was making him scrape the bottom of his pocket so that at some future possible never-never time she might be able to smile without restraint before the cameras.

The long day passed slowly and it grew very hot. Clouds massed heavily, dense and fungoid in shape, over the huddled roofs of the town. But they did nothing to diminish the heat, seeming instead to enclose it and its still, threatening air under a thick muffling lid. The sun had gone, blanked out by sultry vapour.

To an observer Wexford might be thought only to be sitting, like many other inhabitants of Kingsmarkham, waiting for the storm to break. He did nothing. He lay back by the open window with his eyes closed and the warm breathless air came to him just as in another cooler season heat fanned from the grid lower down the wall. No one disturbed him and he was glad. He was thinking.

In Stamford, where it was raining, Inspector Burden went to a country house supposedly occupied by a man named McCloy and found it deserted, its doors locked and its garden overgrown. There were no neighbours and no one to tell him where McCloy had gone.

Detective Constable Loring drove along the promenades of the south coast towns, calling at police stations and paying particular attention to those clubs and cafés and amusement halls where girls come and go and pass each other. He had found a club where Doreen Dacres had been engaged but where no Doreen Dacres had arrived and this comforted him. He even telephoned Wexford to tell him about it, his elation subsiding somewhat when he heard the chief inspector had also found this out three hours before.

The storm broke at five o'clock.

For some time before this heavy clouds had increased and in the west the sky had become a dense purplish-black, a range of mountainous cumulus against which the outlines of buildings took on a curious clarity and the trees stood out livid and sickly bright. In spite of the clammy heat, shoppers began to hurry, but the rain which fell so readily when rainy days preceded it, now, after a fortnight's drought, held off as if it could only be squeezed out as a result of some acute and agonising pressure. It was as though the clouds were not themselves mere vapour but impermeable sagging sacks, purposely constructed and hung to contain water.

The first whispering breeze came like a hot breath and Wexford closed his windows. Almost imperceptibly at first the trees in the High Street pavement began to sway. Most of the merchandise outside greengrocers' and florists' had already been taken in and now it was the turn of the sunblinds to be furled and waterproof awnings to take their place. The air seemed to press against Wexford's windows. He stood against them, watching the dark western sky and the ash-blue cumulus now edged with brilliant white.

The lightning was the forked kind and it branched suddenly like a firework and yet like the limb of a blazing tree. As its fiery twigs flashed out and cut into the inky cloud, the thunder rolled out of the west.

Wexford dearly loved a storm. He liked the forked lightning better than the zig-zag kind and now he was gratified by a second many-branched display that seemed to spring and grow from the river itself, blossoming in the sky above the Kingsbrook meadows. This time the thunder burst with a pistol-shot snap and with an equal suddenness, as if at last those swollen vessels had been punctured, the rain began to fall.

The first heavy drops splashed in coin shapes on the pavement below and in their tubs the pink flowers on the forecourt dipped and swayed. For a brief moment it seemed that the rain still hesitated, that it would only patter dispiritedly on the dust-filled gutters where its drops rolled like quick-silver. But then, urged on as it were by a series of multiple lightning flashes, it hesitated no more and, instead of increasing gradually from the first tentative shower, the water gushed forth in a vast fountain. It dashed against the windows, washing off dust in a great cleansing stream, and Wexford moved away from the glass. The sudden flood was more like a wave than rain and it blinded the window as surely as darkness.

He heard the car splash in and the doors slam. Burden, perhaps. The internal phone rang and Wexford lifted the receiver.

'I've got Cullam here, sir.' It was Martin's voice. 'Shall I bring him up? I thought you might like to talk to him.'

Maurice Cullam was afraid of the storm. That didn't displease Wexford. With some scorn he eyed the man's pale face and the bony, none-too-steady hands.

'Scared, Cullam? Not to worry, we'll all die together.'

'Big laugh,' said Cullam, and he winced as the thunder broke above their heads. 'I don't reckon it's safe being so high up. When I was a kid I was in a house that got struck.'

'But you got out unscathed, eh? Well they say the devil looks after his own. Why have you brought him here, Sergeant?'

'He's bought that refrigerator,' said Sergeant Martin. 'And

a room heater *and* a load of other electrical bits and pieces. Paid cash for them, a couple of quid short of a hundred and twenty pounds.'

Wexford put the lights on and behind the streaming glass the sky looked black as on a winter's night. 'All right, Cullam, where did you get it?'

'I saved it up.'

'I see. When did you buy that washing machine of yours, the one you washed your gear in after Hatton died?'

'April.' As the storm receded and the thunder became a distant grumbling, Cullam's shoulders dropped and he lifted sullen eyes. 'April, it was.'

'So, you've saved another hundred and twenty pounds in just two months. What do you get a week? Twenty? Twenty-two? You with five kids and council house rent to pay? You've saved it in two months? Come off it, Cullam. I couldn't save it in six and my kids are grown up.'

'You can't prove I didn't save it.' Cullam gave a slight shiver as the overhead light flickered off, then on again. A rolling like the banging of many drums, distant at first, then breaking into a staccato crackling, announced the return of the storm to Kingsmarkham. He shifted in his chair, biting his lip.

Wexford smiled as a zig-zag flash changed the gentle illumination of the office into a sudden white blaze. 'A hundred pounds,' he said. 'That's pathetic payment for a man's life. What's yours worth, Sergeant?'

'I'm insured for five thousand, sir.'

'That's not quite what I meant, but we'll let it pass. You see, an assassin is paid according to his own self-valuation. Never mind what the victim's life's worth. If a road sweeper kills the king he can't expect to get the same gratuity as a general. He wouldn't expect it. His standards are low. So if you're going to employ an assassin and you're a mean skinflint you pick on the lowest of the low to do your dirty work. Mind you, it won't be so well done.'

Wexford's last words were drowned in thunder. 'What d'you mean, lowest of the low?' Cullam lifted abject yet truculent eyes.

'The cap fits, does it? They don't come much lower than

you, Cullam. What, drink with a man — drink the whisky he paid for — and then lie in wait to kill him?'

'I never killed Charlie Hatton!' Cullam leapt trembling to his feet. The lightning flared into his face and, covering his eyes with one hand, he said desperately, 'For God's sake can't we go downstairs?'

'I reckon Hatton was right when he called you an old woman, Cullam,' Wexford said in disgust. 'We'll go downstairs when I'm good and ready. You talk and when you've told me where McCloy is and what he paid you, then you can go downstairs and hide your head.'

Still on his feet, Cullam leant on the desk, his head hanging. 'It's a lie,' he whispered. 'I don't know McCloy and I never touched Hatton.'

'Where did the money come from then? Oh, sit down, Cullam. What sort of man are you, anyway, scared of a bit of thunder? It's laughable, afraid of a storm but brave enough to wait in the dark down by the river and bash your friend over the head. Come on now, you may as well tell us. You'll have to sooner or later and I reckon this storm's set in for hours. Hatton had fallen foul of McCloy, hadn't he? So McCloy greased your palm a bit to walk home with Hatton and catch him unawares. The weapon and the method were left to you. Curious, you were so mean, you even grudged him a proper cosh.'

Cullam said again, 'It's all a lie.' He twisted down into the chair, holding his head and keeping it averted from the window. 'Me bash Charlie on the head with one of them stones? I wouldn't have thought of it . . . I wouldn't . . .'

'Then how did you know it was a river stone that killed him?' Wexford pounced triumphantly. Slowly Cullam raised his head and the sweat glistened on his skin. 'I didn't tell you.'

'Nor me, sir,' said the sergeant.

'Jesus,' Cullam said, his voice uneven and low.

The black clouds had parted to show between them shreds of summer sky turned sickly green. Against the glass the unremitting rain pounded.

Stamford police knew nothing of Alexander James McCloy. His name was on the voters' list as occupying Moat Hall, the small mansion Burden had found deserted, but plainly he had left it months before. Burden plodded through the rain from estate agent to estate agent and he at last found Moat Hall, listed in the books of a small firm on the outskirts of the town. It had been sold in December by McCloy to an American widow who, having changed her mind without ever living in the place, had returned it to the agent's hands and departed to spend the summer in Sweden.

Mr McCloy had left them no address. Why should he? His business with them had been satisfactorily completed; he had taken his money from the American lady and disappeared.

No, there had never really been anything in Mr McCloy's behaviour to make them believe he wasn't a man of integrity.

'What do you mean, "really"?' Burden asked.

'Only that the place was never kept decently as far as I could see, not the way a gentleman's house should be. It was a crying shame to see those grounds neglected. Still, he was a bachelor and he'd no staff as far as I know.'

Moat Hall lay in a fold of the hills perhaps a mile from the A.1. 'Was he always alone when you saw him at the house?' Burden asked.

'Once he had a couple of chaps with him. Not quite up to his class I thought.'

'Tell me, were you taken all over the house and grounds to make your survey or whatever you do?'

'Certainly. It was all quite above board — none too clean, but that's by the way. Mr McCloy gave me a free hand to go where I chose, bar the two big outhouses. They were used for stores he said, so there was no point in me looking. The doors were padlocked anyway and I got what I wanted for my purpose from looking at the outside.'

'No stray lorries knocking about, I daresay?'

'None that I saw.'

'But there might have been in the outhouses?'

'There might at that,' said the agent doubtfully. 'One of them's near as big as a hangar.'

'So I noticed.' And Burden thanked him grimly. He was almost certain that he had found him, that he could say, 'Our McCloy was here,' and yet what had he achieved but dredge up a tiny segment of McCloy's life? The man had been here and had gone. All they could do now was to turn Moat Hall upside down in the forlorn hope something remained in the near-derelict place to hint at its erstwhile owner's present refuge.

'Are you going to charge me with murdering him?' Cullam said hollowly.

'You and McCloy and maybe a couple of others when you've told us who they are. Conspiracy to murder, the charge'll be. Not that it makes much difference.'

'But I've got five kids!'

'Paternity never kept anyone out of jail yet, Cullam. Come now, you wouldn't want to go inside alone, would you? You wouldn't want to think of McCloy laughing, going scot-free, while you're doing fifteen years? It'll be the same sentence for him, you know. He doesn't get off any lighter just because he only told you to kill Hatton.'

'He never did,' Cullam said wildly. 'How many times do I have to tell you I don't know this McCloy?'

'A good many times before I'd believe you. Why would you kill Hatton on your own? You don't have to kill a man because he's got more money and a nicer home than you have.'

'I didn't kill him!' Cullam's voice came dangerously near a sob.

Wexford switched off the light and for a moment the room seemed very dark. Then, as his eyes grew accustomed, he saw that it was no darker than on any summer evening after heavy rain. The light had a cold bluish tinge and the air was cooler too. He opened the window and a light fresh breeze clutched at the curtains. Down below on the forecourt the tub flowers had been flattened into a sodden pink mush.

'Listen, Cullam,' he said, 'you were there. You left the bridge ten minutes before Hatton started. It was twenty to eleven when you said goodbye to Hatton and Pertwee and even walking none too fast you should have been indoors at home by eleven. But you didn't get in till a quarter past. The following morning you washed the shirt you'd been wearing, the pullover and the trousers. You knew a river stone had been used to kill Hatton and today you, who get twenty pounds a week and never have a penny to bless yourself with, spent a hundred and twenty quid on luxury equipment. Explain it away. Cullam, explain it away. The storm's blowing over and you've nothing to worry about except fifteen years inside.'

Cullam opened his big ill-made hands, clenched them and leant forward. The sweat had dried on his face. He seemed to be having difficulty in controlling the muscles which worked in his forehead and at the corners of his mouth. Wexford waited patiently, for he guessed that for a moment the man was totally unable to speak. Terror had dried and paralysed his vocal cords. He waited patiently, but without a vestige of sympathy.

'The hundred quid and his pay packet,' Cullam said at last. His tone was hoarse and terrified. 'I . . . I took it off his body.'

CHAPTER TWELVE

'What did he want it for, Charlie-bloody-Hatton? I've been in his place, I've seen what he'd got. You ever seen his wife, have you? Got up like a tart with her new frocks and her jewellery and all that muck on her face, and not a bleeding thing to do all day long but watch that colour telly and ring up her pals. They hadn't got no kids, yelling and nagging at you the minute you get in, crawling all over you in the night because they're cutting their bloody teeth. You want to know when my missus last had a new frock? You want to know when we last had a night out? The answer's never, not since the first baby come. My missus has to buy the kids' clothes down the jumble sale and if she wants a pair of nylons they come off the Green Shield stamps. Bloody marvellous, isn't it? Lilian Hatton's got more coats than a perishing film star but she has to go and spend thirty quid on a new outfit for Pertwee's wedding. A hundred pounds? She wouldn't even miss it. She could use it for spills to light her fags.'

The flood-gates had opened and now Cullam, the reticent, the truculent, was speaking without restraint and from a full heart. Wexford was listening with concentration, but he did not appear to be listening at all. If Cullam had been in a fit state to observe behaviour he might have thought the chief inspector bored or preoccupied. But Cullam only wanted to talk. He was indifferent to listeners. All he required was the luxury of silence and a nearly empty room.

'I could have stuck it all,' he said, 'but for the bragging. "Put it away, Maurice," he'd say. "Your need's greater than mine," and then he'd tell me about the new necklace he'd bought for his missus. "Plenty more where that came from," he'd say. Christ, and I can't find the money to buy my kids new shoes! Two kids I'd got when I'd been married as long as Hatton. Is it fair? Is it right? You tell me.'

'I've listened to the party political broadcast,' said Wexford. 'I don't give a damn for your envy. Envy like yours is a hell of a good motive for murder.'

'Yeah? What would I get for killing him? I wasn't in his will. I've told you what I did. I took the money off his body. Five kids I've got and the milkman don't come till eleven in the morning. You ever tried keeping milk for five kids without a fridge in a heatwave?' He paused and with a shifty, fidgety look, said, 'D'you know what Hatton'd have done that Saturday if he hadn't been killed? Wedding first, Pertwee's wedding, and Hatton all got up in a topper with his tarty wife. Round the shops afterwards, not to buy anything, just to fritter. Charlie told me it wasn't nothing for them to get through twenty nicker poking about in the shops. Bottle of wine here, some muck for her face there. Then they'd have some more booze at the Olive, have dinner. Off to the pictures in the evening and in the best seats. Bit of a contrast from me, isn't it? If I want to relax I go out in the garden, anywhere to get away from the kids' bawling.'

'Are you a Catholic, Cullam?'

That surprised him. He had perhaps been expecting a tougher comment and he hunched his shoulders, muttering suspiciously, 'I haven't got no religion.'

'Don't give me that stuff about children then. Nobody makes you have children. Ever heard of the pill? My God, they knew how to plan families twenty years, thirty years before you were born.' Wexford's voice grew hard as he warmed to a favourite theme. 'Having kids is a privilege, a joy, or it should be, and, by God, I'll get the County down on you if I see you strike that boy of yours on the head again! You're a bloody animal, Cullam, without an animal's . . . Oh! what's the use? What the hell are you doing anyway, cluttering up my office, wasting my time? Cut the sob stuff and tell me what happened that night. What happened when you left Hatton and Pertwee at the bridge?'

Stamford had promised to give Burden all the help they could and they were as good as their word. A sergeant and a constable went back with him to Moat Hall and the locks on the two outhouses were forced.

Inside they found oil on the concrete floor and, imprinted by that oil, a tracery of tyre marks. Apart from that there was nothing to show a suspect occupancy but two crushed cardboard cases in one corner. Both had contained canned peaches.

'No joy here,' said Burden to the sergeant. He threw the flattened cardboard down in disgust. 'I've got things like this in my own garage at home. The supermark et gives them to me to bring my wife's shopping home in on Fridays.'

He came to the doorway and started across the deserted yard. As surely as if he could see them actually arriving, see them now, he pictured the stolen lorries driven in. The big doors would open for them and close on them and McCloy and the men who were 'not quite up to his class' would unload them and store the cargoes here. Back-slapping, laughing immoderately, Charlie Hatton would go into the house for a drink and a 'bite to eat' before driving the lorry away and abandoning it.

'I'd like to go over the house,' he said, 'only breaking and entering's not in my line. We'll have to wait for permission from the expatriate lady in Sweden.'

Cullam got up and wandered to the window. He looked as if he expected Wexford to hinder him, but Wexford said nothing.

'He was flashing all this money about in the Dragon. On and on about it he was when we walked up to the bridge.' Cullam stood by the window, staring fixedly now at the road he had trodden with Hatton and Pertwee. The wet pavements cast back mirror reflections. Wexford guessed the Kingsbrook must have swollen now, its stones submerged under a mill-race. 'Pertwee told me to wait for Charlie Hatton,' Cullam said. 'I wouldn't do that. God, I was sick of him and his money.' Slowly he pushed a hand through his thin tow-coloured hair. 'Anyway, I told you, I wasn't feeling too good. I just walked along the path in the dark.'

Thinking of what you were going home to, Wexford thought, and what Hatton was. There would have been no sound down there but the sibilant trickle of water. Above Cullam, above the web of black branches, a tranquil galaxy, a net of stars. Greed and envy took from a man's heart everything but — well, greed and envy. If Cullam had noticed anything as he walked it would have been the rubbish, the flotsam that the river sucked in and gathered on its journey through the meadows.

'Did you wait for him?'

'Wait, nothing!' Cullam said hotly. 'Why would I? I hated his guts.' Wexford wondered how long since anyone had made so many damaging admissions in his office in so short a space of time. Cullam burst out violently. 'I was sick then. I threw up under the trees. And I felt bloody, I can tell you.' He shuddered a little, but whether at the memory of this vomiting by the water's edge or of something even uglier Wexford could not tell. He watched the man narrowly, not caring for the wariness of his eyes and the way his hands had begun to twitch. 'I'm not used to whisky. A half of bitter's more my line.'

'You're not the only one,' Wexford said sharply. 'What happened then? Did you hear Hatton approach?'

'I'd heard him for a bit by then. I could hear him whistling a long way behind. He was whistling that stupid little old song of his about the man who was scared to go home in the dark.' Wexford looked up and met the shifty eyes. They slid away furtively, the pink lids blinking. Was Cullam a complete clod or did he realise how macabre his words had been? A man would have to be totally deficient in imagination to fail to be struck with a kind of horror and awe.

> 'Mabel, dear,
> Listen here,
> There's robbery in the park . . .'

Burden, who had heard them, had memorised the words and repeated them to his chief. 'Robbery in the park . . .' How did it go on? Something about there being no place like home but he couldn't go home in the dark. It was Wexford's turn to shiver now. In spite of his age, his experience, he felt a cold thrill run through him.

'Then it happened,' Cullam said suddenly. His voice trembled. 'You're not going to believe this, are you?'

Wexford only shrugged.

'It's the truth. I swear it's the truth.'

'Save your swearing for the dock, Cullam.'

'Christ . . .' The man made a sudden effort and the words tumbled out fast. 'The whistling stopped. I heard a sort of sound

. . .' He had no descriptive power, few adjectives but hackneyed obscenities. 'A kind of choking, a sort of — well, God, it was horrible! I felt so bloody bad, anyway. After a bit I got up and — and I went back. I was scared stiff. It was sort of creepy down there. I couldn't see nothing and I — I stumbled over him. He was lying on the path. Could I have a drink of water?'

'Don't be a damned fool,' Wexford snapped.

'You needn't be so rough with me,' Cullam whined. 'I'm telling you, aren't I? I don't have to tell you.'

'You have to, Cullam.'

'I struck a match,' the man mumbled. 'Charlie's head was all bashed in. I turned him over and I got blood on me.' The words slurred and he gabbled. 'I don't know what come over me. I put my hand inside his coat and took hold of that wallet. There was a hundred quid in it, just on a hundred. He was all warm . . .'

Wexford stared at him aghast. 'He was dead, though?'

'I don't know . . . I don't . . . Christ, yes, he was dead! He must have been dead. What are you trying to do to me?' The man put his head in his hands and his shoulders shook. Wexford took hold of his jacket roughly, pushing him so that his head jerked up. The tears on Cullam's cheeks awoke in him a nausea and a rage so fierce that it was all he could do to prevent himself from striking him. 'That's all, everything,' Cullam whispered, shuddering. 'The body rolled down the slope into the water. I ran home then, I ran like hell.' He put his fists into his eyes like a child. 'It's all true,' he said.

'The stone, Cullam, what about the stone?'

'It was laying by him. By his legs. I don't know why but I chucked it back in the water. There was blood on it and hair, bits of hair and — and other bits . . .'

'A bit late in the day to get squeamish, wasn't it?'

Wexford's tone was savage, its effect electric. Cullam sprang to his feet and let out a great cry, drumming his fists on the desk.

'I never killed him, I never, never . . . ! You've got to believe me.'

Burden had just come in, damp and disgruntled, when Wexford erupted bull-like from the lift.

'Where's Martin?'

'Don't ask me. I've just driven close on two hundred miles and I . . .'

'Never mind all that. I've got Cullam upstairs and he's come out with a fine tale.' Controlling his voice with an effort, he gave Burden a swift précis. 'Says he took the money off Hatton's corpse. Maybe that's all he did. I just don't know.'

'But you'll hold him? Keep him here on a charge of stealing the hundred quid and the pay packet?'

'Something like that. Martin can deal with it. I want you and Loring and anyone else going spare over in Sewingbury to turn Cullam's house upside down.'

'In case he's got McCloy's blood money hidden away?'

'Mike, I'm just beginning to wonder,' Wexford said wearily, 'if McCloy isn't a myth, a fiction. Cullam's a damned liar and all we know of McCloy rests on his word alone. Why shouldn't he have fabricated McCloy as a neat little red herring?' He sighed. 'Only he hasn't got any imagination,' he said.

'McCloy exists all right,' Burden said emphatically. 'He's an elusive sort of bird but he exists.'

It was eleven when Wexford got home. They had searched Cullam's house, grubbing through soiled unmade beds, cupboards full of clothes that smelt of food spills, drawers containing a jumble of broken rubbish. They had searched but the only money they had found was two and eightpence in Mrs Cullam's handbag, a white plastic handbag with black grease in its creases. And their only sinister discovery was bruises and contusions on the legs of one of the children . . .

'Give me an ounce of civet, good apothecary,' said Wexford to Clytemnestra, 'to sweeten my imagination.' In the belief that he had told her she was a good dog, Clytemnestra wagged her plumed grey tail. The door opened and Sheila came in. 'What are you doing home on a Wednesday?' said her father ungraciously.

'That thing came off my tooth. I was eating a Milky Way and it collapsed. So I had to come down and see Mr Vigo.' She gave him a disarming smile and kissed his cheek. Her hair was dressed in a pyramid of fat ringlets and she looked like a

Restoration wench, maid to Millamant, scene stealer, fit to be kissed in corners.

'Well, did he fix it up?'

'Mm-hm. On the spot. He said he wouldn't charge me.'

'Charge you? Me, you mean. And I should hope not.'

Wexford grinned, sloughing off the memory of Cullam's filth like a soiled skin. 'Now you've got false teeth,' he said, 'you mustn't expect to eat toffee.'

'I haven't got false teeth. I've just got a crown. D'you want some of my coff-choc? It's Nes and drinking chocolate mixed up. Quite groovy.'

'I don't think so, lovey, thanks all the same.'

'Mr Vigo and I got quite matey,' said Sheila. She dropped on the floor and, lying on her stomach with her elbows on the carpet, looked up into his face. 'He gave me tea in that Chinese room of his. I was scared to move, he's obviously so crazy about all that stuff. His wife came in and banged the door and he was furious because it made the china rattle; he said she just didn't understand.'

'How quaint. What you might call a new one.'

'Oh, Pop, it wasn't like that. When I went the receptionist was just leaving and she walked down into the town with me. She said Mr Vigo had really married for money. She was an heiress and she had a hundred thousand pounds and Mr Vigo wanted money to collect that Chinese stuff. He only stays with his wife now because of the baby. And he goes away most weekends. Sometimes he doesn't come back till quite late on a Monday night. The receptionist thinks he's got a girl friend in London. She seemed a bit jealous. D'you know, I got the idea he sleeps with her too.'

Wexford kept his face unmoved, but for the faintest flicker of what he hoped looked like sophisticated amusement. He wasn't shocked by what he had been told; he was astonished that it should have been said to him by his own daughter. In a way he was proud and grateful. Nearly forty years had passed since he was Sheila's age. Could he have spoken such words to his father? He would rather have died.

Sheila stretched, got up easily. 'Since I'm home,' she said, 'I might as well do my duty. Fancy ten minutes down by the river, dog?'

Wexford said quickly, 'No, not there, sweetheart.' What, allow his child to walk alone by those dark waters? 'I'll take the dog.'

'Really?'

'Go on. Get off to bed. That hair looks as though it'll take a lot of coping with.'

Sheila giggled. 'You'd be surprised.' He stared, somewhat appalled, as she lifted the wig like a hat and dropped it over a cut-glass vase.

'My God, it's a wise father that knows his own child!' He eyed her eyelashes suspiciously, her long fingernails. How many more bits were take-off-able? Wexford, who was hardly ever shaken from his equilibrium by the devious excesses of criminals, was perpetually astonished by his own daughter. Smiling wryly, he fetched the lead and yanked Clytemnestra from the best armchair.

The night air was fresh, washed by the storm into a cool clarity. Hardly a star showed, for the sky was veiled by a lacy wrack, bleached snow-white by the moon that rose in a clear unclouded patch. The meadow grass he had compared to a tapestry had since that earlier walk been cut and the land had become a pale stubbly desert. It was cold for the time of year. When he came to the river he saw that it was much swollen. In places the stones were totally submerged under the racing water.

Wexford whistled up the dog and stepped on briskly. He could see the bridge now, its stones gleaming silver and the hart's tongue ferns between them like shivering slivers of metal. Someone was standing on the parapet, leaning over and looking down. It was some time before Wexford could decide whether it was a man or a woman and when he realised it was a woman he called out a brisk, cheerful good night so that she should not be afraid.

'Good night, Chief Inspector.' The voice was low, ironic, immediately indentifiable. Wexford approached Nora Fanshawe and she turned to face him.

'A fine evening after the storm,' he said. 'How's your mother?'

'She'll live,' the girl said coolly. A reserve that was part distaste blanked her features. Wexford knew that look. He had seen it hundreds of times on the faces of people who fancied that they had said too much to him, opened their hearts too wide. Presumably they imagined their confidences led him to regard them with disgust or pity or contempt. If only they knew that to him their revelations were but bricks in the house he was trying to build, rungs on the ladder of discovery, twisted curve-edged pieces in the current puzzle!

'Nothing fresh come back to her?'

'If you mean about the girl in the car, she says there was no girl. I know when she's telling the truth.'

'People never remember what happened immediately before they got hit on the head,' Wexford said cheerfully, 'especially when their skulls are fractured. It's medical fact.'

'Is that so? I mustn't keep you, Chief Inspector. Did you know your dog's out in the road?'

Wexford retrieved Clytemnestra from the path of a solitary oncoming car. The driver wound down his window and cursed him, adding that for two pins he'd tell the police.

'Blooming thorn in my flesh, you are,' Wexford said to the dog as he clipped the lead on. 'A source of humiliation.' He watched the girl retreat into the Olive and Dove, the moonlight casting her shadow black, straight and attenuated.

CHAPTER THIRTEEN

Detective Constable Loring was delighted at the prospect of a day in London. He was mortally afraid of Wexford who, he felt, treated him with a just but unremitting harshness. Someone had told Loring of the chief inspector's almost paternal fondness for his predecessor, Mark Drayton, and of his disillusionment when Drayton had come to grief. It had been over some mess with a girl and a bribe. Drayton, they told him, had worn his hair long, had been surly and sarcastic and clever and a devil with the women. Loring, therefore had his own hair cropped eccentrically close and was as eager, as bright and cheerful as he could be. Cleverness, he felt, must come hereafter. At present he couldn't compete with Wexford and Burden who were constantly being clever all over the place. As for the women... Loring was healthily keen. It afforded him considerable pleasure to be going to London on a quest for three missing girls. Wistfully he thought how very gratifying it would be to find the right one and perhaps hear an appreciative Wexford call him Peter. Drayton had frequently been favoured by the use of his Christian name.

For all his dreams and his naïveté, Loring was a perfectly competent officer. He made his mistakes and he was frank about them. At twenty-one he was six feet tall, as thin as he had been at fourteen, and desperately anxious for the day to come when he had finally grown out of his acne. For all that — the spots were far less noticeable than he believed — the girls he asked out usually accepted his invitations and the older women he interviewed patted their hair and smiled when he began his questions. With luck, he sometimes thought, when he put on a bit of weight and got rid of those damned spots, he might one day look rather like John Neville. He was surprised and somewhat chagrined by his reception at the Eastcheap hairdresser's.

Carol Pearson was the girl whose disappearance he was investigating and he had already called on her mother in Muswell Hill. A skittish lady of forty with the mental age and taste in dress of eighteen, she had simpered over him and offered him gin. God knew, you were only young once — Mrs Pearson looked as if she intended to be young several times over — and if Carol chose to pop off with her boy friend for a couple of months, she wasn't one to stand in her way. The boy friend was married, so what else could poor Carol do? The fact was she was sick to death of that job of hers, threatening to leave any time. Did Loring know the miserable wages they paid, the fact that the girls practically had to live on their tips? The boy friend had money. He was a travelling salesman, Mrs Pearson said vaguely. But she couldn't recall his name, hadn't been able to tell the police when they asked before. Jack, Carol had called him. She never wrote letters. Easy come, easy go like her mother she was, and Mrs Pearson gave him an ingratiating smile. She'd turn up one of these fine days.

So Loring had taken the tube to Tower Hill, getting lost a couple of times on the way. He walked up Eastcheap and picked out the office of the late Jerome Fanshawe by the brass plate on its marble doorway. Roma, the hairdresser's where Carol Pearson had worked, was diagonally opposite. Loring went in.

Never in his life had he seen anything like that receptionist. She wasn't the sort of girl you would dare to kiss, supposing you wanted to. Her hair was an artfully and deliberately tangled mass of red curls, the face beneath a miracle of paintwork, an artist's achievement of cream and amber light and shade with sooty eyes and blacked-out mouth. She wore a near-ankle-length black skirt, backless red boots and a short red caftan embroidered in gold.

Both her white telephones rang simultaneously as Loring entered. She lifted the receivers one after the other, said into each, 'Good morning. Roma. Will you hold the line one moment?' before resting them side by side on her enormous appointments book. 'Can I help you?'

Loring said he was a police officer and produced his card. She betrayed no surprise. 'One moment, please.' The telephone conversations were consecutively resumed, appointments made in the book. Loring glanced down the salon. Nothing like it had ever been seen in Kingsmarkham where clients still sat isolated in separate cells. Here the walls were lined in what looked like huge slices of pumpernickel. The chandeliers were black and silver mobiles and the floor a seemingly frozen lake of scarlet. Most of the assistants were men, tired worn-looking young men in lightweight suits drifted all over with many-coloured hair.

'If you've come about Carol Pearson,' the receptionist said contemptuously, 'you'll want Mr Ponti. One moment, please.' The left-hand phone had rung again. 'Good morning. Roma. Will you hold the line a moment, please? He's in the gentleman's salon and he's styling so you can't . . . Just *one* moment.' She lifted the second phone. 'Good morning. Roma. Just one . . .'

'Thank you for all your help,' Loring said. He retreated into the street and entered the door to what he would have called the barber's. It was not very different from its Kingsmarkham equivalent. Things in the world of fashion evolve more slowly for men than for women.

Mr Ponti looked more like a master at a public school than a hairdresser. He was tall and thin and he wore a perfectly plain, almost ascetic dark suit. The only indication that he had in fact been 'styling' was the handle of a pair of scissors protruding from his breast pocket and which Loring, so over-powering was the pedagogic impression, had at first taken for the rims of spectacles.

The other stylists leapt aside deferentially as he wove his way along the aisle between the chairs. The daylight from the door showed suntan powder on his cheekbones and now that he was close to, Loring saw him as an actor made up to play some academic part. The stoop was there, the vague though sharp expression, the myopic eyes.

A very faint trace of an Italian accent came through as he spoke. 'Carol?' he said. 'We have had the police here before and I told them, we cannot help.' He took the black leather handbag from Loring and fingered it appreciatively. 'This is very nice quality, very good.' With a shrug, he swept shut a concertina-style folding door that partly closed off the shop. 'Listen, she would not have this. I don't like to be cruel, but she was a cheap little girl. No style, no elegance. Ha!' From the interior of the bag he took out the Woolworth compact and the lipstick in its grazed metal case. 'These she might have, this cheap rubbish.' His long thin nose quivered disdainfully.

Loring thought him an odious man. 'Have you ever had a Mr Jerome Fanshawe among your clients?'

The name was evidently familiar. 'The stockbroker from across the street? I am told he is dead in a car accident.' Loring nodded. 'He has never been here.'

'Sure of that?'

'I never forget a client's name. All my clients are personally known to me.' Ponti snapped the bag shut and leant against the counter, looking bored.

'I'm wondering if Miss Pearson knew him,' Loring said, flinching from the scent of the man's after-shave. 'Did she ever mention him or did you ever see her go into his office?'

'I know nothing.' Ponti slid the door aside an inch and snapped his fingers. 'Those shots of Carol,' he called authoritatively, adding to Loring, 'I showed them to the other policemen. You may care to look at them.' He fixed his pale brown eyes on Loring's own haircut and studied it reflectively and with faint distaste.

The photographs were pushed round the edge of the door and Loring took them. 'I used her once as a model,' said Ponti. 'She was no good, no damn' good at all.'

They looked all right to Loring. He had a simple taste in feminine beauty, demanding no more than that a girl should be pretty and fresh and smiling. For these shots Carol Pearson's hair had been dressed in fantastic pyramids of sausage curl, some of which spiralled to her shoulders. She looked ill-at-ease as if she wore instead of her own hair a Britannia helmet and she seemed to be shrinking beneath the weight, peering upwards with a nervous half-smile. Her eyes were painted ridiculously with diagonal lines radiating from the lower lids and her ear lobes dragged down by encrusted pendants. Under the *maquillage* she was a pretty girl, classically lovely, and Loring recalled sickeningly that it might be she who had come to her death, hideously disfigured, in blood and fire and water.

'No damn' good at all,' the hairdresser said again.

Doreen Dacres had turned up.

It was a curious story Loring heard from her married sister in Finchley. Doreen had gone to take up her club job in

Eastbourne, arrived early and been kept waiting in a deserted lounge. There a well-informed cleaner had enlightened her as to what some of her new duties might consist of and Doreen, taking fright, had debunked into the street.

She had only five pounds in the world. Room and job in London having been abandoned, she took stock of her situation. The married sister had made it clear she wouldn't be welcome as a lodger with her and her husband, and their parents were in Glasgow, a city to which Doreen had sworn she would never return. Finally she had taken her luggage to a boarding house and, nervous that the club might catch up with her, booked herself in as Doreen Day and taken a shop assistant's job in the same name.

It was only when she wanted some clothes sent on that she had contacted her sister, six weeks later, by telephone. Thankfully, Loring crossed her off his list.

His last port of call was the Princess Louise Clinic in New Cavendish Street and he was directed by its porter to the nurses' home. This was a pleasant four-storey Regency house with white pillars flanking a bright blue front door liberally decorated with polished brass. A woman who called herself Home Sister came down to him and, before Loring could speak, she placed one pink finger against her lips.

'Quiet as a mouse, please. We mustn't forget the night staff are all getting their beauty sleep, must we?'

There was deep silence in the hall and a sweet scent far removed from the strong antiseptic of the hospital proper. It made Loring think of young girls, bevies of girls, whose freshly bathed bodies, as they passed through this place, left behind a mingled memory of Jasmine and Russian Leather and French Fern and New Mown Hay. He tip-toed after this stout navy-blue woman, who seemed to him half wardress and half mother superior, into a little lounge where there were chintz-covered chairs and flowers and an old television set.

'The girl who had the room next to Nurse Culross will be the best one to help you,' said Home Sister. 'Her name is Nurse Lewis, but of course it's out of the question that she should be disturbed if she's still sleeping.' She fixed him with a fierce censorious eye. 'Out of the question,' she said again. 'If you were the Home Secretary himself I wouldn't do it.' Apparently she was waiting for some show of defiance, and when Loring merely returned her look meekly, she lost some of her asperity and said, 'I'll make enquiries but I can't promise anything. Meanwhile, perhaps you'd care to look at some books.'

By this she meant magazines. The Princess Louise Nurses' Home was less sophisticated than Vigo's waiting room and it offered instead of *Nova* and *Elle* the *Nursing Mirror* and two copies of *Nursery World* which Loring saw were fifteen years old. Left alone, he stared out into the street.

An annexe to the clinic was a maternity hospital, part of it but distinctly separate from the larger building. While he waited, Loring saw a Bentley draw up and a young girl emerge leaning heavily on the arm of her husband. Her body was huge and unwieldy and evidently she was already in labour. Ten minutes passed and a Jaguar appeared. A similar little tableau took place, but in this case the potential mother was older and her maternity dress even more indicative of the *couturière* from whom it had come. The Princess Louise Clinic was busily fulfilling its function of replenishing the upper classes.

It was nearly five o'clock before the door opened slowly and Nurse Lewis came to him. Her eyes were heavy and she looked as if she had just wakened. She wore no make-up and she looked spotlessly clean, her blouse stiff and crisp from the launderer, her pale, almost cream-fair hair damp and streaked where a coarse-toothed comb had just passed through it.

'I'm sorry if I've kept you. I'm on nights you see.'

'That's all right,' Loring said. 'I work nights myself some-times. I know what it's like.'

Nurse Lewis sat down and her bare legs gleamed. Her pink toes were like a little girl's in a little girl's sandals.

'What did you want to know? I talked to the police before.' She smiled earnestly. 'I told them all I knew about Bridie Culross, but that wasn't much, you see. Bridie didn't make close friends with girls, she was a man's girl.'

'I'd like to hear anything you can tell me, Miss Lewis.' Just let them talk. He had learnt that from Wexford. 'About what sort of girl she was. She had a lot of boy friends?'

'Well, this isn't a teaching hospital so there aren't any

medical students. She'd been here for a year since she qualified and she's been out with all the housemen.'

Loring wrote that down.

'The man she was most keen on — well, I never knew his name. She called him Jay.'

'As if it were an initial, do you mean? Like short for John or James or — Jerome?'

'I suppose so. I told the police all this before, you know. They weren't very interested.'

'You see, we don't usually bother very much about missing girls.'

'Why are you bothering now?'

'Let's leave that for a moment shall we, Miss Lewis? Tell me more about this Jay.'

She crossed her long bare legs. 'I never saw him,' she said. 'He was married, I'm afraid. Bridie didn't worry much about that sort of thing. Oh, and I remember her saying his wife had been a patient here.'

Charming, Loring thought. He visits his sick wife and picks up one of the nurses on his way out.

'I know what you're thinking,' said Nurse Lewis, 'and it wasn't very nice. He'd got lots of money and a nice car and all that. Bridie . . .' She hesitated and blushed. 'Well, Bridie lived with him actually.'

'Lived with him? In his house?'

'I didn't quite mean that.'

'Oh, I see.' Nurses, who ought to be used to the facts of life, were astonishingly prudish, he thought. 'Er — she went to spend a weekend with this man on Saturday, May 18th? In Brighton, wasn't it?'

'That's right, with Jay.' Nurse Lewis was still blushing at the implications of this weekend. 'She didn't come back. I heard Matron say she wouldn't have her back this time if she came.'

'She'd done it before, you mean?'

'Well, she'd been late a good many times and sometimes she didn't bother to come in after a late night. She said she wasn't going to dress operations and cart bedpans around for the rest of her life. She was going to have it soft. That's what she said. I thought she'd gone away with Jay to live with him properly. Well, not properly, but you know what I mean.'

'Tell me, did he give her presents? Did she have a very good black handbag with a Mappin and Webb label? This one?'

'Oh, yes! He gave it to her for her birthday. She was twenty-two. Look . . .' She frowned and leant towards him. 'What is this? You've found her handbag but you haven't found her?'

'We're not sure yet,' said Loring, but he was.

Wexford would be displeased if he went back with just this and no more. Loring would have liked another day in London, but it was hardly worth facing Wexford's rage, the necessary preliminary to granting it. He went into the main hospital building and rang the bell at the enquiry desk. While he waited he looked about him, reflecting that he had never been in a hospital like this one before. His impression was that he was the first person to enter it for a long time with less than five thousand a year and he thought of Stowerton Infirmary where the outpatients sat for hours on hard chairs, where the paint was peeling off the walls and where everyone seemed to be in a hurry.

Here, instead, was an atmosphere of lazy graciousness as in a large private house. A very faint odour of disinfectant was almost entirely masked by the scent of flowers, sweet peas in copper jugs and, on the enquiry desk, a single rose in a fluted glass. The floor was carpeted in dark red Wilton.

Loring glanced up the branched staircase and watched the receptionist descend. He asked for a list of all the patients who had entered the Princess Louise Clinic in the past year and his request was received with a look of outrage.

It took him nearly half an hour, during which he was passed from one official personage to another, before he got the permission he wanted.

The list was long and imposing. Loring had never seen *Debrett* but he felt that this catalogue might have been a section of it. Nearly half the names on it were preceded by a title and among the plain Misters he recognised a distinguished industrialist, a former cabinet minister and a television personality who was a household word. Among the women was a duchess, a ballet dancer, a famous model. Loring couldn't find Dorothy Fanshawe. He searched all through the list again because he had been so certain her name would be there. It wasn't there.

J for Jerome, but J also for John, James, Jeremy, Jonathan, Joseph. Was Bridget Culross's lover the husband of the Hon. Mrs John Frazer-Bennet of Wilton Crescent or the husband of Lady James Fyne of The Boltons? Loring concluded and supposed Wexford would also conclude him to be the late husband of Dorothy Fanshawe.

CHAPTER FOURTEEN

The young Pertwees were honeymooning in Jack's father's house. Their own flat wouldn't be ready for a fortnight and Jack had cancelled the hotel booking. There was nowhere else for them to go and nothing much to do. Jack had taken his annual holiday, so here he was at home. Where else would he be? It was, after all, the only honeymoon he would ever get. Usually in his spare time he did a bit of painting or decorating or went to the dogs or down the Dragon. Marilyn made her dresses and giggled with her girl friends and went to meetings calculated to stir up social strife. These are not occupations for a honeymoon and the young Pertwees felt that to follow their old ways during this period, provided as it were for festive idleness and the indulgence of love, would be a kind of desecration. As Jack put it, you can't stay in bed all day, so they spent most of the time sitting hand in hand in the little-used parlour. Marilyn was only articulate on the subject of politics and Jack was never talkative. Neither of them ever read a book and they were abysmally bored. Each would have died rather than confess this to the other and they knew in their hearts that their silence was no threat of future discord. Everything would be fine once Jack was back at work and they were in their own flat. When there were his workmates to discuss and the furniture and having her mother to tea. Now they filled their silences with sad reflections on Charlie Hatton and although this too was no subject for a honeymoon, their shared memory of him expressed in hackneyed and sentimental phrases passed the time away and, because it was selfless and sincere, strengthened their love.

It was thus that Wexford found them.

Marilyn let him into the house, her only greeting a shrug. He too could be laconic and brusque and when Jack rose clumsily to his feet, Wexford said only, 'I've come to talk to you about McCloy.'

'You talk then. You tell me.'

The girl smiled at that. 'Give us a cig, Jack,' she said, and she gave her husband a fond proud look. 'Yes,' she said, coming up close to Wexford, 'you give us a lecture. We'd like to know, wouldn't we, Jack? We don't mind listening, we've nothing else to do.'

'That doesn't sound too good on your honeymoon.'

'Some honeymoon,' Jack grumbled. 'You think this is the way I'd planned it?'

Wexford sat down and faced them. 'I didn't kill Charlie Hatton,' he said. 'I didn't even know him. You did. You were supposed to be his friend. You've got a funny way showing it.'

A spasm of pain shivered the red from Jack's face. He took his wife's hand and he sighed. 'He's dead. You can't be friends with a dead man. All you've got is his memory to hold on to.'

'Give me a piece of your memory, Mr Pertwee.'

Jack looked him full in the face and now the blood returned, beating under the skin. 'You're always playing with words, twisting, being clever . . .'

His wife cut in, 'Showing your bloody education!'

'Leave it, love. I feel the same, but it's no good. It's . . . You've made up your mind Charlie was a crook, haven't you? It wouldn't be no good me telling you what he was really like, generous, good-hearted, never let you down. But it wouldn't be no good, would it?'

'I doubt if it would help me to find who killed him.'

'He found us our flat,' Jack said. 'D'you know what he did? The bloke that's got it now, he wanted key money. Two hundred he wanted and Charlie put that up. On loan, of course, but he wouldn't take no interest. May the 21st it was. I'll never forget that date as long as I live. Charlie'd been driving all the day before, driving down from the north. But he come here in the morning to say he'd found this flat for us. I was at work but Marilyn got a couple of hours off from the shop and went down there with him. Promised the bloke the money, he did, more like he was her dad than — just a friend.'

May the 21st. The day Hatton had ordered his teeth. Just after the robbery that never was. Here was another example of what Hatton had done with the small fortune he had somehow got out of McCloy.

'I'll let you have it whenever you want, Charlie said. Just

say the word. You should have seen him when we did say the word! I reckon giving things away made him really happy.'

'This place,' said Marilyn, mildly for her, 'well, it's not the same without Charlie Hatton and that's a fact.'

Sentimental twaddle, Wexford thought harshly. 'Where did he get all his money, Mrs Pertwee?'

'I could ask him that, could I? I could just come out with it like that? I may be common working class but I was brought up right. I've got manners. So, for God's sake, leave me out of it.'

'Mr Pertwee?'

He would have to answer, Wexford thought. He had said too much and been too self-controlled to plead distress as an excuse this time. Jack put his fist up to his forehead and leant on his elbow.

'Where did he get it? Two hundred and fifty pounds for his teeth, two hundred for you . . .' How it mounted up! 'Money for his furniture, his wife's clothes, your wedding present, money going week by week into the bank. He was earning twenty pounds a week, Mr Pertwee. What do you earn?'

'Mind your own damn' business.'

'Come on now, love,' said Pertwee miserably. He looked at Wexford, biting his lip. 'Bit more than that,' he said. 'Bit more in a good week.'

'Could you lend your best friend two hundred pounds?'

'My best friend's dead!'

'Don't stall, please,' Wexford said sharply. 'You knew what Hatton's life was, Pertwee. Don't tell me you never asked yourself where all that money came from. You asked yourself and you asked him. How did Hatton get to be a rich man on May 21st?'

And now Pertwee's brow cleared. He sighed and there was a tiny gleam of triumph in his eyes. 'I don't know. You could ask me from now till Doomsday. I can't tell you because I don't know.' He hesitated. 'You asked me about McCloy,' he said. 'Charlie didn't get no money from McCloy on May 21st. He couldn't have.'

Then Wexford questioned him and probed and used all the subtlety years of experience had given him. Pertwee held his wife's hand, shook his head, answered monosyllabically and at last he dried up.

At the special court held to give his case its preliminary hearing, Maurice Cullam pleaded guilty to stealing one hundred and twenty pounds from the dead body of Charlie Hatton and was remanded in custody. Further charges might be preferred against him, Burden intimated.

He didn't believe Cullam was a murderer. His house had been searched from top to bottom but no money had been found. Cullam had no bank account and no more than a few shillings in the Post Office. The only effect of the search was the incidental discovery of such savage bruises on the legs of Samantha Cullam as to necessitate her removal into the care of the county authority. Further charges would be preferred against her father, but they would not be in the nature of murder or larceny.

'What's your next step?' said Dr. Crocker idly, on his way back from examining the little girl's injuries. 'A bastard who'd beat up a kid like that wouldn't stop at murder, if you ask me.'

'It doesn't follow.'

'The trouble with you lot you're always looking for complications. Here's the boss now. I've just been asking Mike here if you've got a vacancy for me on your staff, seeing how I've helped you with your enquiries.'

Wexford gave him a sour look. 'Cullam's no killer.'

'Maybe not. Prefers his victims undersized and female,' and the doctor launched into a heated tirade against the arrested man.

'Oh, I'm sick of the whole bloody thing,' Wexford shouted suddenly. 'I've spent the entire morning trying to pump Pertwee. Sentimental fool! Everyone knows Hatton was a thief and a twister, but Pertwee won't talk because he doesn't want to sully the fellow's memory.'

'It's not a bad principle,' said Burden.

'Any principle's bad, Mike, if putting it into practice means a murderer goes free. Hatton did jobs for McCloy and one weekend in May he started squeezing his old employer. He squeezed him pretty hard, I can tell you. Two hundred pounds for Pertwee, two hundred and fifty for Vigo . . . Oh, I can't go into it all again.'

'So you're giving up?' said the doctor.

Burden looked deeply shocked and he clicked his tongue old-maidishly. But Wexford said calmly, 'I'm going to try another line for the present and I'm relying on you to smooth the path. You're supposed to be a doctor, after all.'

Mrs Fanshawe was alone when they got back to the Infirmary, but she was out of bed. Wrapped in a black nylon negligé — afterwards Crocker called it a *peignoir* — she was sitting in an armchair reading *Fanny Hill*.

'A chief inspector and an inspector and a doctor to see you,' said Nurse Rose. Mrs Fanshawe tucked *Fanny Hill* under her new copy of *Homes and Gardens*. She knew now that Nurse Rose was a nurse and not a maid and that she was in hospital. But that was no reason why the girl should take the attitude that her patient was honoured by this visit. Mrs Fanshawe knew what was due to her. Besides, she was glowing with the self-confidence of someone who, having been distressingly and obtusely disbelieved for days, has now proved her point. Nora was alive; Nora was here, or at least, a couple of miles away in Kingsmarkham. Probably this deputation, sent from whatever authority it was that had stupidly persisted in burying her, had been sent to apologise.

Hastily Mrs Fanshawe grabbed a handful of rings from the jewel case her sister had brought in and it was a lavishly decorated hand that she extended graciously to Wexford.

Wexford saw a discontented face with sagging chin muscles and lines pulling the mouth down at the corners. Mrs Fanshawe's eyes were hard and bright and her voice acid when she said:

'I'm not mad, you see. Everyone thought I was insane when I said my daughter was alive. Now, I expect, they'd like to apologise.'

'Certainly, Mrs Fanshawe. We all apologise.' Apologies cost nothing. He smiled blandly into the petulant face and suddenly he remembered what this woman's daughter had told him. How her father had paid her mother to let him have his women in the house. 'No one thought you were mad,' he said, 'but you'd been in a serious accident.' She nodded smugly and Wexford thought, She's no madder than she's ever been. But what did that amount to? She had never, he considered, been very bright.

Nurse Rose scampered in with two more chairs and she bridled, giggling a little, when all three men thanked her effusively.

'You can get me another cushion,' said Mrs Fanshawe. 'No, not a pillow, a proper cushion. And then you can ring my daughter.'

'In ten minutes, Mrs Fanshawe,' said Nurse Rose, tired but bright as ever.

'Just as you like.' Mrs Fanshawe waited until she was gone and then she said pettishly, 'This is supposed to be a private room, not that anyone would think so the cavalier treatment you get. Half the time you ring the bell they don't come.'

Wexford said dryly, 'You don't find it as comfortable as the Princess Louise Clinic?'

'What's that supposed to mean?'

'I understand you were in the Princess Louise Clinic in Cavendish Street in London last year.'

'You understood wrong then. The only time I've ever been in hospital was when my daughter was born.' She sighed impatiently when the door opened and Nurse Rose entered with tea for four. 'I thought you were under-staffed? These gentlemen are officials. They aren't paying a social call.'

But Dr Crocker said, 'Thank you very much, my dear,' and he ogled Nurse Rose outrageously. 'Will you be mother, Mrs Fanshawe, do the honours?'

The rings clinked as she poured the tea. She eyed him suspiciously. 'Well, my daughter's alive,' she said, 'and I've never been to the Princess Louise Clinic. What else d'you want?'

Wexford just glanced at Burden and Burden said, 'Your daughter's alive but there was a dead girl lying by the wreckage of your car. Any idea who she could be? The name Bridget Culross mean anything to you?'

'Nothing at all.'

'She was a nurse.' Mrs Fanshawe's sniff told him eloquently

what she thought of nurses. 'She was twenty-two and a girl who might be she was dead in the road with your husband.'

'She was never alive in the car with my husband.'

'Mrs Fanshawe,' Wexford said carefully, 'are you quite sure you gave no one a lift from Eastbourne, from Eastover?'

'I am sick of this,' said Dorothy Fanshawe. 'I don't know how many times I've told you. There was no one else in the car.'

He looked at her and he thought, *Would* you tell me? Are you ashamed that your husband flaunted these women at you, paid you? Or is it that you don't care any more, haven't cared for years, and there really was no one in the car?

Dorothy Fanshawe watched her rings winking in the sunlight. She avoided meeting the eyes of these tiresome men. They thought her stupid or a liar. She knew very well what they were getting at. Nora had been talking to them. Nora hadn't the decency and the discretion to keep silent about Jerome's nasty habits.

How stupid these men were! Their faces were all embarrassed and prudish. Did they really suppose she cared what Jerome had done? Jerome was dead and buried deep. Good riddance. All the money was hers and Nora's now, more money than all those foolish-looking men would earn between the lot of them in their lifetimes. As long as Nora didn't do anything stupid like marrying that Michael, there was nothing in the world to worry about.

Dorothy Fanshawe drank her tea and put the cup down with a sharp tap. Then she rang the bell and as the door opened, said:

'We shall want some more hot water.'

She had been going to say please, but she cut the word off and swallowed it. Suddenly Nurse Rose, so plump and pink and young, had looked just like that maid Jerome used to paw about when she was making the beds. She smiled a little, though, for Jerome was dead and there were no maids or nurses or soft young flesh where he had gone.

'Exhumation!' Burden exclaimed. 'You couldn't do it.'

'Well, I could, Mike,' said Wexford mildly. 'I daresay we

could get an order. Only she's been dead so long and the face was in a mess then and . . . God, I could wring Camb's bloody neck!'

'The aunt was so sure,' Burden said.

'We'd best get that Lewis girl down from the Princess Louise Clinic, show her the clothes. But if the girl was Bridget Culross, what was she doing in Fanshawe's car with Fanshawe's wife?'

'I believe Mrs Fanshawe, sir.'

'So do I, Mike. So do I.' Wexford said it again to convince himself. 'I think Fanshawe was capable of taking the girl to his bungalow and sleeping with her while his wife was there. I believe Mrs Fanshawe would have stood it. As to the girl — well, we don't know enough about her to say. But Nora Fanshawe knew nothing of it and Nora Fanshawe was with them until the Saturday. They thought she was going to stay on. So where does Culross come in? And where was she stowed away on the Friday night?'

'It's very disgraceful,' said Burden and he made a face like someone who had been shown a disgusting mess of offal.

'Never mind that. Leave the ethics and concentrate on the circumstantial evidence. The more I hear of them the more I go back to my old idea.'

'Which is?'

'In the light of our fresh information, this: Bridget Culross never knew Fanshawe. His wife was never a patient at the Princess Louise Clinic, therefore he isn't Jay. Probably she went to Eastbourne or Brighton with Jay, rowed with him and tried to get back to London on her own. Maybe she hitch-hiked. A lorry driver put her down on the Stowerton By-pass, she thumbed a lift from Fanshawe — maybe she stepped out into the road, he couldn't stop, hit her head and crashed. How's that?'

Burden looked dubious. 'That means to thumb her lift she would have had to be standing on the soft verge between the two carriageways.'

'And any normal hitch-hiker stands on the nearside and waits for someone coming down the slow lane?'

'Mm-hm. On the other hand we do know that Mrs Fanshawe heard her husband call out 'God!' just before the crash; in fact, that was the last thing he ever did say.'

'I hope,' said Wexford, 'the cry was heard by Providence and interpreted as a plea for forgiveness.' He chuckled sourly. 'So he sees the girl standing on the road, cries out, swerves, hits her. Why did she have only a little loose change in her handbag, no keys, nothing to identify her? Why would a lorry driver put her down on the by-pass instead of in the town?'

'It's your theory, sir.'

'I know it is, damn it!' said Wexford.

But he kept thinking about that lorry driver. Charlie Hatton had passed that way a quarter of an hour before the accident. He couldn't have seen the accident. Could he have seen the girl waiting to thumb a lift? Or could he have been the driver who had left her there? The trouble was Charlie Hatton had been driving in the other direction.

It had been May 20th and on May 21st Charlie Hatton was a rich man. There must be a connection. But where did McCloy come into all this?

Every police force in England and Wales was now looking for Alexander James McCloy, light brown hair, medium height, aged 42, late of Moat Hall, near Stamford in Lincolnshire; because of Burden's recent discoveries they were looking for him in Scotland too.

This time it was Mr Pertwee senior who admitted him into the house. Still hand-in-hand the honeymooners were watching television.

'Christ, do we have to?' Marilyn said crossly when her husband got up and switched off the party political broadcast. 'What d'you want this time?'

Wexford said, 'In November of last year your friend Hatton arranged to have the lorry he drove for his employer Mr Bardsley hi-jacked. When I say arranged, I mean he did so under the instructions of his other employer, Alexander James McCloy. Hatton got a little tap on the head and they tied him up, just to make things look more realistic. Fortunately, Mr Bardsley was insured. He wasn't, though, when it happened again in March. That time he had to stand the loss himself, unaware, of course, that a good percentage of it was finding its way directly into Hatton's pocket.'

He stopped and looked into Jack Pertwee's pale face. Jack returned his stare for an instant and then dipped his face down into his hands.

'Don't you admit nothing, Jack,' said Marilyn fiercely.

'On the 19th of May,' Wexford continued, 'Hatton drove up to Leeds. He'd been ill and he took it slowly, returning on the next day, Monday, May 20th. While he was in Leeds or on the road he encountered McCloy. He encountered him or discovered something about him to McCloy's disadvantage. Enough, anyway, to put him into a position from which he was able to blackmail McCloy to the extent of several thousand pounds.'

'It's a filthy lie,' said Jack in a choking voice.

'Very well, Mr Pertwee. I'd like you to come down to the police station with me, if you please . . .'

'But he's just got married!' interrupted the father.

'Mrs Pertwee may accompany him if she chooses. The situation has arisen that information is being deliberately withheld in a murder enquiry. Are you ready, Mr Pertwee?'

Jack didn't move. Then the hands that clutched his forehead began to tremble. Marilyn put her arms around him protectively, but not gently, and her lips twisted as if she would have liked to spit in Wexford's face.

'Blackmail?' Jack stammered. 'Charlie?' He took his hands away and Wexford saw that he was weeping. 'That's crazy!'

'I don't think so, Mr Pertwee.'

'He couldn't have,' Jack said, mouthing something Wexford didn't quite catch.

'What did you say?'

'I said, he couldn't have. McCloy's inside. You're a copper, aren't you? You know what I mean. McCloy's in prison.'

CHAPTER FIFTEEN

The news from Scotland came through at almost exactly the same time as Jack Pertwee's revelation. Alexander McCloy had been sent to prison for two years on April 23rd, having been found guilty with two other men of organising a break-in at a supermarket in Dundee on early-closing day, and stealing goods to the value of twelve hundred pounds. A caretaker had been slightly injured during the course of the robbery and McCloy would have received a heavier sentence but for his unblemished record.

'So while Hatton was in Leeds that May weekend,' said Wexford in the morning, 'McCloy had already been safely locked up in Scotland for a month.'

'It looks that way,' said Burden.

'And that not only means he wasn't available to be black-mailed, but also that Hatton's source of — well, I was nearly going to say legitimate, income was cut off. In fact, in May Hatton found himself shorter of money than probably at any time since he was married.'

'Mrs Hatton said that when he was ill during the previous week he hesitated about sending for the doctor privately. By that time he'd presumably spent whatever he'd made when they nicked Bardsley's lorry in March.'

'At his rate of expenditure,' Wexford cut in, 'he probably had. It must have given him quite a nasty feeling. Panicked him, I daresay. Can't you imagine him, Mike, looking to the future when he wouldn't be able to stand all those rounds in the Dragon or take his wife frittering on a Saturday afternoon or cut a fine open-handed figure at his friend's wedding?'

'I imagine he quickly looked round for another source of supply.'

'We'll go up to the Stowerton By-pass,' Wexford said, getting up, 'and do some reconnoitring. Our two cases are converging, Mike, and unless I'm mistaken, they're soon going to bump.'

*

'There was no suitcase,' said Sergeant Martin, 'but I want you to look at the clothes she was wearing. They're in a bad way, Miss Lewis. You must try to keep calm.'

She was a nurse and trained to control herself. Martin took her into another room where the burnt torn clothes lay like rubbish heap rags on the table. Each blackened tattered garment lay separate from the others and there was something in this arrangement that suggested a parody of a draper's window.

The bodice of the coat and of the dress were charred fragments, although their skirts were almost intact and patches of orange and yellow showed between the scorch marks. The dead girl's brassière was an ellipse of wire from which every shred of cotton and lace had been burnt away. Margaret Lewis shuddered, keeping her hands behind her back. Then she touched the orange shoes, the white lace stockings as wide-meshed and fine as a hair-net, and she began to cry.

'I gave her those stockings,' she whispered, 'for her birthday.'

Their tops only were charred, but a long brown mark ran down to the knee of one of them where a flame had licked. Martin put his arm under the girl's elbow and led her away.

'I'll tell you everything I can about Bridie,' she said and she gulped the tea Loring had brought her. 'And everything she told me about Jay. She met him in October while she was nursing his wife. The wife was in a long time on account of having a threatened toxaemia and Bridie used to go out with him after he'd visited her. She'd come off duty at eight-thirty, you see, and he'd just about be leaving.

'Well, he dropped her after his wife left the clinic and I thought that was the end of it. But it wasn't. He turned up again in May and the whole thing was on again. Bridie started talking about marrying him. Oh, it was awful, really, and I didn't used to listen much. I wish I had now.'

'Did you ever see him, Miss Lewis?' Martin asked.

Margaret Lewis shook her head. The colour had come back into her cheeks and she wore no make-up to smear when she dabbed at the lids with a spotless handkerchief. 'We weren't working in the same department, you see. Lots of people must have. You'll have to ask the other girls. Bridie said he was quite

old, lots older than her, and that was the one thing that made
her — well, hesitate, if you know what I mean.'

'So you wouldn't know if this is him?' And Martin showed
her a photograph of Jerome Fanshawe. It had been taken by
flash at a company dinner and the face was hard, confident,
heavily jowled, but because of its arrogance and its strength and
despite its age, not unattractive to women.

She looked at it with the distaste of the very young and, not
answering him, said, 'I told you they went to Brighton on the
18th of May?' Loring nodded. 'Bridie was going to be met by
him at Marble Arch. I saw her go off in that yellow coat and
dress. She said she'd have to amuse herself during the daytime
because Jay would be at his conference. That's why he was
going, you see, to be at this conference.

Loring gave another encouraging smile. This was the sort
of thing Wexford wanted. Then he remembered his search
through the clinic's patient list.

'The man we had in mind,' he said carefully, 'we couldn't
find his name among the clinic's patients, you know. His wife
denies she was ever in there.'

The girl touched the photograph and looked up at him in
bewilderment. 'How old is she, for goodness' sake?'

'The wife? Fifty, fifty-five.'

'I'm sorry,' Margaret Lewis blushed. 'I think this has been
my fault. Jay's wife was in the *maternity* department. They're
always separate, you know, the general and the maternity
departments in hospitals. Always. Bridie had done her mid-
wifery and she was nursing Jay's wife when she was ill before
the birth and while she was having the baby.'

Burden was driving. With the accident plan Camb had given
him on his lap, Wexford looked up and said:

'Park in the next lay-by, Mike, and we'll walk.'

An ancient milestone which had always stood on the bank
since this highway was the coaching road to London, by chance
pinpointed the crash spot. From it a slow incline wound down
into the valley.

The northbound and southbound sections of the by-pass,
opened a year before, were separated by a strip of grass on

which grew clumps of thin birch trees. Fanshawe's Jaguar had struck one of these trees, overturned and caught fire. Wexford and Burden waited for two cars and a van to pass and then they crossed the road to the centre strip.

A large area of this grass had been burnt but by now new growth had replaced it and there was nothing but a ragged black stump to show where the crash tree had been.

'First,' said Wexford, 'we'll work on the assumption that the girl was in the car with the Fanshawes, she was Jerome Fanshawe's fancy piece and he was driving her back to London. Who sits where? Mrs Fanshawe in the back and her supplanter next to Don Juan or vice versa?'

'Surely there must have been some amount of pretence, sir,' said Burden, wrinkling his fastidious nose. 'It can't have been all open and above-board. The girl would have sat in the back.'

'It's the seat on the driver's left that's called the suicide seat, Mike, and whereas the girl died, Mrs Fanshawe is still alive. If the girl was there at all, she sat in the front.' Wexford made a sweeping gesture with his right hand. 'Up comes Fanshawe, driving like the maniac he was at eighty or so. Now there's no evidence of a burst tyre and the windscreen didn't shatter. What did Fanshawe see that made him cry out 'God!' and pull the wheel over?'

'Something in the road?'

'Yes, but what? A big piece of metal or a wooden box? He'd have sailed right over cardboard. Anyway, they didn't find anything in the road afterwards.'

'A dog?'

'Fanshawe wouldn't have crashed for the sake of a dog. And he didn't hit one because there was no body.'

'Then he saw the girl herself,' said Burden carefully, 'stepping out of the centre section to wave him down.'

'But we're assuming the girl was *in* the car. Don't you agree with me now that she can't have been?'

Burden walked a little way away from him and stopped by the black birch stump. 'If the girl stepped off here,' he said, taking a couple of paces towards the fast lane, 'and Fanshawe thought he was going to hit her, why didn't he swerve to the *left*, into the middle lane, instead of to the right? The road must have been clear as there were no witnesses to the accident. He swerved inwards, to the right, mounted this centre strip and hit the tree.'

Wexford shrugged. A car in the fast lane leapt past them at seventy. 'Feel like experimenting, Mike?' he said with a grin. 'Just pop out into the road now, wave your arms and see what happens.'

'You can, if you're so keen,' said Burden, involuntarily retreating from the edge. 'I want to stay alive.'

'Funny that girl didn't. Mike, it couldn't have been straight suicide, could it?'

Burden said thoughtfully, 'I suppose it could have at that. Assume she has no connection with Fanshawe, assume she went to the South Coast with another boy friend who ditched her so that she had to hitch a lift as far as here. The driver that brought her to this point might then have dropped her at her own request. She crosses to the centre section, waits until a fast car comes and steps out suddenly in front of it. Of course, that doesn't explain why Fanshawe pulled to the right instead of to the left.'

'And it doesn't explain why everything that might have identified her was *removed* from her handbag. If she was a suicide, there's no possible reason why she should have removed it herself. Anyway, you seem to have forgotten our main reason for coming here. The crash occurred at ten to ten and Hatton passed on the other highway, going in the other direction, at approximately twenty to. Impoverished Hatton, desperate to replenish the empty coffers. Suppose he passed a little later than that and saw the girl step out? Now, if Fanshawe were still alive, if, say, he'd killed the girl without damage to his car, and had simply driven on, Hatton might have blackmailed him. But Fanshawe is dead, Mike.'

Now it was Burden's turn to shrug and look baffled. He eyed the other highway, the southbound section, the hedge that bounded it, the meadows behind that hedge. The road came to a crest some fifty yards to the north of where they stood and above this ridge nothing but the pale milky sky was visible.

'If there was some sort of foul play,' he said thoughtfully, 'if, for instance, the girl was pushed into the road . . . Oh, I know it's fantastic, but haven't you got something of the sort in mind yourself? If she was pushed and Hatton, approaching over the brow of that hill, was a witness, why didn't whoever it was doing the pushing, see him first? His lorry was an outsize very high van and anyone standing here would see the top of it appearing over the crest seconds before its driver could see him. Look, here comes a lorry now.'

Wexford turned his eyes towards the brow of the hill. The lorry's roof loomed above it and it seemed that some seconds passed before the cab came into view.

'It was dark,' he said.

'Anyone standing where we are could see its headlights at precisely the same time as its driver saw him.'

The same thought striking each man simultaneously, they walked towards the crest. Beneath them half Sussex lay spread, broad meadows, green and gold, the dense bluish shadows of woodland and in the folds between, farmhouses and the occasional pointing spire of a church. Through this pastoral landscape the road wound its twin white ribbon, hummocking here, dipping there, and sometimes entirely concealed by the green swelling land.

Not more than twenty yards beyond the crest, the southbound section widened into an arc and in this lay-by the occupants of two cars sat picnicking.

'Perhaps he parked here for a bit,' Burden said. 'Walked up this way for — well, a natural purpose or just because he needed air. He hadn't been well, after all.'

But Wexford looked at the view and said presently, 'Where every prospect pleases, and only man is vile.'

The huge American car with its splayed fins dwarfed every other vehicle in the Olive's car park. Crossing the forecourt with Burden, Wexford saw on closer scrutiny that it was neither new nor well cared for. One of its headlamps was broken and the rust on its chrome rim showed that it had been broken a long time. Scratches marred the bluish-green finish on its wings. Here in this tiny car park in a small country town it was an unwieldy mass of metal that doubtless gave a poor return for the petrol it devoured. It took up an immense amount of space but its seating capacity was small.

'Reminds me of one of those prehistoric monsters,' said Wexford, 'all brawn and no brain.'

'Must have been grand once, though.'

'That's what they said about the dinosaurs.'

They sat in the saloon bar. In the far corner Nora Fanshawe sat on a leather settle beside a huge fair man with a small head. His expression was vapid, his shoulders of Mister Universe proportions. Another dinosaur, Wexford thought, and suddenly he was sure this was the owner of the car.

'We keep running into each other, Miss Fanshawe.'

'You keep running into me,' said the girl dryly. She wore another of her finely tailored, neatly stitched suits, navy blue this time and as slick and business-like as a uniform. 'This is Michael Jameson. You may remember, I mentioned him to you.'

The hand that took Wexford's had a damp palm. 'Nice little place this, if a bit off the map.'

'Depends where you make your maps.'

'Come again? Oh, I see. Ha ha!'

'We were just going,' said Nora Fanshawe. Then her strong masculine voice quavered a little as she said, 'Ready, Michael?' Suddenly she was vulnerable. Wexford knew that wistful pleading look. He had seen it before in the eyes of plain women, the pathetic terror of rejection that, because it deprives them of confidence, makes them plainer.

Jameson got up sluggishly, reluctantly; he winked at Wexford and that wink was as eloquent as words.

'Off to see your mother, Miss Fanshawe?'

The girl nodded and Jameson said, 'The old girl keeps her on her toes.'

'Let's go, Michael.' She linked her arm in his and held it tight. Wexford watched them go, telling himself he was a fool to let the scene upset him. She was gruff, rude, unfeminine. She was also peculiarly honest and she lacked the talent of self-deception. Not for a moment did Wexford doubt that she knew this man was quite unworthy of her, in intelligence, in probity, in character. But he was good looking and she had money.

'A bit of an oaf,' said Burden.

Wexford lifted the curtain and between the fuchsias he saw

Jameson get into the huge car and start the engine. Nora Fanshawe was not the kind of woman who looks on courtesy from men as her right. The car was already in motion before she got herself into the passenger seat. Jameson had not even opened the door for her from the inside.

CHAPTER SIXTEEN

'I want you all to concentrate,' Wexford said. 'Don't tell me it
was a long time ago and you can't remember. It was only about
seven weeks ago. You'll be surprised what you can remember if
you try.'

They were sitting in Lilian Hatton's flat, Wexford confronting the three people on the sofa. Mrs Hatton wore a black
cotton frock and all the jewellery Charlie had ever given her.
Her face was white and tense, still stained by the tears she had
shed when Wexford had revealed her husband's source of
income. Was it a revelation or had she always known? Wexford
couldn't make his mind up about that. For all her short skirt
and her make-up and the equipment in her kitchen, she was
essentially at heart a Victorian wife, helpless, clinging, accepting
all her husband's quirks with unquestioning passivity. She would
no more have asked Charlie if the brooch she wore was bought
with ill-gotten money than her nineteenth-century counterpart
would have asked her lord and master to admit that his presents
to her were the result of cheating at cards. Hers not to reason
why, hers but to accept and praise and adore. Now, as he faced
her, Wexford wondered how this anachronism would fend for
herself in the world Charlie called a battlefield.

'He always talked about fighting for what you wanted,' she
had said wretchedly, 'about being one up on the next man.
Planing his — his stra . . . His stra — something.'

'Strategy?'

'That's it. Like as if he was a general.'

A soldier of fortune, Wexford thought, a mercenary.

The other two knew all right, the young Pertwees. They
had finally admitted as much and now Marilyn said sullenly,
'He was getting back at the big nobs. What does losing a load
mean to them? They're all robbers, anyway. Capitalism's or-
ganised robbery of the working classes. Charlie was only taking
back what was due to him.'

'Having his revenge on society perhaps, Mrs Pertwee?'

331

'Yeah, and why not? When we've got real people's government in this country, folks like Charlie'll get their fair shares and there won't be no crime. Or what you call crime. When we get real socialism.'

'Charlie always voted Conservative,' said Lilian Hatton. 'I don't know, Marilyn, I don't think . . .'

Wexford interrupted them. There was no room for laughter in this flat, yet he wanted to laugh. 'Let's postpone the political discussion, shall we? Mrs Hatton, you've had time to think now and I want you to tell me all you remember about your husband's departure for Leeds on Sunday, May 19th and his return on the 20th.'

She cleared her throat and glanced hesitantly at Jack Pertwee, waiting perhaps for more masculine directions and more masculine support.

'Don't you worry, Lily,' said Marilyn. 'I'm here.'

'I'm sure I don't know what I'd do without you. Well . . . Well, Charlie'd been ill and I didn't want him to go but he would insist.'

'Was he worried about money, Mrs Hatton?'

'Charlie never bothered me with things like that. Oh, wait a minute though . . . He did say the doctor would have to wait to get paid. I remember him saying that. D'you want me to go on about that Sunday?' Wexford nodded. 'Jack and Marilyn came in the evening for a three-handed solo.'

'That's right,' said Marilyn, 'and Charlie rung you from Leeds while we was here.'

Mrs Hatton looked at her admiringly. 'So he did. Yes, he did.'

'What did he say to you?'

'Nothing much. It was mostly — well, asking me how I was and saying he missed me.' She sniffed and bit her lip. 'We didn't like being separated. We couldn't sleep away from each other.'

'More like sweethearts than man and wife they were,' said Jack and he put his arm around her shoulders.

'Did he say he was still feeling unwell?'

'Bit under the weather. He'd have come back that night else.'

'Did he sound pleased, excited?'

'Down in the dumps, if anything.'

'Now I want you to be very exact about this. Precisely what time did your husband come home on the following night, the Monday night?'

She didn't hesitate. 'Ten on the dot. He'd said ten the night before and I'd made him a chicken casserole. Charlie'd bought me a kitchen timer back in March, but it went wrong and had to go back to the shop, and that was the first time I'd used it. I set it for ten and it just started pinging when Charlie put his key in the door.'

'How was he when he came in?'

'In himself, d'you mean? He'd had his sickness back, he said, and he'd had to stop a couple of times on the road. He'd have been back earlier if he hadn't stopped. He wanted to get back earlier, you see, to surprise me.' Emotion overcame her and she breathed quickly, fighting back the tears. 'I . . . He . . . he said it was stifling in the lorry and he'd had to get a breath of fresh air on the Stowerton By-pass. He walked in the fields a bit where it was cool.'

'Think carefully, Mrs Hatton. Did he say he had seen anything of interest while he was in those fields?'

She looked at him in bewilderment. 'No, he only said it had done him good. He felt fine, he said, and I could see he did. On top of the world he was that night, a different man. He was having his meal and we talked about Jack's wedding.' Her voice grew hoarse and she leant heavily against Jack's arm. 'Charlie wanted me to have a whole new outfit, dress, coat, hat, the lot. He said — he said I was his wife and he wanted me to be a credit to him.'

'And you always were, love. Charlie was proud of you.'

'What happened the next day?' said Wexford.

'We had a bit of a lay-in.' She bit her lip. 'Charlie got up at nine and then he phoned a fellow he knew who was leaving his flat. Charlie'd said he'd come down and look at it when he'd had his breakfast and that's what he did. You tell it, Jack, it's your turn.'

Jack eased away his arm and patted the widow's hand.

'Charlie came down to the works but I couldn't get away. I was off doing the wiring in them new houses over Pomfret

way. He said he reckoned he'd found us a flat and I said, take
Marilyn with you. I can see him now, old Charlie, pleased as
punch and grinning like he always did when he was going to do
something for you. Bobbing up and down he was like a monkey
on a stick.' He sighed and shook his head. 'Old Charlie,' he
said.

Impatiently, Wexford turned to the wife. 'You went with
him?'

'Yeah, he came down to Moran's.' Moran's was Kingsmarkham's biggest draper's. 'That old bitch, that manageress,
didn't want me to go at first. Not that there's much trade to
speak of on a Monday morning. I'm leaving in a month anyway,
I said, and if you don't like it you can give me my cards and I'll
go now. Straight out I said it. I'd made her look real small in
front of Charlie and she never said another word. Well, me and
Charlie we went to look at this flat and there was this geezer
who was leaving, a right queer if you ask me, wanted two
hundred quid key money before he'd let us have it. I could have
smacked his face then and there. In a dressing gown he was.
There'll be forced labour for his sort one of these fine days and
I was just going to come out with it when Charlie said that was
all right and we'd find the money somehow. He could see I was
dead keen on the place.'

'He paid over the money?'

'Don't be so daft. He said something about consulting with
Jack, though if I wanted it Jack'd want it too all right, and then
he went. I was fuming. I'll put up the money, Charlie said when
we was outside, and you can pay me back when you're rolling.
How about that, then?'

'Yes,' said Jack, 'how about that?'

'Did Hatton take you back to the shop?'

'Of course he didn't, he wasn't my keeper. He walked up
with me as far as the Olive and then he said he'd got to make
a phone call. He went into that box outside the Olive and I
never saw him again for a couple of days.'

'Why would he make a phone call from a box when he had
his own phone at home?'

The married pair were thinking what he, under other
circumstances, might have thought. A married man with a

phone of his own makes calls from a box to his mistress. Mrs
Hatton looked innocent, subdued, armoured by her memories.
Then Marilyn laughed harshly. 'You're crazy if you're thinking
what I think you are! Charlie Hatton?'

'What do you mean, Marilyn?' the widow asked.

'I'm thinking nothing,' said Wexford. 'Did your husband
come home for his lunch?'

'About half-past twelve. I asked him what he was going to
do with himself in the afternoon and it was then he said he was
going to get his teeth seen to. He kept getting bits of food under
his plate, you see. He was very ashamed of having false teeth
was Charlie on account of being so young and all that. And on
account of me . . . He thought I minded. Me mind? I wouldn't
have cared if . . . Oh, what's the use? I was telling you about
getting his teeth fixed. He'd often said he'd see about getting a
real good set when he could afford it and he said he thought
he'd go to Mr Vigo.'

'I'd sort of recommended him, you see,' Jack put in.

'You?' Wexford said rudely.

Jack lifted his face and flushed a deep wine colour.

'I didn't mean I went to him for my teeth,' he muttered.
'I'd been up at his place once or twice doing electrical work and
I'd sort of described what the place was like to Charlie. Sort of
about the garden and all the old things he's got up there and
that room full of Chinese stuff.'

Mrs Hatton was crying now and she wiped her eyes,
smiling reminiscently through her tears. 'Many's the laugh
Charlie and Jack used to have over that,' she said. 'Charlie said
he'd like to see it. Like to have a dekko, he said, and Jack said
Mr Vigo was rolling in money. Well, he'd have to be a good
dentist to make all that, wouldn't he? So Charlie thought he was
the man for him and he phoned then and there. You'll never
get an appointment for today, I said, but he did. Mr Vigo had
a cancellation and he said he'd see him at two.'

'And then?'

'Charlie came back at four and said Mr Vigo was going to
fix him up with a new set. Mr Vigo was as nice as pie, he said,
no side to him. He'd given him a drink in this said Chinese
room and Charlie said when he was rich he was going to have

stuff like that, rooms full of it and vases and ornaments and —
and a little army of chess men and . . . Oh God, he'll never have
anything where he is!'

'Don't, Lily, don't, love.'

'When did Mr Hatton give you the key money for this flat
of yours?'

'It was a loan,' said Marilyn Pertwee indignantly.

'Lend it to you, then?'

'He come round with it to Jack's dad's place on the
Wednesday.'

'That would have been the 22nd?'

'I reckon. We handed it over to this bloke as had the flat
the next day.' Jack Pertwee stared hard at Wexford. The dull
eyes were glazed now, the face pallid yet mottled. Wexford
could hardly suppress a shiver. God help the man who murdered Charlie Hatton, he thought, if Pertwee gets on to him
before we do.

'Isn't it about time we got shot of that thing?'

Sheila removed Clytemnestra from her father's chair and
contemplated the mass of hairs the dog had moulted on to the
cushion. 'I'm getting a bit fed up with her myself,' she said.
'Sebastian's supposed to be coming for her tonight.'

'Thank God for that.'

'All right if I have the car to take him to the station?'

'What, is he scared to cross those fields alone?' Mabel, dear,
listen here, there's a robbery in the park . . . 'I may want the car.
He's young and healthy. Let him walk.'

'He's got a verruca,' said Sheila. 'He had to walk here and
back when he brought her a fortnight ago. I'd be meeting him
now' — she gave her father a disgruntled look — 'only you've
always got the car.'

'It is my car,' said Wexford absurdly, and then, because it
was a game that he and Sheila played, 'It was my turquoise. I
had it off Leah when I was a bachelor. I would not have given
it . . .'

'For a wilderness of verrucas! Oh, Pop, you're a honey
really. There's Sebastian now.'

Mrs Wexford began calmly laying the table. 'Don't say

anything about his hair,' she said to her husband. 'He's got peculiar hair and you know what you are.'

Sebastian's hair resembled Clytemnestra's, only it wasn't grey. It hung on to his shoulders in shaggy curls.

'I hope the Swoofle Hound hasn't been too much of a bore for you, Mr Wexford.'

Wexford opened his mouth to make some polite denial but Clytemnestra's transports at the sight of her owner made speech impossible for a while. She hurled herself at his long legs and plummeted her body against his jacket, a garment which Wexford incredulously identified as part of the full dress uniform of a commander in the Royal Norwegian Navy.

'You'll stay and have a meal?' said Mrs Wexford.

'If it isn't too much trouble.'

'How was Switzerland?'

'All right. Expensive.' Wexford was beginning to nourish the unkind thought that the holiday would have been even more costly had he had to pay boarding kennels fees, when Sebastian disarmed him by producing from his haversack a large box of chocolates for Mrs Wexford.

'Suchard!' said Mrs Wexford. 'How kind.'

Encouraged, Sebastian made short work of roast beef and Yorkshire pudding, occasionally reaching under the table to fondle Clytemnestra's ears.

'I'll drive you to the station,' said Sheila and she gave her father a confident smile.

'That'd be great. We might take Clytemnestra into that Olive place. She likes beer and it'd be a treat for her.'

'Not in my car, you don't,' said Wexford firmly.

'Oh, Pop!'

'Sorry, sweetheart, but you don't drink and drive.'

Sebastian's expression combined admiration for the daughter and a desire to ingratiate himself with the father. 'We'll walk down.' He shrugged. 'It's such a hell of a way to your station, though.' He eyed the banana custard. 'Yes, thanks, I will have some more. The trouble is I'll have to walk Sheila back, unless she goes home by the road,' he added unchivalrously. 'We heard about your murder even in Switzerland. Down in those fields at the back, wasn't it?'

Wexford seldom talked shop at home. Probably this young man wasn't pumping him and yet . . . He gave a non-committal nod.

'Odd,' Sebastian said. 'I went to the station that way a fortnight ago, across the fields.'

Wexford intercepted his wife's glance, deflected it, said nothing. Sheila said it for him.

'What time was it, Seb? About ten?'

'A bit after that. I didn't meet a soul and I can't say I'm sorry.' He ruffled the dog's curly coat. 'If I hadn't jumped smartly out of the way, Clytemnestra, you mightn't ever have seen your papa again. Big American car nearly ran me down.'

'They do nip into that station approach,' said Sheila.

'Station approach, nothing. This was in the fields. In that lane that leads up to that stile thing. Great green car swept in at about forty and I practically had to dive into the hedge. I took the number actually but what with all the kerfuffle about my holiday I lost the bit of paper I wrote it on.'

'A courting couple?' said Wexford lightly.

'Could have been. I was too busy taking the number to look and I was scared of losing my train.'

'Well we won't go by the fields this time, and I'll trail all the way back by the road if it makes you happy, Pop.'

'You can take the car,' said Wexford. 'Stick to bitter lemon in the Olive, eh?'

CHAPTER SEVENTEEN

'Here's my theory,' said Burden, 'for what it's worth. I've been thinking about it, though, and it's the only possible solution. We've talked a lot about hired assassins but the only hired assassin in this case was Charlie Hatton, hired by Bridget Culross's boy friend.'

'Fertile,' said Wexford, 'but I'd like it amplified.'

Burden shifted his chair a little nearer those of Wexford and the doctor. The wind and the sunlight filled the office with a pattern of dancing leaves. 'Jay is a rich man. He must be if he can afford to pay for three months in that clinic of yours just because his wife's having a difficult pregnancy.'

'Money down the drain,' commented Crocker. 'Do just as well on the N.H.S.'

'He's rich enough to pay someone to do his killing for him. You can bet your life he's a one-time friend of McCloy's. He arranges for Hatton to be waiting on that by-pass at the point where he's going to drop the girl on their way back from this conference.'

'Just what conference, Mike? Have we checked on Brighton conferences that weekend?'

'The National Union of Journalists, the Blake Society and the Gibbonites all met there,' said Burden promptly.

'What are the last lot?' put in the doctor, 'a bunch of monkeys?'

'Not gibbons,' said Burden, unsmiling. 'Gibbon. The *Decline and Fall* man, the historian. I reckon they're just another collection of cranks.'

'And Jay took a girl to Brighton, but left her alone all day while he gossiped about Gibbon?' said Wexford thoughtfully. 'Well, stranger things have happened. Go on.'

'He faked a quarrel with her in the car on the way back to London and turfed her out of the car in a rage. Hatton was waiting for her, hit her over the head, emptied her handbag and made off back to his lorry. The next day Jay paid him his blood money. You can be sure that call Hatton made from a phone box was to Jay, telling him that the deed was done. And no one would have been any the wiser if Hatton hadn't been greedy and started soaking Jay.'

The doctor made a derisive face. 'Pardon me as a mere layman, but that's a load of old rubbish. I'm not saying the girl couldn't have been dead before the car hit her. She could have. But why should Hatton put her in the road? He couldn't be sure a car would come along and hit her. Besides, he could so easily have been seen. And he was a small man. He wouldn't have had the strength to carry her across the southbound highway. Why bother, anyway? If her death was supposed to look like the work of some vagrant maniac, why not kill her behind the hedge and leave her there?'

'What's your idea then?' said Burden sourly.

Crocker looked uppish. 'I don't have to have theories. I'm not paid for this kind of diagnosis.'

'Come down from your perch, Paracelsus,' said Wexford, 'and put yourselves in our shoes for a moment. Have a shot at it.'

'The trouble with you lot is you believe everything you're told. I don't. I know from experience people distort the truth because they're afraid or they have a psychological block or they want to be over-helpful. They leave things out because they're ignorant and when you tell them you want to know everything, they sort out what everything is to them. It's not necessarily everything to the expert who's asking the questions.'

'I know all that,' said Wexford impatiently.

'Then, Mrs Fanshawe says the girl wasn't in the car, not because she's ashamed to admit it but because she's literally forgotten. Of course she was in the car. She hitched a lift a couple of miles before the crash and all that period is a blank to Mrs Fanshawe. Naturally she's not trying to clear the blank. The very word "girl" is a red rag to a bull to her. You're bothered because there were no keys and no other identification in that expensive handbag. She left them in her suitcase and she left that suitcase in Jay's car.'

'Why?'

'So that Jay would have to come back for her. It was on the seat and after a few miles he'd realise and come back. Or so she thought. When he didn't she knew she could get it back all right at a later date. Presumably she knew where Jay lived. *In extremis* it would be an excuse for having it out with him, and confronting the wife.'

'But Jay didn't come back and she got fed-up with waiting, so she hitched a lift from Fanshawe.'

'That's the simple natural solution, isn't it?'

'What you're saying amounts to that Jay is just a more or less harmless philanderer. Why didn't he come forward when we found the girl?'

The doctor gave a sardonic and superior laugh. 'Thanks to a spot of inefficiency on someone's part, you told the Press the dead girl was Nora Fanshawe. Why should Jay stick his neck out? If he'd ditched the girl on the outskirts of Stowerton it was because he never wanted to see her again. He's not likely to pop up and help you with your enquiries.'

Wexford said quietly, 'Where does Charlie Hatton come into all this?'

'If you don't mind, I'll answer that question with a question of my own. What makes you think he didn't have a source of supply completely separate from McCloy or Fanshawe or Jay?'

Wexford looked at Burden and he saw uneasiness creep into the inspector's face. He couldn't allow for this sort of doubt. It was unthinkable. 'He was behind that hedge,' he said stoutly. 'He saw that girl pushed into the road.'

'Get away!'

'Oh, not from the central strip of grass.' Wexford paused for effect. The quivering leaf shadows played, danced and died as the sun went in. 'From a car,' he said, 'she was thrown out of a car.'

The sunlight came and went intermittently. Alone now, Wexford watched the cloud masses drift above the High Street roofs and cast their shadows now on a house front, now on the road itself. The sun blazed briefly, appearing from time to time embedded in a golden nest.

Presently he took his railway timetable from his desk drawer and looked up the afternoon trains to London. There was a fast one at two-fifteen.

The lift was waiting for him, its door invitingly open. By now Wexford had lost all his inhibitions about it. He stepped inside and pressed the ground-floor button. The door closed with a whisper and sank on a sigh.

Someone on the first floor must have summoned it, for it trembled and its floor seemed to rise a fraction. Then it shivered and stopped, Wexford waited for the door to slide but nothing happened.

It was a solid door with neither glass nor grille. Impatiently Wexford tapped his foot. He glanced at the control panel and wondered why the light marked one hadn't come on. Probably it had been summoned and whoever was waiting had got bored and used the stairs. In that case, why wasn't the light on? He stuck his thumb on the ground-floor button. Nothing happened.

Or rather, the worst, what he had always feared, had happened. The damned thing had broken. It had got stuck. Very likely it was between floors. A tremor of panic touched one corner of his brain and he dismissed it with a fierce oath. He tapped smartly on the door.

Was the thing sound-proof? Wexford had never had much faith in sound-proofing methods, having lived during the early part of his career in a series of flats highly commended by their agents for the seaweed board allegedly incorporated in their walls and ceilings. They hadn't stopped him being driven nearly mad by the piano from upstairs and the incessant drumming of children's feet. They couldn't sound-proof a dwelling house, he thought furiously. It would be just like 'them' to succeed in the utterly pointless achievement of sound-proofing a lift. He knocked on the door again and then he pressed the button marked Emergency. If anything, the little black and gilt box settled into an even deeper immobility.

There was a little leather seat, like the extra seats in a taxi, folded into the wall. Wexford pulled it down. It creaked when he sat on it. Glancing about him with simulated ease, he assessed the volume of the lift. Seven by four by four. As far as he could see there was no means of letting air in or carbon dioxide out. He listened. He might have been stone deaf, the silence was so deep.

How long could anybody as big as he remain confined in a

space seven by four by four? He had no idea. It was ten minutes to two. He got up and the seat snapped back into the wall. The sound made him jump. He brought both fists down against the panelling and pounded hard. The lift quivered and that disquieted him. For all he knew it was hanging by a thread.

It might be better to shout. But shout what? 'Help, let me out!' was too humiliating to consider.

'Is there anyone there?' he called, and because that sounded like a medium in a seance, 'Hey, the lift's stuck!'

Under the circumstances, it would be wiser to save his breath. It was possible that most of the rooms were empty. Burden and Martin and Loring were all out. Camb might be sitting downstairs (downstairs!) at his desk. Someone would be sitting there. It was equally certain that his cries were unheard.

With an unpleasant sinking feeling, Wexford faced the fact that unless Burden returned two hours earlier than he had said, it was likely that no one would want to use the lift. Camb was at his post, Martin in Sewingbury. It hadn't escaped Wexford's notice that most of the uniformed branch preferred the stairs. He might be there till tea-time and if so, would he still be alive at tea-time?

Two o'clock. If he didn't get out in five minutes he would miss that train. That didn't matter too much. Without checking at the Princess Louise Clinic, he was almost sure he had the answer. Guesswork perhaps, but inspired guesswork. If he died they would never know . . .

Sick of shouting, he flapped down the seat again. Probably it was only his fancy that the air in the tiny box was growing thick. Panic would not help at all. It was outside the indulgences he allowed himself. Outside them too was the thread of terror that told him he was a rat in a hole, a fox in a stopped earth. Briefly he thought of Sheila. No more of that, that way madness lies . . .

Two-fifteen, Wexford took out his notebook and a pencil. At any rate, he could write it all down.

'I don't know where he gets his crazy ideas,' said the doctor indiscreetly. Burden gave him a neutral smile. 'If I was in your place I'd want to try it out. Have you got something else on this afternoon?'

'Nothing Martin and Loring can't see to without me.'

'Shall we take my car, then?'

'Don't you have a surgery?' asked Burden, who thought the whole plan unorthodox.

'My afternoon off. I rather like this dabbling in forensics.'

Burden didn't. He wondered what Crocker would say if he suggested accompanying him to a patient's bedside. 'All right,' he said reluctantly. 'But not the by-pass, for heaven's sake.'

'Cheriton airfield,' said the doctor.

The place hadn't been used for years. It lay on the far side of Cheriton forest beyond Pomfret and it was a favourite haunt of L-drivers. Teenagers below the permitted age of provisional licence holders got their parents to bring them on to the disused runways where they kangaroo-hopped in comparative safety.

Today it was deserted. The greens between the runways had been ploughed up and used for a turnip and sugar beet crop. Beyond the rows of regularly planted beet the pine forest climbed over gently undulating hills.

'You can drive,' said the doctor. 'I fancy the victim's role.'

'Rather you than I,' said Burden, who was wearing his new Gannex.

He shifted into the driving seat. The runway was as broad as the northbound highway of the Stowerton By-pass.

'Presumably she was a strong healthy girl,' said Crocker. 'You couldn't push anyone like that out of a moving vehicle if she was in full possession of her faculties. He must have hit her on the head first.'

'You're suggesting he had an unconscious girl beside him?'

'They'd had a row and he'd socked her,' said the doctor laconically. 'Now I'm her and I'm unconscious. The road is clear. You wouldn't do it from the fast lane, though, would you? Something might just come whizzing up behind you and that'd be awkward. So it's the middle lane. Go on, move over.'

Burden eased into the centre of the runway. 'That row of beet on the right corresponds to the central strip,' he said. 'Fanshawe swerved to the right to avoid the body.'

'So *he* says.'

'What do I do? Leave the passenger door on the latch?'

'I reckon so. Trickle along and then push me out.'

Crocker rolled himself into a ball, his arms around his knees. Burden didn't dare drive at more than a snail's pace. He was doing five miles an hour. He leaned across, swung the door wide and gave the doctor a light push. Crocker rolled easily into the road, staggered and stood up. Burden stopped.

'You see?' Crocker dusted himself off with a grimace. 'I told you he was crazy. See where I landed? Right in the slow lane. And you'd hardly got the car moving. Our mystery man was going at a fair lick. The girl would have rolled right over to the left, almost on to the grass verge.'

'D'you want to try it in the fast lane, just for the record?'

'Once is enough,' said the doctor firmly. 'You can see what would happen, anyway. The girl mightn't have rolled into the slow lane, but she'd have landed in the *middle of the road*. You just couldn't get a body into the fast lane itself from a moving car.'

'You're right. Necessarily, having been thrown from the left, it would roll towards the left, in which case Fanshawe in the fast lane would have passed cleanly to the right of it.'

'Or if the mystery man was in fact driving in the fast lane and the body landed plumb in that lane, Fanshawe would have swerved to the *left* to avoid it and never hit that tree in the central strip. There's only one possibility and we've proved that's not tenable.'

Burden was sick of being told his job. 'Exactly,' he said hastily. 'If the girl was thrown out to the right and her head was towards the middle lane with her feet towards the central strip, only then might Fanshawe have swerved to the right. He would have swerved instinctively to avoid the head.'

'But that, as we know, is impossible. If you're driving a car you can only throw someone out from the passenger seat on the left, not from one of the back seats, and that means the victim is always going to land way over to the left.'

'I'll go back and tell him,' said Burden thoughtfully, and he let the doctor take the wheel to drive them back along the runway between the lines of green leaves.

'Chief Inspector gone out?' Coming out of Wexford's office, Burden encountered Loring in the corridor.

'I don't know, sir. Isn't he in his office?'

'You imagine he's hiding under his desk, do you, or maybe he's filed himself away in the filing cabinet.'

'I'm sorry, sir.' Loring raised a yellow venetian blind. 'His car's there.'

'I know that.' Burden had come up by the stairs. He went towards the lift, pressed the button to summon it. When he had waited a minute and it hadn't come, he shrugged and walked down to the ground floor. Sergeant Camb turned from the woman who had lost a Siamese cat.

'Mr Wexford? He hasn't gone out.'

'Then where the hell is he?' Burden never swore, even as mildly as that. Camb stared. 'He was going to London. I'd reckoned he'd go on the two-fifteen.'

It was half-past three. 'Maybe he went out the back way.'

'Why should he? He never does unless he's going into court.'

'Blue eyes,' said the woman plaintively, 'and a coffee coloured mark on his neck.'

The sergeant sighed. 'All Siamese cats have blue eyes and brown marks on their backs, madam.' He picked up his pen and said to Burden, 'To tell you the truth, I've been tied up all the afternoon, trying to get hold of the engineers to see to that lift. Inspector Letts said it wouldn't come when he pressed the button. I reckon it's stuck between floors.'

'And I reckon,' said Burden, 'Mr Wexford is stuck in it.'

'My God, you don't mean it, sir?'

'Give me that phone. D'you realise he's been in there nearly two hours? *Give me that phone.*'

It was afternoon visiting at Stowerton Infirmary. It was also consultants' day. That meant an exodus of hundreds of cars which the woman on traffic patrol usually controlled efficiently. Today, however, a huge bluish-green car with battered fins, parked half across the drive, blocked the exit. It was locked, keyless, immovable, and behind it a traffic jam stretched nose to tail from the car park.

In vain four ambulance men had tried to lift it and hump it against the gate of the porter's lodge. Presently Vigo, the orthodontist, got out of his own car to lend a hand. He was bigger and more powerful than any of the ambulance men, but all their combined efforts couldn't shift it.

'Probably belongs to someone visiting a private patient,' said Vigo to the consultant gynaecologist whose car had come to a standstill behind his.

'Better get a porter to ring the private wing.'

'And fast,' said Vigo. 'These people ought to be shot. I've got an appointment at four.'

And it was five to when Nurse Rose knocked on Mrs Fanshawe's door. 'Excuse me, Mr Jameson, but your car's blocking the drive. Could you move it please? It's not just visitors that want to get out.' Her voice took on an awed tone. Outrage had been committed. 'Personal request of Mr Vigo and Mr Delauney. So if you wouldn't mind . . .'

Michael Jameson got up languidly. 'I don't know these guys.' He gave Nurse Rose a long appraising look. 'But I wouldn't want you to get in bad with them, sweetheart. I'll shift it.'

Nora Fanshawe touched his sleeve. 'You'll come back for me, Michael?'

'Sure, don't fuss.' Nurse Rose opened the door for him and he walked out ahead of her. 'Dead bore, this hospital visiting,' the women in the room heard him say.

Mrs Fanshawe had painted her face for the first time since regaining consciousness. Now she touched up her thin lips with scarlet and rubbed at the eyeshadow which had settled in greasy streaks into the folds of her lids. 'Well?' she said.

'Well what, Mother?'

'I take it you're going to marry that waster?'

'I am and you'll have to get used to it.'

'Your father would never have allowed it if he were alive,' said Mrs Fanshawe, twisting her rings.

'If my father were alive, Michael wouldn't want to marry me. I wouldn't have any money you see. I'm being quite frank with you. I thought that's what parents wanted, frankness from their children.' She shrugged and flicked a fair hair from the shoulder of her blue suit. Her voice was ugly, stripped bald of convention and pretence. 'I wrote to him and told him my father was dead.' She laughed. 'He came down here like a shot. I've bought him,' she said. 'I tried the product and liked it and now I'm going to keep it. The principle is that of the mail order catalogue.'

Mrs Fanshawe wasn't shocked. She hadn't taken her eyes from her daughter's face and she hadn't flinched. 'All right,' she said. 'I can't stop you. I won't quarrel with you, Nora.' Her voice didn't waver. 'You're all I've got, all I've ever had.'

'Then there is no reason why we shouldn't be a happy little family, is there?'

'A happy family! Frank you may be, but you're deceiving yourself. He's got his eye on that nurse already.'

'I know.'

'And you think you've bought him!' All Mrs Fanshawe's self-control couldn't stop the bitterness breaking through. 'Buying people! You know where you get it from, don't you? Your father. You're your father all over again, Nora. God knows, I tried to keep you innocent, but he taught you, he taught you people could be bought.'

'Oh, no, Mother,' said Nora Fanshawe equably. 'You taught me. Shall we have some more tea?' And she rang the bell.

At four-fifteen the lift slid down to the ground floor. The door began to slide and Burden felt sick, his bowels turned to water. He couldn't look. The two engineers came down the stairs, running.

The foyer was full of people. Grinswold, the Chief Constable, Inspector Lewis and Letts, Martin, Loring, Camb and, nearest the lift, Dr Crocker.

The door was open. Burden had to look. He stepped forward, pushing people aside.

'Gangway!' said the doctor.

Wexford came out, grey in the face, the doctor's arm about his shoulders. He took two heavy steps.

'Bricked up,' he said, 'like a bloody nun!'

'God, sir. Are you all right?'

'It's all in the book,' Wexford gasped. 'I've got it all down in the book. Nothing . . .' he said, 'nothing like a rarefied atmosphere for making the brain work. Cheaper than going up Everest, that lift.'

And then he collapsed into the sling Crocker and Letts made with their arms.

'I'm just going off duty,' said Nurse Rose, 'and the night staff are in the kitchen, so you won't mind finding your own way, will you?' She peered at him in the dim light of the corridor. 'Didn't you come visiting Mrs Fanshawe? I thought so. You'll know where to go, then. He's in room five, next door but one to hers.'

Burden thanked her. Turning the corner, he came face to face with Mrs Wexford and Sheila.

'How is he?'

'He's fine. No after-effects. They're only keeping him in for the night to be on the safe side.'

'Thank God!'

'You really care about poor old Pop, don't you?' When she smiled, he could have kissed her, she looked so like her father. Crazy, really, that this enchanting perfect face was the copy and the essence of the heavy wrinkled face that had been haunting him all the time he had made out his arrest and read out the charge. He didn't want to seem sentimental and he managed a cheerful grin. 'He's dying to see you,' she said. 'We were just a stop-gap.'

Wexford lay in bed in a room that was just like Mrs Fanshawe's. He had an old red checked dressing gown around his shoulders and a fuzz of grey hair showed between the lapels of his pyjama jacket. A grin curled the corners of his mouth and his eyes snapped.

Tip-toeing, Burden crossed to the bed. Everyone in hospital tip-toes, except the staff, so he did too, glancing nervously about him. The cooking smell and the disinfectant smell with which the corridor was redolent were drowned in here by the carnations Mrs Wexford had brought her husband.

'How are you feeling?'

'Perfectly all right, of course,' Wexford said impatiently. 'All those damned flowers. Makes the place look like a chapel of rest. I'd come out now only that bloody Crocker and his henchmen keep getting at me, sapping my strength.' He sat up with a jerk and scowled. 'Open that beer, will you? Sheila brought those cans in for me. She's a good girl, chip off the old block.'

Burden rinsed the glass from Wexford's supper tray and from the washbasin took the toothglass for himself. 'A private room, eh? Very grand.'

Wexford chuckled. 'Not my idea, Mike. They were heading for the general ward when Crocker remembered Monkey Matthews was in, having his veins done. We came to the conclusion it might be an embarrassment to him after I did him a couple of years ago for stealing by finding. Don't worry, I'll take care to tell him what saving his face has cost me.' He looked round him complacently. 'Eight quid a day, this room. Good thing I wasn't in that lift any longer.' He drank his beer, wiped his mouth with a man-size Kleenex. 'Well, have you done the deed?'

'At five-thirty.'

'Pity I wasn't there.' Suddenly he shivered. 'The skin of my teeth . . .' Then he laughed. 'Teeth!' he said. 'That's funny.'

Footsteps that didn't tip-toe sounded outside and Crocker marched in. 'Who gave you leave to have a booze-up?'

'Sit down, not on the bed. Nurse Rose doesn't like it. We were just going to have a post-mortem. Interested?'

The doctor fetched himself a chair from the empty room next door. He flopped into it. 'I've heard who it is over the grapevine. By God, you could have knocked me down with a feather.'

'I leave that to others,' said Wexford. 'The intemperate fellows who aren't content with feathers. They use stones.' He met the doctor's eyes and saw there the astonishment and the eagerness for enlightenment he loved to see. 'Murderers aren't unknown among the medical profession,' he said. 'What about Crippen? Buck Ruxton? This time it happened to be a dentist.'

350

CHAPTER EIGHTEEN

'It's always a problem,' said Wexford, 'to know where to begin. Where's the beginning? I often think novelists must have my trouble. Well, I know they do. I used to know a chap who wrote books. He said it was easy to end and the middle just happened naturally, but he never knew where to begin. How far do you have to go back in a man's life to find what makes him do things? To his childhood, to his parents, to Adam?'

'Let's not go back that far,' said Burden. 'We'll be here all night.'

Wexford grinned at him. He banged his pillows and pulled their corners round his shoulders. 'I think I'll begin ten years ago,' he said. 'But don't worry. You know how time flies.'

'Vigo wasn't here ten years ago.'

'He was getting married. He married a rich girl, probably not entirely for her money. But the money set him up in practice here and bought his house for him. They had a child.'

'It was mongoloid,' said the doctor. 'Been in an institution since it was six months old. Vigo took it very hard.'

'Who wouldn't?' said Wexford. 'Look at Vigo. What Hitler would have called the perfect Aryan type and clever with it. If you were stud farming humans, wouldn't you choose Vigo as your ideal stallion?' The doctor gave a grudging nod.

'And if you were Vigo, wouldn't you expect to sire splendid progeny?'

'Everyone does.'

'Maybe. Everyone hopes, let's say, and sometimes the most unexpected people are lucky.' He smiled to himself and finished the last drop of beer Sheila had brought. 'I reckon Vigo blamed his wife. Don't tell me that was unfair. Life's unfair. They didn't have any more children for eight years.'

The doctor leant forward. 'They've got a son now,' he sighed. 'Poor kid.'

'If he's poor it's his father's fault,' Wexford snapped. 'Don't give me that sentimental stuff. This is the real beginning. Mrs

Vigo's second pregnancy. She had high blood pressure, she got toxaemia.'

'A threatened toxaemia, surely,' the doctor corrected him pedantically.

'Whatever it was, she was admitted to the Princess Louise Clinic in New Cavendish Street two months before the birth. You can imagine Vigo's feelings, was it going to go wrong again?'

'Toxaemia doesn't lead to mongoloid babies.'

'Oh, shut up!' said Wexford irritably. 'People don't reason in cases like that. He was scared and depressed and he took up with one of the nurses he met when he was visiting his wife. Maybe he'd always been a bit of a philanderer. I've got my own reasons for thinking that.'

'In your notes,' said Burden, who had the book open on his lap, 'you said he dropped Bridget Culross after the child was born healthy and normal.'

'That's conjecture. Let's say he was too taken up with the child — he's crazy about that child — to bother about outside interests. Did you check with the clinic?'

'I did. Mrs Vigo was admitted last October and remained in the clinic until two weeks after the child was born at the end of December. Bridget Culross was on duty in the ward where her room was from November 1st until January 1st.'

Wexford leaned back. 'It had to be someone with a Christian or surname beginning with J, you see. Jerome Fanshawe, we thought at first, but that couldn't be because Mrs Fanshawe was past the age of childbearing. I seriously considered Michael Jameson. It wouldn't at all surprise me to know he's got a wife somewhere.' He lowered his voice. Mrs Fanshawe was two doors down the corridor. 'A Michael Jameson might just as well call himself Jay as Mike and he had the right kind of car. But we'll come to that later. Anyway, it wasn't either of them. It was Jolyon Vigo. With a name like that you'd be glad of a convenient abbreviation sometimes.'

'You say he dropped the girl. Why did he take up with her again?'

'A man has a child,' said Wexford. 'If he worships the child it may, for a while, bring him closer to his wife. But these things wear off. Can the leopard change his spots? The girl thought she'd a chance of getting him to marry her. No doubt, he'd even considered that when he thought his wife wasn't ever going to give him a child. Now he wanted his bit of fun on the side but he wasn't going to lose his son for it. Not on your life. And that's the crux.'

The doctor crossed his legs and shifted his chair a little. 'Where does Charlie Hatton come into all this?'

Wexford didn't answer him directly. Instead he said, 'Vigo and Culross were carrying on their affair intermittently. If it wasn't all that of a regular thing, that's probably because the girl nagged him about marriage and he stalled.'

'You can't possibly know that,' Burden objected.

Wexford said loftily, 'I understand human nature. On the 18th of May Bridget Culross had a long weekend off and, by chance, the Blake Society were also having their weekend conference in Brighton over the next three days. Vigo picked Culross up at Marble Arch and drove her to Brighton in his car, a big Plymouth sedan.'

'How do you know it was the Blake Society? Why not the Gibbonites?'

'Vigo's got Blake drawings all over his hall walls. Did you check their room bookings?'

'They booked in at the Majestic in their own names. Two adjoining rooms. They vacated them on Monday afternoon, Monday May 20th.'

Wexford nodded. 'Perhaps it was their first weekend together. Bridget Culross spent it pressurising Vigo into agreeing to divorce his wife. Or trying to. I don't know what happened. How could I? I'll make a guess that she knew they'd have to pass through Kingsmarkham, or near it, on their way back to London, and she tried to persuade Vigo to take her back with him to the house in Ploughman's Lane and confront his wife together.' He cleared his throat. 'Men don't like that kind of thing,' he said. 'They had a fight. Want to know where? I guess she put the pressure on really hard when they reached the point where the road passes nearest to Kingsmarkham. That's about three miles south of the spot where the body was found. No doubt they got out of the car and my guess is the girl said she'd make her way to Ploughman's Lane on her own if he wouldn't come with her. Vigo's a big powerful man. They struggled, she fell and hit her head. He had an unconscious, perhaps dead, girl on his hands. You see his dilemma?'

'Whatever he did next, his wife would find out, divorce him and get custody of the child,' said Burden.

'Exactly. He began some quick thinking. First remove all identification from the expensive handbag he had given her himself. No doubt, a good many people knew where she had gone, but she had assured him no one knew his name. Vigo's an intelligent man, a medical man who knows something about police methods. They wouldn't search for a girl with a reputation like Bridget Culross's and no near relatives to give a damn. Suppose she was found dead in the road, knocked down by a passing vehicle? It would be assumed she'd quarrelled with her boy-friend, hitched a lift to Stowerton and been knocked down crossing the road or trying to hitch a second lift. He put her on the passenger seat, laying her flat with her head on his lap so as not to mark the seat with blood. Probably he had a newspaper or an old rug to cover his knees, something he could burn when he got home.

'He entered the by-pass where at that time of night and during the week, the road was comparatively clear. Now he wouldn't dare drive too fast — no one could open a car door and throw a body out at any speed — so he kept to the slow lane.'

'What then?'

'Things went according to plan. He drove along at twenty or thirty miles an hour and when there were no other vehicles in sight, he shot the girl out and she landed as he had expected with her head well over into the fast lane . . .'

'Wait a minute,' said the doctor sharply. 'That's not possible. It can't be done. We tried it and . . .'

'Wait a minute by all means,' said Wexford, and in execrable French, *'Pas devant les infirmières.'*

'Tea, coffee, Ovaltine or Horlicks,' said a bright voice whose owner had tapped on the glass panel in the door.

'Ovaltine would be very wholesome,' said Wexford blandly. 'Thank you kindly.'

'A chiel's among ye, taking notes,' said Wexford. 'In other

words, Charlie Hatton.' He sipped his Ovaltine with an inscrut-able expression. 'He had parked his lorry in the lay-by just over the brow of the hill and was taking the air in the field on the other side of the hedge.'

'You mean he saw Vigo push a girl out of his car and did nothing about it?'

'Depends by what you mean by nothing. In my experience the Charlie Hattons of this world aren't over-anxious to get involved with the police even as indignant observers. Hatton did something. He blackmailed Vigo.'

'Can I have a couple of your grapes?' said the doctor. 'Thanks. The only grapes I ever taste are the ones I nick from my patients.' He put one in his mouth and chewed it, seeds and all. 'Did he know Vigo?'

'By sight, I daresay, or else he knew the car. You'll get appendicitis.'

'Rubbish, old wives' tale. Anyhow, I've had it. What happened next?'

Wexford took another Kleenex and wiped his mouth.

'Hatton went home to his wife. Five minutes later Jerome Fanshawe came along, driving like the clappers, spotted the girl in the road too late and shouted out, 'My God!' She was lying remember, with her body and legs in the middle lane and her head over the fast lane. Fanshawe swerved. Wouldn't it be instinctive in those circumstances to avoid the head at all costs? So he swerved to the *right,* mounted the turfed centre section and crashed into a tree. That, I think, sums up the entire intervention of the Fanshawes into this case. For once in his life, Fanshawe was the innocent victim.'

Burden nodded agreement and took up the tale. 'On the following morning,' he said, 'Hatton mulled over the whole business. He made his telephone call about the flat for Pertwee and then went down to see it with the girl Marilyn. Immediately there was a call on his purse. The tenant of the flat wanted two hundred pounds key money.'

'And that clinched it,' said Wexford. 'He left Marilyn at the Olive and Dove and she saw him go into a phone box. We may be sure he was phoning Vigo, making an appointment for the afternoon.'

'I thought you said he made the appointment later from his own home?' said the doctor.

'He *phoned* again from his own home. That was just a blind for his wife. You may be sure he'd already made it clear to Vigo what he wanted and that he would phone again as if legitimately asking for an appointment. Of course it happened that way. If it hadn't, do you suppose Vigo would have agreed to an appointment that same day, only an hour afterwards? He's a busy man, booked up weeks in advance. Charlie Hatton wasn't even a patient of his. I've no doubt that in the morning Charlie told him he wanted hush money out of him and he'd have the best set of false teeth Vigo could provide. Free of charge, of course.'

'It must have been a hell of a shock to Vigo,' said Crocker thoughtfully. 'The night before he'd taken a risk and acted on the spur of the moment. The chances then of its coming out were fairly high, I'd have thought. But Fanshawe's crash was an unforeseen stroke of luck for him. Seeing it in the morning paper and seeing that the girl had been identified as Nora Fanshawe made him safe. By the time the real Nora turned up things would be so confused, the truth would very likely never come out. Who would have imagined his actions had been seen?'

'Naturally he paid up,' said Wexford. 'Paid and paid. My guess is that when he phoned the first time Hatton asked him to draw a thousand pounds immediately from his bank, a sum which he was to give to Hatton, and did give him, during his visit to Ploughman's Lane that afternoon, the afternoon of May 21st. Must have been rather bizarre, mustn't it, that consultation of Hatton's? The mind boggles, as they say. You have to picture the blackmailer lying back in his chair with his mouth open while his victim, desperate, at bay, if you like, probed about, measuring him for his new teeth.'

'On the following day, May 22nd, we know Hatton paid five hundred pounds into his own account, keeping two hundred for the Pertwees' key money and the remaining three hundred for incidental expenses, furniture, clothes and other frivolity. The weekly payments of fifty pounds a time followed at once. I reckon Hatton got Vigo to leave the money in some prearranged hiding place down by the river on Friday nights somewhere along the route Hatton took on his way home from the darts club. And one Friday night . . .'

'Yes, why that particular Friday?'

'Who can say at what point the victim of blackmail reaches the end of his tether?'

'Mrs Fanshawe,' put in Burden unexpectedly. 'You see, that wasn't quite right, what you said about the Fanshawes' intervention having come to an end. Mrs Fanshawe regained consciousness the day before Hatton was killed. It was in the morning papers, just a paragraph, but it was there.'

'You've got something there, Mike. Nora was still missing, but once Mrs Fanshawe could talk, Vigo might believe she'd tell us the girl's body couldn't be that of her daughter. Hatton was an important witness with someone else now to back up his story. Once he'd had all he wanted out of Vigo . . .'

The doctor got up, stood for a moment staring at Wexford's flowers and then said, 'It's a good story, but it's impossible. It couldn't have happened that way.' Wexford smiled at him. Crocker said irritably, 'What are you grinning like that for? I tell you there's an obvious flaw. If anyone throws a body out of a car, even feet first, it's going to fall well over to the left. Vigo would have had to be driving right on the grass section itself for the girl's head to have been in the fast lane. And as to that theory of yours about the head being on his lap to stop bloodstains getting on the passenger seat, it's nonsense. That way her *feet* would have been in the fast lane and Fanshawe would have swerved to the *left* to avoid her head.'

He stopped and gave a defiant snort as the nurse came back with a sleeping pill.

'I don't want that,' said Wexford. He slid down in the bed and pulled up the covers. 'I'll sleep, I'm tired.' Over the top of the sheet he said, 'Nice of you two to come. Oh, and by the way, it's a foreign car. Left-hand drive. Good night.'

CHAPTER NINETEEN

'Electrician,' said Jack Pertwee on the doorstep. 'You've got a switch that wants fixing.'

'Not me,' said the girl. 'I only work here. Wait a bit . . . Is this it?' She fumbled among some loose sheets of paper on a table beneath the mullioned window and her face reddened with indignation. 'You was supposed to come last week.'

'I was off last week. This is my first day back. Don't work yourself up. I've been here before. I can find my own way.'

His first day back. His first job on his first day, the first return to normal routine after the earthquake. Jack didn't know why he had chosen to come here — there were a dozen names who needed him on his list. Perhaps it was because some unformed unrecognised hunger in his subconscious cried for the solace and the refreshment of looking on beautiful things; perhaps because this place was unique in his experience, alien and remote from anywhere he had ever been with Charlie.

But as always when he found himself at the house in Ploughman's Lane, a clumsiness dragged at his feet and his deft fingers began to feel all thumbs. He was like a barbarian who, having entered a forsaken Roman villa, stood dazzled and amazed, overcome by the awe of ignorance. He crossed the hall and pretending to himself that he did not know the precise location of the switch — there was no need to, he was alone now — he opened door after door to peer in wonderment at the treasures within. A muttered 'Pardon me, lady' would have been his defence if one of them had been occupied but there was no one about and Jack looked his fill undisturbed at velvet and silk, dark tables inlaid with ivory, pictures in gilt frames, flowered china holding real flowers, a bust in bronze, a pomander whose orange spicy scent was brought to him on warm sunlight.

Afterwards he was unable to say what had suddenly brought Charlie so vividly to his mind, except perhaps that the memory of his dead friend was never far from it. Maybe this flash of pain, sharper and more real than any he had yet felt, came when he opened the door of the Chinese room. It was here, just inside the door, that his task awaited him and he stepped for a moment on the threshold stunned into immobility by the strange rich colours. It was too early yet for the sun to have reached the back of the house but the reds and golds, the unearthly sea greens and citrus yellows, blazed fiercely enough in shadow. Jack put down his tool bag and gazed about him numbly. He had been here before and yet it seemed to him that he had never seen the room until this moment. It was as if his nerves had been stripped raw and, unprotected, received the impact of these glorious yet intolerable colours in a series of vibrations like electric shocks.

Half in a trance he approached the chessmen that Charlie had called an army and saw in the face of one of them, a red knight, the perfect facsimile of his dead friend's face, sharp, cunning, astute and kind. A longing to possess and preserve it seized him but he was afraid even to touch the delicate carved jade and he heard himself give a low sob.

It was his awed and perhaps childlike descriptions of this house which had, he supposed, led Charlie here. Just as he, Jack, might have gone to the grocer's, so Charlie Hatton had come here to buy the best. Jack's sorrow dissolved in admiration of that audacity. His friend had penetrated this museum too and that not as a servant or a workman but as a customer. Vigo had brought him into this room and drunk with him. Jack could imagine Charlie's cocky poise, his hard brown hands even daring to lift a cup or finger a silk picture while he commented on its quality, its desirability, with brash impudence. Had he recognised himself at the head of that scarlet army? And the Philistines slew Jonathan . . . How are the mighty fallen and the weapons of war perished!

Jack turned away from the sharp little faces that seemed to scrutinise him and, opening his bag, squatted down in front of it. He felt worn out, exhausted at ten in the morning, and the girl's voice behind him made him jump.

'Thought you might fancy a cup of tea.'

He could guess his own expression and he didn't want her to see his face. 'Mr or Mrs about?' he asked. 'I'd better see one of them.'

'Haven't you heard then? She's gone away and taken the boy. The police arrested him yesterday for killing that lorry driver.'

There had been tears in Jack's eyes and now his eyelids burned as they sometimes did after an evening with Charlie in the smoke-filled bar of the Dragon. He was staring into the heap of tools but not seeing them. His brain had become an empty red space. He got to his feet and there was a hammer in his hand, although he couldn't remember selecting it from the heap.

The red light before his eyes split into a spectrum of insane red and gold and sea green that roared as it twisted and leapt about him, as if a kaleidoscope could make sound as varied and as fantastic as its changing pictures. Behind him another, shriller noise echoed. The girl had begun to scream.

'A bull in a china shop,' said Wexford.

He picked his way through the fragments which littered the carpet, stopping occasionally to lift between finger and thumb a sliver of transparent porcelain. His expression was impassive and cold but a little heat entered it as he approached the table where the chessmen had been. Not a piece remained intact, but here and there among the red and white gravel he found a delicate spear with an amputated hand still grasping it, a fragment of ivory lace, a horse's hoof.

Burden was kneeling down, smoothing out torn remnants of the silk pictures. A big rough footprint scarred the scales of the painted fish, the print of the same foot that had ground saké cups to dust.

'Frightening, isn't it?' said Wexford. 'Barbarity is frightening. I'm glad I don't know . . .'

'What all this stuff was worth?' Burden hazarded.

'Not so much as all that. I meant I'm glad I don't know its uniqueness, its age, its quality really; looting must be like this, I suppose, wanton, revengeful.'

'You said Charlie Hatton was a soldier of fortune.'

'Yes. Is there any point in going to talk to his comrade-in-arms? I suppose we have to.'

Jack Pertwee was in the kitchen with Sergeant Martin. He

was sitting down, his arms spread and his body slumped across the table. Wexford shook him roughly and jerked his head back. Their eyes met and for a moment Wexford still held on to the electrician's coat collar, shaking it as might a man who has brought a destructive dog under control. Jack's jowls shook and his teeth chattered.

'You're a fool, Pertwee,' Wexford said scornfully. 'You'll lose your job over this. And for what? For a friend who's dead and can't thank you?'

His voice almost inaudible, Jack said, 'The best . . . The best friend a man ever had. And it was me sent him here.' He clenched his fist, drove it hard against the table.

'Oh, take him away, Sergeant.'

Jack dragged himself to his feet. His fist opened and something fell to the floor, rolled and came to rest at Wexford's feet. The chief inspector stared downwards. It was the red knight's decapitated head. The wicked sharp face, tricked into expression by a ribbon of sunlight, grinned widely and showed its teeth.

'Charlie,' Jack whispered. He tried to say it again but great agonised sobs tore away the name.

Wolf to the Slaughter

I think the Vessel, that with fugitive
Articulation answer'd, once did live,
And merry-make; and the cold Lip I kiss'd
How many Kisses might it take—and give!

For Don

'Tis all Chequer-board of Nights and Days
Where Destiny with Men for pieces plays:
Hither and thither moves, and mates, and slays,
And one by one back in the Closet lays.

The Rubaiyát of Omar Khayyám

CHAPTER ONE

They might have been going to kill someone.

The police would possibly have thought so if they had stopped the car that was going too fast along the darkening road. The man and the girl would have had to get out and explain why they were carrying an offensive weapon. Explanation would have had to come from the man, for the girl could not have answered them. In the gathering dusk, watching the thin rain trickle down the glass, she thought that the raincoats they wore looked like a disguise, gangster garments, and the knife unsheathed for use.

'Why do you carry it?' she asked, speaking for the first time since they had left Kingsmarkham and its street lamps drowned in drizzle. 'You could get into trouble having a knife like that.' Her voice was nervous, although the nerves were not for the knife.

He pressed the switch that worked the windscreen wipers. 'Suppose the old girl turned funny?' he said. 'Suppose she changed her mind? I might have to put the fear of God into her.' And he drew his fingernail along the flat of the blade.

'I don't like it much,' the girl said, and again she did not only mean the knife.

'Maybe you'd rather have stayed at home, with him liable to come in at any minute? It's a miracle to me you ever got around to using his car.'

Instead of answering him, she said carefully, 'I mustn't see this woman, this Ruby. I'll sit in the car out of the way while you go to the door.'

'That's right, and she'll nip out the back. I got the whole thing arranged on Saturday.'

Stowerton was seen first as an orange blur, a cluster of lights swimming through the mist. They came into the town centre where the shops were closed but the launderette still open. Wives who worked by day sat in front of the machines, watching their washing spin round inside the portholes, their faces greenish, tired in the harsh white light. On the corner at the crossroads, Cawthorne's garage was in darkness, but the Victorian house behind it brightly illuminated and from its open front door came the sound of dance music. Listening to this music, the girl gave a soft giggle. She whispered to her companion, but because she had only said something about the Cawthornes having a party, nothing about their own destination and their purpose, he merely nodded indifferently and said:

'How's the time?'

She caught sight of the church clock as they turned into a side street. 'Nearly eight.'

'Perfect,' he said. He made a face in the direction of the lights and the music and raised two fingers in a derisive gesture. 'That to old Cawthorne,' he said. 'I reckon he'd like to be in my shoes now.'

The streets were grey and rain-washed and they all looked the same. Stunted trees grew from the pavements at four-yard intervals and their struggling roots had made cracks in the tarmac. The squat houses, unbroken rows and rows of them, were all garageless and there was a car stuck half-way on the pavement outside nearly every one.

'Here we are, Charteris Road. It's number eighty-two, the one on the corner. Good, there's a light in the front room. I thought she might have done the dirty on us, got cold feet or something and gone out.' He put the knife into his pocket and the girl watched the blade flick back to bury itself in the shaft. 'I shouldn't have liked that,' he said.

The girl said quietly, but with an undercurrent of excitement in her voice, 'Nor should I now.'

The rain had brought night early and it was dark in the car, too dark to see faces. Their hands met as together they fumbled to make the little gold cigarette lighter work. In its flame she saw his dark features glow and she caught her breath.

'You're lovely,' he said. 'God, you're beautiful.' He touched her throat, moving his fingers into the hollow between the horizontal bones. They sat for a moment looking at each other, the flame making soft candlelight shadows on their faces. Then he snapped the lighter closed and pushed open the car door. She twisted the gold cube in her hands, straining her eyes to read its inscription: For Ann who lights my life.

A street lamp on the corner made a bright pool from the kerb to the gate. He crossed it and it threw his shadow black and sharp on this evening of blurred outlines. The house he had come to was poor and mean, its front garden too small to have a lawn. There was just an earth plot, an area ringed with stones, like a grave.

On the step he stood a little to the left of the front door so that the woman who would come to answer his knock should not see more than she need, should not, for instance, see the tail of the green car, wet and glistening in the lamplight. He waited impatiently, tapping his feet. Raindrops hung from the window sills like chains of glass beads.

When he heard sounds of movement from within, he stood stiffly and cleared his throat. The footsteps were followed by sudden illumination of the single diamond pane in the door. Then, as the latch clicked, that pane became a frame for a wrinkled painted face, businesslike but apprehensive, crowned with ginger hair. He thrust his hands into his pockets, feeling a smooth polished hilt in the right-hand one, and willing things to go right for him.

When things went wrong, hideously wrong, he had a terrible sense of fate, of inevitability. It would have happened sometime, sooner or later, this way or the other. They got into their coats somehow and he tried to staunch the blood with his scarf.

'A doctor,' she kept moaning, 'a doctor or the hospital.' He didn't want that, not if it could be avoided. The knife was back in his pocket and all he wanted was air and to feel the rain on his face and to get to the car.

The terror of death was on both their faces and he could not bear to meet her eyes, staring and red as if the blood were reflected in the pupils. Down the path, they held on to each other, staggering past the little bit of earth like a grave, drunk with panic. He got the car door open and she fell across the seat.

'Get up,' he said. 'Get a grip on yourself. We've got to get out of here,' but his voice sounded as far off as death had once seemed. The car jerked and shuddered up the road. Her hands were shaking and her breath rattled.

'You'll be all right. It was nothing — that tiny blade!'

'Why did you do it? Why? Why?'

'That old girl, that Ruby . . . Too late now.'

Too late. A blueprint for last words. Music came out from Cawthorne's house as the car went past the garage, not a dirge but music for dancing. The front door stood open and a great band of yellow light fell across the puddles. The car went on past the shops. Beyond the cottages the street lamps came to an end. It had stopped raining but the countryside was shrouded in vapour. The road was a tunnel between trees from which the water dripped silently, a huge wet mouth that sucked the car along its slippery tongue.

Across the band of light and skirting the puddles, party guests came and went. Music met them, hot dry music in sharp contrast to the night. Presently a young man came out with a glass in his hand. He was gay and full of *joie de vivre* but he had already exhausted the possibilities of this party. The drunk he spoke to in a parked car ignored him. He finished his drink and put the glass down on top of a diesel pump. There was no one to talk to except a sharp-faced old girl, going home, he guessed, because the pubs were shutting. He hailed her, declaiming loudly:

'Ah, make the most of what we yet may spend,
Before we too into the dust descend!'

She grinned at him. 'That's right, dear,' she said. 'You enjoy yourself.'

He was hardly in a fit state to drive. Not at the moment. Besides, to remove his own car would necessitate the removal of six others whose owners were all inside enjoying themselves. So he began to walk, buoyantly and in the faint hope of meeting someone rather special.

It had come on to rain again. He liked the cool feeling of the drops on his hot face. The road to Kingsmarkham yawned at him. He walked along it happily, not at all tired. Far away in the distance, in the throat as it were of this deep wet mouth, he could see the lights of a stationary car.

'What lamp,' he said aloud, 'had destiny to guide
Her little children stumbling in the dark?'

CHAPTER TWO

A high east wind blowing for a day and night had dried the streets. The rain would come again soon but now the sky was a hard bitter blue. Through the centre of the town the Kingsbrook rattled over round stones, its water whipped into little pointed waves.

The wind was high enough to be heard as well as felt. It swept between the alleys that divided ancient shops from new blocks and with a sound like an owl's cry made leafless branches crack against the slate and brick. People waiting for the Stowerton bus going north and the Pomfret bus going south turned up collars to shelter their faces. Every passing car had its windows closed and when cyclists reached the summit of the bridge over that rushing stream, the wind caught them and stopped them for a moment before they battled against it and wobbled down past the Olive and Dove.

Only the daffodils in the florist's window showed that it was April and not December. They looked as sleek and smug behind their protective glass as did the shopkeepers and office workers who were lucky enough to be indoors on this inclement morning. Such a one, at least for the moment, was Inspector Michael Burden, watching the High Street from his well-insulated observatory.

Kingsmarkham police station, a building of startling modernity, commands a view of the town although it is separated from its nearest neighbour by a strip of green meadow. A horse was tethered there this morning and it looked as cold and miserable as Burden had felt on his arrival ten minutes before. He was still thawing out by one of the central heating vents which blew a stream of warm air against his legs. Unlike his superior, Chief Inspector Wexford, he was not given to quotation, but he would have agreed on this bitter Thursday morning, that April is the cruellest month, breeding, if not lilacs, grape hyacinths out of the dead land. They clustered beneath him in stone urns on the station forecourt, their flowers smothered by a tangle of battered foliage. Whoever had planted them had intended them to blossom as blue as the lamp over the canopy, but the long winter had defeated them. Burden felt that he might have been looking upon tundra rather than the fruits of an English spring.

He swallowed the last of the hot sugarless tea Sergeant Camb had brought him. The tea was sugarless because Burden preferred it that way, not from motives of self-denial. His figure remained lean naturally, no matter what he ate, and his greyhound's face thin and ascetic. Conservative in dress, he was wearing a new suit this morning, and he flattered himself that he looked like a broker on holiday. Certainly no one seeing him in this office with its wall-to-wall carpet, its geometrically patterned curtains and its single piece of glass sculpture would have taken him for a detective in his natural habitat.

He restored the tea cup to its saucer of black Prinknash pottery and his gaze to a figure on the opposite pavement. His own sartorial correctness was uppermost in his mind today and he shook his head distastefully at the loiterer with his long hair and his unconventional clothes. The window was beginning to mist up with condensation. Burden cleared a small patch fastidiously and brought his eyes closer to the glass. He sometimes wondered what men's clothes were coming to these days — Detective Constable Drayton was just one example of contemporary sloppiness — but this! An outlandish jacket of spiky fur more suited to an eskimo, a long purple and yellow scarf that Burden could not excuse by connecting it with any university, pale blue jeans and suede boots. Now he was crossing the road — a typical jay walker — and entering the station forecourt. When he bent down and snapped off a grape hyacinth head to put in his buttonhole, Burden almost opened the window to shout at him, but remembered about letting warm air out and stopped in time. The scarf was the last he saw of him, its purple fringe flying out as its wearer disappeared under the canopy.

Might as well be in Carnaby Street, Burden thought, recalling a recent shopping trip to London with his wife. She had been more interested in the cranky-looking people than the shops. When he got home he would tell her there was no need to go fifty miles in a stuffy train when there were funnier sights on her own doorstep. Even this little corner of Sussex would soon be infested with them, he supposed as he settled down at his desk to read Drayton's report on the theft of some Waterford glass.

Not bad, not bad at all. Considering his youth and his inexperience, Drayton was shaping up well. But there were gaps, vital facts omitted. If you wanted anything done in this world, he thought aggrievedly, you mostly had to do it yourself. He took his raincoat from the hook — his overcoat was at the cleaner's. Why not, in April? — and went downstairs.

After days of being almost obscured by muddy footmarks, the foyer's black and white checkerboard floor was highly polished this morning. Burden could see his own well-brushed shoes reflected in its surface. The long ellipse of the counter and the uncomfortable red plastic chairs had that chill clear-cut look wind and dry air give even to an interior.

Also contemplating his reflection in the mirror-like tiles, his bony hands hanging by his sides, sat the man Burden had seen in the street. At the sound of footsteps crossing the floor, he glanced up vaguely to where Sergeant Camb was on the phone. Apparently he needed attention. He had not come, as Burden had formerly supposed, to collect garbage or mend fuses or even sell shady information to Detective Sergeant Martin. It seemed that he was an authentic innocent member of the public in some sort of minor trouble. Burden wondered if he had lost a dog or found a wallet. His face was pale and thin, the forehead bumpy, the eyes far from tranquil. When Camb put the receiver down, he approached the counter with a curious sluggish irritability.

'Yes, sir?' said the sergeant, 'What can I do for you?'

'My name is Margolis, Rupert Margolis,' It was a surprising voice. Burden had expected the local brand of country cockney, something to go with the clothes, anything but this cultured effeteness. Margolis paused after giving his name, as if anticipating some startling effect. He held his head on one side, waiting perhaps for delighted gasps or extended hands. Camb merely gave a ponderous nod. The visitor coughed slightly and passed his tongue over dry lips.

'I wondered,' he said, 'if you could tell me how one goes about finding a charwoman.'

Neither dogs nor wallets, fuses nor undercover information. The man simply wanted his house cleaned. An anti-climax or a salutary lesson in not jumping to obvious conclusions. Burden smiled to himself. What did he think this was? The Labour Exchange? A Citizen's Advice Bureau?

Seldom disconcerted, Camb gave Margolis a genial smile. The enquirer might have found it encouraging, but Burden knew the smile covered a philosophical resignation to the maxim that it takes all sorts to make a world.

'Well, sir, the offices of the Ministry of Labour are only five minutes from here. Go down York Street, past Joy Jewels and you'll find it next to the Red Star garage. You could try there. What about advertising in the local rag or a card in Grover's window?'

Margolis frowned. His eyes were a very light greenish-blue, the colour of a bird's egg and like a bird's egg, speckled with brown dots. 'I'm very bad at these practical things,' he said vaguely, and the eyes wandered over the foyer's gaudy decor. 'You see, normally my sister would see to it, but she went away on Tuesday, or I suppose she did.' He sighed, leaning his whole weight against the counter. 'And that's another worry. I seem to be quite bogged down with care at the moment.'

'The Ministry of Labour, sir,' Camb said firmly. He recoiled, grabbing at fluttering papers, as Detective Constable Drayton came in. 'I'll have to see to those doors. Sheer waste running the heating.' Margolis made no move to go. He watched the sergeant twist the chrome handles, crouch down to examine the ball catch.

'I wonder what Ann would do,' he said helplessly. 'It's so unlike her to go off like this and leave me in a mess.'

His patience rapidly going, Burden said, 'If there aren't any messages for me, Sergeant, I'm off to Sewingbury. You can come with me, Drayton.'

'No messages,' said Camb, 'but I did hear Monkey Matthews was out.'

'I thought he must be,' said Burden.

The car heater was a powerful one and Burden found himself weakly wishing Sewingbury was fifty miles away instead of five. Their breath was already beginning to mist the windows when Drayton turned up the Kingsbrook Road.

'Who's Monkey Matthews, sir?' he asked, accelerating as they passed the derestriction sign.

'You haven't been with us all that long, have you? Monkey's a villain, thief, small-time con man. He went inside last year for trying to blow someone up. In a very small way, mind, and with a home-made bomb. He's fifty-odd, ugly, and he has various human weaknesses, including womanising.'

Unsmiling, Drayton said, 'He doesn't sound very human.'

'He looks like a monkey,' Burden said shortly, 'if that's what you mean.' There was no reason to allow a simple request for official information to grow into a conversation. It was Wexford's fault, he thought, for taking a liking to Drayton and showing it. Once you started cracking jokes with subordinates and being matey, they took advantage. He turned his back on Drayton to stare at the landscape of chilly fields, saying coldly, 'He smokes like a chimney and he's got a churchyard cough. Hangs around the Piebald Pony in Stowerton. Keep on the look-out for him and don't think you won't encounter him because you're bound to.' Better let him hear it and hear it without sentimentality from him than Wexford's highly coloured version. The Chief Inspector enjoyed the peculiar *camaraderie* he had with characters like Monkey and it was all right for him in his position. Let Drayton see the funny side and goodness knew where he would end up. He stole a glance at the young man's dark hard profile. Those cagey contained ones were all the same, he thought, a mass of nerves and complexes underneath.

'First stop Knobby Clark's, sir?'

Burden nodded. How much longer was Drayton going to let his hair grow? For weeks and weeks until he looked like a drummer in one of those pop groups? Of course Wexford was right when he said they didn't want all and sundry picking out an obvious cop from his raincoat and his shoes, but that duffel coat was the end. Line Drayton up with a bunch of villains and you wouldn't be able to tell the sheep from the goats.

The car drew up outside a small shabby jeweller's shop. 'Not on the yellow band, Drayton,' Burton said sharply before the hand brake was on. They went inside. A stout man, very short of stature, with a purple naevus blotching his forehead and the greater part of his bald pate, stood behind a glass-topped table, fingering a bracelet and a ring.

'Nasty cold morning,' Burden said.

'Bitter, Mr Burden.' Knobby Clark, jeweller and occasional receiver of stolen goods, shifted a step or two. He was too short to see over the shoulder of the woman whose trinkets he was pricing. His whole massive head came into view and it resembled some huge root vegetable, a swede perhaps or a kohl rabi, this impression being enhanced by the uneven stain of the birthmark.

'Don't hurry yourself,' Burden said. 'I've got all day.'

He transferred his attention to a display of carriage clocks. The woman Knobby was haggling with was, he could have sworn, utterly respectable. She wore a thick tweed coat that reached below her knees although she was a youngish woman, and the handbag from which she had produced the jewellery, wrapped in a thin plain handkerchief, looked as if it had once been expensive. Her hands shook a little and Burden saw that she wore a wedding ring on each. The shaking might have been due to the intense cold of Knobby's unheated shop, but only nerves could have been responsible for the tremor in her voice, nerves and the natural reluctance of such a woman to be there at all.

For the second time that day he was surprised by a tone and an accent. 'I was always given to understand the bracelet was valuable,' she said and she sounded ashamed. 'All my husband's gifts to me were very good.'

'Depends what you mean by valuable,' Knobby said, and Burden knew that the ingratiating note, the servility that covered granite imperviousness to pleading, was for his benefit. 'I'll tell you what I'll do. I'll give you ten for the lot.'

In the icy atmosphere her quickly exhaled breath hung like smoke. 'Oh, no, I couldn't possibly.' She flexed her hands, giving them firmness, but still they fumbled with the handkerchief and the bracelet made a small clink against the glass.

'Suit yourself,' said Knobby Clark. He watched indifferently as the handbag closed. 'Now, then, Mr Burden, what can I do for you?'

For a moment Burden said nothing. He felt the woman's humiliation, the disappointment that looked more like hurt love than wounded pride. She edged past him with a gentle, 'Excuse me', easing on her gloves and keeping that curious custody of the eyes that is said to be a nun's discipline. Going on for forty, he thought, not pretty any more, fallen on evil days. He held the door open for her.

'Thank you so much,' she said, not effusively but with a faint surprise as if once, long ago, she had been acustomed to such attentions and thought them lost for ever.

'So you haven't seen any of this stuff?' Burden said gruffly, thrusting the list of stolen glass under Knobby's bulbous nose.

'I already told your young lad, Mr Burden.'

Drayton stiffened a little, his mouth muscles hard.

'I think I'll take a look.' Knobby opened his mouth to complain, showing tooth fillings as richly gold as the metal of the clocks. 'Don't start screaming for a warrant. It's too cold.'

The search yielded nothing. Burden's hands were red and stiff when they came out of the inner room. 'Talk about Aladdin's cave in the Arctic,' he grumbled. 'O.K., that'll do for the time being.' Knobby was an occasional informer as well as a fence. Burden put his hand to his breast pocket where his wallet slightly disturbed the outline of the new suit. 'Got anything to tell us?'

Knobby put his vegetable-like head to one side. 'Monkey Matthews is out,' he said hopefully.

'Tell me something I don't know,' Burden snapped.

The swing doors had been fixed when they got back. Now it was difficult to open them at all. Sergeant Camb sat at his typewriter with his back to the counter, one finger poised in the warm air, his expression bemused. When he saw Burden he said as wrathfully as his bovine nature permitted:

'I've only just this minute got shot of him.'

'Shot of who?'

'That comedian who came in when you went out.'

Burden laughed. 'You shouldn't be so sympathetic.'

'I reckon he thought I'd send Constable Peach down to his cottage to clean up for him if he went on long enough. He lives in Quince Cottage down in Pump Lane, lives there with his sister only she's upped and left him to his own devices. Went to a party on Tuesday night and never came back.'

'And he came in here because he wanted a *charwoman*?' Burden was faintly intrigued, but still they didn't want to add to their Missing Persons list if they could avoid it.

'I don't know what to do, he says. Ann's never gone off before without leaving me a note. Ann this and Ann that. Talk about Am I my brother's keeper?'

The sergeant was a loquacious man. Burden could hardly help wondering how much Camb's own garrulity had contributed to Rupert Margolis's long diatribe. 'Chief Inspector in?' he asked.

'Just coming now, sir.'

Wexford had his overcoat on, that hideous grey overcoat which would never be at the cleaner's during cold spells because it was never cleaned. Its colour and its ridged, hide-like texture added to the elephantine impression the Chief Inspector made as he strode heavily down the stairs, his hands thrust into his pockets which held the shape of those fists even when empty.

'Carousel for a spot of lunch, sir?' said Burden.

'May as well.' Wexford shoved the swing door and shoved again when it stuck. With a half-grin, Camb returned smugly to his typewriter.

'Anything come up?' Burden asked as the wind hit them among the potted hyacinths.

'Nothing special,' Wexford said, ramming his hat more firmly on his head. 'Monkey Matthews is out.'

'Really?' said Burden and he put out his hand to feel the first spots of icy rain.

CHAPTER THREE

That Chief Inspector Wexford should be sitting at his rosewood desk reading the *Daily Telegraph* weekend supplement on a Friday morning was an indication that things in Kingsmarkham were more than usually slack. A cup of tea was before him, the central heating breathed deliciously and the new blue and grey folkweave curtains were half-drawn to hide the lashing rain. Wexford glanced through a feature on the beaches of Antigua, pulling down an angle lamp to shed light on the page. His little eyes, the colour of cut flints, held a mocking gleam when they lighted on a more than usually lush advertisement for clothes or personal furnishings. His own suit was grey, double-breasted, sagging under the arms and distorted at the pockets. He turned the pages, slightly bored. He was uninterested in after-shave, hair-cream, diets. Corpulent and heavy, he had always been stout and always would be. His was an ugly face, the face of a Silenus with a snub nose and wide mouth. The classics have it that Silenus was the constant companion for Bacchus, but the nearest Wexford ever got to Bacchus was an occasional pint with Inspector Burden at the Olive and Dove.

Two pages from the end he came upon an article which caught his eye. He was not an uncultured man and the contemporary fashion of investment by buying pictures had begun to interest him. He was looking at coloured photographs, two of paintings and one of a painter, when Burden came in.

'Things must be quiet,' Burden said, eyeing the *Weekend Telegraph* and Wexford's pile of scattered correspondence. He came up behind the Chief Inspector and glanced over his shoulder. 'Small world,' he said. Something in his tone made Wexford look up and raise one eyebrow. 'That bloke was in here yesterday.' And Burden stabbed his finger at the photographed face.

'Who? Rupert Margolis?'

'Painter, is he? I thought he was a Mod.'

379

Wexford grinned. 'It says here that he's a twenty-nine-year-old genius whose picture, "The Dawn of Nothing", has just been bought by the Tate Gallery.' He ran his eye down the page. ' "Margolis, whose 'Painting of Dirt' is contemporaneous with the Theatre of Cruelty, uses coal dust and tea leaves in his work as well as paint. He is fascinated by the marvellous multifarious textures of matter in the wrong place, etcetera, etcetera." Come, come, Mike, don't look like that. Let us keep an open mind. What was he doing in here?'

'Looking for some home help.'

'Oh, we're a domestic service agency now, are we? Burden's Buttling Bureau.'

Laughing, Burden read aloud the paragraph beneath the Chief Inspector's thick forefinger. ' "Some of Margolis's most brilliant work is the fruit of a two-year sojourn in Ibiza, but for the past year he and his sister Anita have made their home in Sussex. Margolis works in a sixteenth-century studio, the converted living room of Quince Cottage, Kingsmarkham, and it is here under the blood-red quince tree that he has given birth after six months' painful gestation to his masterpiece, or 'Nothing' as he whimsically calls it." '

'Very obstetric,' said Wexford. 'Well, this won't do, Mike. We can't afford to give birth to nothing.'

But Burden had settled down with the magazine on his knees. 'Interesting stuff, this,' he said. ' "Anita, a former model and Chelsea playgirl, is often to be seen in Kingsmarkham High Street, shopping from her white Alpine sports car. . . ." I've never seen her and once seen never forgotten, I should think. Listen. "Twenty-three years old, dark and exquisite with arresting green eyes, she is the Ann of Margolis's portrait for which he was offered two thousand pounds by a South American collector. Her devotion to Margolis's interests is the inspiration of some of his best work and it is this which, some say, led to the breaking off six months ago of her engagement to writer and poet Richard Fairfax." '

Wexford fingered his own sample of the glass sculpture which with the desk and the curtains had just been allocated to the station. 'Why don't you buy the *Telegraph* yourself if you're so keen,' he grumbled.

'I'm only reading it because it's local,' Burden said. 'Funny what goes on around you and you don't know it.'

Wexford quoted sententiously, 'Full many a gem of purest ray serene the dark unfathomed caves of ocean bear.'

'I don't know about dark unfathomed caves.' Burden was sensitive to criticisim of his hometown. He closed the magazine. 'She's a gem all right. Dark and exquisite, arresting green eyes. She goes to parties and doesn't come home. . . .'

The glance Wexford gave him was sharp and hard and the query cracked out like a shot. 'What?'

Surprised, Burden looked up. 'I said she goes to parties and doesn't come home.'

'I know you did.' There was a hard anxious edge to Wexford's impatience. The teasing quality present in his voice while they had been reading was quite gone and from facetious mockery he had become suddenly alert. 'I know what you said. I want to know what made you say it. How d'you know?'

'As I said, genius came hunting for a charwoman. Later he got talking to Camb and said his sister had been to a party on Tuesday night and he hadn't seen her since.'

Wexford got up slowly. The heavy lined face was puzzled and there was something else there as well. Doubt? Fear? 'Tuesday night?' he said, frowning. 'Sure it was Tuesday night?'

Burden did not care for mysteries between colleagues. 'Look, sir, he didn't even report her missing. Why the panic?'

'Panic be damned!' It was almost a shout. 'Mike, if her name is Ann and she went missing Tuesday night, this is serious. No picture of *her*, is there?' Wexford flicked expertly through the magazine, having snatched it roughly from Burden. 'No picture,' he said disgustedly. 'What's the betting the brother hasn't got one either?'

Burden said patiently, 'Since when have we got all steamed up because a single girl, a good-looking, probably rich girl, takes it into her head to run off with a boy friend?'

'Since now,' Wexford snapped. 'Since this morning, since this.' The correspondence, Wexford's morning post, looked like a pile of litter, but he found the envelope unerringly and held it out to Burden. 'I don't like this at all, Mike.' He shook out a sheet of thick folded paper. The glass sculpture, indigo blue and translucent, shed upon it a gleaming amorphous reflection like a bubble of ink. 'Things are slack no longer,' he said.

It was an anonymous letter that lay where the magazine had been and the words on it were handwritten in red ball-point.

'You know what a hell of a lot of these we get,' Wexford said. 'I was going to chuck it in the basket.'

A back-sloping hand, large writing, obviously disguised. The paper was not dirty nor the words obscene. The distaste Burden felt was solely on account of its author's cowardice and his desire to titillate without committing himself.

He read it to himself.

A girl called Ann was killed in this area between eight and eleven Tuesday night. The man who done it is small and dark and young and he has a black car. Name of Geoff Smith.

Discarding it with a grimace, he turned to the envelope. 'Posted in Stowerton,' he said. 'Twelve-fifty yesterday. Not very discreet of him, writing it. In our experience, the usual line is to cut words out of newspapers.'

'Assuming the infallibility of handwriting experts?' Wexford scoffed. 'Have you ever heard one of those johnnies give a firm opinion one way or the other, Mike? I haven't. If your recipient hasn't got a sample of your normal handwriting you might just as well save your newspaper and your scissors. Slope backwards if you normally slope forwards, write large if you usually write small, and you're perfectly incognito, safe as houses. No, I'll send this down to the lab but I'll be very much surprised if they can tell me anything I haven't deduced for myself. There's only one thing I haven't deduced for myself. There's only one thing here that'll lead me to my correspondent.'

'The paper,' Burden said thoughtfully. He fingered its thick creamy surface and its silky watermark.

'Exactly. It's handmade, unless I'm much mistaken, but the writer isn't the kind of man to order handmade paper. He's an uneducated chap; look at that "done it".'

'He could work in a stationers,' Burden said slowly.

'More likely work for someone who ordered this paper specially from a stationers.'

'A servant, d'you mean? That narrows the field a lot. How many people around here employ menservants?'

'Plenty employ gardeners, Mike. The stationers should be our starting point and we'll only need to tackle the high-class ones. That leaves out Kingsmarkham. I can't see Braddon's supplying handmade paper and certainly not Grover's.'

'You're taking this whole thing very seriously, sir.'

'I am. I want Martin, Drayton, Bryant and Gates up here because this is one anonymous letter I can't afford to treat as a practical joke. You, Mike, had better see what you can get out of the twenty-nine-year-old genius.'

He sat beside Burden behind the desk when they were all assembled. 'Now, I'm not taking you off your regular work,' he began. 'Not yet. Get hold of the electoral register and make a list of all the Geoffrey Smiths in the district. Particularly in Stowerton. I want them all looked up during the course of the day and I want to know if any of them are small and dark and if any of them has a black car. That's all. No frightening of wives, please, and no insisting on looking into garages. Just a casual survey. Keep your eyes open. Take a look at this paper, Sergeant Martin, and if you find any like it in a stationers I want it brought back here for comparison . . .'

After they had gone, Burden said bitterly, 'Smith! I ask you, Smith!'

'Some people really are called Smith, Mike,' Wexford said. He folded up the colour supplement with Margolis's photograph uppermost and tucked it carefully in a drawer of the rosewood desk.

'If I could only find the matches,' Rupert Margolis said, 'I'd make you a cup of coffee.' He fumbled helplessly among dirty crockery, topless bottles of milk, crumpled frozen food cartons on the kitchen table. 'There were some here on Tuesday night. I came in about eleven and all the lights had fused. That's not unusual. There was an enormous pile of newspapers on here and I picked them up and chucked them outside the back door. Our dustbins are always full. However, I did find the matches then, about fifteen boxes where the papers had been.' He sighed heavily. 'God knows where they are now. I haven't been cooking much.'

'Here,' said Burden and handed him one of the match books the Olive and Dove gave away with drinks. Margolis poured a percolator full of black liquid sprouting mould down the sink. Grounds clung to the sink side and to an aubergine floating in dirty dishwater. 'Now, let me get this straight.' It had taken him half an hour to get the salient facts out of Margolis and even now he was not sure if he had them sorted out. 'Your sister, whose name is Anita or Ann, was going to a party given by Mr and Mrs Cawthorne of Cawthorne's service station in Stowerton on Tuesday night. When you got home at eleven, having been out since three, she was gone and her car also, her white Alpine sports car which is usually parked outside in the lane. Right?'

'Right,' said Margolis worriedly. The kitchen had no ceiling, only a roof of corrugated metal supported by ancient beams. He sat on the edge of the table staring at the cobwebs which hung from them and moving his head gently in time to the movement of those swinging grey ropes, agitated by the rising steam from the coffee pot.

Burden went on firmly. 'You left the back door unlocked for her and went to bed but you were awakened soon afterwards by Mr Cawthorne telephoning to ask where your sister was.'

'Yes. I was very annoyed. Cawthorne's a terrible old bore and I never talk to him unless I have to.'

'Weren't you at all concerned?'

'No. Why should I be? I thought she'd changed her mind and gone off somewhere else.' The painter got down from his perch and ran the cold water tap over two filthy tea cups.

'At about one o'clock,' Burden said, 'you were awakened again by lights passing across your bedroom ceiling. These you assumed to be the lights of your sister's car, since no one else lives in Pump Lane, but you did not get up . . .'

'I went straight off to sleep again. I was tired, you see.'

'Yes, I think you said you'd been in London.'

The coffee was surprisingly good. Burden tried to ignore the incrustations on the cup rim and enjoy it. Someone had been dipping wet spoons in the sugar and at times it had apparently been in contact with a marmalade-covered knife.

'I went out at three,' Margolis said, his face vague and dreamy. 'Ann was here then. She told me she'd be out when I got back and not to forget my key.'

'And had you forgotten it, Mr Margolis?'

'Of course I hadn't,' the painter said, suddenly sharp. 'I'm not crazy.' He drank his coffee at a gulp, and a little colour came into his pale face. 'I left my car at Kingsmarkham station and went to see this man about a show I'm having.'

'A show?' Burden said, bewildered. The word conjured up in his mind visions of dancing girls and dinner-jacketed comedians.

'An exhibition, then,' Margolis said impatiently. 'Of my work. Really, you are a bunch of philistines. I thought so yesterday when nobody seemed to know who I was.' He favoured Burden with a look of dark suspicion as if he doubted his efficiency. 'As I was saying, I went to see this man. He's the manager of the Morissot Gallery in Knightsbridge and when we'd had our talk he rather unexpectedly gave me dinner. But I was absolutely exhausted with all this travelling about. This gallery man's a fearful bore and it got very tedious just sitting there listening to him talking. That's why, when I saw Ann's car lights, I didn't bother to get up.'

'But yesterday morning,' Burden said, 'you found her car in the lane.'

'All wet and revolting with the *New Statesman* plastered across its windscreen.' Margolis sighed. 'There were papers all over the garden. I don't suppose you could send someone to clear them up, could you? Or get the council to?'

'No,' said Burden firmly. 'Didn't you go out at all on Wednesday?'

'I was working,' said Margolis. 'And I sleep a lot.' He added vaguely, 'At odd times, you know. I thought Ann had come and gone. We go our own ways.' His voice rose suddenly to a shrill pitch. Burden began to wonder if he might be slightly mad. 'But I'm lost without her. She never leaves me like this without a word!' He got up abruptly, knocking a milk bottle on to the floor. The neck broke off and a stream of sour whey flowed across coconut matting. 'O God, let's go into the studio if you don't want any more coffee. I don't have a photograph of her, but I could show you my portrait if you think it would help.'

There were probably twenty pictures in the studio, one of them so large that it filled an entire wall. Burden had only once in his life seen a larger and that was Rembrandt's *Night Watch* viewed reluctantly on a day trip to Amsterdam. To its surface, giving a three-dimensional look to the wild cavorting figures, other substances apart from paint adhered, cotton wool, slivers of metal and strips of tortured newspaper. Burden decided that he preferred the *Night Watch*. If the portrait was in the same style as this picture it would not be helpful for the purposes of identification. The girl would have one eye, a green mouth and a saucepan scourer sticking out of her ear.

He sat down in a rocking chair, having first removed from its seat a tarnished silver toast rack, a squashed tube of paint and a wooden wind instrument of vaguely Mediterranean origin. Newspapers, clothes, dirty cups and saucers, beer bottles, covered every surface and in places were massed on the floor. By the telephone dead narcissi stood in a glass vase half-full of green water, and one of them, its stem broken, had laid its wrinkled cup and bell against a large wedge of cheese.

Presently Margolis came back with the portrait. Burden was agreeably surprised. It was conventionally painted rather in the style of John, although he did not know this, and it showed the head and shoulders of a girl. Her eyes were like her brother's, blue with a hint of jade, and her hair, as black as his, swept across her cheeks in two heavy crescents. The face was hawk-like, if a hawk's face can also be soft and beautiful, the mouth fine yet full and the nose just verging on the aquiline. Margolis had caught, or had given her, a fierce intelligence. If she were not already dead in her youth, Burden thought, she would one day be a formidable old woman.

He had an uneasy feeling that one ought always to praise a work when shown it by its creator and he said awkwardly:

'Very nice. Jolly good.'

Instead of showing gratitude or gratification, Margolis said simply, 'Yes, it's marvellous. One of the best things I've ever done.' He put the painting on an empty easel and regarded it happily, his good humour restored.

'Now, Mr Margolis,' Burden said severely, 'in a case like this it's normal practice for us to ask the relatives just where they think the missing person might be.' The painter nodded without turning round. 'Please concentrate, sir. Where do you personally think your sister is?'

He realised that his tone had become more and more stern, more schoolmasterish, as the interview progressed, and suddenly he wondered if he was being presumptuous. Since his arrival at Quince Cottage he had kept the newspaper feature in mind, but only as a guide, as information on the brother and sister that could only have been elicited from Margolis after hours of probing. Now he remembered why that feature had been written and what Margolis was. He was in the presence of genius, or if that was journalist's extravagance, of great talent. Margolis was not like other men. In his fingers and his brain was something that set him apart, something that might not be fully recognised and appreciated until long after the painter was dead. Burden experienced a sense of awe, a strange reverence he could not reconcile with the seamy disorder that surrounded him or with the pale-faced creature that looked like a beatnik and might be a latter-day Rembrandt. Who was he, a country policeman, to judge, to mock and put himself among the philistines? His voice softened as he repeated his question.

'Where do you think she is, Mr Margolis?'

'With one of her men friends. She's got dozens.' He turned round and his opalescent eyes seemed to go out of focus and into some dreamy distance. Did Rembrandt ever come into contact with whatever police they had in those days? Genius was more common then, Burden thought. There was more of it about and people knew how to deal with it. 'Or I *would* think so,' Margolis said, 'but for the note.'

Burden started. Had he also received an anonymous letter? 'What note? A note about your sister?'

'That's the point, there isn't one, and there should be. You see, she's often popped off like this before and she wouldn't disturb me if I was working or sleeping.' Margolis passed his fingers through the long spiky hair. 'And I don't seem to do much apart from working and sleeping,' he said. 'She always leaves a note in a very prominent position, by my bed or propped up somewhere.' Memories seemed to come to him of such former examples of his sister's solicitude. 'Quite a long detailed note usually, where she'd gone and who with and what to do about cleaning the place and — and, well, little things for me to do, you know.' He gave a small doubtful smile which clouded into sourness as the telephone rang. 'That'll be dreary old Russell Cawthorne,' he said. 'He keeps bothering me wanting to know where she is.'

He reached for the receiver and rested his elbow against the chunk of mouldering cheese.

'No, she isn't here. I don't know where she is.' Watching him, Burden wondered exactly what were the 'little things' his sister would recommend him to do. Even so small a thing as answering the telephone seemed to throw him into a state of surly misanthropy. 'I've got the police here, if you must know. Of course I'll tell you if she turns up. Yes, yes, yes. What d'you mean, you'll be seeing me? I shouldn't think you will for a moment. We never do see each other.'

'Oh, yes, you will, Mr Margolis,' Burden said quietly. 'You and I are going to see Mr Cawthorne now.'

CHAPTER FOUR

Thoughtfully Wexford compared the two sheets of paper, one piece with red ballpoint writing on it, the other new and clean. The texture, colour and watermark were identical.

'It was from Braddon's, after all, sir,' said Sergeant Martin. He was a painstaking officer whose features were permanently set in an earnest frown. 'Grover's only sell pads and what they call drawing blocks. Braddon's get this paper specially from a place in London.'

'D'you mean it's ordered?'

'Yes, sir. Fortunately they only supply it to one customer, a Mrs Adeline Harper who lives in Waterford Avenue, Stowerton.'

Wexford nodded. 'Good class residential,' he said. 'Big old-fashioned houses.'

'Mrs Harper's away, sir. Taking a long Easter holiday, according to the neighbours. She doesn't keep a manservant. In fact the only servant she does have is a char who goes in Mondays, Wednesdays and Fridays.'

'Could she be my correspondent?'

'They're big houses, sir, and a long way apart. Waterford Avenue's not like a council estate or a block of flats where everyone knows everyone else. They keep themselves to themselves. This char's been seen to go in and out, but no one knows her name.'

'And if she has a way of snapping up unconsidered trifles like expensive writing paper, her employer and the neighbours don't know about it?'

'All the neighbours know,' said Martin, a little discomfited by the paucity of his information, 'is that she's middle-aged, showily dressed and got ginger hair.'

'Mondays, Wednesdays and Fridays . . . I take it she goes in while her employer's away?'

'And today's Friday, sir. But, you see, she only goes in mornings and she was gone before I got there. "I've just seen

389

her go by", the neighbour said. I nipped up the road smartish but she was out of sight.'

Wexford turned his attention once more to the sheets of paper and to the lab report on that paper. No fingerprints had been found on the anonymous letter, no perfume clung to it; the pen with which it had been written was a cheap ballpoint such as could be bought in every stationers in the country. He had an inventive imagination but he could not visualise the con-catenation of happenings that must have been the prerequisite to this letter. A ginger-haired charwoman, whose own conduct was apparently not above reproach, had seen something or heard something that had led her to write to the police. Such communication would necessarily be alien to a woman of her type, a woman found to be an occasional thief. And yet she, or someone closely associated with her, had written it. Fear or spite might have prompted her action.

'I wonder if it could be blackmail,' Wexford said.

'I don't quite follow you, sir.'

'Because we always think of blackmail being successful or, at any rate, successful for a time. Suppose it isn't successful at all. Suppose our ginger-haired woman tries to put the squeeze on Geoff Smith, but he won't play. Then, if she's vindictive, she carries out her threat.'

'Blackmailers always are vindictive, sir,' Martin said, sagely unctuous. 'A nasty spiteful thing, if ever there was one. Worse than murder, sir.'

An excessive show of respect always grated on Wexford, especially as in this case when it was associated with the imparting of platitudes he had heard a thousand times before. 'Here endeth the first lesson,' he said sharply. 'Answer that, will you?'

Martin leapt to the phone before the end of the second double peal. 'Inspector Burden for you, sir.'

Wexford took the receiver without getting up. The stretched coil lead passed dangerously near his glass sculpture. 'Move that thing,' he said. The sergeant lifted it and stuck in on the narrow window sill. 'Well?' Wexford said into the mouthpiece.

Burden's voice sounded dazed. 'I'm off to have a word with

Cawthorne. Can we spare someone to come down here and fetch Miss Margolis's car? Drayton, if he's not tied up. Oh, and the cottage'll have to be gone over.' Wexford heard his tone drop to a whisper. 'It's a proper shambles, sir. No wonder he wanted a char.'

'We want one, too,' Wexford said crisply, 'a snappy dresser with ginger hair.' He explained. The phone made crackling sounds. 'What's going on?'

'The cheese has fallen into a flower pot.'

'My God,' said Wexford. 'I see what you mean.'

Mark Drayton came down the police station steps and crossed the road. To reach Pump Lane he had to walk the whole length of the High Street and when he came to Grover's the newsagent he stopped for a moment to glance at its window. It seemed incredible to him that Martin had for a moment considered this place as the possible purveyor of handmade paper. It had the shady, almost sordid, aspect of a shop in the slum streets of some great city. A high brick wall towered above it and between it and the florist's next door a brown cobbled alley plunged deep into a dubious hinterland of dustbins and sheds and a pair of garages.

In the shop window the displayed wares looked as if they had been arranged there some years before and since left utterly untended. Easter was not long past and the Easter cards were topical. But it seemed to him that their topicality must be an accident in the same way as a stopped clock must be right twice a day, for there were Christmas cards there as well, some fallen on their sides and filmed with dust.

Dying houseplants stood among the cards. Perhaps they were for sale or perhaps misguidedly intended for decoration. The earth around their roots had shrunk through dehydration, leaving an empty space between soil and pot. A box containing a game of snakes and ladders had come open, so that the coloured board hung from a shelf. The counters lay on the floor among rusty nails, spilt confetti and shed leaves. Drayton thought he had seldom seen anything which could be regarded as an advertisement so repellent and so discouraging to those shoppers who passed this way.

He was going to walk on with a shrug of disgust when, through the dirty glass panel that separated this window from the interior of the shop, he caught sight of a girl behind the counter. He could only see her dimly, the shape of her, and her pale bright hair. But, as he hesitated, his interest faintly aroused, she approached the panel and opening it, reached for a pack of cards which lay to the left of the snakes and ladders box. That she made no attempt to retrieve the counters or blow the dust from the box lid, annoyed him. He was meticulous in his own work, tidy, attentive to the tools of his life and his trade.

Because he felt distaste and a desire to make plain the disapproval of at least one potential customer, he raised his eyes coldly and met hers. At once he knew who she was. A face which had haunted him for four days and which was faintly familiar but not specifically identifiable was confronting him. He stared at her and felt the hot blood rush into his cheeks. She could not know that he had seen her before, or if she did know it, could not be aware of the thoughts, many of them dreamlike, searching, sensuous, which had accompanied his constant evoking of her image on to his mind's eye. She could not know it, but he felt that she must do so, that such vivid violent imaginings could not be contained within the brain that conceived them and must by some telepathic process be communicated to their object.

She gave no sign. Her grey eyes, large and listless, met his only for a moment. Then she took the pack of playing cards, kneeling among the dust and the confetti to reach them, and retreated to serve a waiting customer. Her legs were long and rather too thin. The dust had left circular grey patches on her knees. He watched the panel swing slowly shut behind her, its fingermarked, bluish translucency obscuring all but the blur of her silver-gold hair.

Drayton crossed the alley, avoiding puddles on whose scummy surface spilt oil made a rainbow iridescence. He glanced at the garage doors, wondering why no one painted them when paint was cheap and the making of things clean and fresh so satisfying. From the stall outside the florist's he could smell daffodils. They and the girl he had just seen shared the same quality of untouched exquisite freshness and like the girl they flowered in squalor. The roughly made dirty wooden box was to them what the sordid newsagents was to her, an ugly unfitting background for breathless beauty.

Was everything he saw going to remind him of her? Had he felt like this before Monday night? As he came to the parapet of the bridge and looked down the river path he asked himself the question again. Certainly he had noticed her shopping in the town. She was the sort of girl any man would notice. For months now she had held for him a vague attraction. Then, on Monday night, he had passed this spot and seen her on that path kissing another man. It had given him a strange feeling to watch her, disarmed, vulnerable, abandoned to a passion anyone walking by in the dusk might witness. It showed that she was flesh and blood, subject to sensuality and therefore attainable, accessible to him.

Their figures had been reflected in the dark water, the man's which he had disregarded, and hers, slim, long, quivering. From that moment her image had haunted him, lying just above the surface of his conscious mind to trouble him when he was alone.

His own reflection, sharper and more real in the afternoon light than theirs had been at twilight, stared back at him coldly from the stream. The dark Italianate face with its guarded eyes and its curved mouth showed nothing of his thoughts. His hair was rather long, much too long for a policeman, and he wore a dark grey duffel coat over slacks and sweater. Burden objected to the coat and the hair, but he could find no fault with Drayton's economy of speech, nor with his reserve, although it was a different brand from his own.

The mirrored head and shoulders crumpled and retreated into the parapet of the bridge. Drayton felt in his pockets to make sure he had remembered his gloves. It was a formality only; he seldom forgot anything. He looked back once, but he could only see shoppers, prams, bicycles, a tall brick wall and an alley with wet litter on its cobbles. Then he made his way to the outskirts of the town and Pump Lane.

This by-way into Kingsmarkham's countryside was new to him, but like the other lanes it was just a tunnel between green banks topped with high trees, a roadway scarcely wide enough for two cars to pass. A cow peered at him over the hedge, its feet in primroses. Drayton was not interested in natural history nor given to pastoral reflection. His eye was drawn to the white sports car, parked half on the verge, half on the road, the only man-made thing in sight. The cottage itself was not immediately visible. Then he discerned, among tangled greening hawthorn and white sloe blossom, a small rickety gate. The branches were spiny and wet. He lifted them, drenching his shoulders. Apple trees, their trunks lichened to a sour pulpy green, clustered in front of the house whose shabby whiteness was relieved by the flame-coloured flowers of a tall shrub growing against it, the quince — though Drayton did not know it — from which the cottage took its name.

He slipped on his gloves and got into the Alpine. Possessing little of his own, he nevertheless had a respect for material things. This car would be a delight to own, a pleasure to drive. It irked him that its owner appeared to have used it as a kind of travelling dustbin, throwing cigarette packets and match ends on to the floor. Drayton knew better than to touch more than was needful, but he had to remove the torn newspaper from the windscreen before he could see to drive. Hawthorn boughs scraping the roof hurt him almost as much as if they had scoured his own skin.

The temptation to take the longer way round by Forby had to be resisted. Traffic was not heavy at this time of day and his only excuse would be that he wanted to enjoy himself. Drayton had trained himself stoically to resist temptation. One, he knew, he would soon succumb to, but not such a triviality as this.

There was a yellow and brown spotted fur coat slung across the passenger seat. It had a strong heady scent, the smell of a beautiful woman, evoking in Drayton's mind past and future love. The car moved smoothly forward. He had reached the centre of the High Street before he noticed the needle on the gauge climbing swiftly and alarmingly. It was almost at danger level. There were no service stations in this part of the main road, but he remembered seeing a garage in York Street, just past Joy Jewels and the labour exchange.

When he reached it he got out and lifted the hood. Steam billowed at him and he stepped back.

'Radiator's leaking,' he said to the pump attendant.

'I'll get you some water. She'll be all right if you take her slow. Far to go?'

'Not far,' said Drayton.

The water began to leak out as soon as they poured it in. Drayton was almost within sight of the police station. He passed Joy Jewels with its windows full of rhinestones on crimson velvet and he passed Grover's but he did not look. Poetry was not among his considerable and heterogeneous reading matter, but he would have agreed that man's love is of man's life a thing apart. He would go there later when his work was done.

Cawthorne's garage was an altogether grander affair than the modest place to which Drayton had taken Anita Margolis's car. It commanded Stowerton crossroads. From the roof of the showroom to the pinnacle of the little glass cubicle where Cawthorne sat at the receipt of custom, hung a yellow and scarlet banner: *Treble stamps with four gallons.* These colours matched the paint on the eight pumps and the neon tubing on the arch to the service entrance. Burden could remember when, not so long ago, a copse of silver birches had stood here and he remembered the efforts of the rural preservation society to prevent Cawthorne's coming. The last of the birches huddled by the showroom wall like bewildered aborigines crowded out by a conqueror from the new world.

By contrast the house behind was old. A triumph of the gothic revival, it sported pinnacles, turrets, gables and aggressive drainpipes. Formerly known as Birch House, the home of two spinster sisters, it had been furnished by Cawthorne and his wife with every conceivable Victorian monstrosity. The mantelpieces were fringed and set about with green glass fluted vases, stuffed birds and wax fruit under domes. Cawthorne, after a dubious look at Rupert Margolis, took them into a sitting room and went away to fetch his wife.

'It's the latest fad,' Margolis said morosely. 'All this Victorian junk.' Above the fireplace hung an oleograph of a woman in grecian dress holding a lily. He gave it an angry glance. 'Cawthorne must be sixty and his wife's a hag. They're mad about young people. I expect the young people think they had this stuff for wedding presents.' And he laughed vindictively.

Burden thought he had seldom met anyone so uncharitable, but when Mrs Cawthorne came in he began to see what Margolis meant. She was extravagantly thin and her dress had a very short skirt and very short sleeves. Her hair was tinted primrose and styled like the head of a feather duster.

'Why, hallo, Roo. You are a stranger.' Burden was suddenly sure that she had met Margolis perhaps only once before, and here she was giving him pet names like a character out of *Winnie the Pooh*. A lion hunter. She bounced into a quilted and buttoned armchair, showing a lot of scrawny leg. Margolis took absolutely no notice of her. 'What's all this about Ann, then?'

'We hope you'll be able to help us, Mrs Cawthorne,' Burden said heavily, but it was to her husband that he turned his eyes. He was an elderly, white-moustached man, with a decided military bearing. If the growing fashion among the young of wearing soldier's uniforms spread to older generations, Cawthorne ought to catch on. He would look fine in a hussar's tunic. 'You had a party on Tuesday evening, Mr Cawthorne. Miss Margolis was invited. I understand she didn't turn up.'

'Right,' Cawthorne said briskly. 'She dropped in in the afternoon, said she'd be sure to be here. Never turned up. I've been damned worried, I can tell you. Glad to see you folk have been called in.'

'Yes, and Dickie Fairfax came all the way down from London just to see her.' Mrs Cawthorne moved closer to Margolis's side. 'They used to be friends. Very close friends, I may add.' She fluttered her beaded eyelashes.

'Fairfax, the writer?' Burden had never heard of him until that morning, but he did not wish to be branded a philistine for the second time that day.

Mrs Cawthorne nodded. 'Poor Dickie was rather peeved when she didn't turn up and drifted away around eleven.'

'Left one of my best brandy glasses on a diesel pump,' said Cawthorne gruffly. 'Damned inconsiderate blighter.'

'But he was here all the evening?' Between eight and eleven, Burden thought. That was the crucial time if the anonymous letter was to be trusted.

'He was here all right. Came on the dot of eight and got started in on the hard stuff right away.'

'You are so mean,' Mrs Cawthorne said unpleasantly. 'Mean and jealous. Just because Ann preferred him.' She gave a tinny laugh. 'She and Russell have a sort of thing.' Burden glanced at Margolis but the painter had gone off into a brooding abstraction. Mrs Cawthorne thrust a bony finger into her husband's ribs. 'Or that's what he kids himself.' The blood rushed into Cawthorne's already pink face. His hair was like white wool or the coat of a West Highland terrier.

Suddenly Margolis roused himself. He addressed Burden, rather as if there was no one else in the room.

'Ann gave Dickie the out months ago. There's someone else now. I'm trying to remember his name.'

'Not Geoff Smith, by any chance.' Burden watched the three faces, saw nothing but blankness. He had memorised the message in that letter. *He is small and young and dark and he has a black car. Name of Geoff Smith.* Of course, it wouldn't be his real name. Smith never was.

'All right. That's all for now. Thanks for your help.'

'I don't call that help.' Mrs Cawthorne giggled. She tried to take Margolis's hand but failed. 'You'll be lost without her, Roo,' she said. 'Now, if there's anything Russell and I can do. . . .'

Burden expected Margolis to maintain his silence, or possibly say something rude. He gave Mrs Cawthorne a blind hopeless stare. 'Nobody else has ever been able to do anything,' he said. Then he walked out of the room, his shoulders straight. For a brief moment he had attained Burden's notion of the heights of genius. He followed, Cawthorne behind him. The garage owner's breath smelt of whisky. His was a soldier's face, brave, hearty, a little stupid. The military air about him extended, Burden thought, even to his name. All those years ago his mother had called him Russell because it sounded so well with Cawthorne, auguring great things. General Sir Russell Cawthorne, K.C.B., D.S.O. . . . Burden knew something of his history. The man had never won a battle or even led a troop. He kept a garage.

'I'm looking for a Geoff Smith who might be a friend of Miss Margolis's.'

Cawthorne gave a braying laugh. 'I daresay he might, only

I've never heard of him. She's got a lot of boy friends. Lovely
girl, lovely little driver and a good head for business. I sold her
that car of hers. That's how we met. Haggled, you know, drove
a hard bargain. I admire that. Only natural she'd have a lot of
boy friends.'

'Would you include yourself among them?'

It was grotesque. The man was all of sixty. And yet boy
friend could be applied these days to a lover of any age. It was
in two senses a euphemism.

For a moment it seemed that Cawthorne was not going to
reply and when he did it was not to answer the question.

'Are you married?'

'Yes, I am.'

'Horrible business, isn't it?' He paused and gazed lugubriously at a pump attendant giving green stamps with change.
'Growing old together . . . Horrible!' He braced his shoulders as
if standing to attention. 'Mind you, it's your duty to stay young
as long as you can. Live it up, keep going, go around with
young people. That's half the battle.' The only one he was ever
likely to fight.

'Did you "go around" with Miss Margolis, Mr Cawthorne?'

The garage proprietor brought his face and his whisky
breath closer to Burden. 'Once,' he said. 'Just the once. I took
her out to dinner in Pomfret, to the Cheriton Forest Hotel.
Stupid, really. The waiter knew me. He'd seen me there with
my wife. I was ordering, you see, and he said, "Will your
daughter have smoked salmon too, sir?" '

Why do it, then? Why make such a crass fool of yourself?
Burden had no temptations, few dreams. He got into the car
beside Margolis, wondering why the defenceless put themselves
into the firing line.

There were pictures on the stairs and pictures on the landing.
The light was fading and Sergeant Martin stumbled over a pile
of washing on the floor outside Anita Margolis's bedroom door.

'No letters and no diaries, sir,' he said to Burden. 'I never
saw so many clothes in all my life. It's like a — a draper's shop
in there.'

'A boutique, you mean,' said Drayton.

'Been in many, have you?' Burden snapped. Drayton looked the type who would buy black nylon underwear for his women and not turn a hair. Through the half-open door, propped ajar with a gilt sandal, he caught sight of garments spread on the bed and hung, crammed closely, in two wardrobes. 'If your sister went away of her own accord,' he said to Margolis, 'she'd have taken clothes with her. Is anything missing?'

'I really wouldn't know. It's absolutely useless asking me things like that. Ann's always buying clothes. She's got masses of them.'

'There's just one thing,' Drayton said. 'We can't find a raincoat.'

Martin nodded agreement. 'That's right. Furs and suede things and all sorts, but no woman's raincoat. It was raining cats and dogs on Tuesday night.'

'Sometimes she takes clothes,' said Margolis, 'and sometimes she doesn't. She's quite likely to have gone just as she was and then buy anything she needed.'

Leaving them to finish their search, Burden followed the painter downstairs. 'She had money then?' The woman in the portrait, the woman who possessed this vast and apparently expensive wardrobe, would hardly be content with something off the peg from Marks and Spencer. Or was the lover expected to cough up? In this set-up anything was possible. 'How much money did she have on her?'

'One of her cheques came on Monday. She has this money of her own, you see. My father left all the money to her. He didn't like me and I couldn't stand him, so he left it all to Ann. They pay it out every three months.'

Burden sighed. Anyone else would have spoken of a private income, of payments made quarterly.

'Do you know how much this cheque was for?'

'Of course I do,' Margolis said crossly. 'I'm not a half-wit. It's always the same, five hundred pounds.'

'And she had this cheque with her?' Here, at last, was something for him to get his teeth into. The beginning of a motive loomed.

'She cashed it as soon as it came,' Margolis said, 'and she put the money in her handbag.'

'All five hundred!' Burden gasped. 'You mean she set off for a party with five hundred pounds in her handbag?'

'Bound to have done. She always carried it about with her,' Margolis said casually, as if it were the most natural thing in the world. 'You see, she might be out and see something she wanted to buy and then she'd have the money on her, wouldn't she? She doesn't like paying for things with cheques because then she gets overdrawn, and Ann's rather middle-class in some ways. She gets worried if she's overdrawn.'

Five hundred pounds, even if it was in fivers, would make a big wad in a woman's handbag. Would she be careless about where she opened the handbag and to whom she revealed the contents? The woman was thoroughly immoral too. Decent women had clean tidy homes. They were either married or had jobs or both. They kept their money in the bank. Burden thought he could see just what had happened to Anita Margolis. She had gone into a shop or a garage on her way to the party, opened her bag and its contents had been seen by that villain Smith. A good-looking plausible villain, probably. Young, dark and with a black car. They had gone off together and he had killed her for the money. The letter writer had got wind of it, maybe tried blackmail, blackmail which hadn't worked?

But a casual pick-up would be next to impossible to find. A regular boy friend, especially if he was down on his luck, might fill the bill.

'Have you remembered the name of Fairfax's successor?' he asked.

'Alan Something. He's got no money and he's very provincial. I don't know what she sees in him, but Ann's rather inclined to go slumming, if you know what I mean. Fitz something. Fitzwilliam? It isn't exactly Fitzwilliam but it's something like that. I've only spoken to him once and that was enough.'

Burden said tartly, 'You don't seem to like anyone very much, sir.'

'I like Ann,' Margolis said sadly. 'I tell you who might know. Mrs Penistan, our late char. I should go and ask her, and if she's just pining to come back and clean this place, don't discourage her, will you?'

A chill grey drizzle was falling as they emerged from the cottage door. Margolis accompanied Burden to the garden gate.

'You haven't found a charwoman, then?'

From behind him the painter's voice held a note of childlike pride. 'I put an advertisement in Grover's window,' he said. 'I wrote it on a little card. Only half-a-crown a week. I really can't imagine why people spend all that money on the agony column of *The Times* when this way is so cheap and easy.'

'Quite,' said Burden, stifling an incipient desire to roar and stamp. 'This Mrs Penistan, she hasn't got ginger hair, has she?'

Margolis stood against the hedge, picking the new shoots off a hawthorn bush. These he put into his mouth and began to chew them with evident relish. 'She always wore a hat,' he said. 'I don't know what colour her hair is, but I can tell you where she lives.' He paused for congratulation perhaps on this unlooked-for feat of memory. Burden's expression seemed to gratify him, for he went on, 'I know that because I drove her home once when it was raining. It's in Glebe Road, on the left, past the fifth tree and just before you get to the pillar box. Red curtains downstairs and . . .'

Burden cut him short with a snort of exasperation. If this was genius he had had enough of it. 'I'll find it.' He could have recourse to the electoral register himself. Penistan was surely as rare a name as Smith was common.

CHAPTER FIVE

Mark Drayton rented a room down by Kingsmarkham station. His landlady was a motherly woman who liked to make her lodgers feel at home. She hung pictures on the walls, provided flowered counterpanes and scattered little ornaments about like seeds. As soon as he moved in Drayton put all the vases and ashtrays into the bottom of the cupboard. There was nothing to be done about the counterpane. He wanted the room to look like a cell. Someone — it was a girl — had told him he had a cold nature and he had since cultivated his personality in this direction. He liked to think he was austere and without emotion.

He was very ambitious. When he had first come to Kingsmarkham he had set out to make Wexford like him and he had succeeded. He carried out all Wexford's instructions meticulously, absorbing the Chief Inspector's homilies, lectures, digressions and pleasantries with courteously inclined head. The district was now as familiar to him as his own hometown and he used his library tickets for works on psychology and forensic medicine. Sometimes he read a novel, but nothing lighter than Mann or Durrell. One day he hoped to be a commissioner. He would marry the right wife, someone like Mrs Wexford, good-looking, quiet and gracious. Wexford had a daughter, a pretty girl and clever, they said. But that was a long way off. He had no intention of marrying until he had attained distinguished rank.

His attitude to women was a source of pride to him. Being intensely narcissistic, he had little admiration left over, and his idealism was reserved for his own career. His affairs had been practical and chilly. In his vocabulary love was a banned verb, the most obscene of the four letter words. He had never used it between 'I' and 'you'. If he ever felt anything stronger than a physical need he called it desire with complications.

That, he thought, was what he felt for the Grover girl. That was why he was going into the shop now to buy his evening paper. Maybe she would not be there. Or maybe when he saw her close-to, not through glass or in someone else's arms, it would all fade away. On the whole he hoped that would happen.

The shop squatted under a towering wall of brown brick. It seemed to lurk there as if it had something to hide. A street lamp in a black iron cage stuck out beside its door but the lamp was still unlit. As Drayton opened this door a little bell made a cold tinkle. The interior was dim and it smelt unpleasant. Behind the paperback stand and a rusty refrigerator hung with lop-sided ice-cream posters, he could see the shelves of a lending library. The books were the kind you buy at jumble sales, nineteenth century three-volume novels, explorer's reminiscences, school stories.

A thin dried-up woman was behind the counter, standing under a naked light bulb. Presumably this was her mother. She was serving a customer with tobacco.

'How's the governor?' said the customer.

'Ever so bad with his back,' said Mrs Grover cheerfully. 'Hasn't left his bed since Friday. Did you say Vestas?' Drayton noted with distaste the girlie magazines, the stand of paper patterns (two swinging mini-skirts to cut out and sew in an evening), the ninepenny thrillers, *Ghosty Worlds*, *Cosmic Creatures*. On a shelf among mock-Wedgwood ashtrays stood a pottery spaniel with artificial flowers growing from a basket on his back. The flowers were furred with dust like a grey fungoid growth. 'That's five and three, then. Thanks very much. It's what they call a slipped disc. He just bent over fiddling with the car and — crack!'

'Nasty,' said the customer. 'You thinking of letting your room again? I heard your young man had gone.'

'And good riddance. I couldn't take another one on, dear, not with Mr Grover laid up. Linda and me have got enough on our hands as it is.' So that was her name, Linda. Drayton turned away from *Ghosty Worlds*. Mrs Grover looked at him indifferently. 'Yes?'

'*Standard*, please.'

There was only one left and that was in the rack outside the shop by the advertisement case. Drayton followed her out and paid for his newspaper on the doorstep. He would never go back in there, inefficient, ill-mannered lot! Perhaps he never would have done and his life would have pursued its ordered, uninterrupted course towards its goal. He lingered only for a moment. The lamp had come on and his eyes was caught by a familiar name on one of the cards. Margolis, Quince Cottage, and beneath a plea for a charwoman. The door opened and Linda Grover came out. Even so quickly can one catch the plague . . .

She was as tall as he and her short grey dress made her look taller. The damp wind blew the stuff against her body, showing the shape of her little breasts and the long slender thighs. She had a small head set on a thin neck and her pale hair was drawn back so tightly that it pulled the skin and stretched wide the smooth dove-coloured eyebrows. He had never seen a girl so completely clothed look so naked.

She opened the card case, removed one and replaced it with another. 'Raining again,' she said. 'I don't know where it all comes from.' An ugly voice, half-Sussex, half-Cockney.

'The sky,' said Drayton. That was the only answer to such a stupid remark. He could not imagine why she had bothered to speak to him at all, unless she had seen him that night and was covering embarrassment.

'Very funny.' Her fingers were long and the hand had a wide octave span. He observed the bitten nails. 'You'll get soaked standing there,' she said.

Drayton put up his hood. 'How's the boy friend?' he asked conversationally. Her reaction pleased him. He had flicked her on the raw.

'Is there one?' Her ugly accent grated on him and he told himself it was this and not her proximity which made him clench his hands as he stood looking at the cards offering prams for sale and council flats to be exchanged.

'A good-looking girl like you?' he said, turning sharply to face her. It was not Mann or Durrell, just standard verbal practice, the first preliminary love play. 'Get away.'

Her smile began very slowly and developed with a kind of secrecy. He noticed that she smiled without showing her teeth, without parting her lips, and it devastated him. They stood looking at each other in the rainy dusk. Drizzle spattered the tiers of newspapers. Drayton shifted his gaze rudely and deliberately back to the glass case.

'You're very interested in those cards, I must say,' she said sharply. 'What's so fascinating about a load of second-hand stuff?'

'I shouldn't mind it being second-hand,' he said, and when she blushed he knew she had seen him witness that kiss.

A charwoman with ginger hair. It might be. Everything pointed that way. Mrs Penistan seemed to fill the requirements. She had cleaned for Anita Margolis, why should she not also clean for Mrs Harper of Waterford Avenue? A woman who lived in unsalubrious Glebe Road might steal paper from one employer to write anonymous letters about another. In Glebe Road they were no strangers to crime, even to murder. A woman had been killed down there only last year. Monkey Matthews had once lived there and it was behind one of these squat stuccoed façades that he had mixed up sugar and sodium chlorate to make his bomb.

Burden tapped smartly on the door of the small terraced house. A light came on, a chain was slipped, and before the door opened he saw a little sharp face peering at him through the glass panel.

'Mrs Penistan?'

Her mouth snapped open like a spring trap and there came forth a voluble stream of words. 'Oh, here you are at last, dear. I'd nearly given you up. The Hoover's all ready for you.' She produced it, an enormous, old-fashioned vacuum cleaner. 'I reckon it's a bit of grit caught up in the motor. My boys don't care what muck they bring in on their shoes. Won't be a long job, will it?'

'Mrs Penistan, I haven't come to service your cleaner. I'm not a . . .'

She peered at him. 'Not a Jehovah Witness, I hope?'

'A police officer.' They sorted it out, Mrs Penistan laughing shrilly. Even in her own house, she still wore a hat. The hair which showed under its brim was not ginger but grey. You could neither describe her as middle-aged, nor showily dressed. In addition to the pudding basin hat, she wore a cross-over sleeveless overall, patterned in mauve and black, over a green cardigan. Burden thought she was approaching seventy.

'You won't mind coming in the kitchenette, will you, dear? I'm getting me boys' tea.' On the cooker chips were frying. She lifted out the wire basket, replenished it with a fresh mound of wet cut potatoes. 'How about a nice cuppa?'

Burden accepted the offer and when the tea came it was hot and strong. He sat down on a grubby chair at the grubby table. The frowsty appearance of the place surprised him. Somehow he expected a charwoman's house to be clean, just as a bank manager's account should always be in the black.

'Smith?' she said. 'No, it doesn't ring a bell.'

'Fitzwilliam?'

'No, dear. There was a Mr Kirkpatrick. Would it be him?'

'It might be.' Knowing Margolis, it very well might be.

'Lives in Pomfret somewhere. Funny you should ask about him because it was on account of him I left.'

'How was that, Mrs Penistan?'

'I don't know why I shouldn't tell you. Missing, you said? Well, it don't surprise me. It wouldn't surprise me if he'd done her in like he said he would.'

'He did, did he?'

'Threatened her in my hearing. D'you want to hear about it?'

'I do indeed, but first I'd like to hear about her, what you thought of her, that kind of thing.'

'She was a nice enough girl, mind, no side to her. First day I came I called her Miss and she just screamed out laughing. 'Oh, Mrs P., darling,' she said, 'you call me Ann. Everyone calls me Ann.' One of the free and easy ones she is, takes things as they come. Mind you, they've got money, got wads of it, but they're not always free with it, that kind. The clothes she gives me, you wouldn't believe. I had to let most of them go to my granddaughter, being a bit past wearing them trouser suits and skirts up to me navel.

'She'd got her head screwed on the right way, mind. Very sharp way she'd got with the tradesmen. She always bought the best and she liked to know what she was getting for her money.

You'd have to get up early in the morning to put anything over on her. Different to him.'

'Mr Margolis?'

'I know it's easy to say, but I reckon he's mental. All of a year I was there and he never had a soul come to see him. Paint, paint, paint, all the blessed day long, but when he'd done you couldn't see what it was meant to be. "I wonder you don't get fed up with it," I says to him once. "Oh, I'm very fecund, Mrs Penistan," he says, whatever that may mean. Sounded dirty to me. No, his mind's affected all right.' She piled the chips on to two plates and began cracking eggs which she sniffed suspiciously before dropping them into the pan.

Burden had just begun to ask her about Kirkpatrick's threats when the back door opened and two large bull-necked men in working clothes came in. Were these the boys who didn't care what they brought in on their feet? Both looked years older than Burden himself. With a nod to their mother, they tramped across the kitchen, taking no notice at all of her visitor. Perhaps they also concluded that he had come to service the vacuum cleaner.

'Hang on a minute, dear,' said Mrs Penistan. A plate in each hand, she disappeared into the living room. Burden finished the last of his tea. Presently one of the boys came back for the tea pot, followed by his mother, now all smiles.

'You can't get a word out of them till they've got a meal inside them,' she said proudly. Her son ignored her, marched off, banging doors behind him. 'Now, dear, you wanted to know about Mr Kirkpatrick. Let's see, where are we now? Friday. It would have been last Wednesday week. Mr Margolis had gone down to Devon for a painting holiday. I come in a couple of days before and I says to her, "Where's your brother, then?" "Dartmoor," she says, and *that* I could believe, though Broadmoor was more his mark.' She let out a shrill laugh and sat down opposite Burden, her elbows on the table. 'Well, two days later on the Wednesday there comes a knock at the door in the afternoon. "I'll go," she says and when she opens the door there's this Kirkpatrick. "Good afternoon," she says, sort of cool but in ever such a funny way I can't describe. "Good afternoon," he says and they just stand there looking at each other. Anyway, as I say, there's no side to her and she introduces me very nice. "Penistan?" he says. "That's a real local name. We've got some Penistans living opposite us in Pomfret," and that's how I know where he come from. Well, I was getting on with cleaning the silver so I went back into the kitchenette.

'No more than five minutes later I hear them go upstairs. Must be going to look at his paintings, I thought in my ignorance. There was paintings all over the place, dear, even in the bathroom. About half an hour after that they come down again and I'm beginning to wonder what's in the air. Then I heard them start this arguing.

' "For God's sake don't drool all over me, Alan," she says sharpish. "Love," she says, raising her voice. "I don't know what that is. If I love anyone it's Rupert." Rupert being her mental brother. Well, this Alan, he flies right off the handle and he starts shouting. All sorts of horrible expressions he used as I couldn't repeat. But she didn't turn a hair. "I'm not ending anything, darling," she says. "You can go on having what you've just had upstairs." I can tell you, dear, all the blood rushed to my head. This is the last time you set foot in here, Rose Penistan, I says to myself. My boys are very particular. They wouldn't want me going where there was immorality. I was going to march right in on her and that Kirkpatrick and tell her there and then when I heard him say, "You're asking to get yourself killed, Ann. I might do it myself one of these fine days."

'Anyway, the upshot was that he just went off in a huff. I could hear her calling out after him, "Don't be so silly, Alan, and don't forget we've got a date Tuesday night." '

'Tuesday?' Burden interjected sharply. 'Would that have been last Tuesday?'

'Must have been. People are funny, aren't they, dear? As business-like as they come, she is, and good too in a sort of way. Collected for Oxfam and the sick animals, read the newspaper from cover to cover and very hot about what she called injustice. Just the same, she was carrying on proper with this Kirkpatrick. It's a funny old world.'

'So you left?'

'That very day. After he'd gone she come out into the

kitchenette just as if nothing had happened. All cool and serene she was, smiling and talking about the horrible weather her poor Rupert was having down on the Moor. I don't know what it is, dear, but I reckon that's what they mean when they talk about charm. I couldn't have it out with her. "I'll finish out the week," was all I said, "and then I'll have to give up. This place is getting too much for me." And I never spoke a truer word.'

'Do you work anywhere else, Mrs Penistan? Stowerton, for instance?'

'Oh, no, dear. It wouldn't be worth my while going all that way. Not that my boys wouldn't fetch me in the van. Always thinking of their Mum, they are.' She accompanied him into the hall where they encountered one of her sons, returning to the kitchen with his empty plate. This he deposited silently on the table. Although he still took no notice at all of his mother, beyond pushing her aside as he passed through the doorway, the meal he had 'got inside him' had effected a slight improvement in his temper, for he remarked gloomily to Burden:

'Nasty night.'

Mrs Penistan smiled at him fondly. She lugged the vacuum cleaner out of the way and opened the front door on to squally rain. Strange how it always came on to pour in the evenings, Burden thought. As he walked along Glebe Road with his head lowered and his collar turned up, he reflected on the awkwardness of questioning Kirkpatrick when they had no body and no more proof of death than an anonymous letter.

CHAPTER SIX

Two men called Geoffrey Smith lived in Kingsmarkham, one in Stowerton and two more in Sewingbury. The only dark-haired one was six feet two; the only one under thirty-five had a blond beard; none possessed a black car. The enquiry had been fruitless, as unsatisfactory as the search of Margolis's house. His sister's note had not come to light, but then neither had anything else which might suggest foul play.

'Except the five hundred quid,' said Burden.

'A very nice sum to go on holiday with,' Wexford said firmly. And then, with less certitude, 'Have we worried Margolis in vain, Mike?'

'Hard to say whether he's worried or not. I don't understand the fellow, sir. One minute I think he's pulling my leg and the next — well, he's just like a child. I daresay that's what they mean by genius.'

'Some say there's a knife edge between it and madness, others that it's an infinite capacity for taking pains.'

If there was anything Burden did understand it was taking pains. 'It looks as if he pours that paint and muck on like you or I might slop sauce on fish and chips,' he said. 'All those paintings are beyond me. I'd say they were just another way of conning the public. How much do they charge to go into the Tate Gallery?'

Wexford roared with laughter. 'Nothing, as far as I know. It's free.' He tightened the thin shiny rag he called a tie. 'You remind me of that remark of Goering's,' he said. 'Whenever I hear the word culture I reach for my gun.'

Burden was offended. He went out into the corridor, looking for someone on whom to vent his temper. Bryant and Gates, who had been chatting up the sergeant, tried to look busy as soon as they saw him. Not so Mark Drayton. He was standing a little apart from the others, staring down at his feet and apparently deep in thought, his hands in the pockets of his duffel coat. The sight of his black hair sticking out over the hood lining inflamed Burden still further. He marched up to Drayton, but before he could speak, the young man said casually:

'Can I have a word with you, sir?'

'The only person you need a word with is a barber,' Burden snapped. 'Four words to be precise. Short back and sides.' Drayton's face was impassive, secretive, intelligent. 'Oh, very well, what is it?'

'An advert in Grover's window. I thought we might be interested.' From his pocket he took a neat flat notebook and opening it, read aloud: 'Quiet secluded room to let for evenings. Suit student or anyone wanting to get away from it all. Privacy guaranteed. Apply, 82, Charteris Road, Stowerton.'

Burden's nostrils contracted in distaste. Drayton was not responsible for the advertisement, he told himself, he had only found it. Indeed it was to his credit that he *had* found it. Why then feel that this kind of thing, so squalid, so redolent of nasty things done in nasty corners, was right up his street?

'Grover's again, eh?' said Wexford when they told him. 'So this is their latest racket, is it? Last year it was — er, curious books. This place gets more like the Charing Cross Road every day.' He gave a low chuckle which Burden would not have been surprised to hear Drayton echo. The fellow was a sycophant if ever there was one. But Drayton's olive-skinned face was wary. Burden would have said he looked ashamed except that he could not think of any reason why he should be.

'Remember the time when all the school kids were getting hold of flick knives and we knew for sure it was Grover but we couldn't pin it on him? And those magazines he sells. How would you like your daughter to read them?'

Wexford shrugged. 'They're not for daughters, Mike, they're for sons, and you don't *read* them. Before we get around to convening the purity committee, we'd better do something about this ad.' He fixed his eyes speculatively on Drayton. 'You're a likely lad, Mark.' It irked Burden to hear the Chief Inspector address Drayton, as he very occasionally did, by his christian name. 'You look the part.'

'The part, sir?'

'We'll cast you as a student wanting to get away from it all,

411

shall we, Inspector Burden?' Still viewing Drayton, he added, 'I can't see any of the rest of us capering nimbly in a lady's chamber.'

The first time they went to the door there was no answer. It was a corner house, its front on Charteris Road, its side with a short dilapidated fence, bordering Sparta Grove. While Burden waited in the car, Drayton followed this fence to its termination in a lane that ran between the backs of the gardens. Here the stone wall was too high to see over, but Drayton found a gate in it, locked but affording through its cracks a view of the garden of number eighty-two. On a clothes line, attached at one end to the wall and at the other to a hook above a rear window of the house, hung a wet carpet from which water dripped on to a brick path.

The house was seventy or eighty years old but redeemed from the slumminess of its neighbours by a certain shipshape neatness. The yard was swept — a clean broom stood with its head against the house wall — and the back step had been whitened. All the windows were closed and hung with crisp net curtains. As Drayton contemplated these windows, a curtain in one, probably the back bedroom, was slightly raised and a small wizened face looked out. Drayton put his foot on a projecting hunk of stone and hoisted himself up until his head and shoulders were above the grass-grown top of the wall. The brown simian face was still there. Its eyes met his and there appeared in them a look of terror, surely out of proportion to the offence or to the retribution for that offence the occupants of the house might be supposed to have committed. The face disappeared quickly and Drayton returned to the car.

'There's someone in,' he said to Burden.

'I daresay there is. Apart from the fact that we can't force an entry over a thing like this, making a rumpus would rather defeat the object of the exercise, wouldn't it?'

Theirs was just one of twenty or thirty cars lining Sparta Grove. At this end of the street there were neither garages nor space for them.

'Someone's coming now,' Drayton said suddenly.

Burden looked up. A woman pushing a shopping basket on

wheels was opening the gate of the corner house. Her head was tied up in a coloured scarf and she wore a coat with a huge showy fur collar. As the door closed behind her, he said:

'I know her. Her name's Branch, Mrs Ruby Branch. She used to live in Sewingbury.'

'Is she one of our customers?'

This use, on Drayton's lips, of one of Wexford's favourite terms, displeased Burden. It seemed not so much an accidental echo as a calculated and ingratiating mimicry of the Chief Inspector's racy style. 'We've had her for shoplifting,' he said stiffly, 'larceny as a servant and various other things. This is a new departure. You'd better go in and do your stuff.'

She subjected him to a careful and at first alarmed scrutiny through the glass panel of the door before opening it. The alarm faded and the door gave a few inches. Drayton put his foot on the mat.

'I understand you have a room to let.' He spoke pleasantly and she was disarmed. She smiled, showing excellent false teeth with lipstick on them. The scarf and the coat had not yet been removed and between the feather boa-like sides of her collar he could see a frilly blouse covering a fine bosom. The face was middle-aged — early fifties, Drayton thought — and bravely painted particularly about the eyelids. 'I happened to see your advert in Grover's window, Mrs Er . . . ?'

'No names, no pack drill, dear,' she said. 'Just call me Ruby.'

'O.K., Ruby.'

The door was closed behind him and he found himself in a tiny narrow hall, its floor covered in cheap bright red nylon carpet. On the threshold of the front room he stopped, staring, and his face must have shown his astonishment, for she said quickly:

'Don't take any notice of the bare boards, duckie. I like everything to be spick and span, you see, and I'm just giving the carpet a bit of an airing.'

'Spring-cleaning, eh?' Drayton said. All the furniture had been moved against the walls. There was a three-piece suite, covered in moquette, whose pattern showed what seemed like, but surely could not be, blue fishes swimming through a tangle

of red and pink climbing roses. On a huge television set stood
a naked lady in pink porcelain whose eternally raised right arm
held aloft a lamp in a plastic shade. The wallpaper was
embossed in gilt and the single picture was of the late King
George the Fifth and Queen Mary in full court regalia. 'I can
see you keep it nice,' he said heartily.

'You wouldn't get things nicer in any of your hotels. When
did you think of coming? Any night would be convenient to
me.' She gave him a long look, partly coy, partly assessing.
'You'll be bringing a young lady with you?'

'If you haven't any objection. I thought perhaps this
evening. Say eight till eleven. Would you . . . ?'

'I'll get my things on by eight sharp,' she said. 'If you'll just
tap on the door you needn't bring the young lady in till after
I've gone. Some do feel a bit shy-like. Say a fiver?'

Burden had agreed to give him ten minutes. Things could
hardly have gone more smoothly. He glanced up at the window
and saw the inspector approaching the front door. That she had
seen him too and knew who he was he guessed from the little
gasp of fear that came from her.

'What's going on, then?' she said, her voice dying to a
whimper.

Drayton turned and addressed her severely. 'I am a police
officer and I have reason to believe you are engaged in keeping
a disorderly house . . .'

Ruby Branch sat down on the red and blue sofa, put her
head in her hands and began to cry.

Drayton had expected they would simply take her down to
Kingsmarkham and charge her. It was all cut and dried and
there had been neither denial nor defiance. She had put the
advertisement in Grover's window to make a little extra money.
What with freezes and squeezes, it was a job to make ends meet
. . . Burden listened to it all. His eyes were on the scarf Ruby
Branch had unwound from her head and was using to wipe her
eyes, or perhaps on the ginger curls the removal of that scarf
had revealed.

'You were a blonde last time I saw you, Ruby,' he said.

'Since when do I have to ask your permission when I want
to have my hair tinted?'

'Still working for Mrs Harper in Waterford Avenue, are you?'

She nodded tearfully, then glared at him. 'What business is it of yours who I work for? If it wasn't for you I'd still have my job at the supermarket.'

'You should have thought of that,' Burden said, 'before your little *contretemps* with six dozen packets of soap powder. You always were houseproud and it's been your undoing. Quite a vice with you, isn't it? I see you've been at it again.'

He stared at the bare boards and thence from Ruby's varicose veined legs in their thin black nylons to her suddenly terrified face. To Drayton he said conversationally:

'There's not many working women would find the time to wash a big carpet. Go over it with a damp cloth, maybe. That's what my wife does. Let's go outside and see what sort of a job she's made of it, shall we? It's not a bad morning and I could do with a spot of fresh air.'

Ruby Branch came with them. She tottered in her high-heeled shoes and it seemed to Drayton that she was dumb with terror. The kitchen was neat and fresh and the step so clean that Burden's not very dirty shoe made a black print on it. Of the man seen at the window — husband? lodger? — there was no sign.

Drayton wondered that the clothes line was strong enough to bear the weight of the carpet, for it was soaking wet and looked as if it had been totally immersed in a bath. The high wind hardly caused it to sway. Burden advanced on it curiously.

'Don't you touch it,' Ruby said shrilly. 'You'll have the lot down.'

Burden took no notice of her. He gave the carpet a twitch and suddenly, as she had predicted, the line snapped. Its load subsided with a squelch, half on to the path and half on to the lawn, giving off from its heavy soaking folds a strong animal smell of sodden wool.

'Look what you've done! What d'you want to come out here poking about for? Now I'll have to do it all again.'

'No, you won't,' Burden said grimly. 'The only people who are going to touch that are scientific experts.'

'Just giving it an airing?' Drayton exclaimed.

'Oh, my God!' Ruby's face had become a yellowish white against which the quivering red lips stood out like a double gash. 'I never meant any harm, I was scared. I thought maybe you'd pin it on me, maybe you'd get me for a — a . . .'

'An accessory? That's a good idea. Maybe we shall.'

'Oh, my God!'

Back in the disarranged sitting room, she sat for a moment in petrified silence, twisting her hands and biting what remained of the lipstick from her mouth. Then she said wildly:

'It's not what you're thinking. It wasn't blood. I was bottling raspberries and I . . .'

'In April? Do me a favour,' said Burden. 'You can take your time.' He looked at his watch. 'We've got a very slack morning, haven't we, Drayton? We can sit here till lunchtime for all I care. We can sit here till tomorrow.'

Again she said nothing and in the renewal of silence shuffling footsteps were heard outside in the passage. The door opened cautiously and Drayton saw a little man with thin grey hair. The face was the face he had seen at the window. With its prognathous jaw, its many furrows in dark brown skin, and its bulbous nose and mouth, it was not prepossessing. The terrified expression had undergone a change. The eyes were fixed on Drayton just as they had been previously, but the agony of fear had been replaced by a kind of gloating horror comparable to that of a man shown a five-legged sheep or a bearded lady.

Burden got up and, because the newcomer seemed inclined to make a bolt for it, closed his hand over the door knob.

'Well, if it isn't Mr Matthews,' he said. 'Can't say I think much of your coming-out togs. I thought they made them to measure these days.'

The man called Matthews said in a feeble grating voice, 'Hallo, Mr Burden,' and then automatically, as if he always did say it, just as other men say, 'How are things?' or 'Nice day', 'I haven't done nothing.'

'When I was at school,' said Burden, 'they taught me that a double negative makes an affirmative. So we know where we are, don't we? Sit down, join the gathering. There aren't any more of you, are there?'

Monkey Matthews skirted the room carefully, finally sitting

down as far as possible from Drayton. For a moment nobody said anything. Matthews looked from Burden to Ruby and then, as if unwillingly compelled, back again at Drayton.

'Is that Geoff Smith?' he asked at last.

'You see,' said Ruby Branch, 'he never saw them. Well, come to that, *I* never saw the girl.'

Wexford shook his head in exasperation. His whole body had shaken with fury when Burden first told him, but now his anger had begun to abate, leaving a sour disgust. Four days had passed since Tuesday, four days of doubt and disbelief. Half a dozen men had been wasting their time, working in the dark and perhaps asking the wrong questions of the wrong people. And all because a silly woman had been afraid to go to the police lest the police stop a racket that promised to be lucrative. Now she sat in his office snivelling into a handkerchief, a scrap of cotton and lace streaked with make-up that the tears had washed away.

'This Geoff Smith,' Wexford said, 'when was the first time you saw him?'

Ruby rolled the handkerchief into a ball and gave a deep choking sigh. 'Last Saturday, Saturday the 3rd. The day after I put the advert in. It was in the morning, about twelve. There was a knock at the door and there was this young chap wanting the room for Tuesday night. He was dark and ever so nice-looking and he spoke nice. How was I to know he was a killer?' She shifted in Wexford's yellow chair and crossed her legs. ' "My name's Geoff Smith," he said. Proud of it, he was. I didn't ask him for his name. Well, he said eight till eleven and I said that'd cost him five pounds. He didn't argue so I saw him off the premises and he got into this black car.

'On Tuesday he came back like he said, at eight sharp. But I never saw any car this time and I never saw his girl. He give me five pounds and said he'd be gone by eleven and when I came back he *had* gone. Now, I'd left the room like a new pin, as good as a hotel it was . . .'

'I doubt if the court will look on that as a mitigating circumstance,' Wexford put in coldly.

At this hint of the revenge society intended to take on her, Ruby gave another loud sniff. 'Well,' she gulped, 'they'd messed it up a bit, moved the furniture, and of course I started putting the room to rights . . .'

'D'you mind sparing me all these asides? I'm a detective, not a domestic science examiner.'

'I have to tell you, don't I? I have to tell you what I did.'

'Tell me what you found.'

'Blood,' Ruby said. 'I moved back the sofa, and there it was, a great big stain. I know I ought to have come to you, Mr Wexford, but I panicked. I was dead scared. All those convictions you've pinned on me. They'll get me for an accomplice or whatever it is, I thought. Then, there was him, Geoff Smith. It's all very well you saying you'd have looked after me. You and me, we know what that amounts to. You wouldn't have put a bodyguard on my place night and day. I was scared stiff.' She added in a querulous whimper, 'Still am, come to that.'

'Where does Matthews come into all this?'

'I was all on my own. I kept going to the window to see if I could see a little dark fellow watching the house. He's killed one girl, I thought. The odds are he won't think twice about finishing me off. George and me, we'd always been good friends.' For a moment Wexford wondered who she meant. Then he recalled Monkey's long disused christian name. 'I'd heard he'd come out and I found him in the Piebald Pony.' She put her elbows on Wexford's desk and fixed him with a long supplicating stare. 'A woman needs a man about at a time like this. I reckon I thought he'd protect me.'

'She wanted someone to protect her,' said Monkey Matthews. 'Can I have another fag? I hadn't got nowhere to go, being as my wife won't have me in the house. Mind you, Mr Burden, I don't know as I'd have gone back with Rube if I'd known what was waiting for me.' He banged his thin concave chest. 'I'm no bodyguard. Got a light?' Unashamed, no longer afraid since he had been assured that any possible resemblance between Drayton and Geoff Smith was coincidental, he sat jauntily in his chair, talking with animation.

Burden struck a match to light the fourth cigarette he had had since his arrival and pushed an ashtray pointedly towards him.

'It was blood on the carpet all right,' Monkey said. The

418

cigarette adhered to his lower lip and the smoke made him screw up his eyes. 'I didn't believe her at first. You know what women are.'

'How much blood?' Burden asked tightly as if the very effort of questioning this man hurt him.

'Good deal. Nasty it was. Like as if someone had been playing silly beggars with a knife.' He shuddered, but he cackled at the same time. The cigarette fell. When he had retrieved it, but not before it had marked the carpet, he said, 'Rube was scared stiff of this Smith coming back, wanted to come to you. "That's no bloody good," I said, "not after all this time," but not one to flout the law when it's a matter of real downright crime I thought I'd better give you a hint there was a body knocking about. So I wrote to you. Rube had got some paper about. She always has things nice.'

He gave Burden an ingratiating smile, hideously distorting his face. 'I knew you'd only need a hint to get your hands on him. Anyone who finds fault with our local police, I always say, Mr Wexford and Mr Burden, they're real educated tip-top men. They'd be up in London at the Yard if there was any justice in this world.'

'If there's any justice in this world,' Burden said furiously, 'it'll put you away for the biggest stretch you've ever done for this.'

Monkey contemplated Burden's green glass statuette as if he hoped to identify it with some known form of human or animal life. 'Now don't be like that,' he said. 'I haven't done nothing. You could say I'd put myself out to help you. I never even set eyes on this Geoff Smith, but if he'd come back snooping around, I'd have been up the creek just the same as Rube.' He gave a deep theatrical sigh. 'It was a real sacrifice I made, helping you with your enquiries, and where's it got me?'

The question was rhetorical but Burden answered it sharply. 'A nice comfortable house to kip down in, for one thing. Maybe you're putting the squeeze on this Smith and you only made your "real sacrifice" when he wouldn't play.'

'It's a dirty lie,' said Monkey passionately. 'I tell you I never saw him. I thought that young bloke of yours was him. God knows, I reckoned I could spot a copper a mile off, but then they tog themselves up so funny these days. Rube and me we'd been scared stiff and then there he was, poking his long nose over the wall. I tell you, I thought my number was up. Put the squeeze on him! That's a proper laugh. How could I put the squeeze on him when I never set foot in Rube's place before Wednesday?' More ape-like than ever, he scowled at Burden, his eyes growing bulbous. 'I'll have another fag,' he said in an injured tone.

'When did you write the letter?'

'Thursday morning while Rube was out working.'

'So you were all by yourself?'

'Yes, on my tod. I wasn't putting Mr Geoff Smith through the third degree if that's what you're getting at. I leave that kind of thing to you.' Indignation brought on a coughing fit and he covered his mouth with deeply stained yellowish-brown fingers.

'I reckon you must have D.T.s of the lungs,' Burden said disgustedly. 'What d'you do when you're — er, behind bars? Start screaming like an addict in a rehabilitation centre?'

'It's my nerves,' Monkey said. 'I've been a mass of nerves ever since I saw that blood.'

'How did you know what to put in the letter?'

'If you're going to trap me,' Monkey said with distant scorn, 'you'll have to be more bloody subtle than that. Rube told me, of course. Be your age. Young, dark and got a black car, she says. Name of Geoff Smith. Come in at eight and was due out at eleven.'

His dog-end was stubbed out on the base of the glass sculpture. Lacking for a brief moment its customary cigarette, Monkey's face reminded the inspector of a short-sighted man without his glasses. There was about it something naked yet unnatural.

'O.K.,' he said. 'You know all this about him, because Ruby told you, but you never saw him and you never saw the girl.' At the last word Monkey's indignant eyes wavered. Burden was not sure whether this was from apprehension or because he was in need of further stimulation. He snatched the cigarette box and put it in the drawer. 'How did you know her name was Ann?' he said.

CHAPTER SEVEN

'How did you know her name was Ann?' Wexford asked.

The look Ruby Branch gave him was one of simple incomprehension. She appeared not merely unwilling to answer his question: She was utterly at sea. With Geoff Smith and his description she had been on firm ground. Now he had plunged her into uncharted and, for some reason possibly known to her, dangerous waters. She turned away her eyes and contemplated one of her veined legs as if she expected to see a ladder running up the stocking.

'You never even saw that letter, did you, Ruby?' He waited. Silence was the worst thing, the thing all policemen fear. Speech, no matter how clever and how subtly phrased, is necessarily a betrayal. 'Geoff Smith never told you that girl's name. How did you know? How does Matthews know?'

'I don't know what you're getting at,' Ruby cried. She clutched her handbag and shrank away from him, her mouth trembling. 'All those sarcastic things you say, they go in one ear and out the other. I've told you all I know and I've got a splitting headache.'

Wexford left her and went to find Burden. 'I don't even begin to understand this,' he said. 'Why does Geoff Smith tell her his name? She didn't want to know. 'No names, no pack drill' is what she said to Drayton.'

'Of course it's an assumed name.'

'Yes, I expect it is. He's an exhibitionist who uses an alias for fun, even when no one's interested.'

'Not only does he give his name unasked, he gives his girl friend's too.'

'No, Mike,' Wexford said crossly, 'my credulity won't stretch that far. "My name's Geoff Smith and I'll be bringing Ann with me." Can you visualise it? I can't. Besides, I've been over and over it with Ruby. I'd stake a year's salary on it. He never told her the girl's name and the first time she heard it was from me in there just now.'

'But Monkey knew it,' said Burden.

'And Monkey wasn't even there. I don't think Ruby's lying. She's scared to death and late in the day though it is, she's throwing herself on our mercy. Mike, would Ann Margolis go to a place like that? You know what the paper said. 'Ex-model and Chelsea playgirl!' Why wouldn't she just take her boy friend home with her?'

'She likes slumming,' said Burden. 'Margolis told me that. Smith, so-called, booked the room on Saturday. Anita knew Margolis would be out on Tuesday evening but she probably thought he'd come home fairly early. He didn't know and she didn't know the gallery manager would ask him out to dinner.'

'Yes, it ties up. Have they started going over Ruby's place?'

'Taking it apart now, sir. The carpet's gone down to the lab. Martin's found a neighbour who saw something. Old girl called Collins. She's waiting for us now.'

She was nearly as large as Wexford himself, a stout old woman with a square jaw. Before he began to question her, she launched forth on a long account of her suffering consequent on being Ruby Branch's next-door neighbour. Hardly an evening passed without her having to bang on the common wall between the houses. Ruby worked all day and did her cleaning after six. The television was always full on and often the vacuum cleaner at the same time. Monkey she knew. He had lived there from Ruby's arrival two years before until six months before he went to prison. It was disgusting, a crying scandal. As soon as she saw him come home with Ruby on Wednesday morning she knew trouble would start. Then there was a married niece and her husband from Pomfret way — if they *were* married — who came a couple of times a week, and who got drinking and laughing until the small hours.

'That's who I thought it was I saw leaving on Tuesday,' she said. 'Staggering down the path and holding on to each other. As much as they could do to walk it was.'

'Two of them?' Wexford said, his voice rising. 'You saw two of them?'

Mrs Collins nodded emphatically. 'Yes, there was two. I didn't look long, I can tell you. I was too disgusted.'

'Did you see them come?'

'I was in my kitchen till gone nine. I come into the front and I thought, thank the Lord she's gone out. There was dead silence until half past. I know I'm right about the time on account of looking at the clock. There was something on telly I wanted at twenty-five to. I'd just got up to switch it on when there comes this great mighty crash from next-door. Here we go, I thought, more hi-jinks, and I banged on the wall.'

'Go on,' Wexford said.

'For two pins, I said to myself, I'll go in and have it out with her. But you know how it is, you don't like to make trouble with the neighbours. Besides, there was three of them and I'm not so young as I used to be. Anyway, I got so far as putting my coat on and I was standing just inside the front door, sort of hesitating, when I saw these two come down the path.'

'How well did you see them?'

'Not that well,' Mrs Collins admitted. 'It was through the little glass bit in the door, you see. They was both in macs and the girl had a scarf on her head. His hair was dark, that I do know. I never saw their faces, but they were drunk as lords. I thought the girl was going to fall flat on her face. And she did fall when he got the car door open, fell right across the front seat.' She nodded indignantly, her expression smug and self-righteous. 'I gave them five minutes to get out of the way and then I went next-door, but there was no answer and I saw her come in myself at eleven. What's been going on? I thought. It wasn't the married niece from Pomfret. She never had no car. Couldn't keep money in her pocket long enough to get one.'

'This was a black car you saw them get into, Mrs Collins?'

'Black? Well, it was under one of them street lamps, and you know what they are, make you go all colours.' She paused, searching in her mind. 'I'd have said it was green,' she said.

Linda Grover flushed when Drayton told her to take the advertisement out of the window. The blood poured into her madonna's face and he knew it was because his explanation had been too crude.

'Didn't you realise what it meant?' he said harshly. 'I

should have thought one look at that old tart would have told you she wasn't a legitimate landlady.'

They were alone in the shop. She stood behind the counter, her eyes on his face and her fingers picking at the dog-eared corner of a magazine. 'I didn't know you were a policeman,' she said in a voice which had grown throaty.

'You know now.'

On his way here from Ruby Branch's house he had stopped at the library, not for the sake of the crime section this time, but to look at the big coloured books of paintings by old masters. There, amid the Mantegnas, the Botticellis and the Fra Angelicos, he had found her face under cracked haloes and he had stared at it in a kind of wonder before rage had taken over and he had slammed the book shut so that the librarian looked up with a frown.

'Is that all you came for?' Her first fright was gone and her voice took on an aggressiveness as he nodded. 'All that song and dance about an old advert card?' With a shrug, she walked past him and out of the shop, her body held straight as if she had an invisible weight on her head. He watched her come back, fascinated by the clean, pure curves of jaw and arm and thigh and by the small graceful movements her hands made as she tore Ruby's card into shreds.

'Be more careful next time,' he said. 'We'll be keeping an eye on you.' He saw that he had made her angry, for the colour faded utterly from her face. It was as if she had blushed white. There was a thin silver chain round her neck. As a schoolboy, Drayton had read the Song of Songs, hoping for something salacious. A line came back to him. He had not known what it meant, but now he knew what it meant for him. Thou hast ravished my heart with the chain of thy neck. . . .

'An eye on us?'

'This shop's got a bad enough reputation as it is.' He didn't give a damn about the shop's reputation, but he wanted to stay there, hang it out as long as he could. 'If I were your father with a nice little business like this I wouldn't touch that filth.'

She followed his glance at the magazines. 'Some like them,' she said. Her eyes had returned to his face. He had the notion that she was digesting the fact that he was a policeman and searching for some brand mark he ought to carry about on him. 'If you've finished with the sermon, I've got Dad's tea to get and I'm going to the pictures straight after. Last house is seven thirty.'

'Mustn't keep what's-his-name waiting,' Drayton sneered.

He could see he had nettled her. 'His name's Ray if you must know and he lodged with us,' she said. 'He's gone, left. Oh, come off it. You needn't look like that. I know you saw me with him. So what? It's not a crime, is it? Don't you ever stop being a cop?'

'Who said anything about a crime? I get enough crime in the daytime without the evenings.' He went to the door and looked back at her. The grey eyes were large and luminous and they had a trick of appearing always full of unshed tears. 'Maybe I wished I'd been in his shoes,' he said.

She took a step towards him. 'You're kidding.'

'Men usually kid you about that, do they?'

Her fingers went up to the little insincere smile that was just beginning and she tucked one of the bitten nails between her lips.

'What exactly are you trying to say?'

Now she looked frightened. He wondered if he had been wrong about her and if she were really as inexperienced and innocent as a tempera madonna. There was no gentleness in him and he did not know how to be soft and kind.

'If I'm kidding,' he said, 'I won't be outside the cinema at seven thirty.' Then he slammed the door and the bell tinkled through the old sagging house.

'Believe it or not,' Wexford said, 'Monkey doesn't want to go home. He's had a nice comfortable bed at Ruby's and God knows how many free meals, but he'd rather spend his weekend in what he calls "this contemporary-type nick". He's scared stiff of coming face to face with Ruby. Just as well, since I haven't the faintest idea what to charge him with.'

'Makes a change,' Burden grinned, 'our customers appreciating the amenities. Maybe we could get ourselves in the A.A. Guide, three-star hotel, specially adapted for those with previous convictions. Anything from the lab yet?'

'No, and I'll take my oath there won't be. We've only got Ruby's and Monkey's word that it was blood at all. You saw it, you saw what she'd done to that carpet. Char-ing may be a lowly trade, but Ruby's at the top of it. If I were Mrs Harper I wouldn't grudge a few sheets of handmade paper to get my house cleaned like that. She must have nearly killed herself washing that carpet. The lab say she used every cleanser in the book short of caustic soda. Oh, sure, they can sort out the Chemiglo from the Spotaway. The trouble is they can't sort out the blood, can't even say what group it is.'

'But they're still working on it?'

'Be working on it for days. They've got buckets full of muck from the pipes and drains. I'll be very surprised if they find anything. It's my bet our couple never went anywhere but that room in which they doubtless left a couple of hundred finger-prints . . .'

'All carefully removed by the Queen of the Chars,' Burden finished for him. 'The girl may be still alive, sir.'

'Because they left together and because the man's getting her out of there at all seems to show regret at what he'd done? I've had all the hospitals and all the G.P.s checked, Mike. They haven't had sight nor sound of anyone with stab wounds. And it must have been a stabbing, a blow on the head and that much loss of blood and the victim would never have been able to stand up, let alone stagger to a car. Moreover, if she's alive, where is she? It may only be assault we're up against or unlawful wounding, but whatever it is, we have to clear it up.'

Monkey Matthews gave them a crafty look when they returned to him.

'I've run out of fags.'

'I daresay Detective Constable Bryant will get you some if you ask him nicely. What d'you want. Weights?'

'You're joking,' said Monkey, stuffing a grubby paw into his jacket pocket. 'Forty Benson and Hedges Special Filter,' he said importantly and he brought out a pound note from a rustling mass that might indicate the presence of others like it. 'Better make it sixty.'

'Should last you till breakfast,' said Wexford. 'Rolling in it, aren't you? I can't help wondering if that's Geoff Smith's fee for silence you're sending up in smoke.' Stroking his chin, his head on one side, he looked speculatively into the other's simian face. 'How did you know her name was Ann?' he asked almost lightly and with a deceptive smoothness.

'Oh, you're round the twist,' Monkey said crossly. 'You don't listen to what you're told.'

When they came out of the cinema a light rain was falling, very little more than a clammy mist. Lamps glowed through the translucence, orange, gold and pearl-coloured. The cinema traffic coming from the car park swam out of the mist like subaqueous creatures surfacing with a gurgle and a splash. Drayton took the girl's arm to shepherd her across the road and left it there when they reached the pavement. This, the first contact he had ever had with her body, sent a tremor through him and made his mouth dry. He could feel the warmth from her skin just beneath the armpit.

'Enjoy the picture?' he asked her.

'It was all right. I don't like sub-titles much, I couldn't understand half of it. All that stuff about the woman letting the policeman be her lover if he wouldn't tell about her stealing the watch.'

'I daresay it happens. You don't know what goes on in these foreign places.' He was not displeased that the film had been sexy and that she wanted to talk about the sexiest part of the plot. With girls, that kind of talk was often an indication of intent, a way of getting on to the subject. Thank God, it wasn't the beginning of the week when they'd been showing that thing about a Russian battleship. 'You thinking of nicking any watches?' he said. She blushed vividly in the lamplight. 'Remember what the character in the film said, or what the sub-title said he said. "You know my price, Dolores." '

She smiled her close-lips smile, then said, 'You are awful.'

'Not me, I didn't write the script.'

She was wearing high heels and she was almost as tall as he. The perfume she had put on was much too old for her and it had nothing to do with the scent of flowers. Drayton wondered if her words had meant anything and if the perfume had been specially put on for his benefit. It was hard to tell how calculating girls were. Was she giving him an invitation or was the scent and the pale silvery stuff on her eyelids worn as a uniform might be, the battledress of the great female regiment who read the magazines she sold?

'It's early,' he said, 'only a quarter to eleven. Want to go for a walk down by the river?' It was under the trees there that he had seen her on Monday. Those trees arched dripping into the brown water, but under them the gravel path was well-drained and here and there was a wooden seat sheltered by branches.

'I can't. I mustn't be late home.'

'Some other night, then.'

'It's cold,' she said. 'It's always raining. You can't go to the pictures every night.'

'Where did you go with him?'

She bent down to straighten her stocking. The puddles she had stepped in had made dark grey splashes on the backs of her legs. The way she stretched her fingers and drew them up the calves was more provocative than all the perfume in the world.

'He hired a car.'

'I'll hire one,' Drayton said. They had come to the shop door. The alley between Grover's and the florist's next door was a walled lane that ended in a couple of garages. Its cobbles were brown and wet like stones on a cave floor that the tide has washed. She looked up at the high wall of her own home and at the blank unlit windows.

'You don't have to go in for a bit,' he said. 'Come under here, out of the rain.' There was no more shelter there than in the open street but it was darker. At their feet a little gutter stream flowed. He took her hand. 'I'll hire a car tomorrow.'

'All right.'

'What's the matter?' He spoke harshly, irritably, for he wanted to contemplate her face in repose, not working with anxiety, her eyes darting from one end of the alley to the other and up at the rain-washed wall. He would have liked eagerness, at least complaisance. She seemed afraid that they were watched and he thought of the thin beady-eyed mother and the mysterious father lying sick behind the brick bastion. 'Not scared of your parents, are you?'

'No, it's you. The way you look at me.'

He was nearly offended. The way he looked at her was something calculated and studied, a long, cold and intense stare that a good many girls had found exciting. A stronger desire than he had ever felt was increasing that intensity and making a contrived mannerism real. The poverty of her response almost killed it and he would have turned away from her to walk off alone into the wet night but for the two little hands which touched his coat and then crept up to his shoulders.

'It's you that frighten me,' she said. 'But that's what you want, isn't it?'

'You know what I want,' he said and brought his mouth down on hers, holding her body away from the cold, clammy wall. At first she was limp and unresisting. Then her arms went around him with a fierce abandon and as her lips parted under his, he felt a great thrill of triumph.

Above them a light appeared as a bright orange rectangle on the dark bricks. Before he opened his eyes Drayton felt it like pain on his eyelids.

She pulled away from him slowly with a long 'Aah!' of pleasure, a sigh of pleasure only begun to be cut short. 'They're waiting up for me.' Her breath was light and fast. 'I must go in.'

'Tomorrow,' he said, 'tomorrow.'

She could not find her key at first and it excited him to see her fumbling and hear her swearing softly under her breath. He had caused this sudden gaucheness, this disorientation, and it filled his masculine ego with the joy of conquest.

'Tomorrow, then.' The smile came, shy and tantalising. Then the door closed on her and the bell made its cold harsh music.

When he was alone in the alley and the light from above had gone out, he stood where they had kissed and passed his forefinger across his lips. The rain was still falling and the street lamp glowed with a greenish sulphurous light. He came out into this light and looked at his finger with the long smear of pale lipstick. It was not pink but the colour of suntanned flesh and he fancied that with it she had left on his mouth something of herself, a grain of skin or a trace of sweat. On the front of his coat was a long fair hair. To have these vestiges of her was in itself a kind of possession. Alone in the wet street, he passed his tongue lightly across his finger and he shivered.

A cat came out of the alley and slunk into a doorway, its fur dewed with fine drops. There was no visible sky, just vapour, and beyond the vapour blackness. Drayton put up his hood and walked home to his lodgings.

CHAPTER EIGHT

To the south of Kingsmarkham and overshadowing the eastern and southern sides of Pomfret lie twenty or thirty square miles of pine woods. This is Cheriton Forest. It is a man-made plantation, consisting mostly of firs and larches, and it has a stark un-English beauty, giving to the green plains beneath it the appearance of an Alpine meadow.

A new estate of small white houses has sprung up on the Pomfret side of the forest. With their coloured front doors and their decorations of cedar board they are not unlike chalets. To one of these, a yellow-painted house with a new car port, Detective Sergeant Martin took himself on Sunday morning, looking for a man called Kirkpatrick.

The door was opened promptly by a girl of about seven, a child with large eyes and a cowed look. Martin waited on the doorstep while she went to find her mother. The house was built on an open plan and he could see a little boy, as pale and wary as his sister, playing apathetically on the floor with alphabet bricks. The woman who came at last had a pugnacious face. She had the roseate breathless look of those who suffer from high blood pressure. Her blonde hair was dressed in tight shiny curls and she wore red-rimmed glasses. Martin introduced himself and asked for her husband.

'Is it about the car?' Mrs Kirkpatrick said savagely.

'In a way.'

The children crept up to their mother and stood staring.

'Well, you can see he isn't here, can't you? If he's crashed the car I can't say I'm sorry. I'd say good riddance. I hope it's a total write-off. When he brought it home here last Monday, I said, "Don't think you'll get me to go joy-riding in that thing. I'd rather walk. If I wanted to make an exhibition of myself in a pink and white car with purple stripes I'd go on the dodgems at Brighton," I said.'

Martin blinked at her. He had no idea what she meant.

'The other thing he had,' she said, 'that was bad enough.

431

Great old-fashioned black Morris like a hearse. God knows, we must be the laughing stock of all the neighbours.' She suddenly became aware of the staring listening children. 'How many times have I told you not to come poking your noses into my private business?' she said viciously. The boy wandered back to his bricks, but it took a savage push to move the little girl. 'Now, then,' she said to Martin. 'What's he done? What d'you want him for?'

'Just to talk to him.'

Mrs Kirkpatrick seemed more interested in listening to the sound of her own voice and airing grievances than eliciting reasons from Martin. 'If he's been speeding again,' she said, 'he'll lose his licence. Then he'll lose his job.' Far from being concerned, her voice held a note of triumph. 'A firm like *Lipdew* aren't going to keep on a salesman who can't drive a car, are they? Any more than they're going to give their people great showy cars for them to smash to smithereens just when it takes their fancy. I told him so before he went to Scotland. I told him on Tuesday morning. That's why he never came in for his dinner Tuesday night. But he can't be told. Pig-headed and stubborn he is and now it's got him into trouble.'

Martin backed away from her. A barrage of gunfire would be preferable to this. As he went down the path he heard one of the children crying in the house behind him.

Monkey Matthews was lying on his bed, smoking, when Wexford went into the cell. He raised himself on one elbow and said, 'They told me it was your day off.'

'So it is, but I thought you might be lonely.' Wexford shook his head reprovingly and looked round the small room, sniffing the air. 'How the rich live!' he said. 'Want me to send out for more of your dope? You can afford it, Monkey.'

'I don't want nothing,' Monkey said, turning his face to the wall, 'except to be left alone. This place is more like a goods yard than a nick. I never got a wink of sleep last night.'

'That's your conscience, Monkey, the still, small voice that keeps urging you to tell me something, like, for instance, how you knew the girl's name was Ann.'

Monkey groaned. 'Can't you give it a rest? My nerves are in a shocking state.'

'I'm delighted to hear it,' Wexford said unkindly. 'Must be the result of my psychological warfare.' He went out into the corridor and upstairs to Burden's office. The inspector had just come in and was taking off his raincoat.

'It's your day off.'

'My wife was threatening to cart me off to church. This seemed the lesser evil. How are we doing?'

'Martin's been talking to Mrs Kirkpatrick.'

'Ah, the wife of Anita Margolis's current boy friend.'

Burden sat down by the window. This morning the sun was shining, not after the fashion of fitful April sunshine but with the strength and warmth of early summer. He raised the blind and opened the window, letting in with the soft light the clear crescendo of bells from Kingsmarkham church steeple.

'I think we may be on to something there, sir,' he said. 'Kirkpatrick's away, travelling for his firm in Scotland. He went off on Tuesday and the wife hasn't seen him since. Moreover, he used to have a black car, had it up until last Monday, when his firm gave him a new one, white thing apparently, plastered all over with advertising gimmicks,' he chuckled. 'The wife's a harridan. Thought he'd smashed the car when she saw Martin, but she didn't turn a hair.' His face hardening slightly, he went on, 'I'm not one to condone adultery, as you know, but it looks as if there may have been some justification for it here.'

'Is he small and dark?' Wexford asked with a pained look at the open window. He moved closer to the central heating vent.

'Don't know. Martin didn't care to go into too many details with the wife. It's not as if we've much to go on.' Wexford nodded a grudging approval. 'Ah, well,' Burden said, getting up. 'Margolis may be able to help us there. For an artist he's a rotten observer, but he has *seen* the man.' He reached for his coat. 'Lovely sound those bells.'

'Eh?'

'I said the bells were lovely.'

'What?' said Wexford. 'Can't hear a word you say for the sound of those bloody bells.' He grinned hugely at the ancient joke. 'You might have a look-in on Monkey on your way out. Just in case he's getting tired of holding out on us.'

After careful examination by the police and a session at a

garage to have its radiator repaired, Anita Margolis's Alpine had been restored to its parking place on the grass verge outside Quince Cottage. Burden was not surprised to find it there, but his eyebrows went up as he saw ahead of him the rears of not one white car but two. He parked his own behind them and came out into the sunshine. As he walked up to it he saw that the new arrival was white only in that this was its background colour. Along its sides a band perhaps a foot wide had been painted in bright pink, adorned with sprays of purple flowers. This particular shade of purple had been used for the lettering above it: *Lipdew, Paintbox for a Prettier You.*

Burden grinned to himself. Only a brazen extrovert would enjoy being seen about in this car. He glanced through a side window at the pink seats. They were littered with leaflets and on the dashboard shelf were samples of the stuff the driver peddled, bottles and jars presumably, done up in mauve packages and tied with gold cord.

There could hardly be two cars in Sussex like this. Kirkpatrick must be somewhere about. Burden unlatched the gate and entered the cottage garden. The wind had scattered the petals of quince blossom and underfoot the ground was slippery scarlet. When nobody answered his knock, he went round the side of the house and saw that the doors of the garage where Margolis kept his own car were open and the car gone.

Fat buds on the apple branches brushed his face and all around him he could hear the soft twittering of birds. The atmosphere and appearance of rustic peace were somewhat marred by the ragged sheets of paper, vestiges of Margolis's inexpert tidying up, which still clung to bushes and in places fluttered in the treetops. Burden stopped by the back door. A man in a stone-coloured belted raincoat was standing on a wooden box and peering in at the kitchen window.

Unseen, Burden watched him in silence for a moment. Then he coughed. The man jumped, turned to face him, and came slowly down from his perch.

'There's nobody in,' he said diffidently, and then, 'I was just checking.' The man was undeniably good-looking, pale, dapper and with curling dark brown hair. The chin was small, the nose straight and the eyes liquid and lashed like a girl's.

'I'd like a word with you, Mr Kirkpatrick.'

'How d'you know my name? I don't know you.' Now that they were standing level with each other, Burden noted that he was perhaps five feet eight inches tall.

'I recognised your car,' he said. The effect of this was electric. Two dark red spots appeared on Kirkpatrick's sallow cheekbones.

'What the hell does that mean?' he said angrily.

Burden looked at him mildly. 'You said no one was in. Who were you looking for?'

'That's it, is it?' Kirkpatrick took a deep breath, clenching his fists. 'I know who you are.' He nodded absurdly and with grim satisfaction. 'You're a snooper, what they call an enquiry agent. I suppose my wife put you on to me.'

'I've never seen your wife,' said Burden, 'but I'm certainly an enquiry agent. More commonly called a police officer.'

'I overheard you asking the sergeant where you could hire a car,' Wexford said.

'In my lunch hour, sir,' Drayton replied quickly.

Wexford shook his head impatiently. 'All right, man, all right. Don't make me out an ogre. You can hire an articulated lorry for all I care and you won't do it in your lunch hour, you'll do it now. There are only three firms in the district doing car hire, Missal's and Cawthorne's in Stowerton and the Red Star where you took Miss Margolis's in York Street here. What we want to know is if anyone hired a green car from them last Tuesday.'

After Drayton had gone, he sat down to think it all out and try to solve the enigma of the cars. The man called Geoff Smith had used a black car on Saturday, a green one on Tuesday, if Mrs Collins could be believed. He thought she could. Last night he and Bryant had tested a black car under the pearly lamplight in Sparta Grove and it had remained black. He had looked at it through clear glass and through stained glass. No amount of contriving or exercise of the imagination could make it green. Did that mean that Geoff Smith possessed two cars, or that on Sunday or Monday he had sold the black one and bought a green? Or could it be that because this new car was conspicuous, he had hired the green one for his dubious and clandestine adventure?

Drayton, too, asked himself these questions as the tumultuous ringing of the church bells ceased and he turned the corner into York Street. In the strengthening sunshine the rhinestone ropes glittered at him from the window of Joy Jewels. He thought of the silver chain Linda wore around her neck and simultaneously of that smooth warm skin, silky to his touch.

He had to shake himself and tighten his mouth before going into Red Star Garage. They showed him two ageing red Hillmans and he turned away to catch the bus for Stowerton. There he found Russell Cawthorne in his office. On the one bit of solid wall behind his head was a calendar of a girl wearing three powder puffs and a pair of high-heeled shoes. Drayton looked at it with contempt and a certain unease. It reminded him of the magazines in Grover's shop. Cawthorne sat up stiffly when Drayton told him who he was and gave a brisk nod, the C in C receiving a promising subaltern.

' 'Morning. Sit down. More trouble brewing?'

Affected old bore, Drayton thought. 'I want to ask you about hiring cars. You do hire cars, don't you?'

'My dear boy, I thought you were here in your official capacity, but if you just . . .'

'I am. This is an official question. What colour are they, these hire cars of yours?'

Cawthorne opened a fanlight. The fresh air made him cough. 'What colour are they? They're all the same. Three black Morris Minors.'

'Were any of them hired on Saturday, the 3rd?'

'Now when would that have been, laddie?'

'Last week. There's a calendar behind you.' Cawthorne's face darkened to an even maroon. 'It'll be in the book,' he muttered.

The book looked well-kept. Cawthorne opened it and turned back a few pages, frowning slightly. 'I remember that morning,' he said. 'I lost my best mechanic. Impertinent young devil, treating the place like he owned it. I gave him the push, lost my temper . . .' Drayton fidgeted impatiently. 'About the cars,' Cawthorne said moodily. 'No, they were all in.'

'What about sales? You wouldn't have sold anyone a green car about that time?'

One of the veined, not very steady hands, went up to twitch at his moustache. 'My business hasn't been exactly booming.' He hesitated, eyeing Drayton warily. 'I'll tell you frankly,' he said, 'I haven't made a sale since Mr Grover took delivery of his Mini in February.'

Drayton felt his face grow hot. The name was enough to do it. 'I want to hire a car myself,' he said. 'For tonight.'

Blustering, confident as only the weak can be, Alan Kirkpatrick stood defiantly in Wexford's office. He had refused to sit down and a constantly reiterated, 'Rubbish' and 'I don't believe it' had greeted Wexford's hints as to Anita Margolis's probable death.

'In that case,' Wexford said, 'you won't mind telling us about your movements last Tuesday, the night you had a date with her.'

'A date?' Kirkpatrick gave a short sneering laugh. 'I like the way you put it. I got to know that woman solely because I'm keen on art. The only way to get into that place and look at Margolis's pictures was through her.'

Burden got up from his corner where he had been sitting quietly and said, 'Interested in his work, are you? So am I. I've been trying to remember the name of that thing he's got in the Tate. Perhaps you can refresh my memory.'

That it was so obviously a trap did not derogate from its significance as a question and a question which, if Kirkpatrick were to sustain his role as a seeker after artistic enlightenment, must be answered. His soft mobile mouth twitched.

'I don't know what he calls them,' he muttered.

'Funny,' said Burden. 'Any admirer of Margolis would surely know "Nothing".' For a moment Wexford himself stared. Then he recalled the *Weekend Telegraph* lying close to his hand in the desk drawer. As he listened to the inspector who had suddenly launched into an esoteric review of modern art, he was lost in admiration. Instead of reaching for his gun, Burden had evidently reached for a work of reference. Kirkpatrick, also perhaps overcome, sat down abruptly, his face puzzled and aggressive.

'I don't have to answer your questions,' he said.

'Quite right,' Wexford said kindly. 'As you rightly say, we can't even prove Miss Margolis is dead.' And he nodded sagely as if Kirkpatrick's wisdom had recalled him from sensational dreams to reality. 'No, we'll just make a note that you were probably the last person to see her alive.'

'Look,' said Kirkpatrick, on the edge of his chair but making no move to get up, 'my wife's a very jealous woman . . .'

'Seems to be infectious in your family. I'd have said it was jealousy made you threaten Miss Margolis a couple of weeks ago.' Wexford quoted Mrs Penistan. ' "I might kill you myself one of these fine days". Was last Tuesday one of those fine days? Funny way to talk to a woman you were only interested in because of her brother's painting, wasn't it?'

'That date, as you call it, she never kept it. I didn't go out with her.'

Ruby would know him again. Wexford cursed the paucity of their evidence. He did not think it would be an easy matter to persuade this man to take part in an identification parade. Kirkpatrick's confidence had been slightly shaken by Burden's questions, but as he sat down again some of his bravado seemed to return. With a look that was part impatience, part resignation, he took out a pocket-comb and began to arrange his curly hair.

'We're not interested in your wife's possible divorce proceedings,' Wexford said. 'If you're frank with us there's no reason why it should go further, certainly not to your wife's ears.'

'There's nothing to be frank about,' Kirkpatrick said in a less belligerent tone. 'I was going up North on Tuesday for my firm. It's true I'd arranged to meet Miss Margolis before I went. She was going to show me some of Margolis's — er, early work. He wouldn't have had it if he'd been there but he was going out.' Wexford raised his eyes and met Burden's calm, polite gaze. How green and gullible did this cosmetic salesman think they were? This story which seemed to fill its teller with pride was so near what Wexford called the 'old etching gag' that he could hardly suppress a chuckle of derision. Early work, indeed! 'I was going home first for a meal but I was late and it was seven when I got to Kingsmarkham. Grover's were closing and I remember that girl made a bit of a scene because I wanted my evening paper. There wasn't time to go home then, so I went straight round to Pump Lane. Ann — Miss Margolis, that is — had forgotten all about me coming. She said she was going to a party. And that's all.'

During the latter part of this explanation Kirkpatrick's face had grown red and he fidgeted uneasily.

'It can't have been more than half-past seven, if that,' Wexford said. He was wondering why Burden had gone to the window and was staring down, his expression amused. 'Surely there was time for your artistic researches, especially as you'd missed your evening meal?'

The flush deepened. 'I asked her if I could come in for a bit and then I said I'd take her out for a meal before the party. She had her ocelot coat on ready to go out, but she wouldn't let me in. I suppose she'd just changed her mind.'

Burden turned from the window and when he spoke Wexford knew what he had been scrutinising. 'How long have you had this car?'

'Since last Monday. I sold my own and got this one from my firm.'

'So Miss Margolis had never seen it before?'

'I don't know what you're getting at.'

'I think you do, Mr Kirkpatrick. I think Miss Margolis wouldn't go out with you because she didn't care to be seen about in such a conspicuous car.' The shot had gone home. Again Wexford marvelled at Burden's perspicacity. Kirkpatrick, who blushed easily at mild slights, had now grown white with anger and perhaps with mortification.

'She was a woman of taste,' Burden said. 'I shouldn't be surprised to hear she burst out laughing when she saw all your pink and mauve decorations.'

Apparently this was the salesman's soft spot. Whether he was a connoisseur of modern painting or just a philanderer, there was no room in either image for this ridiculous vehicle. It was the scar of the branding iron, the yellow armband, the shameful card of identity.

'What's so funny about it?' he said aggressively. 'Who the

hell did she think she was, laughing at me?' Indignation began to rob him of caution. 'It doesn't alter my personality, make me into a different man, just because I have to have a car with a slogan on it. I was good enough for her before, my money was good enough to spend on her . . .' He had said too much, and his rage gave place to a sudden recollection of where he was and to whom he was speaking. 'I mean, I'd given her a few samples in the past, I . . .'

'For services rendered, no doubt?'

'What the hell does that mean?'

'You said she showed you her brother's paintings without his knowledge. A kindly act, Mr Kirkpatrick. Worth a pot of nail varnish or some soap, I should have thought.' Wexford smiled at him. 'What did you do, borrow a more innocuous car?'

'I tell you, we didn't go anywhere. If we had, we could have gone in hers.'

'Oh, no,' Wexford said softly. 'You couldn't have used hers. The radiator was leaking. I suggest you got hold of a green car and used this to drive Miss Margolis into Stowerton.'

Still smarting from the derision his car had aroused, Kirkpatrick muttered, 'I suppose someone saw me in Stowerton, did they? Cawthorne, was it? Come on, you may as well tell me who it was.'

'Why Cawthorne?'

Kirkpatrick flushed patchily. 'He lives in Stowerton,' he said, stammering a little over the dentals and the sibilant. 'He was giving that party.'

'You were on your way to Scotland,' Wexford said thoughtfully. 'You must have made a detour to go through Stowerton.' He got up ponderously and went over to the wall map. 'Look, here's the London Road and you'd have to go that way, or east into Kent, if you wanted to by-pass London. Either way, Stowerton was miles off your route.'

'What the hell does it matter?' Kirkpatrick burst out. 'I had the whole evening to kill. There was nothing else to do. I didn't want to land up in Scotland in the small hours. I should have thought the main thing was Ann wasn't with me. My God, she wasn't even in Stowerton, she didn't go to that party!'

'I know,' Wexford said, returning to his chair. 'Her brother knows and Mr Cawthorne knows, but how do you know? You never got back into Sussex till this morning. Now listen, an identification parade would clear the whole thing up. Do you object?'

Suddenly Kirkpatrick looked tired. It could have been mere physical exhaustion or that the strain of lying — and lying ineffectually — was telling badly on him. His good looks were particularly vulnerable to anxiety. They depended on a swagger in the tilt of his head, a laugh on his full mouth. Now there was sweat on his upper lip and the brown eyes, which were his most compelling feature, looked like those of a dog when someone had trodden on its tail.

'I'd like to know what it's in aid of,' he said sullenly. 'I'd like to know who saw me where and what I'm supposed to have been doing.'

'I'll tell you, Mr Kirkpatrick,' said Wexford, drawing up his chair.

'When am I going to get my carpet back?' said Ruby Branch.

'We're not cleaners, you know. We don't do an express service.'

She must be lamenting the days, Burden thought, when women wore veils as a matter of course, as often as not just to go out in the public street. He could remember one his grandmother had had on a toque, a thick, seemingly opaque curtain which when lowered was a perfect disguise for its wearer.

'Pity we're not in Morocco,' he said, 'you could put on your yashmak.'

Ruby gave him a sulky glance. She pulled down the brim of her hat until it almost covered her eyes and muffled her chin with a chiffon scarf.

'I shall be a marked woman,' she said. 'I hope you lot realise that. Suppose I pick him out and he escapes? The jails can't hold them these days. You've only got to look at the papers.'

'You'll have to take your chance on that,' said Burden.

When they were in the car she said diffidently, 'Mr Burden? You never told me whether you're going to do anything about that other thing, that keeping a what-d'you-call-it house?'

'That depends. We shall have to see.'

'I'm putting myself out to help you.'

They drove in silence until they reached the outskirts of Kingsmarkham. Then Burden said, 'Be honest with me, Ruby. What's Matthews ever done for you except take your money and pretty well break up your marriage?'

The painted mouth trembled. There were callouses and the long grey indentations housework makes on the fingers that held the scarf to her lips. 'We've been so much to each other, Mr Burden.'

'That was a long time ago,' he said gently. 'You've got yourself to think of now.' It was cruel what he had to say. Perhaps justice always is and he was used, if not to administering it, at least to leading people to its seat. Now, to find out what he wanted, he would lead Ruby away from it and cruelty would have to be his means. 'You're nearly ten years off your pension. How many of those women you work for would employ you if they knew what you'd been up to? They will know, Ruby. They read the papers.'

'I don't want to get George into trouble.' It took him, as it had Wexford, a moment's reflection before he remembered that George was Monkey's christian name. 'I was crazy about him once. You see, I never had kids, never had what you'd call a real husband. Mr Branch was old enough to be my father.' She paused and with a tiny lace handkerchief dabbed at the tear-stained space between scarf and hat brim. 'George had been in prison. When I found him he seemed — well, so kind of happy to be with me.' In spite of himself, Burden was moved. He could just recall old Branch, doddery and crotchety in advance of his years. 'Four quid George had off me,' she said unevenly, 'and all the drink I'd got in the place and God knows how many good dinners, but he wouldn't lie down beside me. It's not nice, Mr Burden, when you've got memories and you can't help . . .'

'He's not worth your loyalty. Come on now. Cheer up. Mr Wexford'll think I've been giving you the third degree. You never heard that Geoff Smith call the girl Ann, did you? It was all made up to save Monkey.'

'I reckon it was.'

'That's a good girl. Now then, did you search the room at all when you'd found the stain?'

'I was too scared for that. Look, Mr Burden, I've been thinking and thinking about it. George was alone in there for hours and hours on the Tuesday doing that letter while I was out at work. I think he must have found something they'd left behind them.'

'I've been thinking, too, Ruby, and I think great minds think alike.'

When they got to the police station a dozen men were lined up in the yard. None was more than five feet nine and all had hair of shades between mid-brown and coal-black. Kirkpatrick stood fourth from the end on the left. Ruby came hesitantly across the concrete, cautious, absurd in her high heels and with her swathed face. Wexford, who had not heard her story, could hardly keep himself from smiling, but Burden watched her rather sadly. Her eyes flickered across the first three men on the left and came to rest for a brief moment on Kirkpatrick. She came closer and walked slowly down the line, occasionally turning to look over her shoulder. Then she turned back. Kirkpatrick looked afraid, his expression bewildered. Ruby stopped in front of him. A spark of recognition seemed to pass between them and it was as marked on his part as on hers. She moved on, lingering longest of all in front of the last man on the right.

'Well?' said Wexford just inside the door.

'For a minute I thought it was the one on the end.' Wexford sighed softly. 'The one on the end' was Police Constable Peach. 'But then I knew I'd got it wrong. It must be the one with the red tie.'

Kirkpatrick.

'Must be? Why must it be?'

Ruby said simply, 'I know his face, I don't know none of the others. His face is kind of familiar.'

'Yes, yes, I daresay. My face ought to be familiar to you by this time, but I didn't hire your knocking shop last Tuesday.' Under the veil Ruby looked resentful. 'What I want to know is, is he Geoff Smith?'

'I don't know. I wouldn't know him if I saw him now. Ever since then I've been dead scared every time I've seen a dark man in the street. All I know is I saw that fellow with the red tie somewhere last week. Maybe it was Tuesday. I don't know. He knew me too. You saw that?' She made a little whimpering, snivelling sound. Suddenly she was a little girl with an old face. 'I want to go home,' she said, darting a vicious glance at Burden. He smiled back at her philosophically. She was not the first person to make a confession to him and then regret it.

Kirkpatrick came back into Wexford's office, but he did not sit down. Ruby's failure to identify him had restored his confidence and for a moment Wexford thought that he was going to add further touches to the image he had tried to create of himself as a patron or connoisseur of the arts. He picked up the blue glass sculpture and fingered it knowingly while giving Wexford a sullen glance.

'I hope you're satisfied,' he said. 'I think I've been very patient. You could see that woman didn't know me.'

You knew *her,* Wexford thought. You were in Stowerton and although you were not at the party nor in her brother's confidence, you knew Anita Margolis never went there.

Kirkpatrick was relaxed now, breathing easily. 'I'm very tired and, as I say, I've been particularly patient and forthcoming. Not many men who'd just driven four hundred miles would be as accommodating as I've been.' The foot-high chunk of glass was carefully replaced on the desk and he nodded as if he had just subjected it to expert evaluation. You poseur, thought Wexford. 'What I want now is a good sleep and to be left in peace. So if there's any more you want you'd better speak now.'

'Or else hereafter for ever hold our peace? We don't work that way, Mr Kirkpatrick.'

But Kirkpatrick hardly seemed to have heard. 'In peace, as I say. I don't want my family bothered or frightened. That woman not identifying me should settle the matter for good and all. I . . .'

You talk too much, Wexford thought.

'The Vine had struck a Fibre; which about
If clings my being — let the Sufi flout;
Of my base metal may be filed a Key,
That shall unlock the Door he howls without.'

CHAPTER NINE

After the rain the town looked cleansed. The evening sun made the pavements gleam like sheet gold and a thin vapour rose from them. It was mild, warm even, and the air heavy with damp. Excitement made a hard knot in Drayton's chest as he drove up the High Street in Cawthorne's hire car and parked it in the alley. He wanted to fill his lungs with fresh air, not this cloying stuff that made him breathless.

Seeing her was a shock. He had had fantasies about her in the intervening time and he had expected reality to disappoint. She was just a girl he fancied and would possess if he could. It had happened to him a dozen times before. Why then, although the shop was full of customers and pretty girls among them, were they all faceless, all so many zombies? The sensuality which had flooded into him last night outside the shop and had since been transmuted into a clinical tickling calculation, came back like a blow and held him, staring at her, while the doorbell rang in his ears.

Her eyes met his and she gave him the faint secret smile that was just a lifting of the corners of her mouth. He turned away and killed time playing with the paperback stand. The shop had an unpleasant smell, food stench that came perhaps from whatever they ate in those back regions, the sickliness of unwrapped sweets, dirt that filled up the corners where no one tried to reach. On the shelf above his head the china spaniel still carried his pot of dusty flowers. Nobody would ever buy him just as nobody would buy the ashtray and the jug which flanked him. What connoisseur of Wedgwood — what conoisseur of anything, come to that — would even enter this shop?

More and more customers kept coming in. The constant tinkling of the bell set Drayton's nerves on edge. He spun the stand and the coloured covers flickered in a bright senseless kaleidoscope, a gun, a skull under a stetson, a girl who lay in blood and roses. His watch told him that he had been in the shop only two minutes.

Only one customer left now. Then a woman came in to buy a dress pattern. He heard Linda say softly, even scornfully, 'Sorry, we're closed.' The woman began to argue. She had to have it that night, a matter of urgency. Drayton felt Linda's shrug, caught a firm phrase of denial. Was it thus, with this cool dogged patience, that she habitually refused demands? The woman went out, muttering. The blind rattled down the window and he watched her turn the sign.

She came away from the door and walked towards him quite slowly. Because her face had lost its smile and her arms hung stiffly at her sides, he thought that she was about to speak to him, perhaps apologise or state conditions. Instead, without a word or a movement of her hands, she lifted her mouth to his, opening her lips with a kind of sensuous gasp. He matched his mood to hers and for a moment they were joined only by the kiss. Then he took her in his arms and closed his eyes against the parody that mocked him from the book jackets, the orgy of writhing lovers, coupling above, below, beside each other, a massed fertility rite in modern undress.

He released her and murmured, 'Let's go.' She gave a soft giggle which drew from him a low, reluctant laugh. They were laughing, he knew, at their own weakness, their defencelessness under the grip of emotion.

'Yes, let's go.' She was breathing hard. The short staccato giggle she had given had nothing to do with amusement. 'Mark,' she said, faintly interrogative, and then, 'Mark' again, as if the repetition of his name settled something for her. To him it seemed like a promise.

'We'll go to Pomfret,' he said. 'I've got the car.'

'To Cheriton Forest?'

He nodded, feeling a stab of disappointment. 'You've been there before?'

The implication in the question was not lost on her. 'With Mum and Dad on picnics.' She looked at him gravely. 'Not like this,' she said. It might mean so much or so little. It might mean she had never been there with a boy friend, with any man, to make love or just to walk hand in hand. Words were a disguise for thought and for intention.

She got into the car beside him and went through a small

ritual of arranging her skirt, removing her gloves, placing her handbag under the dashboard. What strange compulsion women had with their genteelisms, their attention to their personal furnishings! And how seldom they abandoned themselves. The face which she had put on was not the one he had seen as they came out from their embrace, but a prideful smug mask arranged, as it were, in the framing of the car window so that the world might observe her serenity out in a car with a man.

'Where would you like to eat?' he asked. 'I thought of the Cheriton Hotel, just where the Forest begins?'

She shook her head. 'I'm not hungry. We could have a drink.'

A girl like this, had she ever been in such a place before? Could she resist being seen there? With all his heart he despised her for her origins, her poverty of conversation, the pitiful smallness of her world. And yet her physical presence excited him almost beyond bearing. How was he to endure an hour with her in an hotel lounge, what would they talk about, how could he keep from touching her? He had nothing to say to her. There were rules in this game, prescribed amorous badinage, corresponding to courtship in the ornithological world, a kind of dancing and fluffing out of feathers. Earlier in the evening, before he had come into the shop, Drayton had to some extent rehearsed these preambles, but now it seemed to him that they had passed beyond them. The kiss had brought them to the threshold. He longed for a little gaiety from her, a spark of joy that might change his excitement from lust into something more civilised.

'I don't know,' he said dully. 'The evening I get the car is the first one it hasn't rained for weeks.'

'We couldn't have come here without it.' Ahead of them the lights of Pomfret glimmered in the dusk through the greening trees. 'It's getting dark,' she said.

Driven to despair for something to talk about, he broke a rule. 'We've been questioning a fellow called Kirkpatrick today,' he said. It was unorthodox, perhaps even wrong, to talk police business. 'He's a customer of yours. D'you know him?'

'They don't give their names,' she said.

'He lives around here.' Exactly here, he thought. This must be it. The black escarpment of the forest rose before them and in front of it, lying like boxes dropped in a green meadow, were a dozen white and blue dwellings, styled 'village houses'.

'Oh, look!' she said. 'That car.' There it was on one of the drives, its pink and lilac turned sickly in the light of a porch carriage lamp. 'That's the man you mean, isn't it? Fancy driving around in a thing like that. I nearly killed myself laughing.' Her animation over something so puerile chilled him. He felt his mouth go stiff. 'What's he done?' she asked.

'You mustn't ask me that.'

'You're very careful,' she said and he sensed that her eyes were on him. 'Your bosses, they must think a lot of you.'

'I hope so.' He thought she was smiling at him, but he dared not turn. It came to him suddenly that her silence and her dullness perhaps sprang from the same source as his own and the thought rocked him. The road was dark here where the pinewoods began, too dark for him to take his eyes from it for an instant. In the distance, between black billows of conifers, he could see the lights of the hotel. She put her hand on his knee.

'Mark,' she said, 'Mark, I don't want that drink.'

It was nearly nine when the call from the station came through to Burden's house.

'Ruby Branch is back again, sir.' The voice was Martin's. 'She's got Knobby Clark with her and she wants to see you. I can't get a word out of them.'

He sounded apologetic and as if he expected a reprimand. But all Burden said was, 'I'll be straight down.'

At his throat, he could feel that odd little stricture, that nervous pull, which meant something was going to happen at last. His tiredness went.

Ruby was in the police station foyer, her attitude abject, almost martyred, and on her face an expression of stoicism. Beside her, on a spoon-shaped red chair inadequate to contain his bulky rotund body, sat the fence from Sewingbury. Looking at him, Burden recalled their last encounter. Knobby looked nervous now and he had the air of a suppliant, but on that previous occasion it was he who had been in a position to exercise scornful contempt, to bargain and reject. In his mind's eye, Burden saw again the shy ladylike woman who had come to sell the jewels that were her husband's gifts. His heart hardened and he was seized with a sudden anger.

'Well?' he said. 'What d'you want?'

With a heavy mournful sigh, Ruby surveyed the colourful appointments of the hall where they sat and it was these she seemed to address. 'A nice way to talk when I've taken the trouble to come all this way. It's a real sacrifice I've made.'

Knobby Clark said nothing. His hands were in his pockets and he appeared to be concentrating on retaining his balance on a seat constructed for narrower buttocks than his own. The little eyes in cushions of fat were still and wary.

'What's he doing here?' Burden asked.

An apparently self-appointed spokeswoman for both of them, Ruby said, 'I guessed George'd go to him, them being old buddies. I had a bus ride to Sewingbury after I'd been here.' She paused. 'After I'd been helping you,' she said with heavy meaning. 'But if you don't want to know, that's O.K. by me.' Clutching her handbag, she got up. Her fur collar undulated at the quivering of the big bosom beneath it.

'You'd better come into my office.'

Still silent, Knobby Clark hoisted himself carefully from his chair. Burden could look down easily on to the top of his head. All that remained of his hair was a feathery tuft, again evocative of the stubbly crown on a great misshapen swede.

Intent on wasting no more time, he said, 'Well, let's see it, then. What is it?' He was rewarded by nothing more than a slight tremor in Knobby's mountainous shoulders.

'D'you mind shutting the door?' said Ruby. Here the lights were brighter and her face looked ravaged. 'Show it to him, Mr Clark.'

The little jeweller hesitated. 'Now, look, Mr Burden,' he said, speaking for the first time. 'You and me, we've had no trouble for a long time, have we? Must be seven or eight years.'

'Six,' said Burden crisply. 'Just six next month since you had your little spot of bother over receiving those watches.'

Knobby said resentfully, 'That was when I come out.'

'I don't see the point of it, anyway.' Ruby sat down,

gathering confidence. 'I don't see the point of trying to make him look small. I come here of my own free will . . .'

'Shut up,' Burden snapped at her. 'D'you think I don't know what's been going on? You're narked with your boyfriend, you want to do him down. So you took yourself over to this little rat's shop in Sewingbury and asked him just what Monkey Matthews flogged to him last Thursday. Make him look small! That's a laugh. If he was much smaller we'd trip over him.' He swallowed hard. 'It wasn't public spirit, it was spite. Naturally Clark came with you when you told him we'd got Monkey here. Now you can fill in the rest but spare me the sob stuff.'

'Knobby wants to make sure there won't be no trouble for him,' Ruby said, now reduced to a tearful whimpering. 'He wasn't to know. How was I to know? I left George alone for a couple of hours on Thursday while I was working, making money to keep him in luxury . . .' Perhaps she recalled Burden's caution as to sentimentality, for she went on more calmly, 'He must have found it down the side of one of my chairs.'

'Found what?'

A fat hand returned to a shapeless pocket, emerged and dropped something hard and shiny on to Burden's desk. 'There's a lovely piece of workmanship for you, Mr Burden. Eighteen carat gold and the hand of a master.'

It was a cigarette lighter of gleaming red-gold, the length and breadth of a matchbox but thinner, its sides delicately chased with a design of grapes and vineleaves. Burden turned it over and pursed his lips. On its base was an inscription: 'For Ann who lights my life'.

A big split opened in Knobby's face, the rift in the mangold that has grown too pulpy for its skin. He was smiling. 'Thursday morning it was, Mr Burden.' The bloated hands spread and quivered. "Take a butcher's at this," Monkey says to me. "Where d'you get it?" I says, knowing his reputation. "All that glisters is not gold," I said . . .'

'But if it wasn't gold,' said Burden nastily, 'it could glisten on till kingdom come for all you cared.'

Knobby looked at him narrowly. ' "My old auntie left it me," he says, "my auntie Ann." "Lively old geezer she must have been," I said. "She leave you her cigar case and her hip flask as well?" But that was only my fun, Mr Burden. I never thought it was hot. It wasn't on the list.' His face split again, virtuously this time. 'I gave him twenty for it.'

'Don't be childish. I'm not senile and you're no philanthropist.' Again Burden remembered the woman with the jewels. 'You gave him ten,' he said contemptuously.

Knobby Clark did not deny it. 'It's my loss, Mr Burden. Ten or twenty, it doesn't grow on trees. You won't make anything of it? No trouble, eh?'

'Oh, get out,' Burden said tiredly. Knobby went. He looked smaller than ever, yet he seemed to be walking on his toes. When he had gone Ruby put her ginger head in her hands.

'It's done then,' she said. 'My God, I never thought I'd shop George.'

'Hear the cock crowing in the distance, can you?'

'You're a hard man. You get more like your boss every day.'

Burden was not displeased at this. 'You can go, too,' he said. 'We won't say any more about the other thing. You've wasted enough public time and public money as it is. I should stick to char-ing in future.' He grinned, his good temper almost restored. 'You've got a genius for cleaning up other people's mess.'

'Would you let me see George?'

'No, I wouldn't. Don't push your luck.'

'I didn't think you would.' She sighed. 'I wanted to say I was sorry.' Her face was ugly and painted and old. 'I love him,' she said and her voice sounded very tired. 'I've loved him for twenty years. I don't reckon you can understand that. You and the others, it's a dirty joke to you, isn't it?'

'Good night, Ruby,' he said. 'I've got things to do.' Wexford would have managed things better. He would have said something ironic and tough — and tender. It was as she had said. He, Burden, could not understand, never would, did not want to. To him that kind of love was a closed book, pornography for Grover's library. Presently he went down to see Monkey Matthews.

'You ought to get yourself a lighter, Monkey,' he said through the smoke, viewing the litter of match ends.

'Can't seem to get on with them, Mr Burden.'

'Not even a nice gold one? Or would you rather have the lolly?' He let it lie in the palm of his hand, then raised it to catch the light from the bare bulb. 'Stealing by finding,' he said. 'What a come-down!'

'I don't suppose it's any use asking you how you found out?'

'Not a bit.'

'Ruby wouldn't do that to me.'

Burden hesitated for a second. She had said he was getting like Wexford and he had taken it as a compliment. Perhaps it was not only the Chief Inspector's toughness he could emulate. He opened his eyes wide in wrathful indignation. 'Ruby? I'm surprised at you.'

'No, I don't reckon she would. Forget I said it. Different to that lousy old git, Knobby Clark. He'd sell his own grandmother for cats' meat.' With slow resignation, Monkey lit another cigarette. 'How long'll I get?' he asked.

The car lights were off. He had parked in a clearing surrounded by dense trees, tall black firs and pines, grown for ship's masts and flagpoles. Their trunks looked grey but even these straight shapes were indiscernible a few yards in from the edge of the wood. Beyond them there was neither night nor day, only a dark labyrinth.

He held her in his arms and he could feel her heart beating. It was the only sound. He thought it would be dark when he opened his eyes — their kiss had been long and blind — and the pallid dusk was a shock.

'Let's walk,' he said, taking her hands. They were all right now. It had come right. He did not know why, but instead of triumph there descended upon him a subtle and hitherto unexperienced fear. It was not in any sense a fear of physical inadequacy, nor of psychological failure, but an apprehension rather of some terrible involvement. Until now his sexual adventures had been transient, sometimes gay, never the spur to introspection. But he felt that they had not in any way been a practice or a rehearsal. Indeed the feelings they had evoked and those by which they had been promoted were quite unlike the sensations he now had both in kind and in degree. He was totally engulfed by something new and terrifying. It might almost have been the first time for him.

'It's like a foreign country,' she said.

It was. An uncharted place, alien, with an untranslatable language. That she should feel what he felt, identically, tele-pathically, made him gasp. Then he looked at her and, follow-ing her gaze upwards to the crowns of the trees, knew with a sudden sense of let-down that she meant the forest itself, and not a state of mind.

'Have you ever been in one?'

'No,' she said, 'but it's like that. And it's like last night. Alone with you between high walls. Did you think of that when you brought me here?' They had begun to climb an avenue which, cutting into the hillside so evenly and precisely, resem-bled an incision in thick black flesh or a sewn wound. 'Did you think of that?'

'Perhaps.'

'That was clever of you.' She was breathing shallowly, although the ascent was steep. To the left of them and a little way ahead, a tiny footpath threaded between the trees.

'But there aren't any windows here, are there?' More than anything in the world, more at that moment even than absolute possession of her, he wanted to see that covert smile, that uplifting of the lips without parting them. She had not smiled at all since they had entered the forest and that look of hers was the essence, the very nucleus of her appeal to him. Without it he could kiss her, even achieve that culmination for which this visit had been contrived, but he would lose the savour and the scent and half his pleasure — or perhaps be saved. Already he was the slave of a fetish.

Echoing him, she said softly, 'No windows . . . No one to watch you or stop you.' She added breathlessly, turning to face him so that their bodies and their eyes were close, 'I'm tired of being watched, Mark.'

A little orange square in a wall, a bell that always jangled, a querulous voice calling.

'You're with me,' he said, 'and nobody watches me.' Usually he was subtle, but her nearness deprived him of restraint and brought out the swagger of the male animal. Before he could stop himself the appeal came out. 'Smile for me,' he said in a hard whisper. Her fingers closed on his shoulders, not firmly or passionately but with a light, almost calculatingly seductive pressure. The look in her eyes was quite blank and the invitation in them came entirely from the tremor of half-closed heavy lids. 'Oh, smile . . .'

Then suddenly he was rewarded. A terrible urgency possessed him, but for all that he took her slowly in his arms, watching the smile that was the focal point of all his desire, and then bringing his own mouth down to meet it.

'Not here,' she whispered. 'In the dark. Take me into the dark.' Her response was strong yet fluid. The words, spoken against his lips, seemed to flow into his body like wine and fill him with heat.

The thread of a path beckoned him and he held her against himself, half carrying her into the deep shadows of the forest edge. Above them the pine needles whispered and the sound was like the distant voices of doves. He took off his coat and spread it on the sandy floor. Then he heard her whispering to him words he could not catch but which he knew were no longer hesitant or passive. Her hands reached for him to pull him down beside her.

The darkness was almost absolute and it was this anonymous secret blackness which she seemed to have needed just as he had needed her smile. Her coquetry, her shy silence, had given place to a feverish hunger. That it was neither false nor simulated he knew when she took his face in the long hands that had become strong and fierce. He kissed her throat and her breasts and she gave a long sigh of pleasure. The darkness was a warm river to drown in. They call it the little death, he thought, and then the power to think at all melted away.

CHAPTER TEN

There was scarcely any delay between his knocking and the opening of the cottage door. A bright shaft of sunshine fell upon a black and mauve spotted overall and a sharp red face.

'Turned up again like a bad penny,' said Mrs Penistan. Burden blinked. He hardly knew whether her remark referred to his arrival or her own unexpected appearance. She clarified with one of her shrill laughs. 'I saw Mr M's advert and I took pity on him, said I'd come back till *she* turns up.' Leaning towards him, her broom held aloft like a spear, she whispered confidingly, 'If she turns up.' She stood aside for him to enter. 'Mind the bucket,' she said. 'We're all at sixes and sevens in here. Good thing my boys can't see what I have to contend with. If they set eyes on this place they'd have their mum out before you could say knife.' Remembering the ox-like Penistan men, not surely conspicuous for filial piety, Burden could only give a neutral smile. Their mother thrust her face into his and with a laugh, this time so cheerful as to amount to glee, said, 'Wouldn't surprise me if there was bugs in them walls.' A shrill peal of giggles pursued him into the studio.

Her efforts seemed to have made as yet small improvement in the general dirty disarray. Perhaps she had only just arrived. Nothing had been tidied or dusted and to the normal unpleasant smell had been added a sour stench, possibly coming from the dregs which still remained in the dozen or so empty cups on the tables and the floor. Here, as nowhere else, Ruby's vigour and acumen were needed.

Margolis was painting. In addition to the tubes of oil colour arranged about him were various small pots of unidentifiable matter. One seemed to contain sand, another iron filings. He looked up when Burden entered.

'I've decided not to think about it,' he said with as near an approach to firmness as could be imagined. 'I'm simply getting on with my work. Ann'll be back.' He added as if this clinched the matter, 'Mrs Penistan agrees with me.'

It was hardly the impression Burden had received on the doorstep. Without comment — let the man be cheerful while he could — he held out the lighter. 'Ever seen it before?'

'It's a cigarette lighter,' Margolis said sagely. So might some authoritative archaeologist identify an obscure find in an ancient barrow.

'The point is, is it your sister's?'

'I don't know. I've never seen it before. People are always giving her things.' He turned it over. 'Look, it's got her name on it.'

'It's got Ann on it,' Burden corrected him.

A poised broom preceded Mrs Penistan's entry into the studio. She seemed to find amusement not so much in her employer's remarks as in his very existence, for, standing behind him as he contemplated the lighter, she favoured Burden with a slow deliberate wink.

'Here, let's have a look,' she said. One glance satisfied her. 'No,' she said, 'no.' This time her laughter seemed aimed at his own gullibility or possibly at his supposing Margolis to be capable of identifying anything. Burden envied her ignorance. Not for her the dilemma of wondering how to contend with genius. Here was a man, inept in practical matters, vague in his speech; therefore he was a lunatic, affording mirth and a kind of rough pity. 'She never had nothing like that,' she said firmly. 'Her and me, we used to have our coffee break mid-morning. Always had a cigarette with it, she did. You need one of them lighters, I said, seeing the way she got through umpteen boxes of matches. Get some young fellow to give you one. It was way back around Christmas, you see, and her birthday was in Jan.'

'So she may have had it for her birthday?'

'If she did, she never showed it to me. Never had a gas lighter, neither. My boy could get you one cost price, him being in the trade, I said, but she . . .'

Burden cut her short, his ears painfully anticipating the strident laugh the end of this story, however humourless, would certainly provoke. 'I'll see myself out,' he said.

'Mind the bucket!' Mrs Penistan called after him cheerfully. He went out among the daffodils. Everything was gold this morning, the sunshine, the pale bright flowers of spring and the little object in his pocket.

Kirkpatrick's car was on his driveway. Burden edged past it, his coat brushing the lettering and the mauve flowers.

'He says he's ill,' Mrs Kirkpatrick said in a loud harsh voice.

Burden showed her his card. It might have been an advertising brochure for all the notice she took of it.

'He says he's got a cold.' Into this last word she put an infinite scorn as if a cold were of all afflictions the least credible and the most bizarre. She let Burden in and, leaving him alone with the two wide-eyed silent children, said, 'You might as well sit down. I'll tell him you're here.'

Two or three minutes later Kirkpatrick came down. He was wearing a silk dressing gown under which he appeared to be fully clothed. Burden recalled similarly attired figures, but gayer and more debonair, who featured in those bedroom comedies of the thirties, still ruthlessly acted by local dramatic societies, to whose performances he was sometimes dragged by his wife. The setting of chintz-covered chairs and mock wood panelling enhanced this impression, but Kirkpatrick had a hangdog look. Had this been a real stage, the audience would have supposed him to have forgotten his opening lines. His face was unshaven. He managed a smile for his children and just touched the little girl's long fair hair.

'I'm going to make the beds,' said Mrs Kirkpatrick. It was not, Burden thought, a statement normally capable of being interpreted as a threat, but she succeeded in putting into it an almost sinister menace. Her husband gave her an encouraging nod, smiling as might one who wishes to foster his wife's interest in some unusual intellectual pursuit.

'I'm sorry to hear you're feeling unwell.'

'I expect it's psychological,' Kirkpatrick said. 'Yesterday afternoon upset me a good deal.'

A psychological cold, Burden thought. That's a new one. 'Pity,' he said aloud, 'because I'm afraid you may have to go through the mill again. Don't you think it would be better if we were to stop this farce about your being interested in Miss

Margolis for the sake of her brother's paintings?' Kirkpatrick's gaze travelled to the ceiling. From above violent noises could be heard as if his wife were not so much making the beds as breaking the furniture. 'We know very well you were her lover,' Burden said roughly. 'You threatened to kill her. On your own admission you were in Stowerton on Tuesday night.'

'Not so loud,' Kirkpatrick said, an agonised note in his voice. 'All right. It's all true. I've been thinking — that's why I feel so bloody — I've been thinking I'll have to tell you. It's not *her*,' he said, and he looked at the boy and girl. 'It's my kiddies. I don't want to lose my kiddies.' In a low voice he added, 'They always give custody to the mother, never mind what sort of mother she is.'

Burden gave an impatient shrug. 'Ever seen this before?'

The colour which flooded Kirkpatrick's face was the outward sign of an emotion Burden could not define. Guilt? Horror? He waited.

'It's Ann's.'

'Sure of that?'

'I saw her with it.' Dropping pretence, he said, 'She flaunted it in my face.'

Although it was warm in the office, Kirkpatrick kept his raincoat on. He had come of his own free will, Burden told Wexford, to talk in comparative comfort away from his wife.

'Did you give this lighter to Miss Margolis?' Wexford asked.

'Me? How could I afford a thing like that?'

'Tell me how you know it's hers.'

Kirkpatrick folded his hands and bowed his head.

'It was about a month ago,' he said, his voice scarcely above a whisper. 'I called for her but she was out. Margolis didn't seem to want to know me and I sat out in the car waiting for her to come back. Not this car,' he said with a small painful frown, 'the other one I had, the black one.'

He sighed and went on, his voice still low, 'She came back in hers about half an hour later — she'd been getting it serviced. I got out and went up to her. That lighter you've got there, it was on the shelf in her Alpine and I picked it up. I knew she hadn't had it before and when I saw the inscription,

"For Ann who lights my life", well, I knew her and I knew what sort of terms she'd be on with the giver.' A tiny thread of hysteria crept into his tone. 'I saw red. I could have killed her then. Christ, I didn't mean that!' He passed his hand across his mouth as if by this action he could wipe away the injudicious words. 'I didn't mean that. You know I didn't, don't you?'

Wexford said very smoothly, 'I know very little about you, Mr Kirkpatrick. You seem to have a split personality. One day you tell me Miss Margolis was merely the key into her brother's art gallery, the next that you were passionately jealous of her. Which personality is — er, the dominant one?'

'I loved her,' he said stonily. 'I was jealous.'

'Of course you were,' Wexford said scornfully, 'and you don't know a Bonnard from a bull's foot.'

'Go on about the lighter,' said Burden.

Instead of continuing, the man said wretchedly, 'My wife mustn't know. God, I was mad, crazy, ever to go near that girl.' Perhaps he noticed that Wexford made him no promises of discretion, noticed and understood the implication, for he said wildly, 'I didn't kill her, I don't know anything about it.'

'For a man in love you're not showing much grief, Mr Kirkpatrick. Let's go back to the lighter, shall we?'

Kirkpatrick shivered in the warm room. 'I was jealous as hell,' he said. 'She took the lighter from me and looked at it in a peculiar way.'

'What d'you mean, a peculiar way?'

'As if there was something to laugh at,' he said savagely, 'as if it was all one hell of a big joke.' He passed his hand across his forehead. 'I can see her now in that spotted fur coat, beautiful, free . . . I've never been free like that. She was holding that little bit of gold in her hand. She read out those words on the bottom, read them aloud, and went on laughing. "Who gave it to you?" I said. "He's got a pretty turn of phrase, my generous friend, hasn't he?" she said. "You'd never think of anything like that, Alan. All you ever do is add two and two and make it come to about sixteen." I don't know what she meant.' His fingers had left white marks where they had pressed the skin. 'You talk about showing grief,' he said. 'I loved her all right, or I thought I did. If you love someone you ought to be sorry when they're dead, oughtn't you? But, my God, if I couldn't have her, just me all to myself, I'd rather she was dead!'

'What were you doing in Stowerton on Tuesday night?' Wexford snapped.

'I don't have to tell you that.' He said it limply, not defiantly. Then he unbuttoned his coat as if he had suddenly grown hot.

'I wouldn't do that,' said Burden, 'not if you're going. As you said yesterday we can't keep you here.'

Kirkpatrick stood up. He looked weary to the point of distress. 'I can go?' He fumbled with his coat belt, his fingers jerking. 'There's nothing more I can tell you anyway.'

'Perhaps it'll come to you,' Wexford said. 'I'll tell you what, we'll drop by later in the day.'

'When the children are in bed,' Burden added. 'Maybe your wife knows what you were doing in Stowerton.'

'If you do that,' Kirkpatrick said fiercely, 'you'll lose me my children.' Breathing heavily, he turned his face to the wall.

'He can cool off in there with Drayton for company,' Wexford said over a cup of coffee in the Carousel Café. It was opposite the police station and he preferred it to their canteen. His entry always had the effect of clearing the place of less desirable elements and now they were alone with the espresso machine, the rubber plants and the juke box playing Mantovani.

'Funny Ruby recognising him like that,' said Burden, 'yet not being sure she recognised him as Geoff Smith.'

'I don't know, Mike. According to your moral code and maybe mine too, his behaviour wasn't exactly ethical, but it wasn't suspicious. She wouldn't have taken much notice of him.'

'Enough to know he was short, young and dark. Kirkpatrick's not that short, must be five feet eight or nine. It's the alias that puzzles me. Smith's obvious, but why Geoff? Why not John, for heaven's sake, or William?'

'Maybe Geoffrey is Kirkpatrick's middle name. We'll have to ask him.' Wexford drew his chair in from the gangway. A slim fair girl in skirt and sweater had come into the cafe and was making for a table beyond the room divider. 'Little Miss Grover,' he whispered. 'Let off the lead for once. If her father was up and about she wouldn't have the chance to pop out even for five minutes.'

'I've heard he's a bit of a tyrant,' Burden said, watching the girl. Her expression was dreamy, far away. 'Wonder what he was up to, slipping a disc? It's not as if he did manual work.'

'Save your detecting for what you get paid for,' said Wexford with a grin.

Linda Grover had ordered a raspberry milk shake. Burden watched her suck it up through a straw and look round with faint embarrassment as the straw made gurgling sounds in the dregs. A little drift of pink foam clung to her upper lip. Her hair, soft and satiny as a child's, was yet another golden eye-catcher on this golden day. 'Regular customer of theirs, Kirkpatrick,' he said. 'Buys his evening paper there. I wonder if he bought a knife too?'

'Let's go back and see,' said Wexford. The sun and the warmth made their walk across the street too short. 'Makes all the difference to the place, doesn't it?' he said as they passed up the steps and the cold stone walls of the police station enclosed them.

Drayton sat at one end of the office, Kirkpatrick at the other. They looked like strangers, indifferent, faintly antagonistic, waiting for a train. Kirkpatrick looked up, his mouth twitching.

'I thought you were never coming,' he said desperately to Wexford. 'If I tell you what I was doing in Stowerton you'll think I'm mad.'

Better a madman than a murderer, Wexford thought. He drew up a chair. 'Try me.'

'She wouldn't come out with me,' Kirkpatrick mumbled, 'on account of that damned car. I didn't believe she was going to that party, so,' he said defiantly, 'I went to Stowerton to check up on her. I got there at eight and I waited for hours and hours. She didn't come. God, I just sat there and waited and when she didn't come I knew she'd lied to me. I knew she'd found someone richer, younger, harder — Oh, what the hell!' He gave a painful cough. 'That's all I did,' he said, 'waited.' He lifted his eyes to Burden. 'When you found me yesterday morning at the cottage, I was going to tell her, ask her who she thought she was to cheat on me!'

Black against the sunlight, Drayton stood staring his contempt. What was he thinking? Wexford wondered. That he with his dark glow of virility, a glow that today was almost insolent, could never be brought so low?

'It got dark,' Kirkpatrick said. 'I parked my car by the side of Cawthorne's under a tree. They were making a hell of a racket in there, shouting and playing music. She never came. The only person to come out was a drunk spouting Omar Khayyam. I was there for three hours, oh, more than that . . .'

Wexford moved closer to the desk, folded his hands and rested his wrists on the rosewood. 'Mr Kirkpatrick,' he said gravely, 'this story of yours may be true, but you must realise that to me it sounds a bit thin. Can you produce anyone who might help to verify it?'

Kirkpatrick said bitterly, 'That's my affair, isn't it? You've done your job. I've never heard of the police hunting up witnesses to disprove their own case.'

'Then you have a lot to learn. We're not here to make "cases" but to see right is done.' Wexford paused. Three hours, he thought. That covered the time of arrival at Ruby's house, the time when the neighbour heard the crash, the time when two people staggered from the house. 'You must have seen the party guests arriving. Didn't they see you?'

'I put the car right down the side turning till it got dark, down by the side of the launderette.' His face grew sullen. 'That girl saw me,' he said.

'What girl?'

'The girl from Grover's shop.'

'You saw her at seven when you bought your evening paper,' Wexford said, trying to keep his patience. 'What you were doing at seven isn't relevant.'

A sulky flush settled on Kirkpatrick's face. 'I saw her again,' he said. 'In Stowerton.'

'You didn't mention it before.' This time impatience had got the upper hand and every word was edged with testiness.

'I'm sick of being made to look a fool,' Kirkpatrick said resentfully. 'I'm sick of it. If I get out of this I'm going to chuck in my job. Maybe someone's got to flog soap and powder and

464

lipstick, but not me. I'd rather be out of work.' He clenched his hands. 'If I get out of this,' he said.

'The girl,' said Wexford. 'Where did you see the girl?'

'I was down the side road by the back of the launderette, just a little way down. She was coming along in a car and she stopped at the traffic lights. I was standing by my car, then. Don't ask me what time it was. I wouldn't know.' He drew his breath in sharply. 'She looked at me and giggled. But she won't remember. I was just a joke to her, a customer who'd kept her late. She saw me standing by that thing and it was good for a laugh. *Lipdew!* I reckon she thinks about me and has a good laugh every time she washes her . . .'

Drayton's face had gone white and he stepped forward, his fingers closing into fists. Wexford interposed swiftly to cut off the last word, the word that might have been innocent or obscene.

'In that case,' he said, 'she will remember, won't she?'

CHAPTER ELEVEN

Sunshine is a great healer, especially when it is the first mild sunshine of spring. Paradoxically it cooled Drayton's anger. Crossing the street, he was once more in command of himself and he could think calmly and even derisively of Kirkpatrick. The man was an oaf, a poor thing with a pansy's job, emasculate, pointed at and pilloried by women. He had a pink and mauve car and he peddled cosmetics. Some day a perfume plutocrat would make him dress up in a harlequin suit with a powder puff on his head, make him knock on doors and give soap away to any housewife who could produce a coupon and sing out a slogan. He was a puppet and a slave.

The shop was empty. This must be a time of lull, lunchtime. The bell rang loudly because he was slow to close the door. Sunlight made the shop look frowstier than ever. Motes of dust hung and danced in its beams. He stood, listening to the pandemonium his ringing had called forth from upstairs, running feet, something that sounded like the dropping of a saucepan lid, a harsh bass voice calling, 'Get down the shop, Lin, for God's sake.'

She came in, running, a tea towel in her hand. When she saw him the anxiety went out of her face and she looked petulant. 'You're early,' she said, 'hours early.' Then she smiled and there was something in her eyes he was not sure that he liked, a look of conquest and of complacency. He supposed that she thought him impatient to be with her. Their date was for the evening and he had come at half past one. That was what they always wanted, to make you weak, malleable in their long frail hands. Then they kicked you aside. Look at Kirkpatrick. 'I can't come out,' she said. 'I've got the shop to see to.'

'You can come where I'm taking you,' Drayton said harshly. He forgot his rage at Kirkpatrick's words, the passion of last night, the tenderness that had begun. What was she, after all? A shop assistant — and what a shop! — a shop girl, afraid of her father, a skivvy with a tea cloth. 'Police station,' he said.

Her eyes went very wide. 'You what? Are you trying to be funny or something?'

He had heard the stories about Grover, the things he sold over the counter — and under it. 'It's nothing to do with your father,' he said.

'What do they want me for? Is it about the advert?'

'In a way,' he said. 'Look, it's nothing, just routine.'

'Mark,' she said, 'Mark, you tried to frighten me.' The sun flowed down her body in a river of gold. It's only a physical thing, he thought, just an itch and a rather worse one than usual. Repeat last night often enough and it would go. She came up to him, smiling, a little nervous. 'I know you don't mean it, but you mustn't frighten me.' The smile teased him. He stood quite still, the sun between them like a sword. He wanted her so badly that it took all his strength and all his self-control to turn and say, 'Let's go. Tell your parents you won't be long.' She was gone two minutes, leaving behind her a breath of something fresh and sweet to nullify the smell of old worn-out things. He moved about the shop, trying to find things to look at that were not cheap or meretricious or squalid. When she came back he saw that she had neither changed her clothes nor put on make-up. This both pleased and riled him. It seemed to imply an arrogance, a careless disregard of other people's opinion, which matched his own. He did not want them to have things in common. Enough that they should desire each other and find mutual satisfaction at a level he understood.

'How's your father?' he said and when he said it he realised it was a foolish catch-phrase. She laughed at him.

'Did you mean that or were you fooling?'

'I mean it.' Damn her for reading thoughts!

'He's all right,' she said. 'No, he's not. He says he's in agony. You can't tell, can you, with what he's got? It's not as if there was anything to show.'

'Seems to me he's a slave driver,' he said.

'They're all slave drivers. Better your own dad than some man.' At the door she basked in the sun, stretching her body like a long golden animal. 'When they talk to me,' she said, 'you'll be there, won't you?'

'Sure I'll be there.' He closed the door behind them. 'Don't do that,' he said, 'or I'll want to do what I did last night.' You could want it like mad, he thought, and still laugh. You could with this girl. My God, he thought, my God!

There was, Wexford thought, something between those two. No doubt Drayton had been chatting her up on the way. Only that would account for the look she had given him before sitting down, a look that seemed to be asking for permission. Well, he had always supposed Drayton susceptible and the girl was pretty enough. He had seen her about since she was a child but it seemed to him that he had never before noticed the exquisite shape of her head, the peculiar virginal grace with which she moved.

'Now, Miss Grover,' he said, 'I just want you to answer a few routine questions.' She smiled faintly at him. They ought not to be allowed to look like that, he thought wryly, so demure, so perfect and so untouched. 'I believe you know a Mr Kirkpatrick? He's a customer of yours.'

'Is he?' Drayton was standing behind her chair and she looked up at him, perhaps for reassurance. Wexford felt mildly irritated. Who the hell did Drayton think he was? Her solicitor?

'If you don't recognise the name, perhaps you know his car, You probably saw it outside just now.'

'A funny pink car with flowers on it?' Wexford nodded. 'Oh, I know *him*.'

'Very well. Now I want you to cast your mind back to last Tuesday night. Did you go to Stowerton that evening?'

'Yes,' she said quickly, 'I always do on Tuesdays. I take our washing to the launderette in my dad's car.' She paused, weariness coming into her young fresh face. 'My dad's ill and Mum goes to a whist drive most nights.'

Why play on my sympathies? Wexford thought. The hint of tyranny seemed to be affecting Drayton. His dark face looked displeased and his mouth had tightened. 'All right, Drayton,' he said, not unpleasantly, 'I shan't need you any longer.'

When they were alone, she said before he had time to ask her, 'Did Mr What's-his-name see me? I saw him.'

'Are you sure?'

'Oh, yes. I know him. I'd served him with an evening paper earlier.'

'It wasn't just the car you identified, Miss Grover, not just an empty car?'

She put up one hand to smooth the soft shiny knob of hair. 'I didn't know the car. He used to have a different one.' She gave a nervous giggle. 'When I saw him in it and knew it was his it made me laugh. He thinks such a lot of himself, you see, and then that car . . .'

Wexford watched her. She was far from being at ease. On her answer to his next question, the significant question, so much depended. Kirkpatrick's fate hung upon it. If he had lied . . .

'What time was it?' he asked.

'Late,' she said firmly. Her lips were like two almond petals, her teeth perfect. It seemed a pity she showed them so seldom. 'I'd been to the launderette. I was going home. It must have been just after a quarter past nine.' He sighed within himself. Whoever had been at Ruby's had certainly been there at nine fifteen. I'd stopped at the traffic lights,' she said virtuously. God, he thought, she's like a child, she doesn't differentiate between me and a traffic cop. Did she expect him to congratulate her? 'He'd parked that car down by the side of the garage . . .'

'Cawthorne's?'

She nodded eagerly. 'I saw him in it. I know it was him.'

'Sure of the time?'

He had noticed she wore no watch on the slender wrist.

'I'd just come from the launderette. I'd seen the clock.'

There was nothing more he could do. Perhaps it was all true. They had no body, no real evidence against Kirkpatrick after this. A fatherly impulse made him smile at her and say, 'All right, Miss Grover, you can run along now. Mr Kirkpatrick ought to be grateful to you.'

For a moment he thought the shot had gone home, then he wasn't sure. The look in her big grey eyes was hard to interpret. He thought it might be a relieved happiness, no doubt because he was terminating the interview. Her departure seemed to deprive the office of some of its brightness, although the sun still shone. Her scent remained, a perfume that was too old for her innocence.

'That girl was got at,' Burden said wrathfully.

'You could be right there.'

'We should never have let Kirkpatrick out of here yesterday afternoon.'

Wexford sighed. 'What had we got to hold him on, Mike? Oh, I agree he probably thought up that alibi between yesterday afternoon and this morning. I daresay he went straight round to Grover's when he left here. That girl wasn't at ease.'

'Show me a Grover who wouldn't do anything for money,' Burden said. 'Like father, like daughter.'

'Poor kid. Not much of a life for her, is it? Cooped up all day in that dirty little hole and carting the washing about in the evenings because her mother's playing whist.'

Burden eyed him uneasily. The expression on his chief's face was tolerant, almost tender, and it puzzled him. If he had not known Wexford to be almost as uxorious a husband as himself, he might have believed . . . But, no, there were limits.

'If he was outside Cawthorne's, sir,' he said, 'and if he was there at half-past nine, he's clear and we're wasting our time with him. But if the girl's lying and he did it, he could have disposed of Anita's body practically anywhere between here and the Scottish border. She could be lying in a ditch anywhere you can name in half a dozen counties.'

'And where the body is the weapon is, too.'

'Or he could have gone home to a place he knew and dumped her in the thickest part of those pine woods in Cheriton Forest.'

'But until we know more, Mike, searching for that body is impracticable, sheer waste of time.'

'I wouldn't mind having a go at Kirkpatrick over it,' Burden said with sudden ferocity. 'Having a go at him in his wife's presence.'

'No. We'll give him a rest for a while. The king-size question is, did he bribe that girl?' Wexford grinned sagely. 'I'm hoping she may feel inclined to confide in Drayton.'

'Drayton?'

'Attractive to the opposite sex, don't you think? That sulky brooding look gets them every time.' Wexford's little glinting eyes were suddenly unkind. 'Unless you fancy yourself in the role? Sorry, I forgot. Your wife wouldn't like it. Martin and I aren't exactly cut out to strut before a wanton ambling nymph . . .'

'I'd better have a word with him then.'

'Not necessary. Unless I'm much mistaken, this is something we can safely leave to Nature.'

CHAPTER TWELVE

The lighter had been lying on the desk in the sun and when Wexford picked it up it felt warm to his hand. The tendrils and leaves of its vine design glowed softly. 'Griswold's been getting at me,' he said. At the mention of the Chief Constable's name Burden looked sour. 'According to him, this is not to be allowed to develop into a murder enquiry. Evidence inconclusive and so on. We can have a couple more days to scout around and that's our lot.'

Burden said bitterly, 'The whole place turned upside-down just to get Monkey Matthews another few months inside?'

'The stain on the carpet was from the fruit of Ruby's imagination, Anita Margolis is on holiday, the couple who staggered down the path were drunk and Kirkpatrick is simply afraid of his wife.' Wexford paused, tossing the lighter up and down reflectively. 'I quote the powers that be,' he said.

'Martin's watching Kirkpatrick's house,' said Burden. 'He hasn't been to work today. Drayton's still presumably hanging around with that girl. Do I call them off, sir?'

'What else is there for them to do? Things are slack enough otherwise. As for the other questions I'd like answered, Griswold isn't interested and I can't see our finding the answer to them in two days, anyway.'

Silently Burden put out his hand for the lighter and contemplated it, his narrow lips pursed. Then he said, 'I'm wondering if they're the same questions that are uppermost in my mind. Who gave her the lighter and was it sold around here? Who was the drunk outside Cawthorne's, the man who spoke to Kirkpatrick?'

Wexford opened his desk drawer and took out his *Weekend Telegraph*. 'Remember this bit?' he asked. 'About her breaking off her engagement to Richard Fairfax? I'll bet it was him. Mrs Cawthorne said he left the party around eleven and Cawthorne said he dumped a brandy glass on one of his diesel pumps.'

'Sounds like a poet,' Burden said gloomily.

'Now, then, remember what I said about Goering.' Wexford grinned at the inspector's discomfiture. 'According to Kirkpatrick he was spouting Omar Khayyám. I used to be hot on old Khayyám myself. I wonder what he said?

' "I often wonder what the vintners buy.
One half so precious as the goods they sell?"

'Or maybe he scattered and slayed with his enchanted sword.'

Burden took this last seriously. 'He can't have done that. He got to Cawthorne's at eight and he didn't leave till eleven.'

'I know. I was fooling. Anyway, Griswold says no hunting up of fresh suspects without a positive lead. That's my directive and I have to abide by it.'

'Still, I don't suppose there'd be any objection if I went to enquire at a few jewellers, would there? We'd have a positive lead if anyone remembered selling it to Kirkpatrick or even Margolis himself, come to that.' Burden pocketed the lighter. Wexford's face had a dreamy look, preoccupied but not discouraging, so he said briskly, 'Early closing today. I'd better get cracking before all the shops shut.'

Left alone, the Chief Inspector sat searching his mind for a peculiarly significant couplet. When he found it, he chuckled.

'What lamp has destiny to guide
Her little children stumbling in the dark?'

There ought to be an answer. It came to him at last but it was not inspiring. 'A blind understanding, Heaven replied,' he said aloud to the glass sculpture. Something like that was what they needed, he thought.

Kirkpatrick was leaning against the bonnet of his car which he had parked on the forecourt of the Olive and Dove, watching the entrance to Grover's shop. Ever since breakfast time Detective Sergeant Martin had been keeping his house and his gaudy car under observation. Mrs Kirkpatrick had gone shopping with the children and just as Martin, from his vantage point under

the perimeter trees of Cheriton Forest, was beginning to abandon hope, the salesman had emerged and driven off towards
Kingsmarkham. Following him had been easy. The car was a
quarry even an intervening bus and hostile traffic lights, changing to red at the wrong moment, could not protect for long.

It was a warm morning, the air soft and faintly scented with
the promise of summer. A delicate haze hung over Kingsmarkham
which the sun tinted a positive gold. Someone came out from the
florist's to put a box of stiff purple tulips on the display bench.

Kirkpatrick had begun to polish the lenses of a pair of sun
glasses on the lapel of his sports jacket. Then he strolled to the
pavement edge. Martin crossed the road before him, mingling
with the shoppers. Instead of making directly for the newsagent's, Kirkpatrick hesitated outside the flower shop, looking
at wet velvety violets, hyacinths in pots, at daffodils, cheap now
because they were abundant. His eyes went to the alley wall no
sun ever reached, but he turned away quickly and hurried into
the York Street turning. Martin took perhaps fifteen seconds to
make up his mind. He was only a step from Grover's. The bell
rang as he opened the door.

'Yes?' Linda Grover came in from the door at the back.

Blinking his eyes to accustom himself to the dimness,
Martin said vaguely, 'Just looking.' He knew her by hearsay but
he was sure she didn't know him. 'I want a birthday card,' he
said. She shrugged indifferently and picked up a magazine.
Martin wandered into the depths of the shop. Each time the bell
tinkled he glanced up from the card stand. A man came in to
buy cigars, a woman with a pekingese which snuffled among the
boxes on the floor. Its owner passed the card stand to browse
among the dog-eared books in Grover's lending library. Martin
blessed her arrival. One person dawdling in the shadows was
suspicious, two unremarkable. He hoped she would take a long
time choosing her book. The dog stuck its face up his trouser
leg and touched bare flesh with a wet nose.

They were the only customers when, five minutes later,
Alan Kirkpatrick entered the shop with a red and gold wrapped
parcel under his arm.

Red and gold were the trade colours of Joy Jewels. Scarlet

carpet covered the floor, gilt *papier mâché* torsos stood about on red plinths, each figure as many-armed as some oriental goddess. Pointed, attenuated fingers were hung with glittering ropes of rhinestone. Schitz and quartz and other gems that were perhaps no more than skilfully cut glass made prisms which caught and refracted the flickering sunlight. On the counter lay a roll of wrapping paper, bright red patterned with gold leaves. The assistant was putting away his scissors when Burden came in and held up the lighter between them.

'We don't sell lighters. Anyway, I doubt if anyone round here would stock a thing like that.'

Burden nodded. He had received the same answer at four other jewellers' already.

'It's a work of art,' the assistant said, and he smiled as people will when shown something beautiful and rare. 'Eight or nine years ago it might have come from this very place.'

Eight or nine years ago Anita Margolis had been little more than a child. 'How come?' Burden asked without much interest.

'Before we took over from Scatcherd's. They were said to be the best jeweller's between London and Brighton. Old Mr Scatcherd still lives overhead. If you wanted to talk to him . . .'

'Too long ago, I'm afraid,' Burden cut in. 'It'd be a waste of my time and his.' Much too long. It was April and at Christmas Anita Margolis had been lighting her cigarettes with matches.

He walked up York Street under the plane trees. The misty sun shone on their dappled grey and yellow bark and their tiny new leaves made an answering shadow pattern on the pavement. The first thing he noticed when he came into the High Street was Kirkpatrick's car outside the Olive and Dove. If Martin had lost him . . . But, no. There was the sergeant's own Ford nudging the end of the yellow band. Burden paused on the Kingsbrook Bridge, idling his time away watching the swans, a cob and a pen wedded to each other and to their river. The brown water rippled on gently over round mottled stones. Burden waited.

The girl's face became sullen when she saw Kirkpatrick. She looked him up and down and closed her magazine, keeping her place childishly with one finger poked between the pages.

'Yes?'

'I was passing,' Kirkpatrick said awkwardly. 'I thought I'd come in and thank you.'

Martin selected a birthday card. He assumed a whimsical, faintly sentimental expression so that the woman with the pekingese might suppose he was admiring the verse it contained.

'This is for you, a token of my gratitude.' Kirkpatrick slid his parcel between the newspapers and the chocolate bar tray.

'I don't want your presents,' the girl said stonily. 'I didn't do anything. I really saw you.' Her big grey eyes were frightened. Kirkpatrick leaned towards her, his brown curls almost touching her own fair head.

'Oh, yes,' he said insinuatingly, 'you saw me, but the point is . . .'

She interrupted him sharply, 'It's all over, it's done with. They won't come bothering me any more.'

'Won't you even look inside the box?'

She turned away, her head hanging like a spring flower on a delicate stalk. Kirkpatrick took off the red and gold wrapping, the tissue paper and from a box padded with pink cotton wool, produced a string of glittering beads. They were little sharp metallic stones in rainbow colours. Rhinestones, Martin thought.

'Give it to your wife,' the girl said. She felt at the neck of her sweater until something silvery trickled over her thin fingers. 'I don't want it. I've got real jewellery.'

Kirkpatrick's mouth tightened. He stuffed the necklace into one pocket, the mass of crumpled paper into the other. When he had gone, banging the shop door behind him, Martin went up to the girl, the birthday card in his hand.

She read the legend. "My darling Granny"?' she said derisively and he supposed she was looking at his greying hair. 'Are you sure it's this one you want?' He nodded and paid his ninepence. Her eyes followed him and when he looked back she was smiling a little closed-lip smile. On the bridge he encountered Burden.

'What's this then?' said the inspector, eyeing the card with the same mockery. Drayton, he thought reluctantly, would have

been more subtle. He stared down at the river bed and the
stone arch reflected in brown and amber, while Martin told him
what he had heard.

'Offered her a necklace,' Martin said. 'Showy sort of thing
wrapped up in red and gold paper.'

'I wonder,' Burden said thoughtfully. 'I wonder if he always
shops at Joy Jewels, if he bought a lighter there years and years
ago when it was Scatcherd's . . .'

'Had it engraved recently for this girl?'

'Could be.' Burden watched Kirkpatrick seated at the
wheel of his car. Presently he got out and entered the saloon
bar of the Olive and Dove. 'There goes your man,' he said to
Martin, 'drowning his sorrows. You never know, when he's
screwed up his courage he may come offering his trinkets to the
Chief Inspector. He certainly won't give them to his wife.'

The mist had begun to lift and there was real warmth in the
sunshine. Burden took off his raincoat and laid it over his arm.
He would have one last go at finding where that lighter came
from, make one last enquiry, and if it was fruitless, give up and
meet Wexford for lunch at the Carousel. But was there any
point, was it too long a shot? He could do with a cup of tea first
and the Carousel would already be serving lunches. The thought
came to him that there was a little place, not a hundred yards
from the bridge, a small café where they served good strong tea
and pastries at all hours. He cut up the path between the
cottages and came out in the Kingsbrook Road. Just past the
bend it was, in the ground floor of one of the Georgian houses.

Strange how heavily the mist seemed to lie in this part of
the town, on high ground too and coloured a deep ochreish
yellow. He passed the big houses and stopped on the brow of
the low hill.

Through the clouds of what he now realised to be not mist
but plaster dust, a contractor's board faced him: *Doherty for
Demolition. What Goes Up Must Come Down!* Beyond, where the
block which had housed his cafe had stood, was a cliff-face of
battered wall, roof, floors, façade torn from it. Among the
rubble of what had once been elegant stonework stood a
wooden hut on the threshold of which three workmen sat eating
sandwiches.

Burden shrugged and turned away. The old town was going, gradually and cruelly. Beauty and grace were inconvenient. They pulled down the old buildings, put up splendid new ones like the police station. New buildings needed new drains and new wiring and digging up the roads killed the old trees. New shops replaced the old, rhinestones and gilt goddesses the best jeweller's between London and Brighton . . . That reminded him. It was useless to waste time regretting the past. If he was to get no tea he certainly wasn't going to delay his lunch. One more enquiry first, though.

Mr Scatcherd reminded Burden of a very old and very amiable parrot. The big curving nose came down over a genial mouth and the bird-like impression was sustained by a bright yellow waistcoat and baggy, shaggy trousers suggestive of plumage. The rooms over the shop might have been a perch or an eyrie, they were so airy and lofty, and their windows looked into the tops of whispering greening trees.

He was shown into a living room apparently unchanged since it had been furnished in the eighties. But instead of the drab browns and reds associated with the nineteenth century, here in the plush and velvet was peacock green, glowing puce and blue. A chandelier that hung from the ceiling winked in the blaze of sun like a handful of diamonds dropped and suspended in space. Fat cushions with gold tassels had cheeks of shiny green shot-silk. There were pieces here, Burden thought as he sat down in a brocade wing chair, that Cawthorne would give his sodden blue eyes to possess.

'I usually have a glass of madeira and a biscuit about this time,' said Mr Scatcherd. 'Perhaps you'll do me the honour of joining me?'

'It's very kind of you,' Burden said. The former variety of refreshment he had never sampled and he was still regretting the depredations which had deprived him of his tea as well as the town of its glory. 'I'd like to.'

A sweet smile told him he had been right to accept. 'Just the shade of a garnet,' the old jeweller said when he brought the wine on a japanned tray. 'Not a ruby.' A severity, the didactic crispness of the connoisseur, had entered his rather fluting voice. 'A ruby is quite different. What have you brought me to look at?'

'This.'

The hand that took it was grey and clawed, the nails long but scrupulously clean.

'Could it have come from around here? Or do you only get things like this in London?'

Mr Scatcherd was not listening to him. He had taken the lighter to the window and he was nodding his head precisely while screwing his old eye up against a pocket glass.

' "*Les grappes de ma vigne*",' he said at last. Burden sat up eagerly. 'That's the name of the design, you know. The grapes of my vine. Baudelaire, of course. Perhaps you are not familiar with the poem. Highly appropriate for a lover's gift.' He smiled with gentle pleasure, turning the lighter over. 'And it was a lover's gift,' he said as he read the inscription. 'A pretty greeting for a lady.'

Burden had no idea what he meant. 'You know it?' he said. 'You've seen it before?'

'Several years ago.' The chandelier flashed pink, violet and green prism spots on the walls. 'Seven, eight years.' Mr Scatcherd put away his glass and beamed with satisfaction. The rainbow lights flickered on his bald head. 'I know the design,' he said, 'and I well remember the inscription.'

'But that engraving was done recently!'

'Oh, no. Before I retired, before Joy Jewels took over.' A smile of mocking disparagement curved his mouth and made his eyes twinkle as he spoke the name. 'My dear inspector,' he said. 'I ought to know. I sold the thing.'

CHAPTER THIRTEEN

'Who did he sell it to? Kirkpatrick?'

Burden hung up his raincoat on the office rack and decided to do without it for the rest of the day. He glanced at the lab reports Wexford was studying and said:

'I don't understand it. Old Scatcherd hasn't sold anything for more than seven years and at that time Anita wasn't here, probably didn't even know such a place as Kingsmarkham existed. Kirkpatrick wasn't here either. Those houses where he lives have only been up a year. Besides, Scatcherd's got a wonderful memory for a man of his age and he's never had a customer called Kirkpatrick.'

'Look, Mike,' Wexford said, giving his reports a glance of disgust, 'are we going to be able to find out who did buy this damned lighter?'

'Scatcherd's looking it up in his books. He says it'll take him a couple of hours. But, you know, sir, I'm beginning to think Anita just found it, picked it up in the street and kept it because the inscription was appropriate.'

'Found it!' Wexford roared. 'You mean someone lost it and Anita found it and then she lost it again at Ruby's? Don't be so daft. It's not a key or an old umbrella. It's a valuable article and I reckon it's the key to this whole thing. If it was lost, why wasn't the loss reported to us? No, you get back to old Scatcherd, assist him with your young eyes.' Burden looked pleased at this as Wexford had known he would. 'You never know what you may discover,' he said. 'Cawthorne may have bought it for her or Margolis himself or at any rate someone who owns a green car. In all this we have to remember that however oddly Kirkpatrick may be behaving he doesn't have and never had a green car.'

When Burden had gone he returned to his perusal of the lab reports. He read them carefully, suppressing a disgusted rage. Never in all his experience had he come across anything so negative. The evidence the carpet afforded would have been satisfactory only to the manufacturers of Ruby's favourite detergents. Fingerprints on her car corresponded to those in Anita Margolis's bedroom. They were hers and hers alone. The ocelot coat gave even less information. An analyst had suggested that the scent with which it was redolent might be Guerlain's *Chant d'Aromes*. Wexford, who was good on perfumes, could have told them that himself. In one pocket was a crumpled sheet of trading stamps. She had probably bought her petrol at Cawthorne's. Wexford sighed. Who had brought that car back at one in the morning and where had it been all the evening? Why had her killer, Kirkpatrick or another, called himself Geoff Smith when it would have been so much more natural and indeed expected for him to remain anonymous?

A pile of thick books, some of them ancient and all bound in dark green morocco, was stacked at Mr Scatcherd's feet. Burden stepped over them and sat down in the brocade chair.

'I've been completely through the last three,' Mr Scatcherd said, showing no sign of a diminution of patience. 'That takes us right back to nineteen fifty-eight.' He had perched a pair of gold-rimmed glasses on his parrot's nose and he glanced over the top of them, smiling pleasantly.

Burden shrugged. It was all getting beyond him. Nine years ago Anita Margolis had been fourteen. Did men give valuable gold cigarette lighters — any cigarette lighters, come to that — to girls of fourteen? Not in his world. Whatever world this was in which he found himself, it was a topsy-turvy one of nightmare inconsistency. The lighter had been sold in Kingsmarkham and in Kingsmarkham its recipient had lived and gone out to meet her death. Simple on the face of it, but for ages and times and a host of confusing facts . . .

'I thought it was new,' he said.

'Oh, no. I knew the artist who made it. He's dead now but in his day he was a fine goldsmith. His name was Benjamin Marks but when I called him Ben it was another master I thought of. Perhaps you can guess whom I mean.' Burden looked at him blankly. 'Cellini, inspector,' Mr Scatcherd said almost reverently. 'The great Benvenuto. My Ben was a naturalist too in his way. It was always to Nature that he went for his inspiration. I remember a standard rose, designed for a lady's powder case. You could see the stamens in the heart of each tiny flower. He made this and inscribed it. It was done to a gentleman's order . . .'

'But whose order, Mr Scatcherd? Until I know that I'm no further.'

'We shall find it. It helps my memory to talk about it.' Mr Scatcherd turned the thick watered pages, running a long fingernail down the margins. 'We're coming up to the end of nineteen fifty-eight now. Do you know, each time I come to the end of a book I feel I'm getting warm. I have a faint recollection of Christmas and I seem to remember selling a fine ring at the same time.' The last page. Burden could see a date in December printed at the top of it. He had a wild sensation that if the record of the sale could not be found in this book or the next, Mr Scatcherd would keep on searching, for hours perhaps or days, until he came back to the first entry made by his father in eighteen eighty-six.

The jeweller looked up with a smile but he had worn this continually and Burden could see no particularly encouraging sign of gratification on his wrinkled face. 'Ah, yes, here we are,' he murmured. 'The ring I mentioned. A diamond and sapphire hoop to Mr Rogers of Pomfret Hall. For his wife, no doubt, or that poor daughter of his. There was insanity there, if I remember.' Nodding sagely, he continued his scanning. 'Not the same day, I'm sure. Perhaps the next day . . . Now, inspector, we're getting somewhere.'

Hope surging back, Burden got up to take the book from him but Mr Scatcherd held fast to it. 'Here we are,' he said again, but this time with a note of quiet triumph. 'Gold cigarette lighter to order: *"Les grappes de ma vigne"*, Benjamin Marks; inscribed: "For Ann who lights my life". Not much help to you, I'm afraid. Such a common name. Still, there's an address.'

Burden was unbearably intrigued. 'What name?' he asked excitedly.

'Smith. It was sold on December 15th, 1958 to a Mr Geoffrey Smith.'

No doubt about it, Drayton was taking his duties seriously,

Wexford thought as he came into the Carousel Café for his lunch. Behind the room divider a hooded coat could be seen lying over the back of a chair, one of its sleeves caught on the fleshy leaves of a rubber plant. Drayton's back was towards the door but there was something concentrated and intense in the set of his shoulders. He seemed to be in animated, not to say amorous, conversation with his companion, for their faces were close. It afforded Wexford considerable amusement to see Drayton raise his hand to cup the girl's white chin and to watch her delicate tentative smile. They had not observed him. Indeed, he thought, it would not be stretching a point to say they had eyes only for each other. A bit hard on the girl, he reflected, and he was wondering how much longer this simulated attention would be necessary when Burden found him.

'What are you eating?'

'Shepherd's pie,' said Wexford. 'Must be ten minutes since I ordered.' He grinned. 'I daresay they've had to go out and shoot a shepherd.'

'I've found him,' Burden explained and while he did so the Chief Inspector's expression changed from interest to scowling incredulity.

Burden said apologetically, 'You said yourself, sir, some people really are called Smith.'

'That was a funny,' Wexford growled. 'Where does he live?'

'Sewingbury.' The shepherd's pie came and Burden ordered a portion for himself. 'I don't understand why he isn't on the electoral register. He can't very well be under age.'

'Not unless we're dealing with a little boy buying cigarette lighters for a little girl.' Wexford raised a forkful of his pie to his mouth and made a face. 'I'd like to get our lab to work on this mashed potato,' he said. 'If I'm not mistaken it's been in a packet since it was dug out of the ground.' He pushed the bowl of green pepper salad the Carousel served with everything to the extreme edge of the table. 'Smith could be a foreigner who's changed his name but never got naturalised.'

Burden pondered. He felt he would think better on a full stomach. The mashed potato might be suspect but it was brown and crisp and the savoury smell whetted his appetite. 'We've assumed all the time Smith was a pseudonym,' he said, brightening as the hot steaming plate was set before him. 'Now it suddenly looks as if everything is going to be plain sailing. How about this, sir? Smith's known Anita for years and the friendship was renewed when she and Margolis came to live here. He booked the room on Saturday, going to Ruby's in his black car which he sold the following day or the Monday, exchanging it for a new green one. But when he gave his name to Ruby he had no idea he'd have anything to hide. An attack on Anita was the last thing he planned.' When Wexford nodded, he continued more confidently. 'She broke her date with Kirkpatrick, not on account of his car, but just because she was fed-up with him and because she'd made a new one with Smith. She met Smith somewhere, parked her own car and went to Stowerton with him in his. They quarrelled in Ruby's room, very likely over Kirkpatrick, and he attacked her with a knife or a razor. He managed to get her out of the house and into the car, but she died and he dumped her body or hid it at this place of his in Sewingbury. Later, when there weren't many people about, he collected her car and returned it to Pump Lane.'

'Who knows?' Wexford pushed aside his empty plate. 'It fits. Kirkpatrick comes into it only as a rival and all his worries are genuinely caused by fear of his wife's revenge.'

It was at this point that Burden, reaching for the pepper, saw Drayton. 'Then we can nip that little intrigue in the bud,' he said.

'Before he gets carried away, eh?' Wexford stood up. 'Yes, we'll accept Kirkpatrick's story for the time being. I don't fancy Griswold will consider Smith a new suspect, do you?' How preoccupied Drayton looked, almost entranced. 'I don't know that I want my young men amorously involved with a Grover, except in the line of business.' He crossed to the cash desk to pay the bill and dropped on one knee to tie his shoelace. Beneath the tablecloth he saw a long bare leg pressed against Drayton's knee. Playing footsie, he said to himself. He took his change and, approaching the two in the corner, gave a slight cough. Drayton lifted his face and instead of cold efficiency Wexford saw a dreamy rapture. 'Feel like a trip to Sewingbury, Drayton?'

The boy was on his feet before the words were out and once more the mask was assumed.

'I'm just coming, sir.'

'Finish your coffee.' By God, that girl was a beauty! The kind that bloomed for half a dozen years and then shrivelled like a straw before they were thirty, the golden kind that came to dust.

Geoffrey Smith's flat was one of four in a converted mansion on the far side of Sewingbury, a gracious Georgian house built perhaps at the same time as St Catherine's convent on to which it backed. A stately staircase took them up to a gallery. The wall facing them had once contained several doors but these had been boarded up and now only two remained, the entrances to flats one and two. Number two was on the left. Wexford rang the bell.

The grandeur of the place scarcely fitted in with Burden's theory of a knife or a razor. On the other hand, a customer of Mr Scatcherd's might well live here. All the same, Burden was not prepared for the lofty space which opened before them when the door swung inwards, and for a moment he looked not at the woman who stood on the threshold, but at the vast apartment behind her which led into another as large and ended finally in a pair of immense windows. It was more like a picture gallery — but for its bare walls — than a flat. Light fell from the windows in two huge twin rectangles and she stood in the darker split between them.

As soon as he met her eyes Burden knew that he had seen her before. She was the woman who had tried to sell her jewels to Knobby Clark.

'Mrs Smith?' Wexford said.

Burden had scarcely expected her to welcome them, but her reaction astonished him. There was shock and horror in her eyes. It was as if, he thought, analysing, she had been tortured for years and then, just as the respite had come, someone had threatened her with a renewal of torment.

'What do you mean?' she said, and she enunciated each word separately and slowly.

'I asked you if you are Mrs Smith, Mrs Geoffrey Smith?'

Her tired, once pretty face grew hard. 'Please go,' she said tightly. Wexford gave her one of his tough implacable looks and showed her his card. It had seldom evoked so gratifying a response. The hard look went with a gasp of relief. She smiled wryly, then laughed. 'You'd better come in.' Suddenly she was cordial, the ladylike creature Burden had seen in Knobby Clark's shop. 'I can't think what you want,' she said. He was sure she had not recognised him. 'But I'm evidently not in danger from you. I mean — well, before I knew who you were, I thought you were rather a lot of strange men for a lone woman to let into her home.'

A thin excuse for such a display of disgusted horror. In spite of the sun it was cold inside the flat. In winter it would be unbearable. They could see no sign of a radiator as they tramped through the first huge room and came into the place where the long windows were. Ivory-coloured double doors, the paint chipped on their mouldings, closed behind them. The furniture was much too small and much too new, but not new enough to be smart. No attempt had been made to achieve harmony between furniture and a noble decor. The elegant gleaming windows towered and shone between skimped bits of flowered cotton like society women fallen on evil days.

'I'd like to see Mr Smith. When do you expect him back?'

'I'd like to see him too.' Now her brown-skinned curly face was alight with a curious half-amused rue. The glasses bobbed on her short nose. Since she had discovered who they were all her fear had gone and she looked like a woman infinitely capable of laughter, a great deal of which might be directed against herself. 'Geoffrey divorced me five years ago,' she said.

'Do you know where he is now, Mrs Smith?'

'Not Mrs Smith, Mrs Anstey. Noreen Anstey. I married again.' She gave Wexford a wise elderly look, a look of wide and perhaps unpleasant experience. 'I think you might tell me why you want him.'

'Routine enquiries, Mrs Anstey.' She was the last woman in the world to be fobbed off with that one, he thought. Her eyes clouded with reproach.

'It must be something very mild,' she said, the gentle mocking smile sending sharp wrinkles up around her eyes. 'Geoff is one of the most honest people I ever met. Don't you think he looks honest?'

Wexford was greedy for the photograph and when it was handed to him, a large studio portrait, he almost grabbed it. A swarthy, pleasant face, black hair, a pipe in the mouth. The Chief Inspector was too old a hand at the game to give opinions as to honesty on this evidence. He was still studying it when Burden said:

'Have you ever seen this before?' He put the lighter into her hands. They shook a little as she took it and she gave a gasp of delight, bringing it close to her face. 'My lighter!' He stared at her. 'And I thought it had gone for ever!' She tried to make it ignite, shrugged, her face still radiant. 'Where did you find it? This is wonderful! Won't you have a cup of tea? Do let me make you some tea.'

She sat on the edge of her chair and she reminded Wexford of a child on Christmas morning. Smith's photograph was in her lap, the lighter in her hand. He had guessed her age at thirty-eight or thirty-nine but suddenly she looked much younger. There was a wedding ring on each hand. One was chased and patterned rather like the lighter she held, the other more like a Woolworth curtain ring.

'Now, let's get this clear,' Wexford said. 'This lighter is yours? You said your name was Noreen.'

'So it is.' He was sure he could believe her. Every word she spoke had the clear ring of honesty. 'Noreen Ann Anstey. I always used to be known as Ann. First I was Ann Greystock and that was fine; then Ann Smith which is dull but not so bad. But Ann Anstey? It's terrible, it's like a stammer. So I use my first name.'

'Your first husband gave you the lighter?' Burden put in.

'For Christmas. Let me see — nineteen fifty-eight it must have been.' She hesitated and her smile was rueful. 'We were getting on fine in those days. I lit his life.'

'How did you come to lose it?'

'How does one lose anything? It was last November. I had a handbag with a faulty clasp. I always carried it about with me even though I can't afford to smoke these days.' Wexford just glanced at the bare shabby furniture and then was sorry he had done so. Very little escaped her and now she was hurt.

With a brief frown, she went on, 'One day the lighter was there and the next it wasn't. I'd lost a necklace, a silver thing, the week before. Same old way. Some of us never learn.' She fingered the lighter lovingly and met Burden's censorious eye. 'Oh, I know it's valuable,' she said hastily. 'Everything Geoff gave me was pretty valuable. He isn't rich but he's the soul of generosity. I was his wife and nothing was too good for me. I've sold most of my other stuff...' Pausing, she glanced at him again and he knew she was remembering their encounter. 'I've had to,' she said. 'I'm a teacher at St Catherine's, but I don't manage very well. I don't know why I kept this.' She lifted her shoulders in the manner of one who regrets but regards regret as a waste of time. 'Perhaps because it was so very personal.' Her sudden smile was a flash of philosophy. 'Ah, well, it's nice to have been loved and remember it when it's gone.'

You didn't lose it, Wexford thought. Don't strain my credulity too far. You may have lost it and Anita Margolis may have lost it, but you didn't both lose it and within six months of each other.

'Mrs Anstey,' he said, 'as his divorced wife, you must know where Mr Smith is now.'

'He never paid me — what-d'you-call-it? — alimony. It was enough for me that he gave us the flat to live in.' She caught her lower lip in small white teeth. 'Ah, I see why you want him. Some tax thing because he's an accountant. Well, if anyone's been fiddling his returns it's nothing to do with Geoff.'

'Where can we find him?'

'Back where you come from, Kingsmarkham.' Wexford listened incredulously, recalling the visits they had paid to every Geoff Smith in the district. 'Twenty-two, Kingsbrook Road, Old Kingsbrook Road, that is. He lived in Kingsmarkham before we married and after the divorce he went back there.'

'Have you ever heard him speak of a Miss Anita Margolis?'

The mention of another woman's name did not please her. He could see that by the way the eager smile faded and her hands came tightly together. But she had an answer, an antidote, he thought, for every hint of poison. 'Is she the girl who's been fiddling her tax?'

'Mrs Anstey, has your ex-husband a key to this flat?'

She wrinkled the already lined brown forehead. Her eyes were teak-coloured but glowing with life. It wouldn't matter what she wore, Wexford reflected, you'd never notice. Her personality, her vitality — for Ann who lights up my life — made of her clothes something she put on to keep her warm. For the first time he observed them, a pullover and an old pleated skirt.

'A key?' she said. 'I shouldn't be surprised. If he has, he doesn't use it. Sometimes . . .' She looked up at him under lowered lashes, but not coyly, not artfully, rather as if she doubted his ability to understand. 'Sometimes I wish he would,' she said. 'One doesn't care to mess up someone else's life. It doesn't matter about me. Contrary to the general opinion, there's a whole heap of consolation in knowing one's only getting what one thoroughly deserves. Geoff deserved the best and he got a kick in the teeth. I'd like to know things had got better for him, that's all.' She had been lost and now she seemed to recollect the company she was in. 'You must think I'm crazy talking like this. Sorry. When you're alone a lot you get garrulous with visitors. Sure you won't have that tea?'

'Quite sure, thank you.'

'When you see him,' she said, 'you might give him my — er, best wishes. Still, maybe you don't carry messages and maybe he's forgotten the past.' Her face was full of tiny crinkles, a map of experience, and not all those lines, Wexford thought, were capable of being shrugged away.

'For Ann who messed my life,' said Burden when they were in the car. 'What did he do, sir, come back and nick the lighter because he'd found another girl who might appreciate it?'

'Let's not sentimentalise him, shall we? He made a nasty mess himself — out of the girl he did give it to. I suppose he remembered that he'd once given a present to his wife that was highly appropriate as a gift to another Ann. Not all that generous and high-minded, is he, if he sneaked back to his ex-wife's flat and stole it?'

'At any rate, we don't have to worry about him giving it to Anita Margolis nine years ago. He needn't have given it to her till a few months ago. Probably didn't even meet her till then.'

'Fair enough,' said Wexford. 'I go along with that, don't you, Drayton?'

Burden looked offended that Drayton had been considered worthy of consultation. 'I daresay he killed her with one of those flick knives from Grover's shop,' he said sourly. Drayton's back grew if anything slightly more rigid. Faintly amused, Wexford cleared his throat.

'Take the Stowerton Road,' he said to Drayton. 'We'll show this photo to Ruby Branch.'

She contemplated it and Wexford knew that it was hopeless. Too much time had passed, too many faces had been brought to her notice. The identity parade which should have settled things had merely unsettled her. She gave Wexford the photograph, shaking her ginger curls, and said:

'How many more of you are going to come calling?'

'What's that supposed to mean?'

Ruby shifted on the blue and red sofa and stared bitterly at the uncarpeted floor.

'Fellow called Martin,' she said, 'he's only been gone ten minutes. He's one of your lot, isn't he?' Wexford nodded, mystified. 'First there comes this great big car, pink and mauve with letters on it and this fellow gets out . . .'

'What fellow?' Not Martin, he thought. What the hell was going on?

'No, no, that chap with the red tie in your parade. As soon as I saw his car I remembered where I'd seen him before. Twice I saw him on that Tuesday night. Outside Cawthorne's he was when I went by at ten past eight and I saw him again at eleven, sitting in his car, staring at everyone, like he was going off his head. But I told your bloke Martin all that just now.'

It was all Wexford could do to quell the laugh that rose in his throat. Ruby's painted face was pink with indignation. Trying to sound severe, Wexford said:

'You wouldn't be saying all this because Mr Kirkpatrick asked you to, would you? You wouldn't be led into temptation by a nifty rope of rhinestones?'

'Me?' Ruby drew herself up virtuously. 'I never even spoke to him. He was just getting out of that daft car of his when your man drives up. Back he nips like one o'clock and off down the street. That Martin,' she said, very aggrieved, 'he was nasty to me. Some would call it threatening.'

'And others,' said Wexford, 'would call it saving weaker vessels from their baser instincts.'

At Stowerton crossroads Cawthorne was nowhere to be seen, but his wife, bony knees displayed and ear-rings big as Christmas tree baubles dangling beneath yellow curls, had perched herself on a diesel pump to flirt with an attendant. In the launderette the portholes still whirled.

'You can consider yourself absolved from laundry duty tonight, Drayton,' Wexford said, chuckling.

'I beg your pardon, sir?'

'Miss Grover always comes over here to do her washing on Tuesdays, doesn't she?'

'Oh, yes, sir. I see what you mean.' There was no need for him to flush quite so deeply, Wexford thought. The dark red colour had spread to the back of his neck.

'Kirkpatrick's safe all right,' he said. 'His bribes fell on stony ground.' The metaphor sounded wrong and he added quickly, 'Those two women saw him outside Cawthorne's right enough. He's just a fool who can't leave well alone. It's the inside of a divorce court he's afraid of, not a jail.'

'Straight to the Old Kingsbrook Road, sir?' Drayton asked stiffly.

'Number twenty-two's this end.' As they passed the Methodist church, Wexford leaned forward, a dull leaden weight diving to the pit of his stomach. He had feared this when Mrs Anstey gave him the address, feared it and dismissed his fear as jumping to conclusions.

'Look at that, Mike.'

'As if a bomb had dropped,' Burden said tiredly.

'I know. I feel like that too. Rather nice Georgian houses and the whole block's nearly demolished.' He got out of the car, Burden following him. In the mild afternoon light the last remaining wall stared at them. It was the inside that was displayed, green wallpaper above, then pink, stone-coloured on the ground. A dozen feet from the top an iron fireplace still clung to the plaster, and where the plaster had been stripped, to bare bricks. A great cable wrapped it and the cable was attached to a tractor, lurching through dust. Through the ochreish clouds they could see a painted board, *Doherty for Demolition,* and underneath the slogan, *What Goes Up Must Come Down!*

Burden's eye caught the number on the remaining door-post, twenty-two. He looked disconsolately from the wall to the cable, the cable to the tractor. Then with a jerk of his head he beckoned the tractor driver.

'Police,' Burden said sharply into a red pugnacious face.

'O.K., O.K. Only I've got my work to do, same as anyone else. What were you wanting?'

Burden looked past him to the number on the doorpost.

'There was an accountant here, chap called Smith. D'you know where he went to?'

'Where you'll never find him.' The smirk was unpleasant. 'Underground.'

'Come again?'

'He's dead,' said the tractor driver, rubbing his dusty hands.

CHAPTER FOURTEEN

'He can't be dead,' Burden said aghast.

'Can't he? I'm only telling you what the old girl in the tea-place told me.' Cocking his head towards where the little café had been, the workman fished in his pocket for a large filthy handkerchief and blew his nose. 'Before her place come down it was. Poor Mr Smith, she says, he'd have hated to see the old house go. All he'd got left what with his wife doing him dirt and him all on his own.'

'What did he die of? A broken heart?'

'Something to do with his heart. The old girl could tell you more than I can.'

'You don't know when he died?' Wexford put in.

'A year, eighteen months. The place stood empty ever since and a proper mess it was in.' Burden knew the truth of this. Where the rubble now was he had often sat having his tea and, leaving, had passed boarded-up windows. 'There's the undertakers up on the corner. They'd know. Always go to the nearest, I reckon.'

The man went back to his tractor and, puffing heavily as if determined to move the wall by his own unaided effort, edged the vehicle forward over mounds of brick-filled loam. Burden went over to the undertakers. The cable pulled taut. Wexford stood watching it and listening to the groans of crumbling mortar until the inspector came back.

'He's dead all right,' Burden said, picking his way through the debris. 'Died last February twelvemonth. They remember the funeral. No one there but that old woman and a girl who used to do Smith's typing. Our surefire suspect is in a grave in Stowerton cemetery.'

'What did he die of?'

'Coronary,' said Burden. 'He was forty-two.' A low crunching tremor like the first cracking that precedes an earthquake made him look behind him. In the wall of Smith's house a fissure had appeared, running between green wallpaper and pink. From the centre of this rift brown plaster dust began to vomit down the patchy brick. 'As I see it, sir,' he said, 'the Geoff Smith business is coincidence. We have to forget him and begin again.'

'Coincidence! No, Mike, I won't have that. Its arm isn't that long. A man came to Ruby's house and said he was Geoff Smith and after he'd gone a lighter was found in that house that a man called Geoff Smith had bought eight years before. We *know* those things if we don't know anything else and you can't get away from them. It was in Stowerton and a man called Geoff Smith had lived in the next town, knew the place like you and I know it. The man is dead, was dead when the lighter went missing from Mrs Anstey's flat, dead before Anita came to live here and stone cold dead as a doornail last Tuesday. But to deny he had any connection with the case on the grounds of coincidence is crazy. That way madness lies.'

'Then Mrs Anstey's lying. She sold Anita the lighter — she admits she's sold a lot of stuff — and happened to tell her all about her first husband at the same time. That wouldn't be coincidence, that'd be normal behaviour for her. Anita told her boy friend the name and it stuck in his subconscious.'

'Why should she lie?' Wexford scoffed. 'What would be the point? I ask you, Mike, did she impress you as a liar?'

Burden shook his head doubtfully and began to follow the Chief Inspector back to Drayton and the waiting car. 'I don't believe her when she says she lost the lighter, at any rate,' he said.

'No, but she thinks she did,' Wexford said quickly. 'The truth is, somebody nicked it. Who? An old mate of Smith's? You know what we're going to have to do, don't you? Every friend of Smith's, every friend of Mrs Anstey's and all Anita's associates are going to have to be hunted up just to see if there's the tiniest tie-up between them.'

A shout from behind made them quicken their pace. 'Stand clear!' The tractor gave a final heave, and with a rumble that grew into a roar, the cable sliced through the wall like a grocer's wire cutter through a piece of cheese. Then everything vanished behind a huge yellow cloud. Where the house had been there was now nothing but a pillar of mud-coloured vapour through which could be seen clean blue sky.

'The last of Geoffrey Smith,' said Wexford. 'Come on. I want my tea.'

There was no future in it, Drayton thought. His ambitions had no place in them for such a girl as Linda Grover. Not even a single rung of his ladder could be spared to bear her weight. Now, looking back over the days, he saw that he had been culpable in associating himself at all with a girl whose father was eyed antagonistically by his superior officers, blameworthy for taking her out, appallingly foolhardy to have made himself her lover. The word with its erotic, insinuating associations made him shiver and the shiver was not for his future and his career.

It seemed that she was bribable, corruptible. He knew only that she, like her surroundings, was corrupting. And Wexford knew it too. Wexford had told him, although not knowing just what his prohibition entailed, to leave her alone. This was his chance, to obey, to yield, and in this yielding to put up a resistance to her spell sanctioned by authority.

He took his hooded coat and went down the police station steps. The evening was too warm to put it on. Cawthorne would have to go without his car hire fee tonight. Drayton made his way to the library where he got out a book on abnormal psychology.

It was seven when he came out and the library was closing. Grover's would be closed too and he would be safe if he went back to his lodgings by way of the High Street. The Stowerton to Forby bus came in as he approached the stop and he felt a strange urge to get on it and be carried far away into the anonymous depths of the countryside. Instead of the intellectual concentration abnormal psychology would demand, he wanted to lose himself and his identity; he wanted oblivion in the warm quiet air. But even as he thought this, he knew with a sudden conviction almost amounting to horror that he could not escape like this, that the wide green world was not big enough to contain him and her unless they were together. He grew cold and he began to hurry, like a man quickening his steps to stimulate circulation on a cold day.

Then he saw her. She was getting off the Stowerton bus and a young, good-looking man was helping her down with a wheel-basket full of bundled washing. Drayton saw her smile as she thanked him and it seemed to him that her smile was more coquettish and more seductive than any she had ever given him. Jealousy caught at him like a punch at the throat.

Avoidance was impossible. He had lost the will and the desire to avoid. Wexford's words — that apt crack about laundry duties — he recalled as he might remember a sermon so boring, so spurious that it sent you to sleep. But he was awake now, uncaringly reckless.

'Carry your bag, lady? Or should I say, push it?'

She smiled, a shadow of the look she had given the man on the bus. It was enough. The fetters were back. He seemed to feel their cold enclosing touch.

'My boss said I'd be a laundryman tonight,' he said, and he knew he was gabbling foolishly, wooing her anew as he did each time they met. 'He was right. Who's looking after the shop?'

'Your boss thinks a lot of you,' she said and he detected the proprietory note, the tone of satisfaction. 'I could tell that in the café today.' Her face clouded. 'Dad's up,' she said. 'His back's awful, but he says he can't trust us to mind the business.'

Drayton felt a curious desire to see the father. He sighed within himself. It was not thus that he had envisaged so crucial and significant a meeting, not in these circumstances nor in this place. Ten years hence, he thought, and a nice educated girl; a tall scholarly father with a degree, pearls round the mother's neck; a half-timbered country house with gardens and perhaps a paddock. She unlocked the shop door and the old grey smell came out to meet him.

Grover was behind the counter, shovelling up sweets someone had spilt. His hands looked dirty and there were rust marks round the rim of the jar he held. Drayton had expected him to be older. The man looked no more than forty, if that. There was no grey in the lustreless dark hair and signs of age showed only in his face muscles, screwed up in pain. When he saw his daughter he put down the jar and clapped his hand to the small of his back.

'Your mum's just off to her whist drive,' he said and Drayton thought his voice horrible. 'She wants them things ironed tonight.' He spoke to his daughter as if she were alone with him and he gave her a surly glance.

'You ought to be in bed,' Linda said.

'And let the business go to pot? Fine mess you've got these books in.' Though he was dark and she fair, the resemblance between father and daughter was so strong that Drayton had to turn away deliberately to stop himself from staring. If the man smiled he thought he would cry aloud in anguish. But there was little chance of Grover's smiling. 'This is the end of me taking things easy,' he said. 'I can see that. Back to the grindstone tomorrow.' He came out from behind the counter as if he were going to pounce on her and, indeed, his crooked movements to some extent suggested those of a crippled and cornered animal. 'Then I'll get the car out,' he muttered. 'Don't suppose you've cleaned it since I was laid up.'

'The doctor'll have something to say about that,' she said and Drayton heard weariness in her voice. 'Why don't you go back to bed? I'm here. I'll manage.'

She took his arm as if he were in fact the ancient broken creature Drayton had imagined. Alone in the shop he felt desolate. This was no place for him and as always when here he felt a compulsion to wash his hands. Perhaps she would forget he was there, engulfed as she always was by her domestic duties, and he would be left among the suspect magazines — the hidden knives? — until night came to deepen this darkness. For he knew that he was a prisoner and that he could not leave without her.

It seemed an age before she returned and when she came he felt his face must betray God knew what enslavement, an end-of-his-tether abandonment to longing.

'I had to hang up the washing,' she said. 'Not that it'll dry tonight. I should have taken it in the afternoon like I did last week.' As she came close to him, he put up his hands to her face, touching it as a blind man might. 'No car tonight?' she asked him. He shook his head. 'We'll take Dad's,' she said.

'No,' he said. 'We'll go for a walk.'

He knew that she could drive; she had told Wexford. What puny power remained to him would be utterly lost if he allowed her to drive him about the countryside in her father's car.

'Tomorrow, then,' she said and she looked long into his eyes. 'Promise you will tomorrow, Mark, before Dad gets mobile — and commandeers it.'

He thought that at that moment he would have promised her his own life if she had asked for it. 'Look after me,' she said, a sudden agony in her voice. Upstairs he could hear the crippled man moving. 'Oh, Mark, Mark . . .'

The river beckoned them with its quiet sheltered path.

Drayton took her in his arms on the spot where he had seen that other man kiss her, but he had forgotten this and everything else which had passed before they met. Even the desire for immediate physical gratification was less strong. He had reached a stage when his paramount wish was to be alone with her in silence, holding her to him, and in silence enclosing her mouth with his.

'I think I was justified in calling you out,' Burden said. He stood up to let Wexford take his seat beside him on the window settle. As usual at this time, the saloon bar of the Olive and Dove was crowded.

'Wouldn't keep till the morning, I suppose,' Wexford grumbled. 'Don't sit down. You can get me a beer before you start expounding.'

Burden came back with two beers in tankards. 'Bit crowded and noisy in here, sir, I'm afraid.'

'Not half so crowded and noisy as my place. My daughter Sheila's having a jam session.'

'No,' said Burden with a smile, 'they don't call it that any more.'

Wexford said belligerently from behind his beer, 'What do they call it, then?'

'Search me.'

They moved into a quieter corner. Wexford lifted the hem of a curtain and looked out at the street. It was dark and there were few people about. Half a dozen youths loitered at the entrance to the cinema car park, pushing each other about and laughing.

'Look at all those bloody green cars,' the Chief Inspector said disgustedly. 'For all we know, he's out there, driving around or in the pictures.'

'I think I know who he is,' Burden said quietly.

'Well, I didn't suppose you'd dragged me down here for the sake of the booze. Let's have it.'

Burden looked speculatively at the heavy wrinkled face. Its expression was not encouraging. For a moment he hesitated, fidgeting with his tankard. His idea had come to him, or rather had crystallised, after three hours of arguing it out with himself. When he had formulated it and catalogued the details he had become so excited that he had to tell someone. The obvious someone now sat opposite him, already derisive and certainly prepared to scoff. The Chief Constable had evidently made up his mind that the whole investigation was so much hot air. Just as the cold light of morning is said to dispel fancies of the night before, so the atmosphere of the Olive and Dove, the sudden bursts of raucous laughter and Wexford's doubting look robbed his ingenious solution of everything cogent and left only the ingenuity. Perhaps it would be better if he drank up his drink and went without another word. Wexford was tapping his foot impatiently. Clearing his throat, Burden said lamely:

'I think it's Mrs Anstey's husband.'

'*Smith?* My God, Mike, we've been through that. He's dead.'

'Smith is, but Anstey isn't. At any rate, we've no reason to suppose so.' Burden lowered his voice as someone passed their table. 'I think it could be Anstey. Shall I tell you why?'

Wexford's spiky eyebrows went up. 'It had better be good,' he said. 'We don't know anything about the fellow. She hardly mentioned him.'

'And didn't you think that was funny?'

'Perhaps it was,' Wexford said thoughtfully. 'Perhaps it was.' He seemed to be about to go on. Burden did not wish to have the wind taken out of his own sails and he said hastily:

'Who does she give the impression of being more fond of, the man who divorced her five years ago or the man she's married to now? She regrets that divorce, sir, and she doesn't mind making it clear to three strangers who didn't even want to know. 'It's nice to have been loved and remember it when it's gone,' she said. Are those the words of a happily married woman? Then what was all that about being alone a lot? She's a teacher. A married woman with a job isn't alone a lot. She'd be hardly alone at all.'

'You think she and Anstey are separated?'

'I do,' said Burden with decision. Wexford showed no inclination to laugh and he began to gather confidence.

'We don't believe she lost the lighter, but she believes it. If she didn't lose it but just left it lying about or in her handbag, who's the most likely person to have it in his possession? The errant husband. Very probably Smith divorced her on Anstey's account. That means adultery, and a man who'll commit it once will commit it again.'

'Thus speaks the stern moralist,' said Wexford, smiling. 'I don't know that I'd go along with that. Your point is, of course, that Anstey took up with Anita and gave her the lighter. Mike, it's all right as far as it goes, but you haven't got any real reason for thinking Anstey's left her. Don't forget the Easter holidays are on and a married woman teacher would be alone a lot in the holidays.'

'Then why does she say she's only got her salary to live on?' Burden asked triumphantly. 'It's quite true what she says about selling jewellery. I saw her in Knobby Clark's shop.'

'I'll buy you a drink,' said Wexford, and now he looked pleased.

'Scotch,' said Burden when he came back. 'Very nice. Cheers.'

'To detection.' Wexford raised his glass. 'Where's Anstey now?'

Burden shrugged. 'Around here somewhere. Just getting on with whatever job he does.'

'Since you're so clever, you'll no doubt be able to tell me why a man called Anstey gives the name of his wife's former husband when he goes out on the tiles with another girl? Not just Smith, mind, *Geoff Smith*.'

'I can't tell you that,' Burden said, less happily.

'Or why he killed the girl. What was his motive?'

'When we suspected Kirkpatrick, we assumed the motive was jealousy. We lost sight of the five hundred pounds Anita was carrying in her handbag.'

'In that case, Mike, why didn't he wait until they were back in the car, drive to some lonely place and kill her there? You don't murder a woman in someone else's house by a method which leaves incriminating traces behind, when you could do it, for example, in Cheriton Forest. Which brings me back to another point. Ruby and Monkey both thought he'd go back. It was because they wanted him caught before he could go back that Monkey wrote to me. Why didn't he?'

'Scared, I suppose. We don't know where he is. For all we know he may have gone home, at least for a time.'

Burden shook his head regretfully. 'I don't know,' he said, and he added, repeating himself, 'I can't tell you that.'

'Perhaps Mrs Anstey can. Drink up. They're closing.'

Out in the street Wexford sniffed the soft April air. The sky which had been clear was now becoming overcast and clouds crossed the moon. They came to the bridge. A swan sailed out from the tunnel, into lamplight and then into their twin shadows. Wexford surveyed the almost empty High Street, the pearly white and yellow lamps and the dark holes made by the unlit alleys.

In the high wall that reared ahead of them an open window twenty feet up disclosed a girl leaning out, her arm dangling as over the rail of a stage balcony. On a bracket below was a lamp in an iron cage, and half in its light, half in velvet shadow, stood a man gazing upwards.

'Ah, moon of my delight,' Wexford quoted softly, 'who know'st no wane . . .'

With a sourness he did not bother to hide, Burden said, 'Drayton was told to leave her alone,' and he scowled at the yellow, cloud-scarred moon.

Indeed the Idols I have loved so long
Have done my Credit in Men's Eye much wrong:
Have drowned my Honour in a shallow cup,
And sold my reputation for a Song.

CHAPTER FIFTEEN

In the morning the rain came back. From the look of the sky it seemed to be one of those mornings when it rains from streaming dawn to dripping, fog-filled dusk. Wexford, dialling Sewingbury, held the receiver gripped under his chin and reached out to lower the venetian blind. He was listening to the ringing tone when Drayton came in.

'That Mrs Anstey to see you, sir. I passed her as I came in.'

Wexford put the phone down. 'For once the mountain has come to Mahomet.'

'Shall I bring her up?'

'Just a minute, Drayton.' It was a command, rather sharp and with a hint of admonition. The young man stopped and turned obediently. 'Enjoy yourself last night?'

If possible, Drayton's face became more than ever a cipher, secret, cautious, but not innocent. 'Yes, thank you, sir.' The rain drummed against the window. It had grown quite dark in the office as if night was coming at nine thirty in the morning.

'I don't suppose you've got to know many young people around here yet?' The question demanded an avuncular heartiness but Wexford made it sound menacing.

'Not many, sir.'

'Pity. God knows, my young daughter seems to know enough. Always having a' — no, not a jam session. Burden had corrected him on that. '— a get-together at our place. Quite a decent bunch if you don't mind noise. I daresay you don't.'

Drayton stood, silence incarnate.

'You must join in one of these nights.' He gave the young man a grey cold stare. 'Just you on your own,' he said.

'Yes, sir. I'd like that.'

'Good, I'll get Sheila to give you a tinkle.' Severity had gone and urbanity replaced it. 'Now for Mrs Anstey,' said the Chief Inspector.

The rain gave him a sensation of almost claustrophobic confinement as if he were enclosed by walls of water. He could hear it streaming from the sills and pouring over the naked stone bodies on the frescoes. Pity it never seemed to wash them properly but just left grey trails on shoulders and haunches. He switched on the lights as Burden came in with Mrs Anstey in his wake, each as wet as creatures from the depths of the sea. Mrs Anstey's umbrella hung from her arm and dripped water in a trickle at her heels.

'I had to come,' she said. 'I had an impulse. After you'd gone I got to thinking what on earth you could have meant about some girl you mentioned.' Her laughter sounded itself like water, fresh bubbling, yet a little hesitant. 'I got the first bus.' She shed her grey mackintosh and stripped a hideous plastic hood from her brown hair. There were raindrops on her nose and she wrinkled it as might a little dog. 'Geoff and a girl. I didn't like that. Dog in a manger, aren't I? The fact is, I just have to see him. I've waited long enough. I'm going there now, but I thought I ought to see you first.' Without explanation, she laughed again and this time her laugh held a nervous break. 'Has he got a girl?' she asked and that explained it.

The first bringer of unwelcome news, thought Wexford, has but a losing office. How did it go on? Something about his voice sounding ever after as a sullen warning bell. That didn't matter. Only the present pain mattered. For the first time since he and Burden had discussed Smith's death, his particular duty was brought home to him. He was going to have to tell her. That she was only an ex-wife would, he was sure, make no difference.

'Has he?' she said again and now she was pleading.

'I wasn't able to see him, Mrs Anstey.'

No lying, no prevaricating. None of that would be possible with this woman. Burden had turned his back.

'What is it? There's something bad. . . .' She got up, the plastic thing from her head stretched taut in her fingers. 'He's ill, he's . . .'

'He's dead.' No matter how prepared you were, it was still a shock. You could never be sufficiently prepared. Until the words were said, hope was invincible. 'I'm sorry,' he said quickly. 'I'm very, very sorry. It was a coronary, bit over a year ago. I'm sure it was quick.'

'He can't be dead!' The words were an echo of Burden's.

He could not have been dead for Burden because that made nonsense of a theory; he could not be dead for her because she had a theory too, a theory of re-shaping her life?

'Not dead!' Wexford heard the thin thread of hysteria, the burning electric shock wire.

'Please sit down. I'll get you something to drink.'

With a kind of horror, he watched her feel blindly behind her for the chair she had sat in, find it, kick it away and lurch at the wall. Her fists clenched, she struck her head against the plaster, then the fists themselves came up, pounding and beating on the hard surface.

Wexford took a step towards her. 'Better get one of the W.P.C.s,' he said to Burden. Then she began to scream with a throaty frenzy.

The policewoman took the tea cup from her and replaced the sodden handkerchief with a clean one of her own.

'Bit better now?'

Noreen Anstey nodded. Her face was pink and swollen and her hair, though wet from rain, gave the illusion of being, like her cheeks, soaked with tears. She was all tears, all grief.

Suddenly she said quite coherently, 'I can never ask him to forgive me now.' For a moment she had breath enough only for this. Sobs succeeded it. They were like blood pumping from a vein. 'I won't cry any more.' The sobs were involuntary. Eventually they would subside. 'I'll go to my grave,' she said, 'knowing he never knew I was sorry.' Wexford nodded to the policewoman and she went out with the tea cup and the wet handkerchief.

'He forgave you,' he said. 'Didn't he give you the flat?'

She hardly seemed to hear him. 'He died and I didn't even know.' Wexford thought of the two women at Smith's funeral, the old neighbour and the girl who did his typing. 'You don't even know what I did to him, do you? We'd been married eight years, the perfect couple, the happy couple. That's what everyone said and it was true.' The sobs made a rattle in her throat. 'He used to buy me presents. Unbirthday presents, he called them. You couldn't have that many birthdays. You'd get old too fast.' She covered her eyes, shaking her head from side to side. 'We lived in a house with his office in it. There was a garage next door. I could see it from my window. I'd given up work, teaching was my work. No need when I had Geoff to look after me.' The sentences jerked out, short, ragged, staccato. Wexford moved his chair close and sat looking down into his lap. 'Ray Anstey worked at the garage. I used to watch him. You know the way they lie on their backs with their heads thrown back? My God!' She shivered. 'You don't want to hear all this. I'd better go.' Her things were still wet, the raincoat, the umbrella that had dripped and made a puddle on the floor like a blister. She dabbed feebly at the sides of the chair, feeling for her handbag.

'We'll take you home, Mrs Anstey,' Wexford said gently. 'But not quite yet. Would you like to have a rest? Two questions only and then you can rest.'

'He's dead. Beyond your reach. Why did you want him?'

'I think,' Wexford said slowly, 'that it's your second husband we want.'

'Ray?'

'Where is he, Mrs Anstey?'

'I don't know,' she said tiredly. 'I haven't seen him for months. He left me at the end of last year.'

'You said he worked in a garage. Is he a mechanic?'

'I suppose he is. What else could he do?' Her gloves were on the floor at her feet. She picked them up and looked at them as at two wet dead things, dredged up from the bottom of a pond. 'You wanted him all along?' Her face went a sickly white and she struggled up out of the chair. 'It was my *husband* you wanted, not Geoff?' Wexford nodded. 'What's he done?' she asked hoarsely.

'A girl is missing, probably dead . . .'

'The knife,' she said. Her eyes went out of focus. Wexford took a step towards her and caught her in his arms.

'Where did your sister get her car serviced?' Burden said. Margolis looked up from his late breakfast of coffee, orange juice and unappetising hard-boiled eggs, his expression helplessly apathetic.

'Some garage,' he said, and then, 'It would be Cawthorne's, wouldn't it?'

'Come, Mr Margolis, you must know. Don't you have your own car seen to?'

'Ann looked after that side of things. When it wanted doing, she'd see to it.' The painter turned the eggshells upside down in their cups like a child playing April Fool tricks. 'There was something, though . . .' His long fingers splayed through his hair so that it stood up in a spiky halo. 'Some trouble. I have a remote recollection of her saying she was going to someone else.' He put the tray on the sofa arm and got up to shake crumbs from his lap. 'I wish I could remember,' he said.

'She took it to that Ray, Mr M.,' said Mrs Penistan sharply. 'You know she did. Why don't you pull yourself together?' She shrugged at Burden, turning her little eyes heavenwards. 'He's gone to pieces since his sister went. Can't do nothing with him.' She settled herself beside Margolis and gave him a long exasperated stare. Burden was reminded of a mother or a nanny taking a recalcitrant child to a tea party, especially when she bent over him and, with a sharp clucking of her tongue, pulled his dressing gown over to hide his pyjama legs.

'Ray who?'

'Don't ask me, dear. You know what she was like with her christian names. All I know is she come in here a couple of months back and says. "I've had about as much as I can stand of Russell's prices. I've a good mind to get Ray to do the cars for me." "Who's Ray?" I says, but she just laughed. "Never you mind, Mrs P. Let's say he's a nice boy who thinks the world of me. If I tell you who he is he might lose his job." '

'Did he come here to service the cars?'

'Oh, no, dear. Well, he wouldn't have the facilities, would he?' Mrs Penistan surveyed the studio and the window as if to imply that nothing of practical use to a sane human being could be found in cottage or garden. 'She always took them to him. He lived local, you see. Somewhere local. I'd see her go off but I'd always gone when she got back. *He'd* have been here.' She shoved her elbow into Margolis's thin ribs. 'But he don't listen to what folks tell him.'

Burden left them together, sitting side by side, Mrs Penistan coaxing Margolis to finish his coffee. The heavy rain had made the path slippery and there were wet petals everywhere underfoot. The garage doors were open and for the first time Burden saw Margolis's own car and saw that it was green.

He was beginning to discern a pattern, a way that it could all have been done. Now he thought he could understand why a black car and a green car had been used and where Anita's white car had been until the small hours. A new excitement made him walk jauntily to the cottage gate. He opened it and the hawthorn bush showered him with water as effectively as if someone had put a tilted bucket in its branches.

This is how it must feel to be a psychiatrist, Wexford thought. Noreen Anstey lay on the couch in the rest room, staring at the ceiling, and he sat beside her, letting her talk.

'He always had a knife,' she said. 'I saw it that first day, the first time he came up from the garage. Geoff was working downstairs. I used to take coffee down to him and then I started talking to Ray as well. One day he came up instead.' For a while she was silent, moving her head from side to side. 'God, he was beautiful. Not handsome, beautiful, perfect. Like people ought to be, like I never was. Not very tall, black haired, red mouth like a flower . . .' He didn't want to interrupt, but he had to. He wasn't a real psychiatrist.

'How old is he?'

'Ten years younger than me,' she said and he knew it hurt her to say it. 'He came up that day. We were quite alone and he had this knife, a little flick knife. He took it out of his pocket and put it on the table. I'd never seen one before and I didn't know what it was. We didn't talk much. What was there for us to talk about? We didn't have anything in common. He sat there smiling, making little sort of sly innuendoes.' She almost laughed but it was a gasp Wexford heard. 'I was sick with wanting him.' Her face turned to the wall, she went on, 'I'd had that lighter a few months and I remember lighting a cigarette for Ray. He said, "No, light it in your mouth". He looked at the lighter and he said, "He give you this? Does he give you toys because he can't give you anything else?" That wasn't true, but it must have been the way it looked, the way I looked. "I've got a toy too", he said, and he picked up the knife and held it against my throat. The blade came out. I kept still or it would have cut me. My God, I was a teacher of French in a girl's school. I'd never been anywhere or done anything. You'd have thought I'd have screamed. D'you know, I'd have let him kill me, then? Afterwards, after he'd gone, there was blood on my neck from a little scratch and I knew he'd been looking at it all the time he was making love to me.'

'Smith divorced you?' Wexford said to fill up the great silence.

'He found out. That wasn't difficult. I've never been much good at hiding my feelings. Geoff would have forgiven me and started afresh. He couldn't believe I'd want to marry a man ten years younger than myself, a garage hand . . . I was mad to have him. I knew he was a sadist and a moron. He'd cut me, really cut me since then.' She pulled open her dress. On the left breast, where the flesh swelled under the collarbone, was a small white cicatrice. For all his years of experience, Wexford felt sickness catch at the back of his throat like a fingernail plucking.

'You were always unhappy?'

'I was never *happy* with him.' She said it almost reproachfully. 'I don't think there was a moment when I could say I was *happy*. He loathed Geoff. D'you know what he used to do? He'd give Geoff's name, pretend he was Geoff.' Wexford nodded, guessing this was to come. 'When the phone rang he'd pick it up and say — well, sort of absent-mindedly, "Geoff Smith speaking". Then he'd correct himself and say he'd made a mistake. Once he took some clothes to the cleaners, filthy overalls, and when I went to collect them they couldn't find the ticket. It was made out to Smith, you see. Anything a bit nasty or disreputable he was involved in and he'd always give Geoff's name. A girl came round once — she couldn't have been more than seventeen — and asked if this was where Geoff Smith lived. He'd dropped her and she wanted him back, even though he'd used the knife on her too. She showed me a scar on her neck. I told him he'd go too far one day. He'd kill one of them or she'd go to the police.'

'He's gone too far,' Wexford said.

'He had to see their blood, you see.' She spoke very calmly, without horror. Not for the first time Wexford pondered on the dulling effect of custom, how habit dulled the edge of shock. All pity choked with custom of fell deeds . . . 'I used to think,' she said, 'that one day there'd be a girl who wasn't mesmerised by him but just plain frightened and that maybe she'd turn the knife on him. He wasn't big and strong, you see, not powerful physically. His power was the other sort. I used to take the knives away but he always got new ones. Then he left me.'

'This must have been about the time you lost your lighter.'

Noreen Anstey raised herself on one elbow, then turned and swung her legs on to the floor. 'I've been thinking about that,' she said. 'Ray must have taken it. He took things from Geoff and me when we were still married. I couldn't prove it, but I thought he had, jewellery, things like that.' She sighed, covered her face and then brought her hands down again. 'I suppose Geoff guessed too. There were so many things,' she said, 'we both knew and never put into words. Oh, I'm sorry!' she cried, clenching her fists and pressing them into her lap. 'I'm so bitterly sorry. I want to find where he's buried and lie on his grave and cry into the earth that I'm sorry!'

So many women who were sorry, Wexford thought, Noreen Anstey because she had thrown away love for love's ugly shadow, Ruby Branch because she had betrayed an old crook, and Anita Margolis? The dead have no regrets. She could not be sorry that she had played her dangerous game once too often, played it with a man and a knife.

CHAPTER SIXTEEN

'Have you got a friend who could stay with you?' Wexford asked. 'Mother, sister, a neighbour?'

Noreen Anstey seemed to have shrunk. Deprived of her vitality, she was just a little plain woman wilting into middle-age. 'My mother's dead,' she said. 'Ray lost me most of my friends.'

'A policewoman will go back with you. She'll try and find someone to keep you company.'

'And when you find him?' she asked with wistful bitterness.

'We'll keep in touch, Mrs Anstey. Why do you suppose he ever came to Kingsmarkham?'

She shrugged her shoulders, pulling the creased raincoat tightly around her. Every movement now was a kind of shiver, a hunching and shrinking of her body in a gradual process of contraction. 'If I say to haunt him,' she said, 'you'll think I'm mad. But that would be like Ray. He'd go to — to Geoff and say he'd wrecked two lives, but he'd left me now and all the agony was for nothing. He's a sadist. Then he'd have started it all over again, that business of giving Geoff's name, telling girls he was Geoff and giving them his address.'

'Mrs Anstey, you thought we were friends of your husband, didn't you? When we called and asked if you were Mrs Smith. You thought Anstey had put us on to you.'

She nodded limply.

'He must have known Mr Smith was dead. Would he give his name, knowing he was dead?'

'He might have done. Not to a girl. There wouldn't be any point in that. But if he was going to do something disreputable or underhand, he might then. It would be a joke to him, dishonouring Geoff's memory. And it would be a habit too.'

'I wonder why he stayed.'

'I suppose he liked it here or got a good job that suited him. His idea of heaven would be an easy-going employer who'd pay him well and turn a blind eye if Ray took his customers away from him and serviced their cars on the cheap. That was always one of the ways he got to know his girls.'

Wexford did not want to hurt her more than he need, but he did not think she would sustain any further injury from a recital of Anstey's misdemeanours.

'By going round to their homes while their husbands were at work, I imagine?' he said. 'Sitting in their cars with them, the personal touch?'

'He wasn't doing too well in Sewingbury,' she said. 'People got to know too much about him. Some of these garage proprietors give their mechanics a car or let them borrow one. Ray's boss got hard about that when he smashed up a hire car. No, you can be sure he found a job and a good one.' She turned away from him and covered her eyes. 'If Geoff had been alive,' she whispered. 'Oh, if only he'd been alive! Ray wouldn't have been able to hurt him or me any more. When Geoff had seen him, seen him once and heard he'd left me, he'd have come back to me. I often used to think, he'll find out, he'll know sooner or later. We used to be able to read each other's minds. Married people can. He's lonely too, I thought. He's been lonely longer than I have.' She began to cry softly, the calm gentle tears of a grief beyond consolation. 'It's a fallacy that, about reading thoughts. He was dead.' She spoke evenly, as if she were just talking and not crying as well. 'And I sat and waited for him, quite happy really and peaceful. I didn't long for him or feel passionate or anything. I had peace and I thought, one day, this week, next week, sometime — well, it was never, wasn't it?' Her fingers dabbed the tears. 'May I have my lighter?' she said.

He let her hold it but shook his head at the request. 'In a little while.'

'The name of the design,' she said, 'came from a poem of Baudelaire. Geoff knew I loved that verse. ". . . *et tes seins*",' she quoted, '"*Les grappes de ma vigne.*"' Wexford's French wasn't up to much but he could just understand. She had shown him the scar Anstey, the thief and the sadist, had made with his knife. He turned away his eyes.

It looked as if Russell Cawthorne had a young girl in the office with him. Her back was to the door and she wore a red mac, the glistening hot red of a fire engine with the paint still wet. Burden drove through the rain and up under the trading stamps banner. He and Wexford dived for the office. The girl opened the door for them and illusion snapped, for it was Mrs Cawthorne's face that appeared between the scarlet collar and the frothy yellow hair.

'Better go into the house,' said Cawthorne. He heaved himself up, grunting. 'Come on, troops, run for it!'

In the living-room the Pre-Raphaelite lady contemplated her lily with pitying scorn. She had seen plenty in that room, she seemed to be saying, most of it unedifying. Mrs Cawthorne took off the red coat and stood revealed in lemon wool. Her Christmas tree ear-rings hung to her shoulders. Red and shining, they reminded Wexford of toffee apples.

'Ray Anstey was with me for six months,' Cawthorne said. 'He was a good lad, knew his job.' They sat down among the piecrust tables, the wax fruit, the candelabra. My God, thought Wexford, is it all coming back? Is this the way my Sheila will do up her house when the time comes? 'When he came he said he wanted something temporary. He'd only come here to hunt up a friend, but then he said the friend had died and he'd like to stay on.' Geoff Smith, Wexford reflected, Smith, the injured, the bait, the perpetually fascinating.

'Much of a one for the women?' he asked.

'I wouldn't say that.' Cawthorne gave Burden a sidelong glance. Perhaps he was remembering enquiries into his own proclivities in that direction. He shook himself and added in the tone of a colonel discussing with an officer of equal or even superior rank the naughtiness of a subaltern, 'Good-looking young devil, though.'

Mrs Cawthorne wriggled. Wexford looked at her. He had seen a similar expression in his seventeen-year-old Sheila's eyes when she was discussing with triumph a boy's unsuccessful advance. Here was the same half-smile, the same mock-anger. But surely he wasn't expected to believe . . . ? He was.

'You wouldn't say that?' she enquired archly of her husband. 'Then all I can say is, you don't listen to a word I say.' Cawthorne's sick glare made this seem more than probable.

'Why, the way he looked at me sometimes!' She turned to Wexford. 'I'm used to it, of course. I could see what young Ray was after. Not that he actually said anything. It was more than his job was worth to go chasing the boss's wife.'

Her husband turned his eyes towards the ceiling where he fixed them on a plaster cherub. 'Oh God,' he said softly.

'When did he leave?' Wexford put in quickly.

His wife's insinuation had temporarily thrown Cawthorne off balance. He went to the sideboard and poured himself a whisky before replying. 'Let's see now,' he said when half the drink had gone down. 'It'd be last Saturday week.' The day he booked Ruby's room, Wexford thought. 'I remember thinking what a bloody nerve he'd got.'

'In what way? Because he left you?'

'Not only that. It was the way he did it. Now I'm in the habit of letting any of my staff borrow a car when they're in need and provided they give me fair warning. It's hard on a young kid, wants to take his girl out.' He smiled philanthropically, the friend of youth, and drained his glass. 'Anstey was one of the kind that take advantage. Night after night he'd have one of the cars and it was all the same to him whether I knew or whether I didn't. Well, on that Saturday morning we were a bit short-handed and I noticed Anstey wasn't about. Next thing he came sweeping in in one of the Minors, all smiles and not a word of excuse. Said he'd been to see a friend on business.'

'A Minor?'

'Black Minor Thousand, one of the three I keep for hiring out. You've seen them out the front.' Cawthorne raised a thick eyebrow like a strip of polar bear fur. 'Drink?' Wexford shook his head for both of them. 'Don't mind if I do, do you?' His glass refilled, he went on, ' "Business?" I said. "Your business is my business, my lad," I said, "and just you remember it." "Oh," he said in a very nasty way, "I wonder how much business you'd have left if I didn't have scruples." Well, that was a bit much. I told him he could have his cards and get out.'

The ear-rings swung as Mrs Cawthorne gave a small theatrical sigh. 'Poor lamb,' she said. Wexford did not for a moment suppose she referred to her husband. 'I wish I'd been kinder to him.' There was no doubt what she meant by that. It was grotesque. God help him, he thought. Surely he wasn't going to have another regretful woman on his hands? What value they all put on themselves, all sorry, all wanting to reverse the hands of the clock.

'Scruples,' he said. 'What did he mean by that?'

Again Cawthorne favoured them with that curious narrowing of the eyes.

'Been taking away your business, had he?' Burden put in quickly, remembering Mrs Penistan.

'He was a good mechanic,' Cawthorne said. 'Too good.' This last perhaps reminded him of the whisky, for he poured himself some more, first half-filling the glass, then, with a quick reckless tilt to the bottle, topping it to the brim. He sighed, possibly with pleasure, possibly with resignation at another temptation unresisted. 'What I mean to say is, he was too much of a one for the personal touch.' Mrs Cawthorne's laugh cut off the last word with the shrill screeching whine of a circular saw. 'Ingratiated himself with the customers,' he said, ignoring her. 'Madam this and madam that, and then he'd open the doors for them and compliment them on their driving. Damn it all, it's not necessary for a thousand mile service.'

'Harmless, I should have thought.'

'Call it harmless, do you, when a little squirt like that takes away your business? The next thing I knew — heard by a roundabout route . . .' He scowled, the general in Intelligence. 'I have my spies,' he said absurdly. 'I could see it all. "Why not let me do it privately for you, madam. I'd only charge ten bob." ' He took a long pull at his drink. 'And there's not a damn thing I could do about it, what with my overheads. I'm out of pocket if I charge less than twelve and six. A good half-dozen of my customers he got away from me like that, and good customers too. I taxed him with it but he swore they'd taken to going to Missal's. But there was Mrs Curran, to give you an example, and Mr and Miss Margolis . . .'

'Ah!' said Wexford softly.

Cawthorne went pink and avoided his wife's eye.

'You might think she was flighty,' he said, 'but you didn't know her. It wasn't easy come, easy go with her. Oh, it came easily enough, but young Anita watched the spending of every penny. For all we'd been close friends for a year, she didn't think twice about going to Anstey on the sly. Still came to me for petrol, mind.' He belched and changed it to a cough. 'As if there was anything to be made on juice!'

'Were they friendly?'

'Anita and young Ray? Show me the man under fifty she wasn't friendly with. He'd have to have a hump or a hare lip.' But Cawthorne was over fifty, well over, and his age was his own deformity.

'He left you on the Saturday,' Burden said slowly. 'Where would he go?' It was a rhetorical question. He did not expect Cawthorne to answer it. 'D'you know where he was living?'

'Kingsmarkham somewhere. One of my boys might know.' His sodden face fell and he seemed to have forgotten his former attack on Anita Margolis's character. 'You think he killed her, don't you? Killed little Ann . . .'

'Let's find that address, Mr Cawthorne.'

The ear-rings bounced. 'Is he on the run?' Mrs Cawthorne asked excitedly. Her eyes glittered. 'Poor hunted creature!'

'Oh, shut up,' said Cawthorne and went out into the rain.

CHAPTER SEVENTEEN

They stood in the porch while Cawthorne questioned the men. The rain was passing now and the clouds splitting. Over Kingsmarkham they could see that patches of sky were showing between the great banks of cumulus, a fresh bright sky that was almost green.

'One hundred and eighty-six, High Street, Kingsmarkham,' Cawthorne said, trotting up to them and making a little final spurt for cover. 'That's his headquarters, or was.'

'One eight six,' said Burden quickly. 'Let's see now. The news block's one five eight to one seven four, then the chemist and the florist . . .' He ticked the numbers off on his fingers. 'But that must be . . .'

'Well, it's Grover's the newsagents.' Cawthorne looked as if it was only what he had expected. 'They let one of their attic rooms, you know. A couple of my chaps have lodged there before and when Anstey lost his first billet down the road here, someone suggested Grover's might fill the bill. Mind you, he was only there a month.'

'On our own doorstep!' Wexford said with an angry snort when they were in the car. 'You can see that place from our windows. A fat lot of use our observatory's been to us.'

'It's common knowledge they take lodgers, sir,' Burden said apologetically, but he did not know for whom he was making excuses and he added in his own defence, 'I daresay we've all seen a young dark fellow going in and out. We'd no cause to connect him with this case. How many thousands of little dark chaps are there in Kingsmarkham alone?'

Wexford said grimly, 'He didn't have to go far to see Ruby's ad., did he? He was in the right place to replace his knife, too. What happens now to your theory about the cars? Anstey didn't even own one, let alone swop black for green.'

'Anita got five hundred pounds the day before they went to Ruby's. Mrs Penistan says she was generous. Maybe she bought him a car.'

517

They pulled up on the police station forecourt. Burden turned his head to see a man come out of Grover's with an evening paper. As they went up the steps under the broad white canopy, water dripped from it on to their coat collars.

'Maybe she bought him a car,' Burden said again. 'You could buy a very decent second-hand car for five hundred.'

'We're told she was generous,' Wexford said on the stairs. 'We're also told she was hard-headed and careful with her money. She wasn't an old woman with a kept man. Young girls don't buy cars for their boy friends.'

It was warm and silent in Wexford's office. The chairs were back against the walls and the papers on the rosewood desk neatly arranged. Nothing remained to show that earlier it had been the scene of a tragic drama. Burden took off his raincoat and spread it in front of the warm air grille.

'Kirkpatrick saw her at twenty past seven,' he said. 'She was at Ruby's by eight. That gave her forty minutes to change her coat, get down to Grover's, leave her Alpine there for him to mend at some future time and drive to Stowerton. It could easily be done.'

'When Kirkpatrick saw her she was wearing that ocelot thing. You'd naturally expect her to change into a raincoat in the cottage, but the ocelot was *on the passenger seat of her car*. It's a small point, but it may be important. Then we come to this question of time. Your theory only works if Anita and Anstey already had a green car available. Maybe they did. We shall see. But if, at that juncture in the proceedings, they had to borrow or hire a car, it couldn't be done.'

'It could be done if they used Margolis's car,' said Burden.

Drayton and Martin interrupted them and moved in on the conference. The four of them sat round the desk while Wexford put the newcomers in the picture. He watched Drayton's face grow hard and his eyes stony when Grover's shop was mentioned.

'Right,' he said, looking at his watch. 'We'll give them a chance to close up and then we'll all go over. Grover's more or less bedridden at the moment, isn't he?' He gave Drayton a sharp look.

'Up and about again now, sir.'

'Good,' Wexford nodded. 'Now,' he said to Burden. 'What's all this about Margolis's car? Margolis was in London.'

'He'd left his car at Kingsmarkham station and it *is* a green car. Wouldn't Anita be just the kind of girl to go a couple of hundred yards down York Street to the station approach and borrow her brother's car? They could have got it back by the time he wanted it.'

'Don't forget they thought he'd want it at nine, not eleven. No one knew he'd be dining with this gallery manager.'

'So what?' Burden shrugged. 'If ever there was an easy-going slapdash pair it's Margolis and his sister. If his car wasn't there he'd probably think he hadn't left it there or that it had been stolen. And he'd never do anything about that until he saw her. Anstey dumped her body, returned Margolis's car to the station car park and when everyone was in bed and asleep, filled up the Alpine radiator, taking a can of water with him to be on the safe side, and drove it back to Quince Cottage.'

He expected to see on Wexford's face a look of pleasure and approval comparable to that he had shown the previous night at the Olive and Dove. Everything was beginning to fit beautifully, and he, Burden, had dovetailed it. Why then had Wexford's mouth settled into those dubious grudging creases? He waited for comment, for some sort of agreement that all this was at least possible, but the Chief Inspector said softly:

'I have other ideas, I'm afraid.'

The shop was closed. In the alley water lay in puddles that mirrored the greenish lamplight. Two bins had been moved out in front of the garage doors for the dust collection in the morning. A cat sniffed them, leaving wet paw marks on someone's discarded newspaper.

Drayton had not wanted to come with them. He knew who Ray Anstey was now, the man he had seen her kissing by the bridge, the man who lodged with them and who had borrowed his employer's cars to take her out. Perhaps they had used that very car in which Drayton himself had driven her to Cheriton Forest. He had deceived her with Ann Margolis and she him with a young policeman. It was a roundabout, a changing spinning thing that sometimes came to a long pause. He felt that he had reached a halt and that they must alight from it together, perhaps for life.

But he had not wanted to come. Undesired things would be revealed to him and she who would be questioned might speak of a love he wanted to forget. He stood at the rear while Burden banged on the glass and as he waited it came to him suddenly that it would not have mattered whether Wexford had brought him or not. Where else had he to go in the evenings? He would have come here anyway, as he always came.

It was Grover himself who came to let them in. Drayton expected him to be antagonistic, but the man was ingratiating and the oiliness of his greeting was more repulsive than hostility. His black hair was flattened down and combed to cover a small bald spot and it smelt of violet oil. One hand clamped to the small of his back, he ushered them into the shop and put on a light.

'Ray was here a month,' he said in answer to Wexford's question. 'Cawthorne gave him the push on the Saturday and he left here on the Tuesday. Or so Lin and the wife said. I never saw him, being as I was laid up.'

'I believe he had one of your attic rooms.'

Grover nodded. He was not an old man but he dressed like one. Drayton tried to keep his eyes still and his face expressionless as he noted the unbuttoned cardigan, the collarless shirt and the trousers that had never been brushed or pressed. 'His room's been done,' the newsagent said quickly. 'Lin cleaned it up. He never left nothing behind so it's no use you looking.'

'We'll look,' Burden said lightly. 'In a minute.' His cold eyes skimmed the magazines and then he strolled down to the dark corner where the library was. Grover followed him, hobbling.

'I've got nothing to tell you, Mr Burden,' he said. 'He didn't leave no forwarding address and he'd paid up his next month's rent in advance. There was three weeks to run.'

Burden took a book from the shelf and opened it in the middle, but his face did not change. 'Tell me about Tuesday evening,' he said.

'Tell you what? There's nothing to tell. Lin was in and out all afternoon. We wanted some bread and it's early closing here on Tuesdays — not for us, we don't close. She popped into Stowerton. The wife went to her whist drive around half seven and Lin was off somewhere — the launderette, that was it.' He paused, looking virtuous. Drayton felt angry and bewildered. The anger was for the way Grover used her as a maid of all work. He could not account for the bewilderment unless it was because he could not understand her father's lack of appreciation. 'I never saw Ray all day,' Grover said. 'I was in bed, you see. You'd have thought he'd have looked in on me to say good-bye and thank me for all I'd done for him.'

'Like what?' Burden snapped. 'Providing him with a lethal weapon, that sort of thing?'

'I never gave him that knife. He had it when he first come.'

'Go on.'

'Go on with what, Mr Burden?' Grover felt his back, gingerly probing the muscles. 'I told you I never saw Ray after the Monday. The doctor came before the wife went out and said I was to stop in bed . . .'

'Anyone else call? During the evening, I mean?'

'Only that girl,' Grover said.

Burden blew dust off the book he was holding and replaced it on the shelf. He came close to Grover and stood over him. 'What girl? What happened?'

'I was in bed, you see, and there was this banging on the shop door.' The newsagent gave Wexford a sly yet sullen glance. 'I thought it was you lot,' he said. 'It's all very well the doctor saying not to get out of bed on any account, but what are you supposed to do when someone comes banging fit to break the door in?' He winced, perhaps at the memory of an earlier and more acute pain. 'One of his customers it was. I'd seen her about before. Tall, good-looking piece, but older than my girl. You want to know what she looked like?'

'Of course. We haven't come here for social chit-chat, Grover.'

Standing by the paperback stand, Drayton felt almost sick. Burden's reprimand, far from disconcerting Grover, had provoked a sycophantic grin. His lips closed, he stretched them wide, half-closing one eye. This mockery of a smile seemed the ghost of Linda's own. In fact it was the begetter, and Drayton felt nausea rise in his throat.

'Bit of all right she was,' Grover said, again sketching his wink. 'Kind of white skin and black hair with two curly bits coming over her cheeks.' He seemed to reflect and he wetted his lips. 'Got up in black trousers and a spotted fur coat. "What d'you mean banging like that?" I said. "Can't you see we've closed?" "Where's Ray?" she says. "If he's in his room I'll go up and root him out." "You'll do no such thing," I said. "Anyway, he's not there." She looked proper put out at that so I asked her what she wanted him for. I don't know whether she didn't like me asking or whether she was thinking up some excuse. "I'm going to a party," she says, "and I'm bloody late as it is and now my car radiator's sprung a leak." Mind you, I couldn't see no car. Go up to his room, would you? I thought, and him going steady with my Linda.'

Drayton gave a small painful cough. It sounded like a groan in the silence which had fallen. Wexford looked at him and his eyes were cold.

Grover went on after a pause, ' "In that case you'd best take it to a garage," I said, and then I come out on to the pavement in my dressing gown. There was this white sports job stuck in my sideway with a pool of water underneath it. "I daren't drive it," she said. "I'm scared it'll blow up on me." '

'Did she go away?' Burden asked, discreetly jubilant.

'I reckon she did, but I didn't wait to see. I locked up again and went back to bed.'

'And you heard nothing more?'

'Nothing till the wife came in. I do remember thinking I hoped she'd got that white car of hers out on account of Lin not being able to get mine into the garage if it was there. But I dropped off to sleep and the next thing I knew was the wife getting into bed and saying Lin had come in half an hour before. D'you want to see his room now?'

Frowning slightly, Burden came out of his dark corner and stood under the light that hung above the counter. He glanced down the passage towards the side door that led to the alley. For a moment Drayton thought he had seen someone coming. Linda herself perhaps, and he braced himself to face the shock of her entrance, but Burden turned back to the newsagent and said:

'Where did he do this car servicing of his?'

'In my spare garage,' Grover said. 'I've got the two, you

see. My own car's in one and the other used to be let, but I lost
my tenant and when young Ray said he wanted it I let him have
it.' He nodded smugly. Perhaps this was the favour, or one of
the favours, for which he had claimed Anstey's gratitude. 'I only
charged him five bob a week extra. Mind you, he had plenty of
customers. Been doing the same thing at his old digs, if you ask
me.'

'I'd like to see both garages,' Burden said. 'Keys?'

'The wife's got them.' Grover went into the passage and
took an old overcoat down from a wall hook. 'Or maybe Lin
has. I don't know, I haven't had the car out for the best part of
a fortnight, my back's been so bad.' He got into the coat with
difficulty, screwing up his face.

'Keys, Drayton,' Wexford said laconically.

Half-way up the stairs, Drayton met Mrs Grover coming down.
She looked at him incuriously and would have passed him, he
thought, without a word.

'Can you let me have your garage keys, Mrs Grover?' he
asked. Linda must have told her who and what he was.

'In the kitchen,' she said. 'Lin left them on the table.' She
peered at him short-sightedly. Her eyes were as grey as her
daughter's, but passionless, and if they had ever held tears they
had long been swept away. 'I'm right in thinking you're her
young fellow, aren't I?' Who he was, Drayton thought, but not
what he was. 'She said you and her'd want the car tonight.' She
shrugged. 'Don't let her dad know, that's all.'

'I'll go up, then.'

Mrs Grover nodded indifferently. Drayton watched her go
down the stairs and leave by the side door. The kitchen door
was open and he went in. Out of her parents' presence, his
sickness went, but his heart was beating painfully. The keys lay
on the table, one for each garage and one ignition key, and they
were attached to a ring with a leather fob. Beside them was a
pile of unfolded, unironed linen, and at the sight of it he felt a
return of that bewilderment he had experienced in the shop.
The keys were in his pocket and he had reached the head of the
stairs when a door facing him opened and Linda came out.

For the first time he saw her hair hanging loose, curtaining her shoulders in a pale bright veil. She smiled at him softly and shyly but all the coquetry was gone.

'You're early,' she said as she had said that day when he had come to take her to Wexford. 'I'm not ready.' It came to him suddenly that she, like her mother, had no idea why he was there or that others of his calling were down below in the shop. Perhaps she need not know and the knowledge of what probably lay in one of those garages be kept from her a little longer. 'Wait for me,' she said. 'Wait in the shop. I won't be long.'

'I'll come back later,' he said. He thought he could go back to them without touching her, but he could neither move nor take his eyes from the spell of the tiny wavering smile and the golden cloak of hair.

'Mark,' she said and her voice was breathless. She came towards him trembling. 'Mark, you'll help me out of — out of all this, won't you? The linen on the table, the shop, the chores. He nodded, committing himself to what? To a yet unconsidered rescue? To marriage? 'You do love me, then?'

For once the question was not a signal for evasion and ultimate departure. That she should love him and want his love was to confer upon him an honour and to offer him a privilege. He took her in his arms and held her to him, touching her hair with his lips. 'I love you,' he said. He had used the forbidden verb and his only sensation was a breathless humble longing to give and give to the utmost of his capacity.

'I'd do anything for you,' he said. Then he let her go and he ran down the stairs.

Faded green paint was peeling from the garage doors. From their roof gutters water streamed out of a cracked drainpipe and made a scummy pool around the dustbins. Drayton let himself into the alley by the side door. His hands were shaking because of what had passed upstairs and because here, a few yards from where Grover and the policemen stood, he had first kissed her. He raised his hood against the drizzle and handed the keys to Wexford.

'You took your time about it.'

'We had to look for them,' Drayton muttered. Whether it was that 'we' or the badly told lie that gave rise to that chilly glance Drayton did not know. He went over to the dustbins and began shoving them out of the way.

'Before we open the doors,' Wexford said, 'there's one little point I'd like cleared up.' Although it was not cold, Grover had begun to rub his hands and stamp his feet. He gave the Chief Inspector a sour disgruntled look. 'Inspector Burden was about to ask you what time Miss Margolis, the girl with the white car, called on you. He was about to ask, but something else came up.'

'Let me refresh your memory,' Burden said quickly. 'Between seven thirty and eight, wasn't it? More like half past seven.'

The hunched shivering figure galvanised into sudden life. 'Half seven?' Grover said incredulously. 'You're joking. I told you the wife and Lin came in just after. Half seven, my foot. It was all of ten.'

'She was dead at ten!' Burden said desperately and he turned to appeal to Wexford who, bland and urbane, stood apparently lost in thought. 'She was dead! You're wrong, you mistook the time.'

'Let us open the doors,' said Wexford.

Drayton unlocked the first garage and it was empty. On the concrete floor was a black patch where oil had once been.

'This the one Anstey used?'

Grover nodded, viewing the deserted place suspiciously. 'There's only my car in the other one.'

'We'll look, just the same.'

The door stuck and Drayton had to put his shoulder to it. When the catch gave, Burden switched on his torch and the beam fell on an olive-green Mini.

It was Wexford who opened the unlocked boot and revealed two suitcases and a canvas bag of tools. Muttering, Grover prodded the bag until Burden removed his hand roughly. Through the rear window something could be seen lying on the passenger seat, a stiff bundle, one arm in a raincoat sleeve outflung, black hair from which the gloss had gone.

Wexford eased his bulky body between the side of the car and the garage wall. He pressed his thumb to the handle and opened the door as widely as he could in that confined space. His mouth set, for he could feel a fresh onset of nausea, Drayton followed him to stare over the Chief Inspector's shoulder.

The body which was sprawled before them had a blackened stain of dried blood across the breast of the raincoat and there was blood on the hilt and the blade of the knife someone had placed in its lap. Once this corpse had been young and beautiful — the waxen features had a comeliness and a symmetry about them even in death — but it had never been a woman.

'Anstey,' said Wexford succinctly.

A dark trickle had flowed from one corner of the dead man's mouth. Drayton put his handkerchief up to his face and stumbled out of the garage.

She had come from the side door and her hair was still loose, moving now in the faint wind. Her arms were bare and on them and on her face gooseflesh had arisen, white and rough, like a disease. Incredible that that mouth had once smiled and kissed.

When he saw her Drayton stopped. In the wind and the rain a death's head was confronting him, a skull staring through stretched skin, and it was much more horrifying than what he had just seen in the car. She parted the lips that had smiled for him and been his fetish and gave a scream of terror.

'You were going to save me! You loved me, you'd do anything for me . . . You were going to save me!' He put out his arms, not to enclose her but to ward her off. 'I went with you because you said you'd save me!' she screamed, and flinging herself upon him, tore at his cheeks with the bitten nails that could not wound. Something cold struck his chin. It was the silver chain that Anstey had stolen from his wife.

When Burden pulled her away and held her while she kicked and sobbed, Drayton stood with his eyes closed. He could sort out nothing from her cries and the harsh tumult of words, only that she had never loved him. It was a revelation more unspeakable than the other and it cut into his ears like a knife slitting membrane. He turned from the watching eyes, the man's stern, the girl's unbearable, stumbled from the alley into the backyard and was sick against the wall.

CHAPTER EIGHTEEN

She was waiting in Wexford's office. Two minutes before, down in the foyer, he had been warned of her presence, so he was able to repress natural astonishment and approach her with the aplomb of a Stanley.

'Miss Margolis, I presume?'

She must have been home. After arriving from wherever she had been, she must have called at the cottage to collect the ocelot coat. It was slung across her shoulders over a puce and peacock trouser suit. He noted her tan and the bronze glaze a hotter sun than that of Sussex had given to her dark hair.

'Rupert said you thought I was dead,' she said. 'But he does tend to be unsure of things. I thought I ought to come and clarify.' She sat on the edge of his desk, pushing papers out of her way. He felt like a guest in his own office and he would not have been surprised if she had asked him in just this imperiously gracious tone to sit down.

'I think I know most of it,' he said firmly. 'Suppose I tell you and you correct the more crashing howlers.' She smiled at him with catlike enjoyment. 'You've been in Spain or Italy. Perhaps Ibiza?'

'Positano. I flew back this morning.' She crossed her legs. The trousers had bell bottoms with pink fringes. 'Dickie Fairfax got through a hundred and fifty quid of my money in a week. You might not think it to look at me but I'm very bourgeois at heart. Love's all very well but it's abstract if you know what I mean. Money's concrete and when it's gone it's gone.' She added thoughtfully, 'So I abandoned him and came home. I'm afraid he may have to throw himself on the mercy of the consul.' Black eyebrows met over the bridge of that pretty hawk's nose. 'Perhaps Dickie's name doesn't mean anything to you?'

'Wild conjecture,' said Wexford, 'leads me to suppose that he is the young man who went to the Cawthornes' party and when he found you weren't there, sallied forth to find you, chanting passages from Omar Khayyám.'

'How clever of you!' If she looked at them like this, Wexford thought, and flattered them like that, it was no wonder they came to her purring and let her devour them. 'You see,' she said, 'I had every intention of going to the party but that bloody stupid car of mine broke down. I hadn't a clue there was anything wrong with it until after half past nine when I left for the party. It was boiling like a kettle all the way down the road. Then I thought of Ray. I knew he'd fix it for me . . . Oh, but you were going to do the talking!'

Wexford returned her smile, but not enthusiastically. He was growing tired of young women, their ways, their wiles, their diverse characteristics. 'I can only guess,' he said. 'Anstey was out. Then I think you tried to drive to the party but the car died on you . . .'

'You've left something out. I saw Ray first. I was trying to get the car out of the alley when the Grover girl came along in hers. Ray was in the passenger seat, looking terrible. She said he was drunk but, my God, he looked as if he was dying! She wouldn't let me go near him, so I just backed the car out and left them.'

'He *was* dying,' Wexford said, 'or dead already.' Her eyebrows went up to meet the bronzy fringe but she said nothing. 'You might have come to us, Miss Margolis. You're supposed to have a reputation for being public-spirited.'

'But I did tell you,' she said softly, 'or I told Rupert. When I left Grover's I got about a hundred yards up the road and the car conked out. Well, I got some water from a cottage and filled up the radiator. I sort of crawled about half way to Stowerton and I was sitting in the damn thing cursing my luck when Dickie came along, singing at the top of his voice about being merry with the fruitful grape. We'd had a sort of affair about six months ago, you see, and we sat in the car talking. I had all that money in my bag. Talk about sugar for the horse. He's always on the breadline and when he knew I was flush he said, what about you and me going off to Italy? Well, it is a bloody climate here, isn't it?'

Wexford sighed. She was her brother's sister all right.

'He was terribly sloshed,' she went on artlessly. Wexford thanked God Burden was otherwise engaged. 'We sat about for hours. In the end when he'd sobered up he went back to Cawthorne's for his car and I drove mine home. It must have been about one. Rupert was in bed and he hates being disturbed, so I wrote him a note, telling him where I was going and then I remembered about Ray. Go round to Grover's, I wrote, and see if Ray's all right because I don't like it . . .'

'Where did you leave it?'

'Leave what?'

'The note.'

'Oh, the note. I wrote it on a big sheet of cartridge paper and stuck it in front of a pile of newspapers on the kitchen counter. I suppose it got lost.'

'He threw it away,' said Wexford. 'The lights fused and he threw it away in the dark with the newspapers. He had an idea we might have sent someone to clear it all up for him.' He added thoughtfully, 'We thought it infra dig. Perhaps we should be more humble.'

'Well, it might have saved a lot of trouble,' said Anita Margolis. Suddenly she laughed, rocking back and forth so that the glass sculpture shook precariously. 'That's so like Roo. He thinks the world owes him a regiment of slaves.' She seemed to remember that the question under discussion was no laughing matter and she grew quickly serious. 'I met Dickie in the High Street,' she said, 'and we drove straight to London Airport.'

'Why did you change your coat?'

'Change my coat? Did I?'

'The one you're wearing now was found on the passenger seat of your car.'

'I remember now. It was raining like mad, so I put on the one raincoat I've got, a red vinyl thing. You see, Dickie's car makes such a racket I didn't want him disturbing the peace and waking Rupert, so I arranged to meet him in the High Street.'

She looked at him impishly. 'Have you ever sat for three hours in a car in a soaking wet fur coat?'

'I can't say I have.'

'The proverbial drowned rat,' she said.

'I suppose you fetched your passport at the same time.' She nodded and he asked in some exasperation, 'Don't you ever send postcards, Miss Margolis?'

'Oh, do call me Ann. Everyone does. As to postcards, I might if I was enjoying myself, but what with Dickie getting through simply millions of horrid little *lire,* I never got around to it. Poor Roo! I'm thinking of carrying him off to Ibiza tomorrow. He's so very disturbed and, anyway, I can't wear all my lovely new clothes here, can I?'

She slithered languidly from the desk and, too late to stop it, Wexford saw the hem of her spotted coat catch at fragile glass. The blue sculpture did a nose-dive, rising slightly in the air, and it was her lunge to save it that sent it crashing against the leg of his desk.

'God, I'm terribly sorry,' said Anita Margolis.

She retrieved a dozen of the larger fragments in a half-hearted, well-meaning way. 'What a shame!'

'I never liked it,' Wexford said. 'One thing before you go. Did you ever own that lighter?'

'What lighter?'

'A gold thing for Ann who lights someone's life.'

She bent her head thoughtfully and the big crescents of hair swept her cheeks. 'A lighter I once showed to Alan Kirkpatrick?' Wexford nodded. 'It was never mine,' she said. 'It was Ray's.'

'He serviced the car and left the lighter in it by accident?'

'Mm-hm. I returned it to him the next day. Admittedly, I more or less let Alan think it was mine.' She wriggled her toes in gilt-strapped sandals, grinding glass into Wexford's carpet. 'He was always so jealous, a natural bait for a tease. Have you seen his car? He wanted to take me out in it. Just what do you think I am? I said, an exhibit in the Lord Mayor's show? I do tease people, I'm afraid.'

'You have teased us all,' said Wexford severely.

The letter of resignation had been pushed aside with the other papers on his desk. It was still unopened, a thick white envelope with the Chief Inspector's name on it in a clear upright hand. Drayton had used good paper and he had used ink, not a ballpoint. He liked, Wexford knew, the good things of life, the best and beautiful things. You could get too fond of beauty, seduced and intoxicated.

Wexford thought he understood, but understanding would not stop him accepting that resignation. He only thanked God that it had all come to light in time. Another day and he'd have asked Drayton if he'd care to make one of a group of young people Sheila was organising to the theatre in Chichester. Another day . . .

Anita Margolis had left perfume behind her. *Chant d'Arômes* that Wexford's nose detected better than an analyst's tests. It was a breath of frivolity, expensive, untender, like herself. He opened the window to let it out before the coming interview.

Drayton came in five minutes before the appointed time and Wexford was on the floor, gathering up broken glass. The young man had not caught him at a disadvantage. Wexford, in getting down to this menial task, had considered any occupation preferable to pacing up and down because a raw detective constable had made a fool of himself.

'You're resigning, I see,' he said. 'I think you're doing the wisest thing.'

Drayton's face was almost unchanged, perhaps a little paler than usual. Four red marks showed on each cheek, but the girl's nails had been too short to break the skin. His expression held neither defiance nor humility. Wexford had expected embarrassment. A violent outburst of emotion, long contained, would not have surprised him. Perhaps that would come. For the moment he sensed a self-control so regulated that it seemed like ease.

'Look, Drayton,' he said heavily, 'no one supposes you actually made that girl any promises. I know you better than that. But the whole thing — well, it smells and that's a fact.'

The narrow contained smile might have been the rejoinder to a wary joke. 'The stink of corruption,' Drayton said and his tone was cooler than the smile. Between them the lingering French scent hung like the perfume of a judge's posy, shielding him from contamination.

'I'm afraid we all have to be beyond reproach.' What else was there to say? Wexford thought of the pompous sermon he had prepared and it sickened him. 'My God, Mark!' he burst out, moving around the desk to stand in front of and tower above Drayton. 'Why couldn't you take the hint and drop her when I told you? You knew her, she talked to you. Couldn't you put two and two together? That alibi she gave to Kirkpatrick and we thought he'd got at her — she was alibi-ing herself! It was eight when she saw him, not nine thirty.'

Drayton nodded slowly, his lips compressed.

Splinters of glass crunched under Wexford's shoes. 'She was on her way to Ruby's house when she saw him and Anstey was with her, only Kirkpatrick didn't notice. Grover told us she went out on Tuesday afternoon, to go shopping, he said. That was when she took the washing, in the afternoon, not in the evening.'

'I began to guess that,' Drayton murmured.

'And you said not a word?'

'It was just a feeling of unease, of something not being right.'

Wexford set his teeth. He had almost gasped with annoyance. Some of it was for his own folly in that, while disapproving, he had entered with a certain romantic and conspiratorial delight into Drayton's love affair.

'You were nosing around that place for God knows how long and all the time that fellow's body was lying in the garage. You knew her, you knew her damn' well . . .' His voice rose and he knew he was trying to spark off in Drayton an answering show of passion. 'Didn't natural curiosity make you want to know who her ex-boy friend was? They'd had a lodger for four weeks, a small dark lodger who disappeared on the night of the murder. Couldn't you have told us?'

'I didn't know,' Drayton said. 'I didn't want to know.'

'You have to want to know, Mark,' Wexford said tiredly. 'It's the first rule of the game.' He had forgotten what it was like to be in love, but he remembered a lighted window, a girl leaning out and a man standing in the shadows beneath. It distressed him to know that passion could exist and grief beside it, that they could twist a man's bones and not show on his face. He had no son, but from time to time it is given to every man to be another's father. 'I should go away from here,' he said, 'right away. No need for you to appear in court. You'll forget it all, you know. Believe me, you will.'

'What did she do?' Drayton said very quietly.

'Anstey held the knife to her throat. He relied on a girl's fear and his own attraction to make her acquiescent. She wasn't, you see. She got it away from him and stabbed him in a lung.'

'Was he dead when they got home?'

'I don't know. I don't think she does. Perhaps we never shall know. She left him and ran upstairs to her father, but the next day she couldn't go back. I can understand that. The time would come when her father would want the car and Anstey would be found. Before that happened she hoped for a miracle. I think you were to be that miracle. You were to help her get him away, but we got there first.'

'She had the car keys out ready for me.' He looked down and now his voice was almost a whisper.

'We came half an hour too soon, Drayton.'

The boy's head jerked up. 'I would never have done it.'

'Not when it came to the final crunch, eh? No, you would never have done it.' Wexford cleared his throat. 'What will you do now?'

'I'll get by,' Drayton said. He went to the door and a sliver of glass snapped under his shoe. 'You broke your ornament,' he said politely. 'I'm sorry.'

In the hall he put on his duffel coat and raised the hood. Thus dressed, with a lock of black hair falling across his forehead, he looked like a mediaeval squire who has lost his knight and abandoned his crusade. When he had said good night to Sergeant Camb who knew nothing but that young Drayton was somehow in hot water, he came out into the wet windy street and began to walk towards his lodgings. By a small detour he could have avoided passing Grover's shop, but he did not take it. The place was in total darkness as if they had all moved away and in the alley the cobbles were wet stones on the floor of a cave.

Two months, three months, a year perhaps, and the worst would be over. Men have died from time to time and worms have eaten them, but not of love . . . The world was full of jobs and full of girls. He would find one of each and they would do him very well The daffodils in the florist's window had an untouched exquisite freshness. He would always think of her whenever he saw something beautiful in an ugly setting.

But you got over everything eventually. He wished only that he did not feel so sick and at the same time so very young. The last time he had felt like this was fourteen years ago when his mother had died and that also was the last time he had wept.

PUT
ON BY
CUNNING

For Simon

So shall you hear . . .
Of deaths put on by cunning and forc'd cause;
And, in this upshot, purposes mistook
Fall'n on th'inventors' heads — all this can I
Truly deliver.

Hamlet

Part One

CHAPTER ONE

Against the angels and apostles in the windows the snow fluttered like plucked down. A big soft flake struck one of the Pre-Raphaelite haloes and clung there, cotton wool on gold tinsel. It was something for an apathetic congregation to watch from the not much warmer interior as the rector of St Peter's, Kingsmarkham, came to the end of the second lesson. St Matthew, chapter fifteen, for 27 January.

'For out of the heart proceed evil thoughts, murders, adulteries, fornications, thefts, false witness, blasphemies. These are the things which defile a man. . . .'

Two of his listeners turned their eyes from the pattern the snow was making on a red and blue and yellow and purple 'Annunciation' and waited expectantly. The rector closed the heavy Bible with its dangling marker and opened an altogether more mundane-looking, small black book of the exercise variety. He cleared his throat.

'I publish the banns of marriage between Sheila Katherine Wexford, spinster, of this parish, and Andrew Paul Thorverton, bachelor, of the parish of St John, Hampstead. This is the first time of asking. And between Manuel Camargue, widower, of this parish, and Dinah Baxter Sternhold, widow, of the parish of St Mary, Forby. This is the third time of asking. If any of you know cause or just impediment why these persons should not be joined together in holy matrimony, ye are to declare it.'

He closed the book. Manuel Camargue resigned himself, for the third week in succession, to the sermon. As the congregation settled itself, he looked about him. The same crowd of old faithfuls came each week. He saw only one newcomer, a beautiful fair-haired girl whom he instantly recognized without being able to put a name to her. He worried about this a good deal for the next half-hour, trying to place her, annoyed with himself because his memory had become so hopeless and glasses no longer did much for his eyes.

The name came to him just as everyone was getting up to

leave. Sheila Wexford. Sheila Wexford, the actress. That was who it was. He and Dinah had seen her last autumn in that Somerset Maugham revival, though what the name of the play had been escaped him. She had been at school with Dinah, they still knew each other slightly. Her banns had been called before his but her name hadn't registered because of that insertion of Katherine. It was odd that two people as famous as they should have had their banns called simultaneously in this country parish church.

He looked at her again. She was dressed in a coat of sleek pale fur over a black wool dress. Her eye caught his and he saw that she also recognized him. She gave him a quick faint smile, a smile that was conspiratorial, rueful, gay, ever so slightly embarrassed, all those things expressed as only an actress of her calibre could express them. Camargue countered with a smile of his own, the best he could do.

It was still snowing. Sheila Wexford put an umbrella up and made an elegant dash towards the lychgate. Should he offer her a lift to wherever she lived? Camargue decided that his legs were inadequate to running after her, especially through six-inch deep snow. When he reached the gate he saw her getting into a car driven by a man at least old enough to be her father. He felt a pang for her. Was this the bridegroom? And then the absurdity of such a thought, coming from him, struck him forcefully and with a sense which he often had of the folly of human beings and their blindness to their own selves.

Ted was waiting in the Mercedes. Reading the *News of the World,* hands in woollen gloves. He had the engine running to work the heater and the wipers and the demisters. When he saw Camargue he jumped out and opened the rear door.

'There you are, Sir Manuel. I put a rug in seeing it's got so perishing.'

'What a kind chap you are,' said Camargue. 'It was jolly cold in church. Let's hope it'll warm up for the wedding.'

Ted said he hoped so but the long range weather forecast was as gloomy as per usual. If he hadn't held his employer in such honour and respect he would have said he'd have his love to keep him warm. Camargue knew this and smiled to himself. He pulled the rug over his knees. Dinah, he thought, my Dinah.

Towards her he felt a desire as passionate, as youthful, as intense, as any he had known as a boy. But he would never touch her, he knew better than that, and his mouth curled with distaste at the idea of it, of him and her together. It would be enough for him that she should be his dear companion — for a little while.

They had entered the gates and were mounting the long curving drive that led up to the house. Ted drove in the two channels, now filling once more with snow, which he had dug out that morning. From the smooth, pure and radiant whiteness, flung like a soft and spotless cloth over the hillocks and little valleys of Camargue's garden, rose denuded silver birches, poplars and willows, and the spikes of conifers, dark green and slate-blue and golden-yellow, as snugly clothed as gnomes.

The jam factory came into view quite suddenly. Camargue called it the jam factory, or sometimes the shoebox, because it was unlike any of the houses around. Not mock or real Tudor, not fake or genuine Georgian, but a long box with lots of glass, and at one end, dividing the original building from the newer wing, a tower with a peaked roof like an oast house. Perched on the weathervane, a facsimile of a treble clef in wrought iron, was a seagull, driven inland in its quest for food. It looked as white as the snow itself against the cinder-dark sky.

Ted's wife, Muriel, opened the front door. You entered the house at the lower level, where it was built into the hillside. There was a wide hall here which led through an arch into the dining room.

'It's so cold, sir,' said Muriel, 'that I'm cooking you a proper lunch since you said you wouldn't be going to Mrs Sternhold's.'

'Jolly thoughtful of you,' said Camargue, who no longer much cared what he ate. Muriel took his coat away to dry it. She and Ted lived in a house in the grounds, a period piece and as much unlike the jam factory as could be. Camargue liked her to have her afternoons off and all of her Sundays, but he couldn't be always checking her generous impulses. When he was half-way up the stairs the dog Nancy came down to meet him, wide smiling mouth and eager pink tongue and young strong paws capable of sending him flying. She was his fifth alsatian, a rich roan colour, just two years old.

The drawing room, two of its walls entirely glass, shone with the curious light that is uniquely reflected off snow. The phone began to ring as he stepped off the top stair.

'Were they well and truly called?'

'Yes, darling, the third time of asking. And at St Peter's?'

'Yes. My word, it was cold, Dinah. Is it snowing in Forby?'

'Well, it is but not all that heavily. Won't you change your mind and come? The main roads are all right and you know Ted won't mind. I do wish you'd come.'

'No. You'll have your parents. They've met me. Let them get over the shock a bit before Saturday.' Camargue laughed at her exclamation of protest. 'No, my dear, I won't come today. Muriel's cooking lunch for me. Just think, after Saturday you'll have to have all your meals with me, no excuses allowed.'

'Manuel, shall I come over this evening?'

He laughed. 'No, please.' It was strange how his accent became more marked when he talked to her. Must be emotion, he supposed. 'The villages will be cut off from Kingsmarkham by tonight, mark my words.'

He went into the music room, the dog following him. Up inside the cone-shaped roof of the tower it was dark like twilight. He looked at the flute which lay in its open case on the table, and then reflectively, no longer with pain, at his clawed hands. The flute had been exposed like that to show to Dinah's mother and Muriel would have been too much in awe of it to put it away. Camargue closed the lid of the case and sat down at the piano. He had never been much of a pianist, a second-class concert average, so it brought him no frustration or sadness to strum away occasionally with those (as he called them) silly old hands of his. He played *Für Elise* while Nancy, who adored piano music, thumped her tail on the marble floor.

Muriel called him to lunch. He went downstairs for it. She liked to lay the big mahogany table with lace and silver and glass just for him, and to wait on him. Far more than he had ever been or could ever be, she was aware of what was due to Sir Manuel Camargue. Ted came in as he was having coffee and said he would take Nancy out now, a good long hike in the snow, he said, she loved snow. And he'd break the ice at the edge of the lake. Hearing the chain on her lead rattle, Nancy nearly fell downstairs in her haste to be out.

Camargue sometimes tried to stop himself sleeping the afternoons away. He was rarely successful. He had a suite of rooms in the wing beyond the tower; bedroom, bathroom, small sitting room where Nancy's basket was, and he would sit determinedly in his armchair, reading or playing records — he was mad about James Galway at the moment. Galway, he thought, was heaps better than he had ever been — but he would always nod off. Often he slept till five or six. He put on the Flute Concerto, Köchel 313, and as the sweet, bright, liquid notes poured out, looked at himself in the long glass. He was still, at any rate, tall. He was thin. Thin like a ramshackle scarecrow, he thought, like an old junk-shop skeleton, with hands that looked as if every joint had been broken and put together again awry. *Tout casse, tout lasse, tout passe.* Now that he was so old he often thought in one or other of the two languages of his infancy. He sat down in the armchair and listened to the music Mozart wrote for a cantankerous Dutchman, and by the time the second movement had begun he was asleep.

Nancy woke him, laying her head in his lap. She had been back from her walk a long time, it was nearly five. Ted wouldn't come back to take her out again. Camargue would let her out himself and perhaps walk with her as far as the lake. It had stopped snowing, and the last of the daylight, a curious shade of yellow, gilded the whiteness and threw long blue shadows. Camargue took James Galway off the turntable and put him back in the sleeve. He walked along the passage and through the music room, pausing to straighten a crooked picture, a photograph of the building which housed the Camargue School of Music at Wellridge, and passed on into the drawing room. As he approached the tea tray Muriel had left for him, the phone rang. Dinah again.

'I phoned before, darling. Were you asleep?'

'What else?'

'I'll come over in the morning, shall I, and bring the rest of the presents? Mother and Dad have brought us silver pastry forks from my uncle, my godfather.'

'I must say, people are jolly generous, the second time

round for both of us. I'll have the drive specially cleared for you. Ted shall be up to do it by the crack of dawn.'

'Poor Ted.' He was sensitive to the slight change in her tone and he braced himself. 'Manuel, you haven't heard any more from — Natalie?'

'From that woman,' said Camargue evenly, 'no.'

'I shall have another go at you in the morning, you know, to make you see reason. You're quite wrong about her, I'm sure you are. And to take a step like changing your will without . . .'

His accent was strong as he interrupted her. 'I saw her, Dinah, not you, and I know. Let's not speak of it again, eh?'

She said simply, 'Whatever you wish. I only want what's best for you.'

'I know that,' he said. He talked to her a little longer and then he went downstairs to make his tea. The tranquillity of the day had been marred by Dinah's raising the subject of Natalie. It forced him to think of that business again when he had begun to shut it out.

He carried the teapot upstairs and lifted the folded napkin from the plate of cucumber sandwiches. That woman, whoever she was, had made the tea and brought the pot up, and it was after that that she had looked at Cazzini's golden gift on the wall and he had known. As is true of all honest and guileless people, Camarge resented attempts to practise deceit on him far more than do those who are themselves deceitful. It had been a hateful affront, and all the worse because it had taken advantage of an old man's weakness and a father's affection. Dinah's plea did not at all alter his feelings. It only made him think he should have told the police or his solicitors, after all. But no. He had told the woman that he had seen through her and he had told her what he meant to do, and now he must do his best to forget it. Dinah was what future he had, Dinah would be his daughter and more than daughter.

He sat by the window with the curtains undrawn, watching the snow turn blue, then glow dully white again as the darkness closed in. The moon was coming up, a full, cold, midwinter's moon, a glowing greenish-white orb. At seven he took the tea things down and fed Nancy a large can of dog meat.

By the light of the moon he could see the lake quite clearly from the drawing-room window. To call it a lake was to flatter it, it was just a big pond really. It lay on the other side of the drive, down a shallow slope and ringed with willow trees and hawthorn bushes. Camargue could see that Ted, as good as his word, had been down to the pond that afternoon and broken the ice for air to get in to the fish. There were carp in the pond, some of them very large and very old. Ted's footprints led down to the water's edge and back up again to the drive. He had cast the ice on to the bank in great grey blocks. The moon showed it all up as well as any arc lamp. Nancy's pawprints were everywhere, and in places in the drifts there were signs of where she had plunged and rolled. He stroked her smooth brown head, drawing her against him, gently pushing her to settle down and sleep at his feet. The moon sailed in a black and shining sky from which all the heavy cloud had gone. He opened his book, the biography of an obscure Romanian composer who had once written an étude especially for him, and read for an hour or so.

When it got to half-past eight he could feel himself nodding off again, so he got up and stretched and stood in the window. To his surprise he saw it was snowing once more, snow falling out of the wrack which was drifting slowly over the clear sky and towards where the moon was. The conifers were powdered again, all but one. Then he saw the tree move. He had often thought that by night and in the half-light and through his failing eyes those trees looked like men. Now he had actually mistaken a man for a tree. Or a woman for a tree. He couldn't tell whether it had been Ted or Muriel that he had seen, a trousered figure in a heavy coat moving up now where the path must be towards the birch copse. It must have been one of them. Camargue decided to postpone letting Nancy out for ten minutes. If Ted saw him he would take over and fuss and probably insist on giving the dog a proper walk which she didn't need after all the exercise she had had. If Muriel saw him she would very likely want to come in and make him cocoa.

The figure in the garden had disappeared. Now the moon was no longer so bright. He couldn't remember that he had ever before seen such snow in all the years he had lived in Sussex. In his youth, in the Pyrenees, the snows had come like this with an even more bitter cold. It was remembering those days that had made him plant in this garden all the little fir trees and yews and junipers. . . .

He could have sworn he saw another tree move. How grotesque was old age when the faculties one took for granted like trusted friends began to play on one malicious practical jokes. He called out:

'Nancy! Time to go out.'

She was there at the head of the stairs long before he was. If he had gone first she would have knocked him over. He walked down behind her, propelling her with his toe when she looked anxiously back and up at him. At the foot of the stairs he switched on the outside light to illuminate the wide court into which the drive led. The snowflakes danced like sparks in the yellow light but when he opened the door the sharp cold of the night rushed in to meet him. Nancy bounded out into the whirling snow. Camargue took his sheepskin coat and gloves and a walking-stick from the cloaks cupboard and followed her out.

She was nowhere to be seen, though her paws had ploughed a path down the slope towards the lake. He fastened his coat and pulled the woollen scarf up around his throat. Nancy, though well aware this outing was no regular walk but merely for the purpose of stimulating and answering a call of nature, nevertheless would sometimes go off. If the weather conditions were right, damp and muggy, for instance, or like this, she had been known to go off for half an hour. It would be a nuisance were she to do that tonight when he felt so tired that even on his feet, even with this icy air stinging his face, he could feel drowsiness closing in on him.

'Nancy! Nancy, where are you?'

He could easily go back into the house and phone Ted and ask him to come over and await the dog's return. Ted wouldn't mind. On the other hand, wasn't that yielding to the very helplessness he was always striving against? What business had he to be getting married, to be setting up house again, even recommencing a social life, if he couldn't do such a little thing for himself as letting a dog out before he went to bed? What he would do was return to the house and sit in the chair in the hall and wait for Nancy to come back. If he fell asleep her scraping at the front door would awaken him.

Even as he decided this he did the very opposite. He followed the track she had made down the slope to the lake, calling her, irritably now, as he went.

The marks Ted had made when he broke the ice at the water's edge were already obliterated by snow, while Nancy's fresh tracks were fast becoming covered. Only the stacked ice showed where Ted had been. The area he had cleared was again iced over with a thin grey crust. The lake was a sombre sheet of ice with a faint sheen on it that the clouded moon made, and the willows, which by daylight looked like so many crouched spiders or daddy-long-legs, were laden with snow that clung to them and changed their shape. Camargue called the dog again. Only last week she had done this to him and then had suddenly appeared out of nowhere and come skittering across the ice towards him.

He began breaking the new ice with his stick. Then he heard the dog behind him, a faint crunching on the snow. But when he turned round, ready to seize her collar in the hook of the walking-stick, there was no dog there, there was nothing there but the gnome conifers and the light shining down on the white sheet of the circular courtyard. He would break up the rest of the thin ice, clear an area a yard long and a foot wide as Ted had done, and then he would go back into the house and wait for Nancy indoors.

Again the foot crunched behind him, the tree walked. He stood up and turned and, raising his stick as if to defend himself, looked into the face of the tree that moved.

CHAPTER TWO

The music met Chief Inspector Wexford as he let himself into his house. A flute playing with an orchestra. This was one of Sheila's dramatic gestures, he supposed, contrived to time with his homecoming. It was beautiful music, slow, measured, secular, yet with a religious sound.

His wife was knitting, on her face the amused, dry, very slightly exasperated expression it often wore while Sheila was around. And Sheila would be very much around for the next three weeks, having unaccountably decided to be married from home, in her own parish church, and to establish the proper period of residence beforehand in her father's house. She sat on the floor, between the log fire and the record player, her cheek resting on one round white arm that trailed with grace upon a sofa cushion, her pale gold water-straight hair half covering her face. When she lifted her head and shook her hair back he saw that she had been crying.

'Oh, Pop, darling, isn't it sad? They've had this tremendous obituary programme for him on the box. Even Mother shed a tear. And then we thought we'd mourn him with his own music.'

Wexford doubted very much if Dora, a placid and eminently sensible woman, had expressed these extravagant sentiments. He picked up the record sleeve. Mozart, Concerto for Flute and Harp, K 229; the English Chamber Orchestra, conductor, Raymond Leppard; flute, Manuel Camargue; harp, Marisa Roblès.

'We actually heard him once,' said Dora. 'Do you remember? At the Wigmore Hall it was, all of thirty years ago.'

'Yes.'

But he could scarcely remember. The pictured face on the sleeve, too sensitive, too mobile to be handsome, the eyes alight with a kind of joyous humour, evoked no image from the past. The movement came to an end and now the music became bright, liquid, a singable tune, and Camargue, who was dead, alive again in his flute. Sheila wiped her eyes and got up to kiss her father. It was all of eight years since he and she had lived under the same roof. She had become a swan since then, a famous lady, a tele-face. But she still kissed him when he came and went, putting her arms around his neck like a nervous child. Wryly, he liked it.

He sat down, listening to the last movement while Dora finished her row in the Fair Isle and went to get his supper. Andrew's regular evening phone call prevented Sheila from getting full dramatic value out of her memorial to Camargue, and by the time she came back into the room the record was over and her father was eating his steak-and-kidney pie.

'You didn't actually know him, did you, Sheila?'

She thought he was reproaching her for her tears. 'I'm sorry, Pop, I cry so easily. It's a matter of having to learn how, you know, and then not being able to unlearn.'

He grinned at her. 'Thus on the fatal bank of Nile weeps the deceitful crocodile? I didn't mean that, anyway. Let me put it more directly. Did you know him personally?'

She shook her head. 'I think he recognized me in church. He must have known I come from round here.' It was nothing that she should be recognized. She was recognized wherever she went. For five years the serial in which she played the most beautiful of the air hostesses had been on television twice a week at a peak-viewing time. Everybody watched *Runway,* even though a good many said shamefacedly that they 'only saw the tail-end before the news' or 'the kids have it on'. Stewardess Curtis was famous for her smile. Sheila smiled it now, her head tilted reflectively. 'I know his wife-that-was-to-be personally,' she said. 'Or I used to. We were at school together.'

'A young girl?'

'Thank you kindly, father dear. Let's say young to be marrying Sir Manuel. Mid-twenties. She brought him to see me in *The Letter* last autumn but I didn't talk to them, he was too tired to come round afterwards.'

It was Dora who brought them back from gossip to grandeur. 'In his day he was said to be the world's greatest flautist. I remember when he founded that school at Wellridge and Princess Margaret came down to open it.'

'D'you know what its pupils call it? Windyridge.' Sheila
mimed the blowing of a woodwind, fingers dancing. Then,
suddenly, the tears had started once more to her eyes. 'Oh, to
die like that!'

Who's Who is not a volume to be found in many private
houses. Wexford had a copy because Sheila was in it. He took
it down from the shelf, turned to the C's and read aloud:

'Camargue, Sir Manuel, Knight. Companion of Honour,
Order of the British Empire, Chevalier of the Legion of
Honour. British fluteplayer. Born Pamplona, Spain, 3 June,
1902, son of Aristide Camargue and Ana Parral. Educated
privately with father, then at Barcelona Conservatoire. Studied
under Louis Fleury.

'Professor of Flute, Madrid Conservatoire, 1924 to 1932.
Fought on Republican side Spanish Civil War, escaped to
England 1938. Married 1942 Kathleen Lister. One daughter.
Naturalized British subject 1946. Concert flautist, has toured
Europe, America, Australia, New Zealand and South Africa.
Founded 1964 at Wellridge, Sussex, the Kathleen Camargue
School of Music in memory of his wife, and in 1968 the
Kathleen Camargue Youth Orchestra. Recreations apart from
music: walking, reading, dogs. Address: Sterries, Ploughman's
Lane, Kingsmarkham, Sussex.'

'They say it's a dream of a house,' said Sheila. 'I wonder if
she'll sell, that one daughter? Because if she does Andrew and
I might really consider . . . Wouldn't you like me living just up
the road, Pop?'

'He may have left it to your friend,' said Wexford.

'So he may. Well, I do hope so. Poor Dinah, losing her first
husband that she *adored* and then her second that never was. She
deserves some compensation. I shall write her a letter of
sympathy. No, I won't. I'll go and see her. I'll phone her first
thing in the morning and I'll . . .'

'I'd leave it a day or two if I were you,' said her father.
'First thing in the morning is going to be the inquest.'

'*Inquest?*' Sheila uttered the word in the loaded, aghast tone
of Lady Bracknell. 'Inquest? But surely he died a perfectly
natural death?'

Dora, conjuring intricately with three different shades of

wool, looked up from her pattern. 'Of course he didn't. Drowning, or whatever happened to him, freezing to death, you can't call that natural.'

'I mean, he didn't do it on purpose and no one did it to him.'

It was impossible for Wexford to keep from laughing at these ingenuous definitions of suicide and homicide. 'In most cases of sudden death,' he said, 'and in all cases of violent death there must be an inquest. It goes without saying the verdict is going to be that it was an accident.'

Misadventure.

This verdict, which can sound so grotesque when applied to the death of a baby in a cot or a patient under anaesthetic, appropriately described Camargue's fate. An old man, ankle-deep in snow, had lost his foothold in the dark, slipping over, sliding into water to be trapped under a lid of ice. If he had not drowned he would within minutes have been dead from hypothermia. The snow had continued to fall, obliterating his footprints. And the frost, ten degrees of it, had silently sealed up the space into which the body had slipped. Only a glove — it was of thick black leather and it had fallen from his left hand — remained to point to where he lay, one curled finger rising up out of the drifts. Misadventure.

Wexford attended the inquest for no better reason than to keep warm, the police station central heating having unaccountably broken down the night before. The venue of the inquest (Kingsmarkham Magistrates' Court, Court Two, Upstairs) enjoyed a reputation for being kept in winter at a temperature of eighty degrees. To this it lived up. Having left his rubber boots just inside the door downstairs, he sat at the back of the court, basking in warmth, surreptitiously peeling off various disreputable layers, a khaki green plastic mac of muddy translucency, an aged black-and-grey herringbone-tweed overcoat, a stole-sized scarf of matted fawnish wool.

Apart from the *Kingsmarkham Courier* girl in one of the press seats, there were only two women present, and these two sat so far apart as to give the impression of choosing each to ostracize the other. One would be the daughter, he supposed, one the

bride. Both were dressed darkly, shabbily and without distinction. But the woman in the front row had the eyes and profile
of a Callas, her glossy black hair piled in the fashion of a
Floating World geisha, while the other, seated a yard or two
from him, was a little mouse, headscarfed, huddled, hands
folded. Neither, as far as he could see, bore the remotest
resemblance to the face on the record sleeve with its awareness
and its spirituality. But when, as the verdict came, the geisha
woman turned her head and her eyes, dark and brilliant, for a
moment met his, he saw that she was far older than Sheila,
perhaps ten years older. This, then, must be the daughter. And
as the conviction came to him, the coroner turned his gaze
upon her and said he would like to express his sympathy with
Sir Manuel's daughter in her loss and a grief which was no less
a personal one because it was shared by the tens of thousands
who had loved, admired and been inspired by his music. He did
not think he would be exceeding his duty were he to quote
Samuel Johnson and say that it matters not how a man dies but
how he has lived.

Presumably no one had told him of the dead man's
intended re-marriage. The little mouse got up and crept away.
Now it was all over, the beauty with the black eyes got up too
— to be enclosed immediately in a circle of men. This of course
was chance, Wexford told himself, they were the escort who had
brought her, her father's doctor, his servant, a friend or two. Yet
he felt inescapably that this woman would always wherever she
was be in a circle of men, watched, admired, desired. He got
back into his coverings and ventured out into the bitter cold of
Kingsmarkham High Street.

Here the old snow lay heaped at the pavement edges in
long, low mountain ranges and the new snow, gritty and
sparkling, dusted it with fresh whiteness. A yellowish-leaden sky
looked full of snow. It was only a step from the court to the
police station, but a long enough step in this weather to get
chilled to the bone.

On the forecourt, between a panda car and the chief
constable's Rover, the heating engineer's van was still parked.
Wexford went tentatively through the swing doors. Inside it was
as cold as ever and Sergeant Camb, sitting behind his counter,

warmed mittened hands on a mug of steaming tea. Burden, Wexford reflected, if he had any sense, would have taken himself off somewhere warm for lunch. Very likely to the Carousel Cafe, or what used to be the Carousel before it was taken over by Mr Haq and became the Pearl of Africa.

This was a title or sobriquet given (according to Mr Haq) to Uganda, his native land. Mr Haq claimed to serve authentic Ugandan cuisine, what he called 'real' Ugandan food, but since no one knew what this was, whether he meant food consumed by the tribes before colonization or food introduced by Asian immigrants or food eaten today by westernized Ugandans, or what these would be anyway, it was difficult to query any dish. Fried potatoes and rice accompanied almost everything, but for all Wexford knew this might be a feature of Ugandan cooking. He rather liked the place, it fascinated him, especially the plastic jungle vegetation.

Today this hung and trembled in the steamy heat and seemed to sweat droplets on its leathery leaves. The windows had become opaque, entirely misted over with condensation. It was like a tropical oasis in the Arctic. Inspector Burden sat at a table eating Nubian chicken with rice Ruwenzori, anxiously keeping in view his new sheepskin jacket, a Christmas present from his wife, which Mr Haq had hung up on the palm tree hatstand. He remarked darkly as Wexford walked in that anyone might make off with it, you never could tell these days.

'Round here they might cook it,' said Wexford. He also ordered the chicken with the request that for once potatoes might not come with it. 'I've just come from the inquest on Camargue.'

'What on earth did you go to that for?'

'I hadn't anything much else on. I reckoned it would be warm too and it was.'

'All right for some,' Burden grumbled. 'I could have found a job for you.' Since their friendship had deepened, some of his old deference to his chief, though none of his respect, had departed. 'Thieving and break-ins, we've never had so much of it. That kid old Atkinson let out on bail, he's done three more jobs in the meantime. And he's not seventeen yet, a real little villain.' Sarcasm made his tone withering. 'Or that's what I call him. The psychiatrist says he's a pathological kleptomaniac with personality-scarring caused by traumata broadly classifiable as paranoid.' He snorted, was silent, then said on an altered note, 'Look, do you think you were wise to do that?'

'Do what?'

'Go to that inquest. People will think . . . I mean, it's possible they might think . . .'

'People will think!' Wexford scoffed. 'You sound like a dowager lecturing a debutante. What will they think?'

'I only meant they might think there was something fishy about the death. Some hanky-panky. I mean, they see you there and know who you are and they say to themselves, he wouldn't have been there if it had all been as straightforward as the coroner . . .'

He was saved from an outburst of Wexford's temper by an intervention from outside. Mr Haq had glided up to beam upon them. He was small, smiling, very black yet very Caucasian, with a mouthful of startlingly white, madly uneven, large teeth.

'Everything to your liking, I hope, my dear?' Mr Haq called all his customers 'my dear', irrespective of sex, perhaps supposing it to be a genderless term of extreme respect such as 'excellency'. 'I see you are having the rice Ruwenzori.' He bowed a little. 'A flavourful and scrumptious recipe from the peoples who live in the Mountains of the Moon.' Talking like a television commercial for junk food was habitual with him.

'Very nice, thank you,' said Wexford.

'You are welcome, my dear.' Mr Haq smiled so broadly that it seemed some of his teeth must spill out. He moved off among the tables, ducking his head under the polythene fronds which trailed from polyethylene pots in polystyrene plantholders.

'Are you going to have any pudding?'

'Shouldn't think so,' said Wexford, and he read from the menu with gusto, 'Cake Kampala or ice cream eau-de-Nil — does he mean the colour or what it's made of? Anyway, there's enough ice about without eating it.' He hesitated. 'Mike, I don't see that it matters what people think in this instance. Camargue met his death by misadventure, there's no doubt about that.

Surely, though interest in the man will endure for years, the manner of his death can only be a nine days' wonder. As a matter of fact, the coroner said something like that.'

Burden ordered coffee from the small, shiny, damson-eyed boy, heir to Mr Haq, who waited at their table. 'I suppose I was thinking of Hicks.'

'The manservant or whoever he was?'

'He found that glove and then he found the body. It wasn't really strange but it might look strange the way he found the dog outside his back door and took her back to Sterries and put her inside without checking to see where Camargue was.'

'Hicks's reputation won't suffer from my presence in court,' said Wexford. 'I doubt if there was a soul there, bar the coroner, who recognized me.' He chuckled. 'Or if they did it'd only be as Stewardess Curtis's dad.'

They went back to the police station. The afternoon wore away into an icy twilight, an evening of hard frost. The heating came on with a pop just as it was time to go home. Entering his living room, Wexford was greeted by a large, bronze-coloured alsatian, baring her teeth and swinging her tail. On the sofa, next to his daughter, sat the girl who had crept away from the inquest, Camargue's pale bride.

CHAPTER THREE

He had noticed the Volkswagen parked in the ruts of ice outside but had thought little of it. Sheila got up and introduced the visitor.

'Dinah, this is my father. Pop, I'd like you to meet Dinah Sternhold. She was engaged to Sir Manuel, you know.'

It was immediately apparent to Wexford that she had not noticed him at the inquest. She held out her small hand and looked at him without a flicker of recognition. The dog had backed against her legs and now sat down heavily at her feet, glaring at Wexford in a sullen way.

'Do forgive me for bringing Nancy.' She had a soft low unaffected voice. 'But I daren't leave her alone, she howls all the time. My neighbours complained when I had to leave her this morning.'

'She was Sir Manuel's dog,' Sheila explained.

A master-leaver and a fugitive, Wexford reflected, eyeing the alsatian who had abandoned Camargue to his fate. Or gone to fetch help? That, of course, was a possible explanation of the curious behaviour of the dog in the night.

Dinah Sternhold said, 'It's Manuel she howls for, you see. I can only hope she won't take too long to — to forget him. I hope she'll get over it.'

Was she speaking of the dog or of herself? His answer could have applied to either. 'She will. She's young.'

'He often said he wanted me to have her if — if anything happened to him. I think he was afraid of her going to someone who might not be kind to her.'

Presumably she meant the daughter. Wexford sought about in his mind for some suitable words of condolence, but finding none that sounded neither mawkish nor pompous, he kept quiet. Sheila, anyway, could always be relied on to make conversation. While she was telling some rather inapposite alsatian anecdote, he studied Dinah Sternhold. Her little round sallow face was pinched with a kind of bewildered woe. One might almost believe she had loved the old man and not merely been in it for the money. But that was a little too much to swallow, distinguished and reputedly kind and charming as he had been. The facts were that he had been seventy-eight and she was certainly fifty years less than that.

Gold-digger, however, she was not. She appeared to have extorted little in the way of pre-marital largesse out of Camargue. Her brown tweed coat had seen better days, she wore no jewellery but an engagement ring, in which the ruby was small and the diamonds pinheads.

He wondered how long she intended to sit there, her hand grasping the dog's collar, her head bowed as if she were struggling to conquer tears or at least conceal them. But suddenly she jumped up.

'I must go.' Her voice became intense, ragged, charged with a sincerity that was almost fierce. 'It was so *kind* of you to come to me, Sheila. You don't know how grateful I am.'

'No need,' Sheila said lightly. 'I wanted to come. It was kind of *you* to drive me home. I had a hire car, Pop, because I was scared to drive in the snow but Dinah wasn't a bit scared to bring me back in the snow and the dark.'

They saw Dinah Sternhold out to her car. Ice was already forming on the windscreen. She pushed the dog on to the back seat and got to work competently on the windows with a de-icing spray. Wexford was rather surprised that he felt no compunction about letting her drive away, but her confidence seemed absolute, you could trust her somehow to look after herself and perhaps others too. Was it this quality about her that Camargue had needed and had loved? He closed the gate, rubbed his hands. Sheila, shivering, ran back into the house.

'Where's your mother?'

'Round at Syl's. She ought to be back any minute. Isn't Dinah nice? I felt so sorry for her, I went straight over to Forby as soon as the inquest was over. We talked and talked. I think maybe I did her a bit of good.'

'Hmm,' said Wexford.

The phone started to ring. Andrew, punctual to the minute. 'Oh, darling,' Wexford heard Sheila say, 'do you remember my

telling you about someone I know who was going to marry . . .'
He began picking alsatian hairs off the upholstery.

Father and daughter is not the perfect relationship. According to Freud, that distinction belongs to mother and son. But
Wexford, looking back, could have said that he had been happy
with his daughters and they with him, he had never actually
quarrelled with either of them, there had never been any sort
of breach. And if Sheila was his favourite he hoped this was so
close a secret that no one but himself, not even Dora, could
know it.

Any father of daughters, even today, must look ahead when
they are children and anticipate an outlay of money on their
wedding celebrations. Wexford realized this and had begun
saving for it out of his detective inspector's salary, but Sylvia
had married so young as almost to catch him napping. For
Sheila he had been determined to be well prepared, then
gradually, with wonder and a kind of dismay, he had watched
her rise out of that income bracket and society in which she had
grown up, graduate into a sparkling, lavish jet set whose
members had wedding receptions in country mansions or else
the Dorchester.

For a long time it had looked as if she would not marry at
all. Then Andrew Thorverton appeared, a young businessman,
immensely wealthy, it seemed to Wexford, with a house in
Hampstead, a cottage in the country somewhere that his future
father-in-law suspected was a sizeable house, a boat and an
amazing car of so esoteric a manufacture that Wexford had
never before heard of it. Sheila, made old-fashioned and sentimental by love, announced she would be married from home
and, almost in the same breath, that she and Andrew would be
paying for the entertainment of two hundred people to luncheon in the banquet room of the Olive and Dove. Yes, she
insisted, it must be so and Pop must lump it or else she'd go
and get married in a register office and have lunch at the Pearl
of Africa.

He was slightly humiliated. Somehow he felt she ought to
cut garment according to cloth, and his cloth would cover a
buffet table for fifty. That was absurd, of course. Andrew
wouldn't even notice the few thousand it would cost, and the

bride's father would give her away, make a speech and hang on to his savings. He heard her telling Andrew she would be coming up to spend the weekend with him, and then Dora walked in.

'She won't be supporting her friend at the cremation then?'

Sheila had put the phone down. She was sometimes a little flushed and breathless when she had been talking to Andrew. But it was not now of him that she spoke. 'Dinah's not going to it. How could she bear it? Two days after what would have been their wedding day?'

'At least it's not the day itself,' said Wexford.

'Frankly, I'm surprised Sir Manuel's daughter didn't fix it on the day itself. She's capable of it. There's going to be a memorial service at St Peter's on Tuesday and everyone will be there. Solti is coming and probably Menuhin. Dinah says there are sure to be crowds, he was so much loved.'

Wexford said, 'Does she know if he left her much?'

Sheila delivered her reply slowly and with an actress's perfect timing.

'He has not left her anything. He has not left her a single penny.' She sank to the floor, close up by the fire, and stretched out her long legs. 'Her engagement ring and that dog, that's all she's got.'

'How did that come about? Did you ask her?'

'Oh, Pop darling, of course I did. Wasn't I with her for hours and hours? I got the whole thing out of her.'

'You're as insatiably inquisitive as your father!' cried Dora, revolted. 'I thought you went to comfort the poor girl. I agree it's not like losing a young fiancé, but just the same . . .'

'Curiosity,' quoted Wexford, 'is one of the permanent and certain characteristics of a vigorous intellect.' He chuckled. 'The daughter gets it all, does she?'

'Sir Manuel saw his daughter a week before he died and that was the first time he'd seen her for nineteen years. There'd been a family quarrel. She was at the Royal Academy of Music but she left and went off with an American student. The first Camargue and his wife knew of it was a letter from San Francisco. Mrs Camargue — he wasn't a Sir then — got ill and died but the daughter didn't come back. She didn't come back at all till last November. Doesn't it seem frightfully unfair that she gets everything?'

'Camargue should have made a new will.'

'He was going to as soon as they were married. Marriage invalidates a will. Did you know that, Pop?'

He nodded.

'I can understand divorce would but I can't see why marriage.' She turned her legs, toasting them.

'You'll get scorch marks,' said Dora. 'That won't look very nice on the beach in Bermuda.'

Sheila took no notice. 'And what's more, he was going to cut the daughter out altogether. Apparently, that one sight of her was enough.'

Dora, won uneasily on to the side of the gossips, said, 'I wish you wouldn't keep calling her the daughter. Doesn't she have a name?'

'Natalie Arno. Mrs Arno, she's a widow. The American student died some time during those nineteen years. Dinah was awfully reticent about her, but she did say Camargue intended to make a new will, and since he said this just after he'd seen Natalie I put two and two together. And there's another thing, Natalie only got in touch with her father after his engagement to Dinah was announced. The engagement was in the *Telegraph* on 10 December, and on the 12th he got a letter from Natalie telling him she was back and could she come and see him? She wanted a reconciliation. It was obvious she was scared stiff of the marriage and wanted to stop it.'

'And your reticent friend told you all this?'

'She got it out of her, Dora. I can understand. She's a chip off the old block, as you so indignantly pointed out.' He turned once more to Sheila. 'Did she try to stop it?'

'Dinah wouldn't say. I think she hates discussing Natalie. She talked much more about Camargue. She really loved him. In a funny sort of daughterly, worshipping, protective sort of way, but she did love him. She likes to talk about how wonderful he was and how they met and all that. She's a teacher at the Kathleen Camargue School and he came over last Founder's Day and they met and they just loved each other, she said, from that moment.'

The somewhat cynical expressions on the two middle-aged faces made her give an embarrassed laugh. She seemed to take her mother's warning to heart at last, for she got up and moved away from the fire to sit on the sofa where she scrutinized her smooth, pale golden legs. 'At any rate, Pop darling, it's an ill wind, as you might say, because now the house is bound to be sold. I'd love to get a look at it, wouldn't you? Why wasn't I at school with Natalie?'

'You were born too late,' said her father. 'And there must be simpler ways of getting into Sterries.'

There were.

'You?' said Burden first thing the next morning. 'What do you want to go up there for? It's only a common-or-garden burglary, one of our everyday occurrences, I'm sorry to say. Martin can handle it.'

Wexford hadn't taken his overcoat off. 'I want to see the place. Don't you feel any curiosity to see the home of our former most distinguished citizen?'

Burden seemed more concerned with dignity and protocol. 'It's beneath you *and* me, I should think.' He sniffed. 'And when you hear the details you'll feel the same. The facts are that a Mrs Arno — she's the late Sir Manuel's daughter — phoned up about half an hour ago to say the house had been broken into during the night. There's a pane of glass been cut out of a window downstairs and a bit of a mess made and some silver taken. Cutlery, nothing special, and some money from Mrs Arno's handbag. She thinks she saw the car the burglar used and she's got the registration number.'

'I like these open-and-shut cases,' said Wexford. 'I find them restful.'

The fingerprint man (Detective Constable Morgan) had already left for Sterries. Wexford's car only just managed to get up Ploughman's Lane, which was glacier-like in spite of gritting. He had been a determined burglar, Burden remarked, to get his car up and down there in the night.

The top of the hill presented an alpine scene, with dark-green and gold and grey conifers rising sturdily from the snow blanket. The house itself, shaped like a number of cuboid boxes pushed irregularly together and with a tower in the midst of them, looked not so much white as dun-coloured beside the dazzling field of snow. A sharp wind had set the treble-clef weathervane spinning like a top against a sky that was now a clear cerulean blue.

Morgan's van was parked on the forecourt outside the front door which was on the side of the house furthest from the lane. Some attempt had been made to keep this area free of snow. Wexford, getting out of the car, saw a solidly built man in jeans and anorak at work sweeping the path which seemed to lead to a much smaller house that stood in a dip in the grounds. He looked in the other direction, noting in a shallow tree-fringed basin the ornamental water newspapers had euphemistically called a lake. There Camargue had met his death. It was once more iced over and the ice laden with a fleecy coat of snow.

The front door had been opened by a woman of about forty in trousers and bulky sweater whom Wexford took to be Muriel Hicks. He and Burden stepped into the warmth and on to thick soft carpet. The vestibule with its cloaks cupboard was rather small but it opened, through an arch, into a hall which had been used to some extent as a picture gallery. The paintings almost made him whistle. If these were originals . . .

The dining-room was open, revealing pale wood panelling and dark red wood furnishing, and in the far corner Morgan could be seen at his task. A flight of stairs, with risers of mosaic tile and treads that seemed to be of oak, led upwards. However deferential and attentive Mrs Hicks may have been towards Sir Manuel — and according to Sheila he had been adored by his servants — she had no courtesy to spare for policemen. That 'she' was upstairs somewhere was the only introduction they got. Wexford went upstairs while Burden joined Morgan in the dining room.

The house had been built on various different levels of land so that the drawing room where he found himself was really another ground floor. It was a large, airy and gracious room, two sides of which were made entirely of glass. At the farther end of it steps led down into what must surely be the tower. Here the floor was covered by a pale yellow Chinese carpet on which stood two groups of silk-covered settees and chairs, one suite lemon, one very pale jade. There was some fine *famille jaune* porcelain of that marvellous yellow that is both tender and piercing, and suspended from the ceiling a chandelier of start-lingly modern design that resembled a torrent of water poured from a tilted vase.

But there was no sign of human occupation. Wexford stepped down under the arch where staghorn ferns grew in troughs at ground level and a *Cissus antarctica* climbed the columns, and entered a music room. It was larger than had appeared from outside and it was dodecagonal. The floor was of very smooth, polished, pale grey slate on which lay three Kashmiri rugs. A Broadwood grand piano stood between him and the other arched entrance. On each of eight of the twelve sides of the room was a picture or bust in an alcove, Mozart and Beethoven among the latter, among the former Cocteau's cartoon of Picasso and Stravinsky, Rothenstein's drawing of Parry, and a photograph of the Georgian manor house in which the music school was housed at Wellridge. But on one of the remaining sides Camargue had placed on a glass shelf a cast of Chopin's hands and on the last hung in a glass case a wind instrument of the side-blown type which looked to Wexford to be made of solid gold. Under it was the inscription: 'Presented to Manuel Camargue by Aldo Cazzini, 1949'. Was it a flute and could it be of gold? He lifted the lid of a case which lay on a low table and saw inside a similar instrument but made of humbler metal, perhaps silver.

He was resolving to go downstairs again and send Muriel Hicks to find Mrs Arno, when he was aware of a movement in the air behind him and of a presence that was not wholly welcoming. He turned round. Natalie Arno stood framed in the embrasure of the further arch, watching him with an unfathom-able expression in her eyes.

CHAPTER FOUR

Wexford was the first to speak.

'Good morning, Mrs Arno.'

She was absolutely still, one hand up to her cheek, the other resting against one of the columns which supported the arch. She was silent.

He introduced himself and said pleasantly, 'I hear you've had some sort of break-in. Is that right?'

Why did he feel so strongly that she was liberated by relief? Her face did not change and it was a second or two before she moved. Then, slowly, she came forward.

'It's good of you to come so quickly.' Her voice was as unlike Dinah Sternhold's as it was reasonably possible for one woman's voice to differ from another's. She had a faint American accent and in her tone there was an underlying hint of amusement. He was always to be aware of that in his dealings with her. 'I'm afraid I may be making a fuss about nothing. He only took a few spoons.' She made a comic grimace, pursing her lips as she drew out the long vowel sound. 'Let's go into the drawing room and I'll tell you about it.'

The cast of her countenance was that which one would immediately categorize as Spanish, full-fleshed yet strong, the nose straight if a fraction too long, the mouth full and flamboyantly curved, the eyes splendid, as near to midnight black as a white woman's eyes can ever be. Her black hair was strained tightly back from her face and knotted high on the back of her head, a style which most women's faces could scarcely take but which suited hers, exposing its fine bones. And her figure was no less arresting than her face. She was very slim but for a too-full bosom, and this was not at all disguised by her straight skirt and thin sweater. Such an appearance, the ideal of men's fantasies, gives a woman a slightly indecent look, particularly if she carries herself with a certain provocative air. Natalie Arno did not quite do this but when she moved as she now did, mounting the steps to the higher level, she walked very sinuously with a stressing of her narrow waist.

During his absence two people had come into the drawing room, a man and a woman. They were behaving in the rather aimless fashion of house guests who have perhaps just got up or at least just put in an appearance, and who are wondering where to find breakfast, newspapers and an occupation. It occurred to Wexford for the first time that it was rather odd, not to say presumptuous, of Natalie Arno to have taken possession of Sterries so immediately after her father's death, to have moved in and to have invited people to stay. Did his solicitors approve? Did they know?

'This is Chief Inspector Wexford who has come to catch our burglar,' she said. 'My friends, Mr and Mrs Zoffany.'

The man was one of those who had been in the circle round her after the inquest. He seemed about forty. His fair hair was thick and wavy and he had a Viking's fine golden beard, but his body had grown soft and podgy and a flap of belly hung over the belt of his too-tight and too-juvenile fawn cord jeans. His wife, in the kind of clothes which unmistakably mark the superannuated hippie, was as thin as he was stout. She was young still, younger probably than Camargue's daughter, but her face was worn and there were coarse, bright threads of grey in her dark curly hair.

Natalie Arno sat down in one of the jade armchairs. She sat with elegant slim legs crossed at the calves, her feet arched in their high-heeled shoes. Mrs Zoffany, on the other hand, flopped on to the floor and sat cross-legged, tucking her long patchwork skirt around her knees. The costume she wore, and which like so many of her contemporaries she pathetically refused to relinquish, would date her more ruthlessly than might any perm or pair of stockings on another woman. Yet not so long ago it had been the badge of an élite who hoped to alter the world. Sitting there, she looked as if she might be at one of the pop concerts of her youth, waiting for the entertainment to begin. Her head was lifted expectantly, her eyes on Natalie's face.

'I'll tell you what there is to tell,' Natalie began, 'and I'm afraid that's not much. It must have been around five this morning I thought I heard the sound of glass breaking. I've been sleeping in Papa's room. Jane and Ivan are in one of the spare rooms in the other wing. You didn't hear anything, did you, Jane?'

Jane Zoffany shook her head vehemently. 'I only wish I had. I might have been able to *help*.'

'I didn't go down. To tell you the truth I was just a little scared.' Natalie smiled deprecatingly. She didn't look as if she had ever been scared in her life. Wexford wondered why he had at first felt her presence as hostile. She was entirely charming. 'But I did look out of the window. And just outside the window — on that side all the rooms are more or less on the ground floor, you know — there was a van parked. I put the light on and took a note of the registration number. I've got it here somewhere. What did I do with it?'

Jane Zoffany jumped up. 'I'll look for it, shall I? You put it down somewhere in here. I remember, I was still in my dressing gown . . .' She began hunting about the room, her scarves and the fringe of her shawl catching on ornaments.

Natalie smiled, and in that smile Wexford thought he detected patronage. 'I didn't quite know what to do,' she said. 'Papa didn't have a phone extension put in his room. Just as I was wondering I heard the van start up and move off. I felt brave enough to go down to the dining room then, and sure enough there was a pane gone from one of the casements.'

'A pity you didn't phone us then. We might have got him.'

'I know.' She said it ruefully, amusedly, with a soft sigh of a laugh. 'But there were only those half-dozen silver spoons missing and two five-pound notes out of my purse. I'd left my purse on the sideboard.'

'But would *you* know exactly what was missing, Mrs Arno?'

'Right. I wouldn't really. But Mrs Hicks has been round with me this morning and she can't find anything else gone.'

'It's rather curious, isn't it? This house seems to me full of very valuable objects. There's a Kandinsky downstairs and a Boudin, I think.' He pointed. 'And those are signed Hockney prints. That yellow porcelain . . .'

She looked surprised at his knowledge. 'Yes, but . . .' Her

cheeks had slightly flushed. 'Would you think me very forward if I said I had a theory?'

'Not at all. I'd like to hear it.'

'Well, first, I think he knew Papa used to sleep in that room and now poor Papa is gone he figured no one would be in there. And, secondly, I think he saw my light go on before he'd done any more than filch the spoons. He was just too scared to stop any longer. How does that sound?'

'Quite a possibility,' said Wexford. Was it his imagination that she had expected a more enthusiastic or flattering response? Jane Zoffany came up with the van registration number on a piece of paper torn from an exercise book. Natalie Arno didn't thank her for her pains. She rose, tensing her shoulders and throwing back her head to show off that amazing shape. Her waist could easily have been spanned by a pair of hands.

'Do you want to see the rest of the house?' she said. 'I'm sure he didn't come up to this level.'

Wexford would have loved to, but for what reason? 'We usually ask the householder to make a list of missing valuables in a case like this. It might be wise for me to go round with Mrs Hicks . . .'

'Of *course*.'

Throughout these exchanges Ivan Zoffany had not spoken. Wexford, without looking at him, had sensed a brooding concentration, the aggrieved attitude perhaps of a man not called on to participate in what might seem to be men's business. But now, as he turned his eyes in Zoffany's direction, he got a shock. The man was gazing at Natalie Arno, had probably been doing so for the past ten minutes, and his expression, hypnotic and fixed, was impenetrable. It might indicate contempt or envy or desire or simple hatred. Wexford was unable to analyse it but he felt a pang of pity for Zoffany's wife, for anyone who had to live with so much smouldering emotion.

Passing through the music room, Muriel Hicks took him first into the wing which had been private to Camargue. Here all was rather more austere than what he had so far seen. The bedroom, study-cum-sitting-room and bathroom were all carpeted in Camargue's favourite yellow — wasn't it in the Luscher

Test that you were judged the best-adjusted if you gave your favourite colour as yellow? — but the furnishings were sparse and there were blinds at the windows instead of curtains. A dress of Natalie's lay on the bed.

Muriel Hicks had not so far spoken beyond asking him to follow her. She was not an attractive woman. She had the bright pink complexion that sometimes goes with red-gold hair and piglet features. Wexford who, by initially marrying one, had surrounded himself with handsome women, wondered at Camargue who had a beautiful daughter yet had picked an ugly housekeeper and a nonentity for a second wife. Immediately he had thought that he regretted it with shame. For, turning round, he saw that Mrs Hicks was crying. She was standing with her hand on an armchair, on the seat of which lay a folded rug, and the tears were rolling down her round, red cheeks.

She was one of the few people he had ever come across who did not apologize for crying. She wiped her face, scrubbing at her eyes. 'I've lost the best employer,' she said, 'and the best friend anyone could have. And I've taken it hard, I can tell you.'

'Yes, it was a sad business.'

'If you'll look out of that window you'll see a house over to the left. That's ours. Really ours, I mean — he *gave* it to us. God knows what it's worth now. D'you know what he said? I'm not having you and Ted living in a tied cottage, he said. If you're good enough to come and work for me you deserve to have a house of your own to live in.'

It was a largish Victorian cottage and it had its own narrow driveway out into Ploughman's Lane. Sheila wouldn't have wanted it, he supposed, its not going with Sterries would make no difference to her. He put up a show for Mrs Hicks' benefit of scrutinizing the spot where Natalie Arno said the van had been.

'There weren't many like him,' said Muriel Hicks, closing the door behind Wexford as they left. It was a fitting epitaph, perhaps the best and surely the simplest Camargue would have.

Along the corridor, back through the music room, across the drawing room, now deserted, and into the other wing. Here was a large room full of books, a study or a library, and three bedrooms, all with bathrooms *en suite*. Their doors were all open but in one of them, standing in front of a long glass and studying the effect of various ways of fastening the collar of a very old Persian lamb coat, was Jane Zoffany. She rushed, at the sight of Wexford, into a spate of apologies — very nearly saying sorry for existing at all — and scuttled from the room. Muriel Hicks' glassy stare followed her out.

'There's nothing missing from here,' she said in a depressed tone. 'Anyway, those people would have heard something.' There was a chance, he thought, that she might lose another kind of control and break into a tirade against Camargue's daughter and her friends. But she didn't. She took him silently into the second room and the third.

Why had Natalie Arno chosen to occupy her father's bedroom, austere, utilitarian and moreover the room of a lately dead man and a parent, rather than one of these luxurious rooms with fur rugs on the carpets and duckdown duvets on the beds? Was it to be removed from the Zoffanys? But they were her friends whom she had presumably invited. To revel in the triumph of possessing the place and all that went with it at last? To appreciate this to the full by sleeping in the inner sanctum, the very holy of holies? It occurred to him that by so doing she must have caused great pain to Mrs Hicks, and then he reminded himself that this sort of speculation was pointless, he wasn't investigating any crime more serious than petty larceny. And his true reason for being here was to make a preliminary survey for a possible buyer.

'Is anything much kept in that chest?' he asked Mrs Hicks. It was a big teak affair with brass handles, standing in the passage.

'Only blankets.'

'And that cupboard?'

She opened it. 'There's nothing missing.'

He went downstairs. Morgan and his van had gone. In the hall were Burden, Natalie Arno and the Zoffanys, the man who had been sweeping the path, and a woman in a dark brown fox fur who had evidently just arrived.

Everyone was dressed for the outdoors and for bitterly cold weather. It struck Wexford forcefully, as he descended the stairs towards them, that Natalie and her friends looked thoroughly disreputable compared with the other three. Burden was always well turned-out and in his new sheepskin he was more than that. The newcomer was smart, even elegant, creamy cashmere showing above the neckline of the fur, her hands in sleek gloves, and even Ted Hicks, in aran and anorak, had the look of a gentleman farmer. Beside them Natalie and the Zoffanys were a rag-bag crew, Zoffany's old overcoat as shabby as Wexford's own, his wife with layers of dipping skirts hanging out beneath the hem of the Persian lamb. Nothing could make Natalie less than striking. In a coat that appeared to be made from an old blanket and platform-soled boots so out of date and so worn that Wexford guessed she must have bought them in a second-hand shop, she looked raffish and down on her luck. They were hardly the kind of people, he said to himself with an inward chuckle, that one (or the neighbours) would expect to see issuing from a house in Ploughman's Lane.

That the woman in the fur was one of these neighbours Burden immediately explained. Mrs Murray-Burgess. She had seen the police cars and then she had encountered Mr Hicks in the lane. Yes, she lived next door, if next door it could be called when something like an acre separated Kingsfield House from Sterries, and she thought she might have some useful information.

They all trooped into the dining room where Hicks resumed his task of boarding up the broken window. Wexford asked Mrs Murray-Burgess the nature of her information.

She had seen a man in the Sterries grounds. No, not last night, a few days before. In fact, she had mentioned it to Mrs Hicks, not being acquainted with Mrs Arno. She gave Natalie a brief glance that seemed to indicate her desire for a continuation of this state of affairs. No, she couldn't recall precisely when it had been. Last night she had happened to be awake at five-thirty — she always awoke early — and had seen the lights of a vehicle turning out from Sterries into the lane. Wexford nodded. Could she identify this man were she to see him again?

'I'm sure I could,' said Mrs Murray-Burgess emphatically. 'And what's more, I *would*. All this sort of thing has got to be stopped before the country goes completely to the dogs. If I've got to get up in court and say that's the man! — well, I've got to and no two ways about it. It's time someone gave a lead.'

Natalie's face was impassive but in the depths of her eyes Wexford saw a spark of laughter. Almost anyone else in her position would now have addressed this wealthy and majestic neighbour, thanking her perhaps for her concern and public spirit. Most people would have suggested a meeting on more social terms, on do-bring-your-husband-in-for-a-drink lines. Many would have spoken of the dead and have mentioned the coming memorial service. Natalie behaved exactly as if Mrs Murray-Burgess were not there. She shook hands with Wexford, thanking him warmly while increasing the pressure of her fingers. Burden was as prettily thanked and given an alluring smile. They were ushered to the door, the Zoffanys following, everyone coming out into the crisp cold air and the bright sunlight. Mrs Murray-Burgess, left stranded in the dining room with Ted Hicks, emerged in offended bewilderment a moment or two later.

Wexford, no doubt impressing everyone with his frown and preoccupied air, was observing the extent of the double glazing and making rough calculations as to the size of the grounds. Getting at last into their car, he remarked to Burden — a propos of what the inspector had no idea — that sometimes these cogitations still amazed the troubled midnight and the noon's repose.

573

CHAPTER FIVE

The owner of the van was quickly traced through its registration number. He was a television engineer called Robert Clifford who said he had lent the van to a fellow-tenant of his in Finsbury Park, north London, a man of thirty-six called John Cooper. Cooper, who was unemployed, admitted the break-in after the spoons had been found in his possession. He said he had read in the papers about the death of Camargue and accounts of the arrangements at Sterries.

'It was an invite to do the place,' he said impudently. 'All that stuff about valuable paintings and china, and then that the housekeeper didn't sleep in the house. She didn't either, the first time I went.'

When had that been?

'Tuesday night,' said Cooper. He meant Tuesday the 29th, two days after Camargue's death. When he returned to break in. 'I didn't know which was the old man's room,' he said. 'How would I? The papers don't give you a plan of the bloody place.' He had parked the van outside that window simply because it seemed the most convenient spot and couldn't be seen from the road. 'It gave me a shock when the light came on.' He sounded aggrieved, as if he had been wantonly interrupted while about some legitimate task. His was a middle-class accent. Perhaps, like Burden's little villain, he was a pathological kleptomaniac with personality-scarring. Cooper appeared before the Kingsmarkham magistrates and was remanded in custody until the case could be heard at Myringham Crown Court.

Wexford was able to give Sheila a favourable report on Camargue's house, but she seemed to have lost interest in the place. (One's children had a way of behaving like this, he had noticed.) Andrew's house in Keats Grove was really very nice, and he did have the cottage in Dorset. If they lived in Sussex they would have to keep a flat in town as well. She couldn't go all the way back to Kingsmarkham after an evening performance, could she? The estate agents had found a buyer for her own flat in St John's Wood and they were getting an amazing price for it. Had Mother been to hear her banns called for the second time? Mother had.

The day of the memorial service was bright and sunny. Alpine weather, Wexford called it, the frozen snow sparkling, melting a little in the sun, only to freeze glass-hard again when the sun went down. Returning from his visit to Sewingbury Comprehensive School — where there was an alarming incidence of glue-sniffing among fourteen-year-olds — he passed St Peter's church as the mourners were leaving. The uniform men wear disguises them. Inside black overcoat and black Homburg might breathe equally Sir Manuel's accompanist or Sir Manuel's wine merchant. But he was pretty sure he had spotted James Galway, and he stood to gaze like any lion-hunting sightseer.

Sheila, making her escape with Dinah Sternhold to a hire car, was attracting as much attention as anyone — a warning, her father thought, of what they might expect in a fortnight's time. The Zoffanys were nowhere to be seen but Natalie Arno, holding the arm of an elderly wisp of a man, a man so frail-looking that it seemed wonderful the wind did not blow him about like a feather, was standing on the steps shaking hands with departing visitors. She wore a black coat and a large black hat, new clothes they appeared to be and suited to the occasion, and she stood erectly, her thin ankles pressed together. By the time Wexford was driven away by the cold, though several dozen people had shaken hands with her and passed on, four or five of the men as well as the elderly wisp remained with her. He smiled to himself, amused to see his prediction fulfilled.

By the end of the week Sheila had received confirmation from the estate agents that her flat was sold, or that negotiations to buy it had begun. This threw her into a dilemma. Should she sign the contract and then go merrily off on her Bermuda honeymoon, leaving the flat full of furniture? Or should she arrange to have the flat cleared and the furniture stored before she left? Persuaded by her prudent mother, she fixed on the Wednesday before her wedding for the removal and Wexford, who had the day off, promised to go with her to St John's Wood.

'We could go to Bermuda too,' said Dora to her husband.

'I know it was the custom for Victorian brides to take a friend with them on their honeymoon,' said Wexford, 'but surely even they didn't take their parents.'

'Darling, I don't mean at the same time. I mean we could go to Bermuda later on. When you get your holiday. We can afford it now we aren't paying for this wedding.'

'How about my new car? How about the new hall carpet? And I thought you'd decided life was insupportable without a freezer.'

'We couldn't have all those things anyway.'

'That's for sure,' said Wexford.

A wonderful holiday or a new car? A thousand pounds' worth of sunshine and warmth took priority now, he reflected as he was driven over to Myringham and the crown court. The snow was still lying and the bright weather had given place to freezing fog. But would he still feel like this when it was sunny here and spring again? Then the freezer and the carpet would seem the wiser option.

John Cooper was found guilty of breaking into and entering Sterries and of stealing six silver spoons, and, since he had previous convictions, sent to prison for six months. Wexford was rather surprised to hear that one of these convictions, though long in the past, was for robbery with violence. Mrs Murray-Burgess was in court and she flushed brick-red with satisfaction when the sentence was pronounced. Throughout the proceedings she had been eyeing the dark, rather handsome, slouching Cooper in the awed and fascinated way one looks at a bull or a caged tiger.

It occurred to Wexford to call in at Sterries on his way back and impart the news to Natalie Arno. He had promised to let her know the outcome. She would very likely be as delighted as her neighbour, and she could have her spoons back now.

A man who tried to be honest with himself, he wondered if this could be his sole motive for a visit to Ploughman's Lane. After all, it was a task Sergeant Martin or even Constable Loring could more properly have done. Was he, in common with those encircling men, attracted by Natalie? Could she have said of him too, like Cleopatra with her fishing rod, 'Aha, you're caught'? Honestly he asked himself — and said an honest, almost unqualified no. She amused him, she intrigued him, he suspected she would be entertaining to watch at certain manipulating ploys, but he was not attracted. There remained with him a nagging little memory of how, in the music room at Sterries, before he had ever spoken to her, he had sensed her presence behind him as unpleasing. She was good to look at, she was undoubtedly clever, she was full of charm, yet wasn't there about her something snake-like? And although this image might dissolve when confronted by the real Natalie, out of her company he must think of her sinuous movements as reptilian and her marvellous eyes when cast down as hooded.

So in going to Sterries he knew he was in little danger. No one need tie him to the mast. He would simply be calling on Natalie Arno for an obligatory talk, perhaps a cup of tea, and the opportunity to watch a powerful personality at work with the weak. If the Zoffanys were still there, of course. He would soon know.

It was three o'clock on the afternoon of a dull day. Not a light showed in the Sterries windows. Still, many people preferred to sit in the dusk rather than anticipate the night too soon. He rang the bell. He rang and rang again, was pleased to find himself not particularly disappointed that there was no one at home.

After a moment's thought he walked down the path to Sterries Cottage. Ted Hicks answered his ring. Yes, Mrs Arno was out. In fact, she had returned to London. Her friends had gone and then she had gone, leaving him and his wife to look after the house.

'Does she mean to come back?'

'I'm afraid I've no idea about that, sir. Mrs Arno didn't say.' Hicks spoke respectfully. Indeed, he had far more the air of an old-fashioned servant than his wife. Yet again Wexford felt, as he had felt with Muriel Hicks, that at any moment the discreet speaker might break into abuse, either heaping insults on Natalie or dismissing her with contempt. But nothing like this happened. Hicks compressed his lips and stared blankly at Wexford, though without meeting his eyes. 'Would you care to come in? I can give you Mrs Arno's London address.'

Why bother with it? He refused, thanked the man, asked almost as an afterthought if the house was to be sold.

'Very probably, sir.' Hicks, stiff, soldierly almost, unbent a little. 'This house will be. The wife and me, we couldn't stick it here now Sir Manuel's gone.'

It seemed likely that Natalie had taken her leave of Kingsmarkham and the town would not see her again. Perhaps she meant to settle in London or even return to America. He said something on these lines to Sheila as he drove her up to London on the following morning. But she had lost interest in Sterries and its future and was preoccupied with the morning paper which was carrying a feature about her and the forthcoming wedding. On the whole she seemed pleased with it, a reaction that astonished Wexford and Dora. They had been appalled by the description of her as the 'beautiful daughter of a country policeman' and the full-length photograph which showed her neither as Stewardess Curtis nor in one of her Royal Shakespeare Company roles, but reclining on a heap of cushions in little more than a pair of spangled stockings and a smallish fur.

'Dorset Stores It' was the slogan on the side of the removal van that had arrived early in Hamilton Terrace. Two men sat in its cab, glumly awaiting the appearance of the owner of the flat. Recognition of who that owner was mollified them, and on the way up in the lift the younger man asked Sheila if she would give him her autograph for his wife who hadn't missed a single instalment of *Runway* since the serial began.

The other man looked very old. Wexford was thinking he was too old to be of much use until he saw him lift Sheila's big bow-fronted chest of drawers and set it like a light pack on his shoulders. The younger man smiled at Wexford's astonishment.

'Pity you haven't got a piano,' he said. 'He comes from the most famous piano-lifting family in the country.'

Wexford had never before supposed that talents of that kind ran in families or even that one might enjoy a reputation for such a skill. He looked at the old man, who seemed getting on for Camargue's age, with new respect.

'Where are you taking all this stuff?'

A list was consulted. 'This piece and them chairs and that chest up to Keats Grove and . . .'

'Yes, I mean what isn't going to Keats Grove.'

'Down the warehouse. That's our warehouse down Thornton Heath, Croydon way if you know it. The lady's not got so much she'll need more than one container.' He named the rental Sheila would have to pay per week for the storage of her tables and chairs.

'It's stacked up in this container, is it, and stored along with a hundred others? Suppose you said you wanted it stored for a year and then you changed your mind and wanted to get, say, one item out?'

'That'd be no problem, guv'nor. It's yours, isn't it? While you pay your rent you can do what you like about it, leave it alone if that's what you want like or inspect it once a week. Thanks very much, lady.' This last was addressed to Sheila who was dispensing cans of beer.

'Give us a hand, George,' said the old man.

He had picked up Sheila's four-poster on his own, held it several inches off the ground, then thought better of it. He and the man called George began dismantling it.

'You'd be amazed,' said George, 'the things that go on. We're like a very old-established firm and we've got stuff down the warehouse been stored since before the First War. . . .'

'The Great War,' said the old man.

'OK, then, the *Great* War. We've got stuff been stored since before 1914. The party as stored it's dead and gone and the rent's like gone up ten, twenty times, but the family wants it kept and they go on paying. Furniture that's been stored twenty years, that's common, that's nothing out of the way. We got one lady, she put her grand piano in store 1936 and she's dead now, but her daughter, she keeps the rent up. She comes along every so often and we open up her container for her and let her have a look her piano's OK.'

'See if you can shift that nut, George,' said the old man.

By two they were finished. Wexford took Sheila out to lunch, to a little French restaurant in Blenheim Terrace, a far cry from Mr Haq's. They shared a bottle of Domaine du Parc and as Wexford raised his glass and drank to her happiness he felt a rush of unaccustomed sentimentality. She was so very much his treasure. His heart swelled with pride when he saw people look at her, whisper together and then look again. For years now she had hardly been his, she had been something like public property, but after Saturday she would be Andrew's and lost to him for ever. . . . Suddenly he let out a bark of laughter at these maudlin indulgences.

'What's funny, Pop darling?'

'I was thinking about those removal men,' he lied.

He drove her up to Hampstead where she was staying the night and began the long haul back to Kingsmarkham. Not very experienced in London traffic, he had left Keats Grove at four and by the time he came to Waterloo Bridge found himself in the thick of the rush. It was after seven when he walked, cross and tired, into his house.

Dora came out to meet him in the hall. She kept her voice low. 'Reg, that friend of Sheila's who was going to marry Manuel Camargue is here. Dinah Whatever-it-is.'

'Didn't you tell her Sheila wouldn't be back tonight?'

Dora, though aware that she must move with the times, though aware that Sheila and Andrew had been more or less living together for the past year, nevertheless still made attempts to present to the world a picture of her daughter as an old-fashioned maiden bride. Her husband's accusing look — he disapproved of this kind of Mrs Grundy-ish concealment — made her blush and say hastily:

'She doesn't want Sheila, she wants you. She's been here an hour, she insisted on waiting. She says . . .' Dora cast up her eyes. 'She says she didn't know till this morning that you were a policeman!'

Wedding presents were still arriving. The house wasn't big enough for this sort of influx, and now the larger items were beginning to take over the hall. He nearly tripped over an object which, since it was swathed in corrugated cardboard and brown paper, might have been a plant stand, a lectern or a standard lamp, and cursing under his breath made his way into the living room.

This time the alsatian had been left behind. Dinah Stern-hold had been sitting by the hearth, gazing into the heart of the fire perhaps while preoccupied with her own thoughts. She jumped up when he came in and her round pale face grew pink.

'Oh, I'm so sorry to bother you, Mr Wexford. Believe me, I wouldn't be here if I didn't think it was absolutely — well, absolutely vital. I've delayed so long and I've felt so bad and now I can't sleep with the worry . . . . But it wasn't till this morning I found out you were a detective chief inspector.'

'You read it in the paper,' he said, smiling. ' "Beautiful daughter of a country policeman." '

'Sheila never told me, you see. Why should she? I never told her my father's a bank manager.'

Wexford sat down. 'Then what you have to tell me is something serious, I suppose. Shall we have a drink? I'm a bit tired and you look as if you need Dutch courage.'

On doctor's orders, he could allow himself nothing stronger than vermouth but she, to his surprise, asked for whisky. That she wasn't used to it he could tell by the way she shuddered as she took her first sip. She lifted to him those greyish-brown eyes that seemed full of soft light. He had thought that face plain but it was not, and for a moment he could intuit what Camargue had seen in her. If his looks had been spiritual and sensitive so, superlatively, were hers. The old musician and this young creature had shared, he sensed, an approach to life that was gentle, impulsive and joyous.

There was no joy now in her wan features. They seemed convulsed with doubt and perhaps with fear.

'I know I ought to tell someone about this,' she began again. 'As soon as — as Manuel was dead I knew I ought to tell someone. I thought of his solicitors but I imagined them listening to me and knowing I wasn't to — well, inherit, and thinking it was all sour grapes. . . . It seemed so — so wild to go to the police. But this morning when I read that in the paper — you see, I know you, you're Sheila's father, you won't . . . I'm afraid I'm not being very articulate. Perhaps you understand what I mean?'

'I understand you've been feeling diffident about giving some sort of information but I'm mystified as to what it is.'

'Oh, of course you are! The point is, I don't really believe it myself. I can't, it seems so — well, outlandish. But Manuel believed it, he was so sure, so I don't think I ought to keep it to myself and just let things go ahead, do you?'

'I think you'd better tell me straight away, Mrs Sternhold. Just tell me what it is and then we'll have the explanations afterwards.'

She set down her glass. She looked a little away from him, the firelight reddening the side of her face.

'Well, then. Manuel told me that Natalie Arno, or the woman who calls herself Natalie Arno, wasn't his daughter at all. He was absolutely convinced she was an impostor.'

CHAPTER SIX

He said nothing and his face showed nothing of what he felt. She was looking at him now, the doubt intensified, her hands lifted and clasped hard together under her chin. In the firelight the ruby on her finger burned and twinkled.

'There,' she said, 'that's it. It was something to — to hesitate about, wasn't it? But I don't really believe it. Oh, I don't mean he wasn't marvellous for his age and his mind absolutely sound. I don't mean that. But his sight was poor and he'd worked himself into such an emotional state over seeing her, it was nineteen years, and perhaps she wasn't very kind and — oh, I don't know! When he said she wasn't his daughter, she was an impostor, and he'd leave her nothing in his will, I. . . .'

Wexford interrupted her. 'Why don't you tell me about it from the beginning?'

'Where is the beginning? From the time she, or whoever she is. . . .'

'Tell me about it from the time of her return to this country in November.'

Dora put her head round the door. He knew she had come to ask him if he was ready for his dinner but she retreated without a word. Dinah Sternhold said:

'I think I'm keeping you from your meal.'

'It doesn't matter. Let's go back to November.'

'I only know that it was in November she came back. She didn't get in touch with Manuel until the middle of December — 12 December it was. She didn't say anything about our getting married, just could she come and see him and something about healing the breach. At first she wanted to come at Christmas but when Manuel wrote back that that would be fine and I should be there and my parents, she said no, the first time she wanted to see him alone. It sounds casual, putting it like that, Manuel writing back and inviting her, but in fact it wasn't a bit. Getting her first letter absolutely threw him. He was very

583

— well, excited about seeing her and rather confused and it was almost as if he was afraid. I suggested he phone her — she gave a phone number — but he couldn't bring himself to do that and it's true he was difficult on the phone if you didn't know him. His hearing was fine when he could *see* the speaker. Anyway, she suggested 10 January and we had the same excitement and nervousness all over again. I wasn't to be there or the Hickses, Muriel was to get the tea ready and leave him to make it and she was to get one of the spare rooms ready in case Natalie decided to stay.

'Well, two or three days before, it must have been about the 7th, a woman called Mrs Zoffany phoned. Muriel took the call. Manuel was asleep. This Mrs Zoffany said she was speaking on behalf of Natalie who couldn't come on the 10th because she had to go into hospital for a check-up and could she come on the 19th instead? Manuel got into a state when Muriel told him. I went over there in the evening and he was very depressed and nervous, saying Natalie didn't really want a reconciliation, whatever she may have intended at first, she was just trying to get out of seeing him. You can imagine. He went on about how he was going to die soon and at any rate that would be a blessing for me, not to be tied to an old man *et cetera*. All nonsense, of course, but natural, I think. He was *longing* to see her. It's a good thing I haven't got a jealous nature. Lots of women would have been jealous.'

Perhaps they would. Jealousy knows nothing of age discrepancies, suitability. Camargue, thought Wexford, had chosen for his second wife a surrogate daughter, assuming his true daughter would never reappear. No wonder, when she did, that emotions had run high. He said only:

'I take it that it was on the 19th she came?'

'Yes. In the afternoon, about three. She came by train from Victoria and then in a taxi from the station. Manuel asked the Hickses not to interrupt them and Ted even took Nancy away for the afternoon. Muriel left tea prepared on the table in the drawing room and there was some cold duck and stuff for supper in the fridge.'

'So that when she came Sir Manuel was quite alone?'

'Quite alone. What I'm going to tell you is what he told me

the next day, the Sunday, when Ted drove him over to my house in the morning.

'He told me he intended to be rather cool and distant with her at first.' Dinah Sternhold smiled a tender, reminiscent smile. 'I didn't have much faith in that,' she said. 'I knew him, you see. I knew it wasn't in him not to be warm and kind. And in fact, when he went down and opened the front door to her he said he forgot all about that resolve of his and just took her in his arms and held her. He was ashamed of that afterwards, poor Manuel, he was sick with himself for giving way.

'Well, they went upstairs and sat down and talked. That is, Manuel talked. He said he suddenly found he had so much to say to her. He talked on and on about his life since she went away, her mother's death, his retirement because of the arthritis in his hands, how he had built that house. She answered him, he said, but a lot of things she said he couldn't hear. Maybe she spoke low, but my voice is low and he could always hear me. However . . .'

'She has an American accent,' said Wexford.

'Perhaps that was it. The awful thing was, he said, that when he talked of the long time she'd been away he actually cried. I couldn't see it was important, but he was so ashamed of having cried. Still, he pulled himself together. He said they must have tea and he hoped she would stay the night and would she like to see over the house? He was always taking people over the house, I think it was something his generation did, and then . . .'

Wexford broke in, 'All this time he believed her to be his daughter?'

'Oh, yes! He was in no doubt. The way he said he found out — well, it's so crazy. . . . Anyway, he actually told her he was going to make a new will after his marriage, and although he intended to leave me the house and its contents, everything else was to go to her, including what remained of her mother's fortune. It was a lot of money, something in the region of a million, I think.

'He showed her the bedroom that was to be hers, though she did say at this point that she couldn't stay, and then they went back and into the music room. Oh, I don't suppose you've ever been in the house, have you?'

'As a matter of fact, I have,' said Wexford.

She gave him a faintly puzzled glance. 'Yes. Well, you'll know then that there are alcoves all round the music room and in one of the alcoves is a flute made of gold. It was given to Manuel by a sort of patron and fan of his, an American of Italian origin called Aldo Cazzini, and it's a real instrument, it's perfectly *playable*, though in fact Manuel had never used it.

'He and Natalie went in there and Natalie took one look in the alcove and said, 'You still have Cazzini's golden flute,' and it was at this point, he said, that he knew. He knew for certain she wasn't Natalie.'

Wexford said, 'I don't follow you. Surely recognizing the flute would be confirmation of her identity rather than proof she was an impostor?'

'It was the way she pronounced it. It ought to be pronounced Catzini and this woman pronounced it Cassini. Or so he said. Now the real Natalie grew up speaking English, French and Spanish with equal ease. She learnt German at school and when she was fifteen Manuel had her taught Italian because he intended her to be a musician and he thought some Italian essential for a musician. The real Natalie would never have mispronounced an Italian name. She would no more have done that, he said — these are his own words — than a Frenchman would pronounce Camargue to rhyme with Montague. So as soon as he heard her pronunciation of Cazzini he knew she couldn't be Natalie.'

Wexford could almost have laughed. He shook his head in dismissal. 'There must have been more to it.'

'There was. He said the shock was terrible. He didn't say anything for a moment. He looked hard at her, he studied her, and then he could *see* she wasn't his daughter. Nineteen years is a long time but she couldn't have changed that much and in that way. Her features were different, the colour of her eyes was different. He went back with her into the drawing room and then he said, 'You are not my daughter, are you?''

'He actually asked her, did he?'

'He asked her and — you understand, Mr Wexford, that I'm telling you what he said — I feel a traitor to him, doubting him, as if he were senile or mad — he wasn't, he was wonderful, but. . . .'

'He was old,' said Wexford. A foolish, fond old man, fourscore years. . . . 'He was overwrought.'

'Oh, yes, exactly! But the point is he said he asked her and she admitted it.'

Wexford leaned forward, frowning a little, his eyes on Dinah Sternhold's flushed, intent face.

'Are you telling me this woman admitted to Sir Manuel that she wasn't Natalie Arno? Why didn't you say so before?'

'Because I don't believe it. I think that when he said she admitted she wasn't Natalie and seemed ashamed and embarrassed, I think he was — well, dreaming. You see, he told her to go. He was trembling, he was terribly distressed. It wasn't in him to shout at anyone or be violent, you understand, he just told her not to say any more but to go. He heard her close the front door and then he did something he absolutely never did. He had some brandy. He never touched spirits in the normal way, a glass of wine sometimes or a sherry, that was all. But he had some brandy to steady him, he said, and then he went to lie down because his heart was racing — and he fell asleep.'

'It was next day when you saw him?'

She nodded. 'Next day at about eleven. I think that while he was asleep he dreamt that bit about her admitting she wasn't Natalie. I told him so. I didn't humour him — ours wasn't that kind of relationship. I told him I thought he was mistaken. I told him all sorts of things that I believed and believe now — that eye colour fades and features change and one can forget a language as one can forget anything else. He wouldn't have any of it. He was so sweet and good and a genius — but he was terribly impulsive and stubborn as well.

'Anyway, he started saying he was going to cut her out of his will. She was a fraud and an impostor who was attempting to get hold of a considerable property by false pretences. She was to have nothing, therefore, and I was to have the lot. Perhaps you won't believe me if I say I did my best to dissuade him from that?'

Wexford slightly inclined his head. 'Why not?'

'It would have been in my own interest to agree with him. However, I did try to dissuade him and he was sweet to me as he always was but he wouldn't listen. He wrote to her, telling her what he intended to do, and then he wrote to his solicitors, asking one of the partners to come up to Sterries on February 4th — that would have been two days after our wedding.'

'Who are these solicitors?'

'Symonds, O'Brien and Ames,' she said, 'in the High Street here.'

Kingsmarkham's principal firm of solicitors. They had recently moved their premises into the new Kingsbrook Precinct. It was often Wexford's lot to have dealings with them.

'He invited Mr Ames to lunch with us,' Dinah Sternhold said, 'and afterwards he was to draw up a new will for Manuel. It must have been on the 22nd or the 23rd that he wrote to Natalie and on the 27th — he was drowned.' Her voice shook a little.

Wexford waited. He said gently, 'He had no intention of coming to us and he wasn't going to confide in his solicitor?'

She did not answer him directly. 'I think I did right,' she said. 'I prevented that. I couldn't dissuade him from the decision to disinherit her but I did manage to stop him going to the police. I told him he would make a — well, a scandal, and he would have hated that. What I meant to do was this. Let him make a new will if he liked. Wills can be unmade and remade. I knew Natalie probably disliked me and was jealous but I thought I'd try to approach her myself a month or so after we were married, say, and arrange another meeting. I thought that somehow we'd all meet and it would come right. It would turn out to have been some misunderstanding like in a play, like in one of those old comedies of mistaken identity.'

Wexford was silent. Then he said, 'Would you like to tell me about it all over again, Mrs Sternhold?'

'What I've just told?'

He nodded. 'Please.'

'But why?'

To test your veracity. He didn't say that aloud. If she were intelligent enough she would know without his saying, and her flush told him that she did.

Without digressions this time, she repeated her story. He listened concentratedly. When she had finished he said rather sharply:

'Did Sir Manuel tell anyone else about this?'

'Not so far as I know. Well, no, I'm sure he didn't.' Her face was pale again and composed. She asked him, 'What will you do?'

'I don't know.'

'But you'll do something to find out. You'll prove she *is* Natalie Arno?'

Or that she is not? He didn't say it, and before he had framed an alternative reply she had jumped up and was taking her leave of him in that polite yet child-like way she had.

'It was very good and patient of you to listen to me, Mr Wexford. I'm sure you understand why I had to come. Will you give my love to Sheila, please, and say I'll be thinking of her Saturday? She did ask me to come but of course that wouldn't be possible. I'm afraid I've taken up a great deal of your time . . .'

He walked with her out to the Volkswagen which she had parked round the corner of the street on an ice-free patch. She looked back once as the drove away and raised her hand to him. How many times, in telling her story, had she said she didn't believe it? He had often observed how people will say they are sure of something when they truly mean they are unsure, how a man will hotly declare that he doesn't believe a word of it when he believes only too easily. If Dinah Sternhold had not believed, would she have come to him at all?

He asked himself if he believed and if so what was he going to do about it?

Nothing till after the wedding. . . .

CHAPTER SEVEN

The success or failure of a wedding, as Wexford remarked, is no augury of the marriage itself. This wedding might be said to have failed. In the first place, the thaw set in the evening before and by Saturday morning it was raining hard. All day long it rained tempestuously. The expected crowd of well-wishers come to see their favourite married, a youthful joyous crowd of confetti-hurlers, became in fact a huddle of pensioners under umbrellas, indifferently lingering on after the Over-Sixties meeting in St Peter's Hall. But the press was there, made spiteful by rain and mud, awaiting opportunities. And these were many: a bridesmaid's diaphanous skirt blown almost over her head by a gust of wind, a small but dismaying accident when the bride's brother-in-law's car went into the back of a press photographer's car, and later the failure of the Olive and Dove management to provide luncheon places for some ten of the guests.

The Sunday papers made the most of it. Their pictures might have been left to speak for themselves, for the captions, snide or sneering, only added insult to injury. Dora wept.

'I suppose it's inevitable.' Wexford, as far as he could recall it and with a touch of paraphrase, quoted Shelley to her. 'They scatter their insults and their slanders without heed as to whether the poisoned shafts light on a heart made callous by many blows or one like yours composed of more penetrable stuff.'

'And is yours made callous by many blows?'

'No, but Sheila's is.'

He took the papers away from her and burnt them, hoping none would have found their way into the Burdens' bungalow where they were going to lunch. And when they arrived just after noon, escorted from their car by Burden with a large coloured golf umbrella, there was not a newspaper to be seen. Instead, on the coffee table, where the *Sunday Times* might have reposed, lay a book in a glossy jacket entitled *The Tichborne Swindle*.

In former days, during the lifetime of Burden's first wife and afterwards in his long widowerhood, no book apart from those strictly necessary for the children's school work was ever seen in that house. But when he re-married things changed. And it could not be altogether due to the fact that his wife's brother was a publisher, though this might have helped, that the inspector was becoming a reading man. It was even said, though Wexford refused to believe it, that Burden and Jenny read aloud to each other in the evenings, that they had got through Dickens and were currently embarking on the Waverley novels.

Wexford picked up the book. It had been, as he expected, published by Carlyon Brent, and was a reappraisal of the notorious nineteenth-century Tichborne case in which an Australian butcher attempted to gain possession of a great fortune by posing as heir to an English baronetcy. Shades of the tale he had been told by Dinah Sternhold. ... The coincidence of finding the book there decided him. For a little while before lunch he and Burden were alone together.

'Have you read this yet?'

'I'm about half-way through.'

'Listen.' He repeated the account he had been given baldly and without digressions. 'There aren't really very many points of similarity,' he said. 'From what I remember of the Tichborne case the claimant didn't even look like the Tichborne heir. He was much bigger and fatter for one thing and obviously not of the same social class. Lady Tichborne was a hysterical woman who would have accepted practically anyone who said he was her son. You've almost got the reverse here. Natalie Arno looks very much like the young Natalie Camargue and, far from accepting her, Camargue seems to have rumbled her within half an hour.'

' "Rumbled" sounds as if you think there might be something in this tale.'

'I'm not going to stomp up and down raving that I don't believe a word of it, if that's what you mean. I just don't know. But I'll tell you one thing. I expected you to have shouted you didn't believe it long before now.'

Burden gave one of his thin, rather complacent little smiles.

In his domestic circle he behaved, much as he had during his first marriage, as if nobody but he had ever quite discovered the heights of marital felicity. Today he was wearing a new suit of smooth matt cloth the colour of a ginger nut. When happy he always seemed to grow thinner and he was very thin now. The smile was still on his mouth as he spoke. 'It's a funny old business altogether, isn't it? But I wouldn't say I don't believe it. It's fertile ground for that sort of con trick, after all. A nineteen-year absence, an old man on his own with poor sight, an old man who has a great deal of money . . . By the way, how do you know this woman looks like the young Natalie?'

'Dinah Sternhold sent me this.' Wexford handed him a snapshot. 'Camargue was showing her a family photograph album, apparently, and he left it behind in her house.'

The picture showed a dark, Spanish-looking girl, rather plump, full-faced and smiling. She was wearing a summer dress in the style known at the time when the photograph was taken as 'the sack' on account of its shapelessness and lack of a defined waist. Her black hair was short and she had a fringe.

'That could be her. Why not?'

'A whitely wanton with a velvet brow,' said Wexford, 'and two pitchballs stuck in her face for eyes. Camargue said the eyes of the woman he saw were different from his daughter's and Dinah told him that eyes fade. I've never heard of eyes or anything else fading to black, have you?'

Burden refilled their glasses. 'If Camargue's sight was poor I think you can simply discount that sort of thing. I mean, you can't work on the premise that she's not Natalie Camargue because she looks different or he thought she did. The pronouncing of that name wrong, that's something else again, that's really weird.'

Wexford, hesitating for his figure's sake between potato crisps, peanuts or nothing at all, looked up in surprise. 'You think so?'

The thin smile came again. 'Oh, I know you reckon on me being a real philistine but I've got kids, remember. I've watched them getting an education if I've never had much myself. Now my Pat, she had a Frenchwoman teaching them French from when she was eleven, and when she speaks a French word she pronounces the R like the French, sort of rolls it in her throat. The point I'm making is, it happens naturally now, Pat couldn't pronounce a French word with an R in it any other way and *she never will.*'

'Mm hmm.' While pondering Wexford had absentmindedly sneaked two crisps. He held his hands firmly together in his lap. 'There's always the possibility Camargue *heard* the name incorrectly because of defective hearing while it was, in fact, pronounced in the proper way. What I'm sure of is that Dinah is telling the truth. I tested her and she told the same story almost word for word the second time as she has the first, dates, times, everything.'

'Pass over those crisp things, will you? I don't see what motive she'd have for inventing it, anyway. Even if Natalie were out of the way she wouldn't inherit.'

'No. Incidentally, we must find out who would. Dinah could have had spite for a motive, you know. If Natalie is the real Natalie no one of course could hope to prove she is not, and no doubt she could very quickly prove she *is*, but an inquiry would look bad for her, the mud would stick. If there were publicity about it and there very likely would be, there would be some people who would always believe her to be an impostor and many others who would feel a doubt.'

Burden nodded. 'And there must inevitably be an inquiry now, don't you think?'

'Tomorrow I shall have to pass on what I know to Symonds, O'Brien and Ames,' said Wexford, and he went on thoughtfully, 'It would be deception under the '68 Theft Act. Section Fifteen, I believe.' And he quoted with some small hesitations, 'A person who by any deception dishonestly obtains property belonging to another, with the intention of permanently depriving the other of it, shall on conviction on indictment be liable to imprisonment for a term not exceeding ten years.'

'No one's obtained anything yet. It'll take a bit of time for the will to be proved.' Burden gave his friend and superior officer a dubious and somewhat wary look. 'I don't want to speak out of turn and no offence meant,' he said, 'but this could be the kind of thing you get — well, you get obsessional about.'

Wexford's indignant retort was cut off in mid-sentence by the entry of Jenny and Dora to announce lunch.

Kingsmarkham's principal firm of solicitors had moved their offices when the new Kingsbrook shopping precinct was built, deserting the medieval caverns they had occupied for fifty years for the top floor above the British Home Stores. Here all was light, space and purity of line. The offices had that rather disconcerting quality, to be constantly met with nowadays, of looking cold and feeling warm. It was much the same in the police station.

Wexford knew Kenneth Ames well by sight, though he couldn't recall ever having spoken to him before. He was a thin, spare man with a boyish face. That is, his face like his figure had kept its youthful contours, though it was by now seamed all over with fine lines as if a web had been laid upon the skin. He wore a pale grey suit that seemed too lightweight for the time of year. His manner was both chatty and distant which gave the impression, perhaps a false one, that his mind was not on what he was saying or listening to.

This made repeating Dinah Sternhold's account a rather uneasy task. Mr Ames sat with his elbows on the arms of an uncomfortable-looking metal chair and the tips of his fingers pressed together. He stared out of the window at St Peter's spire. As the story progressed he pushed his lips and gradually his whole jaw forward until the lower part of his face grew muzzle-like. This doggy expression he held for a moment or two after Wexford had finished. Then he said:

'I don't think I'd place too much credence on all that, Mr Wexford. I don't think I would. It sounds to me as if Sir Manuel rather got a bee in his belfry, you know, and this young lady, Mrs — er, Steinhalt, is it? — Mrs Steinhall maybe gilded the gingerbread.' Mr Ames paused and coughed slightly after delivering these confused metaphors. He studied his short clean fingernails with interest. 'Once Sir Manuel was married he'd have had to make a new will. There was nothing out of the way in that. We have no reason to believe he meant to disinherit Mrs Arno.' The muzzle face returned as Mr Ames glared at his fingernails and enclosed them suddenly in his fists as if they offended him. 'In point of fact,' he said briskly, 'Sir Manuel invited me to lunch to discuss a new will and to meet his bride, Mrs — er, Sternhill, but unfortunately his death intervened. You know, Mr Wexford, if Sir Manuel had really believed he'd been visited by an impostor, don't you think he'd have said something to us? There was over a week between the visit and his death and during that week he wrote to me and phoned me. No, if this extraordinary tale were true I fancy he'd have said something to his solicitors.'

'He seems to have said nothing to anyone except Mrs Sternhold.'

An elastic smile replaced the muzzle look. 'Ah, yes. People like to make trouble. I can't imagine why. You may have noticed?'

'Yes,' said Wexford. 'By the way, in the event of Mrs Arno not inheriting, who would?'

'Oh dear, oh dear, I don't think there's much risk of Mrs Arno not inheriting, do you, really?'

Wexford shrugged. 'Just the same, who would?'

'Sir Manuel had — has, I suppose I should say if one may use the present tense in connection with the dead — Sir Manuel has a niece in France, his dead sister's daughter. A Mademoiselle Thérèse Something. Latour? Lacroix? No doubt I can find the name for you if you really want it.'

'As you say, there may be no chance of her inheriting. Am I to take it then that Symonds, O'Brien and Ames intend to do nothing about this story of Mrs Sternhold's?'

'I don't follow you, Mr Wexford.' Mr Ames was once more contemplating the church spire which was now veiled in fine driving rain.

'You intend to accept Mrs Arno as Sir Manuel's heir without investigation?'

The solicitor turned round. 'Good heavens, no, Mr Wexford. What can have given you that idea?' He became almost animated, almost involved. 'Naturally, in view of what you've told us we shall make the most thorough and exhaustive inquiries. No doubt, you will too?'

'Oh, yes.'

'A certain pooling of our findings would be desirable, don't you agree? It's quite unthinkable that a considerable property such as Sir Manuel left could pass to an heir about whose provenance there might be the faintest doubt.' Mr Ames half closed his eyes. He seemed to gather himself together in order to drift once more into remoteness. 'It's only,' he said with an air of extreme preoccupation, 'that it doesn't really do, you know, to place too much credence on these things.'

As the receiver was lifted the deep baying of a dog was the first sound he heard. Then the soft gentle voice gave the Forby number.

'Mrs Sternhold, do you happen to know if Sir Manuel had kept any samples of Mrs Arno's handwriting from *before* she went away to America?'

'I don't know. I don't think so.' Her tone sounded dubious, cautious, as if she regretted having told him so much. Perhaps she did, but it was too late now. 'They'd be inside Sterries, anyway.' She didn't add what Wexford was thinking, that if Camargue had kept them and if Natalie was an impostor, they would by now have been destroyed.

'Then perhaps you can help me in another way. I gather Sir Manuel had no relatives in this country. Who is there I can call on who knew Mrs Arno when she was Natalie Camargue?'

Burden's Burberry was already hanging on the palm tree hatstand when Wexford walked into the Pearl of Africa. And Burden was already seated under the plastic fronds, about to start on his antipasto Ankole.

'I don't believe they have shrimps in Uganda,' said Wexford, sitting down opposite him.

'Mr Haq says they come out of Lake Victoria. What are you going to have?'

'Oh, God. Avocado with Victorian shrimps, I suppose, and maybe an omelette. Mike, I've been on to the California police through Interpol, asking them to give us whatever they can about the background of Natalie Arno, but if she's never been in trouble, and we've no reason to think she has, it won't be much. And I've had another talk with Dinah. The first — well, the only really — Mrs Camargue had a sister who's still alive and in London. Ever heard of a composer called Philip Cory? He was an old pal of Camargue's. Either or both of them ought to be able to tell us if this is the real Natalie.'

Burden said thoughtfully, 'All this raises something else, doesn't it? Or, rather, what we've been told about Camargue's will does. And in that area it makes no difference whether Natalie is Natalie or someone else.'

'What does it raise?'

'You know what I mean.'

Wexford did. That Burden too had seen it scarcely surprised him. A year or two before the inspector had often seemed obtuse. But happiness makes so much difference to a person, Wexford thought. It doesn't just make them happy, it makes them more intelligent, more aware, more alert, while unhappiness deadens, dulls and stupefies. Burden had seen what he had seen because he was happy, and happiness was making a better policeman of him.

'Oh, I know what you mean. Perhaps it was rather too readily assumed that Camargue died a natural death.'

'I wouldn't say that. It's just that then there was no reason to suspect foul play, nothing and no one suspicious seen in the neighbourhood, no known enemies, no unusual bruising on the body. A highly distinguished but rather frail old man happened to go too near a lake on a cold night in deep snow.'

'And if we had known what we know now? We can take it for granted that Natalie's aim — whether she is Camargue's daughter or an impostor — her aim in coming to her father was to secure his property or the major part of it for herself. She came to him and, whether he actually saw through her and denounced her or thought he saw through her and dreamed he denounced her, he at any rate apparently wrote to her and told her she was to be disinherited.'

'She could either attempt to dissuade him,' said Burden, 'or take steps of another sort.'

'Her loss wouldn't have been immediate. Camargue was getting married and had therefore to make a new will after his marriage. She might count on his not wishing to make a new will at once and then another after his marriage. She had two weeks in which to act.'

'There's a point too that, whereas she might have dissuaded him from cutting her out, she couldn't have dissuaded him from leaving Sterries to Dinah. But there don't seem to have been any efforts at dissuasion, do there? Dinah doesn't know of any or she'd have told you, nor did Natalie come to Sterries again.'

'Except perhaps,' said Wexford, 'on the night of Sunday, 27 January.'

Burden's answer was checked by the arrival of Mr Haq, bowing over the table.

'How are you doing, my dear?'

'Fine, thanks.' Any less hearty reply would have summoned forth a stream of abject apology and the cook from the kitchen as well as causing very real pain to Mr Haq.

'I can recommend the mousse Maherere.'

Mr Haq, if his advice was rejected, was capable of going off into an explanation of how this dish was composed of coffee beans freshly plucked in the plantations of Toro and of cream from the milk of the taper-horned Sanga cattle. To prevent this, and though knowing its actual provenance to be Sainsbury's instant dessert, Burden ordered it. Wexford always had the excuse of his shaky and occasional diet. A bowl of pale brown froth appeared, served by Mr Haq's own hands.

Quietly Wexford repeated his last remark.

'The night of 27 January?' echoed Burden. 'The night of Camargue's death? If he was murdered, and I reckon we both think he was, if he was pushed into that water and left to drown, Natalie didn't do it.'

'How d'you know that?'

'Well, in a funny sort of way,' Burden said almost apologetically, 'she told me so.'

'It was while we were up at Sterries about that burglary. I was in the dining room talking to Hicks when Natalie and the Zoffany couple came downstairs. She may have known I was within earshot but I don't think she did. She and Mrs Z. were talking and Natalie was saying she supposed she would have to get Sotheby's or someone to value Camargue's china for her. On the other hand, there had been that man she and Mrs Z. had met that someone had said was an expert on Chinese porcelain and she'd like to get hold of his name and phone number. Zoffany said what man did she mean and Natalie said he wouldn't know, he hadn't been there, it had been at so-and-so's party *last Sunday evening.*'

'A bit too glib, wasn't it?'

'Glib or not, if Natalie was at a party there'll be at least a dozen people to say she was, as well as Mrs Z. And if Camargue was murdered *we will never prove it*. If we'd guessed it at the time it would have been bad enough with snow lying everywhere, with snow falling to obliterate all possible evidence. No weapon but bare hands. Camargue cremated. We haven't a hope in hell of proving it.'

'You're over-pessimistic,' said Wexford, and he quoted softly, 'If a man will begin with certainties, he shall end in doubts, but if he will be content to begin with doubts he shall end in certainties.'

CHAPTER EIGHT

A shop that is not regularly open and manned seems to announce this fact to the world even when the 'open' sign hangs on its door and an assistant can be seen pottering inside. An indefinable air of neglect, of lack of interest, of precarious existence and threatened permanent closure hangs over it. So it was with the Zodiac, nestling in deep Victoriana, tucked behind a neo-Gothic square, on the borders of Islington and Hackney.

Its window was stacked full of paperback science fiction, but some of the books had tumbled down, and those which lay with their covers exposed had their gaudy and bizarre designs veiled in dust. Above the shop was a single storey — for this was a district of squat buildings and wide streets — and behind it a humping of rooms, shapelessly huddled and with odd little scraps of roof, gables protruding, seemingly superfluous doors and even a cowled chimney. Wexford pushed open the shop door and walked in. There was a sour, inky, musty smell, inseparable from secondhand books. These lined the shop like wallpaper, an asymmetrical pattern of red and green and yellow and black spines. They were all science fiction, *The Trillion Project, Nergal of Chaldea, Neuropodium, Course for Umbrial, The Triton Occultation.* He was replacing on the shelf a book whose cover bore a picture of what appeared to be a Boeing 747 coated in fish scales and with antennae, when Ivan Zoffany came in from a door at the back.

Recognition was not mutual. Zoffany showed intense surprise when Wexford said who he was, but it seemed like surprise alone and not fear.

'I'd like a few words with you.'

'Right. It's a mystery to me what about but I'm easy. I may as well close up for lunch anyway.'

It was ten past twelve. Could they hope to make any sort of living out of this place? Did they try? The 'open' sign was turned round and Zoffany led Wexford into the room from which he had come. By a window which gave on to a paved

yard and scrap of garden and where the light was best, Jane
Zoffany, in antique gown, shawl and beads, sat sewing. She
appeared to be turning up or letting down the hem of a skirt
and Wexford, whose memory was highly retentive about this
sort of thing, recognized it as the skirt Natalie had been wearing
on the day they were summoned after the burglary.

'What can we do for you?'

Zoffany had the bluff, insincere manner of the man who
has a great deal to hide. Experience had taught Wexford that
what such a nature is hiding is far more often some emotional
disturbance or failure of nerve than guilty knowledge. He could
hardly have indulged in greater self-deception than when he
had said he was easy. There was something in Zoffany's eyes
and the droop of his mouth when he was not forcing it into a
grin that spoke of frightful inner suffering. And it was more
apparent here, on his home ground, than it had been at
Sterries.

'How long have you known Mrs Arno?'

Instinctively, Jane Zoffany glanced towards the ceiling. And
at that moment a light footstep sounded overhead. Zoffany
didn't look up.

'Oh, I'd say a couple of years, give or take a little.'

'You knew her before she came to this country then?'

'Met her when my poor sister died. Mrs Arno and my sister
used to share a house in Los Angeles. Perhaps you didn't know
that? Tina, my sister, she died the summer before last, and I
had to go over and see to things. Grisly business but someone
had to. There wasn't anyone else, barring my mother, and you
can't expect an old lady of seventy — I say, what's all this in
aid of?'

Wexford ignored the question as he usually ignored such
questions until the time was ripe to answer them. 'Your sister
and Mrs Arno shared a house?'

'Well, Tina had a flat in her house.'

'A room actually, Ivan,' said Jane Zoffany.

'A room in her house. Look, could you tell me why you
want . . . ?'

'She must have been quite a young woman. What did she
die of?'

'Cancer. She had cancer in her twenties while she was still married. Then she got divorced, but she didn't keep his name, she went back to her maiden name. She was thirty-nine if you want to know. The cancer came back suddenly, it was all over her, carcinomatosis, they called it. She was dead in three weeks from the onset.'

Wexford thought he spoke callously and with a curious kind of resentment. There was also an impression that he talked for the sake of talking, perhaps to avoid an embarrassing matter.

'I hadn't seen her for sixteen or seventeen years,' he said, 'but when she went like that someone had to go over. I can't think what you want with all this.'

It was on the tip of Wexford's tongue to retort that he had not asked for it. He said mildly, 'When you arrived you met Mrs Arno? Stayed in her house perhaps?'

Zoffany nodded, uneasy again.

'You got on well and became friends. After you came home you corresponded with her and when you heard she was coming back here and needed somewhere to live, you and your wife offered her the upstairs flat.'

'That's quite correct,' said Jane Zoffany. She gave a strange little skittish laugh. 'I'd always admired her from afar, you see. Just to think of my own sister-in-law living in Manuel Camargue's own daughter's house! I used to worship him when I was young. And Natalie and I are very close now. It was a really good idea. I'm sure Natalie has been a true friend to me.' She re-threaded her needle, holding the eye up against the yellowed and none-too-clean net curtain. 'Please, why are you asking all these questions?'

'A suggestion has been made that Mrs Arno is not in fact the late Sir Manuel Camargue's daughter but an impostor.'

He was interested by the effect of these words on his hearers. One of them expected this statement and was not surprised by it, the other was either flabbergasted or was a superb actor. Ivan Zoffany seemed stricken dumb with astonishment. Then he asked Wexford to repeat what he had said.

'That is the most incredible nonsense,' Zoffany said with a loaded pause between the words. 'Who has suggested it? Who

would put about a story like that? Now just you listen to
me. . . .' Wagging a finger, he began lecturing Wexford on the
subject of Natalie Arno's virtues and misfortunes. 'One of the
most charming, delightful girls you could wish to meet, and as
if she hasn't had enough to put up with. . . .'

Wexford cut him short again. 'It's her identity, not her
charm, that's in dispute.' He was intrigued by the behaviour of
Jane Zoffany who was sitting hunched up, looking anywhere but
at him, and who appeared to be very frightened indeed. She
had stopped sewing because her hands would have shaken once
she moved each out of the other's grasp.

He went back into the shop. Natalie Arno was standing by
the counter on the top of which now lay an open magazine. She
was looking at this and laughing with glee rather than amusement. When she saw Wexford she showed no surprise, but
smiled, holding her head a little on one side.

'Good morning, Mr — er, Wexford, isn't it? And how are
you today?' It was an Americanism delivered with an American
lilt and one that seemed to require no reply. 'When you close
the shop, Ivan,' she said, 'you should also remember to lock the
door. All sorts of undesirables could come in.'

Zoffany said with gallantry, but stammering a little, 'That
certainly doesn't include you, Natalie!'

'I'm not sure the chief inspector would agree with you.' She
gave Wexford a sidelong smile. She knew. Symonds, O'Brien
and Ames had lost no time in telling her. Jane Zoffany was
afraid but she was not. Her black eyes sparkled. Rather ostentatiously, she closed the magazine she had been looking at,
revealing the cover which showed it to belong to the medium
hard genre of pornography. Plainly, this was Zoffany's under-
the-counter solace that she had lighted on. He flushed, seized
it rather too quickly from under her hands and thrust it
between some catalogues in a pile. Natalie's face became
pensive and innocent. She put up her hands to her hair and her
full breasts in the sweater rose with the movement, which
seemed to have been made quite artlessly, simply to tuck in a
tortoiseshell pin.

'Did you want to interrogate me, Mr Wexford?'

'Not yet,' he said. 'At present I'll be content if you'll give me the name and address of the people whose party you and Mrs Zoffany went to on the evening of 27 January.'

She told him, without hesitation or surprise.

'Thank you, Mrs Arno.'

At the door of the room where Jane Zoffany was she paused, looked at him and giggled. 'You can call me Mrs X, if you like. Feel free.'

A housekeeper in a dark dress that was very nearly a uniform admitted him to the house in a cul-de-sac off Kensington Church Street. She was a pretty, dark-haired woman in her thirties who doubtless looked on her job as a career and played her part so well that he felt she *was* playing, was acting with some skill the role of a deferential servant. In a way she reminded him of Ted Hicks.

'Mrs Mountnessing hopes you won't mind going upstairs, Chief Inspector. Mrs Mountnessing is taking her coffee after luncheon in the little sitting room.'

It was a far cry from the house in De Beauvoir Square to which Natalie had sent him, a latter-day Bohemia where there had been Indian bedspreads draping the walls and a smell of marijuana for anyone who cared to sniff for it. Here the wall decorations were hunting prints, ascending parallel to the line of the staircase whose treads were carpeted in thick soft olive-green. The first-floor hall was wide, milk chocolate with white cornice and mouldings, the same green carpet, a *Hortus siccus* in a copper trough on a console table, a couple of fat-seated, round-backed chairs upholstered in golden-brown velvet, a twinkling chandelier and a brown table lamp with a cream satin shade. There are several thousand such interiors in the Royal Borough of Kensington and Chelsea. A panelled door was pushed open and Wexford found himself in the presence of Natalie Arno's Aunt Gladys, Mrs Rupert Mountnessing, the sister of Kathleen Camargue.

His first impression was of someone cruelly encaged and literally gasping for breath. It was a fleeting image. Mrs Mountnessing was just a fat woman in a too-tight corset which compressed her body from thighs to chest into the shape of a sausage and thrust a shelf of bosom up to buttress her double chin. This constrained flesh was sheathed in biscuit-coloured wool and upon the shelf rested three strands of pearls. Her face had become a cluster of pouches rather than a nest of wrinkles. It was thickly painted and surmounted by an intricate white-gold coiffure that was as smooth and stiff as a wig. The only area of Mrs Mountnessing which kept some hint of youth was her legs. And these were still excellent: slender, smooth, not varicosed, the ankles slim, the tapering feet shod in classic court shoes of beige glacé kid. They reminded him of Natalie's legs, they were exactly like. Did that mean anything? Very little. There are only a few types of leg, after all. One never said 'She has her aunt's legs' as one might say a woman had her father's nose or her grandmother's eyes.

The room was as beige and gold as its owner. On a low table was a coffee cup, coffee pot, sugar basin and cream jug in ivory china with a Greek key design on it in gold. Mrs Mountnessing rose when he came in and held out a hand much be-ringed, the old woman's claw-like nails filed to points and painted dark red.

'Bring another cup, will you, Miranda?'

It was the voice of an elderly child, petulant, permanently aggrieved. Wexford thought that the voice and the puckered face told of a lifetime of hurts, real or imagined. Rupert Mountnessing was presumably dead and gone long ago, and Dinah Sternhold had told him there had been no children. Would Natalie, real or false, hope for an inheritance here? Almost the first words uttered by Mrs Mountnessing told him that, if so, she hoped in vain.

'You said on the phone you wanted to talk to me about my niece. But I know nothing about my niece in recent years and I don't — I don't want to. I should have explained that to you, I realize that now. I shouldn't have let you come all this way when I've nothing at all to tell you.' Her eyes blinked more often or more obviously than most people's. The effect was to give the impression she fought off tears. 'Thank you, Miranda.' She took the coffee cup and listened, subsiding back into her chair as he told her the reason for his visit.

'Anastasia,' she said.

The Tichborne Claimant had been recalled, now the Tsar's

youngest daughter. Wexford did not relish the reminder, for wasn't it a fact that Anastasia's grandmother, the one person who could positively have identified her, had refused ever to see the claimant, and that as a result of that refusal no positive identification had ever been made?

'We hope it won't come to that,' he said. 'You seem to be her nearest relative, Mrs Mountnessing. Will you agree to see her in my presence and tell me if she is who she says she is?'

Her reaction, the look on her face, reminded him of certain people he had in the past asked to come and identify, not a living person, but a corpse in the mortuary. She put a hand up to each cheek. 'Oh no, I couldn't do that. I'm sorry, but it's impossible. I couldn't ever see Natalie again.'

He accepted it. She had forewarned him with her mention of Anastasia. If he insisted on her going with him the chances were she would make a positive identification simply to get the whole thing over as soon as possible. Briefly he wondered what it could have been that her niece, while still a young girl, had done to her, and then he joined her at the other end of the room where she stood contemplating a table that was used entirely as a stand for photographs in silver frames.

'That's my sister.'

A dark woman with dark eyes, but nevertheless intensely English. Perhaps there was something of the woman he knew as Natalie Arno in the broad brow and pointed chin.

'She had cancer. She was only forty-five when she died. It was a terrible blow to my poor brother-in-law. He sold their house in Pomfret and built that one in Kingsmarkham and called it Sterries. Sterries is the name of the village in Derbyshire where my parents had their country place. Kathleen and Manuel first met there.'

Camargue and his wife were together among the photographs on the table. Arm-in-arm, walking along some Mediterranean sea front; seated side by side on a low wall in an English garden; in a group with a tall woman so like Camargue that she had to be his sister, and with two small dark-haired smiling girls. A ray of sunlight, obliquely slanted at three on a winter's afternoon, fell upon the handsome moustached face of a man in the uniform of a colonel of the Grenadier Guards. Rupert Mountnessing, no doubt. A little bemused by so many faces, Wexford turned away.

'Did Sir Manuel go to the United States after your niece went to live there?'

'Not to see *her*. I think he went there on a tour — yes, I'm sure he did, though it must be ten or twelve years since he gave up playing. His arthritis crippled him, poor Manuel. We saw very little of each other in recent years, but I was fond of him, he was a sweet man. I would have gone to the memorial service but Miranda wouldn't let me. She didn't want me to risk bronchitis in that terrible cold.'

Mrs Mountnessing, it seemed, was willing to talk about any aspect of family life except her niece. She sat down again, blinking back non-existent tears, held ramrod stiff by her corset. Wexford persisted.

'He went on a tour. Did he make any private visits?'

'He may have done.' She said it in the way people do when they dodge the direct affirmative but don't want to lie.

'But he didn't visit his daughter while he was there?'

'California's three thousand miles from the east coast,' she said, 'it's as far again as from here.'

Wexford shook his head dismissively. 'I don't understand that for nineteen years Sir Manuel never saw his daughter. It's not as if he was a poor man or a man who never travelled. If he had been a vindictive man, a man to bear a grudge — but everyone tells me how nice he was, how kind, how good. I might say I'd had golden opinions from all sorts of people. Yet for nineteen years he never made an effort to see his only child and allegedly all because she ran away from college and married someone he didn't know.'

She said so quietly that Wexford hardly heard her, 'It wasn't like that.' Her voice gained a little strength but it was full of distress. 'He wrote to her — oh, ever so many times. When my sister was very ill, was in fact dying, he wrote to her and asked her to come home. I don't know if she answered but she didn't come. My sister died and she didn't come. Manuel made a new will and wrote to her, telling her he was leaving her everything because it was right she should have his money and her mother's. She didn't answer and he gave up writing.'

I wonder how you come to know that? he asked himself, looking at the crumpled profile, the chin that now trembled.

'I'm telling you all this,' said Mrs Mountnessing, 'to make you understand that my niece is cruel, cruel, a cruel unfeeling girl and violent too. She even struck her mother once. Did you know that?' The note in her voice grew hysterical and Wexford, watching the blinking eyes, the fingers clasping and unclasping in her lap, wished he had not mentioned the estrangement. 'She's a nymphomaniac too. Worse than that, it doesn't matter to her who the men are, her own relations, it's too horrible to talk about, it's too. . . .'

He interrupted her gently. He got up to go. 'Thank you for your help, Mrs Mountnessing. I can't see a sign of any of these propensities in the woman I know.'

Miranda showed him out. As he crossed to the head of the stairs he heard a very soft whimpering sound from the room he had left, the sound of an elderly child beginning to cry.

CHAPTER NINE

A birth certificate, a marriage certificate, an American driving licence complete with immediately recognizable photograph taken three years before, a United States passport complete with immediately recognizable photograph taken the previous September, and perhaps most convincing of all, a letter to his daughter from Camargue, dated 1963, in which he informed her that he intended to make her his sole heir. All these documents had been readily submitted to Symonds, O'Brien and Ames, who invited Wexford along to their offices in the precinct over the British Home Stores to view them.

Kenneth Ames, distant and chatty as ever, said he had personally seen Mrs Arno, interviewed her exhaustively and elicited from her a number of facts about the Camargue family and her own childhood which were currently being verified. Mrs Arno had offered to take a blood test but since this could only prove that she was *not* Camargue's daughter, not that she was, and since no one seemed to know what Camargue's blood group had been, it was an impracticable idea. Mr Ames said she seemed heartily amused by the whole business, a point of course in her favour. She had even produced samples of her handwriting from when she was at the Royal Academy of Music to be compared with her writing of the present day.

'Do you know what she said to him?' Wexford said afterwards, meeting Burden for a drink in the Olive and Dove. 'She's got a nerve. "It's a pity I didn't do anything criminal when I was a teenager," she said. "They'd have my fingerprints on record and that would solve everything".'

Burden didn't smile. 'If she's not Natalie Camargue, when could the change-over have taken place?'

'Provided we accept what Zoffany says, not recently. Say more than two years ago but after the death of Vernon Arno. According to Ames, he would seem to have died in a San Francisco hospital in 1971.'

'He must have been young still.' Burden echoed Wexford's words to Ivan Zoffany. 'What did he die of?'

'Leukaemia. No one's suggesting there was anything odd about his death, though there's a chance we'll know more when we hear from the California police. But, Mike, if there was substitution, if this is an assumed identity, it was assumed for some other reason. That is, it wasn't put on for the sake of inheriting from Carmargue.'

Burden gave a dubious nod. 'It would mean the true Natalie was dead.'

'She may be but there are other possibilities. The true Natalie may be incurably ill in some institution or have become insane or gone to live in some inaccessible place. And the impostor could be someone who needed an identity because keeping her own was dangerous, because, for instance, she was some kind of fugitive from justice. That Camargue was rich, that Camargue was old, that Natalie was to be his sole heir, all these facts might be *incidental*, might be a piece of luck for the impostor which she only later decided to take advantage of. The identity would have been taken on originally as a safety measure, even perhaps as the only possible lifeline, and I think it was taken on at a point where the minimum of deception would have been needed. Maybe at the time the move was made from San Francisco to Los Angeles or much later, at the time when Tina Zoffany died.'

Burden, who seemed not to have been concentrating particularly on any of this, said suddenly, looking up from his drink and fixing Wexford with his steel-coloured eyes:

'Why did she come to this country at all?'

'To make sure of the dibs,' said Wexford.

'No.' Burden shook his head. 'No, that wasn't the reason. Impostor or real, she was in no doubt about what you call the dibs. She'd had that letter from Camargue, promising her her inheritance. She need do nothing but wait. There was no need to re-establish herself in his eyes, no need to placate him. If she'd felt there was she'd have tried it before. After all, he was getting on for eighty.

'And it's no good saying she came back because he was getting married again. No one knew he was getting married till

10 December when his engagement was in the *Telegraph*. She came back to this country in November but she made no attempt to see Camargue until after she read about his engagement. She was here for three or four weeks before that. Doing what? Planning what?'

Admiration was not something Wexford had often felt for the inspector in the past. Sympathy, yes, affection and a definite need, for Burden had most encouragingly fulfilled the function of an Achates or a Boswell, if not quite a Watson. But admiration? Burden was showing unexpected deductive powers that were highly gratifying to witness, and Wexford wondered if they were the fruit of happiness or of reading aloud from great literature in the evenings.

'Go on,' he said.

'So why did she come back? Because she was sentimental for her own home, her ain countree, as you might say?' As Scott might say, thought Wexford. Burden went on, 'She's a bit young for those feelings. She's an American citizen, she was settled in California. If she is Natalie Camargue she'd lived there longer than here, she'd no relatives here but a father and an aunt she didn't get on with, and no friends unless you count those Zoffanys.

'If she's an impostor, coming back was a mad thing to do. Stay in America and when Camargue dies his solicitors will notify her of the death, and though she'll no doubt then have to come here and swear affidavits and that sort of thing, *no one will question who she is*. No one would have questioned it if she hadn't shown herself to Camargue.'

'But she had to do that,' Wexford objected. 'Her whole purpose surely in going to see him was to persuade him not to re-marry.'

'She didn't know that purpose would even exist when she left the United States in November. And if she'd stayed where she was she might never have known of Camargue's re-marriage until he eventually died. What would that announcement have merited in a California newspaper? The *Los Angeles Times*, for instance? A paragraph tucked away somewhere. "Former world-famous British flautist ..."'

'They say flutist over there.'

'Flautist, flutist, what does it matter? Until we know *why* she came here I've got a feeling we're not going to get at the truth about this.'

'The truth about who she is, d'you mean?'

'The truth about Camargue's death.' And Burden said with a certain crushing triumph, 'You're getting an obsession about who this woman is. I knew you would, I said so. What interests me far more is the murder of Carmargue and who did it. Can't you see that in the context of the murder, who she is is an irrelevance?'

'No', said Wexford. 'Who she is is everything.'

The California police had nothing to tell Wexford about Natalie Arno. She was unknown to them, had never been in any trouble or associated with any trouble.

'The litigation in the Tichborne case,' said Burden gloomily, 'went on for three years and cost ninety thousand pounds. That was in 1874. Think what the equivalent of that would be today.'

'We haven't had any litigation yet,' said Wexford, 'or spent a single penny. Look on the bright side. Think of the claimant getting a fourteen-year sentence for perjury.'

In the meantime Kenneth Ames had interviewed two people who had known Camargue's daughter when she was an adolescent. Mavis Rolland had been at the Royal Academy of Music at the same time as Natalie Camargue and was now head of the music department at a girls' school on the South Coast. In her opinion there was no doubt that Natalie Arno was the former Natalie Camargue. She professed to find her not much changed except for her voice which she would not have recognized. On the other hand, Mary Woodhouse, a living-in maid who had worked for the Camargue family while they were in Pomfret, said she would have known the voice anywhere. In Ames's presence Mrs Woodhouse had talked to Natalie about Shaddough's Hall Farm where they had lived and Natalie had been able to recall events which Mrs Woodhouse said no impostor could have known.

Wexford wondered why Natalie had not proffered as witnesses for her support her aunt and that old family friend, Philip

Cory. It was possible, of course, that in the case of her aunt (if she really was Natalie Arno) the dislike was mutual and that, just as he had feared Mrs Mountnessing would recognize her as her niece to avoid protracting an interview, so Natalie feared to meet her aunt lest animosity should make her refuse that recognition. But Cory she had certainly seen since she returned home, and Cory had so surely believed in her as to cling to her arm in the excess of emotion he had no doubt felt at his old friend's obsequies. Was there some reason she didn't want Cory brought into this?

In the early years of broadcasting Philip Cory had achieved some success by writing incidental music for radio. But this is not the kind of thing which makes a man's name. If Cory had done this at all it was on the strength of his light opera *Aimée*, based on the story of the Empress Josephine's cousin, the French Sultana. After its London season it had been enthusiastically taken up by amateur operatic societies, largely because it was comparatively easy to sing, had a huge cast, and the costumes required for it could double for *Entführung* or even *Aladdin*. This was particularly the case in Cory's own locality, where he was looked upon as something of a pet bard. Driving out to the environs of Myringham where the composer lived, Wexford noted in the villages at least three posters announcing that *Aimée* was to be performed yet again. It was likely then to be a disappointed man he was on his way to see. Local fame is gratifying only at the beginning of a career, and it could not have afforded much solace to Cory to see that his more frivolous work was to be staged by the Myfleet and District Operatic Society (tickets £1.20, licensed bar opens seven-thirty) while his tone poem *April Fire* and his ballet music for the *Flowers of Evil* were forgotten.

Parents can of course (as Wexford knew personally) enjoy success vicariously. Philip Cory might be scarcely remembered outside village-hall audiences, but his son Blaise Cory was a celebrity as only a television personality can be. His twice-weekly show of soul-searching interviews, drumming up support for charities, and professing aid for almost anyone out of a job, a home or a marriage, vied for pride of place with *Runway* in the popularity ratings. The name was as much a household word as Frost or Parkinson; the bland, handsome, rather larger-than-life face instantly familiar.

'But he doesn't live here, does he?' said Burden whose *bête noire* Blaise Cory was.

'Not as far as I know.' Wexford tapped the driver on the shoulder. 'Those are the gates up ahead, I think. On the left.'

It had been necessary to keep an eye out, for Moidore Lodge, which was in deep country, was three miles from the nearest village and, Cory had told Wexford on the phone, was invisible from the road. The pillars that supported the gates and on which sat a pair of stone wolves or possibly alsatians — they very much resembled Nancy — were, however, unmistakable. The car turned in and, as the drive descended, entered an avenue of plane trees. And very strange and sinister they looked at this season, their trunks and limbs half covered in olive-green bark, half stripped to flesh colour, so that they appeared, or would have appeared to the fanciful, like shivering forms whose nakedness was revealed through rags. At the end of this double row of trees Moidore Lodge, three floors tall, narrow, and painted a curious shade of pale pea-green, glared formidably at visitors.

To ring the front-door bell it was necessary to climb half a dozen steps, though at the top of them there was no covered porch, nothing but a thin railing on each side. The wind blew sharply off the downs. Wexford, accustomed of late, as he remarked to Burden, to moving amongst those in the habit of being waited on, expected to be let in by a man or a maid or at least a cleaning woman, and was surprised when the door was opened by Cory himself.

He was no bigger than the impression of him Wexford had gained from that glimpse outside St Peter's, a little thin old man with copious white hair as silky as floss. Rather than appearing disappointed, he had a face that was both cheerful and peevish. He wore jeans and the kind of heavy navy-blue sweater that is called a guernsey, which gave him a look of youth, or the look perhaps of *a* youth who suffers from some terrible prematurely ageing disease. Before speaking, he looked them up and down closely. Indeed, they' had passed through the over-heated, dusty, amazingly untidy and untended hall and were in the overheated, dusty rubbish heap of a living room before he spoke.

'Do you know,' he said, 'you are the first policemen I've ever actually had in my house. In any house I've ever lived in. Not the first I've ever *spoken* to, of course. I've *spoken* to them to ask the way and so forth. No doubt, I've lived a sheltered life.' Having done his best to make them feel like lepers or untouchables, Cory cracked his face into a nervous smile. 'The idea was distinctly strange to me. I've had to take two tranquillizers. As a matter of fact, my son is coming. I expect you've heard of my son.'

Burden's face was a mask of blankness. Wexford said, Who hadn't? and proceeded to enlighten Cory as to the purpose of their visit. The result of this was that the old man had to take another Valium. It took a further full ten minutes to convince him there was a serious doubt about Natalie Arno's identity.

'Oh dear,' said Cory, 'oh dear, oh dear, how dreadful. Little Natalie. And she was so kind and considerate to me at poor Manuel's memorial service. Who could possibly have imagined she wasn't Natalie at all?'

'Well, she may be,' said Wexford. 'We're hoping you can establish that one way or the other.'

Looking at the distracted little man on whom tranquillizers seemed to have no effect, Wexford couldn't help doubting if the truth could be established through his agency. 'You want me to come with you and ask her a lot of questions? How horribly embarrassing that will be.' Cory actually ran his fingers through his fluffy hair. Then he froze, listening, and looking for all the world like an alerted rabbit. 'A car!' he cried. 'That will be Blaise. And none too soon. I must say, really, he knew what he was about when he insisted on being here to support me.'

If the father was no larger than Wexford had anticipated, the son was much smaller. The screen is a great deceiver when it comes to height. Blaise Cory was a small, wide man with a big face and eyes that twinkled as merrily as those of Santa Claus or a friendly elf. He came expansively into the room, holding out both hands to Wexford.

'And how is Sheila? Away on her honeymoon? Isn't that marvellous?' Forewarned, astute, one who had to make it his business to know who was who, he had done his homework. 'You know, she's awfully like you. I almost think I should have known if I hadn't known, if you see what I mean.'

'They want me to go and look at poor Manuel's girl and tell them if she's really her,' said Cory dolefully.

His son put up his eyebrows, made a soundless whistle. 'You don't mean it? Is *that* what it's about?'

He seemed less surprised than his father or Mrs Mountness-ing had been. But perhaps that was only because he daily encountered more surprising things than they did.

'Do you also know her, Mr Cory?' Wexford asked.

'Know her? We took our first violin lessons together. Well, that's an exaggeration. Let me say we, as tots, went to the same master.'

'You didn't keep it up, Blaise,' said Cory senior. 'You were never a *concentrating* boy. Now little Natalie was very good. I remember little Natalie playing so beautifully to me when she was fifteen or sixteen, it was Bach's Chaconne from the D minor Partita and she . . .'

Blaise interrupted him. 'My dear father, it is twelve-thirty, and though I seem to remember promising to take you out to lunch, a drink wouldn't come amiss. With the possible exception of Macbeth, you must be the world's worst host.' He chuckled irrepressibly at his own joke. 'Now surely you have something tucked away in one of these glory holes?'

Once more Cory put his hands through his hair. He began to trot about the room, opening cupboard doors and peering along cluttered shelves as if he were as much a stranger to the house as they were. 'It's because I've no one to look after me,' he said distractedly. 'I asked Natalie — or whoever she is, you know — I asked her if she didn't want those Hickses and if she didn't, would they come and work for me? She was rather non-committal, said she'd ask them, but I haven't heard an-other word. How do *you* manage?'

Wexford was saved from replying by a triumphant shout from Blaise Cory who had found a bottle of whisky and one of dry sherry. It was now impossible to refuse a drink especially as

Blaise Cory, with ferocious twinkles, declared that he knew for a fact policemen did drink on duty. The glasses were dusty and fingermarked, not to be too closely scrutinized. Nothing now remained but to fix a time with Philip Cory for visiting Natalie, and Wexford felt it would be wise, in spite of Burden's prejudice, to invite Blaise too.

'Ah, but I've already seen her. And frankly I wouldn't have the foggiest whether she was the late lamented Sir Manuel's daughter or not, I hadn't set eyes on her since we were teenagers. She said she was Natalie and that was good enough for me.'

'You were also at the memorial service?'

'Oh, no, no, no. Those morbid affairs give me the shivers. I'm a *life* person, Mr Wexford. No, I gave Natalie lunch. Oh, it must have been a good five or six weeks ago.'

'May I ask why you did that, Mr Cory?'

'Does one have to have a reason for taking attractive ladies out to lunch apart from the obvious one? No, I'm teasing you. It was actually Natalie who phoned me, recalled our former acquaintance and asked me if I could get a friend of hers a job, a man, she didn't say his name. I'm afraid it was all rather due to my programme. I don't know if a busy man like you ever has a moment to watch it? A poor thing, but mine own. I do make rather bold claims on it — not, however, without foundation *and* results — to aid people in finding — well, niches for themselves. This chap was apparently some sort of musician. Fancied himself on the box, I daresay. Anyway, I couldn't hold out much hope but I asked her to have lunch with me. Now I come to think of it, it was January 17th. I remember because that was the dear old dad's birthday.'

'I was seventy-four,' said Cory senior in the tone of one intending to astonish nobody, as indeed he had.

'And when you met her that day you had no doubt she was the Natalie Camargue you had once known?'

'Now wait a minute. When it came to it, I didn't meet her that day. She cancelled on account of some medical thing she had to have, a biopsy, I think she said. We made a fresh date for the following Tuesday. She kept that and I must say we had a delightful time, she was absolutely charming, full of fun. I was only sorry to have to say I hadn't anything cooking for this bloke of hers. But, you know, I couldn't actually tell you if she was *our* Natalie. I mean, it obviously never occurred to me.' He let his eyes light on Burden as being closer to his own age than the others. 'Would you recognize a lady you hadn't seen since you were nineteen?'

Burden responded with a cold smile which had no disconcerting effect on Blaise Cory.

'It 's all rather thrilling, isn't it? Quite a tonic it must be for the dear old dad.'

'No, it isn't,' said the composer. 'It's very upsetting indeed. I think I'll come back to London with you, Blaise, since I've got to be up there tomorrow. And I think I may stay awhile. I suppose you can put up with me for a couple of weeks?'

Blaise Cory put an arm round his father's shoulders and answered with merry affirmatives. Perhaps it was Wexford's imagination that the twinkle showed signs of strain.

The kind of coincidence that leads to one's coming across a hitherto unknown word three times in the same day or receiving a letter from an acquaintance one has dreamed of the night before was no doubt responsible for the poster in the window of the Kingsbrook Precinct travel agents. *Come to sunny California, land of perpetual spring.* . . . A picture of what might be Big Sur and next to it one of what might be Hearst Castle. Wexford paused and looked at it and wondered what the chief constable would say if he suggested being sent to the Golden West in quest of Natalie Arno's antecedents. He could just imagine Colonel Griswold's face.

Presently he turned away and went back to the police station. He had come from Symonds, O'Brien and Ames. Their handwriting expert had examined the writing of the eighteen-year-old Natalie Camargue and that of the thirty-seven-year-old Natalie Arno and expressed his opinion that, allowing for normal changes over a period of nearly two decades, the two samples had in all probability been made by the same person. Wexford had suggested the samples also be examined by an expert of police choosing. Without making any positive objection, Ames murmured that it would be unwise to spoil the ship with too many cooks.

Wexford thought he saw a better way.

'Mike,' he said, putting his head round the door of Burden's office, 'where can we get hold of a violin?'

CHAPTER TEN

Burden's wife was something of a paragon. She was a history teacher, she was well-read in English literature, she was an excellent cook and dressmaker and now it appeared she was musical too.

'You never told me Jenny played the violin,' said Wexford.

'As a matter of fact,' said Burden rather shyly, 'she used to be with the Pilgrim String Quartet.' This was a local ensemble that enjoyed a little more than local fame. 'I expect we could borrow her Hills if we were very careful with it.'

'Her *what*?'

'Her Hills. It's a well-known make of violin.'

'If you say so, Stradivarius.'

Burden brought the violin along in the morning. They were going to call for Philip Cory at his son's home and drive him to De Beauvoir Place. It was a bright sunny day, the first since the snow had gone.

Blaise Cory lived on Campden Hill, not far from Mrs Mountnessing, and work seemed to have claimed him, for his father was alone in the big penthouse flat. Although he popped a Valium pill into his mouth as soon as he saw them, a night in London had evidently done him good. He was sprightly, his cheeks pink, and he had dressed himself in a dark suit with a thin red stripe, a pink shirt and a burgundy silk tie, more as if he were going to a smart luncheon party than taking part in a criminal investigation.

'In the car he was inclined to be talkative.

'I think I shall write to those Hickses personally. I've no reason to believe they're not well-disposed towards me. I understand they like the country and the thing about Moidore Lodge is, it's in the real country. Charming as poor Manuel's place is, I always used to think there was something Metroland-ish about it. One might as well be living in Hampstead Garden Suburb. Do you know, I thought it would be quite an ordeal facing little Natalie today, but actually I feel rather excited at the prospect. London is such a stimulus, don't you find? It seems to tone up one's whole system. And if she isn't Natalie, there's nothing to be embarrassed about.'

Wexford had no intention of going into the bookshop. The door to the upstairs flat was at the side of the building, a panelled door with a pane of glass in it, set under a porch with a steep tiled roof. As they walked up the path, Wexford leading and Burden bringing up the rear with the violin, the door opened, a woman came out and it immediately closed again. The woman was elderly and so tiny as to be almost a midget. She wore a black coat and a brightly coloured knitted hat and gloves. Cory said:

'Good gracious me! It's Mrs Woodhouse, isn't it?'

'That's right, sir, and you're Mr Cory.' She spoke with a Sussex burr. 'How have you been keeping? Mustn't grumble, that's what I always say. I see Mr Blaise on the telly last night, he's a real scream, just the same as ever. You living in London now, are you?'

'Oh dear, no,' said Cory. 'Down in the same old place.' His eyes widened suddenly as if with inspiration. 'I haven't anyone to look after me. I don't suppose . . .'

'I'm retired, sir, and never had so much to do. I don't have a moment for myself let alone other folks, So I'll say bye-bye now and nice to see you after all this time.'

She scuttled off in the direction of De Beauvoir Square, looking at her watch like the White Rabbit as she went.

'Who was that?' said Burden.

'She used to work for poor Manuel and Kathleen when they lived at Shaddough's Hall Farm. I can't think what she's doing up here.'

The door, though closed, had been left on the latch. Wexford pushed it open and they went up the steep staircase. Natalie had come out on to the landing and was waiting for them at the top. Wexford had thought about her so much, had indeed become so obsessive about her, that since last seeing her he had created an image of her in his mind that was seductive, sinister, Mata Hari-like, corrupt, guileful and serpentine. Before the reality this chimera showed itself briefly for the absurd delusion it was and then dissolved. For here, standing before them, was a charming and pretty woman to whom none of these pejorative expressions could possibly apply. Her black hair hung loose to her shoulders, held back by a velvet Alice band. She wore the skirt Jane Zoffany had been altering and with it a simple white shirt and dark blue cardigan. It was very near a school uniform and there was something of the schoolgirl about her as she brought her face down to Cory's and kissed him, saying with the slightest edge of reproach:

'It's good to see you, Uncle Philip. I only wish the circumstances were different.'

Cory drew his face away. He said in a kind of sharp chirp, 'One must do one's duty as a citizen.'

She laughed at that and patted his shoulder. They all went into a small and unpretentious living room from which a kitchen opened. It was all a far cry from Sterries. The furnishings looked if they had come down to the Zoffanys from defunct relatives who hadn't paid much for them when they were new. Nothing seemed to have been added by Natalie except a small shelf of paperbacks which could only be designated as non-Zoffany because none of them was science fiction.

There was an aroma of coffee and from the kitchen the sound, suggestive of some large hibernating creature snoring, that a percolator makes.

'Do sit down,' said Natalie, 'Make yourselves at home. Excuse me while I see to the coffee.' She seemed totally carefree and gave no sign of having noticed what Burden had brought into the flat. There's no art, thought Wexford, to find the mind's construction in the face.

The coffee, when it came, was good. 'The secret', said Natalie gaily, 'is to put enough in.' Uttering this cliché, she laughed. 'I'm afraid the British don't do that.'

She surely couldn't be enjoying herself like this if she was not Natalie, if there was any chance of her failing the test ahead of her. He glanced at Burden whose eyes were on her, who seemed to be studying her appearance and was recalling perhaps newspaper photographs or actual glimpses of Camargue. Having taken a sip of his coffee into which he ladled three spoonfuls of sugar, Cory started at once on his questioning. He would have made a good quizmaster. Perhaps it was from him that Blaise had inherited his talents.

'You and your parents went to live at Shaddough's Hall
Farm when you were five. Can you remember what I gave you
for your sixth birthday?'

She didn't hesitate. 'A kitten. It was a grey one, a British
Blue.'

'Your cat had been run over and I gave you that one to
replace it.'

'We called it Panther.'

Cory had forgotten that. But Wexford could see that now
he remembered and was shaken. He asked less confidently:
'Where was the house?'

'On the Pomfret to Cheriton road. You'll have to do better
than that, Uncle Philip. Anyone could have found out where
Camargue lived.'

For answer he threw a question at her in French. Wexford
wasn't up to understanding it but he gave Cory full marks for
ingenuity. There was more to this old man than at first met the
eye. She answered in fluent French and Cory addressed her in
what Wexford took to be Spanish. This was something he was
sure Symonds, O'Brien and Ames had not thought of. But what
a sound test it was. Momentarily he held his breath, for she was
not answering, her face had that puzzled foolish look people
have when spoken to in a language they know less thoroughly
than they have claimed.

Cory repeated what he had said. Burden cleared his throat
and moved a little in his chair. Wexford held himself perfectly
still, waiting, knowing that every second which passed made it
more likely that she had been discovered and exposed. And
then, as Cory was about to speak for the third time, she broke
into a flood of fast Spanish so that Cory himself was taken
aback, uncomprehending apparently, until she explained more
slowly what it was that she had said.

Wexford drank his coffee and she, looking at him mischie-
vously, refilled his cup. On Burden she bestowed one of her
sparkling smiles. Her long hair fell forward, Cleopatra-like, in
two heavy tresses to frame her face. It was a young face,
Wexford thought, even possibly too young for the age she
professed to be. And wasn't it also *too Spanish*? Natalie Camargue's mother had been English, typically English, her father

half-French. Would their daughter look quite so much like one of Goya's women? None of the evidence, convincing though it was, was as yet conclusive. Why shouldn't an impostor speak Spanish? If the substitution had taken place in Los Angeles she might even be Mexican. Why not know about the kitten and its name if she had been a friend of the true Natalie and had set out to absorb her childhood history?

'What was the first instrument you learned to play?' Cory was asking.

'The recorder.'

'How old were you when you began the violin?'

'Eight.'

'Who was your first master?'

'I can't remember,' she said.

'When you were fifteen you were living at Shaddough's Hall Farm and you were on holiday from school. It was August. Your father had just come back from a tour of — America, I think.'

'Canada.'

'I do believe you're right.' Cory, having been determined almost from Wexford's first words on the subject to consider her an impostor, grew more and more astonished as the interrogation went on. 'You're right, it was. God bless my soul. Do you remember my coming to dinner with your parents? I and my wife? Can you remember that evening?'

'I think so. I hadn't seen you for about a year.'

'Before dinner I asked you to play something for me and you did and . . .'

She didn't even allow him to finish.

'I played Bach's Chaconne from the D minor Partita.'

Cory was stunned into silence. He stared at her and then turned on Wexford an affronted look.

'It was too difficult for me,' she said lightly. 'You clapped but I felt I'd made a mess of it.' The expressions on the three men's faces afforded her an amused satisfaction. 'That's proof enough, isn't it? Shall we all have a drink to celebrate my reinstatement?' She jumped up, took the tray and went into the kitchen, leaving the door open.

It was perhaps this open door and the sound of their hostess humming lightheartedly that stopped Cory from rounding on Wexford. Instead he raised his whiskery white eyebrows almost into his fluffy white hair and shook his head vigorously, a gesture that plainly said he felt he had been brought here on a wild-goose chase. If she wasn't Natalie, Wexford thought, there was no way she could have known about that piece of music. It was impossible to imagine circumstances in which the true Natalie would have spoken of such a thing to the false. If she had done so it would presuppose her having recounted every occasion on which she had played to a friend, listing every friend and every piece of music, since it could never have been foreseen that this particular piece would be inquired about. That Cory would ask this question, a question that had no doubt come into his mind because of his reference to the Bach Chaconne on the previous day, could only have been guessed at by those who had been present at the time, himself, Burden and Blaise.

So one could almost agree with her and acclaim her reinstated as Camargue's heir. She had passed the test no impostor could have passed. He looked at her wonderingly as she returned to the room, the contents of the tray now exchanged for a couple of bottles and an ice bucket. If she was, as she now seemed undoubtedly to be, Natalie Arno, how had Camargue possibly been deceived in the matter? This woman would never have mispronounced a word or a name in a foreign language known to her. And if Camargue had indeed accused her of doing so, it had been in her power to correct that misapprehension at once and to furnish him with absolute proof of who she was. For now Wexford had no doubt that if Camargue had asked her she would have recalled for him the minutest details of her infancy, of the family, of esoteric domestic customs which no one living but he and she could have known. But Camargue had been an old man, wandering in his wits as well as short-sighted and growing deaf. That tiresome woman Dinah Sternhold had wasted their time, repeating to him what was probably only one amongst several of a dotard's paranoid delusions.

Burden looked as if he was ready to leave. He had reached down to grasp once more the handle of the violin case.

'Would you play that piece of music for us now, Mrs Arno?' Wexford said.

If she had noticed the violin, as she surely must have done, she had presumably supposed it the property of Cory and unconnected with herself, for with his question her manner changed. She had put the tray down and had been about to lift her hands from it, but her hands remained where they were and slightly stiffened. Her face was unaltered, but she was no longer quite in command of the situation and she was no longer amused.

'No, I don't think I would,' she said.

'You've given up the violin?'

'No, I still play in an amateurish sort of way, but I'm out of practice.'

'We'll make allowances, Mrs Arno,' said Wexford. 'The inspector and I aren't competent to judge, anyway.' Burden gave him a look implying that *he* might be. 'If you'll play the violin so as to satisfy Mr Cory I will myself be satisfied that Sir Manuel had — made a mistake.'

She was silent. She sat still, looking down, considering. Then she put out her hand for the violin case and drew it towards her. But she seemed not quite to know how to open it, for she fumbled with the catch.

'Here, let me,' said Burden.

She got up and looked at the tray she had brought in. 'I forgot the glasses. Excuse me.'

Burden lifted out the violin carefully, then the bow. The sight of it restored Cory's temper and he touched one of the strings lightly with his finger. From the kitchen came a sudden tinkle of breaking glass, an exclamation, then a sound of water running.

'You may as well put that instrument away again,' said Wexford quietly.

She came in and her face was white. 'I broke a glass.' Wrapped round her left hand was a bunch of wet tissues, rapidly reddening, and as she scooped the sodden mass away, Wexford saw a long thin cut, bright red across three fingertips.

CHAPTER ELEVEN

It should have been the beginning, not the end. They should have been able to proceed with a prosecution for deception and an investigation of the murder of Sir Manuel Camargue. And Wexford, calling on Symonds, O'Brien and Ames with what he thought to be proof that Natalie Arno was not who she said she was, felt confident he had a case. She might speak French and Spanish, she might know the most abstruse details about the Camargues' family life, but she couldn't play the violin and that was the crux. She had not dared to refuse so she had deliberately cut her fingers on the tips where they must press the strings. Kenneth Ames listened to all this with a vagueness bordering on indifference which would have alarmed Wexford if he hadn't been used to the man's manner. He seemed reluctant to disclose the address of Mrs Mary Woodhouse but finally did so when pressed.

She lived with her son and daughter-in-law, both of whom were out at work, in a council flat on the Pomfret housing estate. While Wexford talked to her, explaining gently but at some length what he suspected, she at first sat still and attentive, but when the purpose of his visit became clear to her, she pushed her brows together and struck out her underlip and picked up the work on which she had been engaged before he arrived. This was some sort of bed cover, vast in size, of dead-white cotton crochet work. Mrs Woodhouse's crochet hook flashed in and out as she expended her anger through her fingers.

'I don't know what you're talking about, I don't know what you mean.' She repeated these sentences over and over whenever he paused for a reply. She was a small, sharp-featured old woman whose dark hair had faded to charcoal colour. 'I went to see Mrs Arno because she asked me. Why shouldn't I? I've got a sister living in Hackney that's been a bit off-colour. I've been stopping with her and what with Mrs Arno living like only a stone's throw away, it's only natural I'd go and see her, isn't it? I've known her since she was a kiddy, it was me brought her up as much as her mother.'

'How many times have you seen her, Mrs Woodhouse?'

'I don't know what you mean. Hundreds of times, thousands of times. If you mean been to her place like this past week, just the twice. The time you saw me and two days previous. I'd like to know what you're getting at.'

'Were some of those "hundreds of times" last November and December, Mrs Woodhouse? Did Mrs Arno go and see you when she first arrived in this country?'

'I'll tell you when I first saw her. Two weeks back. When that solicitor, that Mr Ames, come here and asked me the same sort of nonsense you're asking me. Only he knew when he was beaten.' The crochet hook jerked faster and the ball of yarn bounced on Mary Woodhouse's lap. 'Had I any doubt Mrs Arno was Miss Natalie Camargue?' She put a wealth of scorn into her voice. 'Of course I hadn't, not a shadow of doubt.'

'I expect Mrs Arno asked you a great many questions, didn't she? I expect she asked you to remind her of things in her childhood which had slipped her mind. The name of a grey kitten, for instance?'

'Panther,' said Mrs Woodhouse. 'That was his name. Why shouldn't I tell her? She'd forgotten, she was only a kiddy. I don't know what you mean, asking me things like that. Of course I've got a good memory, I was famous in the family for my memory. Mr Camargue — he was Mr Camargue then — he used to say, Mary, you're just like an elephant, and people'd look at me, me being so little and thin, and he'd say, You never forget a thing.'

'I expect you understand what conspiracy is, don't you, Mrs Woodhouse? You understand what is meant by a conspiracy to defraud someone of what is theirs by right of law? I don't think you would want to be involved in something of that kind, would you? Something which could get you into very serious trouble?'

She repeated her formula fiercely, one hand clutching the crochet hook, the other the ball of yarn. 'I don't know what you mean. I don't know what you're talking about.'

Mavis Rolland, the music teacher, was next on his list to be seen. He had the phone in his hand, he was about to dial the school number and arrange an appointment with her when Kenneth Ames was announced.

It was as warm in Wexford's office as it was in the Kingsbrook Precinct, but Ames removed neither his black, waisted overcoat nor his black-and-grey check worsted scarf. He took the chair Wexford offered him and fixed his eyes on the northern aspect of St Peter's spire just as he was in the habit of contemplating its southern elevation from his own window.

The purpose of his call, he said, was to inform the police that Symonds, O'Brien and Ames had decided to recognize Mrs Natalie Kathleen Camargue Arno as Sir Manuel Camargue's rightful heir.

In fact, said Ames, it was only their regard for truth and their horror of the possibility of fraud that had led them to investigate in the first place what amounted to malicious slander.

'We were obliged to look into it, of course, though it never does to place too much credence on that kind of mischief-making.'

'Camargue himself . . .' Wexford began.

'My dear chap, according to Mrs Steinbeck, according to *her*. I'm afraid you've been a bit led up the garden. Lost your sense of proportion too, if I may say so. Come now. You surely can't have expected my client to play you a pretty tune on that fiddle when she'd got a nasty cut on her hand.'

Wexford noted that Natalie Arno had become 'my client'. He was more surprised than he thought he could be by Ames's statement, he was shocked, and he sat in silence, digesting it, beginning to grasp its implications. Still staring skywards, Ames said chattily:

'There was never any real doubt, of course.' He delivered one of his strange confused metaphors. 'It was a case of making a mare's nest out of a molehill. But we do now have incontrovertible proof.'

'Oh yes?' Wexford's eyebrows went up.

'My client was able to produce her dentist, chappie who used to see to the Camargue family's teeth. Man called Williams from London, Wigmore Street, in point of fact. He'd still got his records and — well, my client's jaw and Miss Natalie Camargue's are indisputably one and the same. She hasn't even lost a tooth.'

Wexford made his appointment with Miss Rolland but was obliged to cancel it next day. For in the interim he had an unpleasant interview with the chief constable. Charles Griswold, with his uncanny resemblance to the late General de Gaulle, as heavily built, grave and intense a man as Ames was slight, shallow and *distrait,* stormed in upon him on the following morning.

'Leave it, Reg, forget it. Let it be as if you had never heard the name Camargue.'

'Because an impostor has seduced Ames into believing a pack of lies, sir?'

'*Seduced?*'

Wexford made an impatient gesture with his hand. 'I was speaking metaphorically, of course. *She is not Natalie Arno.* My firm belief is that ever since she came here she's been employing a former servant of the Camargue family to instruct her in matters of family history. As for the dentist, did Symonds, O'Brien and Ames check on him? Did they go to him or did he come to them? If this is a conspiracy in which a considerable number of people are involved. . . .'

'You know I haven't the least idea what you're talking about, don't you? All I'm saying is, if a reputable firm of solicitors such as Symonds, O'Brien and Ames will accept this woman and permit her to inherit a very significant property, we will accept her too. And we'll forget way-out notions of pushing old men into frozen lakes when we have not a shred of evidence that Camargue died anything but a natural death. Is that understood?'

'If you say so, it must be, sir.'

'It must,' said the chief constable.

Not the beginning but the end. Wexford had become obsessional about cases before, and the path these obsessions took had been blocked by just such obstacles and opposition. The feeling of frustration was a familiar one to him but it was none the less bitter for that. He stood by the window, cursing under his breath, gazing at the opaque pale sky. The weather had become raw and icy again, a white mist lifting only at midday and then hanging threateningly at tree height. Sheila was coming back today. He couldn't remember whether she was due in at ten in the morning or ten at night and he didn't want to know. That way he couldn't worry too precisely about what was happening to her aircraft in the fog, unable to land maybe, sent off to try Luton or Manchester, running short of fuel. . . . He told himself sternly, reminded himself, that air transport was the safest of all forms of travel, and let his thoughts turn back to Natalie Arno. Or whoever. Was he never to know now? Even if it were only for the satisfaction of his own curiosity, was he never to know who she was and how she had done it? The switch from one identity to another, the impersonation, the murder. . . .

After what Griswold had said, he dare not, for his very job's sake, risk another interview with Mary Woodhouse, keep his appointment with Mavis Rolland, attempt to break down the obduracy of Mrs Mountnessing or set about exposing that fake dentist, Williams. What could he do?

The way home had necessarily to be via the Kingsbrook Precinct, for Dora had asked him to pick up a brace of pheasants ordered at the poulterers there. Proximity to the premises of Symonds, O'Brien and Ames angered him afresh, and he wished he might for a split moment become a delinquent teenager in order to daub appropriate graffiti on their brass plate. Turning from it, he found himself looking once more into the window of the travel agents.

A helpful young man spread a handful of brochures in front of him. What had been Dora's favourites? Bermuda, Mexico, anywhere warm in the United States. They had discussed it endlessly without coming to a decision, knowing this might be the only holiday of such magnitude they would ever have. The poster he had seen in the window had its twin and various highly coloured siblings inside. He glanced up and it was the skyscraper-scape of San Francisco that met his eyes.

The fog had thickened while he was in there. It seemed to lay a cold wet finger on the skin of his face. He drove home very slowly, thinking once more about Sheila, but as he put his key into the front door lock the door was pulled open and there she was before him, browner than he had ever seen her, her hair bleached pale as ivory.

She put out her arms and hugged him. Dora and Andrew were in the living room.

'Heathrow's closed and we had to land at Gatwick,' said Sheila, 'so we thought we'd come and see you on our way. We've had such a fabulous time, Pop, I've been telling Mother, you just have to go.'

Wexford laughed. 'We are going to California,' he said.

Part Two

CHAPTER TWELVE

The will, published in the *Kingsmarkham Courier,* as well as in the national press, showed Sir Manuel Camargue to have left the sum of £1,146,000 net. This modest fortune became Natalie Arno's a little more than two months after Camargue's death.

'I shouldn't call a million pounds modest,' said Burden.

'It is when you consider all the people who will want their pickings,' Wexford said. 'All the conspirators. No wonder she's put the house up for sale.'

She had moved into Sterries, but immediately put the house on the market, the asking price being £110,000. For some weeks Kingsmarkham's principal estate agents, Thacker, Prince and Co., displayed in their window coloured photographs of its exterior, the music room, the drawing room and the garden, while less distinguishable shots of it appeared in the local press. But whether the house itself was too stark and simplistic in design for most people's taste or whether the price was too high, the fact was that it remained on sale throughout that period of the year when house-buying is at its peak.

'Funny to think that we know for sure she's no business to be there and no right to sell it and no right to what she gets for it,' said Burden, 'and there's not a damn thing we can do about it.'

But Wexford merely remarked that summer had set in with its usual severity and that he was looking forward to going somewhere warm for his holiday.

The Wexfords were not seasoned travellers and this would be the farthest away from home either had ever been. Wexford felt this need not affect the preparations they must make, but Dora had reached a point just below the panic threshold. All day she had been packing and unpacking and re-packing, confessing shamefacedly that she was a fool and then beginning to worry about the possibility of the house being broken into while they were away. It was useless for Wexford to point out that whether they were known to be in San Francisco or

Southend would make little difference to a prospective burglar. He could only assure her that the police would keep an eye on the house. If they couldn't do that for him, whom could they do it for? Sylvia had promised to go into the house every other day in their absence and he set off that evening to give her a spare key.

Wexford's elder daughter and her husband had in the past year moved to a newer house in north Kingsmarkham, and it was only a slightly longer way round to return from their home to his own by taking Ploughman's Lane. To go and look at the house Camargue had built, and on the night before he set out to prove Natalie Arno's claim to it fraudulent, seemed a fitting act. He drove into Ploughman's Lane by way of the side road which skirted the grounds of Kingsfield House. But if Sterries had been almost invisible from the roadway in January and February, it was now entirely hidden. The screen of hornbeams, limes and planes that had been skeletons when last he was there, were in full leaf and might have concealed an empty meadow rather than a house for all that could be seen of it.

It was still light at nearly nine. He was driving down the hill when he heard the sound of running feet behind him. In his rear mirror he saw a flying figure, a woman who was running down Ploughman's Lane as if pursued. It was Jane Zoffany.

There were no pursuers. Apart from her, the place was deserted, sylvan, silent, as such places mostly are even on summer nights. He pulled into the kerb and got out. She was enough in command of herself to swerve to avoid him but as she did so she saw who it was and immediately recognized him. She stopped and burst into tears, crying where she stood and pushing her knuckles into her eyes.

'Come and sit in the car,' said Wexford.

She sat in the passenger seat and cried into her hands, into the thin gauzy scarf which she wore swathed round her neck over a red and yellow printed dress of Indian make. Wexford gave her his handkerchief. She cried some more and laid her head back against the headrest, gulping, the tears running down her face. She had no handbag, no coat or jacket, though the dress was sleeveless, and on her stocklingless feet were Indian sandals with only a thong to attach them. Suddenly she began to speak, pausing only when sobs choked her voice.

'I thought she was wonderful. I thought he was the most wonderful, charming, gifted, *kind* person I'd ever met. And I thought she liked me, I thought she actually wanted my company. I never thought she'd really noticed my husband much, I mean except as my husband, that's all I thought he was to her, I thought it was *me.* . . . And now he says . . . oh God, what am I going to do? Where shall I go? What's going to become of me?'

Wexford was nonplussed. He could make little sense of what she said but guessed she was spilling all this misery out on to him only because he was there. Anyone willing to listen would have served her purpose. He thought too, and not for the first time, that there was something unhinged about her. You could see disturbance in her eyes as much when they were dry as when they were swollen and wet with tears. She put her hand on his arm.

'I did everything for her, I bent over backwards to make her feel at home, I ran errands for her, I even mended her clothes. She took all that from me and all the time she and Ivan had been — when he went out to California they had a relationship!'

He neither winced nor smiled at the incongruous word, relic of the already outdated jargon of her youth. 'Did she tell you that, Mrs Zoffany?' he asked gently.

'He told me. Ivan told me.' She wiped her face with the handkerchief. 'We came down here on Wednesday to stay, we meant to stay till — oh, Sunday or Monday. The shop's a dead loss anyway, no one ever comes in, it makes no difference whether we're there or not. She invited us and we came. I know why she did now. She doesn't want him but she wants him in love with her, she wants him on a string.' She shuddered and her voice broke again. 'He told me this evening, just now, half an hour ago. He said he'd been in love with her for two years, ever since he first saw her. He was longing for her to come and live here so that they could be together and then when she did come she kept fobbing him off and telling him to wait and now . . .'

'Why did he tell you all this?' Wexford interrupted.

She gulped, put out a helpless hand. 'He had to tell someone, he said, and there was no one but me. He overheard her talking to someone on the phone like he was her lover, telling him to come down once we'd gone but to be discreet. Ivan understood then. He's broken-hearted because she doesn't want him. He told his own wife that, that he doesn't know how he can go on living because another woman won't have him. I couldn't take it in at first, I couldn't believe it, then I started screaming. She came into our room and said what was the matter? I told her what he'd said and she said, "I'm sorry, darling, but I didn't know you then". She said that to *me*. "I didn't know you then," she said, "and it wasn't anything important anyway. It only happened three or four times, it was just that we were both lonely." As if that made it better!'

Wexford was silent. She was calmer now, though trembling. Soon she would begin regretting that she had poured out her heart to someone who was almost a stranger. She passed her hands over her face and dropped her shoulders with a long heavy sigh.

'Oh God. What am I going to do? Where shall I go? I can't stay with him, can I? When she said that to me I ran out of the house, I didn't even take my bag, I just ran and you were there and — oh God, I don't know what you must think of me talking to you like this. You must think I'm out of my head, crazy, mad. Ivan says I'm mad, "If you're going to carry on like that," he said, "a psychiatric ward's the best place for you." ' She gave him a sideways look. 'I've been in those places, that's why he said that. If only I had a friend I could go to but I've lost all my friends, in and out of hospital the way I've been. People don't want to know you any more when they think you've got something wrong with your mind. In my case it's only depression, it's a disease like any other, but they don't realize.' She gave a little whimpering cry. 'Natalie wasn't like that, she knew about my depression, she was *kind*. I thought she was, but all the time. . . . I've lost my only friend as well as my husband!'

Her mouth worked unsteadily from crying, her eyes were red. She looked like a hunted gypsy, the greying bushy hair hanging in shaggy bundles against her cheeks. And it was plain from her expression and her fixed imploring eyes that, because of his profession and his manner and his having caught her the way he had, she expected him to do something for her. Wreak vengeance on Natalie Arno, restore an errant husband or at least provide some dignified shelter for the night.

She began to speak rapidly, almost feverishly. 'I can't go back there, I can't face it. Ivan's going home, he said so, he said he'd go home tonight, but I can't be with him, I can't be alone with him, I couldn't bear it. I've got my sister in Wellridge but she won't want me, she's like the rest of them. . . . There must be somewhere I could go, you must know somewhere, if you could only. . . .'

There flashed into Wexford's mind the idea that he could take her home with him and get Dora to give her a bed for the night. The sheer nuisance this would be stopped him. They were going on holiday tomorrow, their flight went at one p.m, which meant leaving Kingsmarkham for Heathrow at ten. Suppose she refused to leave? Suppose Zoffany arrived? It just wasn't on.

She was still talking non-stop. 'So if I could possibly be with you there are lots of things I'd like to tell you. I feel if I could only get them off my chest I'd be that much better and they'd help you, they're things you'd want to know.'

'About Mrs Arno?' he said sharply.

'Well, not exactly about her, about *me*. I need someone to listen and be sympathetic, that does you more good than all the therapy and pills in the world, I can tell you. I can't be alone, don't you understand?'

Later he was to castigate himself for not giving in to that first generous impulse. If he had done he might have known the true facts that night and, more important, a life might have been saved. But as much as the unwillingness to be involved and to create trouble for himself, a feeling of caution prevented him. He was a policeman, the woman was a little mad. . . .

'The best thing will be for me to drive you back up the hill to Sterries, Mrs Zoffany. Let me. . . .'

'No!'

'You'll very probably find your husband is ready to leave and waiting for you. You and he would still be in time to catch the last train to Victoria. Mrs Zoffany, you have to realize he'll get over this, it's something that will very likely lose its force now he's brought it into the open. Why not try to . . . ?'

'No!'

'Come, let me take you back.'

For answer, she gathered up her skirts and draperies and half jumped, half tumbled out of the car. In some consternation, Wexford too got out to help her, but she had got to her feet and as he put out his arm she threw something at him, a crumpled ball. It was his handkerchief.

She stood for a little while a few yards from him, leaning against the high jasmine-hung wall of one of these sprawling gardens. She hung her head, her hands up to her chin, like a child who has been scolded. It was deep dusk now and growing cool. Suddenly she began to walk back the way she had come. She walked quite briskly up the hill, up over the crown of the hill, to be lost amid the soft, hanging, darkening green branches.

He waited a while, he hardly knew what for. A car passed him just as he started his own, going rather fast down the hill. It was a mustard-coloured Opel, and although it was much too dark to see at all clearly, the woman at the wheel looked very much like Natalie Arno. It was a measure, of course, of how much she occupied his thoughts.

He drove home to Dora who had packed for the last time and was watching Blaise Cory's programme on the television.

CHAPTER THIRTEEN

Wexford was driving on the wrong side of the road. Or that was how he put it to himself. It wasn't as bad as he had expected, the San Diego Freeway had so many lanes and traffic moved at a slower pace than at home. What was alarming and didn't seem to get any better was that he couldn't judge the space he had on the right-hand side so that Dora exclaimed, 'Oh, Reg, you were only about an inch from that car. I was sure you were going to scrape!'

The sky was a smooth hazy blue and it was very hot. Nine hours' flying had taken its toll of both of them. Stopped at the lights — traffic lights hung somewhere up in the sky here — Wexford glanced at his wife. She looked tired, she was bound to, but excited as well. For him it wasn't going to be much of a holiday, unless you agreed with those who say that a change is as good as a rest, and he was beginning to feel guilty about the amount of time he would have to spend apart from her. He had tried to explain that if it wasn't for this quest of his they wouldn't be coming here at all, and she had taken it with cheerful resignation. But did she understand quite what he meant? It was all very well her saying she was going to look up those long-lost friends of hers, the Newtons. Wexford thought he knew just how much they would do for a visitor, an invitation to dinner was what that would amount to.

He had just got used to the road, was even beginning to enjoy driving the little red automatic Chevette he had rented at the airport, when the palms of Santa Monica were before them and they were on Ocean Drive. He had promised Dora two days here, staying in luxury at the Miramar, before they set off for wherever his investigations might lead them.

Where was he going to begin? He had one meagre piece of information to go on. Ames had given it to him back in February and it was Natalie Arno's address in Los Angeles. The magnitude of his task was suddenly apparent as, once they had checked in and Dora had lain down in their room to sleep, he stood under the eucalyptus trees, looking at the Pacific. Everything seemed so big, a bigger sea, a bigger beach, a vaster sky than he had ever seen before. And as their plane had come in to land he had looked down and been daunted by the size of the sprawling, glittering, metallic-looking city spread out there below them. The secret of Natalie Arno had appeared enormous in Kingsmarkham; here in Los Angeles it was surely capable of hiding itself and becoming for ever lost in one of a hundred million crannies.

But one of these crannies he would explore in the morning. Tuscarora Avenue, where Natalie had lived for eight years after coming south from San Francisco, Tuscarora Avenue in a suburb called Opuntia. The fancy names suggested to Wexford that he might expect a certain slumminess, for at home Vale Road would be the site of residential elegance and Valhalla Grove of squalor.

The shops were still open. He walked up Wilshire Boulevard and bought himself a larger and more detailed street plan of Los Angeles than the car hire company had provided.

The next morning when he went out Dora was preparing to phone Rex and Nonie Newton. A year or two before she met Wexford Dora had been engaged to Rex Newton; a boy-and-girl affair it had been, they were both in their teens, and Rex had been supplanted by the young policeman. Married for thirty years now, Rex had retired early and emigrated with his American wife to California. Wexford hoped wistfully that they would be welcoming to Dora, that Nonie Newton would live up to the promises she had made in her last letter. But he could only hope for the best. By ten he was on his way to Opuntia.

The names had misled him. Everything here had an exotic name, the grand and tawdry alike. Opuntia wasn't shabby but paintbox bright with houses like Swiss chalets or miniature French chateaux set in garden plots as lush as jungles. He had previously only seen such flowers in florist's shops or the hothouses of public gardens, oleanders, bougainvilleas, the orange-and-blue bird-of-paradise flower, emblem of the City of the Angels. No wind stirred the fronds of the fan palms. The sky was blue, but white with smog at the horizon.

Tuscarora Avenue was packed so tightly with cars that two drivers could hardly pass each other. Wexford despaired of finding a niche for the Chevette up there, so he left it at the foot of the hill and walked. Though there were side streets called Mar Vista and Oceania Way, the sea wasn't visible, being blocked from view by huge apartment buildings which raised their penthouse tops out of a forest of palm and eucalyptus. 1121 Tuscarora, where Natalie Arno had lived, was a small squat house of pink stucco. It and its neighbours, a chocolate-coloured mini-castle and a baby hacienda painted lemon, reminded Wexford of the confections on the sweets trolley at the Miramar the previous night. He hesitated for a moment, imagining Natalie there, the light and the primary colours suiting her better than the pallor and chill of Kingsmarkham, and then he went up to the door of the nearest neighbour, the chocolate-fudge-iced 1123.

A man in shorts and a tee-shirt answered his ring. Wexford, who had no official standing in California, who had no right to be asking questions, had already decided to represent himself as on a quest for a lost relative. Though he had never before been to America, he knew enough of Americans to be pretty sure that this kind of thing, which might at home be received with suspicion, embarrassment and taciturnity, would here be greeted with warmth.

The householder, whose shirt campaigned in red printed letters for the Equal Rights Amendment, said he was called Leo Dobrowski and seemed to justify Wexford's belief. He asked him in, explained that his wife and children had gone to church, and within a few minutes Wexford found himself drinking coffee with Mr Dobrowski on a patio hung with the prussian-blue trumpets of morning glory.

But in pretending to a family connection with Tina Zoffany he had made a mistake. Leo Dobrowski knew all about Tina Zoffany and scarcely anything about Natalie Arno or any other occupants of 1121 Tuscarora. Hadn't Tina, in the two years she had lived next door, become Mrs Dobrowski's closest friend? It was a pleasure, though a melancholy one, for Mr Dobrowski at last to be able to talk about Tina to someone who *cared*. Her brother, he thought, had never cared, though he hoped he wasn't speaking out of turn in saying so. If Wexford was Tina's uncle, he would know what a sweet lovely person she had been and what a tragedy her early death was. Mrs Dobrowski herself had been made sick by the shock of it. If Wexford would care to wait until she came back from church he knew his wife had some lovely snapshots of Tina and could probably let him have some small keepsake of Tina's. Her brother had brought all her little odds and ends to them, wouldn't want the expense of sending them home, you could understand that.

'You sure picked the right place when you came to us,' said Mr Dobrowski. 'I guess there's not another family on Tuscarora knew Tina like we did. You have ESP or something?'

After that Wexford could scarcely refuse to meet the church-going wife. He promised to come back an hour later. Mr Dobrowski beamed his pleasure and the words on his tee-shirt — 'Equality of rights under the law shall not be denied or abridged by the United States or any state on account of sex' — expanded with his well-exercised muscles.

The occupants of 1125 — this time Wexford was a cousin of Natalie's and no nonsense about it — were new to the district and so were those who lived further down the hill in a redwood-and-stucco version of Anne Hathaway's cottage. He went to 1121 itself and picked up from the man he spoke to his first piece of real information, that the house had not been bought but was rented from Mrs Arno. Who was there in the neighbourhood, Wexford asked him, who might have known Mrs Arno when she lived here? Try 1122 on the opposite side, he was advised. In an ever-changing population, the people at 1122, the Romeros, had been in residence longest.

Natalie's cousin once more, he tried at 1122.

'You English?' said Mrs Donna Romero, a woman who looked even more Spanish than Natalie and whose jet-black hair was wound on to pink plastic rollers.

Wexford nodded.

'Natalie's English. She went home to her folks in London. That's all I know. Right now she's somewhere in London, England.'

'How long have you been living here?'

'I just love your accent,' said Mrs Romero. 'How long have

we been here? I guess it'd be four years, right? We came the summer Natalie went on that long vacation up the coast. Must've been the summer of '76. I guess I just thought the house was empty, no one living there, you know, you get a lot of that round here, and then one day my husband says to me, there's folks moved into 1121, and that was Natalie.'

'But she'd lived there before?'

'Oh, sure she lived there before but we didn't, did we?' Donna Romero said this triumphantly as if she had somehow caught him out. 'She had these roomers, you know? There was this guy she had, he was living here illegally. Well, I guess everyone knew it, but my husband being in the Police Department — well, he had to do what he had to do, you know?'

'You mean he had him deported?'

'That's what I mean.'

Wexford decided he had better make himself scarce before an encounter threatened with the policeman husband. He contented himself with merely asking when this deportation had taken place. Not so long ago, said Mrs Romero, maybe only last fall, as far as she could remember.

It was now noon and growing fiercely hot. Wexford reflected that whoever it was who had first described the climate of California as perpetual spring hadn't had much experience of an English April. He went back across the road.

The presence on the drive of 1123 of a four-year-old manoeuvring a yellow and red truck and a six-year-old riding a blue bicycle told him Mrs Dobrowski was back. She greeted him so enthusiastically and with such glistening if not quite tearful eyes that he felt a thrust of guilt when he thought of her conferring later with the man at 1121 and with Patrolman (Lieutenant? Captain?) Romero. But it was too late now to abandon the role of Tina's uncle. He was obliged to listen to a catalogue of Tina's virtues while Mrs Dobrowski, small and earnest and wearing a tee-shirt campaigning for the conservation of the sea otter, pressed Tina souvenirs on him, a brooch, a pair of antique nail scissors, and a curious object she said was a purse ashtray.

At last he succeeded in leading the conversation to Natalie by saying with perfect truth that he had seen her in London before he left. It was immediately clear that Mrs Dobrowski hadn't approved of Natalie. Her way of life had not been what Mrs Dobrowski was used to or expected from people in a nice neighbourhood. Turning a little pink, she said she came from a family of Baptists, and when you had children you had standards to maintain. Clearly she felt that she had said enough on the subject and reverted to Tina, her prowess as what she called a stenographer, the sad fact of her childlessness, the swift onset of the disease which had killed her. Wexford made a second effort.

'I've often wondered how Tina came to live here.'

'I guess Natalie needed the money after Rolf Ilbert moved out. Johnny was the one who told Tina Natalie had a room for rent.'

Wexford made a guess. 'Johnny was Natalie's — er, friend?'

Mrs Dobrowski gave him a grim smile. 'I've heard it called that. Johnny Fassbender was her lover.'

The name sounded German but here might not be. When Wexford asked if he were a local man Mrs Dobrowski said no, he was Swiss. She had often told Tina that one of them should report him to the authorities for living here without a residence permit, and eventually someone must have done so, for he was discovered and deported.

'That would have been last autumn,' Wexford said.

'Oh, no. Whatever gave you that idea? It was all of three years ago. Tina was still alive.'

There was evidently a mystery here, but not perhaps one of pressing importance. It was Natalie's identity he was primarily concerned with, not her friendships. But Mrs Dobrowski seemed to feel that she had digressed too far for politeness and moved rapidly on to her visitor's precise relationship to Tina. Was he her true uncle or uncle only by marriage? Strangely, Tina had never mentioned him. But she had mentioned no one but the brother who came over when she died. She, Mrs Dobrowski, would have liked Ivan to have stayed at her house while he was in Los Angeles but hadn't known how to broach this as she had hardly exchanged a word with Natalie all the years they had lived there. Wexford pricked up his ears at that. No, it was true, she had never set foot inside 1121 or seen Natalie closer than across the yard.

Wexford noted that what she called the yard was, by Kingsmarkham standards, a large garden, dense with oleanders, peach trees and tall cacti. In order not to offend Mrs Dobrowski, he was obliged to carry off with him the brooch as a keepsake. Perhaps he could pass it on to the Zoffanys.

'It's been great meeting you,' said Mrs Dobrowski. 'I guess I can see a kind of look of Tina about you now. Around the eyes.' She gathered the four-year-old up in her arms and waved to Wexford from the porch. 'Say hello to Ivan for me.'

In the heat of the day he drove back to the Miramar and took Dora out to lunch in a seafood restaurant down by the boardwalk. He hardly knew how to tell her he was going to have to leave her alone for the afternoon as well. But he did tell her and she bore it well, only saying that she would make another attempt to phone the Newtons. In their room she dialled their number again while he consulted the directory, looking for Ilberts. There was no Rolf Ilbert in the Los Angeles phone book or in the slimmer Santa Monica directory, but in this latter he did find a Mrs Davina Lee Ilbert at a place called Paloma Canyon.

Dora had got through. He heard her say delightedly, 'Will you really come and pick me up? About four?' Considerably relieved, he touched her shoulder, got a wide smile from her, and then he ran out to the lift, free from guilt at least for the afternoon.

It was too far to walk, half-way to Malibu. He found Paloma Canyon without difficulty and encouraged the car up an impossibly steep slope. The road zig-zagged as on some alpine mountainside, opening up at each turn bigger and better views of the Pacific. But otherwise he might have been in Ploughman's Lane. All super residential areas the world over are the same, he thought, paraphrasing Tolstoy, it is only the slums that differ from each other. Paloma Canyon was Ploughman's Lane with palms. And with a bluer sky, daisy lawns and an architecture Spanish rather than Tudor.

She wasn't the wife but the ex-wife of the man called Rolf Ilbert. No, she didn't mind him asking, she would be only too glad if there was anything she could do to get back at Natalie

Arno. Would he mind coming around to the pool? They always spent their Sunday afternoons by the pool.

Wexford followed her along a path through a shrubbery of red and purple fuchsias taller than himself. She was a tall thin woman, very tanned and with bleached blonde hair, and she wore a sky-blue terry-cloth robe and flat sandals. He wondered what it must be like to live in a climate where you took it for granted you spent every Sunday afternoon round the pool. It was extremely hot, too hot to be down there on the beach, he supposed.

The pool, turquoise blue and rectangular with a fountain playing at the far end, was in a patio formed by the balconied wings of the lemon-coloured stucco house. Davina Lee Ilbert had evidently been lying in a rattan lounging chair, for there was a glass of something with ice in it and a pair of sunglasses on the table beside it. A girl of about sixteen in a bikini was sitting on the rim of the fountain and a boy a bit younger was swimming lengths. They both had dark curly hair and Wexford supposed they must resemble their father. The girl said 'Hi' to him and slipped into the water.

'You care for iced tea?' Mrs Ilbert asked him.

He had never tasted it but he accepted. While she was fetching it he sat down in one of the cane peacock chairs, looking over the parapet to the highway and the beaches below.

'You want to know where Rolf met her?' Davina Ilbert took off her robe and stretched out on the lounger, a woman of forty with a good if stringy figure who had the discretion to wear a one-piece swimsuit. 'It was in San Francisco in '76. Her husband had died and she was staying with friends in San Rafael. The guy was a journalist or something and they all went into the city for this writers' conference that was going on, a cocktail party, I guess it was. Rolf was there.'

'Your former husband is a writer?'

'Movie and TV scripts,' she said. 'You wouldn't have heard of him. Whoever heard of script writers? You have a serial called *Runway* on your TV?'

Wexford said nothing, nodded.

'Rolf's done some of that. You know the episodes set at Kennedy? That's his stuff. And he's made a mint from it, thank

God.' She made a little quick gesture at the balconies, the fountain, her own particular expanse of blue sky. 'It's Natalie you want to know about, right? Rolf brought her back to LA and bought that house on Tuscarora for her.'

The boy came out of the pool and shook himself like a dog. His sister said something to him and they both stared at Wexford, looking away when he met their eyes.

'He lived there with her?' he asked their mother.

'He kind of divided his time between me and her.' She drank from the tall glass. 'I was really dumb in those days, I trusted him. It took me five years to find out and when I did I flipped. I went over to Tuscarora and beat her up. No kidding.'

Wexford said impassively, 'That would have been in 1976?'

'Right. Spring of '76. Rolf came back and found her all bruised and with two black eyes and he got scared and took her on a trip up the coast to get away from me. It was summer, I don't suppose she minded. She was up there two, three months? He'd go up and join her when he could but he never really lived with her again.' She gave a sort of tough chuckle. 'I'd thrown him out too. All he had was a hotel room in Marina del Rey.'

The sun was moving round. Wexford shifted into the shade and the boy and girl walked slowly away into the house. A humming bird, no larger than an insect, was hovering on the red velvet threshold of a trumpet flower. Wexford had never seen one before. He said:

'You said "up the coast". Do you know where?'

She shrugged. 'They didn't tell me their plans. But it'd be somewhere north of San Simeon and south of Monterey, maybe around Big Sur. It could have been a motel, but Rolf was generous, he'd have rented a house for her.' She changed her tone abruptly. 'Is she in trouble? I mean, real trouble?'

'Not at the moment,' said Wexford. 'She's just inherited a very nice house and a million from her father.'

'Dollars?'

'Pounds.'

'Jesus, and they say cheating never pays.'

'Mrs Ilbert, forgive me, but you said your former husband and Mrs Arno never lived together again after the summer of '76. Why was that? Did he simply get tired of her?'

She gave her dry bitter laugh. '*She* got tired of him. She met someone else. Rolf was still crazy about her. He told me so, he told me all about it.'

Wexford recalled Jane Zoffany. Husbands seemed to make a practice of confiding in their wives their passion for Natalie Arno. 'She met someone while she was away on this long holiday?'

'That's what Rolf told me. She met this guy and took him back to the house on Tuscarora — it was hers, you see, she could do what she wanted — and Rolf never saw her again.'

'*He never saw her again?*'

'That's what he said. She wouldn't see him or speak to him. I guess it was because he still hadn't divorced me and married her, but I don't know. Rolf went crazy. He found out this guy she was with was living here illegally and he got him deported.'

Wexford nodded. 'He was a Swiss called Fassbender.'

'Oh, no. Where d'you get that from? I don't recall his name but it wasn't what you said. He was English. Rolf had him deported to England.'

'Did *you* ever see her again?'

'Me? No, why would I?'

'Thank you, Mrs Ilbert. You've been very frank and I'm grateful.'

'You're welcome. I guess I still feel pretty hostile towards her for what she did to me and my kids. It wouldn't give me any grief to hear she'd lost that house and that million.'

Wexford drove down the steep hill, noticing attached to a house wall something he hadn't seen on the way up. A printed notice that said 'No Solicitors'. He chuckled. He knew very well that this was an American equivalent of the 'nice' suburb's injunction to hawkers or people delivering circulars, but it still made him laugh. He would have liked to prise it off the wall and take it home for Symonds, O'Brien and Ames.

Dora was out when he got back to the Miramar and there was a note for him telling him not to wait for dinner if she wasn't back by seven-thirty. Rex Newton, whom he had rather disliked in the days when they had been acquaintances, he now blessed. And tomorrow he would devote the whole day exclusively to Dora.

CHAPTER FOURTEEN

From the map it didn't look as if there was much in the way of habitation in the vicinity of Big Sur, and Wexford's idea that Natalie Arno's trail might therefore easily be followed was confirmed by an elderly lady in the hotel lobby. This was a Mrs Lewis from Denver, Colorado, who had spent, it appeared, at least twenty holidays in California. There was hardly a house, hotel or restaurant, according to Mrs Lewis, between San Simeon in the south and Carmel in the north. The coast was protected, Wexford concluded, it was conserved by whatever the American equivalent might be of the National Trust.

The Miramar's enormous lobby had carpet sculpture on the walls. Although it was probably the grandest hotel Wexford had ever stayed in, the bar was so dark as to imply raffishness or at least that it would be wiser not to see what one was drinking. In his case this was white wine, the pleasant, innocuous, rather weak chablis which must be produced here by the millions of gallons considering the number of people he had seen swilling it down. What had become of the whisky sours and dry martinis of his reading? He sat alone — Dora and Mrs Lewis were swapping family snaps and anecdotes — reflecting that he should try to see Rolf Ilbert before he began the drive northwards. Ilbert was surely by now over Natalie and would have no objection to telling him the name of the place where she had stayed in the summer of 1976. Wexford finished his second glass of wine and walked down past the sculptured carpet palms to phone Davina Ilbert, but there was no reply.

In the morning, when he tried her number again, she told him her ex-husband was in London. He had been in London for two months, researching for a television series about American girls who had married into the English aristocracy. Wexford realized he would just have to trace Natalie on what he had. They drove off at lunchtime and stopped for the night at a motel in Santa Maria. It was on the tip of Wexford's tongue to grumble to Dora that there was nothing to do in Santa Maria, miles from the coast and with Route 101 passing through it. But then it occurred to him that a visitor might say exactly that about Kingsmarkham. Perhaps there was only ever something obvious to do in the centre of cities or by the sea. Elsewhere there was ample to do if you lived there and nothing if you didn't. He would have occupation soon enough and then his guilt about Dora would come back.

Over dinner he confided his theory to her.

'If you look at the facts you'll see that there was a distinct change of personality in 1976. The woman who went away with Ilbert had a different character from the woman who came back to Los Angeles. Think about it for a minute. Camargue's daughter had led a very sheltered, cared-for sort of life, she'd never been out in the world on her own. First there was a secure home with her parents, then elopement with and marriage to Arno, and when Arno died, Ilbert. She was always under the protection of some man. But what of the woman who appears *after* the summer of '76? She lets off rooms in her house to bring in an income. She doesn't form long steady relationships but has casual love affairs — with the Swiss Fassbender, with the English man who was deported, with Zoffany. She can't sell the house Ilbert bought for her so she lets it out and comes to England. Not to creep under her father's wing as Natalie Camargue might have done, but to shift for herself in a place of her own.'

'But surely it was a terrible risk to go to Natalie's own house and live there as Natalie? The neighbours would have known at once, and then there'd be her friends . . .'

'Good fences make good neighbours,' said Wexford. 'There's a lot of space between those houses, it's a shifting population, and if my idea is right Natalie Camargue was a shy, reserved sort of woman. Her neighbours never saw much of her. As to friends — if a friend of Natalie's phoned she had only to say Natalie was still away. If a friend comes to the house she has only to say that she herself is a friend who happens to be staying there for the time being. Mrs Ilbert says Ilbert never saw her after she came back. Now if the real Natalie came back it's almost impossible Ilbert never saw her. Never was alone with her maybe, never touched her, but never saw her? No, it was

the impostor who fobbed him off every time he called with
excuses, with apologies, and at last with direct refusals, allegedly
on the part of the real Natalie, ever to see him again.'

'But, Reg, how could the impostor know so much about the
real Natalie's past?'

He took her up quickly. 'You spent most of last evening
talking to Mrs Lewis. How much do you know about her from,
say, two hours' conversation?'

Dora giggled. 'Well, she lives in a flat, not a house. She's a
widow. She's got two sons and a daughter. One of the sons is a
realtor, I don't know what that is.'

'Estate agent.'

'Estate agent, and the other's a vet. Her daughter's called
Janette and she's married to a doctor and they've got twin
girls and they live in a place called Bismarck. Mrs Lewis has
got a four-wheel-drive Chevrolet for the mountain roads and a
holiday house, a log cabin, in the Rockies and . . .'

'Enough! You found all that out in two hours and you're
saying the new Natalie couldn't have formed a complete dossier
of the old Natalie in — what? Five or six weeks? And when she
came to England she had a second mentor in Mary Woodhouse.'

'All right, perhaps she could have.' Dora hesitated. He had
had a feeling for some hours that she wanted to impart — or even
break — something to him. 'Darling,' she said suddenly, 'You
won't mind, will you? I told Rex and Nonie we'd be staying at the
Redwood Hotel in Carmel and it so happens, I mean, it's a
complete coincidence, that they'll be staying with Nonie's
daughter in Monterey at the same time. If we had lunch with
them once or twice — or I did — well, you won't mind, will you?'

'I think it's a wonderful idea.'

'Only you didn't used to like Rex, and I can't honestly say
he's changed.'

'It's such a stupid name,' Wexford said unreasonably.
'Stupid for a man, I mean. It's all right for a dog.'

Dora couldn't help laughing. 'Oh, come. It only just misses
being the same as yours.'

'A miss is as good as a mile. What d'you think of my theory
then?'

'Well — what became of the old Natalie?'
'I think it's probable she murdered her.'

The road came back to the sea again after San Luis Obispo. It was like Cornwall, Wexford thought, the Cornish coast gigantically magnified both in size and in extent. Each time you came to a bend in the road another bay opened before you, vaster, grander, more majestically beautiful than the last. At San Simeon Dora wanted to see Hearst Castle, so Wexford drove her up there and left her to take the guided tour. He went down on the beach where shade was provided by eucalyptus trees. Low down over the water he saw a pelican in ponderous yet graceful flight. The sun shone with an arrogant, assured permanence, fitting for the finest climate on earth.

There wasn't much to San Simeon, a car park, a restaurant, a few houses. And if Mrs Lewis was to be believed, the population would be even sparser as he drove north. The Hearst Castle tour lasted a long time and they made no more progress that day, but as they set off next morning Wexford began to feel something like dismay. It was true that if you were used to living in densely peopled areas you might find the coast here sparsely populated, but it wasn't by any means *unpopulated*. Little clusters of houses — you could hardly call them villages — with a motel or two, a store, a petrol station, a restaurant, occurred more often then he had been led to believe. And when they came to Big Sur and the road wandered inland through the redwood forest, there were habitations and places to stay almost in plenty.

They reached the Redwood Hotel at about eight that night. Simply driving through Carmel had been enough to lower Wexford's spirits. It looked a lively place, a considerable seaside resort, and it was full of hotels. Another phone call to Davina Ilbert elicited only that she had no idea of Ilbert's London address. Wexford realized that there was nothing for it but to try all the hotels in Carmel, armed with his photograph of Natalie.

All he derived from that was the discovery that Americans are more inclined to be helpful than English people, and if this is because they are a nation of salesmen just as the English are a nation of small shopkeepers, it does little to detract from the overall pleasant impression. Hotel receptionists exhorted him on his departure to have a good day, and then when he was still at it after sundown, to have a nice evening. By that time he had been inside every hotel, motel and lobby of apartments-for-rent in Carmel, Carmel Highlands, Carmel Woods and Carmel Point, and he had been inside them in vain.

Rex Newton and his American wife were sitting in the hotel bar with Dora when he got back. Newton's skin had gone very brown and his hair very white, but otherwise he was much the same. His wife, in Wexford's opinion, looked twenty years older than Dora, though she was in fact younger. It appeared that the Newtons were to dine with them, and Newton walked into the dining room with one arm round his wife's waist and the other round Dora's. Dora had given them to understand he was there on official police business — what else could she have said? — and Newton spent most of his time at the table holding forth on the American legal system, American police, the geography and geology of California and the rival merits of various hotels. His wife was a meek quiet little woman. They were going to take Dora to Muir Woods, the redwood forest north of San Francisco, on the following day.

'If he knows so much,' Wexford grumbled later, 'he might have warned you there are more hotels up here than in the West End of London.'

'I'm sorry, darling. I didn't ask him. He does rather talk the hind leg off a donkey, doesn't he?'

Wexford didn't know why he suddenly liked Rex Newton very much and felt even happier that Dora was having such a good time with him.

For his own part, he spent the next day and the next making excursions down the coast the way they had come, visiting every possible place to stay. In each he got the same response — or worse, that the motel had changed hands or changed management and that there were no records for 1976 available. He was learning that in California change is a very important aspect of life and that Californians, like the Athenians of old, are attracted by any new thing.

Nonie Newton was confined to bed in her daughter's house with a migraine. Wexford cut short his inquiries in Monterey to get back to Dora, who would have been deserted by her friends. The least he could do for her was take her on the beach for the afternoon. He asked himself if he hadn't mismanaged everything. The trip wasn't succeeding either as an investigation or as a holiday. Dora was out when he got back, there was no note for him, and he spent the rest of the day missing his wife and reproaching himself. Rex Newton brought her back at ten and, in spite of Nonie's illness, sat in the bar for half an hour, holding forth on the climate of California, seismology and the San Andreas Fault. Wexford couldn't wait for him to be gone to unburden his soul to Dora.

'You could always phone Sheila,' she said when they were alone.

'Sure I could,' he said. 'I could phone Sylvia and talk to the kids. I could phone your sister and my nephew Howard and old Mike. It would cost a great deal of money and they'd all no doubt say hard cheese very kindly, but where would it get me?'

'To Ilbert,' she said simply.

He looked at her.

'Rolf Ilbert. You said he does part of the script for *Runway*. He's in London. Even if he's not working on *Runway* now, even if she's never met him, Sheila's in a position to find out where he is, she could easily do it.'

'So she could,' he said slowly. 'Why didn't I think of that?'

It was eleven o'clock on the Pacific coast but seven in London, and he was lucky to find her up. Her voice sounded as if she were in the next room. He knew exactly what her voice in the next room would sound like because his hotel neighbours had had *Runway* on for the past half-hour.

'I don't know him, Pop darling, but I'm sure I can find him. Nothing easier. I'll shop around some likely agents. Where shall I ring you back?'

'Don't call us,' said her father. 'We'll call you. God knows where we'll be.'

'How's Mother?'

'Carrying on alarmingly with her old flame.'

He would have laughed as he said that if Dora had shown the least sign of laughing.

*

656

Because it wasn't his nature to wait about and do nothing he spent all the next day covering what remained of the Monterey Peninsula. Something in him wanted to say, forget it, make a holiday of the rest of it, but it was too late for that. Instead of relaxing, he would only have tormented himself with that constantly recurring question, where had she stayed? It was awkward phoning Sheila because of the time difference. All the lines were occupied when he tried at eight in the morning, tea time for her, and again at noon, her early evening. When at last he heard the ringing there was no answer. Next day, or the day after at the latest, they would have to start south and leave behind all the possible places where Natalie Arno might have changed her identity. They had only had a fortnight and eleven days of it were gone.

As he was making another attempt to phone Sheila from the hotel lobby, Rex Newton walked in with Dora. He sat down, drank a glass of chablis, and held forth on Californian vineyards, migraine, the feverfew diet and the gluten-free diet. After half an hour he went, kissing Dora — on the cheek but very near the mouth — and reminding her of a promise to spend their last night in America staying at the Newtons' house. And also their last day.

'I suppose I'm included in that,' Wexford said in a rather nasty tone. Newton was still not quite out of earshot.

She was cool. 'Of course, darling.'

His investigation was over, failed, fruitless. He had rather hoped to have the last two days alone with his wife. But what a nerve he had and how he was punished for it!

'I'm hoist with my own petard, aren't I?' he said and went off to bed.

The Newtons were flying back that morning. It would be a long weary drive for Wexford. He and Dora set off at nine.

The first of the *Danaus* butterflies to float across the windscreen made them both gasp. Dora had seen one only once before, Wexford never. The Milkweed, the Great American Butterfly, the Monarch, is a rare visitor to the cold British Isles. They watched that one specimen drift out over the sea, seeming to lose itself in the blue meeting the blue, and then a cloud of its fellows were upon them, thick as autumnal leaves that strow the brooks in Vallombrosa. And like leaves too, scarlet leaves veined in black, they floated rather than flew across the span of California One, down from the cliffs of daisies, out to the ocean. The air was red with them. All the way down from Big Sur they came, wings of cinnabar velvet, butterflies in flocks like birds made of petals.

'The Spanish for butterfly is *mariposa*,' said Dora. 'Rex told me. Don't you think it's a beautiful name?'

Wexford said nothing. Even if he managed to get hold of Sheila now, even if she had an address or a phone number for him, would he have time to drive back perhaps a hundred miles along this route? Not when he had to be in Burbank or wherever those Newtons lived by nightfall. A red butterfly came to grief on his windscreen, smashed, fluttered, died.

They stopped for a late lunch not far north of San Luis Obispo. He tried in vain to get through to Sheila again and then Dora said she would try. She came back from the phone with a little smile on her lips. She looked young and tanned and happy, but she hadn't been able to reach Sheila. Wexford wondered why she should look like that if she hadn't been talking to anyone. The Newtons would have been back in their home for hours by now. He felt that worst kind of misery, that which afflicts us as the result entirely of our own folly.

The road that returned from inland to the coast wound down through yellow hills. Yuccas pushed their way up through the sun-bleached grass and the rounded mountains were crowned with olives. The hills folded and dipped and rose and parted to reveal more hills, all the same, all ochreish in colour, until through the last dip the blue ocean appeared again. Dora was occupied with her map and guide book.

There was a little seaside town ahead. A sign by the roadside said: Santa Xavierita, height above sea level 50.2 metres, population 482. Dora said:

'According to the book there's a motel here called the Mariposa. Shall we try it?'

'What for?' said Wexford crossly. 'Half an hour's kip? We have to be two hundred miles south of here by eight and it's five now.'

'We don't have to. Our plane doesn't go till tomorrow night. We could stay at the Mariposa, I think we're meant to, it was a sign.'

He nearly stopped the car. He chuckled. He had known her thirty-five years but he didn't know her yet. 'You phoned Newton back there?' he said but in a very different tone from the one he would have used if he had asked that question ten minutes before. 'You phoned Newton and said we couldn't make it?'

She said demurely, 'I think Nonie was quite relieved really.'

'I don't deserve it,' said Wexford.

Santa Xavierita had a wide straggly street with a dozen side turnings at right angles to it, as many petrol stations, a monster market, a clutch of restaurants and among a dozen motels, the Mariposa. Wexford found himself being shown, not to a room, but to a little house rather like a bungalow at home in Ramsgate or Worthing. It stood in a garden, one of a score of green oases in this corner of Santa Xavierita, and up against its front door was a pink and white geranium as big as a tree.

He walked back between sprinklers playing on the grass to the hotel reception desk and phoned Sheila on a collect call. In London it was two in the morning, but by now he was unscrupulous. Sheila had got Ilbert's address. She had had it for two days and couldn't understand why her father hadn't phoned. Ilbert was staying at Durrant's Hotel in George Street by Spanish Place. Wexford wrote down the number. He looked round for someone to inform that he intended to make a call to London.

There was no sign of the little spry man called Sessamy who had checked them in. No doubt he was somewhere about, watering the geraniums and fuchsias and the heliotrope that smelt of cherries. Wexford went back to find Dora and tell her the news, such as it was. She was in the kitchen of their bungalow, arranging in a glass bowl, piling like an Arcimboldo still life, the fruit they had bought.

'Reg,' she said, turning round, a nectarine in her hand, 'Reg, Mrs Sessamy who owns this place, she's English. And she says we're the first English people to stay here since — a Mrs Arno in 1976.'

CHAPTER FIFTEEN

'Tell me about it,' Wexford said.

'I don't know anything about it. I don't know any more than I've told you. Your Natalie Arno stayed here in 1976. After we've eaten we're to go and have coffee with Mrs Sessamy and she'll enlighten you.'

'Will she now? And how did you account for my curiosity? What did you tell her about me?'

'The truth. The idea of you being a real English policeman almost made her cry. She was a GI bride, I think, she's about the right age. I honestly think she expects you to turn up in a blue uniform and say 'ere, 'ere, what's all this about? and she'd love it!'

He laughed. It was rare for him to praise his wife, almost unknown for him to call her by an endearment. That wasn't his way, she knew it and wouldn't have wanted it. It would have bracketed her with those he loved on the next level down. He put his hand on her arm.

'If something comes of all this,' he said, 'and one of us gets sent back here at the government's expense, can I come too?'

There was, of all things, a Lebanese restaurant in the main street of Santa Xavierita. They walked there and ate delicate scented versions of humous and kebab and honey cake. The sun had long gone, sunk almost with a fizzle into that blue sea, and now the moon was rising. The moonlight painted the little town white as with frost. It was no longer very warm. In the gardens, which showed as dark little havens of lushness in aridity, the sprinklers still rotated and sprayed.

Wexford marvelled at his wife and, with hindsight, at his own ignorant presumption. Instead of allowing herself to be a passive encumbrance, she had made him absurdly jealous and had hoodwinked him properly. By some sixth sense or some gift of serendipity, she had done in an instant what had eluded him for nearly a fortnight — found Natalie Arno's hideout. And like

660

Trollope's Archdeacon of his wife, he wondered at and admired the greatness of that lady's mind.

The Sessamys lived in a white-painted frame building, half their home and half the offices of the motel. Their living room was old-fashioned in an unfamiliar way, furnished with pieces from a thirties culture more overblown and Hollywood-influenced than that which Wexford himself had known. On a settee, upholstered in snow-white grainy plastic, a settee that rather resembled some monstrous dessert, a cream-coated log perhaps, rolled in coconut, sat the fattest woman Wexford had ever seen. He and Dora had come in by way of the open French windows, as she had been instructed, and Mrs Sessamy struggled to get to her feet. Like a great fish floundering to raise itself over the rim of the keeper net, she went on struggling until her guests were seated. Only then did she allow herself to subside again. She gave a big noisy sigh.

'It's such a pleasure to see you! You don't know how I've been looking forward to it ever since Mrs Wexford here said who you was. A real bobby! I turned on the waterworks, didn't I, Tom?'

Nearly forty years' domicile in the United States had not robbed her of a particle of her old accent or given her a hint of new. She was a Londoner who still spoke the cockney of Bow or Limehouse.

'Bethnal Green,' she said as if Wexford had asked. 'I've never been back. My people all moved out to one of them new towns, Harlow. Been there, of course. Like every other year mostly we go, don't we, Tom?'

Her husband made no reply. He was a little brown monkey of a man with a face like a nut. He suggested they have a drink and displayed a selection of bottles ranged behind a small bar. There was no sign of the promised coffee. When Dora had apologetically refused bourbon, rye, chablis, Hawaiian cocktail, Perrier, grape juice and gin, Mrs Sessamy announced that they would have tea. Tom would make it, the way she had taught him.

'It's such a pleasure to see you,' she said again, sinking comfortably back into white plastic. 'The English who come here, mostly they stop up at the Ramada or the Howard Johnson. But you picked the old Mariposa.'

'Because of the butterflies,' said Dora.

'Come again?'

'*Mariposa* — well, it means butterfly, doesn't it?'

'It does?' said Tom Sessamy, waiting for the kettle to boil. 'You hear that, Edie? How about that then?'

It seemed the policy of the Sessamys to question each other frequently but never to answer. Mrs Sessamy folded plump hands in her enormous lap. She was wearing green trousers and a tent-like green and pink flowered smock. In her broad moon face, in the greyish-fair hair, could still be seen traces of the pretty girl who had married an American soldier and left Bethnal Green for ever.

'Mrs Wexford said you wanted to know about that girl who lived here — well, stopped here. Though she must have been here three months. We thought she'd go on renting the chalet for ever, didn't we, Tom? We thought we'd got a real sinecure.'

'I'd heard it was up around Big Sur she stayed,' said Wexford.

'So it was at first. She couldn't stick it, not enough life for her, and it was too far to drive to Frisco. You can get up to San Luis in twenty minutes from here by car. She had her own car and he used to come up in a big Lincoln Continental.'

'Ilbert?'

'That's right, that was the name. I will say for her she never pretended, she never called herself Mrs Ilbert. Couldn't have cared less what people thought.'

Tom Sessamy came in with the tea. Wexford who, while in California, had drunk from a pot made with one teabag, had seen tea made by heating up liquid out of a bottle or by pouring warm water on to a powder, noted that Tom had been well taught by his wife.

'I never did fancy them bags,' said Edith Sessamy. 'You can get tea loose here if you try.'

'Hafta go to the specialty shop over to San Luis,' said Tom.

Mrs Sessamy put cream and sugar into her cup. 'What more d'you want to know about her?' she said to Wexford.

He showed her the photograph. 'Is that her?'

She put on glasses with pink frames and rhinestone decoration. Mrs Sessamy had become Californian in all ways but for her tea and her speech. 'Yes,' she said, 'yes, I reckon that's her.' Her voice was full of doubt.

'I guess that's her,' said Tom. 'It's kinda hard to say. She kinda wore her hair loose. She got this terrific tan and wore her hair loose. Right, Edie?'

Edith Sessamy didn't seem too pleased by her husband's enthusiastic description of Natalie Arno. She said rather sharply, 'One man wasn't enough for her. She was two-timing that Ilbert the minute he was off to L.A. For instance, there used to be a young fella hung about here, kipped down on the beach, I reckon you'd have called him a beachcomber in olden times.'

'Kinda hippie,' said Tom.

'She carried on with him. I say he slept on the beach, that summer I reckoned he slept most nights in Natalie's chalet. Then there was an English chap, but it wasn't long before she left she met him, was it, Tom?'

'Played the guitar at the Maison Suisse over to San Luis.'

'Why did she leave?' Wexford asked.

'Now that I can't tell you. We weren't here when she left. We were at home, we were in England.'

'Visiting with her sister over to Harlow,' said Tom.

'She was living here like she'd stay for the rest of her life when we left. That'd have been the end of July, I reckon. Tom's cousin from Ventura, she come up to run the place like she always does when we're off on our holidays. She kept in touch, I reckon we got a letter once a week. I remember her writing us about that woman who got drowned here, don't you, Tom? But she never mentioned that girl leaving. Why should she? There was guests coming and going all the time.'

'You weren't curious yourselves?'

Edith Sessamy heaved up her huge shoulders and dropped them again. 'So if we were? There wasn't much we could do about it, six thousand miles away. She wasn't going to tell Tom's cousin why she upped and went, was she? When we come back we heard that's what she'd done, a moonlight flit like. Ilbert come up the next day but the bird was flown. She went off in her car, Tom's cousin said, and she'd got a young chap with her, and she left that poor mug Ilbert to pay the bill.'

Wexford woke up very early the next morning. The sun was perhaps the brightest and the clearest he had ever seen and the little town looked as if it had been washed clean in the night. Yet Edith Sessamy had told him that apart from a few showers the previous December they had had no rain for a year. He bathed and dressed and went out. Dora was still fast asleep. He walked down the narrow straight road bordered with fan palms, feather dusters on long tapering handles, that led to Santa Xavierita state beach.

The sky was an inverted pan of speckless blue enamel, the sea rippling blue silk. Along the silver sand a young man in yellow tee-shirt and red shorts was jogging. Another, in swimming trunks, was doing gymnastic exercises, sit-ups, press-ups, toe-touching. There was no one in the water. In the middle of the beach was a chair raised up high on stilts for the use of the lifeguard who would sit on it and halloo through his trumpet at over-venturesome swimmers.

Wexford's thoughts reverted to the night before. There was a question he ought to have asked, that he had simply overlooked at the time, because of the crushing disappointment he had felt at the paucity of Edith Sessamy's information. Disappointment had made him fail to select from that mass of useless matter the one significant sentence. He recalled it now, picking it out as the expert might pick out the uncut diamond from a handful of gravel.

Two hours later, as early as he decently could, he was waiting in the motel's reception area by the counter. Ringing the bell summoned Tom Sessamy in shortie dressing gown which left exposed hairless white legs and long white feet in sandals of plaited straw.

'Hi, Reg, you wanna check out?'

'I wanted to ask you and your wife a few more questions first if you'll bear with me.'

'Edie, are ya decent? Reg's here ta pick your brains.'

Mrs Sessamy was rather more decent than her husband in an all-enveloping pink kimono printed with birds of paradise.

She sat on the white sofa drinking more strong black tea, and on her lap on a tray were fried eggs and fried bacon and hash browns and English muffins and grape jelly.

'It's been such a pleasure meeting you and Dora, I can't tell you.' She had told him at least six times already, but the repetition was somehow warming and pleasant to hear. Wexford returned the compliment with a few words about how much they had enjoyed themselves.

'You wanna cup of Edie's tea?' said Tom.

Wexford accepted. 'You said last night a woman was drowned here. While you were away. D'you know any more than that? Who she was? How it happened?'

'Not a thing. Only what I said, a woman was drowned. Well, it was a young woman, a girl really, I do know that, and I reckon I heard she was on holiday here from the East somewhere.'

'You hafta talk to the cops over to San Luis,' said Tom.

'Wait a minute, though — George Janveer was lifeguard here then, wasn't he, Tom? I reckon you could talk to George.'

'Why don't I call George right now?' said Tom.

He was dissuaded from this by his wife since it was only just after eight. They would phone George at nine. Wexford wasn't pressed for time, was he? No, he wasn't, not really, he had all day. He had a 200-mile drive ahead of him, of course, but that was nothing here. Edith Sessamy said she knew what he meant, it was nothing here.

He walked slowly back. At last a clear pattern was emerging from the confusion. The pieces fluttered and dropped into a design as the coloured fragments do when you shake a kaleidoscope. Camargue too had been drowned, he thought.

Just after nine he went back and paid his bill. Tom said apologetically that he had phoned George Janveer's home and talked to Mrs Janveer who said George had gone to Grover City but she expected him back by eleven.

'Oughta've called him at eight like I said,' said Tom.

Wexford and Dora put the cases in the car and went to explore what they hadn't yet seen of Santa Xavierita. Wouldn't it be best, Wexford asked himself, to head straight for San Luis Obispo and call on the police there and see what facts he could get out of them? But suppose he couldn't get any? Suppose, before they imparted anything to him, they required proof of who he was and what he was doing there? He could prove his identity, of course, and present them with bona fides but it would all take time and he hadn't much left. He had to be at Los Angeles international airport by six in time for their flight home at seven. Better wait for Janveer who would know as much as the police did and would almost certainly talk to him.

Mrs Janveer was as thin as Edith Sessamy was fat. She was in her kitchen baking something she called devil's food and her overweight black labrador was sitting at her feet, hoping to lick out the bowl.

It was after eleven and her husband still hadn't come back from Grover City. Maybe he had met a friend and they had got drinking. Mrs Janveer did not say this in a shrewish or condemnatory way or even as if there were anything to be defensive about. She said it in exactly the same tone, casual, indifferent, even slightly complacent, she would have used to say he had met the mayor or gone to a meeting of the Lions.

Wexford was driven to ask her if she remembered anything about the drowned woman. Mrs Janveer put the tin of chocolate cake mixture into the oven. The dog's tail began to thump the floor. No, she couldn't say she remembered much about it at all, except the woman's first name had been Theresa, she recalled that because it was hers too, and after the drowning some of her relations had come out to Santa Xavierita, from Boston, she thought it was, and stayed at the Ramada Inn. She put the mixing bowl under the tap and her hand to the tap. The dog let out a piteous squeal. Mrs Janveer shrugged, looking upset, and slapped the bowl down in front of the dog with a cross exclamation.

Wexford waited until half-past eleven. Janveer still hadn't come. 'Considering what I know now,' he said to Dora, 'they're bound to send me back here. It's only time I need.'

'It's a shame, darling, it's such bad luck.'

He drove quickly out of the town, heading for the Pacific Highway.

CHAPTER SIXTEEN

The difference between California and Kingsmarkham was a matter of colour as well as temperature. The one was blue and gold, the sun burning the grass to its own colour; the other was grey and green, the lush green of foliage watered daily by those massy clouds. Wexford went to work, not yet used to seeing grass verges instead of daisy lawns, shivering a little because the temperature was precisely what Tom Sessamy had told him it could fall to in Santa Xavierita in December.

Burden was waiting for him in his office. He had on a lightweight silky suit in a shade of taupe and a beige silk shirt. No one could possibly have taken him for a policeman or even a policeman in disguise. Wexford, who had been considering telling him at once what he had found out in California, now decided not to and instead asked him to close the window.

'I opened it because it's such a muggy stuffy sort of day,' said Burden. 'Not cold, are you?'

'Yes, I am. Very cold.'

'Jet lag. Did you have a good time?'

Wexford grunted. He wished he had the nerve to start the central heating. It probably wouldn't start, though, not in July. For all he knew, the chief constable had to come over himself on 1 November and personally press a button on the boiler. 'I don't suppose there've been any developments while I was away?' he said.

Burden sat down. 'Well, yes, there have. That's what I'm doing in here. I thought I ought to tell you first thing. Jane Zoffany has disappeared.'

Zoffany had not reported her missing until she had been gone a week. His story, said Burden, was that he and his wife had been staying at Sterries with their friend Natalie Arno, and on the evening of Friday, 27 June his wife had gone out alone for a walk and had never come back. Zoffany, when pressed, admitted that immediately prior to this he and his wife had quarrelled over an affair he had had with another woman. She had said she was going to leave him, she could never live with him again, and had left the house. Zoffany himself had left soon after, taking the 10.05 p.m. train to Victoria. He believed his wife would have gone home by an earlier train.

However, when he got to De Beauvoir Place she wasn't there. Nor did she appear the next day. He concluded she had gone to her sister in Horsham. This had apparently happened once before after a quarrel. But Friday 4 July had been Jane Zoffany's birthday, her thirty-fifth, and a birthday card came for her from her sister. Zoffany then knew he had been wrong and he went to his local police station.

Where no one had shown much interest, Burden said. Why should they? That a young woman should temporarily leave her husband after a quarrel over his infidelity was hardly noteworthy. It happened all the time. And of course she wouldn't tell him where she had gone, that was the last thing she had wanted him to know. Burden only got to hear of it when Zoffany also reported his wife's disappearance to the Kingsmarkham police. He seemed genuinely worried. It would not be putting it too strongly to say he was distraught.

'Guilt,' said Wexford, and as he pronounced the word he felt it himself. It was even possible he was the last person — the last but one — to have seen Jane Zoffany alive. And he had let her go. Because he was off on holiday, because he didn't want to inconvenience Dora or upset arrangements. Of course she hadn't taken refuge with her sister or some friend. She had had no handbag, no money. He had let her go, overwrought as she was, to walk away into the dusk of Ploughman's Lane — to go back to Sterries and Natalie Arno.

'I had a feeling we ought to take it a bit more seriously,' Burden said. 'I mean, I wasn't really alarmed but I couldn't help thinking about poor old Camargue. We've got our own ideas about what kind of a death that was, haven't we? I talked to Zoffany myself, I got him to give me the names of people she could possibly have gone to. There weren't many and we checked on them all.'

'And what about Natalie? Have you talked to her?'

'I thought I'd leave that to you.'

'We'll have to drag the lake,' said Wexford, 'and dig up the garden if necessary. But I'll talk to her first.'

The effect of her inherited wealth was now displayed. A new hatchback Opel, mustard-coloured, automatic transmission, stood on the gravel circle outside the front door. Looking at her, staring almost, Wexford remembered the skirt Jane Zoffany had mended, the old blanket coat. Natalie wore a dress of some thin clinging jersey material in bright egg-yellow with a tight bodice and full skirt. Around her small neat waist was tied a belt of yellow with red, blue and purple stripes. It was startling and effective and very fashionable. Her hair hung loose in a glossy black bell. There was a white gold watch on one wrist and a bracelet of woven white gold threads on the other. The mysterious lady from Boston, he thought, and he wondered how you felt when you knew your relatives, parents maybe, and your friends thought you were dead and grieved for you while in fact you were alive and living in the lap of luxury.

'But Mr Wexford,' she said with her faint accent — a New England accent? 'But, Mr Wexford, Jane never came back here that night.' She smiled in the way a model does when her mouth and not her eyes are to show in the toothpaste ad. 'Her things are still in the room she and Ivan used. Would you like to see?'

He nodded. He followed her down to the spare rooms. On the carved teak chest stood a Chinese bowl full of Peace roses. They went into the room where he had once before seen Jane Zoffany standing before the long mirror and fastening the collar of a Persian lamb coat. Her suitcase lay open on the top of a chest of drawers. There was a folded nightdress inside it, a pair of sandals placed heel to toe and a paperback edition of Daphne du Maurier's *Rebecca*. On the black-backed hairbrush on the dressing table and the box of talcum powder lay a fine scattering of dust.

'Has Mrs Hicks left you?'

'In the spirit if not the flesh yet, Mr Wexford. She and Ted are going to Uncle Philip.' She added, as if in explanation to someone who could not be expected to know intimate family usage, 'Philip Cory, that is. He was just crazy to have them and it's made him so happy. Meanwhile this place is rather neg-

lected while they get ready to leave. They've sold their house
and I think I've sold this one at last. Well, practically sold it.
Contracts have been exchanged.' She chatted on, straightening
the lemon floral duvet, opening a window, for all the world as
if he too were a prospective purchaser rather than a policeman
investigating an ominous disappearance. 'I'm having some of
the furniture put in store and the rest will go to the flat I've
bought in London. Then I'm thinking of going off on vacation
somewhere.'

He glanced into the adjoining bathroom. It had evidently
been cleaned before Muriel Hicks withdrew her services. The
yellow bath and basin were immaculate and fresh honey-coloured towels hung on the rail. Without waiting for permission,
he made his way into the next room, the one Natalie had
rejected in favour of using Camargue's very private and personal territory.

There were no immediately obvious signs that this room
had ever been occupied since Camargue's death. In fact, it
seemed likely that the last people to have slept here were Dinah
Sternhold's parents when they stayed with Camargue at Christmas. But Wexford, peering quickly, pinched from the frill that
edged one of the green and blue flowered pillows, a hair. It was
black but it was not from Natalie's head, being wavy and no
more than three inches long.

This bathroom too lacked the pristine neatness and cleanliness of the other. A man no more than ordinarily observant
might have noticed nothing, but Wexford was almost certain
that one of the blue towels had been used. On the basin, under
the cold tap, was a small patch of tide mark. He turned as
Natalie came up softly behind him. She was not the kind of
person one much fancied creeping up on one, and he thought,
as he had done when he first met her, of a snake.

'That night,' he said, 'Mrs Zoffany ran out of the house and
then afterwards her husband left. How long afterwards?'

'Twenty minutes, twenty-five. Shall we say twenty-two and
a half minutes, Mr Wexford, to be on the safe side?'

He gave no sign that he had noticed the implicit mockery.
'He walked to the station, did he?'

'I gave him a lift in my car.'

Of course. Now he remembered that he had seen them. 'And after that you never saw Mrs Zoffany again?'

'Never.' She looked innocently at Wexford, her black eyes very large and clear, the lashes lifted and motionless. 'It's the most extraordinary thing I ever came across in my life.'

Considering what he knew of her life, Wexford doubted this statement. 'I should like your consent to our dragging the lake,' he said.

'That's just a polite way of saying you're going to drag it anyway, isn't it?'

'Pretty well,' he said. 'It'll save time if you give your permission.'

Out of the lake came a quantity of blanket weed, sour green and sour smelling; two car tyres, a bicycle lamp, half a dozen cans and a broken wrought-iron gate as well as a lot of miscellaneous rubbish of the nuts and bolts and nails variety. They also found Sir Manuel Camargue's missing glove, but there was no trace of Jane Zoffany. Wexford wondered if he had chosen the lake as the first possible place to search because of the other drownings associated with Natalie Arno.

It was, of course, stretching a point to touch the garden at all. But the temptation to tell the men to dig up the flowerbed between the lake and the circular forecourt was very great. It was, after all, no more than three or four yards from the edge of the lake and the soil in it looked suspiciously freshly turned and the bedding plants as if they had been there no more than a day or two. Who would put out bedding plants in July? They dug. They dug to about three feet down and then even Wexford had to admit no body was buried there. Ted Hicks, who had been watching them for hours, now said that he had dug the bed over a week ago and planted out a dozen biennials. Asked why he hadn't said so before, he said he hadn't thought it his place to interfere. By then it was too late to do any more, nine on a typical English July evening, twilight, greyish, damp and cool.

Wexford's phone was ringing when he got in. The chief constable. Mrs Arno had complained that he was digging up the grounds of her house without her permission and without a warrant.

'True,' said Wexford, because it was and it seemed easier to confess than to get involved in the ramifications of explaining. A scalding lecture exploded at him from the mouthpiece. Once again he was overstepping the bounds of his duty and his rights, once again he was allowing an obsession to warp his judgement. And this time the obsession looked as if it were taking the form of a vindictive campaign against Mrs Arno.

Had her voice on the phone achieved this? Or had she been to Griswold in person, in the yellow dress, holding him with her glowing black eyes, moving her long pretty hands in feigned distress? For the second time he promised to persecute Natalie Arno no more, in fact to act as if he had never heard her name.

What changed the chief constable's mind must have been the systematic searching of the Zodiac. Two neighbours of Ivan Zoffany went independently to the police, one to complain that Zoffany had been lighting bonfires in his garden by night, the other to state that she had actually seen Jane in the vicinity of De Beauvoir Place on the night of Sunday, 29 June.

The house and the shop were searched without result. Zoffany admitted to the bonfires, saying that he intended to move away and take up some other line of work, and it was his stock of science-fiction paperbacks he had been burning. Wexford applied for a warrant to search the inside of Sterries and secured one three days after the dragging of the lake.

CHAPTER SEVENTEEN

The house was empty. Not only deserted by its owner but half-emptied of its furnishings. Wexford remembered that Natalie Arno had said she would be going away on holiday and also that she intended having some of the furniture put in store. Mrs Murray-Burgess, that inveterate observer of unusual vehicles, told Burden when he called at Kingsfield House that she had seen a removal van turn out of the Sterries drive into Plough-man's Lane at about three on Tuesday afternoon. It was now Thursday, 17 July.

With Wexford and Burden were a couple of men, detective constables, called Archbold and Bennett. They were prepared not only to search but to dismantle parts of the house if need be. They began in the double garage, examining the cupboards at the end of it and the outhouse tacked on to its rear. Since Sterries Cottage was also empty and had been since the previous day, Wexford intended it to be searched as well. Archbold, who had had considerable practice at this sort of thing, picked the locks on both front doors.

The cottage was bare of furniture and carpets. Like most English houses, old or new, it was provided with inadequate cupboard space. Its walls were of brick but were not cavity walls, and at some recent period, perhaps when Sir Manuel and the Hickses had first come, the floors at ground level had been relaid with tiles on a concrete base. No possibility of hiding a body there and nowhere upstairs either. They turned their attention to the bigger house.

Here, at first, there seemed even less likelihood of being able safely to conceal the body of a full-grown woman. It was for no more than form's sake that they cleared out the cloaks cupboard inside the front door, the kitchen broom cupboard and the small room off the kitchen which housed the central-heating boiler and a stock of soap powders and other cleansers. From the first floor a great many pieces had gone, including the pale green settee and armchairs, the piano and all the furniture from Camargue's bedroom and sitting room. Everywhere there seemed to be blank spaces or marks of discolouration on the walls where this or that piece had stood. The Chinese vase of Peace roses, wilted now, had been stuck on the floor up against a window.

Bennett, tapping walls, discovered a hollow space between the right-hand side of the hanging cupboard and the outside wall in Camargue's bedroom. And outside there were signs that it had been the intention on someone's part to use this space as a cupboard for garden tools or perhaps to contain a dustbin, for an arch had been built into which to fit a door and this arch subsequently filled in with bricks of a slightly lighter colour.

From the inside of the hanging cupboard Bennett set about unscrewing the panel at its right-hand end. Wexford wondered if he were getting squeamish in his old age. It was with something amounting to nausea that he stood there anticipating the body falling slowly forward as the panel came away, crumpling into Bennett's arms, the tall thin body of Jane Zoffany with a gauzy scarf and a red and yellow dress of Indian cotton for a winding sheet. Burden sat on the bed, rubbing away fastidiously at a small powder or plaster mark that had appeared on the hem of his light fawn trousers.

The last screw was out and the panel fell, Bennett catching it and resting it against the wall. There was nothing inside the cavity but a spider which swung across its webs. A little bright light and fresh air came in by way of a ventilator brick. Wexford let out his breath in a sigh. It was time to take a break for lunch.

Mr Haq, all smiles and gratified to see Wexford back, remarked that he was happy to be living in a country where they paid policemen salaries on which they could afford to have holidays in California. With perfect sincerity, he said this made him feel more secure. Burden ordered for both of them, steak Soroti, an innocuous beef stew with carrots and onions. When Mr Haq and his son were out of earshot he said he often suspected that the Pearl of Africa's cook hailed from Bradford. Wexford said nothing.

'It's no good,' said Burden, 'we aren't going to find anything in that place. You may as well resign yourself. You're too much of an optimist sometimes for your own good.'

'D'you think I want the poor woman to be dead?' Wexford retorted. 'Optimist, indeed.' And he quoted rather crossly, 'The optimist proclaims that we live in the best of all possible worlds. The pessimist fears this is true.'

'You want Natalie Arno to be guilty of something and you don't much care what,' said Burden. 'Why should she murder her?'

'Because Jane Zoffany knew who she really is. Either that or she found out how the murder of Camargue was done and who did it. There's a conspiracy here, Mike, involving a number of conspirators and Jane Zoffany was one of them. But there's no more honour among conspirators than there is among thieves, and when she discovered how Natalie had betrayed her she saw no reason to be discreet any longer.' He told Burden what had happened when he encountered Jane Zoffany in Ploughman's Lane on 27 June. 'She had something to tell me, she would have told me then only I didn't realize, I didn't give her a word of encouragement. Instead she went back to Sterries and no doubt had the temerity to threaten Natalie. It was a silly thing to do. But she was a silly woman, hysterical and unstable.'

The steak Soroti came. Wexford ate in silence. It was true enough that he wanted Natalie Arno to have done something, or rather that he now saw that charging her with something was almost within his grasp. Who would know where she had gone on holiday? Zoffany? Philip Cory? Would anyone know? They had the ice cream eau-de-Nil to follow but Wexford left half of his.

'Let's get back there,' he said.

It had begun to rain. The white walls of Sterries were streaked with water. Under a lowering sky of grey and purple cloud the house had the shabby faded look which belongs particularly to English houses built to a design intended for the Mediterranean. There were lights on in the upper rooms.

Archbold and Bennett were working on the drawing room, Bennett having so thoroughly investigated the chimney as to clamber half-way up inside it. Should they take up the floor? Wexford said no, he didn't think so. No one could hope to conceal a body for long by burying it under the floor in a house which was about to change hands. Though, as Wexford now told himself, it wasn't necessarily or exclusively a body they were looking for. By six o'clock they were by no means finished but Wexford told them to leave the rest of the house till next day. It was still raining, though slightly now, little more than a drizzle. Wexford made his way down the path between the conifers to check that they had closed and locked the door of Sterries Cottage.

In the wet gloom the alsatian's face looking out of a ground-floor window and almost on a level with his own made him jump. It evoked strange ideas, that there had been a time shift and it was six months ago and Camargue still lived. Then again, from the way some kind of white cloth seemed to surround the dog's head . . .

'Now I know how Red Riding Hood felt,' said Wexford to Dinah Sternhold.

She was wearing a white raincoat with its collar turned up and she had been standing behind the dog, surveying the empty room. A damp cotton scarf was tied under her chin. She smiled. The sadness that had seemed characteristic of her had left her face now. It seemed fuller, the cheeks pink with rain and perhaps with running.

'They've gone,' she said, 'and the door was open. It was a bit of a shock.'

'They're working for Philip Cory now.'

She shrugged. 'Oh well, I suppose there was no reason they should bother to tell me. I'd got into the habit of bringing Nancy over every few weeks just for them to see her. Ted loves Nancy.' She took her hand from the dog's collar and Nancy bounded up to Wexford as if they were old friends. 'Sheila said you'd been to California.'

'For our summer holiday.'

'Not entirely, Mr Wexford, was it? You went to find out if what Manuel thought was true. But you haven't found out, have you?'

He said nothing, and she went on quickly, perhaps thinking she had gone too far or been indiscreet. 'I often think how strange it is she could get the solicitors to believe in her and Manuel's old friends to believe in her and the police and people who'd known the Camargues for years, yet Manuel who wanted to believe, who was pretty well geared up to believe anything, saw her on that one occasion and didn't believe in her for more than half an hour.' She shrugged her shoulders again and gave a short little laugh. Then she said politely as was her way, 'I'm so sorry, I'm keeping you. Did you want to lock up?' She took hold of the dog again and walked her out into the rain. 'Has she sold the house?' Her voice suddenly sounded thin and strained.

Wexford nodded. 'So she says.'

'I shall never come here again.'

He watched her walk away down the narrow lane which led from the cottage to the road. Raindrops glistened on the alsatian's fur. Water slid off the flat branches of the conifers and dripped on to the grass. Uncut for more than a week, it was already shaggy, giving the place an unkempt look. Wexford walked back to the car.

Burden was watching Dinah Sternhold shoving Nancy on to the rear seat of the Volkswagen. 'It's a funny thing,' he said. 'Jenny's got a friend, a Frenchwoman, comes from Alsace. But you can't call her an Alsatian, can you? That word always means a dog.'

'You couldn't call anyone a Dalmatian either,' said Wexford.

Burden laughed. 'Americans call alsatians German Shepherds.'

'We ought to. That's their proper name and I believe the Kennel Club have brought it in again. When they were brought here from Germany after the First World War there was a lot of anti-German feeling — hence we used the euphemism "alsatian". About as daft as refusing to play Beethoven and Bach at concerts because they were German.'

'Jenny and I are going to German classes,' said Burden rather awkwardly.

'What on earth for?'

'Jenny says education should go on all one's life.'

Next morning it was heavy and sultry, the sun covered by a thick yellow mist. Sterries awaited them, full of secrets. Before he left news had come in for Wexford through Interpol that the woman who drowned in Santa Xavierita in July 1976 was Theresa or Tessa Lanchester, aged thirty, unmarried, a para-legal secretary from Boston, Massachusetts. The body had been recovered after having been in the sea some five days and identified a further four days later by Theresa Lanchester's aunt, her parents both being dead. Driving up to Sterries, Wexford thought about being sent back to California. He wouldn't mind a few days in Boston, come to that.

Archbold and Bennett got to work on the spare bedrooms but without positive result and after lunch they set about the study and the two bathrooms.

In the yellow bathroom they took up the honey-coloured carpet, leaving exposed the white vinyl tiles beneath. It was obvious that none of these tiles had been disturbed since they were first laid. The carpet was replaced and then the same procedure gone through in the blue bathroom. Here there was a shower cabinet as well as a bath. Archbold unhooked and spread out the blue and green striped shower curtain. This was made of semi-transparent nylon with a narrow machine-made hem at the bottom. Archbold, who was young and had excellent sight, noticed that the machine stitches for most of the seam's length were pale blue but in the extreme right-hand corner, for about an inch, they were not blue but brown. He told Wexford.

Wexford, who had been sitting on a window-sill in the study, thinking, watching the cloud shadows move across the meadows, went into the blue bathroom and looked at the curtain and knelt down. And about a quarter of an inch from the floor, on the panelled side of the bath, which had been covered for nearly half an inch by the carpet pile, were two minute reddish-brown spots.

'Take up the floor tiles,' said Wexford.

Would they find enough blood to make a test feasible? It appeared so after two of the tiles had been lifted and the edge of the one which had been alongside the bath panelling showed a thick dark encrustation.

CHAPTER EIGHTEEN

'You might tell me where we're going.'

'Why? You're a real ignoramus when it comes to London.' Wexford spoke irritably. He was nervous because he might be wrong. The chief constable had said he was and had frowned and shaken his head and talked about infringements of rights and intrusions of privacy. If he was wrong he was going to look such a fool. He said to Burden, 'If I said we were going to Thornton Heath, would that mean anything to you?'

Burden said nothing. He looked huffily out of the window. The car was passing through Croydon, through industrial complexes, estates of small red terraced houses, shopping centres, big spreadeagled roundabouts with many exits. Soon after Thornton Heath station Wexford's driver turned down a long bleak road that was bounded by a tall wire fence on one side and a row of sad thin poplars on the other. Thank God there were such neighbours about as Mrs Murray-Burgess, thought Wexford. A woman endowed with a memory and a gimlet eye as well as a social conscience.

'An enormous removal van,' she had said, 'a real pantechnicon, and polluting what's left of our country air with clouds of the filthiest black diesel fumes. Of course I can tell you the name of the firm. I sat down and wrote to their managing director at once to complain. William Dorset and Company. I expect you've seen that slogan of theirs, "Dorset Stores It", it's on all their vans.'

The company had branches in north and south London, in Brighton, Guildford, and in Kingsmarkham, which was no doubt why both Sheila and Natalie Arno had employed them. Kingsmarkham people moving house or storing furniture mostly did use Dorset's.

Here and there along the road was the occasional factory as well as the kind of long, low, virtually windowless building whose possible nature or use it is hard for the passer-by to guess at. Perhaps all such buildings, Wexford thought as they turned into the entrance drive to one of them, served the same purpose as this one.

It was built of grey brick and roofed with red sheet iron. What windows it had were high up under the roof. In the concrete bays in front of the iron double doors stood two monster vans, dark red and lettered 'Dorset Stores It' in yellow.

'They're expecting us,' Wexford said. 'I reckon that's the office over there, don't you?'

It was an annexe built out on the far side. Someone came out before they reached the door. Wexford recognized him as the younger of the two men who had moved Sheila's furniture, the one whose wife had not missed a single episode of *Runway*. He looked at Wexford as if he thought he had seen him somewhere before but knew just the same that he was mistaken.

'Come in, will you, please? Mr Rochford's here, our deputy managing director. He reckoned he ought to be here himself.'

Wexford's heart did not exactly sink but it floundered a little. He would so much rather have been alone, without even Burden. Of course he could have stopped all these people coming with him, he had the power to do that, but he wouldn't. Besides, two witnesses would be better than one and four better than two. He followed the man who said his name was George Prince into the office. Rochford, a man of Prince's age and in the kind of suit which, while perfectly clean and respectable, looks as if it has been worn in the past for emergency manual labour and could be put to such use again if the need arose, sat in a small armchair with an unopened folder on his knees. He jumped up and the folder fell on the floor. Wexford shook hands with him and showed him the warrant.

Although he already knew the purpose of the visit, he turned white and looked nauseous.

'This is a serious matter,' he said miserably, 'a very serious matter.'

'It is.'

'I find it hard to believe. I imagine there's a chance you're wrong.'

'A very good chance, sir.'

'Because,' said Rochford hopefully and extremely elliptically, 'in summertime and after — well, I mean, there's been nothing of that sort, has there, George?'

Not yet, thought Wexford. 'Perhaps we might terminate this suspense,' he said, attempting a smile, 'by going and having a look?'

'Oh yes, yes, by all means. This way, through here. Perhaps you'll lead the way, George. I hope you're wrong, Mr Wexford, I only hope you're wrong.'

The interior of the warehouse was cavernous and dim. The roof, supported by girders of red iron, was some thirty feet high. Up there sparrows flitted about and perched on these man-made branches. The sunlight was greenish, filtering through the tinted panes of high, metal-framed windows. George Prince pressed a switch and strip lighting came on, setting the sparrows in flight again. It was chilly inside the warehouse, though the outdoor temperature had that morning edged just into the seventies.

The place had the air of a soulless and shabby township erected on a grid plan. A town of caravans, placed symmetrically a yard or two apart and with streets crossing each other at right angles to give access to them. It might have been a camp for refugees or the rejected spill-over of some newly constituted state, or the idea of such a place in grim fiction or cinema, a settlement in a northern desert without a tree or a blade of grass. Wexford felt the fantasy and shook it off, for there were no people, no inhabitants of this container camp but himself and Burden and George Prince and Rochford padding softly up the broadest aisle.

Of these rectangular houses, these metal cuboids ranked in rows, iron red, factory green, camouflage khaki, the one they were making for stood at the end of the topmost lane to debouch from the main aisle. It stood up against the cream-washed wall under a window. Prince produced a key and was about to insert it into the lock on the container door when Rochford put out a hand to restrain him and asked to see the warrant again. Patiently, Wexford handed it to him. They stood there, waiting while he read it once more. Wexford had fancied for minutes now that he could smell something sweetish and foetid but this became marked the nearer he got to Rochford and it was only the stuff the man put on his hair or his underarms. Rochford said:

'Mrs N. Arno, 27a De Beauvoir Place, London, N1. We didn't move it from there, did we, George? Somewhere in Sussex, didn't you say?'

'Kingsmarkham, sir. It was our Kingsmarkham branch done it.'

'Ah, yes. And it was put into store indefinitely at the rate of £5.50 per week starting from 15 July?'

Wexford said gently, 'Can we open up now, sir, please?'

'Oh, certainly, certainly. Get it over, eh?'

Get it over. . . . George Prince unlocked the door and Wexford braced himself for the shock of the foul air that must escape. But there was nothing, only a curious staleness. The door swung silently open on oiled hinges. The place might be sinister and evocative of all manner of disagreeable things, but it was well-kept and well-run for all that.

The inside of the container presented a microcosm of Sterries, a drop of the essence of Sir Manuel Camargue. His desk was there and the austere furnishings from the bedroom and sitting room in his private wing, the record player too and the lyre-backed chairs from the music room and the piano. If you closed your eyes you could fancy hearing the first movement from the Flute and Harp Concerto. You could smell and hear Camargue and nothing else. Wexford turned away to face the furniture from the spare bedrooms, a green velvet ottoman in a holland cover, two embroidered footstools, sheathed in plastic, a pair of golden Afghan rugs rolled up in hessian, and under a bag full of quilts and cushions, the carved teak chest, banded now with two stout leather straps.

The four men looked at it. Burden humped the quilt bag off on to the ottoman and knelt down to undo the buckles on the straps. There was a rattly intake of breath from Rochford. The straps fell away and Burden tried the iron clasps. They were locked. He looked inquiringly at Prince who hesitated and then muttered something about having to go back to the office to check in his book where the keys were.

Wexford lost his temper. 'You knew what we'd come for. Couldn't you have checked where the keys were before we came all the way down here? If they can't be found I'll have to have it broken open.'

'Look here. . . .' Rochford was almost choking. 'Your warrant doesn't say anything about breaking. What's Mrs Arno going to say when she finds her property's been damaged? I can't take the responsibility for that sort of. . . .'

'Then you'd better find the keys.'

Prince scratched his head. 'I reckon she said they were in that desk. In one of the pigeonholes in that desk.'

They opened the desk. It was entirely empty. Burden unrolled both rugs, emptied the quilt bag, pulled out the drawers of the bedside cabinet from Camargue's bedroom.

'You say you've got a note of where they are in some book of yours?' said Wexford.

'The note says there in the desk,' said Prince.

'Right. We break the chest open.'

'They're down here,' said Burden. He pulled out his hand from the cleft between the ottoman's arm and seat cushion and waved at them a pair of identical keys on a ring.

Wexford fitted one key into the lock on the right-hand side, turned it, and then unlocked the left-hand side. The clasps opened and he raised the lid. The chest seemed to be full of black heavy-duty polythene sheeting. He grasped a fold of it and pulled.

The heavy thing that was contained in this cold glossy slippery shroud lurched against the wooden wall and seemed to roll over. Wexford began to unwrap the black stuff and then a horrible thing happened. Slowly, languidly, as if it still retained life, a yellowish-white waxen arm and thin hand rose from the chest and loomed trembling over it. It hung in the air for a moment before it subsided. Wexford stepped back with a grunt. The icy thing had brushed his cheek with fingers of marble.

Rochford let out a cry and stumbled out of the container. There was a sound of retching. But George Prince was made of tougher stuff and he came nearer to the chest with awe. With Burden's help, Wexford lifted the body on to the floor and stripped away its covering. Its throat had been cut and the wound wadded with a bloody towel, but this had not kept blood off the yellow dress, which was splashed and stained with red all over like some bizarre map of islands.

Wexford looked into the face, knowing he had been wrong, feeling as much surprise as the others, and then he looked at Burden.

Burden shook his head, appalled and mystified, and together they turned slowly back to gaze into the black dead eyes of Natalie Arno.

CHAPTER NINETEEN

'*Cui bono?*' said Kenneth Ames. 'Who benefits?' He made a church steeple of his fingers and looked out at St Peter's spire. 'Well, my dear chap, the same lady who would have benefited had you been right in your preposterous assumption that poor Mrs Arno was not Mrs Arno. Or to cut a tall story short, Sir Manuel's niece in France.'

'You never did tell me her name,' said Wexford.

He did not then. 'It's an extraordinary thing. Poor Mrs Arno simply followed in her father's footmarks. It's no more than a week ago she asked me if she should make a will and I naturally advised her to do so. But, as was true in the case of Sir Manuel, she died before a will was drawn up. She too had been going to get married, you know, but she changed her mind.'

'No, I didn't know.'

Ames made his doggy face. 'So, as I say, the beneficiary will be this French lady, there being no other living relatives whatsoever. I've got her name somewhere.' He hunted in a drawer full of folders. 'Ah, yes. A Mademoiselle Thérèse Lerèmy. Do you want her precise address?'

The transformation of Moidore Lodge was apparent long before the house was reached. The drive was swept, the signboard bearing the name of the house had been re-painted black and white, and Wexford could have sworn the bronze wolves (or alsatians) had received a polish.

Blaise Cory's Porsche was parked up in front of the house and it was he, not Muriel Hicks, who opened the door. They send for him like other people might send for their solicitor, thought Wexford. He stepped into a hall from which all dust and clutter had been removed, which even seemed lighter and airier. Blaise confided, looking once or twice over his shoulder:

'Having these good people has made all the difference to the dear old dad. I do hope you're not here to do anything which might — well, in short, which might put a spanner in the works.'

'I hardly think so, Mr Cory. I have a question or two to ask Mrs Hicks, that's all.'

'Ah, that's what you people always say.' He gave the short, breathy, fruity laugh with which, on his show, he was in the habit of receiving the more outrageous of the statements made by his interviewees. 'I believe she's about the house, plying her highly useful equipment.'

The sound of a vacuum cleaner immediately began overhead as if on cue, and Wexford would have chosen to go straight upstairs but he found himself instead ushered into Philip Cory's living room.

Ted Hicks was cleaning the huge Victorian french windows, the old man, once more attired in his boy's jeans and guernsey, watching him with fascinated approval. Hicks stopped work the moment Wexford came in and took up his semi-attention stance.

'Good morning, sir!'

'Welcome, Chief Inspector, welcome.' Cory spread out his meagre hands expansively. 'A pleasure to see you, I'm sure. It's so delightful for me to have visitors and not be ashamed of the old place, not to mention being able to find things. Now, for instance, if you or Blaise were to require a drink I shouldn't have to poke about looking for bottles. Hicks here would bring them in a jiffy, wouldn't you, Hicks?'

'I certainly would, sir.'

'So you have only to say the word.'

It being not yet ten in the morning, Wexford was not inclined to utter any drink-summoning word but asked if he might have a talk in private with Mrs Hicks.

'I saw in the newspaper about poor little Natalie,' said Cory. 'Blaise thought it would upset me. Blaise was always a very *sensitive* boy. But I said to him, how can I be upset when I don't know if she was Natalie or not?'

Wexford went upstairs, Hicks leading the way. Moidore Lodge was a very large house. Several rooms had been set aside to make a dwelling for the Hickses without noticeably depleting the Cory living space. Muriel Hicks, who had been cleaning

Cory's own bedroom with its vast four-poster, came into her own rooms, drying her newly washed hands on a towel. She had put on weight since last he saw her and her pale red hair had grown longer and bushier. But her brusque and taciturn manner was unchanged.

'Mrs Arno was going away on her holidays. She says to me to see to the moving when the men came next day. It wasn't convenient, we were leaving ourselves and I'd got things to do, but that was all the same to her, I daresay.' Her husband flashed her an admonitory look, implying that respect should be accorded to *all* employers, or else perhaps that she must in no way hint at ill of the dead. Her pink face flushed rosily. 'Well, she said that was the only day Dorset's could do it, so it was no use arguing. She'd had a chap there staying the weekend. . . .'

'A *gentleman*,' said Hicks.

'All right, Ted, a gentleman. I thought he'd gone by the Sunday, and maybe he had, but he was back the Monday afternoon.'

'You saw him?'

'I *heard* him. I went in about six to check up with her what was going and what was staying, and I heard them talking upstairs. They heard me come in and they started talking French so I wouldn't understand, and she laughed and said in English, 'Oh, your funny Swiss accent!' By the time I got upstairs he'd hid himself.'

'Did you hear his name, Mrs Hicks?'

She shook her head. 'Never heard his name and never saw him. She was a funny one, she didn't mind me knowing he was there and what he was to her like, but she never wanted me nor anyone to actually see him. I took it for granted they both went off on their holidays that same evening. She said she was going, she told me, and the car was gone.'

'What happened next day?'

'The men came from Dorset's nine in the morning. I let them in and told them what to take and what not to. She'd left everything labelled. When they'd gone I had a good clear-up. There was a lot of blood about in the blue bathroom, but I never gave it a thought, reckoned one of them had cut theirselves.' Wexford remembered the deliberate cutting of Natalie's fingertips in the bathroom in De Beauvoir Place and he almost shuddered. Muriel Hicks was more stolid about it than he. 'I had a bit of a job getting it off the carpet,' she said. 'I saw in the paper they found her at Dorset's warehouse. Was she . . . ? I mean, was *it* in that chest?'

He nodded.

She said indifferently, 'The men did say it was a dead weight.'

Blaise Cory walked out to the car with him. It was warm today, the sky a serene blue, the leaves of the plane trees fluttering in a light frisky breeze. Blaise said suddenly and without his usual affected geniality:

'Do you know Mrs Mountnessing, Camargue's sister-in-law?'

'I've seen her once.'

'There was a bit of a scandal in the family. I was only seventeen or eighteen at the time and Natalie and I — well, it wasn't an affair or anything, we were like brother and sister. We were close, she used to tell me things. The general made a pass at her and the old girl caught them kissing.'

'The general?' said Wexford.

Blaise made one of his terrible jokes. 'Must have been caviare to him.' He gave a yelp of laughter. 'Sorry. I mean old Roo Mountnessing, General Mountnessing. Mrs M told her sister and made a great fuss, put all the blame on poor little Nat, called her incestuous and a lot of crap like that. As if everyone didn't know the old boy was a satyr. Camargue was away on a tour of Australia at the time or he'd have intervened. Mrs Camargue and her sister tried to lock Nat up, keep her a sort of prisoner. She got out and hit her mother. She hit her in the chest, quite hard, I think. I suppose they had a sort of brawl over Natalie trying to get out of the house.'

'And?'

'Well, when Mrs Camargue got cancer Mrs Mountnessing said it had been brought on by the blow. I've heard it said that can happen. The doctors said no but Mrs M. wouldn't listen to that and she more or less got Camargue to believe it too. I've always thought that's why Natalie went off with Vernon Arno, she couldn't stand things at home.'

'So that was the cause of the breach,' said Wexford. 'Camargue blamed her for her mother's death.'

Blaise shook his head. 'I don't think he did. He was just confused by Mrs M. and crazy with grief over his wife dying. The dear old dad says Camargue tried over and over again to make things right between himself and Nat, wrote again and again, offered to go out there or pay her fare home. I suppose it wasn't so much him blaming her for her mother's death as her blaming herself. It was guilt kept her away.'

Wexford looked down at the little stocky man.

'Did she tell you all this when you had lunch with her, Mr Cory?'

'Good heavens, no. We didn't talk about that. I'm a *present* person, Chief Inspector, I live in the moment. And so did she. Curious,' he said reflectively, 'that rumour which went around back in the winter that she was some sort of impostor.'

'Yes,' said Wexford.

It was not a long drive from Moidore Lodge to the village on the borders of St Leonard's Forest. It was called Bayeux Green, between Horsham and Wellridge, and the house Wexford was looking for bore the name Bayeux Villa. Well, it was not all that far from Hastings, there was another village nearby called Doomsday Green, and very likely the name had something to do with the tapestry.

He found the house without having to ask. It was in the centre of the village, a narrow, detached, late nineteenth-century house, built of small pale grey bricks and with only a small railed-in area separating it from the pavement. The front door was newer and inserted in it was a picture in stained glass of a Norman soldier in chain mail. Wexford rang the bell and got no answer. He stepped to one side and looked in at the window. There was no sign of recent habitation. The occupants, at this time of the year, were very likely away on holiday. It seemed strange that they had made no arrangements for the care of their houseplants. Tradescantias, peperomias, a cissus that climbed to the ceiling on carefully spaced strings, a Joseph's coat, a variegated ivy, all hung down leaves that were limp and parched.

He walked around the house, looking in more windows,

and he had a sensation of being watched, though he could see no one. The two little lawns looked as if they had not been cut for a month and there were weeds coming up in the rosebed. After he had rung the bell again he went to the nearest neighbour, a cottage separated from Bayeux Villa by a green-grocer's and a pair of garages.

It was a comfort to be himself once more, to have resumed his old standing. The woman looked at his warrant card.

'They went off on holiday — oh, it'd be three weeks ago. When I come to think of it, they must be due back today or tomorrow. They've got a caravan down in Devon, they always take three weeks.'

'Don't they have friends to come in and keep an eye on the place?'

She said quickly, 'Don't tell me it's been broken into.'

He reassured her. 'Nobody's watered the plants.'

'But the sister's there. She said to me on the Saturday, my sister'll be staying while we're away.'

This time he caught her off guard. He came up to the kitchen window and their eyes met. She had been on the watch for him too, creeping about the house, looking out for him. She was still wearing the red and yellow dress of Indian cotton, she had been shut up in there for three weeks, and it hung on her. Her face looked sullen, though not frightened. She opened the back door and let him in.

'Good morning, Mrs Zoffany,' he said. 'It's a relief to find you well and unharmed.'

'Who would harm me?'

'Suppose you tell me that. Suppose you tell me all about it.'

She said nothing. He wondered what she had done all by herself in this house since 27 July. Not eaten much, that was obvious. Presumably, she had not been out. Nor even opened a window. It was insufferably hot and stuffy and a strong smell of sweat and general unwashedness emanated from Jane Zoffany as he followed her into the room full of dying plants. She sat down and looked at him in wary silence.

'If you won't tell me,' he said, 'shall I tell you? After you left me on that Friday evening you went back to Sterries and found the house empty. Mrs Arno had driven your husband to the station. As a matter of fact, her car passed me as I was driving down the hill.' She continued to eye him uneasily. Her eyes had more madness in them than when he had last seen her. 'You took your handbag but you left your suitcase; didn't want to be lumbered with it, I daresay. There's a bus goes to Horsham from outside St Peter's. You'd have had time to catch the last one, or else maybe you had a hire car.'

She said stonily, 'I haven't money for hire cars. I didn't know about the bus, but it came and I got on.'

'When you got here you found your sister and her husband were leaving for their summer holiday the next day. No doubt they were glad to have someone here to keep an eye on the place while they were gone. Then a week later you got yourself a birthday card. . . .'

'No.' She shook her head vehemently. 'I only posted it. My sister had bought a card for me and written in it and done the envelope and everything. She said, here, you'd better have this now, save the postage. I went out at night and posted it.' She gave a watery vague smile. 'I liked hiding, I enjoyed it.'

He could understand that. The virtue for her would be twofold. To some extent she would lose her identity, that troubling self, she would have hidden here from herself as successfully as she had hidden from others. And there would be the satisfaction of becoming for a brief while important, of causing anxiety, for once of stimulating emotions.

'What I don't see,' he said, 'is how you managed when the police came here making inquiries.'

She giggled. 'That was funny. They took me for my sister.'

'I see.'

'They just took it for granted I was my sister and they kept on talking about Mrs Zoffany. Did I have any idea where Mrs Zoffany might be? When had I last seen her? I said no and I didn't know and they had to believe me. It was funny, it was a bit like . . .' She put her fingers over her mouth and looked at him over the top of them.

'I shall have to tell your husband where you are. He's been very worried about you.'

'Has he? Has he *really*?'

Had she, during her semi-incarceration, watched television,

heard a radio, seen a newspaper? Presumably not, since she had not mentioned Natalie's death. He wouldn't either. She was safe enough here, he thought, with the sister coming back. Zoffany himself would no doubt come down before that. Would they perhaps get her back into a mental hospital between them? He had no faith that the kind of treatment she might get would do her good. He wanted to tell her to have a bath, eat a meal, open the windows, but he knew she would take no advice, would hardly hear it.

'I thought you'd be very angry with me.'

He treated that no more seriously than if the younger of his grandsons had said it to him. 'You and I are going to have to have a talk, Mrs Zoffany. When you've settled down at home again and I've got more time. Just at present I'm very busy and I have to go abroad again.'

She nodded. She no longer looked sullen. He let himself out into Bayeux Green's little high street, and when he glanced back he saw her gaunt face at the window, the eyes following him. In spite of what he had said, he might never see her again, he might never need to, for in one of those flashes of illumination that he had despaired of ever coming in this case, he saw the truth. She had told him. In a little giggly confidence she had told him everything there still remained for him to know.

In the late afternoon he drove out to the home of the chief constable, Hightrees Farm, Millerton. Mrs Griswold exemplified the reverse of the Victorian ideal for children; she was heard but not seen. Some said she had been bludgeoned into passivity by forty years with the colonel. Her footsteps could sometimes be heard overhead, her voice whispering into the telephone. Colonel Griswold himself opened the front door, something which Wexford always found disconcerting. It was plunging in at the deep end.

'I want to go to the South of France, sir.'

'I daresay,' said Griswold. 'I shall have to settle for a cottage in north Wales myself.'

In a neutral voice Wexford reminded him that he had already had his holiday. The chief constable said yes, he remembered, and Wexford had been somewhere very exotic, hadn't he? He had wondered once or twice how that sort of thing would go down with the public when the police started screaming for wage increases.

'I want to go to the South of France,' Wexford said more firmly, 'and I know it's irregular but I would like to take Mike Burden with me. It's a little place *inland* —' Griswold's lips seemed silently to be forming the syllables St Tropez, '— and there's a woman there who will inherit Camargue's money and property. She's Camargue's niece and her name is Thérèse Lerèmy.'

'A French citizen?'

'Yes, sir, but . . .'

'I don't want you going about putting people's backs up, Reg. Particularly foreign backs. I mean, don't think you can go over there and arrest this woman on some of your thin suspicions and. . . .'

But before Wexford had even begun to deny that this was his intention he knew from the moody truculent look which had replaced obduracy in Griswold's face that he was going to relent.

CHAPTER TWENTY

From the city of the angels to the bay of the angels. As soon as they got there the taxi driver took them along the Promenade des Anglais, though it was out of their way, but he said they had to see it, they couldn't come to Nice and just see the airport. While Wexford gazed out over the Baie des Anges, Burden spoke from his newly acquired store of culture. Jenny had a reproduction of a picture of this by a painter called Dufy, but it all looked a bit different now.

It was still only late morning. They had come on the early London to Paris flight and changed planes at Roissy-Charles de Gaulle. Now their drive took them through hills crowned with orange and olive trees. Saint Jean-de-l'Éclaircie lay a few miles to the north of Grasse, near the river Loup. A bell began to chime noon as they passed through an ivy-hung archway in the walls into the ancient town. They drove past the ochre-stone cathedral into the Place aux Eaux Vives where a fountain was playing and where stood Picasso's statue 'Woman with a Lamb', presented to the town by the artist (according to Wexford's guide book) when he lived and worked there for some months after the war. The guide book also said that there was a Fragonard in the cathedral, some incomparable Sevres porcelain in the museum, the Fondation Yeuse, and a mile outside the town the well-preserved remains of a Roman amphitheatre. The taxi driver said that if you went up into the cathedral belfry you could see Corsica on the horizon.

Wexford had engaged rooms for one night — on the advice of his travel agent in the Kingsbrook Precinct — at the Hotel de la Rose Blanche in the *place*. Its vestibule was cool and dim, stone-walled, stone-flagged, and with that indefinable atmosphere that is a combination of complacency and gleeful anticipation and which signifies that the food is going to be good. The chef's in his kitchen, all's right with the world.

Kenneth Ames had known nothing more about Mademoiselle

Lerèmy than her name, her address and her relationship to
Camargue. It was also known that her parents were dead and
she herself unmarried. Recalling the photograph of the two little
girls shown him by Mrs Mountnessing, Wexford concluded she
must be near the age of Camargue's daughter. He looked her
up in the phone book, dialled the number apprehensively
because of his scanty French, but got no reply.

They lunched off seafood, bread that was nearly all crisp
crust, and a bottle of Monbazillac. Wexford said in an ab-
stracted sort of voice that he felt homesick already, the hors
d'oeuvres reminded him of Mr Haq and antipasto Ankole. He
got no reply when he attempted once more to phone Thérèse
Lerèmy, so there seemed nothing for it but to explore the town.

It was too hot to climb the belfry. On 24 July Saint-Jean-
de-l'Éclaircie was probably at its hottest. The square was
deserted, the narrow steep alleys that threaded the perimeter
just inside the walls held only the stray tourist, and the morning
market which had filled the Place de la Croix had packed up
and gone. They went into the cathedral of St Jean Baptiste,
dark, cool, baroque. A nun was walking in the aisle, eyes cast
down, and an old man knelt at prayer. They looked with proper
awe at Fragonard's 'Les Pains et Les Poissons', a large hazy
canvas of an elegant Christ and an adoring multitude, and then
they returned to the bright white sunshine and hard black
shadows of the *place*.

'I suppose she's out at work,' said Wexford. 'A single
woman would be bound to work. It looks as if we'll have to
hang things out a few hours.'

'It's no hardship,' said Burden. 'I promised Jenny I
wouldn't miss the museum.'

Wexford shrugged. 'O.K.'

The collection was housed in a sienna-red stucco building
with Fondation Yeuse lettered on a black marble plaque.
Wexford had expected it to be deserted inside but in fact they
met other tourists in the rooms and on the winding marble
staircase. As well as the Sevres, Burden had been instructed to
look at some ancient jewellery discovered in the Condamine,
and Wexford, hearing English spoken, asked for directions from
the woman who had been speaking correctly but haltingly to an

695

American visitor. She seemed to be a curator, for she wore on one of the lapels of her dark red, near-uniform dress an oval badge inscribed Fondation Yeuse. He forced himself not to stare — and then wondered how many thousands before him had forced themselves not to stare. The lower part of her face was pitted densely and deeply with the scars of what looked like smallpox but was almost certainly acne. In her careful stumbling English she instructed him where to find the jewellery. He and Burden went upstairs again where the American woman had arrived before them. The sun penetrating drawn Venetian blinds shone on her flawless ivory skin. She had hands like Natalie Arno's, long and slender, display stands for rings as heavy and roughly made as those on the linen under the glass.

'We may as well get on up there,' said Wexford after they had bought a *flacon* of Grasse perfume for Dora and a glazed stoneware jar in a Picasso design for Jenny. 'Get on up there and have a look at the place.'

The two local taxis, which were to be found between the fountain and the hotel de la Rose Blanche, were not much in demand at this hour. Their driver spoke no English but as soon as Wexford mentioned the Maison du Cirque he understood and nodded assent.

On the north-eastern side of the town, outside the walls, was an estate of depressing pale grey flats and brown wooden houses with scarlet switchback roofs. It was as bad as home. Worse? ventured Burden. But the estate was soon left behind and the road ran through lemon groves. The driver persisted in talking to them in fast, fluent, incomprehensible French. Wexford managed to pick out two facts from all this, one that Saint-Jean-de-l'Éclaircie held a lemon festival each February, and the other that on the far side of the hill was the amphitheatre.

They came upon the house standing alone at a bend in the road. It was flat-fronted, unprepossessing but undoubtedly large. At every window were wooden shutters from which most of the paint had flaked away. Big gardens, neglected now, stretched distantly towards olive and citrus groves, separated from them by crumbling stone walls.

'Mariana in the moated grange,' said Wexford. 'We may as well go to the circus while we're waiting for her.'

The driver took them back. The great circular plain which was the base of the amphitheatre was strangely green as if watered by a hidden spring. The tiers of seating, still defined, still unmistakable, rose in their parallel arcs to the hillside, the pines, the crystalline blue of the sky. Wexford sat down where some prefect or consul might once have sat.

'I hope we're in time,' he said. 'I hope we can get to her before any real harm has been done. The woman has been dead nine days. He's been here, say, eight. . . .'

'If he's here. The idea of him being here is all based on your ESP. We don't know if he's here and, come to that, we don't know who he is or what he looks like or what name he'll be using.'

'It's not as bad as that,' said Wexford. 'He would naturally come here. This place, that girl, would draw him like magnets. He won't want to lose the money now, Mike.'

'No, not after plotting for years to get it. How long d'you reckon we're going to be here?'

Wexford shrugged. The air was scented with the herbs that grew on the hillsides, sage and thyme and rosemary and bay, and the sun was still very warm. 'However long it may be,' he said enigmatically, 'to me it would be too short.' He looked at his watch. 'Martin should have seen Williams by now and done a spot of checking up for me at Guy's Hospital.'

'Guy's Hospital?'

'In the course of this case we haven't remembered as often as we should that Natalie Arno went into hospital a little while before Camargue died. She had a biopsy.'

'Yes, what *is* that?'

'It means to look at living tissue. It usually describes the kind of examination that is done to determine whether certain cells are cancerous or not.'

Once this subject would have been a highly emotive one for Burden, an area to be avoided by all his sensitive acquaintances. His first wife had died of cancer. But time and his second marriage had changed things. He responded not with pain but only with an edge of embarrassment to his voice.

'But she didn't have cancer.'

'Oh, no.'

697

He sat down in the tier below Wexford. 'I'd like to tell you what I think happened, see if we agree.' On the grass beside him the shadow of Wexford's head nodded. 'Well, then. Tessa Lanchester went on holiday to that place in California, Santa – what was it?'

'Santa Xavierita.'

'And while she was there she met a man who played the guitar or whatever in a restaurant in the local town. He was living in America illegally and was very likely up to a good many other illegal activities as well. He was a con man. He had already met Natalie Arno and found out from her who her father was and what her expectations were. He introduced Tessa to Natalie and the two women became friends.

'He persuaded Tessa not to go back home to Boston but to remain longer in Santa Xavierita learning all she could about Natalie's life and past. Then he took Natalie out swimming by night and drowned her and that same night left with Tessa for Los Angeles in Natalie's car with Natalie's luggage and the key to Natalie's house. From then on Tessa became Natalie. The changes Natalie's body had undergone after five days in the sea made a true identification impossible and, since Tessa was missing, the corpse was identified as that of Tessa.

'Tessa and her accomplice then set about their plan to inherit Camargue's property, though this was somewhat frustrated by Ilbert's intervening and the subsequent deportation. Tessa tried in vain to sell Natalie's house. I think at this time she rather cooled off the plan. Otherwise I don't know how to account for a delay of more than three years between making the plan and putting it into practice. I think she cooled off. She settled into her new identity, made new friends and, as we know, had two further love affairs. Then one of these lovers, Ivan Zoffany, wrote from London in the autumn of 1979 to say he had heard from his sister-in-law who lived near Wellridge that Camargue was about to re-marry. That alerted her and fetched her to England. There she was once more able to join forces with the man who had first put her up to the idea. They had the support and help of Zoffany and his wife. How am I doing so far?'

Wexford raised his eyebrows. 'How did they get Williams and Mavis Rolland into this? Bribery?'

'Of course. It would have to be a heavy bribe. Williams's professional integrity presumably has a high price. I daresay Mrs Woodhouse could be bought cheaply enough.'

'I never took you for a snob before, Mike.'

'It's not snobbery,' said Burden hotly. 'It's simply that the poorer you are the more easily you're tempted. Shall I go on?'

The shadow nodded.

'They hesitated a while before the confrontation. Tessa was naturally nervous about this very important encounter. Also she'd been ill and had to have hospital treatment. When she finally went down to Sterries she blundered, not in having failed to do her homework — she knew every fact about the Camargue household she could be expected to, she knew them like she knew her own family in Boston — but over the pronunciation of an Italian name. Spanish she knew — many Americans do — French she knew, but it never occurred to her she would have to pronounce Italian.

'The rest we know. Camargue told her she would be cut out of his will, so on the following Sunday she made a sound alibi for herself by going to a party with Jane Zoffany. *He* went down to Sterries, waited for Camargue in the garden and drowned him in the lake.'

Wexford said nothing.

'Well?'

As befitted a person of authority sitting in the gallery of an amphitheatre, Wexford turned down his thumbs. 'The last bit's more or less right, the drowning bit.' He got up. 'Shall we go?'

Burden was still muttering that it had to be that way, that all else was impossible, when they arrived back at the Maison du Cirque. Ahead of them a bright green Citroen 2 CV had just turned into the drive.

The woman who got out of it, who came inquiringly towards them, was the curator of the Fondation Yeuse.

CHAPTER TWENTY-ONE

The sun shone cruelly on that pitted skin. She had done her best to hide it with heavy make-up, but there would never be any hiding it. And now as she approached these two strangers she put one hand up, half covering a cheek. Close to, she had a look of Camargue, all the less attractive traits of the Camargue physiognomy were in her face, too-high forehead, too-long nose, too-fleshy mouth, and added to them that acne-scarred skin. She was sallow and her hair was very dark. But she was one of those plain people whose smiles transform them. She smiled uncertainly at them, and the change of expression made her look kind and sweet-tempered.

Wexford introduced them. He explained that he had seen her earlier that day. Her surprise at being called upon by two English policemen seemed unfeigned. She was astonished but not apparently nervous.

'This is some matter concerning the *musée* — the museum?' she asked in her heavily accented English.

'No, mademoiselle,' said Wexford, 'I must confess I'd never heard of the Fondation Yeuse till this morning. You've worked there long?'

'Since I leave the university — that is, eighteen years. M. Raoul Yeuse, the Paris art dealer, he is, was, the brother of my father's sister. He has founded the museum, you understand? Excuse me, monsieur, I fear my English is very bad.'

'It is we who should apologize for having no French. May we go into the house, Mademoiselle Lerèmy? I have something to tell you.'

Did she know already? The announcement of the discovery of the body at Dorset's would have scarcely appeared in the French newspapers until three days ago. And when it appeared would it have merited more than a paragraph on an inside page? A murder, in England, of an obscure woman? The dark eyes of Camargue's niece looked merely innocent and inquiring. She led them into a large high-ceilinged room and opened

700

latticed glass doors on to a terrace. From the back of the Maison du Cirque you could see the green rim of the amphitheatre and smell the scented hillsides. But the house itself was shabby and neglected and far too big. It had been built for a family and that family's servants in days when perhaps money came easily and went a long way.

Now that they were indoors and seated she had become rather pale. 'This is not bad news, I hope, monsieur?' She looked from one to the other of them with a rising anxiety that Wexford thought he understood. He let Burden answer her.

'Serious news,' said Burden. 'But not personally distressing to you, Miss Lerèmy. You hardly knew your cousin Natalie Camargue, did you?'

She shook her head. 'She was married. I have not heard her husband's name. When last I am seeing her she is sixteen, I seventeen. It is many years...'

'I'm afraid she's dead. To put it bluntly, she was murdered and so was your uncle. We're here to investigate these crimes. It seems the same person killed them both. For gain. For money.'

Both hands went up to her cheeks. She recoiled a little.

'But this is terrible!'

Wexford had decided not to tell her of the good fortune this terrible news would bring her. Kenneth Ames could do that. If what he thought was true she would be in need of consolation. He must now broach the subject of this belief of his. Strange that this time he could be so near hoping he was wrong...

Her distress seemed real. Her features were contorted into a frown of dismay, her tall curved forehead all wrinkles. 'I am so sorry, this is so very bad.'

'Mademoiselle Lerèmy...'

'When I am a little girl I see him many many times, monsieur. I stay with them in Sussex. Natalie is, was, nice, I think, always laughing, always very gay, have much sense of *humeur*. The world has become a very bad place, monsieur, when such things as this happen.' She paused, bit her lip. 'Excuse me, I must not say "sir" so much, is it not so? This I am learning to understand...' She hesitated and hazarded, 'Lately? Recently?'

Her words brought him the thrill of knowing he was right
— and sickened him too. Must he ask her? Burden was looking
at him.

The telephone rang.

'Please excuse me,' she said.

The phone was in the room where they were, up beside the
windows. She picked up the receiver rather too fast and the
effect on her of the voice of her caller was pitiful to see. She
flushed deeply and it was somehow apparent that this was a
flush of intense fearful pleasure as well as embarrassment.

She said softly, 'Ah, Jean . . . We see each other again
tonight? Of course it is all right, it is fine, very good.' She made
an effort, for their benefit or her caller's, to establish formality.
'It will be a great pleasure to see you again.'

He was here all right then, he was talking to her. But where
was he? She had her back to them now. 'When you have finished
your work, yes. *Entends*, Jean, I will fetch — pick up — pick you
up. Ten o'clock?' Suddenly she changed into rapid French.
Wexford could not understand a word but he understood *her*.
She had been speaking English to a French speaker so that her
English hearers would know she had a boy friend, a lover. For
all her scarred face, her plainness, her age, her obscure job in
this backwater, she had a lover to tell the world about.

She put the phone down after a murmured word or two, a
ripple of excited laughter. Wexford was on his feet, signalling
with a nod to Burden.

'You do not wish to ask me questions concerning my uncle
and my *cousine* Natalie, monsieur?'

'It is no longer necessary, mademoiselle.'

The taxi driver had gone to sleep. Wexford woke him with a
prod in his chest.

'La Rose Blanche, *s'il vous plaît*.'

The sun was going down. There were long violet shadows
and the air was sweet and soft.

'He's a fast worker if ever there was one,' said Burden.

'The material he is working on could hardly be more
receptive and malleable.'

'Pardon? Oh, yes, I see what you mean. Poor girl. It's a

terrible handicap having all that pitting on her face, did you notice? D'you think he knew about that? Before he came here, I mean? The real Natalie might have known — you usually get that sort of acne in your teens — but Tessa Lanchester wouldn't have. Unless she picked it up when she was gathering all the rest of her info in Santa Xavierita.'

'Mrs Woodhouse might have known,' said Wexford. 'At any rate, he knew she was unmarried and an heiress and no doubt that she worked in the museum here. It was easy enough for him to scrape up an acquaintance.'

'Bit more than an acquaintance,' said Burden grimly.

'Let's hope it hasn't progressed far yet. Certainly his intention is to marry her.'

'Presumably his intention was to marry that other woman, but at the last she wouldn't have him and for that he killed her.' Burden seemed gratified to get from Wexford a nod of approval. 'Once he'd done that he'd realize who the next heir was and come here as fast as he could. But there's something here doesn't make sense. In putting her body in that chest he seems to have meant to keep it concealed for months, possibly even years, but the paradox there is that until the body was found death wouldn't be presumed and Thérèse Lerèmy wouldn't get anything.'

Wexford looked slyly at him. 'Suppose he intended by some means or other to prove, as only he could, that it was Natalie Arno and not Tessa Lanchester who drowned at Santa Xavierita in 1976? If that were proved Thérèse would become the heir at once and in fact *would have been* the rightful possessor of Sterries and Camargue's money for the past six months.'

'You really think that was it?'

'No, I don't. It would have been too bold and too risky and fraught with problems. I think this was what was in his mind. He didn't want the body found at once because if he then started courting Thérèse even someone as desperate as she might suspect he was after her money. But he wanted it found at some time in the not too distant future or his conquest of Thérèse would bring him no profit at all. What better than that the presence of a corpse in that warehouse should make itself apparent after, say, six months? And if it didn't he could always send the police an anonymous letter.'

'That's true,' said Burden. 'And there was very little to connect him with it, after all. If you hadn't been to California we shouldn't have known of his existence.'

Wexford laughed shortly. 'Yes, there was some profit in it.' They walked into the hotel. Outside Burden's room where they would have separated prior to dressing, or at least sprucing up, for dinner, Burden said, 'Come in here a minute. I want to ask you something.' Wexford sat on the bed. From the window you could see, not the square and the fountain but a mazy mosaic of little roofs against the backdrop of the city walls. 'I'd like to know what we're going to charge those others with. I mean, Williams and Zoffany and Mary Woodhouse. Conspiracy, I suppose – but not conspiracy to murder?'

Wexford pondered. He smiled a little ruefully. 'We're not going to charge them with anything.'

'You mean their evidence will be more valuable as prosecution witnesses?'

'Not really. I shouldn't think any of them would be a scrap of use as witnesses of any kind. They didn't witness anything and they haven't done anything. They all seem to me to be perfectly blameless, apart from a spot — and I'd guess a very small spot — of adultery on the part of Zoffany.' Wexford paused. 'That reconstruction of the case you gave me while we were at the amphitheatre, didn't it strike you there was something unreal about it?'

'Sort of illogical, d'you mean? Maybe, bits of it. Surely that's because they were so devious that there are aspects which aren't clear and never will be?'

Wexford shook his head. 'Unreal. One can't equate it with what one knows of human nature. Take, for instance, their foresight and their patience. They kill Natalie in the summer of 1976 and Tessa impersonates her. Fair enough. Why not go straight to England, make sure Natalie is the beneficiary under Camargue's will and then kill Camargue?'

'I know there's a stumbling block. I said so.'

'It's more than a stumbling block, Mike, it's a bloody great barrier across the path. Think what you — and I — believed they did. Went back to Los Angeles, ran the risk of being suspected by the neighbours, exposed by Ilbert — returned to and settled in what of all cities in the world was the most dangerous to them. And for what?'

'Surely she stayed there to sell the house?'

'Yet she never succeeded in selling it, did she? No, a delay of three-and-a-half years between the killing of Natalie and the killing of Camargue was too much for me to swallow. I can come up with just one feeble reason for it — that they were waiting for Camargue to die a natural death. But, as I say, that's a feeble reason. He might easily have lived another ten years.' Wexford looked at his watch. 'I'll leave you to your shaving and showering or whatever. A wash and brush-up will do me. Laquin won't be here before seven.'

They met again in the bar where they each had a Stella Artois. Wexford said:

'Your suggestion is that Tessa came to England finally because, through Zoffany's sister-in-law, she heard that Camargue intended to marry again. Doesn't it seem a bit thin that Jane Zoffany's sister should come to know this merely because she lives in a village near the Kathleen Camargue School?'

'Not if she was set by the others to watch Camargue.'

Wexford shrugged. 'The others, yes. There would be five of them, our protagonist and her boy friend, the Zoffanys and Jane Zoffany's sister. Five conspirators working for the acquisition of Camargue's money. Right?'

'Yes, for a start,' said Burden. 'There were finally more like eight or nine.'

'Mary Woodhouse to give Tessa some advanced coaching, Mavis Rolland to identify her as an old school chum, and Williams the dentist.' Wexford gave a little shake of the head. 'I've said I was amazed at their foresight and their patience, Mike, but that was nothing to the trouble they took. That staggered me. All these subsidiary conspirators were persuaded to lie, to cheat or to sell their professional integrity. Tessa studied old samples of Natalie's handwriting, had casts made of her jaw, took lessons to perfect her college French and Spanish — though she neglected to polish up her Italian — while one of the others made a survey of the lie of the land round Sterries and of Camargue's habits. Prior to this Zoffany's sister-in-law was sending a secret agent's regular dispatches out to Los

Angeles. Oh, and let's not forget — Jane Zoffany was suborning her neighbours into providing a fake alibi. And all this machinery was set in motion and relentlessly kept in motion for the sake of acquiring a not very large house in an acre of ground and an *unknown sum of money* that, when the time came, would have to be split between eight people.

'I've kept thinking of that and I couldn't believe in it. I couldn't understand why those two had chosen Camargue as their prey. Why not pick on some tycoon? Why not some American oil millionaire? Why an old musician who wasn't and never had been in the tycoon class?'

Burden supplied a hesitant answer. 'Because his daughter fell into their hands, one supposes. Anyway, there's no alternative. We know there was a conspiracy, we know there was an elaborate plan, and one surely simply comments that it's impossible fully to understand people's motivations.'

'But isn't there an alternative? You said I was obsessed, Mike. I think more than anything I became obsessed by the complexity of this case, by the deviousness of the protagonist, by the subtlety of the web she had woven. It was only when I saw how wrong I'd been in these respects that things began to clear for me.'

'I don't follow you.'

Wexford drank his beer. He said rather slowly, 'It was only then that I began to see that this case wasn't complicated, there was no deviousness, there was no plotting, no planning ahead, no conspiracy whatsoever, and that even the two murders happened so spontaneously as really to be unpremeditated.' He rose suddenly, pushing back his chair. Commissaire Mario Laquin of the Compagnies Republicaines de Securité of Grasse had come in and was scanning the room. Wexford raised a hand. He said absently to Burden as the commissaire came towards their table, 'The complexity was in our own minds, Mike. The case itself was simple and straightforward, and almost everything that took place was the result of accident or of chance.'

It was a piece of luck for Wexford that Laquin had been transferred to Grasse from Marseilles some six months before, for they had once or twice worked on cases together and since then the two policemen and their wives had met when M. and Mme Laquin were in London on holiday. It nevertheless came as something of a shock to be clasped in the commissaire's arms and kissed on both cheeks. Burden stood by, trying to give his dry smile but succeeding only in looking astonished.

Laquin spoke English that was almost flawless. 'You pick some charming places to come for your investigations, my dear Reg. A little bird tells me you have already had two weeks in California. I should be so lucky. Last year when I was in pursuit of Honorat L'Eponge, where does he lead me to but Dusseldorf, I ask you!'

'Have a drink,' said Wexford. 'It's good to see you. I haven't a clue where this chap of ours is. Nor do I know what name he's going under while here.'

'Or even what he looks like,' said Burden for good measure. He seemed cheered by the presence of Laquin whom he had perhaps expected to speak with a Peter Sellers accent.

'I know what he looks like,' said Wexford. 'I've seen him.'

Burden glanced at him in surprise. Wexford took no notice of him and ordered their drinks.

'You'll dine with us, of course?' he said to Laquin.

'It will be a pleasure. The food here is excellent.'

Wexford grinned wryly. 'Yes, it doesn't look as though we'll be here to enjoy it tomorrow. I reckon we're going to have to take him at the Maison du Cirque, in that wretched girl's house.'

'Reg, she has known him no time at all, a mere week at most.'

'Even so quickly can one catch the plague. . . . You're right, of course.'

'A blessing for her we're going to rid her of him, if you ask me,' said Burden. 'A couple of years and he'd have put her out of the way as well.'

'She implied he was working here . . .'

'Since Britain came in the European Economic Community, Reg, there is no longer need for your countrymen to have work permits or to register. Therefore to trace his whereabouts would be a long and laborious business. And since we know that later on tonight he will be at the Maison du Cirque . . .'

'Sure, yes, I know. I'm being sentimental, Mario, I'm a fool.' Wexford gave a grim little laugh. 'But not such a fool as to warn her and have him hop off on the next plane into Switzerland.'

After *bouillabaisse* and a fine *cassoulet* with brie to follow and a small armagnac each, it was still only nine. Ten-thirty was the time fixed on by Wexford and Laquin for their visit to the house by the amphitheatre. Laquin suggested they go to a place he knew on the other side of the Place aux Eaux Vives where there was sometimes flamenco dancing.

In the evening there was some modest floodlighting in the square. Apparently these were truly living waters and the fountain was fed by a natural spring. While they dined tiers of seating had been put up for the music festival of Saint Jean-de-l'Éclaircie, due to begin on the following day. A little warm breeze rustled through the plane and chestnut leaves above their heads.

The flamenco place was called La Mancha. As they passed down the stairs and into a kind of open, deeply sunken courtyard or cistern, a waiter told Laquin there would be no dancing tonight. The walls were made of yellow stone over which hung a deep purple bougainvillea. Instead of the dancers a thin girl in black came out and sang in the manner of Piaf. Laquin and Burden were drinking wine but Wexford took nothing. He felt bored and restless. Nine-thirty. They went up the stairs again and down an alley into the cobbled open space in front of the cathedral.

The moon had come up, a big golden moon flattened like a tangerine. Laquin had sat down at a table in a pavement cafe and was ordering coffee for all three men. From here you could see the city walls, part Roman, part medieval, their rough stones silvered by the light from that yellow moon.

Some teenagers went by. They were on their way, Laquin said, to the discotheque in the Place de la Croix. Wexford wondered if Camargue had ever, years ago, sat on this spot where they were. And that dead woman, when she was a child . . .? It was getting on for ten. Somewhere in St Jean she would be meeting him now in the little green Citroen. The yellow hatchback Opel was presumably left in the long-term car park at Heathrow. He felt a tautening of tension and at the same time relief when Laquin got to his feet and said in his colloquial way that they should be making tracks.

Up through the narrow winding defile once more, flattening themselves tolerantly against stone walls to let more boys and girls pass them. Wexford heard the music long before they emerged into the Place aux Eaux Vives. A Mozart serenade. The serenade from *Don Giovanni*, he thought it was, that should properly be played on a mandolin.

Round the last turn in the alley and out into the wide open square. A group of young girls, also no doubt on their way to the discotheque, were clustered around the highest tier of the festival seating. They clustered around a man who sat on the top, playing a guitar, and they did so in the yearning, worshipping fashion of muses or nymphs on the plinth of some statue of a celebrated musician. The man sat aloft, his tune changed now to a Latin American rhythm, not looking at the girls, looking across the square, his gaze roving as if he expected at any moment the person he waited for to come.

'That's him,' said Wexford.

Laquin said, 'Are you sure?'

'Absolutely. I've only seen him once before but I'd know him anywhere.'

'I know him too,' said Burden incredulously. 'I've seen him before. I can't for the life of me think where, but I've seen him.'

'Let's get it over.'

The little green 2CV was turning into the *place* and the guitarist had seen it. He drew his hand across the strings with a flourish and jumped down from his perch, nearly knocking one of the girls over. He didn't look back at her, he made no apology, he was waving to the car.

And then he saw the three policemen, recognizing them immediately for what they were. His arm fell to his side. He was a tall thin man in his late thirties, very dark with black curly hair. Wexford steadfastly refused to look over his shoulder to see her running from the car. He said:

'John Fassbender, it is my duty to warn you that anything you say will be taken down and may be used in evidence . . .'

CHAPTER TWENTY-TWO

They were in the Pearl of Africa, having what Wexford called a celebration lunch. No one could possibly feel much in the way of pity for Fassbender, so why not celebrate his arrest? Burden said it ought to be called an elucidation lunch because there were still a lot of things he didn't understand and wanted explained. Outside it was pouring with rain again. Wexford asked Mr Haq for a bottle of wine, *good* moselle or a riesling, none of your living waters from Lake Victoria. They had got into sybaritic habits during their day in France. Mr Haq bustled off to what he called his cellar through the fronds of polyethylene Spanish moss.

'Did you mean what you said about there having been no conspiracy?'

'Of course I did,' Wexford said, 'and if we'd had a moment after that I'd have told you something else, something I realized before we ever went to France. The woman we knew as Natalie Arno, the woman Fassbender murdered, was never Tessa Lanchester. Tessa Lanchester was drowned in Santa Xavierita in 1976 and we've no reason to believe either Natalie or Fassbender even met her. The woman who came to London in November of last year came solely because Fassbender was in London. She was in love with Fassbender and since he had twice been deported from the United States he could hardly return there.'

'How could he have been deported twice?' asked Burden.

'I wondered that until the possibility of dual nationality occurred to me and then everything about Fassbender became simple. I'd been asking myself if she had two boy-friends, an Englishman and a Swiss. There was a good deal of confusion in people's minds over him. He was Swiss. He was English. He spoke French. He spoke French with a Swiss accent. He was deported to London. He was deported to Geneva. Well, I'll come back to him in a minute. Suffice it to say that it was after he had been deported a second time that she followed him to London.'

He stopped. Mr Haq, beaming, teeth flashing and spilling, was bringing the wine, a quite respectable-looking white medoc. He poured Wexford a trial half-glassful. Wexford sipped it, looking serious. He had sometimes said, though, that he would rather damage his liver than upset Mr Haq by sending back a bottle. Anyway, the only fault with this wine was that it was at a temperature of around twenty-five degrees Celsius.

'Excellent,' he said to Mr Haq's gratification, and just stopped himself from adding, 'Nice and warm.' He continued to Burden as Mr Haq trotted off, 'She had a brief affair with Zoffany during Fassbender's first absence. I imagine this was due to nothing more than loneliness and that she put it out of her head once Zoffany had departed. But he kept up a correspondence with her and when she needed a home in London he offered her a flat. Didn't I tell you it was simple and straightforward?

'Once there, she saw that Zoffany was in love with her and hoped to take up their relationship (to use Jane Zoffany's word) where it had ended a year and a half before. She wasn't having that, she didn't care for Zoffany at all in that way. But it made things awkward. If she had Fassbender to live with her there, would Zoffany be made so jealous and angry as to throw her out? She couldn't live with Fassbender, he was living in one room. The wisest thing obviously was to keep Fassbender discreetly in the background until such time as he got a job and made some money and they could afford to snap their fingers at Zoffany and live together. We know that Fassbender was in need of work and that she tried to get him a job through Blaise Cory. The point I'm making is that Zoffany never knew of Fassbender's existence until he overheard Natalie talking on the phone to him *last month*.

'I suspect, though I don't know for certain, that there was no urgency on her part to approach Camargue. Probably she gave very little thought to Camargue. It was the announcement of his engagement that brought her to get in touch with him — perhaps reminded her of his existence. But there was no complex planning about that approach, no care taken with the handwriting or the style of the letter, no vetting of it by, say, Mrs Woodhouse....'

Young Haq came with their starter of prawns Pakwach. This was a shocking pink confection into which Burden manfully plunged his spoon before saying, 'There must have been. It may be that the identity of the woman we found in that chest will never be known, but we know very well she was an impostor and a fraudulent claimant.'

'Her identity is known,' said Wexford. 'She was Natalie Arno, Natalie Camargue, Camargue's only child.'

Pouring more wine for them, Mr Haq burst into a flowery laudation of various offerings among the entrées. There was caneton Kioga, wild duck breasts marinated in a succulent sauce of wine, cream and basil, or T-bone Toro, tender steaks *flambés*. Burden's expression was incredulous, faintly dismayed. Fortunately, his snapped 'Bring us some of that damned duck,' was lost on Mr Haq who responded only to Wexford's gentler request for two portions of caneton.

'I don't understand you,' Burden said coldly when Mr Haq had gone. 'Are you saying that the woman Camargue refused to recognize, the woman who deliberately cut her hand to avoid having to play the violin, whose antecedents you went rooting out all over America — that woman was Camargue's daughter all the time? We were wrong. Ames was right, Williams and Mavis Rolland and Mary Woodhouse and Philip Cory were right, but we were wrong. Camargue was wrong. Camargue was a senile half-blind old man who happened to make a mistake. Is that it?'

'I didn't say that,' said Wexford. 'I only said that Natalie Arno was Natalie Arno. Camargue made no mistake, though it would be true to say he misunderstood.' He sighed. 'We were such fools, Mike — you, me, Ames, Dinah Sternhold. Not one of us saw the simple truth, that though the woman who visited Camargue was not his daughter, she was not his daughter, if I may so put it, for just one day.'

'You see,' he went on, 'an illusion was created, as if by a clever trick. Only it was a trick we played upon ourselves. We were the conjurors and we held the mirrors. Dinah Sternhold told me Camargue said the woman who went to see him wasn't his daughter. I jumped to the conclusion — you did, Dinah did, we all did — that therefore the woman *we* knew as Natalie Arno wasn't his daughter. It never occurred to us he could be right and yet she might still be his daughter. It never occurred to us that the woman he saw might not be the woman who claimed to be his heir and lived in his house and inherited his money.'

'It wasn't Natalie who went there that day but it was Natalie before and always Natalie after that?' Burden made the face people do when they realize they have been conned by a stratagem unworthy of their calibre. 'Is that what you're saying?'

'Of course it is.' Wexford grinned and gave a rueful shake of the head. 'I may as well say here and now that Natalie wasn't the arch-villainess I took her for. She was cruel and devious and spiteful only in my imagination. Mind you, I'm not saying she was an angel of light. She may not have killed her father or plotted his death, but she connived at it afterwards and she had no scruples about taking an inheritance thus gained. Nor did she have any scruples about appropriating other women's husbands either on a temporary or a permanent basis. She was no paragon of virtue but she was no Messalina either. Why did I ever think she was? Largely, I'm ashamed to say, because Dinah Sternhold told me so.

'Now Dinah Sternhold is a very nice girl. If she blackened Natalie's character to me before I'd even met her, I'm sure it was unconscious. The thing with Dinah, you see, is that odd though it undoubtedly seems, she was genuinely in love with that old man. He was old enough to be her grandfather but she was as much in love with him as if he'd been fifty years younger. Have you ever noticed that it's only those who suffer most painfully from jealousy that say, "I haven't a jealous nature"? Dinah said that to me. She was deeply jealous of Natalie and perhaps with justification. For in marrying her, wasn't Camargue looking to replace his lost daughter? How then must she have felt when that lost daughter turned up? Dinah was jealous and in her jealousy, all unconsciously, without malice, she painted Natalie as a scheming adventuress and so angled the tale of the visit to Camargue to make her appear at once as a fraudulent claimant.'

'I'd like to hear your version of that visit.'

Wexford nodded. The duck had arrived, modestly veiled in a thick brown sauce. Wexford took a sip of his wine instead of a long draught, having decided with some soul-searching that it would hardly do to send for a second bottle. He sampled the duck, which wasn't too bad, and said after a few moments:

'The first appointment Natalie made with her father she couldn't keep. In the meantime something very disquieting had happened to her. She discovered a growth in one of her breasts.'

'How d'you know that?'

'A minute scar where the biopsy was done showed at the post-mortem,' said Wexford. 'Natalie went to her doctor and was sent to Guy's Hospital, the appointment being on the day she had arranged to go down to Sterries. She didn't want to talk to her father on the phone — I think we can call that a perfectly natural shrinking in the circumstances — so she got Jane Zoffany to do it. Shall I say here that Natalie was a congenital slave-owner and Jane Zoffany a born slave?

'Well, Jane made the call and a new date for the 19th. Natalie went to the hospital where they were unable to tell her whether the growth was malignant or not. She must come into their Hedley Atkins Unit in New Cross for a biopsy under anaesthetic.

'Now we're all of us afraid of cancer but Natalie maybe had more reason than most of us. She had seen her young husband die of leukaemia, a form of cancer, her friend Tina too, but most traumatic for her, her mother had died of it and died, it had been implied, through her daughter's actions. Moreover, at the time she had only been a few years older than Natalie then was. Small wonder if she was terrified.

'Then — due no doubt to some aberration on the part of the Post Office — the letter telling her she was to go into the Hedley Atkins Unit on 17 January didn't arrive till the morning before. This meant she couldn't go to Kingsmarkham on the 19th. I imagine she was past caring. All that mattered to her now was that she shouldn't have cancer, shouldn't have her beautiful figure spoilt, shouldn't live in dread of a recurrence or an early death. Jane Zoffany could deal with her father for her, phone or write or send a telegram.'

From staring down at his empty plate, Burden now lifted

his eyes and sat bolt upright. 'It was Jane Zoffany who came down here that day?'

Wexford nodded. 'Who else?'

'She too is thin and dark and about the right age. . . . But why? Why pose as Natalie? For whatever possible purpose?'

'It wasn't deliberate,' Wexford said a shade testily. 'Haven't I said scarcely anything in this case was deliberate, planned or premeditated? It was just typical silly muddled Jane Zoffany behaviour. And what months it took me to guess it! I suppose I had an inkling of the truth, that wet day in the garden at Sterries, when Dinah said how strange it was Natalie could get the solicitors and Camargue's old friends to believe in her, yet Camargue who wanted to believe, who was longing to believe, saw her *on that one occasion* and didn't believe in her for more than half an hour. And when Jane Zoffany said how the police had taken her for her own sister and then stuck her hand up over her mouth — I knew then, I didn't need to be told any more.'

'But she did tell you more?'

'Sure. When I talked to her last night. She filled in the gaps.'

'Why did she go down to Sterries at all?' asked Burden.

'Two reasons. She wanted to see the old man for herself — she'd been an admirer of his — and she didn't want his feelings hurt. She knew that if she phoned and told him Natalie had yet again to keep a hospital appointment he'd think she was making excuses not to see him and he'd be bitterly hurt. For nineteen years his daughter had stayed away from him and now that she had come back and they were on the brink of a reunion, he was to be fobbed off with a phone call — and a second phone call at that. So she decided to go down and see him herself. But not, of course, with any idea of posing as Natalie, nothing of that sort entered her head. It's just that she's a rather silly muddled creature who isn't always quite mentally stable.'

'You mean,' said Burden, 'that she came down here simply because it seemed kinder and more polite to call in person? She came to explain why Natalie couldn't come and — well, sort of assure him of Natalie's affection for him? Something like that?'

'Something very much like that. And also to get a look at

the man who had been acclaimed the world's greatest flautist.'
Wexford caught Mr Haq's eye for their coffee. 'Now Camargue,' he said, 'was the first person to cast a doubt on Natalie's
identity, it was Camargue who started all this, yet it was
Camargue himself who took Jane Zoffany for his daughter
because it was *his daughter that he expected to see.*

'He had waited for nineteen years — eventually without
much hope. Hope had reawakened in the past five weeks and
he was keyed up to a pitch of very high tension. He opened the
door to her and put his arms round her and kissed her before
she could speak. Did she try to tell him then that he had made
a mistake? He was deaf. He was carried away with emotion. She
has told me she was so confused and aghast that she played
along with him while trying to decide what to do. She says she
was embarrassed, she was afraid to disillusion him.

'She humoured him by speaking of the Cazzini gold flute
— which Natalie had possibly mentioned to her but which was
in any case clearly labelled — and having no knowledge of
Italian, she mispronounced the name. We know what happened then. Camargue accused her of imposture. But it was no
dream of Camargue's, no senile fantasy, that his visitor confessed. Jane Zoffany freely admitted what she had been longing
to admit for the past half-hour — but it did her no good.
Camargue was convinced by then this was a deception plotted
to secure Natalie's inheritance and he turned her out of the
house.

'And that, Mike, was all this so-called imposture ever
amounted to, half an hour's misunderstanding between a well-
meaning neurotic and a "foolish, fond old man." '

While Burden experimented yet again with ice cream eau-de-
Nil, Wexford contented himself with coffee.

'Natalie,' he said, 'came out of hospital on January 20th
and she was so elated that the biopsy had shown the growth to
be benign that instead of being angry she was simply amused
by Jane's activities. As I've said, she had a very lively sense of
fun. I think it must have tickled her to imagine the pair of them
at cross-purposes, the wretched Jane Zoffany confessing and the
irate Camargue throwing her out. What did it matter, anyway?

She hadn't got cancer, she was fit and well and on top of the world and she could easily put that nonsense with her father right again. Let her only see if she could get a job out of Blaise Cory for her Johnny and then she'd see her father and patch things up.

'Before she could get around to that Camargue had written to her, informing her she should inherit nothing under the new will he intended to make.'

'Which led her,' said Burden, 'to plan on killing him first.'

'No, no, I've told you. There was no planning. Even after that letter I'm sure Natalie was confident she could make things smooth with her father. Perhaps she even thought, as Dinah says *she* did, that this could best be effected after the marriage. Natalie was not too concerned. She was amused. The mistake she made was in telling Fassbender. Probably for the first time Fassbender realized just how potentially wealthy a woman his girl friend actually was.'

'Why do you say for the first time?'

'If he'd known it before,' Wexford retorted, 'why hadn't he married her while they were both in California? That would have been a way of ensuring he didn't get deported. She was an American citizen. In those days, no doubt, she would have been willing enough to marry him, so if they didn't it must have been because he couldn't see there was anything in it for him. But now he did. Now he could see there was a very pleasant little sinecure here for the rest of their lives if only she wasn't so carefree and idle as to cast it all away.

'That Sunday Natalie went to a party with Jane Zoffany. She went because she liked parties, she liked enjoying herself, her whole life had been blithely dedicated to enjoying herself. There was no question of establishing an alibi. Nor, I'm sure, did she know Fassbender had taken himself off down to Kingsmarkham to spy out the land and have a look at the house and the affluence Natalie was apparently so indifferent to. It was on the impulse of the moment, in a sudden frenzy of — literally — taking things at the flood, that he seized Camargue and forced him into the water under the ice.'

For a moment they were both silent. Then Burden said:

'He told her what he'd done?'

A curious look came into Wexford's face. 'I suppose so. At any rate, she knew. By the time of the inquest she knew. How much she cared I don't know. She hadn't seen her father for nineteen years, but still he was her father. She didn't care enough to shop Fassbender, that's for sure. Indeed, you might say she cared so little that she was prepared to take considerable risks to *defend* Fassbender. No doubt, she liked what she got out of it. Life had been a bit precarious in the past four years, hadn't it? Once rid of Ilbert, it was a hand-to-mouth affair, and one imagines that while she was in De Beauvoir Place she was living solely on the rent from her house in Los Angeles. But now she had Sterries and the money and everything was fine. I'd like to think it was his murdering her father that began the process of going off Fassbender for Natalie, but we've no evidence of that.'

'What I don't understand is, since she *was* Natalie Arno, why did she play around half pretending she wasn't? It was a hell of a risk she was taking. She might have lost everything.'

'There wasn't any risk,' said Wexford. 'There wasn't the slightest risk. If she wasn't Natalie there might be many ways of apparently proving she was. But since she was Natalie it could never possibly be proved that she was not.'

'But why? Why do it?'

Burden had never had much sense of humour. And lately, perhaps since his marriage, Wexford thought, this limited faculty had become quiescent. 'For fun, Mike,' he said, 'for fun. Don't you think she got enormous fun out of it? After all, by that time she believed there was no question of our associating Camargue's death with foul play. What harm could she do herself or Fassbender by just ever so slightly hinting she might be the impostor Dinah Sternhold said she was? And it must have been fun, I can see that. It must have been hilarious dumbfounding us by answering Cory's questions and then really giving me hope by nicking her fingers with a bit of glass.

'I said we were fools. I reckon I was an arch fool. Did I really believe an impostor would have had her instructor with her on the very morning she knew we were coming? Did I really believe in such an enormous coincidence as Mary Woodhouse leaving that flat by chance the moment we entered it? What fun

Natalie must have got out of asking her old nanny or whatever she was to come round for a cup of coffee and then shooing her out when our car stopped outside. Oh, yes, it was all great fun, and as soon as it had gone far enough she had only to call in her dentist and prove beyond the shadow of a doubt who she was. For Williams is genuinely her dentist, a blameless person of integrity who happens to keep all his records and happens to have been in practice a long time.' Wexford caught Mr Haq's eye. 'D'you want any more coffee?'

'Don't think so,' said Burden.

'I may as well get the bill then.' Mr Haq glided over through the jungle. 'Once,' Wexford said, 'she had proved herself Natalie Arno to the satisfaction of Symonds, O'Brien and Ames, everything was plain sailing. The first thing to do was sell Sterries because it wouldn't do to have Fassbender show his face much around Kingsmarkham. But I think she was already beginning to go off Fassbender. Perhaps she saw that though he hadn't been prepared to marry her in America, even for the reward of legal residence there, he was anxious to do so now she was rich. Perhaps, after all, she simply decided there was no point in marrying. She hadn't done much of it, had she? Once only and she'd been a widow for nine years. And what would be the point of marrying when she now had plenty of money of her own and was happily independent? Still, this sort of speculation is useless. Suffice it to say that she had intended to marry Fassbender but she changed her mind. They quarrelled about it on the very eve of their going away on holiday together, and in his rage at being baulked of possession of the money he had killed for, had been to prison for, he attacked her and cut her throat.

'The body he put into that chest, which he locked, knowing it would be removed by Dorset's on the following day. Then off he went in the yellow Opel to Heathrow to use one of the two air tickets they had bought for their holiday in the South of France.'

Wexford paid the bill. It was modest, as always. By rights he ought, months ago, to have run Mr Haq in for offences under the Trade Descriptions Act. He would never do that now. They walked out into the High Street where the sun had unaccountably begun to shine. The pavements were drying up, the heavy grey clouds rushing at a great rate away to the horizon. At too great a rate, though, for more than temporary disappearance.

The Kingsbrook tumbled under the old stone bridge like a river in winter spate. Burden leaned over the parapet. 'You knew Fassbender when we came upon him in that place in France,' he said. 'I've been meaning to ask you how you did. You hadn't seen him in America, had you?'

'Of course I hadn't. He wasn't in America while I was. He'd been back here for over a year by then.'

'Then where had you seen him?'

'Here. Back at the very start of this case. Back in January just after Camargue died. He was at Sterries too, Mike. Can't you remember?'

'You saw him too,' Wexford went on. 'You said when we spotted him, "I've seen him somewhere before."'

Burden made a gesture of dismissal. 'Yes, I know I did. But I was mistaken. I couldn't have seen him, I was mixing him up with someone else. One wouldn't forget that name.'

Instead of replying, Wexford said, 'Fassbender's father was a Swiss who lived here without ever becoming naturalized. I don't know what his mother was or is, it hardly matters. John Fassbender was born here and has dual nationality, Swiss and British, not at all an uncommon thing. Ilbert had him deported to this country in 1976 but of course there was nothing to stop him going back into America again on his Swiss passport. When Romero shopped him three years later he was sent back to Switzerland but he soon returned here. Presumably, he liked it better here. Maybe he just preferred the inside of our prisons – he'd seen enough of them.'

'He's got a record, has he?'

Wexford laughed. 'Don't happen to have your German dictionary on you, do you?'

'Of course I don't carry dictionaries about with me.'

'Pity. I don't know why we've walked all the way up here. We'd better take shelter, it's going to rain again heavens hard.'

He hustled Burden down the steps into the Kingsbrook Precinct. A large drop of rain splashed against the brass plate of Symonds, O'Brien and Ames, a score more against the travel agency's window, blurring the poster that still invited customers to sunny California.

'In here,' said Wexford and pushed open the door of the bookshop. The dictionaries section was down at the back on the left-hand side. Wexford took down a tome in a green-and-yellow jacket. 'I want you to look up a word. It won't be much use to you in your studies, I'm afraid, but if you want to know where you saw Fassbender before you'll have to find out what his name means.'

Burden put the book down on the counter and started on the Fs. He looked up. 'Spelt Fassbinder, a barrel maker, a maker of casks . . .'

'Well?'

'A cooper. . . .' He hesitated, then said slowly, 'John Cooper, thirty-six, Selden Road, Finsbury Park. He broke into Sterries the night after the inquest on Camargue.'

Wexford took the dictionary away from him and replaced it on the shelf. 'His father called himself Cooper during the war — Fassbender wasn't generally acceptable then, on the lines of Beethoven and German Shepherds, one supposes. Fassbender held his British passport in the name of Cooper and his Swiss as Fassbender.

'That burglary was the only bit of planning he and Natalie did and that was done on the spur of the moment. It was a desperate measure taken in what they saw as a desperate situation. What alerted Natalie, of course, was Mrs Murray-Burgess telling Muriel Hicks she'd seen a suspicious-looking character in the Sterries grounds and that without a doubt she'd know him again. The only thing was, she couldn't quite remember which night. Natalie and Fassbender knew which night, of course. They knew it was the night Camargue drowned. So they faked up a burglary. Natalie slept in her late father's room, not to keep away from the amorous marauding Zoffany, still less to wound the feelings of Muriel Hicks, but to be in a room where she could credibly have heard breaking glass and seen the van's number.

'She had to have seen that to facilitate our rapidly getting our hands on Fassbender. Then Mrs Murray-Burgess could do her worst — it was a burglar she had seen and not a killer. In the event, he served four months. He came out in June, with two months' remission for good conduct.'

'I only saw him once,' said Burden. 'I saw him down the station here when we charged him.'

'With nicking six silver spoons,' said Wexford. 'Come on, the rain's stopped.'

They went outside. Once more a bright sun had appeared, turning the puddles into blinding mirrors.

Burden said doubtfully, 'It was a bit of a long shot, wasn't it? I mean, weren't they — well, over-reacting? They were supposing in the first place that Mrs Murray-Burgess would come to us and secondly that if she did we'd connect the presence of a man in the Sterries garden on an unspecified night with an old man's accidental death.'

'There was more to it than that,' said Wexford with a grin. 'She'd seen me, you see.'

'Seen you? What d'you mean?'

'At the inquest. You said at the time people would think things and you were right. Someone must have told Natalie who I was, and that was enough. I only went there because our heating had broken down, I was looking for somewhere to get warm, but she didn't know that. She thought I was there because at that early stage we suspected foul play.'

Burden started to laugh.

'Come,' said Wexford, 'let us shut up the box and the puppets, for our play is played out.'

And in the uncertain sunshine they walked up the street to the police station.